THE LAST
CAVALIERS

THE LAST CAVALIERS

GILBERT MORRIS

BARBOUR
PUBLISHING

Thumbnail covers: Faceout Studio, www.faceoutstudio.com
Thumbnail photography: Steve Gardner, Pixelworks Studios

Published by Barbour Publishing, Inc., P.O. Box 719, Uhrichsville,
Ohio 44683, www.barbourbooks.com

Our mission is to publish and distribute inspirational products offering
exceptional value and biblical encouragement to the masses.

 Member of the
Evangelical Christian
Publishers Association

Printed in the United States of America.

the CROSSING

PART ONE : THE RETURN 1855—1858

CHAPTER ONE

I feel like a bag of sticks in a bunch of gaudy Christmas baubles." Daniel Harvey Hill, normally of a dry and caustic humor, still glanced at his wife with a look of tenderness in his eyes.

"Don't you dare call me gaudy, Harvey," Isabella Morrison Hill retorted, "after you practically forced me to buy this material for this dress." She was a pretty woman, as were her two sisters who accompanied them in the carriage.

Isabella was the older sister, with ash brown hair and dark eyes set in a small oval face. Her younger sister, Mary Anna, had a more quiet beauty. Her hair was a darker, thicker chestnut brown and her brown eyes were soft and warm. The youngest sister, Eugenia, was vivacious, with sparkling eyes and a bow-shaped mouth that looked as if she were always smiling. All three sisters were small-boned, petite women.

On this fine snowy day of December 12, 1855, D. H. Hill, in his somber black suit, had indeed almost disappeared in the finery worn by his wife and two sisters-in-law. His wife, Isabella, wore a scarlet dress that showcased her tiny waist, with a touch of white fur on her collar and cuffs and hem. Anna Morrison wore a festive holly green trimmed with frosty white lace. Her bonnet was velvet and framed her face perfectly. Eugenia Morrison Barringer

9

wore a daring winter white trimmed with black velvet. Instead of a traditional bonnet, she sported a skullcap hat bordered by rich black sable, and her black gloves and hem were trimmed with the same expensive fur.

"You look lovely, my dear," Hill said gruffly. "You all do. Very festive. Puts me right in the Christmas spirit." His looks belied his words; he was a rather severe-looking man with sandy hair and a stubborn chin.

"Wonderful!" Eugenia, the saucy one, said. "So you won't be so grumpy, brother?"

"I'm never grumpy. I'm just matter-of-fact."

"Here's the bookseller's," Anna said, always the peacemaker. "Perhaps we may find a thesaurus, and each of us can pinpoint our particular dispositions. For myself, I do agree that brother Daniel is always factual and to the point."

"Pointy, you mean," Eugenia said merrily. "As for me, I believe I am of a spirited disposition. Isabella is good-humored and personable, and you, Anna, are reserved and of an intellectual nature."

"Boring, you mean?" Anna asked, her eyes twinkling.

"Never, sister," Eugenia said. "You're much too smart to be boring. So, shall we go in? If we don't settle all of this soon, we'll be late for Uncle William's party." Their driver opened the carriage door and pulled down the steps.

Anna started to step out and was surprised to see a hand extended to her and a gentle voice ask, "May I be of assistance, Miss Morrison?"

"Why, yes, Major Jackson. How wonderful to see you!" In spite of her reserve, Anna flushed slightly and her eyes lit up.

He helped her out of the carriage then gallantly handed down the other ladies.

D.H. shook his hand heartily. "Thomas, it is very good to see you. It's been far too long. You do look well."

Thomas Jonathan Jackson was thirty years old. For almost four years now he had been at Virginia Military Institute as professor of natural and experimental philosophy—at which he was an indifferent teacher at best—and instructor of artillery tactics—at which he was uncannily expert. He still wore the uniform he had worn during the Mexican War, where he had learned his artillery skills and, along the way, had been breveted a major for gallantry at Chapultepec, where he showed conspicuous courage and bravery. This uniform was not, however, made to show him off; it was a rather dusky blue, much worn and mended, double-breasted with two modest rows of buttons and the one oak leaf of a major on his shoulder flashes. The breeches were shiny at the knee, and the red stripe down the side was much faded. He wore his old cavalry boots and army-issued blue-caped greatcoat.

He was about five-ten and weighed one hundred seventy-five pounds. His complexion was smooth, his forehead broad, his nose aquiline. His hair was dark brown, soft, and had a tendency to curl. Jackson's most striking feature, however, was undoubtedly his eyes. They were of a lightning blue, such a bright color that they seemed almost to glow at times when he was feeling strong emotion. One of the nicknames the cadets at the Virginia Military Institute had given him was "Old Blue Light." His manner was always dignified and somewhat stiff, with an undoubtedly military bearing. In spite of this he was a forthright man, natural and unaffected. When he spoke to a person, his full attention and that frank gaze were fixed unerringly upon them.

"Thank you, D.H.," he answered. "As do you. But I must say that you lovely ladies positively brighten the day—even the whole town. Miss Morrison, that particular shade of green becomes you very much. Mrs. Hill, you look so much like a Christmas spirit that I wish it was Christmas today. Mrs. Barringer, as always, you are positively sparkling."

The ladies murmured their thanks.

D.H. asked, "Thomas, are you going to the bookseller's? Or have you already been?"

Jackson had a brown-wrapped parcel under his arm. For a moment he looked slightly uncomfortable. "No, this is a picture. That is, a daguerreotype. Of me." Next door to the bookseller's was a photographer's studio.

"Really?" Anna exclaimed. "Oh, may we see it?"

"I—I wouldn't deny you any pleasure, Miss Morrison," Jackson answered, obviously flustered. "But I think that would not be a very great pleasure. Besides, it—it is wrapped securely for my trip home."

Now Anna was embarrassed. "Of course, Major Jackson, it must stay—wrapped. I wasn't thinking."

Jackson bowed slightly. "But if you are going to Parson's Books and Reading Rooms, may I beg to accompany you all? I didn't have any particular book in mind, but I love to browse around."

"Please do, Major," Eugenia insisted prettily. "We are going to dinner at Uncle William's tonight, and we wanted to stop and get him a book for Christmas. We were thinking about *A Christmas Carol*. Don't you think he's much like old Mr. Fezziwig?" The sisters' uncle William Graham was a merry gentleman, a Whig of the old school who wore antique knee breeches, ruffled shirts, silk stockings, and heeled shoes with silver buckles.

Thomas smiled broadly and his eyes burned brightly. "So he is! A delightful old gentleman, if I recall. It has been, I think, two years since I've seen him."

"He looks the same," Eugenia said mischievously. "He always looks the same. I think he was born looking like Mr. Fezziwig."

"Then *A Christmas Carol* it must be," D.H. said. "Though he will never get the joke. My dear?" He offered Isabella his arm, and Jackson gallantly escorted both Mary Anna and Eugenia into the shop.

It was much like booksellers' shops everywhere, comfortably crowded with books both careworn and brand-new. The shop smelled like aged leather and old paper.

Mr. Parsons was a short, balding man with glasses perched on the edge of his nose and a perpetual slight squint, probably from reading almost continuously for at least forty-two of his forty-five years. He welcomed them and urged them to take tea or coffee in one of the reading rooms. Mr. Parsons was not a grasping man; he loved books so much that he had included two parlors attached to his shop that were far too inviting to promote quick sales. He barely made a profit on his shop, but he didn't care. He loved reading and avid readers and encouraged his customers to sit in one of the comfortably overstuffed chairs by the fireplace to peruse the books at their leisure.

The group wandered about the shop, Jackson to find Shakespeare and Hill in search of Dickens.

Eugenia was heard to exclaim, "Oh, look sisters! It's the newest *Godey's Ladies' Book!*"

The three sisters crowded around the magazines then went into the nearest parlor to spread them out on the library table so they could all look at them together. Jackson selected a copy of Shakespeare's sonnets then followed the ladies. The parlor was a large room, with four armchairs grouped comfortably around a brisk, crackling fire. The library table was large enough to accompany twelve people, and the sisters were grouped at one end, excitedly talking about the newest ladies' fashions. Jackson helped himself to hot tea from a sideboard then sat down by the fire.

Soon D.H. joined him, with his newly purchased copy of *A Christmas Carol*. Hill and Jackson had been friends for almost ten years now, because they had served together in the Mexican War. Hill, who in 1851 had been professor of mathematics at Washington College in Lexington, had recommended Jackson to the post at VMI that he had been awarded. The previous year, in 1854, Hill had joined the faculty of Davidson College, near Charlotte, North Carolina. In the last year he and Jackson had not corresponded much, both because Hill had moved and because of the tragic death of Jackson's wife, Elinor. She had died in November of 1854, giving birth to a stillborn son.

Hill settled into the armchair next to Jackson.

Jackson looked up and smiled, a sad and lonely smile that had been his customary expression for more than a year.

"How have you been, Thomas?" Hill asked quietly.

Jackson sighed. "It has been very difficult, I admit, D.H. I miss my Ellie more than I can say."

Hill shook his head. "I cannot imagine the trial, Thomas. I am so truly sorry."

"God has given me comfort, but you're right. It is indeed a trial. I know that Ellie and my son are waiting for me in Paradise. . . and sometimes I wish I could join them." He stared into space for a moment then continued, "But I have found solace in my work, and in my home."

"You are still living with Mr. Junkin?" Hill asked. When Elinor and Thomas had married in August of 1853, her father had built onto the family home for them.

"Yes, and he is a pillar of strength. And my sister-in-law, Margaret, has also been a great help to me," Jackson answered. "Sometimes I wonder at the enduring faith and love that seems to strengthen women more than men."

"I agree," D.H. said. "I also think Isabella is much stronger than I am, in so many ways."

Jackson brightened a bit. "She and her sisters are all such lovely ladies. A man would be blessed to have a wife from the Morrison family."

"So true, my friend," Hill agreed.

Carelessly Thomas commented, "I'm surprised that Miss Anna has not married. She is such a lovely lady, so intelligent and engaging."

"She is, and she has had two offers that I know of," Hill said. "But she wasn't the least bit interested. It seems that it must be very difficult for a man to persuade her to have him."

"Mmm," Jackson hummed noncommittally. "Most of the time the things that are hardest to obtain are the more precious to have."

With some negotiations about exactly how many *Godey's Ladies' Books* to buy, and whether or not to also purchase *Bleak House*, which Isabella had never read, the group finished their book shopping and returned to the carriage.

Once again Jackson escorted Anna, but Eugenia was walking with Isabella, still talking excitedly about their new magazines. Anna asked, "Won't you let us drive you home, Major?"

"Thank you, but no, I prefer to walk. In spite of the cold, it is a lovely day."

It was true; Lexington looked like an idyllic greeting card. The small village had feathery pillows of snow, but the sun was shining beatifically. Far on the horizon were more snow clouds, but they only served to accentuate the brightness of the late afternoon. The walks had been shoveled by industrious boys who earned a nickel from the town's treasury. They had done a fine job, pushing the snow up into neat snowbanks bordering the streets.

Anna agreed. "It is a beautiful afternoon. But I'm afraid if I walked too far I might muss my hem." Her hooped skirt was floor-length, as was fashionable, and it took particular care to hold it up without exposing a glimpse of a forbidden ankle.

Jackson smiled down at her. "In that case, Miss Morrison, I would be obliged, like that gentleman Sir Walter Raleigh, to cast my cloak at your feet. But I'm afraid it would be a sorry carpet for you." Jackson's blue caped coat, like his clothes, was worn and thin.

"I would still be honored, sir," Anna said. "I would be glad to tread on your cloak any time."

He handed her up into the carriage, and D.H. stopped at the open carriage door. "Thomas, won't you join us for dinner? Not tomorrow—Isabella and I have a prior engagement—but what about on Friday night? Rufus and Eugenia and Anna and I would, I think, make a merry party."

"That you would, D.H.," Jackson gravely agreed. Glancing at Anna he added, "It would be a very great pleasure, and I will be sure to bring my cloak."

The Hills, Anna, and Eugenia and her husband, Rufus Barringer, were staying at the Col Alto Manor House. All of them had relatives in Lexington, but instead of imposing on them for their Christmas visit, they had decided that it would be much easier to stay at this comfortable boardinghouse.

Col Manor had been built in 1827 and was a gracious two-story home with spacious bedrooms, two parlors for guests' use, and an elegant dining room. Col Alto was very well-known, too, for its fine food and was one of the locals' favorite places to eat.

Thomas Jackson joined them in the dining room, which was sumptuously lit with dozens of candles. It was a large room, but the tables were so discreetly located that it gave each party a feeling of privacy. Two enormous fireplaces faced each other across the room, and on this frosty night, the fires, continually tended by servants, snapped and sparked. The smoky scent of aged Virginia oak mingled with the delicious aromas of food cooked fresh and served hot. The D.H. Hill party was seated at a table in a corner, with the fireplace pleasantly distant enough so that they could feel the warmth but not to excess.

D.H. Hill introduced Thomas to Rufus Barringer, Eugenia's husband, whom Thomas had never met.

Barringer was a neat, compact man, balding, with light brown hair and a fine-trimmed mustache and beard. His blue eyes seemed to continually twinkle with good humor, and his mouth was wide and appeared, like his wife's, to be always on the verge of a smile. He was a man of good humor and patience, which served him well in his marriage to the spirited Eugenia Morrison. Barringer said, "Sir, I have heard of your famous artillery expertise, both in the Mexican War and at Virginia Military Institute. It's a pleasure to meet you."

"You're too kind," Jackson said. "But I must agree that both the study and the practice of artillery gives me a great deal of pleasure—much more, I'm afraid, than the study of natural and experimental philosophy."

"I admit to considerable ignorance," Barringer said. "My study has been confined almost exclusively to the law. What, exactly, is natural and experimental philosophy, sir?"

"I don't know," Jackson answered, deadpan.

There was a long silence at the table, and then the entire party—except for Jackson, who only smiled—laughed.

They were a merry party that evening. Jackson and the other two men were wearing the only acceptable fine evening attire—dark suits, black ties, and white ruffled shirts. The women, in contrast, looked like colorful little birds in a drab wood. Isabella looked regal in royal blue, Anna glowed in a deep rose, and Eugenia wore a golden brown that made her complexion look like pure ivory. The candlelight cast a rich aura over them; as was the fashion, their shoulders were bare and their hair was gracefully swept up. Isabella wore a golden comb, and Anna and Eugenia wore dainty tortoiseshell. Anna rarely wore jewelry, but on this festive night, she wore pearl drop earrings that her uncle William Graham had given her years before, stating that they were such purity as became her naturally.

The party was seated at a round table, which served well, in that the matching of Anna and Thomas was not so obvious.

Thomas Jackson exerted himself to be lighthearted company, but he was obviously still mourning the loss of his wife. Often when there was a pause in the conversation, his face took on a distant look, his fire blue eyes dimmed, and he stared into the distance as if searching for something far away. But throughout the long and delicious meal, he was for the most part amusing and perfectly cheerful.

Rufus Barringer questioned him about his service in the Mexican War, with his brother-in-law, D.H. Hill, as a fellow soldier.

"I prefer to remember the pleasant things about Mexico, and there were many," Jackson answered. One corner of his mouth gave a tiny tug. "The senoritas were particularly cordial. Not, of course," he added with a mischievous air, "to Major Hill, as he was engaged to you at this time, Mrs. Hill, and he never compromised his affections and loyalties to you. He was, however, uncommonly fond of quince. . .and that did get us into some trouble, as I recall."

Over Hill's protestations, Eugenia asked slyly, "And so this was a Senorita Quince, Major Thomas?"

"Eugenia, really," Anna scolded her. "That is—there was not a Senorita Quince, was there, Major Jackson?"

"No, no, there was not," Jackson hastily replied. "Quince is a fruit. It looks like a pear, but it is much more tart and crisp. All of us loved them, because they were so refreshing in that hot, dry climate. Once, I'm afraid, this hunger for them forced me and Major Hill to climb an adobe garden wall for fresh quince, and I believe we came closer to getting killed by the owner of the home than we ever were in battle. And there was a senorita involved. . .at least she made a good deal of noise, and I think that her father thought that we were more interested in her than in the less dangerous fruit. I think that is the fastest that I've seen D.H. move, climbing back across that garden wall."

Isabella glowered. "And you, Harvey, did you know this senorita? Is that how you came to know about the quince tree?"

"No! No!" he vigorously protested. "It was all Jackson's fault. He had seen the very tip-top of the tree the day before, and he said the gardener would never miss two or three of the fruits. But as it happened, he did object most strenuously."

CROSSING

"But after all this, did you get any fruit, Major Jackson?" Anna asked, smiling.

"We did, but it was at a high price. D.H. skinned his knee terribly in our shameful retreat, and I fell off the wall on the other side and twisted my ankle so badly I could hardly get my boot on the next day. But the quince was very good," he added, his blue eyes light and fiery as he glanced slightly at Anna, "and so I may say it was worth it. Most of the time, the things that are hardest to obtain are the more precious to have."

The First Presbyterian Church was a solemn edifice, two stories of graceful Greek Revival architecture of white sandstone, with five lofty columns guarding the entrance and a great steeple with a clock tower. Thomas Jackson had joined the church in 1851. Before he joined he had visited with Dr. William S. White, the pastor, many times and had found him to be a dedicated scholar of the Bible and servant of the Lord.

Once again Thomas found himself escorting Miss Morrison as she and her sisters and brothers-in-law attended church with him. He wondered again at Anna. She was an attractive, modest, intelligent woman of a quiet, sweet wit, and it was unusual for a woman of such family and virtues to remain unmarried by the age of twenty-four. He had known her for five years now, having met her several times, as he had been a popular visitor to D.H. Hill's home when he had been at Washington College. He had always thought her a mildly pretty woman and an interesting one, but he had been so very much in love with Elinor Junkin that no other woman touched his mind except in passing.

Even now as he thought of Ellie, his thoughts, mind, and heart wandered. It had been over a year, and yet the grief and the feeling of loss was still so raw that, unknowing, he drew in a deep, ragged breath, stopped walking, and stared off at the distant blue hills to the east. The Blue Ridge Mountains were wreathed in mysterious smoke as always, and he longed to lose himself in that far place where, it seemed, everything and everyone must be immortal—forever beloved, unhurt, and undying. . . .

❧

Anna stopped as Major Jackson paused and watched him with sympathy, for the expression on his face bore some sadness.

She recalled the first time she had met him. It was at D.H. Hill's house, on one of Thomas's many visits to the Lexington house where D.H. and Isabella had entertained on any opportunity permitted. Thomas was generally her escort by default, as Isabella was engaged to D.H. and her younger sister, Eugenia, had many suitors to escort here anywhere and everywhere. Anna admired Major Jackson. He was a true man, it seemed to her, and a strong and genuine person.

In fact, she wrote to one of her acquaintances:

> *More soldierly looking than anything else, his erect bearing and military dress being quite striking; but upon engaging in conversation, his open, animated countenance, and his clear complexion, tinged with the ruddy glow of health, were still more pleasing. . . . His head was a splendid one, large and finely formed, and covered with soft, dark brown hair, which, if allowed to grow to any length, curled; but he had a horror of long hair for a man. . .he was at all times manly and noble looking, and when in robust health he was a handsome man.*

When Thomas had announced his engagement to Elinor Junkin, Anna had appeared to wish him the best goodwill, as did her family. She never spoke of her private feelings to anyone. Her sisters did know that she admired Major Jackson, but Anna was reserved, so they never dreamed of intruding upon her by questioning her of her feelings about his marriage. Through those two years of Jackson's marriage, and the death of his wife and his subsequent mourning, Anna had conducted herself with great aplomb; but whenever she saw him again, she had a sparkle in her soft eyes. She spoke of him often to her sisters and to D.H., but it was always impersonal, regarding the last time they had seen him or reminiscing about old times.

Anna was reluctant to interrupt his reverie, but it was almost time for the service to begin. Softly she said, "Major Jackson?"

He came alive again, from that far-off land, and they went into the church, arm in arm.

Anna hoped that one day he would look at her with that same tender regard she had seen as he stared at the faraway Blue Ridge Mountains.

D.H., Isabella, Rufus, Eugenia, and Anna left Lexington on Monday, December 17, a week before Christmas. At the train station, Thomas Jackson discreetly asked Anna if he might correspond with her, strictly as a loyal friend. Anna agreed heartily.

Over the next months, Thomas wrote her nice little letters, about the goings-on at VMI and the coming spring and the beauty of the Shenandoah Valley. In summer he wrote about the great riches of his farm—corn, tomatoes, snap beans, peas, turnips, carrots, squash, celery, and beets. He wrote, mildly and oddly noncommitally, about the growing tensions between North and South on the question of secession.

Anna saw nothing more of Thomas Jackson until July 1856. Virginia Military Institute planned a particularly extravagant July Fourth celebration. Urged by Uncle William Graham and many of their cousins, D.H. Hill and Isabella decided to take a large party to Lexington to celebrate.

Without fanfare, Thomas escorted Anna to the festivites. They watched the fireworks and the immaculate artillery performances by the VMI cadets. As the merriments were winding down, he turned to her and said, "Although I realize it might be forward of me, I have a gift for you. Would it be too presumptuous to ask you to receive it?"

"Not at all, sir," she answered, blushing in spite of herself. She took his arm and he led her to his horse, which was in the institute's stables.

Out of his saddlebag he drew a brown-wrapped parcel. He handed it to her, then closed his hands over both of hers as she grasped it. "I would very much prefer if you would keep it until you go home and then unwrap it," he said quietly.

"Of—of course, Major Jackson," she answered. "Certainly. I thank you very much, and I'm sure that it is a gift I shall cherish."

"I hope so." He led her back to her family.

They returned home, the Hills and Barringers and Anna back to Col Alto, Thomas Jackson back to Junkin Home.

Anna did not open her gift that night. She was tired and slightly drained, and she thought that whatever it was, she would appreciate it much more when she felt well and energetic. And she had the most curious feeling about the gift—great anticipation on the one hand and a sort of dread that it would be disappointing on the other. Though she was extremely curious, she still could not bring herself to open the gift. She told herself that she could deal with the emotion—whichever extreme it was—if she were at home.

The next day was July 5, the day they were to return back home to North Carolina. Anna had packed the brown-wrapped parcel tightly and securely in her trunk, between her brown velvet day dress and her green velvet evening dress. Major Thomas Jackson did not come to the railroad station to see them off, as he had said his good-byes the night before.

The next day at Cottage Home in North Carolina, Anna finally summoned the courage to open her package. It was Major Jackson, his daguerreotype from that December. There was no note attached. To her, he looked very handsome, and his light blue eyes had a hint of sadness in them. But they seemed to look forward, to new days, instead of the grief of the last year. She was extremely happy with her gift and treasured it, though she kept it in a bureau drawer because she felt it would be too much anticipation of the future to keep it displayed by her bedside.

On that same evening, July 6, she received a telegram. Major Thomas Jackson had written to tell her that he was gone to Europe, on a grand tour including Belgium, France, Germany, Switzerland, England, and Scotland. He hoped that she would be amenable to him corresponding with her. A few days later she began receiving his letters, which she answered immediately.

Once he wrote in more flowery language than she had ever heard him use:

CROSSING

I would advise you never to name my European trip to me unless you are blest with a superabundance of patience, as its very mention is calculated to bring up with it an almost inexhaustible assemblage of grand and beautiful associations. . . .

Anna wrote back that she did, indeed, possess much patience.

He returned in October. His letters had grown steadily more personal and even showed some affection. So though Anna expressed surprise, she wasn't really shocked when he shambled up on his horse, unannounced, to call at Cottage Home. After visiting with her family, Thomas asked if he might speak to Anna alone.

There were many endearments expressed, although neither Anna nor Thomas recorded all of them. On one knee, holding her hand and looking up at her with a forgotten warmth and hope in his eyes, he asked, "Miss Anna, would you do me the greatest honor and consent to become my wife?"

"I will," she answered with tears in her eyes. "And sir, you do *me* great honor."

Anna Morrison had been kissed a very few times before, but Major Thomas Jackson's kiss celebrating their engagement was the sweetest, and the most poignant, she had ever known.

They were married at Cottage Home on July 16, 1857.

CHAPTER TWO

Yancy Tremayne leaned over the bank, as motionless as the stones in the stream below. He had held that position for ten minutes, but now with a flash of movement, he grabbed a fish and flung it on the bank behind him. He whooped with triumph, for it was the biggest fish he had ever caught; it was fifteen pounds at least, a striped bass. He strung it out and started back to the camp.

Even at the young age of twelve, he was half a head taller than any of the Cheyenne boys his age, and he already had matured more so that he had taken on a sort of manhood. He had dark eyes and an olive tint to his skin, and his hair was as black as the darkest thing in nature. He had a straight English nose and a cleft in his chin exactly as did his father, Daniel. Like all the Cheyenne, Yancy wore buckskin breeches, moccasins, and a buckskin vest with intricate beading. He had taken that off when he was fishing so that it wouldn't get wet.

He hurried back, for he always liked to bring his trophies directly to his father. Suddenly a Cheyenne boy named Hinto jumped out onto the path. Hinto was the son of the Cheyenne chief, White Buffalo. Hinto was his eldest son and was much indulged. Although he had handsome features, as did the Cheyenne people, he tended toward chubbiness and was a bully. He was sixteen years old and much bigger than Yancy. Now he blocked Yancy's way. "I'll take that fish, Yancy."

"No, you won't! This is my fish."

Hinto grabbed the fish, and Yancy let it go. Hinto turned, and Yancy picked up a smooth round river stone and hit him in the head, knocking him flat. Yancy picked up the fish and looked at Hinto, noting that he wasn't hurt badly or unconscious, only befuddled. "You go catch your own fish," he taunted then ran lightly down the path.

He reached the camp made of tepees covered with buffalo hide, which were scattered over an open meadow, but he ran by them like a fleeing deer and circled back to the riverbank. There his father had built a log cabin, insulated with river mud daub. It had only one room, with a loft where Yancy slept, and he headed there to find his father.

❧

Daniel Tremayne sat outside, rocking in a chair he had made from Lake Essee's fine oak timber.

"Look at the fish I caught!" Yancy cried, holding up his prize.

"That is a right nice fish you got there." Daniel, at the age of thirty-two, was over six feet tall and was very lean and muscular. Ordinarily he wore a fur cap, but the summer was hot, so he wore nothing on his head. His long reddish blond hair was tied back with a rawhide thong. His face was handsome in a rugged way; his jaw was lean, and his cheekbones sharp. In the bright sun he had sun-squints at the corners of his blue eyes. He had a small scar beside his mouth, and a livid red one ran from his left jawbone down to his shoulder blade. His buckskin vest was much finer than Yancy's, for the beading was from the V-shaped front all the way to the shoulders and was very intricate. His buckskin breeches had a long fringe, and his knee-high moccasins were also beaded. He reached out and took the fish, holding the mouth with his thumb. "This fellow ought to feed us until we get sick of eating fish."

Yancy was pleased with his father's praise. He was telling his father how he had caught it, relating every second, when they were interrupted by White Buffalo and his son Hinto, who had a bloody forehead.

White Buffalo growled, "Look what your boy did, Tremayne."

Daniel got to his feet and looked at the son of the chief. "What happened, Hinto?"

"While I wasn't looking, Yancy came up behind me and hit me with a rock."

"That's a lie!" Yancy argued, and stood up very straight to face Chief White Buffalo, his fists clenched by his sides. "He took my fish away from me, and when he turned around I hit him with a rock. I had to to get my fish back. He's a thief!"

White Buffalo was tall and well formed, a strong man. Since he was war chief, very rarely did anyone press him or argue with him. He crosssed his arms and frowned darkly at Yancy.

Daniel Tremayne grew alert. He knew the man had a fiery temper and was an expert with any weapon. White Buffalo carried only a knife at his side now, but he was always dangerous.

"You should teach your son how brothers behave," White Buffalo muttered.

"I'll take care of my son, you take care of yours, White Buffalo. Hinto stole Yancy's fish, and he had a right to get it back."

White Buffalo was angry to the core. He had never liked Daniel Tremayne, who was a far better shot with a rifle than he was. Also, when they were much younger and before White Buffalo became chief, they had a fight during which the two had bloodied each other thoroughly. It was, in fact, because White Buffalo had insulted Daniel's half-breed wife, Winona. In that altercation Daniel had emerged the victor.

Now White Buffalo grunted, "Your boy isn't a true Cheyenne, and you aren't of the people yourself. The boy's mother was only half Cheyenne. The other half was white trapper." He spat on the ground disdainfully.

"He's Cheyenne enough to make his way," Daniel said quietly and civilly.

White Buffalo had said what he came to say. "Tremayne, why don't you go to your own people? Neither of you belong here. Neither of you are true Cheyenne." He turned abruptly and walked away, followed by Hinto, who looked back and made a childish face at Yancy.

Daniel watched them leave until they disappeared over the path toward the Cheyenne camp. Then he sat back in his rocking chair and motioned for Yancy to sit down on the rough bench beside him. "Yancy, there's something we need to talk about."

Yancy sat and waited, his eyes fixed on his father. He was disturbed by the reference to his white blood. It was something that the pure-blooded Indian boys taunted him about often. His mother had been only half Cheyenne. Her father had been Pierre Charbeau, a fur trapper. The Cheyenne felt only disdain for anyone not of pure blood, although they did not—like the Comanche or the Sioux—torment or sometimes kill the mixed breeds. They just didn't include them, which was difficult for the mixed breeds in the tribe. The Cheyenne creed meant very strong and loyal family ties to their own, and to be left out of this close circle was painful.

The Cheyenne had been, perhaps, more accepting of Winona because she tried hard to fit in with them. She could raise a good tepee, she could fish, she made wonderful soft buckskin breeches and shirts and vests. Her skill in beading was the best in the village; often the chieftains bought beads at the trading post at Cantonment and paid her in fish and deer meat and rabbit to do her beading on their garments.

She had lived alone, because her mother had died when she was fifteen and her father had disappeared during trapping season, going off to the distant Ouachita Mountains, never to return. When Daniel Tremayne had first met the Cheyenne, she had been seventeen. He had loved her the minute he set eyes on her. They had married, in the Cheyenne way, and a year later she had Yancy. When Yancy was ten, she contracted cholera and died.

Now as Daniel remembered her he was saddened, because this place had always been Winona's home; but he knew that it wasn't his home, nor was it meant to be Yancy's home. "Yancy, we're going to be leaving this place."

Yancy stared at his father, his dark eyes suddenly narrowing. "Why would we do that? These are our people."

"No, they're not, as you just heard. When your mother was

alive, we were a part of the Cheyenne people because of her. But you and I. . .we don't belong here."

"But, Father, these are my people, the Cheyenne! You've always taught me to be proud of my mother and what my Cheyenne blood meant!"

"Yes, Yancy, and I believe I've done the right thing. I always want you to be proud of your mother and your blood." He shrugged slightly. "Maybe if your mother had lived and I had completely adopted the way of the Cheyenne, it would've been different. But I am a white man, and though I loved your mother very much, we lived as white people. Just look at our cabin. I could never live in a tepee that you could just pick up and move from one day to the next. I don't have the wandering plains thoughts that your mother's people do. I need roots, and family, and a feeling of being permanent. And though you don't realize it, you sometimes show me you feel the same way."

Yancy looked as though he might cry, though he never had and certainly never would—at least not in front of anyone. "But, Father, where would we go?"

"I've thought about this for a long time, son, and we have to go back to my people," Daniel answered quietly and with some sorrow. "My parents are getting old, if they're still alive. I have many regrets, because I ran away from home. . .and I wasn't much older than you are now. I want us to go back to them and be a family again. That is, if they'll have us."

"Why wouldn't they have you, Father?" Yancy asked curiously. His father had often told him stories and the history of the Cheyenne, but he had rarely mentioned his own family.

"Because my people belong to a group called the Amish, and they feel that a son should obey his father. Well, I didn't do that. I ran away because I was tired of their rules and their boring lives. But now it seems to me that they do know what true love, and real family, can be."

"But I don't want to leave, Father! I want to be a Cheyenne. I *am* Cheyenne!" Yancy protested, his dark eyes glinting, his olive skin taking on an angry copper glow.

Daniel Tremayne sighed heavily, for this was as hard as he had known it would be. Yancy had known nothing his whole life but Indian ways. It was a life of freedom for young boys, and Yancy had reveled in it. The tribe didn't have much contact with whites, and Yancy knew very little about that world.

Daniel had been avoiding making a decision, but this incident with Hinto and White Buffalo settled the thing in his mind. His blue eyes looked into the distance, watching the scarlet sunset over the lake. He was quiet for a time, and Yancy, too, watched the sun as it seemed to be inextricably drawn down to the quiet red waters. "You know, Yancy, White Buffalo's people have been lucky," Daniel said thoughtfully. "We found a good place to settle, a fertile place, with a lake full of good fish, with woods and grass and herbs. There are deer, turkey, quail, dove, and wild hogs that make easy hunting here." He sighed deeply. "But it's destined not to last. The white men have pushed and shoved and maneuvered the Indians from everywhere in the West. I've told you that they made us move down here from the north, and many of the Cheyenne didn't find a place that was nearly as good to live as here, at Lake Essee." The Cheyenne had named the lake *E 'se'he*, which meant "sun," but the white men had corrupted it to *Lake Essee*. "And the day will come that they'll push the Cheyenne away from here. We can't stay with them. They are a dying people. And we are not of their own."

"They'll fight," Yancy said angrily.

"Yes, they will, courageously," Daniel agreed. "And they'll die."

Yancy stared at his father and saw that there was no point arguing, for when Daniel Tremayne's mind was made up, that was the end of it. It was part of his strength. "When will we leave?" asked Yancy, resigned.

"We'll leave right away, son." He rose and he put his hand on the boy's shoulder, saying gently, "One day when you're a man, you'll see I've made the right decision."

"When I'm grown up, I will come back to the Cheyenne!"

Daniel almost smiled, for the rebellion in his son was very familiar to him. It was exactly the way he had been when he was a young man. "That may very well be. But until then, you and I will be together. No matter what happens, you are my son, and I'm very proud of you. I will always love you, and I will never forsake you.

So we'll see what comes—and even if we find no other people, we'll be a family always."

It took almost three months for Daniel and Yancy to travel from the Oklahoma plains to the Shenandoah Valley in Virginia. Even though Lake Essee had been like an oasis in the desert, in no way could it compare to the valley. To the west were the Allegheny Mountains, gentle and eternal, old mountains with tops rounded from the ages. To the east were the Blue Ridge Mountains, smoky, quiet, mysterious. Fertile, green, serene, even in the blazing heat of August, the Shenandoah Valley lay like a priceless emerald that stretched from southern Virginia to Maryland. Every view was scenic. Every scene was green. All the green was rich.

Daniel and Yancy stopped on a small rise overlooking a large farm. The farmhouse was substantial, three stories, with gables in the attic and a wide veranda surrounding the house. There were several outbuildings—an enormous barn, stables, a housing for a huge windmill, two sheds for farm equipment, and a carriage house. Behind and to the west was a great pasture filled with fat cows, and to the east were horses feeding contentedly. Beyond were fields, rich with harvest; cornfields; hay; wheat; tobacco; barley; and soybeans. It all gave the impression of a great richness, though it was a richness that had nothing to do with money.

"This is my home," Daniel said softly. "This is where I grew up."

Throughout the entire journey, Yancy had grown more and more sullen. Now all he said was, "It's a big farm. Must be lots of hard work."

"It is," Daniel agreed. "But I think it might be worth it. And it's not just the farming. The valley is good hunting and good fishing, even in wintertime. I think you'll like it, Yancy."

"I dunno," he muttered. "I already miss home."

"But this is our home now," Daniel said. "We'll be fine." Daniel hoped this was true. He had sent a telegram to his parents from Oklahoma City, saying that he was coming home and was bringing their grandson. He hoped they had received it. He knew they would never answer it, for the Amish wouldn't contemplate using something as modern and complicated as a telegraph.

As they rode toward the farmhouse, Daniel said rather uncertainly, "You'll find my parents are very religious. They are what's called Amish people."

"What does that mean? Amish?"

"They are people that sort of set themselves apart from others. They believe that they should live very simply and quietly. They are good Christian people, but their rules are much stricter than some others."

"Why didn't you tell me anything about this before?" Yancy demanded. "You've never said anything about God, or even about the Cheyenne gods!"

"I know," Daniel said with some discomfort. "It's because I'm still not sure where I am with the Lord, even now. But I do know that we need to come home." Daniel stopped in front of the house and slipped off his horse.

A woman came through the screened door and stood on the porch, watching him. She was a small woman but held herself so straight she seemed taller than she actually was. At the age of sixty-three, her hair was still black, but with one silver wing from her left temple back to the bun she wore. Her hair was thick and healthy. Since the Amish women never cut their hair, it reached below her waist when it was down. She had sharp features—a straight nose and a strong jaw, but her blue eyes were kind. She wore the dress of Amish women. They wore plain dark dresses with collarless high necks. Over their shoulders they wore a *holsz duch*, a triangular shawl pinned to their apron in front. All of their fastenings were straight pins, for buttons were forbidden. All Amish women wore prayer caps, usually made of white organza. "So you've finally come home, Daniel," she breathed. Then she held out her arms.

Daniel rushed to her, and they held each other for a long time. Then he held her out at arm's length and said, "You're looking well, Mother. I've missed you."

"I am well," she answered, "and I've missed you, too, Daniel. So this is Yancy?"

"Yes, this is your grandson. Yancy, this is your grandmother, Zemira."

"Hello, ma'am," Yancy said awkwardly, dismounting and taking off his slouch hat.

Zemira Tremayne smiled. "He favors you, Daniel."

"Maybe, but he favors his mother more." Daniel looked toward the house and asked, "Is Father inside?"

"No, son, he's over there." Zemira gestured toward a grove of oak trees, adding, "He went to be with the Lord two years ago."

Daniel glanced at the small cemetery then dropped his gaze, unable to meet his mother's eyes. He had left home because he'd been unable to live within the *Ordnung*, the set of rules and regulations that define the Amish lifestyle. He remembered how he had never fit into the strict confines demanded by the community. He remembered and regretted the heated arguments he had with his father, and now he burned with shame. "I'm so sorry about the way I treated you and Father. I wanted to ask his forgiveness for running away like I did."

"He forgave you without being asked," Zemira said. "Your father was never a man to hold a grudge. You hurt him badly when you left, saying hard words to him, Daniel. I was afraid he'd not be able to deal with it, but he did. He came to me one day about six months after you left and told me, 'If you ever see Daniel again and I'm not here, tell him I loved him even if we didn't agree.'"

"I was wrong to leave that way, Mother, and I want to make it up to you any way that I can. If you'll let us come back, I'll try and be a good son to you."

Zemira grasped both of his hands in hers, lifted her head, and looked straight into Daniel's eyes. "Of course you are welcome, Daniel. You are my son, and you are my family." Then she turned to Yancy, saying, "I expect you're hungry, Yancy. Come in the house, and I'll see what we've got to eat."

Daniel and Yancy followed her into the house, and Daniel ran his eyes over the front parlor as she led them through to the kitchen. "Nothing has changed, Mother. It's just like it was the day I left."

The Amish made all of their furniture, and like everything about them, it was simple and plain. Two settees, facing each other from either side of the fireplace, had straight backs with thin cushions. There were two straight chairs and two rocking chairs. One round table in the corner served as a tea table.

Daniel got a small lump in his throat when they passed through the dining room. The dining table was fine, made of maple, long enough to seat twelve. All of the chairs were handmade, ladder-back, and Daniel's father, Jacob, had even indulged in a small scroll on the topmost crosspiece.

Daniel had helped him make this furniture. Or at least Jacob had pretended that Daniel was helping. He had been small, maybe five or six years old. Jacob had given him a piece of sandpaper and had told him to sand small pieces of wood. Now Daniel wondered if anything he had sanded was actually included in the furniture. In the crosspieces of the chairs, perhaps.

They went into the kitchen, where there was an oak worktable with four stools. "Here, Yancy, Daniel, you sit down. I have some leftovers from dinner today. Sol Raber and Shadrach Braun were here today, helping with the farm, and I fixed this for them."

"So how have you been managing the farm by yourself, Mother?" Daniel asked.

Zemira set down a platter of roast beef and a big bowl of mashed potatoes that had been kept on the woodstove, which still had coals enough to keep it warm. "You know this, Daniel," she answered matter-of-factly. "You are not my only family. This community is my family, too, and since your father died, everyone in the valley has helped me."

The Amish were indeed loyal to everyone in their community. Anytime anyone needed help—with money, with children, with work, with the farm—the entire community helped. The settlement in the Shenandoah Valley was relatively small, now with twenty-two family farms, though that number was growing as they married and bought more land. But when Jacob Tremayne had died, all of the able men of the twenty-two families took turns taking care of the Tremayne farm and holdings. Zemira was still strong, and she herself still tended to the milking, the cows, the horses, the kitchen garden, and the cornfield. But the men of the Amish community had helped with plowing, sowing, seeding, harvesting, selling the goods at market, and with firewood and tending the livestock in the bitter winters. Zemira told Daniel of all the men and boys who had helped her for the last two years since Jacob had died.

Yancy was quiet as he listened to his father and his grandmother. The roast beef and potatoes were delicious, and he ate hungrily.

As they were finishing up, Zemira asked, "What do you want to do, Daniel? Will you be going back to hunting and trapping?"

"No, Mother, I don't want to do that." Daniel hesitated, but he had rehearsed what he wanted to say, so he forged ahead. "I want to come back and join the community. I want to work this farm. I want us to be a family."

Zemira gave Daniel a direct look. "Do you think so, Daniel? You never took discipline well. It will be difficult for you."

"I'll give it my best," Daniel said firmly.

"You'll have to prove yourself. You know what that will be like."

"It'll be hard, but if you'll have me, I'll be grateful."

"So be it then." Zemira turned to Yancy. "What about you, Yancy? What do you think of learning to live with us?"

Yancy shook his head. "I don't know. I don't really know much about you—about the Amish. But I'll tell you the truth, ma'am. It doesn't sound like I'll like it much."

"Call me Grandmother," Zemira said softly. "And I'll help you, Yancy. It'll be so good to have family here again."

"You'll have to help me, too, Mother," Daniel said. "I know I want to be here, but I'm still not sure where I stand with the Lord, and with Amish ways. It's been so long. . . ."

"It's never too long, or too late, with the Lord, Daniel," Zemira said. "You'll see."

CHAPTER THREE

Rebecca! What are you doing? Daydreaming about a husband?"

Shadrach Braun leaned up against the doorjamb and sipped his lemonade. It was August, and it was hot. He had been out working in the fields and had come in to cool off for a bit before they finished up and had to put the stock away. He was dressed as all Amish men dressed for work—dark trousers, plain white shirt, suspenders, straw hat. He was not a big man but was tightly muscled, with dark hair and dark blue eyes that sometimes looked like a muddy green.

In the parlor his three sisters sat on low hickory benches, and his mother sat in her favorite rocking chair. Lois, the youngest sister at thirteen, and her sister, Judith, who was one year older, were plying their needles industriously, sewing pillowcases. Their mother, Adah, was making a chair cushion.

Rebecca, the eldest sister, had dropped her pillowcase onto her lap and was staring out the window dreamily. She turned as Shad spoke. "Maybe I was just meditating on things of the Lord, Shad. That would be better than sewing another one of these dumb pillowcases."

Shad grinned. "I doubt very much that you were thinking of God. You don't meditate nearly as much as you should, at least according to the bishop." He came to sit by her. She was his favorite sister as he was her favorite brother, perhaps because the two of them were much alike.

Rebecca Braun was an attractive woman of twenty-eight. She wore the traditional unadorned garb of Amish women—a dark dress, white fichu, and white apron. Her devotional cap covered most of her coal black hair. Her eyes mirrored Shad's, a dark blue with a hazel green tint. She had an oval face with a mouth that was full and attractive but too broad for actual beauty.

"So did you leave the fields to come in here and see if I've magically produced a suitor this morning, Shad?" she asked pertly.

Shad shook his head in feigned disgust. "You're never going to get a husband, Becky. Look, Lois is only thirteen and she's got her hope chest full, and Judith's just a year older and her hope chest is packed full. Yours looks suspiciously empty, and you're years older than them."

Rebecca shrugged her trim shoulders. "I know. But if I should find a man that I would want to marry—which is highly unlikely, considering what I have to choose from—but anyway, if that happens I'll just steal my sisters' hope chests. I'm the eldest; I have the right, don't I?"

Both of her sisters protested loudly and shrilly.

Adah said, "Oh, do be quiet, girls. Can't you tell by now when your sister is teasing you?" Adah was a tiny woman, with red hair and green eyes. Though she was modest and quiet, she was fully capable of taking her children in hand.

Shad watched Rebecca. A mischievous grin played on her wide mouth as her sisters kept complaining to their mother. Rebecca was a self-sufficient, self-contained woman, but with a lively spirit. She had a temperament that could swing from hearty laughter to deep, honest anger. And she had a wry sense of humor that was sometimes embarrassing to her family.

"Don't worry, Judith, Lois. Becky's too picky. Your hope chests are safe." Shad told Rebecca, "You turned down Chris Finebaum, and every girl in the community was after him. Dorcas Chupp stole him from right under your nose."

"He's boring." Rebecca yawned ostentatiously, patting her mouth. "I don't want to spend the rest of my life with a man that can't talk about anything but crops and the weather. I want a man who is entertaining."

"Oh, you want to be entertained? You should marry a juggler like that one that came with the medicine show last year."

"Father is put out with you," Judith said. She had red hair and green eyes, much like her mother. At fourteen she was already a serious young girl who was thinking forward to the time when her courtship would begin. "He says you're frivolous."

"That's right," Lois agreed piously. "Father has always told you to take the young men in the community more seriously, Becky."

"That's the trouble. They are too dead serious, deadly bore serious."

"Shad!" Judith said accusingly. "Tell her!"

"I do try," Shad replied with mock seriousness. "I've tried to teach my sister how to catch a husband. It doesn't take. Now she's twenty-eight years old and has run off three good men that I know of."

"Three." Adah sighed regretfully. "And they were all so fond of you, Rebecca."

"Oh, they managed to get over me soon enough," Becky said cheerfully. "All three of them married only a few months after I ran them off."

"For shame, Becky. Shad has a point and you know it," Judith put in. "A good Amish girl marries early and has children."

Shad shrugged. "You all might as well face up to it. Becky isn't your typical Amish woman."

Lois was still naive in many ways. "Becky, don't you want to find a good man and get married?"

Becky picked up the pillowcase and put in two stitches, apparently thinking over the question. "I haven't so far. Perhaps God will send me a husband. He would have to, to make me want to get married."

"Becky, I just don't understand you," Judith exclaimed. "It seems like you *want* to be an old spinster!"

"Oh, don't worry about me. If all else fails I can always catch me an English." *English* was what the Amish called someone outside of the Amish community. "If that's what happens, just pray he is so weak I can persuade him to join our church." She got up and tossed the pillowcase in the cedar trunk that constituted as her hope chest which, truth to tell, was pitifully empty. "I'm going out to see the new baby goat. If a suitable man comes by, be sure to tell him my demands for a husband. He's got to be able to take orders from his wife; if he's an English, he's got to become Amish; and he's got to be entertaining." She winked at Shad and left the room.

"She'll never get a husband, Mother." Shad sighed. "You and Father will have her on your hands for the rest of your life."

The next day Rebecca decided to take her dog, Hank, into the woods to look for herbs. In spite of the fact that she was not really the ideal Amish woman—she was an indifferent cook, disliked putting up canned goods and preserves, cared little for sewing, and often went barefoot when it was considered scandalous—she was a very good nurse and was good at herbalism.

She had filled her basket and several sacks with black sage, which was good for tea to calm the nerves. She had also found a good bit of burdock that was good for purifying the blood. Some said it was also good for a rattlesnake bite, but Becky didn't hold too much with that and hoped she never had to test it in that way.

She sang softly as she made her way home. The Amish didn't believe in using musical instruments. They thought they were frivolous. But they did sing, and Becky had a good voice. She sang a very old hymn from the traditional Amish hymnal, the *Ausbund*. It dated back to the 1700s, and all of the hymns were in German.

Suddenly Hank ran off barking, which he rarely did, so she became curious. "What have you stirred up, Hank?" She followed him and came to a wide creek that was covered with a log jam— the beginnings of a beaver dam. Hank stood on the bank, barking monotonously, at the beavers, Becky presumed. Looking across the stream, she saw a large growth of redroot, which made an excellent tea that was good for relaxation, tending to sleep. She had discovered that it was also good for excessive menstruation, diarrhea, and dysentery, and the leaves and the tender stems could be eaten raw in salads.

Carefully Becky started across the creek, stepping on one half-submerged log to another. She was a sure-footed woman, but one of the logs suddenly rolled over and threw her off balance and she fell into the creek. The log continued rolling until it came to rest across her thighs. It was heavy, and since the stream was shallow, it was only halfway in the water and there was no chance that it would float off. It seemed securely anchored right across her.

Becky knew she wouldn't drown, but it would be a long time before she was missed. Her family wouldn't know where to look, for she had just told them she was going to look for herbs, not the direction she was going. In fact, she hadn't planned that at all. She had merely wandered along and picked the herbs that she found.

Even though it was August and the heat was oppressive, the stream was cold. She knew that even in the blistering heat of summer a person could get chilled and shocked if they were submerged too long in cold water. She struggled and struggled, but the log didn't move at all.

The minutes passed slowly, and after almost an hour of trying desperately to free herself, her legs ached with the weight of the log, and she knew that she couldn't fight anymore. She was exhausted.

Becky began to pray with all the faith she had.

As the sun fell down into the deep woods to the west, Becky began to shiver, and at the same time she was growing drowsy. She knew this wasn't good, that it was a sign that she was slowly going into shock. She heard Hank, now somewhere in the distance, baying. He had a distinctive call, starting deep in his chest and ending up with a high howl. He bayed on and on, for a long time it seemed to Becky, and then suddenly he stopped.

Wonder what old Hank's doing. . . . He's too lazy to tree a raccoon. Barking at squirrels or something? she thought sleepily.

Then he bounded up, long ears flapping, tongue hanging out the side of his mouth. He splashed right into the water and started licking Becky's face.

She scratched his head, murmuring, "Dumb ol' dog."

"Not so dumb," a deep voice said somewhere behind her. "Came and got me. You've got yourself in a right predicament, haven't you, ma'am?" A man wearing buckskins and riding a bay mare came into her sight at the stream's edge. He dismounted, and she saw he was tall, with a sun-bronzed face and chiseled features.

"Hello," she said lamely. "And yes, I have gotten myself into a predicament. I was going to get"—she motioned weakly toward the other side of the stream—"that redroot. Can you get me out of this?"

He waded out into the stream. "I can. When I lift the log, pull your legs out." He reached around the log that pinned her legs, grunted, and lifted one end.

Becky waited until the pressure eased, then she leaned back and pushed with her hands until her legs came free. When she was clear of the log, he dropped it heavily. Becky sat up and then tried to stand but found that her legs were numb; she could barely move them. So she just sat. "Just give me a minute," she said then shivered.

"Ma'am, you're already freezing. You don't need to sit in this cold water anymore. If you'll allow me. . . ?" He reached out both arms and she nodded with relief, reaching up to him.

He picked her up easily and then carried her to sit her sidesaddle on his horse. "It's so warm today that I didn't carry a coat with me. We need to get you home, ma'am. May I ask your name?" He led the horse through the woods toward the clearing.

"I'm Rebecca Braun," she answered weakly, clutching herself and rubbing her arms, trying to warm up. "H–hello, Mr. Tremayne."

"You know me?" he asked with surprise.

"I remember you. It's been a long time. Let's see. . .I was, I think, eleven years old when you left."

He looked her up and down. Then a light of recognition came into his eyes. "Oh, yes. Becky Braun. Black hair, skinny little girl."

"That was me. Still have the black hair, not so skinny."

"Still pretty hair," Daniel commented.

They came into the sunshine. Immediately Becky felt the welcome warmth of the afternoon August sun. Her cap had disappeared—into the stream, she guessed. Woefully she tried to wring out her long, dripping hair. "Thank you, but I must look like a drowned cat," she muttered.

He looked up at her and grinned crookedly. In the strong light she could clearly see the scar beside the right side of his mouth and the other on his neck. He looked well-worn and tough. "Mmm, you are kinda soggy, ma'am. You getting warmer?"

"Yes, the sun feels so good," she answered, but helplessly she shivered again.

Suddenly he gave a leap and got on the horse behind her. He reached around her and grabbed the reins, and she was very aware of the pressure of his body against hers as he embraced her to try to warm her.

She stiffened and started to protest, but then she reflected that he was the type of man that if he wanted to give her a bear hug, he would just do it. She stayed quiet and relaxed. "Why did you stay away so long, Mr. Tremayne?" she asked curiously.

"Nothing but foolishness."

"I see. My father says you're not a steady man."

"He's right. Or he *was* right. I've decided to become a solid, responsible man."

"Have you?" She turned to face him, and he met her with a steady gaze. "I heard that you have a son. Is your wife with you?"

He answered quietly, "I was married to a woman named Winona. She was half Cheyenne. She died two years ago."

"I'm sorry; that must be very difficult," she said softly. "What's your son's name?"

"Yancy. He's twelve now. So you're married, I suppose?"

Facing away from him, a small smile played on her lips. "Why do you suppose that?"

"It's been a long time, but if I remember right, most Amish girls get married young. Sometimes around fifteen, sixteen."

"And I'm older than that?"

"I think so."

"You think right," she said lightly. "It seems that I have never been able to find the right man for me."

The horse stumbled slightly and his grip tightened around her waist. Becky found herself enjoying it.

"No? Why not?"

"For two very good reasons, Mr. Tremayne. The first is that all of them seemed to be very boring."

Daniel found this amusing, and she felt him laugh slightly. "What's the other reason?" he asked.

"I haven't found a man I would like to share a bed with for the next fifty years."

Daniel did laugh aloud then. "Well, that's speaking right out! I like a woman that says what she means. What would you say if I asked to call on you?"

Becky twisted around to face him again to see if he was still laughing, but now he was serious. "I don't know. I don't know you well enough."

"Thought that was the point," Daniel said lightly. "How are you going to get to know how wonderful I am if you don't let me call on you?"

"I'll say one thing. . .you aren't boring, Mr. Tremayne," Becky said. "All right. You can come sit on the porch, and my whole family will sit with us, and they will watch every move you make and listen to every word you say. I'm sure you remember how the courting goes around here."

"I do, I'm sorry to say. But what about the other thing—the bed thing?"

She answered primly, "We'll have to see about that."

"Yes, ma'am, we sure will," he agreed heartily.

Rebecca couldn't remember being more fascinated with a man like she was with Daniel Tremayne. There was a rough handsomeness about him and a strength that she recognized instantly. She also liked him for his plain speaking.

Finally they came up to her house. Daniel dismounted and then helped Becky down.

Simon Braun came out and exclaimed, "What in the world happened, daughter?"

"I fell in the creek, Father, and got trapped under a log. Mr. Tremayne heard Hank barking and came and got me out."

Simon stared at Daniel then said, "It's been a long time, Daniel. I remember you when you were just a boy."

"Yes, sir, I remember you and Mrs. Braun, too. She always had sugar cookies for us when we came to visit with Shadrach. And speaking of him—hello, Shad." The rest of the family had come outside. Daniel shook hands with Shadrach.

He said, "It's been a while, Daniel. We were glad to hear that you're back. And what's this? You had to rescue my sister from some scrape she'd gotten herself into?" He rolled his eyes at the sight of Becky.

Rebecca was in no hurry to go inside. She stood there, dripping and bedraggled, listening with interest to the men's conversation. Her mother had hurried back in to fetch her a towel, and slowly Rebecca folded her long hair into it and dabbed it.

"I'm real glad to be back, too," Daniel answered. "Especially just in time to rescue Miss Braun." He spoke to the entire family. "I want you all to know that I'm so grateful to you for helping my mother with the farm after my father died. Thank you, all of you. And I want you to know that I'm going to stay, and I'm going to take care of her and the farm now. I'm trying very hard to become a good, steady man."

"I told Mr. Tremayne that you wanted to find a steady man for me as a husband, Father, and he's assured me that he is now," Becky said lightly. "So I invited him to come sit on the porch and court me." She enjoyed the look of shock that came across her parents' and her sisters' faces. She saw that Shad was amused.

"So she has," Daniel agreed with equanimity. "But I know it'll take time for me to prove myself, both to you and to Miss Tremayne. I understand she has some high standards where a husband is concerned."

For a moment Rebecca was afraid he would mention her comment about sharing a bed with a man for fifty years. She was vastly relieved when he gave her a surreptitious wink and said no more about it.

Simon looked bemused. "Well—I suppose—if Becky wants to see you, then you're welcome, Daniel."

"Good. Thank you, sir. I'll be back. Probably before you really want me to." He mounted, nodded to the ladies, slapped his hat securely back on his head, then turned and dashed off.

"Well, I do declare," Adah breathed. "He's a man that knows what he wants, isn't he? Rebecca, have you been very forward?"

"No, ma'am," Becky replied, her eyes dancing. "He's the one who's forward."

"Better get used to his ways, Mother," Shad said, grinning. "Looks to me like he's hoping to be your son-in-law."

CHAPTER FOUR

August in the valley was hot, but it was nothing like the Oklahoma plains, Yancy reflected. Even though they had lived by a lake, surrounded by thick woods and rich grasses and herbs, it had still been scorching, dusty, and bone-dry from April to September. Yancy liked the Shenandoah Valley. Even on the hottest days it was cool in the deep shades of the woods and on the large veranda of the farmhouse, where he sat now, yawning in the first gentle light of dawn.

Zemira was cooking breakfast, but the kitchen and dining room did get steamy in the summertime, so Yancy's grandfather had built an oak table and chairs so they could have meals outside in the fresh breezes.

Although Yancy did like the valley, there wasn't much more about living here that he cared for. In the year since he and Daniel had returned, he had adjusted to farm life. He didn't mind the hard work, for he wasn't lazy; and in some ways he had come to appreciate the verdant fields, the rich harvests, the satisfaction of making something out of one's own land. But the Amish were very strict in all things, and sometimes he felt as if he were suffocating.

He was thirteen years old—he had longings and desires for things he could barely name, and not all of them had to do with his newfound appreciation for girls. Sometimes he wished he could just be free again, not under scrutiny by an entire community, not have to go to Amish school, able to do what he wanted when he wanted. . .much like when they had lived with the Cheyenne.

Zemira came out onto the porch carrying a tray. It had a tin coffeepot, steaming, and cups and saucers and sugar and fresh cream on it. There was a basket, too, covered with a linen cloth. She set it on the table by Yancy and then put her hands on her hips. "Don't eat it all."

Yancy sniffed then grinned. "Friendship Bread." He lifted one corner of the cloth on the basket.

She slapped his hand lightly and then put her hands back on her hips. "Don't eat it all," she repeated sternly. "You'll ruin your breakfast that's good for you. It'll be ready in a minute or two, and when I come back with it, there had better be plenty of that bread left for me and your father."

Amish Friendship Bread was a rich bread that required a complicated starter, and then took ten days to make. It had milk, flour, sugar, heavy double cream, vanilla, cinammon, and nuts. The reason it was called Friendship Bread was because it was traditional, when one presented it as a gift to good friends, to include the starter along with a loaf of the bread.

She bustled back into the house. Yancy fixed himself a cup of coffee, very sweet with lots of cream, and ate two generous pieces of the mouthwatering bread. He sipped his coffee; then, with a guilty look around, he crammed another piece into his mouth, chewing quickly. Then he tried to rearrange the bread so it looked like it was piled up higher than after his raid. He was, after all, only thirteen.

Zemira returned with a very large tray that held plates, silverware, napkins, and four covered bowls with scrambled eggs, bacon, grits, and biscuits. She set three places then sat down with Yancy. "We'll go ahead and bless," she said. "Your father's milking, and I'm not sure when he'll be here." They both bowed their heads in silence. The Amish did not believe in praying aloud; they thought that it could induce pride.

Yancy watched her out of the corner of his eye until she raised her head. The first thing she did was look at the Friendship Bread.

"You ate three pieces," she said accusingly. "The biggest ones."

"I can't help it, Grandmother. I love it more than anything," he said lightly, helping himself to large portions of all the breakfast dishes.

"Humph. Only Friendship Bread you've ever had, I guess."

"Still the best."

She shrugged a little. "I can see it hasn't ruined your appetite," she said begrudgingly. Although she grumbled at Yancy, she kept a batch of Friendship Bread, in different stages, going all the time now, so he wouldn't run out.

They ate in companionable silence for a while. Yancy was very comfortable with his grandmother; he liked her a lot and was still forming a growing attachment to her. They had lived with her for about a year, but Yancy's affections weren't easily given. This was a part of his mother's Cheyenne blood. The Cheyenne were extremely loyal to family but rarely formed affectionate attachments outside it. Zemira was his grandmother, but he was just now learning to love her.

She was watching him shrewdly as these thoughts flitted through his mind. Then she asked, "Yancy, are you very unhappy here?"

Carefully, slowly, he buttered a biscuit, his eyes downcast. He took a deliberate bite and chewed. Then he answered, "It's hard for me, Grandmother. It's so different, and a lot of times I just don't understand what the People are doing. I mean, what's the matter with buttons, for goodness' sake? And what's the matter with having a blue buggy, with blue cushions, instead of all black? And so what if my moccasins are beaded?"

"Yancy, I know you've been told that the Amish truly believe in simple living, plain dress, and keeping to the old ways," Zemira answered. "Those things separate us from the world, from the evils of the world. It helps to keep us pure in the eyes of the Lord."

"My mother made my moccasins," he said stubbornly. "There was nothing wrong with my mother. She wasn't evil. And neither am I."

Zemira sighed. "I hate to tell you this, Yancy, but you must understand—we all have the seed of sin in us. All of us. And that's why we need Jesus to save us from this evil that is born in us, that we have inherited from Adam and Eve, when sin first entered this world. And that is why we try to keep ourselves pure in these ways, to combat that evil that is in all of us."

Yancy answered steadily, "I know, I know, I've heard all that in church, Grandmother. It's just that I can't see that for me to wear a shirt with buttons and moccasins with beads makes me evil."

Zemira took a sip of coffee, eyeing him over the rim with her sharp blue eyes. "Is that why you're unhappy here, Yancy? Because you know, we've been very lenient. We've let you wear the clothes you want, let you hunt with your gun, though it's against our beliefs. We let you do whatever you want instead of doing chores, even let you skip the sing. I don't understand that; most young people look forward to that time of being together."

Yancy snorted. "Skip the sing? Singing in German, which I don't speak, with no instruments? Sitting across the tables from the girls and taking turns singing—which, again, I can't do—and then barely talking to a girl before her father and brothers swoop in like bobcats and hustle her off like I'm a criminal or something? Can't imagine why I'd miss all that."

"It is very different from the life you've known, Yancy, but it's a good life. It's a clean, orderly, rewarding life."

He shook his head. "Good life for some, I guess, but I don't think it's for me."

"Your father thought that, too, when he was your age, and was on *rumspringa*. He left because he thought this life wasn't for him. But he came back to us."

"I know, Grandmother. And I know he's happy now." Yancy played with some leftover eggs on his mostly empty plate then asked moodily, "So what did you mean? What's rumspringa?"

Zemira hesitated for a few moments, staring into her coffee cup. "We've debated about telling you this, because your father thought it might just—confuse you. But you're a smart young man, Yancy, and old for your years, so I think you should know." She lifted her head and continued. "The Amish realize that young people must have some leniency, some. . .leeway. And so we give them a time, called rumspringa, which means 'running around.'

The church rules are relaxed, and it's understood that in these times there will be a certain amount of misbehavior. It's neither condoned nor overlooked, but it's understood at the end of this period, the young person will be baptized into the church, will marry, and will settle down in the community."

"So this is letting me run around?" Yancy asked with astonishment. "This is running wild? Seems to me like I'm watched like I'm a prisoner most of the time."

"We let you wear your own clothes, which violates the Ordnung," Zemira answered gently. "And as I said, we pretty much let you decide what you're going to do every day. We don't hold you to chores, and we let you ride around all day without questioning you if you wish to. In other words, we're letting you make your own decisions."

Yancy stared at her. "What if I decide to leave? To go back to the Cheyenne?"

"Would you do that? Leave your family?"

He dropped his gaze. "No, ma'am. I don't want to leave Father. . . or you. You're the only reason I haven't gone stark raving crazy."

She reached over and patted his hand. "I love you very much, Yancy, and you can't know how glad I am that you and your father are here. I've been very lonely since your grandfather died. To have family again is precious to me."

He kept his head low, his gaze averted, and Zemira could sense his discomfort. She withdrew her hand then asked lightly, "Has your father told you about our family? The Tremaynes?"

"Not much. He—I think he feels bad about leaving, about Grandfather and all."

"So he does. But he's making up for it now, and your grandfather loved him always. Anyway, his great-grandfather Tremayne, and my great-grandfather Fisher, along with the other families, came to the valley in the 1730s. They found a good land, a fruitful land, and established our community. All of the families here can trace their land back to that time. When they started, there were only eight families. Now there are twenty-two, and we're still growing. It was a good thing, to find this place," she said dreamily. "It's been a good home."

"It is a good home," Yancy agreed quietly. "I do like the valley, very much."

She smiled warmly at him. "When our great-grandfathers came here, there were several tribes of Indians. Mostly Kiowa, but also Iroquois, Shawnee, and Algonquin. And our great-grandfathers made fast friends with them. We traded with them, we sometimes cared for their sick, we attended their funerals, and we even broke bread with them. But then when the English—the *Long Knives*, the Kiowas called them—began to come into the valley in greater numbers, the Indians slowly left, going west. And our forefathers regretted it. They felt that they had lost people that belonged in the valley, even though they regarded them as heathens. You see, Yancy, the Amish never judge others who are not of the People. We believe we should always show them God's love. So whatever you do, Yancy, we will love you. Always."

Yancy climbed up on the buggy, sitting beside Daniel on the driver's bench.

Zemira sat on one of the benches in the back.

"Can I drive, Father?"

"Sure, Yancy. You're a good hand with a buggy, just like you are at riding."

"We're going to the Keims' house, is that right?"

"That's right. That's where church this Sunday will be."

The Amish had church services every other Sunday. Each Sunday, services were at a different home in the community, for the Amish didn't believe in building church buildings. They took this from the verse Acts 17:24, "God that made the world and all things therein, seeing that he is Lord of heaven and earth, dwelleth not in temples made with hands."

Each congregation of the church owned community property in the form of tables, chairs, benches, and wagons to transport them from farm to farm as the services were held in each home. The men from the congregation moved them every other Sunday for services.

Yancy spoke to the mare, and she started out with a sassy little toss of her head. He liked the look of her and the way she high-stepped. She had spirit, so he had to keep her on a tight rein, but for Yancy that only made the driving better. He had no use for a plodding, slow-moving horse and kept the mare at a fast trot.

"Good mare," Daniel commented. "Now who is she?"

Yancy took care of the farm horses. "This is Fancy," Yancy answered. "I named her that 'cause there's nothing else around here that is," he added mischievously. "She's the one that has that fine little foal, Midnight. He's young, but I've already started training him. Grandmother says he's a showy horse, too showy for the Amish."

"Guess that's true," Daniel agreed. "The Amish have a simple life."

Yancy shook his head. "Their church services sure aren't. First a short sermon, then singing, then prayers, then a long sermon, then a longer sermon, then more singing, then the longest sermon. Last week over at the Beilers' house it lasted for over four hours. How are you supposed to stay awake for all that?"

Daniel said regretfully, "I had the same problem, son, when I was your age. Guess the sermons do get a little long-winded, and those benches are downright uncomfortable. The Methodists have seats with backs on them instead of those backless ones that the People like. For the life of me, I can't see that a comfortable seat would be a sin."

"I was just saying stuff like that to Grandmother, Father," Yancy said soberly. "Like, why can't I wear my own clothes to church? I hate these stupid breeches. They're itchy and too short. And these shoes are like wood blocks on your feet. They hurt."

"It's a matter of respect, Yancy. The Amish wear simple clothes. You notice all the men dress alike, and so do the women, pretty much. And we let you wear your clothes all the time, except for church."

After a rather awkward silence, Yancy said, "Yeah, I know. Grandmother told me about rumspringa today. You're letting me off easy for now."

Daniel studied his son's face. In profile, he strongly showed his mother's heritage. He had a thin nose, very high cheekbones, the slight copper tint of the Cheyenne. His eyes were dark and penetrating. Even at thirteen, he was beginning to lose his childish awkwardness and fill out, lean and muscled. His hair was glossy black, and he wore it longer than the Amish, with the back brushing his collar and a lock that fell over his forehead. Sometimes Daniel thought that the only thing Yancy had inherited from him was the cleft in his chin. "You're so much like your mother. . ." he murmured absently. Then he roused and said, "Rumspringa, yes. But it's not just me and your grandmother, Yancy. It's the bishop, the deacon, the secretary, and the preachers. They all watch out for the young people in the community."

A redtail hawk suddenly crossed the road in front of them. Yancy watched it longingly until it disappeared. "Sometimes I wish I was a hawk. They don't have bishops watching them and don't have to go to sings and wear hard shoes that hurt their feet."

Daniel grinned and slapped Yancy on the shoulder. "Even hawks have their hard times, too."

"Guess so. Good hunters though."

"Yes, they are, but living by hunting is hard, Yancy. You and I both know that."

Yancy was silent.

Daniel hesitated then said in a light tone, trying not to sound dictatorial, "I know it's hard, Yancy, but I'd like for you to try to be more friendly. There are some good young people here."

Yancy protested, "But all the girls think about is courting and getting ready to marry. Who wants to think about getting married when they're thirteen?"

"Girls do," Daniel said drily. "But you don't have to think about that right now. And the other young men are interested in the same things you are—fishing, riding, even racing."

"But no gambling," he said disdainfully. "I know the other fellows like to fish, and they're interested in horses. It's just that I'm used to doing all those things alone." It was the Cheyenne way.

Daniel decided to say no more. Actually, he was proud of the way that Yancy had surrendered such a free life for one of close confinement. Yancy hadn't complained much. In fact, he said very little at all about their circumstances. He kept to himself. Daniel didn't realize that that was something else Yancy had inherited from him.

So it was something of a surprise when Yancy asked carelessly, "So, Father, are you going to marry that lady?"

Daniel replied steadily, "You know her name. It's Becky, and yes, I am."

"You've been sitting on the Brauns' porch for a year now, sipping lemonade and all of them watching you like that redtail hawk we just saw looking for a mouse. When are you going to ask her?"

"I had to take the time, son, to make the Brauns see that I'm a dependable man now, that I've settled down, and that I'll be a good husband," Daniel explained patiently. "When I feel the time is right, I'll ask her. So how do you feel about it?"

Yancy shrugged. "Okay, I guess. She's pretty nice. But she's not my mother."

"No, she's not," Daniel said quietly. "But she would be a good mother. I know she would."

～

Yancy drew the mare to a halt by the corral.

The lot before the barn was already crowded with buggies, and two men were working, unhitching the horses and turning them into the corral. Sunday services and dinner was an all-day thing.

Yancy helped his grandmother down and she immediately went to a group of women who were standing by the house, in the shade of great oak trees. Daniel and Yancy started unhitching Fancy from the buggy, who pranced and snorted as if to say, *I could go another twenty miles if I had to!* Yancy loved her, for she was also a good saddle horse.

A young boy Yancy knew came running up. "Hey, Yancy! Why weren't you at the sing last Sunday? So when are we going fishing? You promised to take me." The boy was Seth Glick, and he was twelve years old.

Seth had met Yancy at the Amish school, which was a one-room schoolhouse with children from six years old to fourteen, the age limit of Amish education. Seth tagged along after Yancy every chance he got.

Yancy shrugged. "Hi, Seth. Whenever we can get together. Not sure."

"That's what you said before," he said. "You promised, Yancy."

"I know, I know. We will. . .sometime."

The boy, his shoulders rounded and head drooping, went toward the barn. In the smaller houses the young boys often sat in the barn for services, and one of the preachers would go out there for the service. Yancy had sat in the barn once, but Daniel had found out that he had sneaked out, stolen Fancy, and gone riding. Since then Daniel made him sit in the house with him and the other men. The women were separated from the men, often in different rooms.

As they finished leading Fancy into the enclosure, Daniel said, "You ought to take the boy fishing, Yancy."

"He doesn't know the first thing about fishing. He talks too loud and too much. He'd scare away every fish in the stream."

"Then it'd be a chance for you to help him. You could teach him. He's looking for a friend, Yancy."

Yancy looked surprised. "I never thought of that."

Daniel clapped Yancy on the back. "Friends are good things to have. Everyone needs them, even you. Make some friends. You'll be happier here."

The congregation, which was about a hundred people including the children, moved toward the house. Many people spoke to Daniel. In the last year, he had established himself as a good man, a good neighbor, and a fine, upstanding member of the community.

Yancy usually spoke back to those who greeted him, but quietly and with few words.

Yancy was thinking about his clothing—mostly about his shoes that hurt his feet and wishing for his soft moccasins.

Carelessly his eyes roamed over the congregation. All the women, even the pretty young girls, looked alike in their dowdy clothing. He had learned that the manner of dress was set out by the Ordnung, which to Yancy was simply a list of too-strict rules that everyone in the local Amish community had to obey.

The men also wore identical clothing, almost like uniforms, which consisted of a long black collarless frock coat with no lapels and split tails, with hook-and-eye closings. All wore vests fastened with hooks and eyes. They wore trousers with no flies and wide front flaps that fastened along the side. In the winter, the men and boys wore wide-brimmed felt hats, but it was close enough to summer that most of the hats were straw.

Yancy had discovered the width of an Amish hat brim meant something. The broader the brim, the more conservative the wearer and the less willing he would be to change. Those who were more liberal and had wilder spirits trimmed their hats to make them at least a *little* different. But no matter what, they all had to conform to the Ordnung.

On Sundays, Yancy, too, conformed. He wore black homespun pants, a linsey-woolsey shirt with no buttons, and the hated heavy black shoes. He had, however, flatly refused to wear a straw hat. "They're girlie hats," he had complained.

"I wear one," Daniel had said mildly.

"And you look girlie," Yancy had retorted. "I'm not wearing one. I'll wear my old slouch hat. That covers my head good enough."

The men's congregation had been set up in the Keims' large parlor. The furniture had been removed, and backless benches had been brought in. The women were in the connecting dining room, with the young women. The young men were in the barn. The smallest children were with their mothers, but during the service they often wandered over to their fathers. As long as they were not disruptive, they were allowed to go back and forth as they would, since the service was so long and it was understood that small children grew restless.

As did Yancy. He studied the congregation with little interest or excitement. It was the same group that he had been meeting with for almost a year now. He knew their names but hadn't grown close to any of them.

The service began as usual with a relatively short sermon by one of the preachers. It was followed by scripture reading and silent prayer. Other preachers went to the barn. Following this came a longer sermon by the bishop. The service always included hymns, without any musical instruments. Even harmony was not permitted.

CROSSING

Yancy sat silently as the sermon moved along tediously, struggling to keep from dozing off.

Finally the service ended. The men worked to put the benches and tables outside and to move the Keims' furniture back in. The women went to the kitchen and then outside to set the tables for Sunday dinner, as was customary. Hosting a Sunday service was demanding, but everyone in the congregation brought food, and they always made sure that any cleaning after services and dinner was done.

This was the one good thing about the services to Yancy— plenty of good food. Fried chicken, roast beef, all sorts of vegetables and casseroles, pies and cakes—all in plenty, enough to satisfy even ravenous teenagers. The men were all seated and the women began to serve them, replenishing their bread baskets; and the butter, tea, and lemonade cooled in the stream.

A young woman, Hannah Lapp, refilled Yancy's lemonade. She was thirteen and was in school with him. She was a pretty girl with sandy brown hair, dark brown eyes with perfect winging brows, and a beautiful complexion. She was a little shy, but she and Yancy had talked some, during lunches and recess. She tended to hover close by him at Sunday dinners. "Are you coming to the sing next Sunday, Yancy?" she asked softly.

"Hope not," he answered shortly.

"You should come. There'll be lots of games and good things to eat."

Yancy shrugged. "That doesn't make up for having to sit through a sing—when you can't sing and you don't even know what you're supposed to be singing."

"I could teach you some of them," Hannah said. "Not all of them are long and hard German words."

"If I cared," Yancy said harshly. "Which I don't."

Rebecca Braun was across from Yancy, serving up fresh bread. She gave him a stern look, but he ducked his head and ate steadily.

"Oh—I—of course not," Hannah said lamely. "I'm—sorry." Quickly she moved along to the next man, to refill his glass.

After the meal, when everyone was meeting and talking in companionable groups, Becky came to sit beside Yancy, as he was still sitting on the bench at the table by himself.

"You weren't very nice to Hannah, Yancy," she said quietly. "I thought you were more of a gentleman."

"Guess not," Yancy muttered. "But I don't see how it's any of your concern, ma'am."

"I think it is my business, Yancy, because I'm going to marry your father. I know I won't be like your mother. But I would like to look at you as my son. And so I would like to know that my son is a kind man, a man that I can be proud of."

Yancy stiffened. "You're right—you're not my mother. You'll never be my mother. And besides, my father hasn't asked you to marry him yet."

"No, he hasn't, but that's because of me. I wanted to wait until I could be sure that he was the kind of man I wanted to marry. A good man, an honorable man that could make a good home for me."

"And?" Yancy demanded.

"And he's that man," Becky said simply. "But there's something else I've been watching and waiting for."

"What's that?"

"I wanted to see if you would be a good older brother to my children."

This amused Yancy so much that despite himself, he smiled. This woman was the one person he saw of the Amish, besides his grandmother, who was different from the others. Becky Braun and Zemira Tremayne always spoke their minds directly, without hesitation or decoration. "So, do you think I'll be good with your children?"

"No. Not right now, I don't."

Her abruptness startled Yancy. "Why wouldn't I be a good brother? Is it because I'm part Indian?"

"No, that's not it."

"What is it then?"

"You haven't learned how to be kind." Becky paused and her eyes were fixed on Yancy with such an intensity that he couldn't turn his gaze away from hers. She had a way of drawing people's attention and keeping them fixed when she spoke. "You were short with Hannah, without need. You should be gentler with people, Yancy."

Yancy was irritated. "I guess you better not marry my father then, if I'm not what you want in a son."

"I know you could be." Becky smiled suddenly, reached out, and pushed a lock of Yancy's coal black hair from his forehead, where it had fallen. "I know you will be. I don't need to wait any longer. So come with me."

"Where are we going?"

"Just come with me and don't ask questions." Becky led Yancy through the crowd to the end of one of the tables, where Daniel sat with Becky's family. They all looked up as they approached, and Daniel got to his feet. "Hello, Becky. I see you've corralled my son. Won't you sit down?"

Becky stopped directly in front of Daniel and looked up at him. "Not just now, Mr. Tremayne. I need to know. . .do you still want to marry me?"

A silence fell over the group, and Yancy saw that his father was taken totally off guard. Astonishment marked Daniel's face and then he turned red. But he answered solidly, "I do want to marry you, Rebecca Braun."

"All right." Becky smiled. "We're engaged then, but I don't want to wait a year." A year was the common period most young couples waited before marriage. Now Becky turned to her father and said firmly, "Father, I know it's not the Amish way, but Daniel and I are older. He's proved himself to be a good man. We'd like your permission to get married in one month."

Simon Braun wasn't a man who was easily shocked, as he'd grown accustomed to Becky's "wild ways" as he called them. He frowned and said, "Daughter, I know when you've made up your mind, a whole string of plow mules couldn't drag you from it. But would you do me a favor, here and now? You know that we don't condone marriage except for November and December, because of the harvest. Won't you at least wait until then?"

Becky said stubbornly, "No, Father—"

Daniel took her hand, tucked it into his arm, and said, "Yes, Mr. Braun, we'll be glad to wait until harvest is over. November will be fine."

"But—" Becky began, looking up at him beseechingly.

Daniel put one finger on her lips. "Shush, bride. Let me win this one."

She took a deep breath then laughed. She had a good laugh, a rich laugh. "All right, groom. But you'd better count this one dear. You won't win many."

"You sure won't, Mr. Tremayne," Simon Braun said, sighing and shaking his hand. "You surely won't."

CHAPTER FIVE

July 1857 was a bountiful harvest, almost more than anyone could ask for. The Tremayne fields of hay, wheat, and corn were bursting. The pantry and the root cellar were overrun from the kitchen garden with peas, squash, tomatoes, carrots, and potatoes. Other women from the community came on Saturdays to help Becky and Zemira can them, as Becky and Zemira also went to their farms to help them with the riches of their lands.

Becky and Zemira sat on the veranda, sipping lemonade and shelling peas. The front veranda faced east, and often they could see the Blue Ridge Mountains, mostly just a grayish smoke on the horizon, but sometimes they could make out the dreamy peaks.

"I've never been there," Zemira murmured. "Jacob and I thought that we might go to the mountains once. But somehow home never let us go."

"Home is good," Becky said quietly. "Sometimes it's better just to stay close. At least, that's how I feel now. I couldn't ask for any other happiness."

Zemira glanced at her sharply. "Becky, daughter, are you with child?"

Becky's finely etched black eyebrows arched in surprise. "I—I think so. But it's so early, I haven't even told Daniel. How did you know, Grandmother?"

Zemira smiled. "I think the Lord tells me things. It's not like I hear His voice; it's just a *knowing*. So how far along are you?"

"I've been telling myself not to hope too much," Becky answered. "It would just be a couple of weeks. But like you, Grandmother, I feel like I just. . .*know*."

"Women do." Zemira nodded. "Women generally do."

They shelled peas in silence for a while, their nimble fingers stripping the tough, stringy stems and separating them into bite-sized chunks.

"You and Daniel have been worried, haven't you?" Zemira asked softly.

Becky didn't answer; she ducked her head and shelled peas energetically.

"It's all right," Zemira continued. "I know you've wondered, though Daniel wouldn't say anything. You've been married eight months now, and I know it makes you anxious to wait. Jacob and I were married for almost forty years and had only one son. And Daniel didn't come along until we'd been married for fourteen years. I know you and he have thought about that." Zemira sighed deeply. She wouldn't tell of the two stillborn sisters Daniel had, one in 1818 and one in 1820. Daniel hadn't been born until 1823.

"It's—it's not just you, Grandmother," Becky said hesitantly. "It's my family, too. I mean, I was born, but then it was eight years until Shadrach was born, and then another six until Judith, and a year later Lois. Daniel and I—it's just that we both want children so badly, and we both want four, maybe five. I don't know if I'll— that is, if time—if we can—"

Zemira dropped her hands and gazed at her daughter-in-law sternly. "Child, you talk foolishness. My son has become a good man, a fine man, constant in the Lord and walking in His will. You are a good and faithful Christian woman. God will bless you. I've no doubt in my mind."

Becky ducked her head. "Yes. Yes, you're right, Grandmother, as always. I'm very proud of Daniel, and I'm so blessed to have him for a husband."

Zemira nodded emphatically. "I'm so proud of him, too. He's a good son, and a good husband, and a good father." She bent to her work again. "But he did have his wanderings. And I think that Yancy may, too. You wouldn't know it from the way Daniel is now, but Yancy is so much like him, when Daniel was in rumspringa."

"You see that in Yancy? That same rebelliousness?"

Zemira glanced at her. "Has Daniel ever told you about his time then? When he left home?"

"No, he hasn't, and I haven't wanted to intrude on him to ask. Whatever happened then, he's a different man now."

"That's the truth, daughter," Zemira agreed. "And I have to say that Yancy is much better behaved than Daniel was then. Maybe it's just a young man's restlessness. He does get into scuffles with the young men, and the girls say he's very forward with them."

Becky laughed. "The young men that he's bested say that, and I think the young girls that complain about him are the ones that don't get his attention. He's a very good-looking young man, you know, and he is strong and quick and probably very desirable to young women."

"I suppose so," Zemira said grumpily, "but the bishop is out here every week, it seems, complaining about another one of his scrapes. It's getting harder to find excuses for him."

Becky answered, "But you do find excuses for him, as I do. All we can do is pray, Grandmother. Pray that he stays with us and finds God. Until then, we must find more excuses."

It was a fruitful year and a bountiful harvest. Even the winter seemed benevolent. They had picturesque snows for Thanksgiving and Christmas and bright, brisk days for the New Year.

Becky and Zemira had been right. Becky was expecting, and though it was an easy winter in the valley, it was hard for her and Daniel. She was due in April and it seemed as if the baby— and the spring—would never come.

But the times of the seasons always come, and the spring of 1858 was glorious. The long days were delightfully warm and the nights refreshingly cool. Rain came just as and when it should. Even

Yancy didn't mind working the fields; the days were so pleasant and the planting was easy.

Early in the evening of April 16, the family was gathered in the parlor. A small, comfortable fire crackled, and the last sweet rays of the sun shone strong through the large windows. Daniel and Yancy were playing checkers while Zemira and Becky quilted.

Becky had never before been a very good seamstress, but Zemira was very skilled. Once Becky had applied herself to quilting under Zemira's expert teaching, she had come to enjoy it.

Leaning back, she rubbed her eyes then sat motionless for a few moments, her eyes closed.

Zemira eyed her shrewdly. Once, when Zemira was young, she had been the best midwife in the community. But after her second stillborn daughter, she had refused to ever consider it again. Still, the founts of knowledge of men and women run deep and are hard to ignore.

Rebecca lifted her head with a small smile. "Daniel?"

"Yes, dearest?"

"I think it's time for you to go fetch Esther Raber."

Daniel jumped up, knocking the straight chair he was sitting in halfway across the room.

This made Yancy jump up in alarm, and his chair fell over.

"Stop!" Becky said, holding up one hand and laughing. "It's no emergency, you know. This little one has taken a sweet time coming, and for all we know it may be tomorrow or the next day before he or she decides to put in an appearance. It's fine, Daniel."

Zemira pursed her lips. "It's a girl, Daniel. And I do think you might step lively to get Mrs. Raber."

Daniel turned and bolted from the room, followed by Yancy.

"Just—wait! Don't kill your silly selves!" Becky called after them. "Grandmother, why did you scare them like that? How do you know?"

"Normally I don't say much about what's between a mother and her child and God. But you're precious to me, daughter, and I have to say that I think this little girl is going to be born before midnight, even though I see you're in real early light pains. Anyway, why don't we go on upstairs and get you fixed up in bed? And I'll have

everything ready by the time Esther gets here. All I can say is"—
she grunted a little, helping Becky rise from the straight-backed
bench—"that I hope that silly, loud, little Leah Raber doesn't insist
on following Yancy over here. I declare right here and now, I think
she'd kidnap him and hold him prisoner if she thought it would
make him marry her."

"Can't blame her," Becky said, smiling. "He is a handsome
young man."

"Doesn't excuse her. She's like a little gnat, always buzzing
around him. So, daughter, what are you going to name her?"

"I'm going to be cautious and wait until we see what it is,
Grandmother, even though I have faith in you. And anyway, I
think I will let Daniel make the final decision when he sees her."

"Her?" Zemira repeated mischievously as they struggled up the
stairs.

"Or him," Becky added quickly then bent over with a sudden
sharp pain. "All right, all right, her," she whispered. Looking up at
Zemira, she grinned. "Guess she's going to take after me."

It took about an hour for Daniel and Yancy to bring Esther back
to the farm, and by that time Rebecca was already in hard labor,
though it was perfectly natural and normal. After an examination,
Esther, a kind, gentle woman with warm, dark eyes, came out into
the hallway and said, "It looks like we're going to have a baby soon,
Daniel. Please go downstairs. . .and don't worry. Both Becky and
the baby look very, very good."

"But how do you know? What do you mean? What—?"

Esther was kind, but she could be firm when she had to be,
particularly with wayward daughters like Leah and distraught
fathers-to-be like Daniel. "You must trust me," she said firmly. "I
know, and certainly Zemira knows. She was the best midwife in
the community."

"Huh?" Daniel said, bewildered.

"Never mind. Just go downstairs, stay calm, and wait."

Yancy and his father went downstairs and waited, but they
certainly were not calm. They paced in the parlor, they paced in the

dining room, and finally they went out and paced on the veranda. The night was beautiful, with a full silver moon and a spangling of stars spanning the sky. They didn't notice. The only thing they noticed was when they accidentally ran into each other, and then they muttered distractedly, "Uh, sorry." They even ran into poor Hank a couple of times, who was sitting at the top of the steps, watching them blundering around with worried eyes.

In the still night, they heard a baby's cry. It was eleven minutes to eleven.

Esther's step sounded on the stairs, and they rushed into the house like mad bulls.

"Come on up," she said, smiling widely. "They're fine."

They ran up the stairs and then, slowing down and almost tiptoeing, they went into the bedroom.

Rebecca sat up in bed. She looked tired, and her hair was dripping with sweat, but she smiled. "Look, Daniel! Just look! Isn't she beautiful?"

"She. . .she? It's a girl?" Daniel murmured, standing by the bed. "Thank the Lord! She's—all right?" he asked Esther anxiously.

Zemira soundlessly came up to stand beside him. She beamed down at the baby. "She's perfect, just perfect. She reminds me of—of—" She choked slightly, then finished in a low voice, "Of you, of course, Daniel. Of you."

The baby was awake and seemed to stare right up at her father. She had reddish blond hair and light blue eyes, just like Daniel. Most babies just look like babies, but Yancy thought that she did indeed resemble Father.

Becky held her up for Daniel to hold. He took her as if she were the most precious thing in the world. "A little girl. . .a girl. . . Oh, thank you, wife."

"Thank you, husband. So what shall we call her?"

"Well, we did talk about that. I know it's kind of a mouthful, but I still like it. Callie Josephine? Callie after my grandmother and Josephine after your grandfather Joseph?"

"Callie Josephine it is," Becky said, settling wearily back into her pillows. "What do you think about your new sister, Yancy?"

It gave Yancy a warm feeling for Becky to call the baby his

sister instead of his half sister. Over the last two years he had come to love Becky, though he could never call her Mother. But this did give him a tie to the baby, for them to name her after his great-grandmother Callie. Grandmother had told him a lot about her mother. She had been a strong, loving woman.

Yancy answered, "Well, she's—uh, little. And she's all red. But she's got pretty-colored hair, like Father's."

Becky laughed. "The red will go away, and she'll have a beautiful complexion, just like her grandmother Zemira. And yes. . ." she finished softly, "she is very much like her father."

Part Two: The Prelude 1858

CHAPTER SIX

Three cadets scurried across the compound, headed for the classroom building. They were fifteen minutes late. They were students of Virginia Military Academy, better known as VMI. This institution was joined to Washington College in the small Virginia town of Lexington.

Sandy Owens, a tall, lanky boy of fifteen with hazel eyes and the sandy reddish hair that his nickname would indicate, led the three. Behind him was Charles Satterfield, a short, stocky fifteen-year-old with jet black hair and warm, brown eyes. Peyton Stevens, the third member of the group, was a handsome blond boy with china blue eyes and the look of aristocracy about him. He was sixteen but could have passed for eighteen. He wasn't as flustered as the other two boys, knowing he wouldn't be in a great deal of trouble since his father was a senator and had gotten him out of every trouble he had managed to get into.

Their awkward hurry was jarring with their splendid appearance. They wore the distinguished uniforms of the Virginia Military Institute, and with that uniform went the unbreakable rule that they be spotless and without fault. The cadets wore the gray tunic with tails. Finely embroidered "frogs"—so named for the three-lobed fleurs-de-lis—adorned the collar and the face of the tunics. At each frog was a button, a silver image of the seal of the state of Virginia. Their breeches were spotless white, and if they were not spotless, the cadet was immediately sent to the barracks to don acceptable pants. In formal dress, they wore snowy white crossbelts with a silver buckle. They proudly wore forage caps with thick silver cords around the brim.

The cadets' finery particularly troubled Sandy Owens; he was something of a ladies' man, and he despised his uniform getting spoiled. It was all too easy for the spotless white breeches to get soiled when riding, or in musket drill, or particularly in cannon drill. He avoided all contact with dirt and grime with great perseverance.

Charles, whom everyone affectionately called Chuckins, had a worried look on his face. He was a good-natured boy who took teasing very well, which was surprising considering he came from an extremely wealthy family. He showed no signs of the usually spoiled scion, however. Now he muttered nervously, "We're going to catch it, Sandy! You know what old Tom Fool will do to us for being so late!"

Sandy grunted. "Whatever happens, you better not let Major Jackson hear you call him Tom Fool. He knows more than we think he knows. I don't know who started calling him Tom Fool, but they're crazy, 'cause he ain't no fool."

"You're right about that," Peyton languidly agreed. He was breathing easily, and he kept his eye fixed on the great Gothic institute that rose before them. "They say that he ate those Mexicans alive during the war, with the artillery. He sure does know what he's doing with artillery pieces." In spite of his apparently languid and lazy appearance, Peyton Stevens dearly loved musket practice and artillery practice. He was very good with both rifles and cannons.

"We know, we know, his artillery class is the best," Chuckins agreed, breathing hard because he had been trotting to keep up with Sandy and Peyton. "It's just this natural and experimental philosophy class. He just recites it from memorization. Puts me to sleep every time, no matter how hard I pinch myself!"

"We have to stay awake, and we have to figure out a way to get into that classroom with a good excuse," Peyton said. "Otherwise we'll all get demerits." Suddenly he stopped walking.

Then Sandy stopped and Chuckins ran into him.

"What we need is a good, sound alibi," Peyton said thoughtfully. "What's the biggest lie you can think of, Sandy?"

"Uh—my grandmother died?"

"Your grandmothers have died four or five times," Peyton scoffed. "How about this? Chuckins, you ate too much dinner and it made you sick. Sandy and I had to take you to the infirmary."

Perplexed, Chuckins asked, "But what would I be doing coming to class if I was sick?"

"You weren't as sick as you thought," Peyton answered smoothly. "And you're so loyal to VMI that you insisted on coming to class, sick or not."

"Hey, that might work!" Chuckins exclaimed, his hazel eyes fixed on the forbidding gray sandstone building looming up before them. "I think I feel my sickness coming back on. Maybe you better help me in."

"That's it, Chuckins," Sandy said. "Here, Peyton, grab his arm. Poor boy is sicker than anybody knows."

Slowing their pace, the three cadets moved toward the classroom building. As they did, Sandy Owens said, "You know, I feel sorry for Major Jackson."

"Why would you feel sorry for him?" Peyton asked.

"You know he got married. Well, his first wife died along with his baby."

"Yeah, but he got married again right away," Peyton said. "He didn't let any grass grow under his feet. That woman he married, Elinor Junkin, she's the daughter of Dr. Junkin that was the president of Washington College. For sure she has money. I imagine she set up the Major pretty well."

Sandy looked at him with surprise. "But Peyton, didn't you hear? Last month Major and Mrs. Anna Jackson lost their baby. A little girl that they had named Mary Graham. She lived almost a month then died. I think maybe that's why he's been so much more stern this last month."

Peyton looked repentant. "No, I hadn't heard. That's—hard. That's hard for a man."

CROSSING

They marched on silently, but they were young, and the tragedies of life had not yet become real for them.

As they neared the classroom building, Chuckins said weakly, "I'm feeling sicker, boys. Let's go in."

The three, moving more slowly, entered the building and trudged down the hall until they came to a door that led into the classroom. They tried the door—but it was sturdily locked. They weren't too surprised, because Major Jackson often did this when he wasn't in a very good mood.

Soon the man himself opened the door and stepped out into the hallway. "Yes, gentlemen? I believe you are—" He ostentatiously pulled a watch from his pocket and stared at it, then looked up. "You are eighteen minutes late." He still wore his dusty major's uniform from the Mexican War. He had grown a fine mustache and beard, and right now they bristled. His eyes were as cold and icy blue as the darkest winter midnight.

"Yes. . .sir. . .Major. . .sir," Chuckins said weakly. "I was sick. Sandy and Peyton took me to the infirmary."

Major Jackson stared at him unforgivingly, raking him from head to toe.

"Uh—but—" Sandy started stuttering.

"Chuckins feels better now, though, Major Jackson," Peyton said smoothly. "He didn't want to miss class."

Jackson's blue-light gaze transferred to Peyton, and even he shifted uncomfortably. "Who is Chuckins?" Jackson demanded.

Charles Satterfield came to backbreaking attention and said stiffly, "It's me, sir. I'm Cadet Charles Satterfield."

"Well, Cadet, you are late for class, and being ill, you've also made your friends late for class. Two demerits for you, one for each of you, Cadet Owens, Cadet Stevens. If you don't want any further punishment, be on time for artillery tomorrow," Jackson said coldly. "Dismissed." He went back into the classroom and again locked the door firmly.

The three cadets stood still in shock for long moments. Then Sandy blew out a long, "Wheeew! We set him off this time, no fooling!"

They turned to walk back down the hall. "And I got two

demerits," Chuckins wailed. "That's not fair! I didn't think of it. You did, Peyton!"

"Relax. I've already got four demerits," Peyton said carelessly. "It's not like they won't graduate you, Chuckins. You're a good little cadet. You'll be fine."

"Well, I'm never listening to you two again," Chuckins grunted. "I'm gonna be right on time for artillery tomorrow."

"Me, too," Sandy agreed.

After a while, Peyton said, "Yeah, me, too."

Sandy Owens, Chuckins Satterfield, and Peyton Stevens were on time, even early, for artillery class the next day. With much self-righteousness, they sat in the front row, their eyes fixed, without wavering, on Major Jackson.

"Understand that learning to load and fire a cannon has no importance whatsoever if you don't learn to *aim* a cannon. . . . Any fool can fire a big gun, but it takes a smart man to hit what he's aiming for."

The cadets sat listening as Major Jackson lectured, and none of them wiggled, for they had learned that his eyes would glow dangerous blue fire if they did. Also, as unassuming as he was in his natural and experimental philosophy classes, he was the polar opposite in his artillery classes. He was authoritative, commanding, and knowledgeable to the point of being almost mystical. In the Mexican War, one of his sergeants had said that it was almost as if he had single-handedly invented artillery.

"Now, gentlemen, we will go out and take practice in the art of artillery. I will appreciate it that you understand that the cannon is an instrument. It is an *art* as much as a skill. Some of it has to be born in you, for it's not just the mathematics and the angle and the azimuth and the wind speed. You've got to have the eye. The eye, gentlemen! So let's go see if any of you boys are blessed with the eye." Jackson stepped off the podium and left the room.

In perfect order the cadets lined up two by two, marching behind him.

Before VMI was given the opportunity to obtain the services

of the renowned Major Thomas Jackson, they had only conducted dumb-fire exercises of the cannons, relying on live-fire for the muskets. But former Lieutenant Thomas Jackson, of General Winfield Scott's army in Mexico fighting Santa Anna, had made quite a name for himself. He and one man, a sergeant of artillery, had managed to break down the great fortress of Chapultepec single-handedly, with one cannon. They held the line until reinforcements arrived from his commander, Captain John Magruder. General Winfield Scott had taken special notice of Lieutenant Jackson, and so because of conspicuous bravery, he had been brevetted to the rank of major.

Because Major Thomas Jackson had gained quite a bit of fame and notoriety for his artillery work and he had persuaded the commandant of VMI that live fire of cannon was essential for the training of the cadets, he had been granted extremely special privileges for his artillery class. The college had, in effect, dug out a large trench, so that the cannons would fire into a hillside and not a fallible target. Four cannons had been purchased for the institute, and every month more powder and balls were bought for Major Thomas's enthusiastic students.

The low ground of open field was to the west of the classroom building. The cannons were placed into a twelve-foot gully that rose above them. Six-foot-tall bales of hay, with circles painted on them vaguely representing men advancing, served as targets. To the rear was a shed filled with ammunition and supplies. The targets were set up in the field, and the underclassmen among the cadets began to open the shed and bring out the powder and shells.

Major Jackson stood rigidly as they did this, staring at the targets as if they were an oncoming battalion.

Peyton Stevens, the only cadet that had ever dared to initiate a conversation with Jackson, stood close by him. "Sir," he asked speculatively, "do you think there will be a war? The papers all say so."

"I'm more interested in what God says than what the papers say, Cadet Stevens. But I pray daily that there will not be a war," Jackson answered.

The irrepressible Stevens would not be quiet and asked intently,

"Would you fight with the Union, sir?" This was a constant question with Southern men—what would they do in case the South seceded?

"I ask God every day of my life to bring North and South together without shedding of blood. I love this country, Cadet Stevens, and it would break my heart to see brother fighting against brother on the field of battle."

And at that Peyton Stevens grew quiet.

Anna Jackson looked across the tea table at her sister Eugenia. Anna was pale, and there were dark shadows under her eyes. She had borne Thomas a daughter on April 30, and they had named her Mary Graham Jackson, but she was weak and ill and had died on May 25.

Eugenia had been here with her sister since the birth. It was the end of June, and Anna assured her that she was fine and Eugenia could return home. Eugenia herself had two healthy children, which, oddly, made her feel a little guilty. It didn't, however, diminish her true sorrow for her sister. Eugenia smiled a little. "You know, Anna, I never told you this, but I was absolutely astonished when you married Major Jackson."

"Why would you be astonished, Eugenia?"

"He's so *different* from you. You're so lively—and he seems so stately, I suppose you'd say."

Anna nodded a little. "He does appear that way. You were always prettier than I, and the young men were fighting to see who would squire you around. While you were doing that, I was spending time with Thomas."

"He's just so different from most men. Does he still worry about his health?"

Anna appeared somewhat disturbed with this. She hesitated before answering, "I'm afraid he's *too* concerned with his health. He seems to me to be absolutely strong and healthy, but he has some odd ideas. He stands straight up for long periods in order to keep perfect alignment of his organs, or so he believes. He will only study his books in the daytime, because he thinks that artificial light like candles harms his eyesight."

"My, that *is* strange."

"Yes, it is. I suppose you've noticed that he keeps a lemon with him at all times? Very rarely do you see him for a long period without his biting the end off and sucking the juices out."

"I don't see how he does that. I should think it would make his mouth pucker."

"He thinks it helps his health. He's really two men, Eugenia; it's almost as if he leads a double life."

"What do you mean?"

"I don't think you know him, and the people of Lexington have never really known my husband. He's so formal and stiff at times in public, but there are other times, especially when we're alone, when he is so gay and carefree no one would recognize him."

"I can't imagine him being gay and lighthearted."

"Oh yes! Why just yesterday he was talking to one of the little girls that belonged to one of the neighbors. He was saying a poem for her, and what poem do you guess it was?"

"I'd guess Wordsworth or Shakespeare."

"No indeed, it was quite different from their work." She smiled and quoted the small poem:

"I had a little pig,
I fed him on clover.
When he died,
He died all over."

"Oh, that's funny! Did he make it up himself?"

"He wouldn't admit it, but I'm sure he did. So as you see, he's really two men. The austere major and professor in the classroom, sometimes very stern and harsh. But when we're alone, it's a different story."

Eugenia said in a low voice, "I know you've grieved terribly over the loss of Mary Graham, sister. Yet Thomas, to a stranger, seems to be just as strong and sure as ever he was."

Anna put down her teacup and grasped her sister's hand in hers. "He suffers, Eugenia. He suffers as much or more than I do.

You remember, he and Ellie lost a son."

"I know. I remember."

Anna's voice choked with tears. "Pray for us both, Eugenia. Thomas and I will forever grieve for the loss of our baby. Don't doubt Thomas. Just because he doesn't show it doesn't mean he doesn't feel it."

"Of course I will pray, sister. I'll pray without ceasing for you both."

"Thank you, my darling sister. And I'll forever be grateful for your coming to me in this difficult time. God bless you on your journey home, and bless you and your husband and children."

When Thomas came in the door, Anna was there to meet him. He put his arms around her very gently. "Ah, my *esposita*, you're so much prettier than any of those ugly cadets I have to face all day!" He kissed her then held her at arm's length. "That's a new dress, isn't it?"

They had decided only to go into mourning for one month for their lost daughter. Jackson had not said much, but he had mourned for more than a year when he lost his first wife, Ellie, and their son. He didn't want to go down that dim gray road again for so long. Anna had tacitly agreed.

Now she looked down at the dress and touched the skirt. It was a pretty peach color, trimmed with green, with a wide hoop skirt. Since she had dressed for dinner, it was off the shoulder, and she wore a small gold pearl necklace and drop earrings. Sadly, she remembered that she hadn't worn the dress since before she had gotten pregnant. But she smiled a little and answered, "No, Thomas, you've seen it about a dozen times."

"I suppose I'm no expert on women's fashion," he said, taking off his jacket and hanging it on the hall tree.

"No, if something doesn't shoot bullets or a cannonball, you don't pay much attention."

He smiled. "I pay attention to you, dearest."

She took his arm. "Yes, you do, husband. Come along, dinner is on the table."

CROSSING

The two went into the dining room. The table was covered in fresh-baked bread, roasted beef, fresh corn off the cob, English peas, and pickled beets.

Thomas sat down across from Anna and they bowed their heads. He said, "Lord, we thank You for this food which is Your provision. I pray that You will bless it, and that You will give us wisdom and insight and will make us love You more each day. In the name of Jesus, Amen."

Thomas reached out and picked up the bowl of green peas. He filled his plate to overflowing. He had formed the habit of eating only one vegetable no matter how many were on the table.

Anna exclaimed, "Thomas, you're not going to fill up on those peas and eat nothing else!"

Jackson answered patiently, "Now, Anna, you know that's the way I like to eat. I like to have one single kind of food, and I like to drink plain water."

"Thomas, you know I'm afraid that's not healthy for you. You should eat meat, vegetables, and bread at every meal."

"Foolish ideas! All of my ideas about health are sound."

"You mean even that you think one side of you is heavier than the other?"

"Sure enough, I figured it all out."

"How could you weigh just one side of yourself, Thomas?"

"I did."

"That's the reason you raise one hand up to arm's length?"

"Yes, it lets the blood flow down and lightens that arm."

Anna suddenly giggled. "Thomas—Thomas, my love! You do have interesting ideas."

Jackson grinned at her, which made him look a great deal younger. Indeed, if his cadets had seen him, they would've been astonished at how young he looked as he took his wife's hand. "That's the reason you fell in love with me, because I'm such an interesting fellow."

The two finished their meal and went for a walk in the garden, for Anna was very proud of her flowers. They waited until the daylight faded and then they went inside.

"I wish you would read to me tonight, Anna," Jackson said.

"All right, what would you like?"

"I would like to hear *Macbeth*."

"Oh, Thomas, that's a horrible play! It's full of blood and killing and horrible things."

"It's a work of genius. Mr. Shakespeare knew much of human nature. If you please, my dear, let's have *Macbeth*."

And so it was that they settled down in the drawing room. Thomas sat bolt upright in a straight-backed chair, but Anna curled up in a settee while reading the tragedy of *Macbeth*. She was a wonderful reader, and this to Thomas was the choice hour of his day. He dearly loved for Anna to read to him.

Anna sighed when she finished. "And so they all died. Some with honor, some not."

"Marvelous insight Shakespeare had," Jackson said thoughtfully. "Not a very godly man, though."

"You don't think Shakespeare was a Christian?"

"I can't think so. He didn't seem to have a very good idea of the goodness of the Lord God. But he did know humans, my dear. He did know the spirit of man."

"Perhaps you're right; he knew about men and women and their weaknesses and trials and tribulations."

Jackson came to sit by her and took her hand.

She closed the book and for a while they watched the dying fire. "Thomas?"

"Yes, my dear?"

"I've been meaning to ask something of you. Would you consider finding a young man to help me around the house?"

He turned to her then touched her face gently. "Is Hetty not enough help for you now, dearest?"

Since the death of the baby, Anna had very little interest in the housekeeping and especially the chores around the house, such as watering the garden, looking after her flower garden, and keeping the lawn. Hetty, her maid, kept house and cooked, but there was much more to maintaining a home than that.

"No, I think we need a young man. This old house often needs so many repairs, such as watching the well, making repairs on the outbuildings, and caring for the horses. You're so tired when you get home. I would like to have you to myself when you come home, instead of working so hard around here."

"I never gave it a thought, but I'm glad you mentioned it. I'll look around and find some young fellow who can help us out."

He reached out to her, and she came into his arms. Holding her tightly, he whispered in her ear, "I love you, *esposa*! The day I stop loving you will be the day I die."

"Oh, Thomas, my dearest. I wish everyone could see this side of the Iron Major. . . ."

CHAPTER SEVEN

As Daniel and Becky moved down the rows of the garden, the heat made a thin film in the windless air. The afternoon sun was warm, but all of summer's scorch was out of it. Now the deep haze of fall had come so that the land lay quietly, waiting for the harvest.

Daniel picked a large crimson tomato from the vine then took a big bite of it. The juice ran down his chin. He munched on the tomato. It was obvious he was at ease with the world.

"If you don't stop eating those tomatoes, we won't have any left for the table."

"Don't ever put off pleasures, wife," Daniel said cheerfully. He reached out and hugged her. She looked up at him, and he kissed her on the lips. "Becky, my love, you're sweeter than the tomatoes."

"You choose the strangest times to get romantic, Daniel."

"Anytime is a good time to find romance."

"Ah, yes. *Love among the Tomatoes.* That would make a good title of a dime novel."

Contentedly they picked tomatoes until their baskets were full. Then they returned to the house.

As they seated themselves on the veranda, through the open windows they could hear Zemira in the parlor, talking to Callie Jo. Zemira adored her granddaughter and begged Becky and Daniel to leave her in her care. Now, through the faint sounds, Daniel and Becky could hear that Zemira was reciting the alphabet to Callie Jo. "And *H* is for horse. We have five horses, and when you get bigger, your brother, Yancy, will teach you to ride just as fine as he does. . . ."

Becky and Daniel exchanged amused glances. "She's four months old, and already she's learning the alphabet," Becky said, laughing.

"And riding horses," Daniel added. In their chairs side by side, he reached out and took her hand.

"You know, Daniel," Becky said quietly, "I'm worried about Yancy."

Daniel sighed. "I know. He's not happy. I don't think he really hates being a farmer. I just think it's not for him."

"I think you have to grow up on a farm to like it."

"You may be right. I grew up on one and I hated it—until now, at least. But when I was young that was the real reason I ran away from home."

"Yes, and I wonder about Yancy. Sometimes I'm afraid we'll wake up one morning and *he'll* be gone."

"I know," Daniel said. "In some ways I know he does take after me. I guess I need to have a talk with him. The problem is you can talk *at* Yancy, but you can't really tell if you're talking *to* Yancy. He hardly ever says a word, and you can never tell what that boy's thinking. Gets that from his Indian mother, I guess. I have to go into town tomorrow, but maybe tomorrow evening Yancy and I can go for a ride and I'll see if I can get him to talk to me then."

They had time for a short ride after Daniel got back from town and Yancy had finished his chores. He had twice as much to do when his father went into town, but he never complained.

Daniel was riding a gelding named Reuben that doubled as a cart horse, and Yancy was riding Fancy. They went through the back of the property, into the pine woods that bordered the stream. Both of them were quiet. The only sounds were the jingles and creaks of the saddle and gear and the crickets cheeping and frogs calling. The air was crisp with the evergreen scent. It was gentle riding, just meandering along, enjoying the evening and the woods and the whisper of the stream.

Finally when the shadows grew long and longer, Daniel said, "We'd better be getting back. It'll be dark soon, and tonight's the new moon."

Yancy looked up. "So it is. I always thought it was funny that we call it the *new moon* when you can't see it at all. Wonder why that is?"

"I don't know, son. That is one thing that I regret, for you at least. The Amish education leaves much to be desired, I'm afraid, unless you're planning on farming for the rest of your life. And I don't think that's what you want to do, is it?"

Reluctantly Yancy answered, "No, sir. I just feel like I can't breathe. There are so many chores and rules, and everyone is watching you to make sure you don't do anything different from everybody else. Every day is packed full of work till nighttime and then there's nothing really to do even if you had time to do it. It's a hard life."

"It's not for everyone," Daniel agreed. "I didn't think it was for me when I was your age, either, so I can't blame you."

"Are you sorry you ran away?" Yancy asked curiously.

"Sorry? No, I'm not sorry, because then I never would have met your mother, and I wouldn't have you." They were riding side by side now, on the old bridle path that led from the stream up to the house. Daniel glanced at Yancy and saw the thoughtful look on his face. Then he added, "You know, Yancy, you've worked really hard on the farm, and I guess I've known all along that you didn't like it much. You're a hard worker, and a good worker, and I'm very proud of you."

"Thank you, sir." Yancy was quiet for a while, staring into the deepening twilight. Then he asked, "Do you think about Mother a lot?"

"Every day, son. Guess I always will."

"Did you love her in a different way than you love Becky?"

"Yes, I did. It was different. Just like I love you in a different way than I love Callie Jo. I think that's the way it's supposed to be.

We have different kinds of love."

Yancy nodded.

Daniel said, "You know, Yancy, I was in town today, and I was thinking about what a good worker you are. I thought about maybe trying to find you a job in town. I was in Mason's Grocer and Dry Goods, and I asked him about any jobs around town. He told me something interesting. Major Thomas Jackson at VMI is looking for a boy to help his wife around the house. I think you'd do a real good job for Mrs. Jackson."

"Really?" Yancy asked with interest. "Who is Major Jackson? What does he do?"

"He's famous, in a way. He made quite a name for himself in the Mexican War. Evidently he is a very courageous, smart, and hardworking soldier. At VMI he's teaching natural and experimental philosophy, and also artillery, which I understand he is extremely good at."

"What kind of work would it be, do you think?"

"Taking care of the horses, helping in the garden, running errands, keeping the grounds. Mrs. Jackson lost a baby, you see, last May. I expect she doesn't feel like doing much of anything at all, so I assume you'd be responsible for driving the maid and cook into town for supplies, keeping the carriage and buggy up. . .things like that. Think you'd like to give it a try?"

"I sure would, sir," Yancy replied. "Don't think I want to get away from you and Becky and Grandmother, but I would like to get off the farm some, try something new."

Daniel nodded. "You'd still be living here, and under the Ordnung, but it would give you more freedom. Tomorrow you can take Fancy and go see Major Jackson."

It was the last week in August, and though the evenings had cooled down, the midday sun was still high and hot. But a fine breeze blew, ruffling Yancy's coal black hair and refreshing him as he rode onto the manicured grounds of Virginia Military Institute.

Straight ahead of him was the lofty edifice of the institute that served as classrooms, offices, and the cadets' barracks. A four-story building made of gray sandstone, it was designed in the Gothic tradition. On either side of the arched entryway were two tall turrets, topped by the institute's flag on one and the flag of the state of Virginia on the other. All of the windows were mullioned. The top of the fortresslike building was lined with mock battlements.

For a moment Yancy wondered how in the world he was going to find Major Jackson, but then he heard the sound of cannons firing and realized this must be Major Jackson's artillery class. He couldn't see the cannons or the men, but he did see faint trails of smoke rising from behind and to the left of the institute building, so he followed that trail.

It led down a gradual slope to a slight ravine. There, a large group of cadets were lined up behind four cannons, each of them with four recruits attending. Nearby, standing very erect, was a man in a blue uniform. Yancy realized he must be Major Jackson, but he didn't approach him; he was curious about the firing of the cannons.

They were still smoking, and the four cadets surrounding the big guns were watching Major Jackson attentively. He had lifted binoculars to his face to look at the targets, which were about three hundred yards away on the side of an earthen breastwork. "Not bad, men. Artillery up!" he shouted.

The four cadets that had been at the guns joined the ranks of the other cadets, and three new teams of four ran to each of the guns.

"Ready your guns!" Jackson shouted. He had a curious, high-pitched voice, though it didn't sound feminine, and it carried clearly on the air.

Two cadets stood in front at each side of the cannons, two at the rear. One of the boys in front took a long pole that had what looked like an enormous corkscrew on one end, rammed it down the barrel, twisted it, and slowly worked it all the way up the muzzle. This was called the "wormer." The other cadet took another long pole with a roll of canvas on the end, dipped it into a bucket of water, and swabbed the entire barrel, which was called "sponging." This was to kill any live sparks from the last charge.

Jackson called, "Advance the round!"

CROSSING

The cadet in the rear to the right of the gun picked up a burlap sack. In it was a twelve-pound ball and two and one-half pounds of black powder. He seated it in the barrel, and the sponger turned his pole around and jammed it down the barrel, all the way to the back. Then all four of the cadets stood at the rear of the gun.

Jackson ordered, "Come to the ready!"

One of the cadets inserted a brass spike into the hole for the fuse, puncturing the canvas bag. Then another inserted a wire fuse attached to a long lanyard. Each member of the crew moved back, the crew captain holding the lanyard and stepping carefully until there was tension on it.

"Clear, sir!" each captain shouted.

"Fire!" Jackson roared.

The explosion was extremely satisfying to Yancy, as it seemed to be to each boy there. All of them had bright eyes, and excitement was clear on their faces.

After Jackson checked the targets with his binoculars, his eyes were bright, burning blue, too. "Good men," he said. "Artillery up!"

And so they began again.

At the very back of the field, Yancy dismounted and stood, stroking Fancy, for she skittered a little at each round though she didn't panic or bolt. He watched the entire class, which lasted about another hour. He was fascinated.

Finally, Jackson walked back and forth at the front of the two rows of cadets, talking to them quietly enough that Yancy couldn't hear. Then they came to attention, and he called, "Dismissed." The group broke up and headed back toward the institute, Jackson several steps behind them.

Yancy took a deep breath then hurried over to Major Jackson, leading Fancy. "Sir?" he called when he got within earshot. "Sir? May I have a word with you?"

Jackson halted and turned his eyes toward Yancy. Yancy thought that he had never seen such a deep penetrating gaze in all of his life. "Yes, what is it, young man?" Jackson asked, not unkindly.

"I—sir—I heard you are looking for a young fellow to do some work for you?"

"So I am. Who told you about it?"

"My father. He heard it from Mr. Mason. From Mason's Grocery and Dry Goods."

"What's your name and who are your people?" Jackson demanded, stopping his stride and turning to look at Yancy attentively. Though Jackson was courteous, he still made Yancy very nervous. His gaze was so intent, and he had such a distant air.

"I'm—my name's Yancy Tremayne, Major. My father is Daniel Tremayne. We live in the Amish settlement just south of town."

Jackson nodded. "All right. Walk with me, and tell me about yourself."

Yancy fell into step with Major Jackson. He didn't tell his whole life story; he just told him that he and his father had returned to the Amish after his father had been away for many years. He told him that the Tremaynes had lived on the farm since the 1730s, and that though he didn't despise farmwork, he hoped to find a job in Lexington and work outside the community.

Jackson searched him, his eyes taking in his homespun trousers and his simple muslin pullover shirt, and then he looked at his feet. "You're wearing moccasins."

"Yes, sir. My mother was half Cheyenne. So I guess you know that means I'm one-fourth Indian," Yancy said evenly.

"Guess I do," Jackson said drily. "Nice moccasins. So I assume you know how to take care of horses?"

It took Yancy a scant moment to shift into the change in conversation, but then he answered eagerly, "Oh yes, sir, because that's what I love to do! I mean—"

"No, you said it, Yancy, a man does best that which he loves to do," Jackson said quickly. "And that is a fine mare you've got there, looks healthy and well cared for. But what about everything else? Other chores, hard work around a house?"

"I work hard at the farm, sir. I'm handy with tools, I'm strong, and usually I can—sort of figure out how to fix things. Like repairing a roof, or putting up a fence. And I've been to four barn raisings, so I've learned some carpentry."

"All right." Jackson nodded. "Then I want you to wait for me. I've got some things to do in my office. My horse is in the institute stables over there. The stable boy will show her to you. You go on over there, clean my tack, and brush her down and pretty her up, show me a little bit of what you can do. By the time you're through with that I'll be ready to go home. I'll take you and introduce you to my wife. As far as I'm concerned you can have a trial period. You can work for a week, and by that time we should know if we can get along with each other."

On 8 East Washington Street in Lexington was a modest two-story house that Jackson had bought. The front steps crowded up against the street, but as they rode up, Yancy could see a generous garden, stables, carriage house, and washhouse in the back.

Jackson went up the side street, where a path led right up to the stable.

"I'll take care of the horses, Major Jackson," Yancy said eagerly. "I know you'll want to talk to Mrs. Jackson before you introduce me."

"Good, good," Jackson murmured, nodding his head. The words and gesture were very familiar to those who knew him. He dismounted, handed the reins to Yancy, and hurried into the house.

Yancy hitched up Fancy, then began unsaddling Major Jackson's horse, which was an unassuming mare by the name of BeBe. In the stall next to her was a big gray gelding who whinnied in recognition when he led BeBe in and then poked his nose out of the stall to watch Yancy curiously. Yancy unsaddled the mare and brushed her down. It didn't take very long, for he had curried her very well at the institute and they hadn't ridden hard to Jackson's home, so he finished quickly. After that he petted the gelding and talked to both horses. He loved horses, and they loved him.

Yancy was standing at the gelding's stall, rubbing his soft nose and murmuring to him, when Jackson came to get him. "I see you've made Gordo's acquaintance," he said.

"That's his name? Gordo?"

"Actually, it's Cerro Gordo. Named after a place in Mexico, where I saw my first action," Jackson said. "This old goat"—he rubbed the horse's nose—"didn't have anything to do with it. I just liked the name, and I'll always remember it."

"I'd like to know about the Mexican War," Yancy said wistfully.

"Would you?" Jackson retorted, swiveling his shrewd gaze to Yancy's face.

"Yes, sir."

"I have two books, memoirs from men who were there," Jackson said. "Maybe you'd like to borrow them?"

"Oh yes, sir. I—I like to read, but the Amish don't encourage it too much. Except the Bible, of course."

"Good of them. Everyone must study the Bible with great energy," Jackson said sternly. "But reading books is a good thing, Yancy. I'm glad you want to read. Shows me something of what you're made of. So, would you like to come meet my wife now?"

"Yes, sir."

Jackson led him into the house. It was modestly furnished, not spare but with good wool rugs, plenty of lamps, and comfortable, gently worn furniture in the parlor.

On a settee was seated a pretty lady, somewhat thin, with thick chestnut hair and warm brown eyes.

"My darling, this is Yancy," Jackson said. "Yancy, this is my wife, Anna."

Yancy did his best to make a sort of bow, not daring to extend his hand. "Ma'am," he murmured.

"I'm so glad to meet you, Yancy," she said in a soft voice. "Already I feel I know you a little, because Thomas has told me about you. Please, won't you be seated?"

Awkwardly Yancy perched on the edge of a straight chair by the fireplace.

"As I said, Yancy is reputed to be good with tools and on a farm, and I've already seen that he's very good with horses," Jackson said, seating himself by his wife. "And he's been working on an Amish farm, and I know that must be hard work."

"Yes, sir," Yancy said faintly.

Anna looked at him intently then smiled a little as she seemed to recognize his nervousness. "The Amish, you know. . .I've heard of them, but I know very little about them," she said. "Perhaps you and I can talk about them sometime."

"Yes, ma'am, even though I—I mean, I—it's kind of new to me, too, so I don't know much about it," Yancy said.

CROSSING

"Then perhaps we can learn together," she said lightly. "Now, you see, the most important thing to Thomas is if you can take good care of the horses and the cart and the carriage and make sure the pump and the drains are working properly. But the most important thing to me, Yancy, is my garden. I think it must be different from farming, but perhaps not so much. And so it doesn't really matter if you don't know much about the Amish, as long as you know about horses and gardening."

Suddenly Yancy smiled at her; he didn't smile very often, but she was so gentle and so obviously wanted him to be at ease that it made him want to reassure her. "Ma'am, I don't know much about flowers and things, but I can learn. And I'm not afraid of any hard work. I'll be glad to do anything around here that needs doing. If I don't know how to do it, I'll find someone who does, and I'll get him to teach me."

Anna and Jackson glanced at each other; and Yancy was surprised at the softness and the warmth with which the stern major looked at his wife.

Then Anna looked back at Yancy. "I think you'll do well, Yancy. I'm sure that we'll be glad that the Lord sent you here. I'll be glad to have the help, and it will be nice to have a young person around the house."

Suddenly Jackson reached out and took her hand.

Yancy saw the sadness in her then and remembered that Daniel had told him of their losing their daughter four months ago. "I will work hard, ma'am, Major," Yancy promised. "I don't know much about the Lord and all, but I do want you to be glad I'm here. I'll work hard to earn that."

Jackson called up, "How's it going, Yancy?"

Yancy was on the roof of the stable. It had a tin roof, and the seams had expanded and loosened during the hot summer. With cold rain and snow coming, Yancy wanted to make sure the roof was snug and secure, so he was adding extra nails along the seams and sealing them with tar. It was hot work, and hard work, but he didn't mind. He wanted BeBe and Gordo to be comfortable this winter.

He looked down and smiled at the major. "Fine, sir, it's going very well. I think I can finish this by tomorrow."

Jackson nodded. "Come down here. I have something for you."

"Yes, sir."

Yancy climbed down the ladder, rubbing his dirty hands against his breeches.

"Here are your wages for the week." He held out two silver dollars.

With great pleasure Yancy took the coins and put them in his pocket. "Thank you, Major. It's been a good week. I like working for you and Mrs. Jackson," he said with a touch of uncharacteristic shyness.

"You have done a good job, Yancy. You are indeed a hard worker. What will you do with your money?"

"Give it to my family, sir."

"Good, good. Be back at eight o'clock on Monday, Yancy."

"Yes, sir, I'm looking forward to it."

"Carry on."

"Sir." Yancy climbed back up onto the roof of the stable.

CHAPTER EIGHT

One thing that Yancy loved about the Amish was their food. As he sat down to dinner with his family, his mouth watered. Zemira and Becky had prepared chicken and corn soup, biscuits, pork ribs and kraut, tomato fritters, and potato salad. Also, they had cheese cubes, pickles, and fresh, crunchy celery straight from the kitchen garden, the last of the season. Steaming on the sideboard for dessert was apple strudel, a jug of fresh cream standing by.

Daniel and Yancy took their seats, and then as was traditional for the Amish, the women seated themselves. Zemira sat down while Becky put Callie Jo in her high chair. Zemira had saved the well-made wooden tray chair for years, wrapped up carefully in an old quilt in the attic. It looked new, but her husband, Jacob, had made it more than thirty years ago for Daniel when he was a baby.

"Now we will bless," Daniel said.

They all bowed their heads for the silent blessing. As always, Yancy surreptitiously watched his father until he raised his head. Of course, most of the time Zemira caught him, but she didn't fuss. She merely gave him an amused, slightly conspiratorial look.

As soon as they began to eat, the conversation began. Dinnertime was usually lively, for the Amish worked hard all day at different tasks and it was a time for catching up on everything around the farm. Today, however, which was Saturday, they only wanted to hear from Yancy about Major and Mrs. Jackson. He had been working for them for more than a month now, and though the Amish considered themselves a separate people, they were always eager to hear about news from town and the outside world.

"So, Yancy, tell us all about Major Jackson and Mrs. Jackson and what has gone on this last week," Becky prodded him. "But first—how is Mrs. Jackson? I know you've told us that she still seems sad at times. It's been, um, six months since she lost the little girl? I can't imagine how long it would take to get over something like that. . . ." Her voice trailed off, and all eyes at the table went to Callie Jo.

As if she were aware of the attention, she grinned, her two top teeth and two bottom teeth shining. She had a bowl of creamed celery on her tray, and she buried one chubby hand in it, waved joyously, and smeared it all over her face.

Zemira, Becky, Yancy, and Daniel burst out laughing. Becky hurried to clean her face and spoon some of the celery properly into her mouth.

Yancy answered, "Mrs. Jackson is better. It seems like she gets a little better every week. Yesterday she even laughed. It's the first time I've heard her laugh."

"About what?" Becky asked curiously.

Yancy grinned. "We were out in the garden. I was down on my knees in one of the flower beds, turning the soil and mulching, and I guess Major Jackson didn't realize I was there. So he comes home and finds Mrs. Jackson, sitting on a bench, reading a book. He starts telling her about this new cadet; his name is Percy Smith. He's a distant cousin of Superintendent Smith's, and they're all under orders to sort of help him along. So during artillery class, Major Jackson lets him be a gun captain, but of course the other guys have to do all the worming and swabbing and priming and loading; all he's got to do is pull the lanyard when Major Thomas yells, 'Fire!'

"But it seems like this Percy Smith is kind of a muffin, 'cause on the first battery he pulls the lanyard, then jumps straight up in the air, covers his ears, and yells, 'Ooohh!' And Major Jackson acted it out, jumping up and screeching like a little girl. Mrs. Jackson laughed and laughed. And I did, too, but I was quiet about it, because I knew Major Jackson would be embarrassed if he knew I'd heard him and seen him."

The others were fascinated. Daniel said thoughtfully, "You know, I've never met Major Jackson, but his reputation seems to be of a rather stern, stiff military man of great dignity."

"So he is," Yancy agreed, "except with Mrs. Jackson. You wouldn't believe how different he is with her. Course, he's very gallant with all ladies, but with her he's kind and soft and smiles a lot and calls her pet names. He doesn't mind who sees, either. It's just that yesterday he was such a big clown that I figured he might mind me seeing that."

Becky nodded with understanding. "He sounds like a wonderful husband. And so the loss of his daughter hasn't affected his mind or his health too adversely?"

Yancy shrugged. "He never seems to be really upset about anything, except his health."

"And so he is in bad health?" Zemira asked.

"I don't know about that. He doesn't really look sick, but he's always complaining of some kind of ailment. Last week he was complaining of an inflammation in his ear and in his throat. He also said he had neuralgia, whatever that is."

"I suppose he goes to the doctor quite often," Becky said sympathetically.

"No, I heard Mrs. Jackson urging him to go, but Major Jackson just said, 'I can prescribe medicine just as well as those fellows.' He showed me once what he was taking, a whole cabinet full of bottles. One was chloroform liniment, and the bottles were labeled—things like ammonia, glycerin, and nutritive silver."

"That sounds awful, and dangerous, too," Daniel said.

"He doesn't act sick, but he talks a lot about his ailments. I told you how he sucks on lemons all the time. Nobody knows where he gets them in the wintertime, but he always has a bunch of them. He thinks they help his digestion or something."

"But he is a Christian man, I heard," Daniel said cautiously.

"Yeah, he is. He talks about the Lord and the Bible all the

time," Yancy answered. "And Mrs. Jackson, too. They're always quoting the Bible."

Zemira, Becky, and Daniel exchanged glances. The Amish didn't believe in quoting scripture excessively. As with vocal prayer, they considered it very forward and smacking of pride. Of course, Yancy didn't know this, and the adults had no intention of confusing him by explaining it to him now.

"He sounds like a good Christian man," Becky said generously. "One that I'm proud for you to work for."

Yancy ducked his head and murmured, "I'm proud to work for him, too."

Very early on Monday morning, Yancy left the farm for the Jackson home in Lexington. It was the second week in October, but they hadn't had a frost yet. It was chilly but not really cold. On this day he rode Fancy because his father had told him they wouldn't need her. He got there at about seven thirty, unsaddled Fancy and put her in her stall next to Gordo, and brushed her down good. Then he went in the back way to the kitchen.

Hetty, Mrs. Jackson's maid, was making coffee. She was a good-natured but no-nonsense woman, chubby, with dark eyes that crinkled into tiny slits when she laughed. Hetty had been with Mary Anna Jackson for many years. " 'Bout time," she grumbled.

"I'm early," he countered. "Mmm, coffee smells good. Can I have some?"

"I don't know if we've got enough sugar and cream for you," she said, hands on hips. "You make such a syrup out of it."

"It's good for me." Yancy grinned. "A pretty girl told me at church yesterday that I'm a growing boy."

"Bet pretty girls tell you lots of things," Hetty said. "My daddy always told me don't believe everything you hear. He was a smart man."

"Bet he was. Bet his daughter is, too."

"Humph. What are you kissing me up for today?"

"Lunch, maybe?" Yancy suggested.

"Like I don't fix lunch for you every single time you're here," she said, sauntering out of the kitchen. "Dunno why I baby you, I truly don't. You're sure no baby. . . ."

Yancy finished his coffee quickly then went to the parlor.

It was the routine—Mrs. Jackson waited for him in the parlor to tell him his duties for the day. He knocked and she said softly, "Come in, Yancy."

He went in, where Mrs. Jackson sat by a small fire. To his surprise, she was wearing a plain skirt with no hoops and a plain white shirt.

Always before she had worn the elaborate dresses that were fashionable for ladies, with wide hoop skirts, lace trim, and lace caps topping full ringlets. Today Anna's hair was bound up tightly in a bun, and a wide-brimmed straw hat lay on the settee by her side. "Good morning," she said.

"Good morning, ma'am. What can I do for you today?"

She smiled. She had a sweet face and kind eyes. As Yancy had noted, she seemed to have overcome her grief for her lost baby slowly over the last month. "Today I want you to work on my flower garden, Yancy. And I'm feeling so well today that I'm going to work, too. My fall flowers are looking so wonderful that I know I'll enjoy working in the garden, as I did before—before."

"That's good, ma'am. I'll enjoy the company for a change."

Anna put on her hat and some leather work gloves, and they went out the back to the garden. Though the Jacksons had only owned the house for a short time, the garden had been created many years before by the previous owners. Anna Jackson loved gardening, so she was constantly making changes in the plantings and renewing the beds. There had also been a rather large kitchen garden in one corner. But Major Jackson had bought a farm just outside of Lexington, and as was everything else in the Shenandoah Valley, it was fruitful and grew all the fresh vegetables they could ever need.

Much of Yancy's time had been spent in this garden, uprooting the old vegetables and tilling and retilling the soil and fertilizing to prepare for flowers. Today, Anna pointed to six shallow crates full of colorful flowers. Yancy had seen them before—his grandmother had them in her front yard—but he didn't know what they were.

"Pansies," Anna said to his unspoken question. "I dearly love them." One crate held solid-colored orange flowers, one white, one yellow, one red, one purple with black markings around the center of the flower, and one with yellow petals and purple markings.

"They are pretty," Yancy agreed, stooping down to caress one of the showy yellow and purple ones. "It's funny; these two-colored ones have little faces."

"You're perceptive," Anna said. "That's exactly what all of the expert botanists call it. They're wonderful flowers. If you have the soil conditioned just right, they bloom even in snow."

"Really?"

"Yes. They look fragile and delicate, but they're actually very strong."

"Mmm, like some ladies," Yancy said, rising and looking at her. He looked down at her, for she was a full foot shorter than he was.

Anna Jackson looked slightly surprised and then pleased. "I'd like to border the flower beds with them. Come, and I'll show you which color goes where and exactly how to plant them."

They worked steadily. Yancy, at the largest flower bed, worked carefully placing the tiny little plants closely around the border. Anna, down on her knees, worked at a small corner bed that had only three sides.

Yancy found himself humming a hymn, a doleful tune, as most of the Amish hymns were. He had no idea what the words said because it was in German, but it had been a hymn they had sung at church the day before.

Anna came to stand over him. "What is that tune, Yancy?" He looked up at her face. Her cheeks were rosy, though she didn't look hot; she looked happy. It was the first time he had seen a complete peaceful happiness on her face.

"I don't know, ma'am. Almost all of the Amish hymns are in German. For all I know, we're singing about sauerkraut and pretzels."

Anna laughed, a sweet, pleasing sound. "I rather doubt that, Yancy. It sounds much too sad for that. You're not sad, are you?"

"Oh no, ma'am. It's just the songs. They all sound sad, and the few that are in English are real sad."

CROSSING

Anna considered this. "So—are your people very somber and grave?"

Yancy thought for a few moments. "Not really, ma'am. I guess they're just like everyone else. Some of them are serious, some of them laugh a lot; sometimes anyone can be sad and serious and other times happy and light. They're just people. Except they dress funny."

"Yancy!" Anna chided him.

"Sorry," he said unrepentantly. "But they try to make me wear a hat that looks just like yours, Mrs. Jackson. It looks real pretty on you, but you're not going to catch me breathing and wearing a straw hat with a wide brim." Yancy wore leather slouch hats with a wide brim and beaded hatband that his mother had made.

"I suppose," she said, struggling to keep a straight face, "that I would feel such reluctance if someone tried to make me wear my husband's forage cap. It simply wouldn't do."

"No, ma'am," Yancy agreed heartily. "It would not do."

Anna knelt by him and they worked side by side for a while. The flower bed was the largest in the garden. Yancy had, in deference to Mrs. Jackson, memorized all the flowers that were blooming this fall—chrysanthemums, marigolds, nasturtiums, dahlias, and now they were adding pansies as a border.

After they had worked for a time, Anna sat up and pulled a heavy round yellow chrysanthemum bloom up to her face. "They're beautiful, but they have no scent. And you know, at Cottage Home in North Carolina we had a white chrysanthemum. It was so unusual. It looked just like a daisy. But it was hardy and fall-blooming. I wish I had one here, but I haven't seen one since I left home."

"You know, ma'am, I think my grandmother has some of those," he said thoughtfully. "There's three big bushes of them in the backyard by the kitchen garden that just started blooming. I'll ask her. I'm sure she'd love for you to have some plants."

"Why, thank you, Yancy," Anna said with pleasure. "I would dearly love to have white daisy-mums in my garden."

They worked until noon, and then had a surprise. Major Jackson rode up and hurried through the backyard to embrace

Anna. As Major Jackson and Anna had gotten more accustomed with Yancy, they had begun to show more affection in front of him. He always made a point to discreetly ignore them, and he knew this made them feel comfortable with him.

"Hello, sir," Yancy said, rising. "I'll go take care of BeBe. "

"Don't unsaddle her," Jackson instructed him. "We're just going to have a quick lunch and then you and I are going back to the institute. So you go ahead and saddle up Fancy."

"Me, sir?" Yancy said with surprise. "But why?"

"You'll see," he said over his shoulder as he walked Anna into the house. "It's a special day."

CHAPTER NINE

The parade ground in front of the institute was filled with cadets, not wearing their dress uniforms but in trousers and shirts that looked like work clothes. They stood around in groups, laughing or kicking and throwing balls.

Major Jackson and Yancy rode in and stabled the horses.

"Bring your rifle," Jackson ordered Yancy.

Without question Yancy took his rifle out of the saddle holster, and they headed out to the field.

Jackson yelled, "Cadet Sims!"

Cadet Erwin Sims, at eighteen, was already tall and deep-chested. He had a voice like a foghorn. "Yes, sir!" he said, running up to the major.

"Assemble the men," Jackson said.

He turned and bellowed out, "All cadets, file in under Major Jackson!"

As the cadets came running toward them, Yancy leaned his musket up against an unused hitching post. He saw that Major Jackson was looking at him with a direct expression. "Would you care to race with our cadets, Mr. Tremayne?"

"Yes, sir, I like to race."

"Fine, get in line there. Line them up, Mr. Sims, and I'll give the signal to start. You will be going to the other side of the institute, from this hitching post to that elm tree straight ahead and back. The winner gets a week off of all duties."

The cheer went up, and as Yancy took his place at the end of the line, he saw he was receiving some angry glances.

The cadet next to him said, "What are you doing here? You're not a cadet."

Yancy didn't answer, merely breathed deeply to prepare.

Jackson called, "Ready—set—go!"

Yancy broke into a burst of speed and ran with all of his might for the tree. It was a short race so he didn't have to worry about getting winded. He was the first one to arrive at the tree, and he whirled and ran back. He had learned in racing to give his very best at the last part of the race, and he outdid himself and crossed the line. He looked back to see the closest cadet was still thirty yards back.

The cadets all came in huffing from lack of breath.

Jackson had a slight smile. "Well, Mr. Tremayne, you're quite a runner."

"The Cheyenne boys race a lot," he said in a low voice. "It was something that the men thought helped us grow and learn."

"I don't know if you know it," Jackson addressed the cadets, "but Mr. Tremayne here lived with the Cheyenne Indians until he was twelve years old. The Indians are known to be great runners."

"Major Jackson, I don't think I ought to get any prize," Yancy said. "I'm not one of the cadets."

Jackson nodded with approval. "Very well. Mr. Hooper, you are the next in line and you're relieved of all duty for the next week. Now, we are going to see what kind of marksmen we have. Go down to the artillery field and get your muskets."

The small arms were stored in the same shed that held the cannon armaments. The boys, whooping and yelling, ran down to the gully that housed the shed and the cannons.

Jackson nodded for Yancy to get his musket. Together they walked down to the artillery field. "That's a fine rifle, Mr. Tremayne."

"Thank you, sir. My father gave it to me. It's an Enfield rifle musket."

"I see you take good care of it, too. You have your cartridges and rounds and caps?"

"Yes, sir."

"Want to try your hand against my cadets?"

"Well—but. . .they might not like it, sir. I don't think they much liked that I won the race."

"Then they need to grow up and act like men and improve themselves and not worry what the man next to them is doing," Jackson snapped impatiently. "Take the second team, so you can see how we drill."

"Yes, sir."

"Teams of five!" Jackson roared. "Step up, men!"

The cadets started jostling around, ranging themselves in fives.

Yancy quickly joined three of the cadets in the second line, and then Cadet Sims joined the four. To Yancy's surprise, both he and the cadet on his other side grinned at him.

On his left was a rather chubby cadet, with a good-natured smile. "Can you shoot as good as you can run?" he asked.

"I dunno," Yancy answered honestly. "Never thought about it much."

"Silence in the ranks!" Jackson ordered, and both boys fell silent, staring straight ahead.

There were twenty-three cadets, and the five targets had been set up at fifty yards.

Jackson waited until all of the cadets were assembled in their teams. When they were all quiet, he called out, "Company! Loading nine times!"

Yancy watched and listened carefully and realized that this meant nine commands required to load and fire the muskets. Jackson barked them out quickly, and Yancy observed the first team, memorizing each movement and each command.

Finally Jackson yelled, "Fire!"

Five loud explosions sounded, then the cadets held their muskets upright by their sides.

Jackson took his binoculars out and surveyed the targets in silence. He nodded briskly. "Not bad, men. Hart, Preston, bull's-eye. Manning, Bridges, and Rogers in the red. Team one, ready for battle command?"

"Yes, sir!" the first five cadets called.

"One minute!" Jackson announced. He took out his pocket-watch, glanced at it, waited a few seconds, then commanded, "Load and fire at will!"

A good rifleman was supposed to be able to load and fire in twenty seconds, and get off three rounds in a minute. The speed was important, but so was the repetition of the drill. Many greenhorns, in the excitement of battle, would shoot while their rammers were still in the barrel. The rammer would travel yards away—and then the rifleman had no way to reload his weapon.

Major Jackson drilled the cadets as much as he could with live rounds, begging and scraping the institute for ammunition. If they didn't have it, he dumb-show drilled them. Almost all of his cadets could fire three rounds in a minute. As could the five cadets on the firing line.

At one minute Jackson called, "Cease fire!" and they had all loaded and shot three times. Jackson ordered Cadet Hart to collect the targets and reset with new ones.

This took a little time, so the friendly cadet next to Yancy spoke to him again in a low voice. "Hi, I'm Charles Satterfield."

"Yancy Tremayne."

"How do you know Major Jackson?"

"I work for him and Mrs. Jackson at their house."

Satterfield's brown eyes widened. "You work for him? On purpose?"

Yancy nodded his head. "He's not like this at home, with Mrs. Jackson. He's different."

"Different? But—"

"Cadet Satterfield, if I catch you making noise on my field just once more you're going to be cleaning every cadet's musket tonight!" Jackson barked.

Satterfield shot to attention. "Yes, sir! No, sir! It won't happen again, sir!"

"Next team, get ready for commands!" Jackson ordered.

Yancy and the four cadets put their muskets upright next to their sides.

Although Yancy had only observed the "Company! Loading

nine times!" routine, he was very quick and picked it up easily. He was even quicker than the cadets. His shot was dead bull's-eye.

The four cadets were in the red.

In battle drill, Yancy just managed to fire four times in a minute, with every shot a bull's-eye.

Jackson studied his target carefully then handed it to Yancy. "Here, you ought to take this and show it to your father," he said in a low voice.

Yancy took the target and said slowly, "No, Major. This isn't the kind of thing my family is proud of. Amish, you know."

Jackson nodded with understanding. "Still, you should be proud. Would you like to try a big gun when we get through with muskets?"

Yancy grinned up at him. "I surely would, sir. They look like even more fun."

Jackson smiled one of his rare, short smiles. "Oh, they are, Mr. Tremayne. They are."

As soon as all of the cadets had done their musket drills, they started bringing out the ammunition and supplies for the four cannons.

Yancy watched three teams shoot three rounds each this time. Firing a cannon didn't have any more steps than firing a musket, but it was a good deal more dangerous. He especially observed how careful the cadets were never to step in front of the muzzle and how far they stood back when the gun captain pulled the long lanyard that fired the piece.

Once again he teamed up with the four cadets he had shot the muskets with. The four seemed to just naturally team up together, and they had sort of hung around Yancy when forming the cannon teams. He was relieved; the cadet that had gotten so mad at him at the race was a big, arrogant eighteen-year-old named Franklin Hart, and his dark eye had lit on Yancy more than once during their drills.

Yancy got to be the wormer, then the sponger/rammer, then the primer on their three shots. Cadet Sims was the gun captain; evidently this was a position that was earned and not automatically rotated. Yancy did all right; he was slightly slower than the others, and once he stepped in front of the muzzle when he was sponging.

One of the other cadets—he later found out it was Peyton Stevens—ducked under the gun and pushed Yancy hard. Then he stood up and with a charming smile said, "Don't want to be standing there, Cheyenne. Sorry about the shove."

"It's all right. Better than getting shoved by a six-pound ball," Yancy said. His gun crew did well, hitting the target with all three rounds.

When the drills were finished and the cadets were returning to the barracks, the four young men he had been shooting with introduced themselves. Cadet Sims was senior, at eighteen, Peyton Stevens was sixteen, and Sandy Owens and Charles Satterfield were fifteen. They shook hands all around.

"Thanks for helping me out today," Yancy told them.

"No, you helped us out in the musket drill," Satterfield said.

"Right, Chuckins," Stevens said lazily. "At least today you didn't fire your rammer."

"Oh I only did that once, the second time we drilled," Chuckins grumbled. "Old Blue Light was yelling at me and made me nervous."

"Old Blue Light? Is that what you call him?" Yancy asked, glancing at Major Jackson.

"Among other things," Cadet Sims said. "So are you coming to VMI, Yancy?"

Yancy shook his head. "No, I couldn't do that. No, I just work for Major Jackson, and I guess he just wanted to bring me today to have some fun."

"Hard to think of races and gun drills as fun," Sandy Owens grumbled. He couldn't run very fast, and he hated the dirt and grime and noise and smell of the musket drills. He secretly, however, did love artillery drill, even if it did get his breeches dirty. He was the best in his class at it.

"Really?" Yancy said in surprise. "I thought it was great." He saw Major Jackson motioning to him, and he hurriedly said, "I've gotta go now. Thanks again, cadets, for the day."

He joined Major Jackson and they went to the stables and saddled up. Jackson didn't say anything, and Yancy didn't either.

CROSSING

They had ridden awhile before Major Jackson said, "That was quite a show you put on there, Mr. Tremayne."

"I didn't mean to show off, sir. It's just that from about the time Indian boys can walk, they race, and their fathers teach them to use a rifle. That's the kind of life I had. It just comes natural, I guess. And you know, I didn't do so good with the cannon."

Jackson answered, "You did real well for your first time. Better than most all of those boys did on their first times. So your father is the one who taught you to shoot like that?"

"Yes, sir."

"But it takes a lot of practice, and a lot of discipline, to get that accurate and that fast."

Yancy shrugged a little. "It doesn't seem like a discipline to me, sir. I love it. Not just hunting, but as you say, target practice and speed practice. My father and I used to compete. He always won. Course we don't do that anymore," he added with a touch of sadness.

"But don't you stop, Mr. Tremayne," Jackson said sternly. "Don't you stop. You're young and tough and good at what you do. You'd make a good soldier."

Yancy was pleased and relished a rare compliment from a man he admired. Then he sighed. "You know, Major Jackson, that the Amish are against any kind of violence. They won't fight in a war."

"Yes, I've heard that."

"I've wondered about that myself sometimes," Yancy said hesitantly. "The Bible says, 'Thou shalt not kill.' "

"I've read that many times. I have a friend who is a scholar in the Hebrew language. I asked him about that commandment. He told me that the word used in our Bible for *kill* is literally *murder* in the original Hebrew text. 'Thou shalt not murder.' "

"What's the difference, sir?"

"You murder someone out of gain, or anger, or jealousy. You take the life to serve yourself. But those who serve as soldiers, they are giving their lives for their country, to preserve it. In most cases they are fighting to save their people from godless armies. So, I tell myself I will not murder, but I will defend my country."

"Yes, sir," Yancy said quietly, thinking, *And I would, too.*

～

Every Amish community had a bishop, a deacon, and a secretary. When all three of them showed up at a house, it was generally a grave situation. Daniel wasn't very surprised when he opened the door and invited them in.

The bishop was Gideon Lambright, who had performed Daniel and Becky's marriage ceremony. Today, in constrast to that day, he seemed tall and stern, his beard and white hair bristling. He had come along with Joshua Middleton, the short, forty-four-year-old deacon, who was normally a jolly man but today was somber. Also accompanying them was Sol Raber, another deacon. He and Daniel had become good friends, but now he seemed distant.

Daniel led them into the parlor where Becky and Zemira waited. "Will you sit down, gentlemen?" he said.

"Thank you, Mr. Tremayne," Lambright answered. He took a chair and the other two flanked him.

"Would you like for us to leave, Bishop?" Becky asked, motioning to herself and Zemira.

Daniel stood by Becky's chair.

"I would like for the whole family to be here." Bishop Lambright took a deep breath and continued, "This isn't a pleasant task that we have, I'm afraid. But it must be done. There is some serious difficulty concerning your son, Yancy."

"Is there a charge being brought against him?" Daniel asked at once. He was facing the men squarely, and there was a light of challenge in his eyes. He had been expecting a visit such as this and forced himself to show no signs of temper.

Bishop Lambright shook his head. "There are no charges against him at this time, Mr. Tremayne, nothing like that. It's just that we have decided that it is highly unseemly for your son to work for Major Jackson. You know well our stand on war and that none of our men are allowed to serve as soldiers."

"But Yancy isn't serving as a soldier. He is just working for the major."

"We understand that he is also taking part in military exercises, using the musket, firing the cannon."

"I fail to see any harm in that," Daniel said firmly.

"But we do see the harm. It wasn't so bad when all your son was doing was working at Major Jackson's home. But now he is mingling with the soldiers at the institute, and he is shooting cannons. I understand he is even learning to use the saber. Please, Mr. Tremayne, you must bring the boy home, here, to work on the farm. Or to find a trade for him."

Daniel was angry, and he knew it wouldn't be good for him to speak what was on his heart.

Becky, however, spoke up. "You must understand, Bishop, that Yancy led a completely different life with the Indians—a life that included hunting, fishing, and using guns. And after all, he is still in rumspringa. He's only fifteen years old."

"I'm well aware of this, Mrs. Tremayne," Bishop Lambright said, not unkindly. "But the fact remains that Yancy is not hunting and fishing. He is learning the tools and the ways of war. And that we cannot allow."

Becky, Zemira, and Daniel all exchanged glances. Daniel took up the argument. "But most of the time he is working at Major Jackson's home, helping Mrs. Jackson. Surely you can find no fault in this?"

"Major Jackson has exposed him to these weapons of war and has influenced his conduct for the worse," Lambright said. "Yancy needs to be here, with the People."

"Major Thomas Jackson is an honorable, Christian—" Daniel began angrily.

Becky laid her hand on his arm, and he was silent. "Do I understand," Becky said in a quiet voice, "that you want us to make Yancy quit this job he loves and bring him back here? And if we don't, will the three of us be punished?"

"Mrs. Tremayne, you and your husband, and of course you, Zemira, have done nothing wrong. But surely you understand the consequences for the boy, if he persists in this course."

That ended the conversation and the three left.

After they were gone, Daniel turned and the expression on his face was bleak. "I can't do this to Yancy, make him leave the Jacksons and come back here," he said. "I think if I did, he'd just take off and leave us. Like I did," he said bitterly.

"Of course we won't do that!" Becky said. "I know we shouldn't disagree with the bishop, but it's not right. It's just not right. You shouldn't *force* people into the community. That's just another form of aggression. You must let them decide for themselves. Yancy has a right to do what he wants, whether it is the Amish way or the English. You know, Daniel, that we don't shun the members of our families who have gone the way of the English. Look at your cousins, Caleb Tremayne's family. Sol Raber is still good friends with him."

Daniel nodded. "I know. I agree. But—Mother? Are you afraid that the leadership may order us to shun Yancy if we don't make him stay home?"

Zemira said firmly, "I don't know, and I don't care. Yancy is a good boy. If I would have had this choice with you, Daniel, I never would have tried to force you into our ways, as Becky said. I think that we must let Yancy do whatever seems right to him, and never in this life will I turn my back on him."

And that settled the matter for the three of them.

When Yancy came home from work, Daniel called him aside and related what Bishop Lambright had said. Then he told him what he, Becky, and Zemira thought.

"What do you think I should do?" Yancy asked worriedly.

"Whatever your heart tells you, as long as it's honorable," Daniel answered, patting Yancy's shoulder. "And I know it will be. We trust you. Follow your heart, and whatever you decide your family will be with you."

The next day Yancy went to work at the Jacksons' home. He and Mrs. Jackson worked more out in the garden, planting the new daisy-mum that he had brought her from Zemira's yard. Anna had been delighted. And they were busy weeding and turning over the soil and mulching, preparing the beds for the long winter.

After a while Anna took a break, getting lemonade for them from the kitchen. She invited Yancy to sit down in the shade for a few minutes. Even though it was the middle of October, the midafternoon was still warm for gardening work.

They sat in silence, as Yancy had very little to say all day. He was tired, as he hadn't really slept.

Finally Anna put her head to one side and asked, "Yancy, what's wrong? Are you not feeling well today?"

"No, ma'am, it's not that," he said, ducking his head. "It's—it's a problem. At home."

"Is it something you can tell me about?" she asked softly.

He hesitated for a long time then looked up at her. His dark eyes were troubled. "I don't know, ma'am. I wouldn't want to trouble you."

"Nonsense," she said. "I would like to help, if I could."

Slowly he explained to her his dilemma. "And so, I'm certain to be shunned if I don't go back and just stay on the farm."

"What do your parents say?" Anna asked.

"They told me to do whatever I feel is right," he answered. "Even my grandmother says I should pray and ask God for what is right for me. Even *she's* not trying to force me to be Amish."

"She sounds like a very wise woman."

"She is. I wish I was as close to God as she is. But I'm still not sure about Him, either."

"You're young," Anna said sturdily, "and you'll find Him. In the meantime, I will pray for you, Yancy. So you'll know in your heart what you must do."

That night, again, he lay awake at home, staring at the faint starlight on the ceiling. His father had told him that he could take as long as he needed to think about his decision. Yancy didn't pray much, and when he did, he felt like he was talking to the ceiling. And so it was on this night.

But close to the dawn, he finally made his decision in his heart and knew his course was set. He dozed for a while then rose early, as always, to go to the Jacksons' house.

When he arrived and took Fancy into the stables, he saw that the new hay for the stall beds had been delivered. He decided to go ahead and muck out the stalls and replace the hay before he checked in with Mrs. Jackson. He had arrived early, anyway.

He started shoveling out the soiled hay bed in the first stall, working energetically. He even started whistling. Since he had made his decision, his heart felt lighter. He knew he had chosen the right course.

Yancy wasn't really surprised to see Major Jackson come into the stable, for both of the Jacksons' horses were still there, so he knew the major hadn't yet gone to VMI.

"Hello, Yancy," Jackson said pleasantly.

"Good morning, Major Jackson. Want me to saddle Bebe or Gordo for you?"

"Not just yet. I'd like to speak with you for a few minutes. Will you come into the kitchen? Hetty has made fresh coffee for us."

"Yes, sir," Yancy said, a little mystified. He and Mrs. Jackson often had coffee or tea or lemonade for a little break, but Major Jackson had never sought him out for a break in work.

Yancy followed Major Jackson into the kitchen, where they seated themselves comfortably on the high stools at the worktable. Yancy almost always had lunch in here, talking with Hetty. Although the Jacksons had made no specific provisions for Yancy's meals—in fact, he almost always brought food from home—more often than not Hetty would fix him lunch, usually leftovers from breakfast and last night's dinner. Sometimes Yancy wondered whether Major and Mrs. Jackson knew this, but then he decided that they were generous people and probably didn't mind.

They sipped their fresh hot coffee for a few moments, and then Jackson said, "My wife tells me that you've had some trouble at home with the Amish leadership."

Yancy shifted uncomfortably on his stool but didn't drop his gaze. The blue glare of Jackson's stare hardly allowed one to look away. "I'm sorry if I bothered Mrs. Jackson," he said. "I didn't mean to, sir."

Jackson gave a dismissive wave. "You didn't bother her, Mr. Tremayne. She told me out of concern for you and your welfare. And I have an interest in that, too."

"You do?" Yancy gulped. "Well—thank you, sir."

"And so, have you been able to come to any conclusions about the course you should follow?" Jackson asked.

"Yes, sir, I have," Yancy answered. "I'd like—I'd like to keep working for you, sir. There's just one thing I'd like to ask. It's kind of a big favor, but I was hoping you might understand."

Jackson nodded. "And what is that?"

"You see, sir, if I keep working for you and disobey the bishop, it—it puts my family in a bad way. They support my decision, sir, but the bishop could still sort of put them in disgrace. They wouldn't be shunned." He grinned unevenly. "Guess that's what's going to happen to me. But still, they would be out of favor with the leadership of the community. So what I was going to ask is if maybe there's a room for me out at your farm, sir. Even if it's just in the loft of the barn or in the carriage house, I could make do. It would just be so much better for my family if I wasn't actually living at the farm."

Jackson leaned back, crossed his arms, and studied Yancy for a long time.

Yancy didn't flinch at his scrutiny; he met his icy gaze solidly.

"That's a hard decision for a boy of fifteen, Yancy. Are you sure this is what you want to do?"

"Yes, sir. And it's not really so hard," he added. "There's no law that says I can't go back and visit them anytime I want. Even if I'm supposed to be shunned, if they decide not to do it, no one's going to go tell on them to the bishop."

"I see. All right, Mr. Tremayne, now let me tell you of something that I think the Lord is leading me to do. You see, Anna and I prayed last night for you, to see if there was something we might do to help you. I believe you're an honest, hardworking, gifted young man, and that is something that I believe should be encouraged always. So I have a proposition that I'd like you to consider."

"What's that, sir?"

Jackson leaned across the table. "How would you like to attend VMI?"

Yancy's eyes widened. "Me? Go to VMI? But—how?"

"One of the alumni has established a charity scholarship program for promising young men who can't afford to attend the institute," Jackson answered. "I believe that if I submit you as a candidate, with my recommendation, you'll be accepted. It would pay for your tuition and your uniforms, provide a small allowance for food and other necessaries, and you would live in the barracks."

Yancy was stunned. "But—you really think I can qualify? I've had very little education, sir."

"Very little formal education, I know," Jackson agreed. "But I've observed that you're very quick, you're intelligent, and you pay attention. I know it will be difficult, but"—he sighed dramatically—"it couldn't possibly be harder for you than it was for me at West Point, Mr. Tremayne. I did it. I have every confidence that you can do it."

Yancy jumped off the stool and reached across the table. Jackson took his hand, and Yancy pumped it enthusiastically. "Yes, sir! I can! I will! And how can I ever thank you, sir?"

"Don't thank me, Mr. Tremayne," Jackson said. "It will be all to my satisfaction to see you become the soldier I know you will be. And the time is coming, I think, that it will be good soldiers that we need."

Part Three: The Foundation 1859—1860

CHAPTER TEN

Broad bands of yellow sunlight streamed through the window, illuminating the snowy white tablecloth on the modest four-seater dining room table at Major Thomas Jackson's house. Anna put the good Blue Willow china on the table; she liked to have a fine table setting when Thomas was home. She looked over the two table settings with satisfaction, with Thomas at the head and her sitting at his right hand. They always sat close together when they dined alone.

Hetty brought in scrambled eggs, grits, and bacon, and then fresh bread and marmalade. She sighed. "I know Major Jackson is only going to eat one thing. Wonder what it'll be today? All the biscuits, or all the bacon, or all the eggs?"

Hetty also served as the Jacksons' cook, but sometimes Anna Jackson cooked, too. She enjoyed it, although ladies such as those in the Morrison family rarely did any cooking. But this morning she had done the scrambled eggs all by herself, and it lent a rosy hue to her normally pale cheeks.

"I'll tell him I cooked everything," Anna said with a touch of amusement. "Maybe then I can make him feel guilty enough to eat a little of everything."

"You can try it, Miss Anna," Hetty said resignedly. "But he'll likely outfox you." She huffed back into the kitchen.

Anna poured two cups of hot coffee, then put sugar in one and set that one in Jackson's place. Then she went down the hall to her husband's study. Politely she knocked—she would never burst in on him uninvited—and called, "Thomas, Thomas, time for breakfast." She returned to the dining room.

In a few moments he appeared at the door, buttoning up his uniform tunic.

She smiled at him. Just then Anna wanted to tell him how happy she was just to see him in the morning, but somehow she could never form that in feeling or proper words. *How do I tell this man that when he isn't here I'm lonely and have a great emptiness? How do I tell him the minute I see him coming I feel safe and secure?*

For so long Anna Jackson had buried her feelings for Thomas Jackson, as she had when he had married Eleanor Junkin. Then, she could never admit to herself that she was in love with a man who was betrothed to another woman; and she could never, would never, entertain the thought that it was through that woman's death that she had married Thomas Jackson. In a way it held her back from expressing her deepest, most secret feelings. But Thomas Jackson was such an affectionate, loving husband that she thought he probably wouldn't profit from her confessions anyway. He knew she loved him.

When he came into the dining room, he put his arms out and she went to him. He held her tightly for a moment, neither of them speaking. He kissed her cheek. "You're better than any breakfast."

Anna said, "I know you, Thomas Jackson. You have eating on your mind, no matter how pretty your words. Let's sit down and eat this food before it gets cold."

They sat down and bowed their heads, and Jackson prayed a simple prayer of thanksgiving. Anna knew that he prayed about everything. Once he told her that he prayed over a glass of water when someone gave him one. Anna knew when he was offered any kind of help he always thanked God for it.

"Now, that bad habit you have of only eating one thing off the table won't work today," Anna said firmly. "I made everything this morning, and I want you to eat some of all of it."

"Why, I could fill up on these good biscuits you made. Look, you made eight of them. I can eat seven and you can eat one. Then you can fill up on all the eggs and grits."

Anna smiled and reached out and took two of the biscuits off the platter, put them on Jackson's plate, then said, "Eat those with your eggs."

She watched as he scraped some eggs on his plate then gave her the rest. He flatly refused the grits, insisting his plate was full, much more than he could eat. They ate in silence for a few moments, and in spite of Anna's best intentions, Jackson ate his two biscuits, got two more, and ignored his eggs. Anna gave up.

Then she said, "Thomas, the news about the North and their antislavery program threatening our cotton states has gotten so heated. What will we do if the South secedes?"

Jackson said quietly, "God hasn't told me, esposa. But He doesn't need to tell me until the problem comes. 'Take therefore no thought for the morrow,' the scripture says. 'Sufficient unto the day is the evil thereof.'"

"I can't help thinking about it. All these riots all over the country! It frightens me. I would like to know I have the courage to face a war."

Jackson reached over and took her hand. "I was talking to young Mr. Murphy just last week. After Sunday school he came up to me and said he'd like to talk to me for a few moments, so I took him aside into the church office. 'Major Jackson, I have a problem.' Of course I asked what it was. He said, 'I hear of people who die so easily it is like going from one room to another. If we go to war, I don't think I can face death like that. I just don't have dying grace.'"

Anna asked, "What did you tell him, Thomas?"

"I told him that he didn't need dying grace, and he asked me why that was. I said, 'Because you're not dying. When it comes your time to die or my time to die, that's when God will give us dying grace. Until that time comes, don't worry about it.' So, my dear, don't worry about it."

Anna always marveled at how her husband could simplify theological problems. He loved nothing better than talking about the deep, profound, and often mysterious things of the Bible.

CROSSING

Basically he saw things in a very simplistic manner that she envied. To him the scripture was very clear and very personal.

"I had a dream last night of having a baby," Anna said dreamily. "But then I worried that it might be too hard to bring a child into this world when it seems there is such trouble ahead."

"Why, Anna, don't you know that Adam might have said something like that to Eve when they were driven out of the garden of Eden? 'Eve, let's not have any children, for it might be too difficult.' " He took a bite of the last biscuit and chewed it thoughtfully. "There never was a time free of trouble. People are afraid of what might happen, but we must trust the Lord, and we must be wise." He smiled. "If God wants to send us another child, He will do so." He rose then and said, "It is time to go to church. Let's go hear what the Lord will teach us this morning."

Yancy rode up to the farmhouse and dismounted. With satisfaction he petted Midnight. He was three years old this month. Grandmother, muttering about "showy, proud horses," had given Yancy the foal after he had been at the farm for only a month. Yancy had trained him for two years now, and it had been difficult, for Midnight was a high-spirited, proud horse. But when Yancy had been a young boy, the Cheyenne had taught him to train shaggy wild mustangs, and he had developed a special knack for turning them into superb saddle horses. And so he had done with Midnight. But he would tolerate no rider except Yancy.

Before he went in he wanted to savor the cool October afternoon, the dry fall scent of the grass and fields, and the high pale sun set in a light blue sky. Hank, coming from the shade of the oak trees in the back of the house and alerted to his presence, bayed once, then loped up in welcome, ears flopping and tongue lolling. Yancy bent to pet him, scratching his ears and murmuring, "Dumb ol' dog. How are you doing, dumb ol' dog? Huh?"

Now he stood for a moment, absolutely still, remembering the richness of the farm. He was alive to the world that was about him, whether well-known or strange. He was sixteen years old now and one inch over six feet, and weighed one hundred and eighty pounds. He was one inch taller than his father, and this amazed him each time he thought of it.

Yancy hadn't worn his VMI uniform home, though it had been the proudest thing he had ever done to have worn it for a year. It wouldn't have been suitable to the Amish, however, for they seemed to freeze every time they saw any man in uniform. So every time he visited home, he wore his old work clothes, this time a pair of heavy wool brown pants and a dark blue wool shirt. He had the sleeves rolled up, and it showed his forearms, which were now strong and thickly corded with muscle. He had given up his silver-trimmed VMI forage cap for his old wide-brimmed slouch hat. In deference to the Amish he had even taken off the bead-trimmed band his mother had made.

Hearing Hank's welcome bark, Becky came out onto the veranda. Holding out her arms, she cried, "Yancy! Yancy, come in! We've missed you so much!"

He went into the parlor, where Becky and Zemira had their quilting rack down.

Zemira looked up to him, her bright dark eyes glowing with pleasure. "You've come back again! I suppose you got hungry."

"I'm always hungry for your cooking, Grandmother." He went to her, bent over, and kissed her smooth cheek. "You're getting prettier every time I see you," he teased.

"Go away from here with that nonsense!" She waved him away with a little laugh.

"Becky, are you all right? You look big as a house."

Becky laughed. "Yes, I'm well. But you have an odd way of framing a compliment, Yancy."

"But that's the way mothers-to-be are supposed to look, aren't they? And you're glowing, you look so pretty. So, Grandmother, are you going to feed me or what? I'm starved!"

"You can have some leftovers, but save an appetite," Zemira said sternly. "For supper I'm going to cook a meal that will make your hair curly."

"I always wanted curly hair." Yancy drew up a chair and sat down. He was soon eating heartily of lunch—cold ham, fresh white bread, jacket potatoes, pickles, and cabbage slaw. "This is wonderful!" Yancy said. "I don't get anything like this at VMI."

"Of course you don't. You're not supposed to get home cooking anywhere but at home," Zemira said. "Now, tell us everything you have been doing."

"It would bore you to death." Yancy smiled. "I get up in the morning, and I have to make sure my bed is made and everything is put away. I have to be sure that all the younger cadets get their rooms clean and their beds made. We then all go out to eat breakfast. Then we have classes, and then lunch. Then we go back to classes, and then supper. Nothing good like this, though."

Becky asked earnestly, "And how are your classes going, Yancy?"

He chewed thoughtfully. "It's hard. They're hard. Stuff I don't know, and stuff I have to work on real hard to catch up. But Major Jackson has helped me. He said he was like me when he went to West Point. He was behind and he had to study extra all the time. He doesn't favor me in class—it would be against his sense of honor to do that—but he helps me figure out how to study. He even talked Peyton Stevens into being my tutor, and he helps me a lot."

"Who's Peyton Stevens?" Zemira asked curiously. "I think I've heard that name before."

"Maybe so," Yancy said. "His father is Virginia Senator Peyton Stevens, Sr. Peyton is Jr. But he's not pompous or anything. He's real smart. He's just kinda lazy, I guess. But Major Jackson talked him into helping me with my studies, and he's helped me with everything, from English literature, to mathematics, to European history. . . ."

They heard a soft call from upstairs, and Zemira stood up. "That's Callie Jo waking up from her nap. I'll go get her."

"I'll get her," Becky offered.

"No ma'am, I'm not too old to climb those stairs and get my granddaughter," Zemira said over her shoulder as she left the room.

"You'll never be old, Grandmother," Yancy called after her. He told Becky, "I've never known anyone like her. She's sure not what I expected when we came here. I was afraid she was going to be this mean old Amish woman that never smiled."

"Nice surprise for you. She's very fond of you, Yancy. I think it's been good for her—and me, too—that you are here."

"You sure?" he asked gravely. "Even though you're supposed to be shunning me, and all of you are not exactly in the good graces of Bishop Lambright?"

Becky smiled warmly at him. "Well, you know, Yancy, shunning is not necessarily absolutely ignoring a person. Of course no one expects you to attend church or the sing, but neither are they angry with you or are they going to openly shame you. I don't think anyone in the community would refuse to speak to you, and certainly no one thinks that we shouldn't still be your family."

Callie Jo came toddling through the door, pulling Zemira by the apron. "Nance! Nance!" she cried, holding up her arms and running to Yancy.

He stood up, hoisted her high over his head, and turned around in circles. She squealed with delight. Then he sat back down with her on his lap.

"Hi, Nance," she lisped.

Yancy looked up at Zemira and Becky. "No one here had better ever tell my nickname to anyone at VMI," he said darkly. "Ever."

"Okay, Nance," Becky said. "It'll be our secret."

Yancy kissed Callie Jo's flushed cheeks. She was two years old now, with thick strawberry blond hair and light blue eyes like Daniel. "Hello, Jo-Jo. Did you know that I brought you a present?"

"Present?" she said, her eyes lighting up.

"Yep. It's out in my saddlebag. Wanna come with me to get it?"

"Yep."

He picked her up and went outside, where Midnight was still hitched to the post in the front yard. He snorted and danced a little when he came out.

"Minnite," Callie Jo said and pointed.

"That's right. You're a very smart little girl."

He pulled a book out of the saddlebag. "See here? This is for you."

"Book!" she announced. "My book! Read me!"

It was a picture book of Bible stories. Yancy sat with Becky and Zemira in the parlor and went through the entire book with her.

Then she said, "Froo with book. Go ride Minnite?"

"You're a mighty little girl for such a big horse."

"Pleez, Nance?" she begged, her blue eyes big and round as

saucers. Yancy had been taking her for rides since she turned one year old.

Yancy told Becky, "You heard her. I'm under orders."

Becky smiled. "Be careful. Hold her tight."

"Always," Yancy said. He left the house carrying Callie Jo and headed toward Midnight. He stepped into the saddle and put her in front of him, letting her hold the reins. The beautiful black stallion galloped away lightly, and Yancy reveled in the thrill of the moment.

❧

It was riotous fall in the valley, with the leaves of the hardwoods turned all the warm shades of red, orange, and yellow imaginable. As always, the evergreens cast their emerald glow over the land.

The three young men made their way through the thick forest just behind the Tremayne farm.

Suddenly, Yancy stopped, threw his rifle up, and pulled the trigger.

"You got him!" Clay Tremayne said. "I didn't even see that little beast."

"I didn't see him either!" Clay's brother Morgan exclaimed. He picked up the squirrel. "You got him right through the head, Yancy. Don't you ever miss?"

Yancy shrugged. "Not much. Well—no. I don't."

"Liar," Morgan scoffed.

"Have you seen me miss?"

"No. But that doesn't mean that you don't, when no one is watching."

They all laughed.

"We've got about enough of these things, haven't we?" Morgan said, holding up his game bag. "Let's go back and get Aunt Zemira to cook us up a great big supper of squirrel and dumplings."

They shouldered their rifles and started back to the farmhouse.

There were two families of Tremaynes in the Shenandoah Valley: The Enoch Tremaynes, as they were called, were the Amish Tremaynes. The Luther Tremaynes were English and lived in Lexington.

In the 1730s the Tremayne family moved to the Shenandoah Valley from Pennsylvania. There were two brothers, Enoch Tremayne, the eldest, and Luther Tremayne, who was the younger. Enoch stayed with the Amish and was Yancy's great-great-great-grandfather. Luther fell in love with an English, became a Methodist, and left the Amish. Luther was Clay's and Morgan's great-great-great grandfather. Basically the Tremaynes were somewhat distant cousins by now, but the two families had stayed close. They all called each other "Cousin" or "Aunt" or "Uncle," whatever seemed appropriate to their respective ages. Clay and Morgan called Yancy "Cousin," and Zemira "Aunt," and Daniel "Uncle."

In the golden afternoon glow, Clay suddenly straightened, pointed, and yelled, "Look, Yancy! There's one!"

Like lightning Yancy shouldered his rifle and sighted. Then he lowered it and muttered, "No, there was not one. What are you playing at, Clay?"

Clay laughed. "Told you you'd miss when no one's watching."

"Idiot," Morgan grumbled as they trudged on, but his tone was unmistakably affectionate.

He and Clay were brothers but were different in almost all aspects. Clay was twenty-three, two years younger than his brother, as tall as Morgan and more lightly built. Morgan had auburn hair and blue eyes, while Clay had dark-colored hair and gray eyes. Clay was high-spirited, a prankster, sometimes loud and boisterous. Morgan was thoughtful, quiet, serious. Since they had been old enough to stand, they had fought each other, verbally and physically. Though Clay seemed the more vigorous of the two, Morgan had always had a quiet, intent strength, while Clay was more suited to fighting like a windmill. Somehow Morgan had always managed to keep his rowdy young brother in check, but now that they were older, Morgan sometimes lost his grip on what Clay was doing. Clay was sly.

"Say, Yancy," Clay said, "Now that you're such a big VMI man and all, swaggering around with Major Thomas Jackson, we ought to go out and celebrate."

"Celebrate what?"

"You, man! It's time you put your pretty-boy uniform away and have a good time for a change!"

"Clay," Morgan said, "you don't want to be teaching him any bad manners."

Clay grinned mischievously. "Don't pay any attention to him. He's just an old milksop. I know a young girl about your age, Yancy. We'll go out and I'll teach you how to handle women."

Morgan warned, "He'll just get you into trouble, Yancy. I'm telling you, I don't care what he says, you'll just get into trouble."

Clay slapped Morgan on the shoulder so hard it almost staggered him. "You know, you're the good brother and I'm the bad one. I guess we're like Isaac and Ishmael. I always like what the Bible said about Ishmael, that he'd be a wild man. That's in Genesis 16:12." He glanced at Yancy and said, "That's my favorite scripture, because that's me." He turned back to his brother and said, "You're the good man and I'm the wild man, Morgan. Nothing you can do to change it."

"Of course there is, dummy. You say that all the time and you know you can change anytime you want to," Morgan insisted. He told Yancy, "If you want to do something, we'll go hunting or fishing. My sister plays the piano beautifully, too. You can come for supper and a concert. But don't go with Clay because he'll lead you astray."

"If I possibly can, I will." Clay laughed. "You better watch out for me. I'm a wild man, Yancy Tremayne!"

The next day was Sunday, so after his father and Becky and Zemira had left for church, Yancy headed back to VMI. About halfway to town he saw a buggy pulled over on the side of the road. He looked closer and saw that it was the Lapps' carriage. Almost all of the Amish buggies looked alike—black with unpainted and unadorned wooden wheels—but Yancy's powers of observation were sharp, and he also knew the gelding pulling the buggy. It was a big bay named Acer, and he belonged to Hannah Lapp's family.

The buggy was pulled to the side of the road, leaning precariously. One of the wheels was awry. The wheel lock had obviously come off, and the wheel tilted drunkenly to one side.

There were two horses hitched to the rear of the buggy and two men standing in the front. Between their thick shoulders, Yancy could see a white Amish prayer cap.

Quickly Yancy cantered up to them, dismounted, and said, "So, is there some trouble here?"

The two men turned, and Yancy recognized Boone Williams and Henry Cousins. They were both tall men, older than Yancy. The two worked at the sawmill in town, where Yancy had met them when fetching lumber for the farm. He had also seen them loitering on the street corners in town, spitting tobacco and furtively watching women who walked by.

Boone sneered at him. He was a burly man with thick, coarse brown hair and muddy brown eyes to match. "Go on your way, Tremayne. There's nothing here that you need to worry about."

Cousins laughed coarsely. He was a thickset man with bulging muscles and had obviously been drinking. "You heard him. Move on, Injun. We saw this squaw first."

They were standing too close to Hannah; Cousins's shoulder almost touched her face. She had her eyes downcast, but Yancy could see her hands, twisting nervously, and the way she cringed backward away from them.

Instantly Yancy made a decision. One of the tactics he learned from Major Jackson was to hit your enemy quick and hard and put him out if you can with the first blow.

Yancy kicked out and his boot caught Cousins in the ankle, which drove the big man off balance. He yelled as he went down, and immediately Boone roared and threw himself toward Yancy.

Yancy whipped out the knife he always carried and held it steadily pointed at Boone's barrel chest. "On your way, Boone. You, too, Cousins. You're not hurt. But if you two stick around you will be."

Cousins got up and snarled, "You won't always have that knife, Tremayne!"

"You're wrong. I'll always have it," Yancy said evenly. "Now get out of here before I use it on you."

The two glared at Yancy, then mounted and rode off, cursing him.

Yancy turned back around and said rather uncomfortably, "Hello, Hannah."

With a sob she threw herself into his arms.

He jerked with surprise but then patted her awkwardly and said, "It's okay. It's okay. They're gone now."

She clung to him desperately and cried, "That's—they scared me. I don't know what they wanted. Probably nothing. . .but—my brother went for a new wheel lock, and I stayed, and I shouldn't have, it was so stupid of me. . . ."

He held her out at arm's length. "It's not your fault, Hannah. Never think that this happened because of anything you did. It was their fault, not yours."

Woefully she gazed into his eyes, and he noticed that she was still just as pretty as she had ever been. Her ash brown hair had come loose in soft ringlets from her prayer cap. Her cheeks, though tear-stained, were still soft, and she had a flawless complexion. Her long lashes were wet with tears. Gently he reached out and smoothed one ringlet away from her face.

The gesture seemed to bring her back to the present. She straightened and pulled away from him, almost imperceptibly. Then she calmly folded her hands and composed her distraught features. The change in her attitude was subtle but unmistakable. She was distancing herself from him.

With a sigh, he stepped back. "So you said your brother was with you?"

"Yes, he was driving. When the wheel lock came off, he decided to walk to the Keim farm and see if they have another one."

"I'm sure they do. Mr. Keim has a good carpentry shop there," Yancy said lamely.

"Yes, he does."

"How—how have you been?" Yancy hadn't seen Hannah for almost a year, because of course he stopped going to church when he joined VMI and the bishop decreed that he must be shunned. He reflected that she hadn't changed at all; she still looked frail and vulnerable and naive. He knew, however, that he had hardened and toughened, and it showed on his face.

"I've been very well," Hannah answered softly. "You look fine, Yancy. You're very tan, I see. Were you out in the sun much this summer? Um—shooting, or drilling or something?"

"Something," he agreed. "But you know. Indian."

"Yes. Of course."

"Yes. Okay, well, I'll just hitch up Midnight and wait with you until your brother gets here."

"Thank you."

Yancy led Midnight to the back of the buggy and tied him up. Then, his hands stuck in his pockets, he went back to the front of the buggy where Hannah silently waited. As she regarded him, he saw that she had completely regained her composure. Her gaze was not hostile, but neither was it welcoming. She just seemed placid and sure of herself.

Yancy swallowed hard and decided to plunge in. "You know, Hannah, I've thought about you a lot. I thought—I thought that we were becoming good friends." Hannah had always shown particular interest in Yancy at Sunday dinners, constantly serving him more lemonade, more biscuits, more butter.

She sighed. "It's been a long time, you know, Yancy. A lot has happened. You're very different now than you were then."

He nodded. "Guess I am." He looked up and squinted in the afternoon sun. "I hear a wagon. Maybe it's your brother."

It was Amos Lapp, Hannah's oldest brother. He was a tall, muscular man with straw blond hair and a stern jaw. He reined the wagon up and nodded at Yancy.

"Hello, Amos," Yancy said. "I happened by and thought I'd wait with Hannah until you got back."

"That was very good of you, Yancy. Thank you. The Keims had a wheel block and also let me bring an extra wheel in case it's warped." He jumped out of the wagon.

Yancy looked closely at the wheel on the buggy. "It looks true, though. Can I help you fix it?"

"It would be easier with two."

"Glad to help."

"I'll pick up the wagon if you just slip the wheel back on the axle, Yancy. Then we'll see if the new block will hold it."

"Sure." Yancy noticed that Amos picked the wheel up as if it was made of feathers. Yancy straightened the wheel over the axle and then Amos let it down. Together they fit the wheel lock over it and hammered it in until the wheel was secure.

After they were finished, Amos said, "Thank you, neighbor. I appreciate the help, and for staying with my sister while I was gone."

"Glad to do it," Yancy said, holding out his hand.

Amos looked down at it then looked up at Yancy gravely. "I'm sorry," he said.

Some of the arbitrary rules of the Ordnung dictated certain conditions of shunning. The Amish could offer help to those who were shunned and could accept help from them. But they couldn't, for example, offer them rides or accept any from them. And they couldn't shake hands with them.

"It's all right. I understand," Yancy said hastily. He turned to Hannah. "Hannah, I was wondering—that is, I thought—"

"I'm sorry, too, Yancy, but no," she said so softly he could barely hear her. And then she turned her back.

Yancy didn't go home the next weekend. He stayed at the institute, doing some extra studies—he always had to work twice as hard as the other boys because of his lack of education when he was young. He washed all his clothes and cleaned the barracks room—twice— and busied himself with other work so that he wouldn't think too much about Hannah Lapp. Seeing her again had sharply reminded him that he had begun to develop feelings for her. In the last year since he had joined VMI, he had been so busy that he was able to block most things out of his mind except his classes and training. But when he had seen her in such awful circumstances, it had awakened all those emotions that he had with such determination put aside.

He had awakened before dawn on Sunday morning, ventured out in the bitterly cold gray predawn, and went for a short ride on Midnight. He found no joy in it though. He and Midnight both got chilled, and there was an icy fog that lay around the grounds of the institute, turning everything in sight a dull gray. He led Midnight back to the stables and began to give him a thorough brushing-down. After that, on the livery potbellied stove, he heated up a pot of hot mash. It was a mixture of oats, grits, and barley soup. It was Midnight's favorite treat.

Major Jackson came into the livery and came right to Midnight's stall. "That smells as good as my breakfast did this morning," he said, stroking Midnight's velvety nose. "This is a fine horse, Cadet Tremayne. No wonder you spoil him."

"Thank you, sir," Yancy said listlessly.

Jackson eyed him shrewdly. "You have anything planned for this morning, Cadet?"

"No, sir."

"Good, good. I want to ask you a question. Are you a Christian, sir?"

Yancy looked up, directly into his burning blue gaze. "I don't rightly know, Major. I pray, but it doesn't seem to do much good, for me or anything else. So I'm just not sure."

"Good answer, Cadet," Jackson said briskly. "Honest and to the point. One day you'll be able to answer with one word—yes. But for now, I'd like you to come with me this morning."

"Where to, Major Jackson?"

"To Sunday school."

"Yes, sir." Yancy was puzzled. Normally no one at the institute saw Major Jackson on weekends. Of course, since Yancy had worked for him and Mrs. Jackson, he was a little more familiar with them than the other cadets. But during the time Yancy had worked for the family, Major Jackson had never asked him to go to church. He wondered now if the major had noticed how low he had been for the past week.

Quickly Yancy saddled Midnight up again and they went into town, into the fine First Presbyterian Church of Lexington. Between the sanctuary and a private residence was the "Lecture Room." Major Jackson and Yancy dismounted and hitched there, a modest one-room addition to the church.

"Here we are, Cadet Tremayne," Jackson said. "I started this Sunday school in 1851, when I first came to Lexington and to the institute. We've had a wonderful time in the last eight years."

He opened the door. Yancy followed him and stopped suddenly as he saw that the room was filled with black people. Many of them were children, some of them young people, but there were also several adults.

Jackson went to the podium at the front of the room. "We have a guest today. This is Yancy Tremayne, one of our cadets from the institute. I thought you might want to meet one of our fine young men."

Yancy was speechless, for he had never dreamed of such a thing. He had remembered hearing Mrs. Jackson speak of a Sunday school, but it had never occurred to him that it was for black people. He took a seat and listened as Jackson taught the lesson. Yancy was once again amazed at how complex this man was. When he had heard of Jackson's fighting ability in Mexico, he pictured him being a man with a murderous spirit in battle. Here he was speaking gently, and one could see the affection that the children had for him, which he returned. After the lesson, they questioned him with spirit and intelligence about the lesson. They called him "Marse Major."

After the lesson and the singing were over, Jackson and Yancy left.

"That's a very fine thing, Major. I didn't know you did it."

"It was something the Lord told me to do. It gives me a great deal of pleasure. I feel sorry for these people because they have a hard way, and I believe the children should be taught just as well as white people, in all things. Ignorant people are sad people, and it's a waste."

Yancy asked hesitantly, "Major, do you think that slavery is wrong?"

Jackson sighed deeply. "I believe that all men should love God and His son, Jesus Christ. I believe that all men should be treated with dignity and respect and courtesy."

Yancy waited for Major Jackson to expand on this equivocal answer but he did not.

They rode on silently. At the cross street that led to Major Jackson's house, he bade Yancy farewell and turned toward home, and Anna.

CHAPTER ELEVEN

Late at night on May 24, 1856, armed raiders went into men's homes and took them to a dark place, and eventually, to their deaths. The condemned men were proslavery settlers in Pottawatomie, Kansas, and their names were James Doyle, William Doyle, Drury Doyle, Allen Wilkinson, and William Sherman. The killers who kidnapped them followed an antislavery crusader named John Brown. They hacked the five men to death with sabers. Later John Brown claimed to have no part in the killings, though he observed them. And he did say that he approved of them.

John Brown's long journey from the Pottawatomie Massacre to Harpers Ferry, Virginia, was a long and convoluted one. Along the way he went from Kansas to Missouri and all over New Engand and to Canada and the Midwest and finally back to Kansas. He met such notable sympathizers as William Lloyd Garrison, Henry David Thoreau, Ralph Waldo Emerson, Harriet Tubman, and Frederick Douglass. However, none of these stalwart men and women were with him on October 16, 1859, when he led eighteen of his followers in the attack on the Harpers Ferry Armory. He had two hundred .52 caliber Sharp's rifles and nine hundred and

CROSSING

fifty pikes contributed by Northern abolitionists. It was his feverish dream that all the slaves in Virginia would join them in the uprising and no blood would be shed except in self-defense.

At first they met no resistance. They cut the telegraph wires and easily captured the armory, which was only defended by one watchman. Then they spread out and took hostage slaveowners from nearby farms, including Colonel Lewis Washington, great-grandnephew of George Washington. Along the way they spread the news to the local slaves that their liberation was at hand.

But then a Baltimore & Ohio train came to the station. The train's baggage master, Hayward Shepherd, tried to warn the passengers that the station had been taken by gunmen. Brown's men called for him to halt and then opened fire. He was shot in the belly, and he spent the next twelve hours begging for water. . .until he died. He was a free black man and had a good reputation in Harpers Ferry. His death was much mourned, by black and white alike.

By 7:00 a.m. on October 17, John Brown's dream had become a nightmare. Local farmers, shopkeepers, and militia pinned down the raiders by firing from the heights behind the town. Some local men were killed by Brown's men. The raid became a pitched battle, with Brown outgunned and outnumbered. Brown was trapped in the arsenal.

By the morning of October 18, Harpers Ferry Armory was surrounded by United States Marines. In command was Colonel Robert E. Lee of the army. A young army lieutenant by his side was J. E. B. "Jeb" Stuart.

Colonel Lee turned to him. "Lieutenant Stuart, take the message in to Brown, if you please."

Stuart, a heavy-set, muscular young man with a full beard and piercing eyes, jumped off his horse, saluted smartly, and said, "Yes, sir!" Waving a white handkerchief, he reached the door of the arsenal and called out, "Surrender now, sir! If you surrender now, your lives will be spared!"

Brown shouted, "No! No, I prefer to die here!"

The Marines used sledgehammers and a battering ram to break down the door. In three minutes Brown was captured, along with his captives.

In those three days, Brown had killed four men and had wounded nine. Ten of Brown's men were killed, including two of his sons.

❧

With the last week in November, winter had come to the Shenandoah Valley. The days were bright and cold, the nights frosty and starry. There was no hint of snow in the air yet, but the wise longtime inhabitants of the valley felt it coming, smelled it coming, in the biting morning air.

Yancy was in Major Jackson's office. The two of them were going over plans for an overnight out in the woods to toughen up the cadets.

A knock sounded on the door.

"Come in," Jackson ordered.

The door opened.

"Lieutenant Stuart," Jackson said, "it's good to see you." He stood up, smiling one of his rare shy smiles.

Jeb Stuart stepped inside in his blue uniform, the uniform of the United States Army. He came over immediately to shake hands with Jackson. The two men knew each other slightly and had a mutual admiration for each other. "This is Cadet Yancy Tremayne. Cadet Tremayne, this is Lieutenant Jeb Stuart."

Yancy took his hand, and Stuart clapped down on him like a vice and spoke the words expected. He had taken off his hat and had jauntily tucked it under his arm. His full head of auburn hair was a mass of curls, as was his beard.

He turned back to Jackson. "I have orders for you, Major Jackson." Stuart reached in his pocket and pulled out an envelope.

Jackson opened it, read it, and looked up. "Do you know what these orders say?"

"Yes, sir, I do. You and a number of your cadets are ordered to go to the execution of John Brown."

Jackson nodded, pointing toward a chair. Stuart took his seat and Jackson resumed his, sitting bolt upright as always. Yancy deferentially stayed behind Jackson's chair, hoping he wouldn't send him out.

"I see these orders come from Governor Wise to Commander Smith," Jackson said. Francis Smith was the superintendent of VMI.

Stuart replied, "The governor decided it was the politic thing to do. This whole John Brown uprising has become a powder keg. And the pride of Old Dominion is the Virginia Military Institute. Since Southerners believe Brown incited slave insurrection in the South, but particularly in Virginia, the governor thinks that it would be better for the superintendent of VMI to be in charge of the execution, rather than the army."

"It's hard to believe that responsible men and women in the North actually helped this madman," Jackson said disdainfully. "The situation between North and South was bad enough as it is. Armed insurrection against Harpers Ferry, and all those senseless deaths. . . No good can come of it, no good at all."

"I agree, Major Jackson. Brown's trial was nothing short of a circus sideshow, with all the newspapers, North and South, competing against each other to see who could shout loudest and longest about who's right and who's wrong," Stuart grunted. "Makes me very proud that I'm a soldier and not a politician and not a journalist."

Jackson nodded agreement. "What is it like, with Brown?"

Stuart shrugged. "He's quiet. He glares with those fiery eyes of his. The old man doesn't have any nerves, I'll give him that."

John Brown's futile attempt to free the slaves had been in October, lasting for three days, the sixteenth through the eighteenth. He had been imprisoned in Charles Town since then.

Stuart continued, "Anyway, as you see there, Major Jackson, his execution is slated for December 2, so you've got some preparations to make." He rose and the two men enthusiastically shook hands again.

Stuart turned to Yancy, his blue eyes alight. "When I was in the livery I saw a fine black stallion, and one of the cadets told me that it belonged to a young man named Tremayne. Are you that lucky young man by any chance?"

Yancy smiled. "Yes, sir, I am. His name is Midnight."

"That horse is the only horse I've ever seen that I think someone riding him might beat me in a race."

"Midnight would beat you, sir, on any mount."

Stuart laughed, a hearty, rich sound. "I like a man who believes in his horse. Maybe we'll have a chance to try that out sometime, Cadet Tremayne." He turned back to Jackson. "I assume Cadet Tremayne will be accompanying you to Charles Town, Major?"

"He will. He's proven to be a very good aide," Jackson answered.

"Then I will see you there, Cadet," Stuart said, holding his hand out to give his usual bone-crushing handshake again. "Though I fear it will not be such a pleasant day as this."

Jackson and twenty-one VMI cadets arrived in Charles Town on November 28. Although Jackson had never made any official appointments, the two cadets whom he depended on most were Yancy Tremayne and Peyton Stevens.

Stevens, in spite of his languid ways, was a good and conscientous cadet and would make a good soldier. He rode a magnificent gold Palomino with a blond mane and tail named, appropriately, Senator. Yancy rode high-stepping Midnight, and between them Major Jackson slouched along on Cerro Gordo. They were an unlikely trio, with Peyton and Yancy in their fine, showy VMI gray and white uniforms and Jackson tightly wound up in his dusty blue coat. There could be, however, no question of who was in command.

The streets were crowded with people talking loudly, groups of men arguing on the street corners, paperboys shouting the latest penny press. The troop rode slowly through and kept in wonderful trim until they reached the town square.

"Courthouse," Jackson said succinctly.

Immediately Yancy held up his hand and shouted, "Company, halt!"

The mounted cadets stopped immediately with barely a sound.

Jackson, with Yancy and Peyton behind him, rode to a hitching post in front of the courthouse and dismounted. They stopped to survey this shabby building that had come to the center of attention of an entire nation.

It was a coupled courthouse, old, with gray and white pillars with the paint flecking off. The windows were of thick, wavy glass, and they were forlorn and dusty. The United States flag on the pole in front was faded and tattered.

Next door was a jail with worn, uneven bricks, with moss growing in between. It, too, was old and dismal looking, the last home John Brown would ever know. As they watched, they saw a plump man, who was evidently the jail master, holding court outside, his thumbs stuck in his suspenders self-importantly. He was talking to some journalists and some others who were obviously just curious.

"He's having his day in the sun," Jackson muttered. "I tell you, cadets, this whole thing has been shameful from beginning to end. I'm going in to see the sheriff about our accomodations. You wait, and don't let any of the boys wander over there to listen to that fool."

That night Jackson wrote to Anna:

Charles Town, Nov. 28, 1859
I reached here last night in good health and spirits. Seven of us slept in the same room. I am much more pleased than I expected to be; the people here appear to be very kind. There are about one thousand troops here, and everything is quiet so far. We don't expect any trouble. The excitement is confined to more distant points. Do not give yourself any concern about me. I am comfortable, for a temporary military post.

The gallows had been erected on a hill just outside of Charles Town. Facing it squarely were two artillery pieces, each manned by seven VMI cadets. Behind them, mounted, were the seven remaining cadets. Yancy and Peyton again flanked Major Jackson. They waited in perfect silence, the gunners at the ready. It was feared by the governor that Brown's fanatical followers might make a last-ditch attempt to rescue him. Charles Town and Execution Hill were ringed with militiamen.

Below them one thousand militiamen waited to escort John Brown to his execution. They led him out of the jail. His steel gray hair and beard bristled aggessively, yet he shufffled slowly in ugly carpet slippers, for he had been injured when he was captured and he was ill. A jail was no place to get healthy and gain strength. Although his step was tentative, his face showed no weakness. He handed a piece of paper to the plump jailer, who took it and started to read it, but Brown spoke in a low tone to him and he folded it and put it in his pocket.

Brown stared around at the soldiers surrounding him and the others waiting in the roadway beyond. He blinked a little, for the sun was incongruously bright and cheerful. It was a cold, crisp day. "I had no idea Governor Wise thought my murder was so important," he said bitterly.

With his jailer on one arm and the sheriff on the other, he went to the waiting wagon. They helped him up into it, and calmly he seated himself on the coffin between the seats. The driver cracked a whip over two white farm horses, and slowly they crawled out of the town and up the hill to the waiting gallows. The wagon finally reached the hollow square of troops, one thousand of them. It filed past the artillery and the VMI cadets.

In a low voice Yancy called, "Attention!"

The standing cadets stood at a perfect formal stance.

The old man lifted his head and gazed at the distant hills, sweet and blue and faraway, and the meeting place of the Shenandoah and Potomac rivers. Yancy heard him say, "This is a beautiful country. I never truly had the pleasure of seeing it before."

"None like it," the sheriff answered.

The prisoner mounted the scaffold first. He turned and stared straight at the cadets and the artillery pieces. Yancy thought his eyes glinted fiercely as he gazed into the gaping mouths of the cannons. Two men fitted a white hood over his face while another adjusted the rope.

One man gently nudged him in the direction of the rope, and in a muffled but calm voice he said, "I can't see, gentlemen. You must lead me."

The sheriff and a guard led him to the trap, where he stood in his carpet slippers and waited. The militia that had accompanied him from the jail traipsed about below, a confusion of stamping feet and muffled commands.

The sheriff asked Brown, "You want a private signal, now, just before?"

"It's no matter to me. If only they would not keep me waiting so long."

The militia went on and on, trying to get themselves into order, and the minutes, it seemed to Yancy, went on endlessly. He felt slightly sick. But some of the younger cadets glanced at each other in secret amusement at the citizen soldiers' stumbling.

Although they had made no sound, Jackson growled, "Gentlemen."

Every cadet immediately became perfectly motionless and expressionless.

Finally the militia were arrayed, and Execution Hill became quiet.

John Brown murmured to his jailer, "Be quick, Avis."

The noose was tightened, the ax parted the rope, the hatch swung open, and John Brown was dead.

Still the field was quiet.

Then Major J. T. L. Preston of VMI shouted loudly, "So perish all such enemies of Virginia! All such enemies of the Union! All such enemies of the human race!"

The soldiers were ordered at ease. Men went forward and took his body down. Nails sounded in the coffin.

The jailer took out the piece of paper that John Brown had handed him, his last words:

> *I, John Brown, am now quite certain that the crimes of this guilty land will never be purged away, but with blood. . . .*

The cadets were very quiet as they returned to their rooms in town. The citizens of Charles Town had been very generous, taking them into their homes and feeding them and making sure they were as comfortable as they could be under the circumstances.

Yancy, Peyton Stevens, Charles Satterfield, and Sandy Owens rode together after the company was dismissed. Chuckins and

Sandy had attended the cannons. They had all been very close to the scaffold, close enough to hear everything that had been said and see all the inner workings of a hanging.

Chuckins said in a tired voice, "I didn't know it was going to be like that. It wasn't what I thought it was going to be at all."

Sandy asked, "What did you think it was going to be, Chuckins?"

"I don't know. Not so—sad. I think the man was crazy, and I think he was wrong, wrong, wrong in what he did, and I know that he's massacred people here and in Kansas. But somehow this—this cold, bloodless. . ." His voice petered out.

"I know what you mean, Chuckins," Peyton said quietly. "No guts, no glory, no thrill of battle or ringing trumpets or great men shouting commands or fiery martyrdom. Just a kind of whimper."

Sandy sighed. "I've seen dead people before, but that's the first time I've seen an execution. And you're right, Peyton, I've no stomach for it at all. I'm glad it's over."

After a few moments Yancy muttered, "I don't think anything is over. I don't think anything ended today except John Brown's life. I think because of it, the trouble has just begun."

CHAPTER TWELVE

On this unrestful year of 1859, Christmas came on the last Sunday of the month, so the Virginia Military Institute let classes out on Friday, December 23. Yancy hurried home early that morning, anxious to see his family. At about noon it began snowing, a soft swirl of big flakes that slowly covered the landscape in a delicate fluffy white quilt. Midnight's steps puffed up big pillows of snow as he turned up the road to the farm.

Hurriedly Yancy hitched Midnight up to the post at the front porch and jumped the steps up onto the veranda. He heard Hank howling, and before he could knock, Daniel came out onto the porch.

"Son! You made it for Christmas!" He held out his arms and gave Yancy a suffocating bear hug.

Zemira, Becky, and Callie Jo came out on the porch, hugging Yancy over and over. Hank blundered out and jumped on everyone. Becky was now so big that Yancy could barely put his arms around her. He bent over and kissed her on both cheeks. Grinning, he said, "You still look beautiful."

Sassily she replied, "I suppose if I'm as big as a barn I'd better still look pretty."

Daniel laughed. "And you do, Beck. Come on, let's get into the

140

parlor. We've got a big warm fire and lots of food."

"That sounds good, Father, but I don't want to leave Midnight out in the snow. I'll stable him and be right back," Yancy said.

Zemira said, "That's good, Yancy. Everything's fresh in the kitchen, but it'll take us a few minutes to set the table."

Daniel went with Yancy. Together they led Midnight to the stables, unsaddled him, and brushed him down. It went quickly with the both of them.

"We'll fix him some of his special mash after we eat," Daniel said. "And since it's Christmastime maybe we'll treat the other horses, too."

"That we will," Yancy murmured. He went to each of the stalls—Fancy, Reuben, Stamper, and Reddie—petted them all and murmured nonsense horse talk to them.

They went back to the house. Yancy noticed that the table and chairs from the veranda were now in the parlor so they could eat by the immense fire. Becky and Zemira had prepared a plain homey meal, for the feasts would commence on Christmas Day, and the following day, December 26, which was for family visiting. On this night they had an immense beef potpie, corn fritters, pickled beets and onions, and fried turnips with greens. For dessert Becky had prepared apple cake, a complicated recipe that she had perfected. For a woman who had never cared much about cooking, Zemira had taught her so well that she now loved it.

As they ate they talked about the farm, the livestock, and the horses.

Zemira said, "Becky's father has offered to exchange a billy goat and a nanny goat for one of our roosters and two sitting hens. I think it's a good trade. Callie Jo likes goat milk. Maybe the new one will, too."

"I like goat cheese, too," Yancy offered.

"You like everything," Daniel scoffed.

"Like his father," Becky said indignantly. "I think you'd eat grass if Mother Zemira cooked it for you."

"When he was six years old he ate it without me cooking it," Zemira said airily. "He saw the horses grazing and decided it might be good."

"Did he get sick?" Becky asked incredulously.

"No, not at all. That's why I don't bother to cook it for him," Zemira answered.

"Well for me, if I'm ever reduced to eating grass, I'm going to hurry home from the war and have some Friendship Bread," Yancy grunted.

A silence descended on them for a moment. The only sound was Callie Jo in her high chair, chewing noisily on a piece of beef from the potpie.

Finally Yancy broke the awkward silence and said, "I know, I know, we don't talk about war. But at the institute that's just about all we talk about. You know that the Southern states are going to secede from the Union. It's going to happen."

Daniel sighed deeply, almost a groan. "We know, and you're wrong, son, we do talk about it. We think about it all the time, because we love you and we understand what will happen if there's a war. I don't suppose that maybe you'd think about coming back to us? Neither the North nor the South will bother the Plain People. They leave us to ourselves and leave our lands to us."

With slow deliberation Yancy put down his knife and fork, wiped his mouth with his napkin, and pushed his plate away. "I can't do that. I've chosen my way. I love you all"—he looked at everyone clearly—"but this is my life. This is the life I want. I want to be a soldier."

"But son, this is a big mistake, in these days and times," Daniel blustered. "You're so young. You're only sixteen! You can come back to us before there's some kind of awful war and then, afterwards, see what you want to do! There's no need for you to—"

Zemira reached over and took Daniel's hand in hers. "Don't make a mistake with him, Daniel," she said quietly. "The boy's a man, and he's decided his way, for the time being. All we can do is love him and offer him a home, no matter what."

For a few moments Daniel's square jaw tightened, but then he closed his eyes and nodded. "I know, Mother. I know. All right then, Yancy. So, what are the English saying out there?"

"Ah, us English talk too much," Yancy said, grinning. "The North says we're a bunch of devils because we own slaves. The

South says the North is a bunch of devils because they just want to take us over and steal our lands and our rights."

"I still read the newspapers, in spite of what my mother says," Daniel said mischievously. Zemira made a face at him. "I read where the North has conferred a sort of sainthood on John Brown, and the South has made him out to be the devil incarnate." He studied Yancy's face, which was expressionless, and then he added, "You haven't said anything about him and his execution, Yancy. What did you and all the cadets think about him?"

Yancy replied, "We didn't think about him much at all, you know. We didn't know him. We didn't know anything about him. We only witnessed his execution."

"That must have been very hard," Becky said sympathetically.

"It was, in one way," Yancy said thoughtfully. "In another way it made us all want to—to—fight, to offer our lives in a meaningful way, to want our lives to count for something. John Brown was a sick old man that died a sorry death. Even though we knew he stood for something, we all believe that we would rather die fighting for a noble cause, standing up for our beliefs and dying a death with glory."

"There is no death with glory in war," Zemira said solidly. "There is only death, bloody and unnecessary death."

"I understand you, Grandmother," Yancy said quietly. "But I would much rather take the chance of a death with honor, facing it with courage, so that it means something to my country."

After supper Yancy and Daniel made sure the livestock were warm, dry, and well fed in the barn and stables. They banked the fires in the bedrooms and kitchen stove and brought in plenty of firewood for the morning fires. By 7:00 they were tired, and everyone went to bed.

Yancy was having a confused dream in which he and Hannah Lapp were frantically running up and down stairs. . .when he realized that people were running up and down the stairs. He jumped out of bed and pulled on his clothes, murkily realizing that when people were running about in the middle of the night it must be an emergency.

CROSSING

When he stepped outside of his bedroom, he saw that his father was indeed running up the stairs with a basin of hot water and several white cloths over his arm. "It's the baby," Daniel said breathlessly.

"But I thought it wasn't due till the second week of January," Yancy said anxiously.

"So we all thought, but it seems the baby thinks otherwise," Daniel answered, heading toward his bedroom, balancing the steamy basin carefully.

"Should I go get Esther Raber?" Yancy asked.

"Mother says there isn't time," Daniel replied tensely. "Go down to the kitchen and make sure there's more boiling water. And watch Callie Jo if she wakes up." He went into the master bedroom, kicking the door shut behind him.

Yancy hurried downstairs and built up the fire in the kitchen iron stove. He filled up two copper pots and set them on the stove to start them boiling. Then he ran upstairs to the nursery, where Callie Jo was sleeping. Silently he slipped in and watched her in the crib that he and his father had built for her. She slept soundly, peacefully.

He hurried back downstairs to stare at the pots of water. Hank was in the kitchen, and even he was anxious, sitting and staring at Yancy and then going around and around in circles before lying down on his rag rug in front of the stove. Then he got up and started circling the kitchen again.

Clearly this was a fruitless occupation for both of them, so Yancy went upstairs, grabbed his boots, coat, and warm felt slouch hat and went back down. He took Hank out to pace on the veranda.

It was a beautiful December night. The sky was so thick with stars that it seemed like a mirror to the snow-spangled earth. The air was clear and biting, with a clean, brisk scent to it. Yancy inhaled deeply.

Then began an odd, seemingly aimless round in the silent snowy December night. He paced with Hank; he went to the kitchen to check on pots of water that eventually boiled; he went upstairs to check on Callie Jo, who slept peacefully on.

Once, on one of these roundabouts, he couldn't stand it any

longer. He tiptoed to the master bedroom and pressed his ear to the door. He could hear, through the thick oak, his grandmother's soft murmur and his father's low mutterings. No sound came from Becky.

Yancy had much experience with childbearing—or of hearing it, at least. In the Cheyenne camp any woman who was bearing a child was the concern of the entire community. In the tepees their cries were clearly heard. Men bore them with no sign of distress; they accepted it as a part of giving life.

Now Yancy remembered that he'd heard nothing when Becky gave birth to Callie Jo, until she uttered her first baby cries. But now the silence seemed to be ominous, as was this entire night. He wondered if things were going terribly wrong.

Slowly he went back downstairs and led Hank out onto the veranda. There he stood at the head of the steps, staring across to the east. Comically, Hank sat down beside him, sighing a doggy sigh and sorrowfully looking out.

Yancy took off his hat and held it to his heart. He spoke out loud. "Father God, I know I'm not a—a—oh, I don't know what I am. But I know what You are, and I know that my father and Grandmother and Becky are Your protected and beloved children. I pray for Becky right now, and for that baby. You love them, I know You do. Save them. Make them well. Make them strong. Thank You."

As always, Yancy felt nothing at all, but he was glad he had prayed anyway. He resumed pacing.

At one minute after midnight he heard loud raucous stomping on the stairs, and his father rushed out onto the veranda. He hugged Yancy so hard he thought he'd suffocate. Hank started howling. "It's a boy, a boy, a big fine boy, and Becky's fine, just fine," Daniel shouted. "C'mon, you have to see your new brother, Yancy. In fact, he kinda looks like you! Hurry, hurry, Becky's got to go to sleep and the baby's tired, too. They had a hard time, but they're both fine. . . ."

They ran upstairs, taking them two at a time, now uncaring that their stout boots made such a rowdy man's noise. Yancy followed his father into the bedroom.

Becky was soaked with sweat, with purple shadows etched under her eyes. But she looked happy, and her smile was beatific. "Your brother, Yancy. We've decided to name him David." She held him up.

Yancy took the tiny bundle into his arms. His face was red and wrinkled, like an old man's. But he had a great thatch of black hair, and his eyes were dark as he sighted around his new world. He was colored like Becky, of course, with a fine complexion, not darkened like Yancy's, but Yancy was still proud. "David," Yancy repeated softly. "Does he have a middle name?"

Becky and Daniel glanced at each other. "Yancy," Becky said. "Yancy is his middle name."

In spite of the growing dark clouds on the horizon that separated North and South, that Christmas holiday at the Tremayne farm was joyous.

All day, Christmas Eve had been a sort of catch-as-catch-can day, for Becky was still very weak, and the baby, though he was healthy, demanded constant attention for the first critical hours.

But that night, all of the Tremaynes, David Yancy included, slept soundly. Just before dawn, Zemira woke up and, after checking on Becky and the baby, started Christmas cooking. Now the family was reaping those riches at Christmas Day dinner.

"Mother, you've outdone yourself," Daniel said enthusiastically. "I think this is the best, biggest, and most wonderful feast I've ever had. How in the world did you do it?"

"Humph," Zemira grunted. "Didn't you know that Yancy helped me cook almost all of it?"

"What!" Daniel said in surprise. "But he's been doing all the chores and taking care of the livestock. How could he have possibly helped you?"

Since the birth of David had been of some difficulty to Becky, she had stayed in bed until joining the family for Christmas dinner. Yancy had assured Daniel that he would take care of the farm, while he took care of Becky and the baby. Daniel had stayed almost continually in their room, bringing Becky broth and cool water and fresh milk and continually changing the baby and bathing him so that he'd be clean and comfortable.

But on Christmas Eve and Christmas Day, Yancy had indeed found time to help Zemira in the kitchen. The Amish didn't believe in a conspicuous, tawdry celebration of Christmas—to them it was a time to meditate upon the birth of the Christ child and of scripture. But they did believe in celebrating the riches of their heritage, which included the wonderful and tasteful foods of the Amish.

Now Yancy grinned crookedly. "I've chopped vegetables. I've kneaded dough. I've tenderized meat. I've timed boiling pots of vegetables. I've worked flour and salt and pepper and spices and vegetables into gravy. I've stuffed a turkey. I've made four batches of corn bread. Take my word for it, Father. I thought studying and classes and artillery and gunnery and marksmanship and mathematics and history and philosophy were hard. They're nothing compared to helping in Grandmother's kitchen."

David Tremayne was a robust, bawling, demanding baby, exactly the opposite of Callie Jo. Sitting in her high chair at the Christmas feast, she pointed to him with her spoon. "He loud," she said plaintively. "He loud."

Becky was holding him, and discreetly she put the squalling child under her shawl to nurse him. He immediately grew silent. "Now he's quiet, Callie Jo," she said soothingly. "Eat your porridge."

"Porrith," she repeated happily and began to, somewhat messily, spoon it into her mouth. She loved oatmeal with cream and brown sugar.

"Good Christmas," Yancy said happily. "Never thought I'd get a present of a little brother. Thought the Amish didn't go in for gifts and such for Christmas."

"So they don't," Daniel said. "But David was a surprise. Showy gift for the Plain People, he is."

"Maybe we should name him Christmas," Yancy said mischievously.

"I think not," Becky said sturdily. "I'd just as soon name him Tinsel or Holly or Plum Pudding."

"Hmm. . .Plum Pudding Tremayne," Daniel said meditatively. "There's a thought."

CROSSING

"No, it's not," Zemira said sternly. "That is what I would call no thought at all."

As they continued the easy banter while finishing up the sumptious meal, Yancy could only be thankful for this special time with his family and hope the coming war—for he was certain it was coming—would not take this all away.

The Amish considered Decmber 26 a day of feasting, of celebrating and visiting among families and the community. At dawn that day, Daniel had ridden around to all of the Amish farms to spread the joyous news of his son David and also to let them know that Becky was still unable to travel around visiting.

By two o'clock that afternoon, the Tremayne farm had received representatives of eighteen families of the community. The food that they had brought overran the kitchen and was starting to crowd even the roomy root cellar.

Every family had been joyous at the arrival of David Yancy, hugging Daniel and shaking his hand vigorously, kissing Becky gently, kissing Zemira. . .and nodding politely to Yancy. Finally he had seen that his being there, and being shunned, was paining his parents and Grandmother, and he decided to go for a long ride on Midnight. He disappeared at about three o'clock.

They wandered aimlessly along the stream, seeing deer and raccoons and opossums and squirrels scurrying along on their errands. Yancy was amazed at all of the tracks in the snow. For once, Yancy wasn't zeroing in on a single track to hunt; he was merely observing all the wildlife. Now he saw that they, too, had purpose and family life and homes. It affected him oddly. Never before had he seen prey as anything but animals to be killed and eaten—or merely to be killed as nuisances. Now he saw that they had an intrinsic design to their lives, with mates and children and an urge to hunt for food and shelter.

"Aw, c'mon, Midnight, I must be getting tired and crazy. I'm feeling sorry for that last nasty 'possum we saw that had six babies on her back. Let's go on home. If we're still overrun with Amish, I'll sleep in the stable with you." Yancy turned him toward home, and Midnight knew the way. Midnight huffed great icy clouds of breath, while Yancy's was a thin stream of mist. He was bone-tired and bent and yawned over the saddle.

It was actually about eight o'clock, three hours after dark, when Yancy and Midnight returned to the stables at the Tremayne farm. Midnight led the way into the stables and stopped before his stall. Sleepily Yancy jumped off and, by an automatic mechanism stemming from hundreds of repetititons, unsaddled him and brushed him down. Gratefully he saw that his father had left a pot of hot mash on the stove, and he fed all five horses on this frosty night.

He went into the farmhouse through the back door, through the kitchen, into the back hall. To his dismay he heard people—men—laughing. . .but then he recognized the raucous roar of his cousin Clay. He hurried into the parlor.

The Caleb Tremayne family had all come to welcome the newest Tremayne. Caleb Tremayne was now forty-seven years old, as was his wife, Bethany. Caleb was a burly man, with dark hair and intense dark brown eyes. Clay had inherited his father's looks. But Morgan took after his mother; she had auburn hair, with light blue eyes, and was of a slender frame, tall and willowy. Clay was as tall as Morgan but more muscular.

And then, to their everlasting surprise, Caleb and Bethany had a "late-in-life" baby, but then, adding more to their surprise, they were late-in-life twins. They called them Brenda and Belinda, and they were born in the spring of 1854. Now just over five years old, they seemed to be foundlings that all the Tremaynes were both delighted and bemused by. They looked like picture-book angels, with strawberry blond curls and heaven blue eyes and perfect little faces. Only their mother and father could tell them apart; even Clay and Morgan got them confused. But then, because of the difference in their ages, it wasn't too surprising that they had spent very little time with their sisters. Clay had dubbed them Bree and Belle, but most of the time he just called both of them Bluebell.

Yancy greeted them all happily. He loved the Caleb Tremayne family. They seemed to be a very happy, stable, loving family, in spite of Clay's mischievousness. He sat down and took Belinda on one knee and Brenda on the other.

Clay was standing, leaning against the mantelpiece and sipping coffee. "Where have you been, Yancy? Hiding?"

"Yes," he answered expressionlessly.

There was a tense silence that Caleb Tremayne finally broke, with a covert glance at Daniel. "Being shunned must be hard—on everyone."

Zemira, seated by Becky, dropped her head and sighed. But Becky straightened her shoulders and said sturdily, "Yancy is strong, and he makes good decisions. Daniel and Grandmother and I have decided to respect that, and him, no matter what."

"I admire you all," Bethany Tremayne said softly. "But still it must be hard. Is it not, Yancy?"

He shrugged carelessly, but his words were not. "What I'm wondering is when—or if—I'm just going to be accepted as an English. As you all are. I know, Uncle Caleb, that the Amish do business with you, that your family is respected, that you're recognized as a leader of the Lexington community by the Amish and the English alike. How—how long will it take before I'm accepted just for who I am?"

Caleb and Daniel exchanged dark glances. Slowly Caleb answered, "Our family has been English for three generations now. Times change, and people change. Who knows? Next year you may be regarded as just one of the English members of the Amish family. We're not the only ones, you know. There are English Rabers, Fishers, and even an English Lambright, a distant relative of Bishop Lambright. One day you will be treated with affection and respect, Yancy, if you earn it as an honorable man."

"I will," Yancy said. "I have to."

The twins were staring at him, trying to fathom this serious grown-up conversation, when at this moment Callie Jo grew jealous and decided to object to their sitting on her brother's lap. She toddled over and yanked on Belinda's bright curls. "My bruvver," she pouted.

The twins' eyes grew round but they said nothing.

"Here now, none of that," Daniel said, hurrying over to pick her up and settle her into his lap. "You have to learn to share.

Especially now that you've got a new baby brother."

"Why?" Callie Jo demanded.

"Because it's the right thing to do."

"Why?"

"Because the Bible tells us to do unto others as you would have them do unto you. So you must love everyone and share with them."

"Why?"

Daniel frowned. "Because I think it's past your bedtime, and so we must save this Bible lesson for later." He stood up, holding Callie Jo, who looked as if she were going to rebel, but then she threw her head onto Daniel's shoulder and closed her eyes.

"I'm too tiwed," she lisped.

"I thought so. If you would all excuse me," Daniel said.

Belinda and Brenda looked at each other in the most uncanny way, perfect echoes of the other's expressions. "Callie Jo's tired," Belinda said.

"Yes, she's tired," Brenda agreed. Solemnly they watched Daniel carry her to the stairs.

Clay, standing propped against the mantel, observed idly, "Does anyone else think that's scary?"

Belinda's and Brenda's heads swiveled to him. Belinda said, "What do you mean, Clay? Who's scary?"

Brenda echoed, "Who's scary?"

"Never mind, Bluebells. Forget I said anything."

"Yes, forget it, girls. Sometimes your brother Clay speaks out of turn," Bethany Tremayne said. "As in, since you were born," she added pointedly to him. "Clay cried all the time, Morgan never cried, and it seemed as if Belinda and Brenda began talking the day after they were born and haven't stopped since. And that brings me to your darling David. He seems to be a very good baby."

"He wasn't at first, but he's beginning to settle into his routine now, I think," Becky said, looking down and rocking the brand-new cradle very gently. David's dark eyes were open, and he seemed to stare up at her as if assessing his mother. "He hasn't cried or fussed all day, and he's definitely been a very busy boy."

Caleb Tremayne rose. "Forgive us, Becky; we've stayed far too long. But the hospitality of your house, Zemira"—he bowed in her direction—"makes us so comfortable. As soon as you're feeling stronger, Becky, you and your family have an open invitation to dinner at our home."

They all rose, and Yancy kissed the girls on their cheeks before setting them down. "Thank you, Uncle Yancy," they echoed.

Clay shook Yancy's hand. "Next Saturday is the New Year, cousin. If you're going to be an English, you'd better come to town and celebrate like one."

"Better not," Morgan grumbled, shaking Yancy's hand in his turn. "Every New Year since he turned fourteen has been nothing but trouble."

Clay clapped Morgan on the back. "Come with us, Morgan, and act your age for once, instead of like a seventy-year-old man! So meet us at Mason's Grocer and Dry Goods. You can't come to the house. Mother would probably chain us to chairs. How about it?"

Slowly Yancy nodded. "Might do me some good, to have some fun for a change. I'll be there. If you're coming, Morgan," he added. "I know there's no way I can handle this wild man by myself."

"I'll come," Morgan agreed. "I wouldn't mind celebrating a little. But I'll keep a close watch on you, Clay. You're not going to get either me or Yancy in trouble. I'll promise you that."

"We'll see," Clay said with a mischievous grin.

The trouble was that Morgan wasn't there. When Yancy went into Mason's to find the two, he found Clay sitting in a straight chair by the iron stove.

His feet propped against an upturned bucket, Clay was eating a pickle and had a handful of crackers and cheese. "Have some of these crackers and cheese, Yancy. They make the pickle go down really good."

"Think I will." Yancy fished a pickle out of the barrel then took a hunk of cheese and some crackers out of a jar. "You buying?"

Clay answered, "Sure. I know you boys at VMI don't make much money, marching around so pretty and shooting at dirt." Clay's great-grandfather had, wisely, decided to spin cotton instead of grow it. He had built a cotton mill, which had been built up until it was the largest in the valley. By this time the Caleb Tremaynes didn't actually work; they were presidents and vice presidents of the mill, gentlemen with the income of merchants, but that didn't actually sully their hands with manual labor. And the Caleb Tremaynes were very well off indeed.

Yancy bristled. "You don't want to insult me about the institute, Clay. I'm not going to take kindly to it."

Clay laughed. "Calm down, cousin. I've lived here all my life. I know how all the institute boys take offense at the least little thing. And they say I make trouble for myself? You boys growl at one wrong syllable."

"Right. Don't make a wrong syllable," Yancy grunted. "Even though I'm not wearing it, I still revere the uniform."

Yancy was wearing his buckskin breeches, moccasins, an undyed, rough linsey-woolsey shirt, and a vest that had been intricately beaded by his mother. He had a canvas rain-proof overcoat that his father had given him.

Clay, in contrast to Yancy, was wearing the typical well-bred gentlemen's clothes—a black suit, white linen finely-ruffled shirt with silk tie, and black boots. He looked immaculate, with his black hair combed back and curling over his collar. His chiseled features, his mouth shaped by good humor, and his sparkling dark eyes all added to his fine looks.

"Yes, suh, Cadet, I heah you," Clay finally said after giving him a careful once-over. Then he gave Yancy a mock salute. "And by the way, don't you have any gentlemen's clothes?"

"These are Cheyenne clothes. They're better than gentlemen's clothes. Except for VMI uniforms," Yancy said succinctly. "Anyway, where's Morgan?"

Clay shook his head in mock shame. "Mama Morgan had to go home. He got word one of his favorite cows is about to have a calf. It's out of season, and she's having trouble with it. You know Morgan, he's more worried about cows and horses and dogs and cats than he is with people."

"Well then, why don't we wait till tomorrow, when we can celebrate with Morgan?" Yancy asked diffidently.

"No, no! You know what the Bible says, 'Don't put off tomorrow what you can do today.' "

"I don't believe it says that," Yancy scoffed.

Clay shrugged. "Then it ought to. Come on, let's settle up with these pickles and crackers." Rising, he went up to the counter, tapped on it, and called, "Mr. Mason! Mrs. Mason! Hello?"

A large, round woman came through the curtains from the back of the store and chugged along to the money drawer. "There is no need," she huffed, "for calling out so sharp and yelling like a wild Indian." When she caught sight of Yancy, her big blue eyes widened in surprise. "Oh, I do beg your pardon. Are you, sir, a wild Indian?"

"No, I'm a tame one," Yancy said with a smile. He came forward, his hand held out. "How do you do, ma'am. I'm Yancy Tremayne."

She stepped back and primly folded her hands in front of her apron. "How do you do, sir. I am Mrs. Mason, and it is my pleasure to meet you. I'm aware that you are being shunned by the Amish. However, that is not why I refuse to shake your hand. You, Mr. Tremayne, and you, Clay Tremayne, smell like pickles, and I don't wish to smell like pickles or to take money that smells like pickles. I insist you come back to the kitchen and wash your hands and face before I take your money. . .or your hands."

"Aw, come on, Delilah, I'll buy some of that rum bay cologne so you'll let me kiss your hand," Clay teased as they headed back toward the curtained kitchen.

"I have not given you leave to call me by me first name, sir, and certainly you're not going to kiss my hand. And if I did sell you the bay rum you would simply smell like bay rum and pickles. Now, wash up and put the money in the cash drawer. Also, I suggest that you freshen your breath, so that everyone you meet won't think you've been putting up pickles. I'm going out back to pick the fresh herbs for the afternoon customers," she said and majestically sailed out the back door.

"What a woman," Yancy said admiringly.

"Maybe if you get lucky we can find you a Delilah tonight," Clay said, grinning.

Just east of the township of Lexington was an old road that

ran from north to south. The Indians that had originally colonized the Shenandoah Valley called it the Great Warriors Trail. Then the Quakers and Amish had come in, and they called it the Valley Pike. The other colonists—the Long Knives, the English—called it the Great Wagon Road. They had come to the verdant valley from Pennsylvania and northern Virginia. Finally the state of Virginia had macadamized it, which made it the quickest and most comfortable road in the state, and then it was called the Valley Turnpike. It ran the length of the valley from Tennnessee to Maryland.

Although Yancy had traveled many miles across America, he had never ventured east of Lexington. Virginia Military Institute was north and slightly west of town, and that had been the border of his wanderings beyond the Tremayne farm. Now as they rode the turnpike he saw that there were outposts and stores and farms as they rode northeast. "Where are we going, anyway?"

"We're riding the Great Valley Road," Clay answered grandly. "Been here more than one hundred and fifty years."

"History's not my favorite subject," Yancy grumbled. "Might as well go back to the institute and read a book."

"Ahh, but one thing you're never going to find in your history book," Clay retorted, "and that would be Star's Starlight Saloon. Right up ahead."

Yancy looked ahead, then, as he was accustomed, he sniffed. He could see faint points of light ahead, and his sensitive hearing picked out noise—nothing of definition, just cacaphonic sounds that did not fit the night—and a very slight man-scent. He looked at Clay and repeated, "Star's Starlight Saloon? Kind of redundant, isn't it?"

Clay stared at him, one sardonic eyebrow raised. "Redundant? So you're such a grand gentleman after all?"

Yancy blushed, though Clay couldn't see it in the dark, and his voice sounded proud. "*Grammar for the Southern Gentleman*— 'redundant: superfluous repetition.' "

Clay laughed long and heartily. "I congratulate you, cousin. You've become an interesting man. You look like a savage Indian and converse like a gentleman. The women are going to eat you alive."

They proceeded to Star's Starlight Saloon, hitched their horses, and went through the double oak-and-glass doors.

Yancy stopped inside to look around and let his senses take everything in. The first of his senses that was assaulted was the most sensitive, as always—his sense of smell. The place smelled of unwashed men, horse manure mixed with mud, strong acrid cigar smoke, cheap perfume, and whiskey. He heard a tinny piano playing "Camptown Races." Underneath the murmur of the crowd, he heard men placing bets and calling hands. His sharp gaze swept across the room, taking in the hard men and half-dressed women, and he saw that Clay had already crossed to the bar, ordered a drink, and was embracing a full-figured blond lady who giggled and embraced him with obvious recognition.

Yancy moved to join him, and then his gaze, stunned, was fixed on a young woman standing at the piano, who was obviously getting ready to sing. She looked like Hannah Lapp. Or rather she looked like a somewhat vulgar copy of Hannah Lapp, but she still gave Yancy a small shock. She was small-boned, with ash brown hair streaked with blond. She had dark eyes and the same narrow shoulders as Hannah, with an erect bearing. She wore a very low-cut dress, and her hair was mussed, with tousles of curls hanging over her shoulders. But primly she crossed her hands and nodded to the pianist. He began a reedy "Ben Bolt."

Oh don't you remember sweet Alice, Ben Bolt
Sweet Alice whose hair was so brown. . .

She sang earnestly, but her voice was drowned out by the din in the saloon, which did not lessen. Still, Yancy could hear her high fluted voice clearly.

Who wept with delight when you gave her a smile,
And trembled with fear at your frown. . . .

The rest of the song was so sad and dreary that Yancy blocked it out, but he listened and watched the girl until she finished. Men crowded around her.

Then Clay appeared in front of him with his blowsy blond

woman. "This is the famous Star," he said, his eyes glinting. "Star can make any man happy. Including you, Yancy. Here you go."

He handed Yancy a bottle, but Yancy hesitated. "Here, handsome," Star said, tipping the bottle toward him. "It's smooth, it'll make you happy, and it's on the house," she said silkily.

"Like you," Clay said, planting a kiss on her reddened lips.

"Only for you, Clay, my young devil," she replied. "Just for you."

"You should be so lucky, Yancy," he leered. "Maybe when you're old enough to be a real man."

Star looked him up and down. "Indian, ain't ya? Handsome Indian, too. Some places don't welcome Indians 'cause the drink makes 'em crazy. But Clay here speaks for you, so I know you'll behave."

"Thank you, ma'am," Yancy said and took another swig. "And thanks for the good whiskey. It's smooth and it makes me happy, 'specially since it's on the house."

"Good manners, too, just like a real gentleman, even if he is a savage," Star said admiringly.

"You got that all wrong, Star," Clay said. "I'm the savage." He started kissing her passionately, and Yancy politely looked away. He took another swig of the whiskey then decided that he wanted to meet the pretty singer.

"Miss Star, ma'am?" he interrupted, slightly nudging Clay on the arm.

"What, cuz?" Clay asked lazily, looking up.

"Who is that lady that was singing just now?" Yancy asked.

Star looked around. "Oh, her? She's one of my very best girls. Here, just wait a minute. . . ." She disentangled herself from Clay and sashayed through the crowd. Pushing aside the men that surrounded the girl, she took her by the arm, whispered, and pointed.

The girl nodded and followed Star back to where Clay and Yancy stood at the bar. Star grabbed Clay's arm again, and the girl stopped and looked Yancy up and down. Then, as elegantly as any well-bred young woman, she curtsied.

Instinctively, as Major Thomas Jackson had taught him to do with ladies, he bowed. "How do you do, ma'am," he said. "May I introduce myself? I am Yancy Tremayne, at your service."

She smiled up at him and put one delicate hand to her half-exposed breast. "Well then, Mr. Yancy Tremayne, suh," she said with an exaggerated Virginia accent, "muh name is whatevuh you would like it to be." She curtsied low again.

Star, Clay, and the girl burst into raucous laughter. "Don't take it amiss, cousin," Clay said with amusement. "These *ladies* are playful, and sometimes as gentlemen we don't quite get the joke."

"I don't get the joke," Yancy said darkly.

The girl took his arm gently and stared up into his eyes. She really was much like Hannah Lapp, except for her blatant worldliness. Her lips were reddened; her eyes were lined with kohl, and now that he was close to her, he could see the coldness in them. She looked hard, and he was sure she looked older than she really was. The skin of her throat and breast was smooth, but she already had tough lines around her eyes and mouth.

"What is your name, ma'am?" he asked with all the gentleness he could muster.

"Hmm. Let's see. . . Your name is Yancy? Then my name is Nancy," she said with cold amusement.

Clay laughed drunkenly. "And he's riding a horse named Fancy! Oh, this is rich!"

They all laughed for a ridiculously long period of time over this poor joke. Yancy had forgotten that he was riding Midnight, not Fancy. He took another drink, sat down on a barstool, and pulled Nancy—or whatever her name was—down on his lap. He kissed her. . .a lot.

Time melted; time meant nothing. His sense of smell, and hearing, and sight, and even feeling was dulled.

Drunkenly he looked up at a loud and annoying ruckus and saw Clay on the floor. Three men were working him over, one holding his arms and the other two landing blows on his chest and face. Yancy shoved Nancy aside, stood up on a barstool, and jumped into the melee. He felt his right fist connect with someone's cheekbone, and then he kicked and felt a shinbone shatter. With his left fist he grabbed someone's throat and squeezed, feeling the life slowly leaking out in short, frantic breaths.

The last thing he heard was, "That's enough! You're all under arrest!"

He felt a stunning blow against his forehead, and everything went night black.

CHAPTER THIRTEEN

Yancy woke up, to his very great sorrow. His head felt like a busted melon; his eyes felt like there were great thumping hammers behind them. His mouth tasted like he had eaten cow dung, and his lips were dry and cracking and felt oddly fat. His body ached, from his fingertips to his toes. He tried very hard to go back to sleep, but such succor evaded him.

He sat up, groaning like an old man. He saw a roughhewn ceiling very close to his head, and he saw that he was on a top bunk. Though the world swirled around him, he bent over to look into the bottom bunk.

His cousin Clay lay there, one knee-booted leg hung over the side negligently. He snored.

Very, very slowly and with much care, Yancy turned so that his legs hung off the bunk. Then, holding his breath, he jumped to the floor. He felt that he landed on steel spikes, from the pain that shot from his feet all the way up to, it seemed, the tips of his hair. Then the nausea hit him, and barely registering that the chamber pot was right by a row of steel bars, he bent over it and was horribly sick. Finally, shakily he stood up, wiped his sore mouth, and mumbled, "So this is jail. I don't like it much."

He started to try to climb back into his bunk, when his cousin's voice sounded, remote and reedy, "Not jail that made you sick, cousin. Sorry 'bout that."

"But what happened?" Yancy asked, bewildered. "I remember that girl named Nancy, and I remember you arguing with three big ol' guys."

"I dunno," Clay answered, "but I think the three big ol' guys won."

A deputy came down the hall and banged on the bars.

Yancy winced at the clanging noise that seemed to burst his eardrums.

"Clay Tremayne, Yancy Tremayne, let's go. You've been bailed out. Come on with me before I change my mind."

Even though Daniel Tremayne and Morgan Tremayne had only the remotest family connection, they looked oddly alike as they stood in the sheriff's office. Both of them stood, their legs planted far apart, their arms crossed, their faces severe. Daniel, of course, was eleven years older and his face was more chiseled and worn. Morgan had fair, fine features and coloring, but his demeanor was so dignified and offended as to seem like the most righteous of preachers.

As they entered, Yancy was as low as low, but Clay seemed airy and unconcerned, even though he pressed his right hand hard to his abdomen. "Hello, brother," he said. "The good news is that they didn't break my nose. The bad news is that I think they broke one of my ribs."

Morgan frowned darkly. "I ought to leave you here. Clay, that boy is sixteen years old. How could you do this? Are you ever going to grow up?"

"Sixteen?" Clay was genuinely surprised. "He doesn't look sixteen, and he sure doesn't fight like he's sixteen. Didn't realize it. Sorry, cousin. I don't think I would have led you into the den of iniquity if I'd known it."

"I may be sixteen, but I still make my own decisions," Yancy grunted. "It's not your fault, Clay. I made up my own mind."

Daniel uncrossed his arms and lifted Yancy's face with one finger. "Not very pretty, son. Black eye and busted lip. Anything else hurt?"

"Everything else," Yancy answered sullenly, "but especially my shin." He pulled up his breeches leg and pulled down his moccasins. There was a big black bruise on his right leg. "Someone kicked me."

"Probably one of those evil women," Clay said, grinning, but then he grimaced and grabbed his ribs again.

"Shut up, Clay," Morgan said. "Don't you ever get tired of this every year?"

"Yes," Clay answered smartly. "But by the time next December rolls around I'll probably forget how tired I am of it."

Morgan rolled his eyes and muttered something unintelligible. Then he took his brother's arm very gently. "C'mon, dummy. No, no, I'm not going to take you home for Mother to work you over. I'll take you to your place and get the doctor." Morgan looked over his shoulder as he helped his brother out the door. "Are you two all right, Uncle Daniel? Is there anything else I can do?"

Daniel shook his head. "No, thank you, Morgan. I'm indebted to you for coming to get me."

"No, sir, there is no debt," Morgan said firmly. "We're family. Call on me and mine anytime for anything."

They went out the door and Yancy's sharp ears caught the low sound of Clay still grumbling.

Yancy pulled himself up straight and gazed into his father's stern blue eyes. "Sir? Are you going to punish me?"

"Before I answer, I need to ask you some questions."

"Yes, sir," Yancy answered solidly.

Daniel narrowed his eyes and studied Yancy's fractured face carefully. "So, did you have fun?"

Yancy hesitated for long moments then answered, "It seemed like fun last night. But it's no fun now, no sir."

"I see. But was it worth it?"

Again Yancy thought carefully. "No sir, it was not. Now that I realize I have to face you, and Becky, and Grandmother, and—and—Major Jackson, I know it wasn't worth it. Not at all. I'm so very sorry, Father."

Daniel nodded. "It's good for a man to take responsibility for his actions."

Yancy looked up at his father with appealing, vulnerable dark eyes. "Sir, will you forgive me?"

Daniel laid his hands on his son's shoulders. " 'Neither do I condemn thee.' Just don't do it again, for my sake and your sake and Becky's sake and Grandmother's sake."

"Don't worry, I'm going to find some other way that doesn't hurt so much to have fun. But sir, what do you mean about not condemning me? What was that?"

Daniel answered, "It's a Bible verse, and it means that I can't condemn you for anything that you've done, son. I've made my own mistakes, and I've seen my own sins. I can't condemn you or anyone else. I just want to protect you and try to help you to have a good life. That's all. And I'm hoping that a black eye and a fat lip will help you learn that lesson."

"Do you think my nose is broken?" Yancy asked anxiously.

Daniel chuckled. "No, I think your pride is, which may be a very good thing. Just remember always, son, 'Pride goeth before destruction, and an haughty spirit before a fall.' And that's even worse than a broken nose."

❧

Slowly they rode home, Yancy dreading every hoofbeat that brought him closer. It was a dreary day, with the sun hidden behind looming snow clouds. He shivered in the biting air, and it seemed as if every inch of his body ached. His left eye was swollen shut, and his lips felt like raw meat. He fully expected Becky and Grandmother to be very angry with him, but he was wrong.

Becky met them on the veranda and threw her arms around him to hug him. "Oh, Yancy, you look awful! And with you so handsome, too!"

They went in and then Zemira hugged him. "You are your father's son, that's sure enough," she said drily. "Come on in. Lie down on the sofa in the parlor. Daniel, take a rag and go get some icicles to put on that eye. Otherwise it'll be swollen for days." She bustled around, getting quilts to put over Yancy and pillows for his head.

Becky said, "I'll go heat up some soup. I know you're probably starving, Yancy, but I doubt you'll be able to chew anything much for a day or two."

CROSSING

Zemira finished making Yancy comfortable then pulled up a straight chair close to the sofa. "Looks like you and Clay had quite a party," she said with a glimmer in her dark blue eyes.

"Seems like I remember something about a party," he sighed, speaking with difficulty because of his sore mouth. "But then it seems like it wasn't very much fun, for a party." He looked up at her woefully. "Grandmother—I'm so, so sorry. I know I've disappointed everyone so much. I can't tell you how sorry I am. And I thought—I thought that you'd be really mad at me."

She smiled and gently smoothed back the lock of his hair that always seemed to fall over his forehead. "Being angry with you is not going to teach you anything. If you were younger, Daniel would probably feel obliged to punish you in some way. But in spite of the fact that you're only sixteen, in the last year you've taken on a man's job and a man's burdens. And since you have a repentant attitude, we see that you're taking responsibility for your actions. So there is no need for us to be angry with you, Yancy. I suspect you're angry enough at yourself."

"You're right about that, Grandmother," he agreed caustically. "Talk about acting like a fool. I know you're not supposed to swear to things, but right here and now I'm telling you I'm going to try very hard not to get myself in such a stupid position again."

"Good boy," she said softly.

Daniel came in with a rag with crushed icicles in it. "Here, Yancy, lay that down on your eye. Maybe after a while the swelling will go down and it'll open back up."

"Thanks." Gingerly he put it on his eye. "Father? Would you sit down for a minute? I want to ask you both something."

"Sure," Daniel said. He stoked up the fire to a comfortable roar then pulled another straight chair up by Zemira's.

"Father, I've been thinking about what you said, about not condemning me because—maybe because you've seen—you've been in some—kind of—"

Daniel put up his hand and then winked at his mother. "Son, I've been there, and worse. Your grandmother may not know the details, but she knows me, always has. So don't worry you're going to surprise her with some dark secret about my past."

"I should say not," Zemira grumbled. "Just come out with it, Yancy. I got over being shocked by what men do a long, long time ago."

"Okay," he said and took a deep breath. "I can understand, Father, that you may have been like me when you were younger and feel like you can't be angry with me because of that. But Grandmother, I know you've never done stupid, wrong things like I've done. So—so what did you mean? About teaching me something by not getting mad at me? It seems like you'd have the right to, if you get my meaning."

Zemira shook her head. "Jesus said, 'He that is without sin among you, let him first cast a stone. . . .' I'm not without sin. No one is, except Jesus. Only He has the right to condemn anyone for sin. And as far as teaching you, Yancy, we only want you to learn one thing from us. That's Christ's love. In the scriptures it's called charity. 'Charity suffereth long, and is kind; charity envieth not; charity vaunteth not itself, is not puffed up. . . .' All of that means that when you love a person with Christ's love, you seek out and do what's best for them. For me to be angry with you would not be Christlike. For me to show you love and be kind is like our Jesus Christ. And that you will remember a long time, Yancy, much longer than any selfish anger. I love you, and I forgive you, and Jesus loves you and will forgive you."

Uneasily Yancy shifted then turned the compress on his eye. Already some of the swelling was going down. "I understand, Grandmother. But I have one big worry left. I know Major Jackson is a good Christian man, and I know he knows a lot about the Bible and Jesus and all that. But I don't think that in his position he's going to be able to forgive me. I'm so afraid I'll get expelled."

Zemira reached over and took his hand. Softly she said, "Yancy, no one ever said there are no consequences for sin; there always are. And you're right. Major Jackson's position regarding you, under the circumstances, is very different from your family's position. But why don't we, right now, get Becky, and all of us will pray for you, that God might spare you and allow you to stay on the path you have chosen? It may be that in His great mercy and understanding, He will spare you this shame."

"Knowing how you feel about soldiers, you'd do that for me, Grandmother?" Yancy asked.

"Of course, because I have the Lord's charity in my heart, and the Lord is kind and merciful and understanding," she answered firmly. "And will you pray with us, Yancy?"

He closed his eyes and a single tear rolled down his cheek. "I can't. Right now I would feel like the worst kind of hypocrite and like a liar. But please—please—do pray for me."

"Always," Daniel said. "Always, son."

Major Thomas Jackson's classes at VMI always began at 8:00 a.m., and as he was always a punctual man, he always arrived at his office at 7:30 a.m. to prepare. On this Monday, January 2, 1860, Yancy Tremayne was waiting for him in the hallway. When Major Jackson came up the stairs, Yancy came to strict attention.

Because of his shame, he hadn't worn his VMI uniform; he was dressed in plain brown wool trousers and a cream-colored linsey-woolsey shirt. He clutched his plain wide-brimmed hat in his hand, turning the brim over and over nervously.

When Major Jackson reached him, Yancy saluted and muttered, "Major Jackson, sir! Cadet Tremayne at your service."

Jackson looked him up and down sternly, and Major Thomas Jackson's severe once-over was stern indeed. "You are out of uniform, Cadet, and you are also out of countenance."

"Yes, sir!"

"Come into my office."

He unlocked the door, led Yancy in, and seated himself behind his desk. Yancy stood at attention, and Jackson did not put him at ease.

"What have you done?" Jackson asked abruptly.

Yancy took a deep breath, his back as stiff as a board, his arms aching at attention at his sides. He sighted somewhere beyond Jackson's right shoulder. His eye was still swollen but had opened, and his lip had gone down somewhat, but his speech was still slurred. As clearly as he could speak, he said, "Sir! I got drunk, running with the wrong crowd. Then I got into a fight and got arrested. My father bailed me out, sir."

Jackson's blue-light eyes glowed balefully. "I see. And so this wrong crowd, they got you into this trouble, and you couldn't help yourself?"

"No, sir. I—I misspoke, sir. I made my own decisions, went my own way, and chose to do the things I did. The—the wrong things."

"You see that now, do you?" Jackson asked sharply.

"Yes, sir."

"And how do you propose to undo the wrong things you did?"

Yancy dropped his head wearily. "I can't, sir. I know that now. It's done. All I can do is apologize. I've gone to my family and begged their forgiveness. And now, sir, I ask you to forgive me and give me another chance. I want to redeem myself."

"How will you do that?"

Yancy lifted his head and stood at strict attention again. "I will be a better cadet, sir. I will work harder, I will study harder, and whatever punishment you feel is appropriate, I will bear. I will regain my honor and my integrity, sir."

Jackson rose and looked out the window, out at the parade ground of the institute. "This is a proud and honorable school, sir, and you have a charitable scholarship here. You have betrayed that trust."

Yancy almost choked but managed to say, "Yes, sir, I know that, all too well. Please, if you will give me another chance, I promise you I will make you proud. I will make the institute proud. I know I have it in me, sir. I know I can achieve, and achieve excellence."

For long moments Jackson stood at the window, staring out. Finally he turned around. "Cadet Tremayne," he said quietly.

Yancy met his ice blue gaze.

"All of us fail," he said firmly, "but the test of our faith and our military life is when we fail, do we just lie there or do we get up and start over again? Do we fight much harder so as to regain the ground we have lost? I'll be watching you, Cadet Tremayne. You know everyone here at the institute has heard about this disgrace. You'll have to work much harder, and longer, to regain your honor and the respect of the faculty and staff and that of your fellow cadets. If you can do it, you will indeed be a fine addition to the institute and a fine soldier."

"I will, sir," Yancy said with a lump in his throat. "I will fight hard."

Jackson nodded. "Then go get into your uniform and go to class." He turned back to the window.

As Yancy left he thought, *I won't quit! No matter how hard it gets, I will never quit!*

Part Four: The Beginning 1860—1861

CHAPTER FOURTEEN

Yancy kept the promise he made to himself on that dreary January day. He didn't quit, no matter how hard it got and how many long hours he had to work. For the next year he was the model cadet. He never missed a class. His rifle skills could hardly be improved, but he still practiced every chance he got. Since his artillery skills needed to be honed, he worked with the cannons every spare minute he had. Of course the only time he had live fire was during artillery class, so he practiced all by himself in dumb show, mouthing the commands, from worming, to sponging, to loading, to priming, to the complicated geometry in aiming, to inserting the fuse, then to firing.

Night had almost taken over the artillery field, but Yancy told himself he had one, maybe two more drills he could do before full dark. Muttering to himself, he went through the repetitive motions as fast and as thoroughly as he could manage. Finally he ordered himself to fire and pulled on an invisible lanyard.

Behind him he heard single, slow applause and a low chuckle. He turned to see Major Jackson smiling and clapping.

It was such an unusual sight that Yancy was speechless for a moment, but then he dropped his head and blushed. "Guess I look pretty silly, huh, Major?"

"Not at all, not at all, Cadet," he said. He came forward and held out his hand for Yancy to shake. "I'm very proud of you, Cadet Tremayne. I might wish all the cadets have the dedication that you show."

"Not all the cadets have to make up for the mistakes I've made, sir."

"One mistake is all that I know of, Yancy," he said gruffly. "And you've more than made up for it. Look, here it is Saturday night and I think you're the only cadet here at the institute. And working at artillery skills at that."

"Yes, sir. Believe me, I've stayed out of saloons and away from—from—ladies—er—"

"I'm not that old, Cadet. I think I know what you mean. Sometimes some ladies can get us gentlemen into trouble. We must always mind the ladies."

Yancy grinned. "You know, that's exactly what my father always says—to mind the ladies."

"Your father sounds like a wise man," Jackson said. "So it's almost too dark to see the targets. Are you going in now?"

"Sir, if you'll excuse me, I'd like to go through just one more drill. Just one more," he answered anxiously.

Jackson asked curiously, "Why? Why is one more so important?"

"Well, sir, it's like this. Today is September 1, 1860."

"Yes," Jackson agreed, puzzled.

"And so tomorrow is my birthday. I'm going to be seventeen."

Jackson nodded. "You seem older. I forget you're so young."

"Most people do, I think. Maybe it's because I'm so tall. Anyway, last January, when I got myself into so much trouble, one of the things I decided was that I was going to get in one hundred artillery drills, all by myself, before my birthday."

"Yes?"

"And sir, that last one was ninety-nine."

"I see," Jackson said gravely. "Well, Cadet Tremayne, it's so dark now I'm not sure I could sight a target with eagle eyes. But why don't we do just one more drill. You're the gun captain. I'll worm, sponge, and prime."

"Sir? You—you want me to be your gun captain?"

"Said so, didn't I? Let's go!" They went through a perfect drill, with Major Jackson worming, sponging, and priming.

Yancy aimed, set the fuse, and instead of mouthing the words, stood tall and shouted, "Fire!" then pulled his invisible lanyard.

"One hundred," Jackson said with satisfaction.

"Yes, one hundred, sir. And thank you, sir."

"My pleasure. And by the way, Cadet Tremayne. . ."

"Yes, sir?"

"On Monday I'll make you a gun captain. Think about the crew you want."

"Sir! Yes, sir! Thank you, sir!"

"Good, good. You've earned it, Cadet."

Yancy picked up the "worm" and the sponge and started toward the storage shed. To his surprise Major Jackson walked with him. "You know, Cadet, I've been watching you carefully this year. I wanted to make sure that I didn't make a mistake in recommending you for your charity scholarship."

"You didn't, sir," Yancy said firmly.

"I'm sure of that now. It takes time to earn trust once it's been broken. You have done that. Not only with rifles and artillery but with your studies. You're nineteenth in a class of one hundred and forty-two. That's quite an accomplishment, Cadet Tremayne, because I know you had no formal education before you came here."

"No, sir," Yancy said. "But my barracks mates have helped me a lot. Especially Cadet Stevens."

Jackson said, "He's a good man, a good soldier. He looks like the worst kind of fop but he's solid. He kind of reminds me of. . ." His voice faded out.

"Lieutenant Jeb Stuart," Yancy supplied. "In fact, Peyton met Lieutenant Stuart in Charles Town before John Brown's execution. He's sort of Peyton's hero."

Jackson said drily, "I can see how he would be. Lieutenant Stuart is a very interesting man."

"Interesting, yes," Yancy agreed. "And by the way, sir, I already know three men I want on my gun crew. My barracks mates— Peyton Stevens, Charles Satterfield, and Sandy Owens."

Jackson nodded. "Very good, Cadet Tremayne. You'll need three more. Any ideas on that?"

"Not yet, sir, but I'll know by Monday." Yancy shut the door to the storage shed, and they walked up through the parade grounds to the stables.

Yancy looked up. The Milky Way was like a diamond shawl thrown across the sky. In this luminous starlight they could see their way. There was no moon. "Major Jackson?" Yancy murmured, staring overhead.

"Yes?"

"Do you know why, when there's no moon, it's called the new moon?"

Jackson looked up and studied the sky. "Cadet, you just happened to ask me something that I know. After the full, the moon gets positioned between the earth and the sun, and the dark side is toward the earth. So after the fullest moon, there's a time when it's born again that we can't see. It's brand-new, and we won't see it until the earth has turned just right to catch the tiniest glimpse of it."

"Born again, and then a glimpse," Yancy repeated softly.

"That's right. Just like life, and love, and learning to live in God's will," Jackson said. "It's not something that just happens. It takes time and dedication." He glanced at Yancy. "Just like you've shown this year, Cadet. Think about that."

"Yes, sir, I will," Yancy said soberly. "I will."

Peyton Stevens lay on his bunk with his forage cap upside down between his booted feet. Negligently he held a deck of cards and with two fingers flipped one into the cap. "Fourteen," he said.

"Shut up," Sandy Owens said irritably. He was on the other lower bunk, frowning over a book.

Stevens flipped another card, perfectly sailing through the air and settling neatly into his cap. "Fifteen."

"Stevens, we all know you're so brilliant you don't have to study, but not all of us are as smart as you are," Yancy said from the bunk above him. He was diligently memorizing from his physics textbook. "Why don't you go outside to the parade ground to show off your card skills? Or go to town and call on one of those girls who is always chasing you around?"

"Boring. And boring," Stevens said lazily. He flipped another card. "Sixteen."

"Shut up," Charles Satterfield grumbled from above Sandy Owens's bunk.

"Whoa, Chuckins, getting kind of bossy, aren't you?" Stevens said, grinning. "What are you trying to study anyway?"

"History of the Founding Fathers," he answered. "But all that's going through my head is your dumb 'fourteen, fifteen, sixteen.' "

"Take my word for it, Chuckins, what's going on today is going to make more history than all the Founding Fathers put together," Stevens said. It was November 6, 1860, and it was the day of the presidential election.

Abruptly Yancy shut his book and turned over on his back. Putting his hands behind his head, he stared at the blank ceiling. "So what do you think this election means, Peyton? What do you think will happen?"

Peyton flicked another card into his cap but didn't count it. "I don't know everything, you know. Just what my father says." His father was a United States senator from Virginia.

"So? What does he say?" Sandy asked impatiently.

Apparently carelessly Peyton replied, "The Democrats have three weak candidates that will split the Southern vote. Abraham Lincoln will probably win. He is undoubtedly antislavery and altogether against secession. If he wins, there will most likely be a war."

And so Abraham Lincoln did win, and the rumblings of war did sound in the air of the United States of America. Between his election in November and the first of February 1861, the cotton states held conventions and voted to secede—South Carolina, Mississippi, Florida, Alabama, Georgia, Louisiana, and Texas. That month delegates from those states met at Montgomery, Alabama, and voted to found a new nation. They called it the Confederate

States of America. Its first president was Jefferson Davis.

Secession and war were the topics at VMI—except in Major Thomas Jackson's classes. He flatly refused to allow any discussion other than the class texts. Even during artillery practice he sternly corrected any cadet that mentioned Virginia's possible involvement in the growing hostilities.

But then April came, and it seemed to Yancy as if everyone, both North and South, had gone mad.

In the first week of April, Abraham Lincoln decided to send a naval relief expedition to Fort Sumter in Charleston, South Carolina, and, carefully avoiding dealing with the Confederacy, notified the state authorities. The fort was a federal naval base and always had been. The problem was that now the Confederacy regarded it as the property of the Confederate States of America, and that government gave the order for the North to immediately surrender the fort. If they did not surrender, Montgomery ordered the dashing Creole commander, General P. G. T. Beauregard, to reduce the fort by arms—to, in fact, start a war.

On April 12, 1861, Beauregard made his demand to Major Robert Anderson and his seventy-five men. He rejected the demand. The Confederate guns opened on the fort, firing all that day and into the night. The next day the garrison yielded.

Responding to the frenzy of outrage in the North, on the fifteenth, the president called for seventy-five thousand volunteers to subdue the rebellious South. This resulted in a fury of patriotism in the Confederate states.

On April 17, Virginia seceded from the Union. Within three weeks, three other states of the Upper South had seceded: Arkansas, Tennessee, and North Carolina. The eleven states of the Confederate States of America was complete.

Major Thomas Jackson was in his element, for a Presbyterian synod was meeting in Lexington. It was Saturday, April 20, and the Jackson home was packed with ministers. The sound of their voices speaking and laughing was meat to Jackson.

Anna came to him once and whispered, "You're in your

element, Thomas. You love nothing more than to argue over the Bible with ministers."

"We're not arguing. We're discussing. It is edifying. You know, esposita, at one point in my life I wished desperately that God would call me to be a minister, but the call never came. So here I am a poor soldier. I can at least give comfort and hospitality to those who are."

Anna smiled. She put her hand on Thomas's arm and said, "In your own way, my dear, you are a minister of the Word, too. Remember one of my favorite chapters in the scripture?"

"Second Corinthians, chapter five," Jackson answered.

"Verse twenty: 'Now then we are ambassadors for Christ. . . .' " Anna said confidently. "You are not only an ambassador, you are a minister. Not only do you teach your cadets, you minister to them, too. Now, please excuse me and I'll go to the kitchen to see about my ministry—providing enough coffee and tea to these gentlemen. It's like trying to keep a battalion supplied," she said with a smile.

In the hot kitchen, Hetty was boiling two big pots of water when Yancy came in the door with three pounds of coffee, a pound of Indian tea, and a pound of chamomile tea. "Hello, Mrs. Jackson. More coffee and tea for the gentlemen." Sometimes on weekends he still helped Anna at the house with her garden and with repairs and with the horses.

"And just in time, too," she sighed. "I think both the coffee samovar and the teapots are empty. Yancy, you look splendid in your uniform. And let me see. . ." She stepped up to him and looked up into his face. "You have, I think, grown another inch or two."

"Guess so, ma'am," he agreed. "I'm a couple of inches taller than my father now, and he's right at six feet."

"And is he as handsome as you are?" Anna asked innocently.

At the stove, Hetty's broad face broke out in a smile.

Yancy replied, "Yes, ma'am—I mean, no, ma'am—wait, that's not right—"

Anna took pity at the woeful confusion on Yancy's face. "I'm sorry, Yancy, that was not a fair question, and I didn't mean to trick you. Well, perhaps I did, but anyway, I was going to ask you to go into the parlor and bring in the samovar and the tea wagon. It's too hot in this kitchen, and I don't want you to wilt in your uniform. It looks so very crisp and clean and fresh."

"Yes, ma'am. Thank you ma'am," Yancy said, still with some confusion, and hurried out of the kitchen.

Indeed, the house was buzzing with activity. Ministers gathered in groups of two or three in spirited discussions; sometimes one man would hold forth to a large group of men in the parlor, sitting and standing—and all of them sipping coffee or tea. Yancy counted them; there were twenty-three men crowded into the Jacksons' modest home. He was kept busy refreshing the coffee samovar and the teapots.

Once, on one of his countless trips from the kitchen to the parlor, he heard the knocker at the front door. He answered it to see a tall man, distinguished looking, wearing a somber black suit and a tall top hat. "Good afternooon, sir, may I help you?" Yancy asked, thinking that he was another minister.

The man looked him up and down in an assessing way.

Yancy was not in full uniform dress with his crossbelts and sword, but he was wearing his gray tunic, and his white trousers were—as Anna had noticed—spotless and flawlessly pressed with a knife-edge crease.

Yancy must have passed muster, because the man removed his hat and made a slight bow. "You are, I believe, one of our excellent cadets from Virginia Military Institute."

Yancy, having learned much etiquette from Peyton Stevens, returned his own cool bow. "Yes, sir. I am Cadet Tremayne, sir."

"My name is Evans, Henry Evans. I am from Governor Letcher's office." Solemnly they shook hands. "May I have an audience with Major Jackson, Cadet Tremayne? It is a matter of some importance and of a private nature." His glance wandered toward the parlor, where the spirited discussions and some laughter sounded.

Yancy stepped back and extended his white-gloved hand for Mr. Evans to come in. "Please wait here, Mr. Evans. I'll tell Major Jackson that you're here."

Yancy found Jackson listening to a minister who was holding forth to a group of six men concerning dispensations. Discreetly he went up to Jackson and whispered, "Sir, there is a Mr. Henry Evans who would like a private word with you. He's from Governor Letcher's office."

A shadow passed over Jackson's face, and he nodded. He had told Yancy he had been expecting a summons of some kind ever since the seventeenth when Virginia had seceded. "Very well. Where is he?"

"In the foyer, sir."

"Good, good," Jackson said absently, and slipped out of the parlor.

Major Jackson and Evans made their introductions and niceties. Then Evans commented, "It sounds as if you're having a party, Major."

"No, it is a group of Presbyterian ministers."

"A group of ministers? They sound like men at a prize fight."

Jackson smiled briefly. "Perhaps so, but I can assure you we are much less inclined to hostility than just honest debate."

Evans nodded. "There is a sad lack of honest debate these days, sir. Which brings me to the governor's business with you." Evans reached into his inner pocket and brought out an envelope. "Orders for you, Major."

Jackson took the envelope and read it, then nodded. "Thank you, Mr. Evans. Am I to understand that these orders are effective immediately?"

"Yes, sir. You'll go into active duty at once."

"Sir, please tell Governor Letcher that his orders will be obeyed to the letter."

"God bless you, sir." After a few more polite words, Evans took his leave.

Jackson went back into the house. Anna wasn't in the parlor or the dining room where the ministers were, so he went into the kitchen where he found her there with Hetty, still boiling water and making more coffee and tea. He went to her and said softly, "Let's go out in the garden for a few minutes."

She looked surprised. "With all our guests?"

"Yes, my dearest."

Anna grew sober. She followed him out to a stone bench in her garden, and they sat down together.

He put his arm around her. "I just got my orders from Governor Letcher, esposa."

She stiffened slightly, but her voice was calm and even. "And what are your orders, Thomas?"

"The best cadets from the institute are called to duty in Richmond. I am to command them."

She nodded. "When are you to go?"

Somewhat sadly he replied, "Tomorrow, I'm afraid. I had hoped to have the Sabbath for church affairs and some rest, but Governor Letcher has ordered us to muster and go to Richmond immediately."

She leaned against him and rested her head on his shoulder.

He lightly kissed her cheek and whispered, "I hate to leave you! God knows I do!"

Anna couldn't answer. His arms tightened on her and they rested together in silence for a few moments.

Finally he said, "I must go dismiss our guests. There is much to do. I'm going to send Yancy to the institute to alert the cadets, and then I'll go talk to them."

Yancy rode to the institute, and for an hour rousted everybody out. Most of them were wearing their uniforms, but the ones who weren't started to change. "Don't bother with uniforms right now. The major just wants to talk to you."

Finally all the cadets were turned out on the parade ground, and Major Jackson walked up. He spoke loudly, "Attention!" and the line stiffened and fell silent.

Yancy kept his eyes on Jackson's face, and he could see that there was some sort of a portent in the major's expression. His features were usually mild and benign, but not now. There was something hard, almost harsh in it.

He stopped in front of the cadets and said, "I have received orders from Governor Letcher. All of the cadets seventeen and older will march to Richmond tomorrow to serve with the Army of Virginia. I'll be your commanding officer. I want you to be ready to march at 1:00. You know what field packs are. Be sure and bring your rifles and plenty of ammunition. Write letters to your families tonight, and I'll arrange a special mail pickup tomorrow. I'll be back early in the morning to see how you're proceeding, and all of our institute officers will be available to help you in any way we can. That's all for now. Dismissed."

Yancy went up to Jackson and said, "Sir, since my family is so close, may I go tonight and tell them good-bye? I'll be back in plenty of time to make up my field pack and for muster tomorrow."

"You may, Cadet Tremayne," Jackson answered. "Give them my best wishes."

It was almost nine o'clock at night before Yancy got to the farm. He was afraid that everyone might be asleep, and waking them up to tell them his news would make it seem so much more melodramatic than it really was. After all, it wasn't as if Richmond was a battle zone. The capital of the Confederate States of America had been moved from Montgomery to Richmond, and so it was the center of the government. Yancy was a little unclear as to what exactly the cadets would be doing, but it seemed unlikely that they would be marching to war.

For now, at least.

As he rode up he was relieved to see the lamps lit in the parlor. Someone was up, at least. He dismounted and tied Midnight to the hitching post. "I'm not going to unsaddle you, boy," he said, rubbing his nose. "We can't stay long."

He went up on the veranda and knocked lightly on the door then stuck his head in. Hank gave one long bay then came galloping out to meet him. "It's just me," he called. "Yancy." He gave Hank a friendly ear rub then went into the parlor.

His father had risen, but Becky and Zemira were still sitting on the settees by a small friendly fire.

"Of course we knew it was you," Zemira said drily. "Who else would it be gallivanting around in the middle of a Saturday night?"

"Not me. . .not for a long time anyway," Yancy replied, kissing her on one smooth cheek. "And I'm not gallivanting. I came out because I have some news."

Slowly Daniel sat back down. All three of them suddenly looked grave.

Yancy sat down by Zemira. He knew there was no way to soften it or sugarcoat it, so he just said it. "The top cadets at VMI have been detached to Richmond to serve with the Army of Northern Virginia. Major Jackson is our commander."

There was a long heavy silence, finally broken by Becky. "I suppose we all knew something like this would happen, considering what's been going on in the last few months. I just suppose we didn't expect it quite so soon. And somehow I thought that maybe the cadets at the institute might be spared unless it was some kind of last resort."

Yancy merely looked at her, a tinge of regret shadowing his feelings.

Daniel said in a low voice, "You would volunteer, wouldn't you? If you hadn't been called up?"

"Yes, sir," he answered without hesitation. "And depending on the nature of our duty in Richmond—and what Major Jackson does—I still may."

Zemira sighed heavily, almost a moan. "I could see it in you, Yancy. I knew. I saw that you'd decided to be a soldier. And we always told you that we would respect your decisions, and we do. But I have to tell you that it grieves me, it truly does."

"I'm sorry," Yancy said lamely.

"Don't be sorry," Becky said, though she sounded sad. "Of course no one wants loved ones in a war. But as your grandmother said, Yancy, we respect your decisions. And I for one am very proud of you. You've grown to be a strong man this last year. You made a promise to us and yourself and you've kept it. The Lord honors those who keep their word and turn from their mistakes. I'll pray that He will bless you, watch over you, protect you, and bring you back to us safe and sound."

"Please, all of you pray for me, every day," Yancy said slowly. "I know I'm going to need it."

"We will, son," Daniel said. "Always."

Yancy nodded and rose. "I can't stay. We all have a lot to do. We're moving out tomorrow afternoon. Can I go say good night to Callie Jo and David? I won't wake them."

"Of course, you must," Becky said. "Go on up."

Quietly Yancy went up to the nursery. Callie Jo looked like a little doll as she slept with her thumb stuck in her mouth. He bent over and kissed her forehead. She stirred just a little but didn't wake up.

David had turned one last Christmas Eve. Yancy took one of his tiny fists, and in his sleep David wrapped his hand around one finger. "Be good, brother," Yancy whispered.

Then he hesitated, because he realized that what he had really been doing was telling his brother and sister good-bye. It hit him then that he may not see them again, and he drew in a sharp breath. For a moment he felt a deep searing fear. But then he bowed his head and prayed silently. *Lord, help me overcome this fear. Please help me to know the right thing to do. Help me find courage. And help me find You.*

Major Jackson went to the institute before dawn to help with the preparations, to prepare his cadets for their first march. It was still early morning when he rode back home, but he stopped at First Presbyterian Church and sent his pastor, Dr. White, to the barracks to pray for his young soldiers. Then he went home and had a late breakfast with Anna.

After breakfast he and Anna went into the parlor and sat close together on the settee. "Let's read the fifth chapter of Second Corinthians," he said.

It was one of Anna's favorite passages. Together, from memory, they said in unison, " 'For we know that if our earthly house of this tabernacle were dissolved, we have a building of God, an house not made with hands, eternal in the heavens.' "

Thomas read the entire chapter aloud, and then he prayed. Humbly he entreated God for peace, for his country and countrymen and cadets, for Anna and their home and the servants.

And then, as soldiers must do, he left to go to war.

CHAPTER FIFTEEN

Jackson led his cadets into Richmond. Wearing his old dusty blue uniform, he rode into town on his shambling gray gelding, Cerro Gordo. Following him as color bearers, Yancy rode Midnight and Peyton Stevens rode his showy palomino, Senator. The contrast between Jackson's humble appearance and his sharp-dressed and trim cadets was striking, but as always, Jackson had a marshal air of authority and competence, so there was no doubt who was in command.

Jackson installed the cadets into a small camp at the fairgrounds, about a mile from the center of the city. Then he called Yancy and Peyton aside. "Until we get settled in and find out exactly what is required of us here, I want you two to be my aides-de-camp and couriers. Right now I'm going to the capitol to speak with Governor Letcher, and you'll accompany me."

"Yes, sir!" they answered, at stiff attention.

They rode back into town, to the Virginia State capitol, situated on Shockoe Hill, overlooking the James River. It was a graceful building, said to be designed by Thomas Jefferson. Modeled after a simplified Roman temple, with soaring columns and an airy porch, it was dignified and stately.

But on this day it more resembled a kicked-over anthill than a peaceful temple. Horses and carriages surrounded the building on all sides. Men, some dressed as gentlemen and some dressed as soldiers and some dressed as laborers, hurried in and out. More groups of men crowded the front in groups of threes and fours and more, and the timbre of their loud conversations could be said to be almost frantic. Young boys, presumably couriers, ran to and fro, weaving nimbly among the crowds, their piping voices calling for their addressees.

The milling crowd of wagons, carriages, and horses around the building made it impossible for them to tether the horses anywhere. Jackson dismounted and told Yancy, "Just stay out of the way as much as you can. I'm going to try to wade through all this to-do and see if I can get an audience with Governor Letcher. Wait here, and try not to get stampeded."

Yancy's Midnight and Peyton's Senator were big, spirited horses and could easily make their own way through a crowd, because other horses shied away from their high-stepping, aggressive gaits. "Let's put old Gordo between them," Yancy said, almost shouting at Peyton in the din of the throng. "Then I think we can get them to crowd out those two carts and those saddle horses and get them hitched up there by the watering trough."

Peyton didn't even try to answer. He just nodded.

They maneuvered the horses around with some trouble, but once Midnight and Senator picked up the scent of the water, they practically shoved everyone and everything aside to get to the trough. They were thirsty, and all three horses had good, long drinks. There was about one foot left of a hitching post, and they tethered the horses. Then Peyton and Yancy went to stand in the shade of the capitol, keeping in sight of the horses.

Though it was April, the sun was hot and bright, and they were very warm in their formal uniforms. They watched the crowds coming and going. All of the streets of Richmond had been just as busy and buzzing.

Peyton finally commented, "This city looks like bedlam."

Yancy agreed. "So far everywhere we've seen has been like everyone's gone mad. The only difference here at the capitol is that there's no ladies. I couldn't believe the way the ladies were crowding the streets talking. I've never seen that before." It was extremely rare to see Southern women gathered together on the streets.

Peyton smiled, a lazy, thoroughly charming, boyish grin. "I was glad to see that, you know. There are some very beautiful ladies in Richmond." Peyton's family owned an enormous mansion on the banks of the James River.

Slyly Yancy said, "Might know you'd have noticed that, Peyton. But you better be a proper gentleman or Old Blue Light will tan your hide, no mistake."

"Don't I know it, and there's no way I'd take that chance. I'm not missing out on this war for anything," Peyton said with uncharacteristic passion. "And I'm going to do whatever it takes to stay with Major Jackson, even if I have to get my father to pull some strings and appoint me personally to him."

Yancy considered this. "You know they're going to activate him, probably soon. So you're saying you'd resign your commission to the institute and join the army?"

"Yes, I will," Peyton answered sturdily. "What about you, Yancy? Have you thought about it?"

"No, this month has been so crazy that I guess I hadn't looked that far in the future. But I'm sure going to think about it."

Peyton sighed and wiped sweat from his aristocratic brow. "You might have plenty of time to do that now. There's no telling how long Major Jackson may have to wait to see the governor."

But he was wrong. Jackson returned just a few minutes later. Wordlessly he mounted up and motioned Yancy and Preston to do the same. They made their way through the city and back to the fairgrounds. Jackson didn't speak until they reached the camp, and then he ordered them to muster the men.

When they were assembled, he addressed them with his typical lack of drama. But he was an intense man, and Yancy could sense his purpose and will and drive as a soldier. The cadets didn't make a sound as he spoke.

"Cadets, I've just met with Governor Letcher. The Virginia Volunteers are men and boys from all walks of life. They are dedicated and loyal and want to serve Virginia and the Confederacy, but they have no training. Some of the commanding officers assigned to them have a military background; some have not. It's been decided that you men have the best training available, so you will be assigned as drill masters. You will teach them the orders, the march, the formations, and the small-arms drill."

There was some murmuring then among the cadets, most of them smiling with satisfaction. Yancy knew, indeed, that they had received the best education and training available in the South.

Jackson allowed them a few minutes to digest this, and then he continued, "Tomorrow you will receive your assignments. I know that all of you will do your duty to the utmost of your abilities; and I know that the men you train will benefit to a great extent from your knowledge." He made a half turn, his hands behind his back as if to leave, but then he turned, and even the cadets in the back rows could surely see the unearthly light in his fiery blue eyes. "I'm proud of you all. Very proud. Dismissed."

Basically, the cadets were snatched up. In two days they were drilling men in every vacant lot and little-used back street in Richmond. This left Major Jackson with very little to do, because the cadets were so expert and so disciplined that they had no need of oversight. Still, he visited each drill team every day. And though he was staying with friends in town, he came to the camp at the fairgrounds every night to get updates on the status of the volunteers the cadets were training. Each drill team had been assigned a captain, and each captain gave Jackson a daily report.

Yancy had been appointed captain of a drill team which included his friends, Peyton Stevens, Sandy Owens, and Charles Satterfield. On the second night he reported to Major Jackson in his officer's tent which had been established, though he was staying in town. Standing at strict attention he said, "Sir, I have learned more about the company that I have been assigned to, Raphine Company. Almost all of the men are from that little town in Rockbridge County. They were recruited and organized by Captain Reese Gilmer, whom you met yesterday. Since he formed the company, sir, they elected him as their captain, and he was confirmed by Secretary of War Walker when they reported for duty."

Jackson, seated at his camp desk with a single candle for light, nodded and muttered, "Good, good. And how do you find Captain Gilmer?"

"Sir?" Yancy asked, mystified.

"How do you find him? As a man, as a soldier, as an officer?"

"But sir, I don't know the man. I only met him yesterday. And—and—he is my superior officer. He's a captain."

Jackson gave Yancy a cold, appraising look, and those ice blue eyes made him straighten and stand even more stiffly. "You, sir, are a drill team captain, and even though this does not outrank an army captain, in this peculiar situation you are his teacher and he is your student. And, Cadet, you are going to have to learn to be a judge of men. Not to judge them for their sins—no, no, no man ever has that right—but to see them, to instinctively know if they are honest and true and men of their word, and to try and estimate their intentions and abilities. In war, this is not only important, but it is crucial, both in summing up your allies and your enemies. And so give me your first impressions of Captain Gilmer."

Yancy swallowed hard. "Major Jackson, I believe he is an honorable man, anxious to serve Virginia and the Confederacy. He is humble enough to know that he hasn't had the training that we have had, and so he eagerly learns all of our drills. But he still maintains a dignified control over his men and has an officer-like demeanor. He is anxious both for himself and his men to prove themselves brave and unwavering soldiers in this war."

"Good, good," Jackson said, scribbling notes. "And, Cadet Tremayne, take notice of any particular men who distinguish themselves, whether in zeal or determination or marksmanship. I shall expect that in your further reports."

"Yes, sir."

Jackson looked up at him in the dim candle glow. "Cadet Tremayne, did you know that Robert E. Lee was appointed general of all forces in Virginia?"

Yancy's face lit up. "No, sir, we had not heard. This is good news, sir."

"Good news indeed. I had the privilege of serving under him in Mexico, and he has proved himself to be a good friend to me ever since then. And this means that things will change and quickly."

Yancy hesitated, for Major Jackson was a private man who always kept his counsel to himself. But then he reflected that the major had offered him this information, and therefore this opening. Summoning his courage, he asked, "Sir, please explain to me what you mean. Will the Virginia Volunteers be called up soon? Maybe immediately?"

Somewhat to Yancy's surprise, Jackson didn't reprimanded him for his impertinence, and he did not hesitate. "Yes, they will. I'm certain. So drill them hard, Cadet Tremayne. Train them on orders and formations and the march, but especially drill them on small-arms battle and the bayonet. Soon even these young men will be facing battle, and I know that with the training of the institute, they will give a good accounting and serve out the enemy with all fury."

Major Thomas Jackson was not a man to be content babysitting raw recruits when the Confederacy was at war. Governor John Letcher was a Rockbridge County man and knew Jackson well. Jackson had come to the attention of Robert E. Lee when serving under him in Mexico, and several years earlier Lee had highly recommended him for a position at the University of Virginia. Jackson had also met other influential friends in Richmond, and he diligently sought his friends' backings to get a position and a post in the army.

His strategy worked. A mere six days after he had arrived in Richmond, Governor Letcher proposed Jackson for the rank of colonel to command the Virginia Infantry. The state convention promptly approved it.

Jackson was sent to Lee, who was very glad indeed to see him and eager to put him to work. They had a meeting, and General Lee assigned him to his new post—Harpers Ferry.

That night, Jackson went to the fairgrounds. Diligent to the last, he wanted his status reports, which he turned in daily to the secretary of war. And he wanted to say good-bye to his cadets.

He was somewhat surprised to see about a dozen cadets waiting for him outside his tent. When he rode up they formed into two rows and came to attention.

Yancy stepped forward. "Colonel Jackson, sir, our drill captains have their reports ready. And also, these men would like to speak to you."

Jackson nodded curtly. "Come in, Cadet Tremayne."

Yancy went into the tent with Jackson, standing at attention as he settled himself behind the camp desk with the candle on it.

"At ease, Cadet. Now, what's all this about?"

Yancy relaxed a bit, took a moment to frame his words, and then said, "Colonel Jackson, I would like to join the Virginia Volunteers. In particular, I hope to join you. We've heard that you're going to form the 1st Brigade, and I would like to enlist."

"Good, good," Jackson murmured under his breath. Then he looked up at Yancy, his eyes sparkling with an inner light. "And is that what all of the cadets out there wish to speak to me about? To join up?"

"Yes, sir."

"Very well then. I'm going to swear you in, Cadet Tremayne. And from now on, you will be Sergeant Tremayne, assigned to my staff as my aide and courier."

"Sir! Thank you, sir!"

"And as my staff assistant you will swear in any such able-bodied cadets as wish to join the 1st Virginia Brigade, and you will document their inductions."

"Yes, sir!"

"Good, good. Now I'll swear you in. Attention!"

Yancy snapped back to attention.

"Repeat after me, cadet:

" 'I, Yancy Tremayne, of the county of Rockbridge, state of Virginia, do solemnly swear that I will support, protect, and defend the Constitution and the government of the Confederate States of America against all enemies, whether domestic or foreign; that I will bear true faith, allegiance, and loyalty to the same, any ordinance, resolution, or laws of any state, convention or legislature to the contrary notwithstanding; and further, that I will faithfully perform all the duties which may be required of me by the laws of the Confederate States of America; and I take this oath freely and voluntarily without any mental reservations or evasions whatsoever.' "

The remainder of the document read:

> *Subscribed and sworn to me*
> *In duplicate this 28th day of April, 1861.*
>
> *The above named has dark complexion, black hair and*
> *black eyes, and is six feet, two inches high.*
> *Colonel Thomas J. Jackson, C.S.A.*

When Yancy and Colonel Jackson finished dutifully filling out the solemn document, Jackson said, "I'm going to make out your certificate of induction. Pay attention."

"Yes, sir."

Again by hand Jackson filled out the form:

> *The Fairgrounds*
> *Richmond, Virginia*
> *April 28th, 1861*
>
> *This is to certify that I have this day sworn Yancy*
> *Tremayne into the service of the Confederate States of*
> *America as a volunteer in the 1st Brigade, Virginia Infantry*
> *serving in the Army of Virginia.*
> *Thomas J. Jackson*
> *Colonel, C.S.A.*

"You got all that, Sergeant?" Jackson demanded.

Yancy swelled until he thought he would burst. "Yes, sir!"

"Then for your first duty as my aide, you're going to have to copy these two documents fair. Then you're going to have to swear in all those recruits out there and make two copies of each document. Meanwhile, direct each drill captain to me to make a daily report on our Virginian Volunteers here in Richmond. After that, report back to me and I will brief you on our upcoming posting. And after I brief you, then you will brief each new member of the 1st Brigade of our first mission."

"Yes, sir!" Yancy said snappily.

Jackson regarded him shrewdly. "You know, Sergeant Tremayne, that the 1st Brigade is going to be formed from the 2nd, 4th, 5th, 27th, and 33rd Virginia Infantry Regiments."

"Yes, sir?" Yancy answered curiously.

"But you're the first volunteer for the 1st Brigade."

"I'm proud to be, sir. And thank you again for my promotion. I won't let you down."

❧

Yancy immediately returned to the cadets and organized the drill team captains to report to Colonel Jackson. Then he set up a camp table outside Jackson's tent and began the tedious task of swearing in the cadets who were joining the Virginia Volunteers, although all of them wished to request the 1st Virginia Brigade.

The first cadet he signed in was Charles Satterfield. Chuckins signed the handwritten forms and watched as Yancy painstakingly made out duplicate forms. Penmanship was not Yancy's strong point and his spelling was not stellar, so he kept having to refer back to the originals that Colonel Jackson had made out for him.

"There's no printed forms for this?" Chuckins asked.

"There were plenty when the call went out for volunteers," Yancy answered, "but they were almost all used up. Colonel Jackson has a few left, but he wants to keep them in case it takes any time to get new printed forms to us. He told me to make handwritten copies for us, the cadets that are signing up."

"I could help you with those forms," Chuckins said.

"Yeah, you're the best in penmanship, I know," Yancy replied thoughtfully.

"And you know, I've already memorized those forms," Chuckins said diffidently.

"What?"

Chuckins shrugged. "Memorized them. I dunno. It's just something I can do."

Gladly Yancy said, "Go find a chair, report back here, and help me out. I'll take their oaths and induct them, and you can write them in."

It was almost one o'clock in the morning when Yancy reported back to Colonel Jackson. Of the fourteen cadets that had volunteered, Jackson called in Yancy, Peyton Stevens, Sandy Owens, and Charles Satterfield. They stood at uncomfortable attention in his tent.

"At ease," Jackson said.

They assumed the at ease position, relaxing their postures and holding their hands behind their backs.

Jackson, seated at his desk, frowned darkly. There was no seating for the cadets, which seemed to dissatisfy him. He rose and started pacing, his hands clasped behind him. "Gentlemen, I am not in the habit of addressing men in a personal manner. However, I have found that you four cadets have been exemplary, both in scholastics and in the military disciplines. Therefore I have made decisions concerning your positions, especially regarding the 1st Virginia Brigade, for which you have volunteered."

The four cadets nodded solemnly but did not speak.

Jackson paced. "Sergeant Tremayne, I've already given you your posting. Since you have such a magnificent horse, we're also inducting Midnight into the 1st Brigade. And, Stevens, I'm giving you a promotion to sergeant, as aide-de-camp and courier. But this is provisional if your horse, Senator, also joins the 1st Brigade."

Yancy had rarely seen Jackson's humor at home, but no other VMI cadet had probably ever witnessed it.

Peyton Stevens appeared nervous. "Sir, yes, sir. I'm—I'm—my horse is happy—that is, we volunteer."

"Mr. Owens," Jackson continued.

"Yes, sir!"

"I know that getting gunpowder and grease on your breeches causes you great distress. But you are one of the best gunners in the institute. The Rockbridge Artillery has been assigned to the 1st Brigade, and it is my wish that you would serve with them."

It was true that Sandy Owens was something of a dandy, and he hated for his dynamic VMI uniform to get soiled or wrinkled. But that was for the carefree days when he was a cadet in the finest military school in the South, and these were days of war. He was best at artillery, and he loved artillery best. "Thank you,

CROSSING

Colonel Jackson," he said quietly. "I would be honored to serve with Reverend Pendleton." Colonel W. N. Pendleton was the commanding officer of the Rockbridge Artillery, and he was also an Episcopal rector. Sandy attended his church.

"So that brings us to you, Mr. Satterfield," Jackson said. He sat down at the desk and shuffled through the pile of papers there.

Chuckins was obviously so nervous he could barely talk. "Y–yes, sir. Me. Th–that brings us to m–me."

Jackson's eyes sparked blue ice, and his set mouth had a slight tinge of amusement. He looked down and went through two more pages then looked up. "These documents are written in a fine hand."

"Th–thank you, sir."

"And there are no errors in the copy, none at all. That's very unusual."

Chuckins swallowed hard. "I—I had them memorized, sir. The forms."

"I see. It seems to me, Mr. Satterfield, that you would make a fine clerk. As it happens, I need a clerk on my staff."

"Sir! May I volunteer for your staff?" Chuckins asked anxiously.

"You may, and I accept. I'm promoting you to sergeant, and I'm appointing you as my chief clerk."

"Colonel, thank you, sir, thank you!"

"You may not thank me when you see the paperwork it takes to sustain a brigade," Jackson said drily. "All right, men, now I want to brief you on our posting. Please keep in mind that the regiments that will form the 1st Brigade have not been briefed yet. I prefer to keep my counsel to myself, for the most part, until I know I have a staff I can trust. I've known you men for a few years, and I feel I can trust you as I already know that you're capable of discretion."

Yancy knew Jackson thoroughly believed that the fewer people that knew the movements of his men, the fewer chances the enemy had to learn them.

Jackson continued, "General Lee has assigned us to Harpers Ferry."

The cadets exchanged puzzled looks.

"Yes, the same Harpers Ferry that John Brown took," Jackson said somberly. "We all witnessed his execution. The reason he took Harpers Ferry is that it is both a strategic and tactical target. Tactical because it's a United States arsenal. The arsenal, with its ordnance manufacture, consists in a complex of government buildings, including an armory, an arsenal, and an enginehouse. And it's a strategic target because a main stem of the Baltimore & Ohio railroad runs right through the town. In fact, it has double tracks, running east-west and west-east. Tons and tons of coal from the Appalachian mines in the Midwest run through that line to the East. And there's a bridge across the Potomac at Harpers Ferry that runs through Maryland on its way to Baltimore and Washington. And that means supplies going to the Federal army."

Owens, Stevens, and Satterfield all looked at Yancy. He seemed to have been elected the speaker for them, since he was in some ways closer to Colonel Jackson because he had worked for the Jacksons. "Sir, if I may ask, what will be the 1st Brigade's responsibility there? What is our mission?"

Jackson didn't grin, but his habitually stern expression lightened to one of amusement. "We're going to kidnap a railroad."

Colonel Thomas Jackson, commanding officer of the Confederate troops stationed at Harpers Ferry, Virginia, lodged a formal complaint with the president of the B & O Railroad, John W. Garrett of Baltimore. The trains disturbed his men at night, and Colonel Jackson demanded that they come through Harpers Ferry at about noon. Mr. John W. Garrett was hardly in a position to to argue with the Confederate officer who held the major railroad bridge over the Potomac. The loaded trains began running west-east from 11:00 a.m. to 1:00 p.m.

But then there were the empties returning east-west at night, and again Colonel Jackson complained and demanded that the dual tracks be scheduled so that the trains ran only around the noon hour. Again he was accommodated, and for two hours a day Harpers Ferry was the busiest railroad hub in America.

At noon on May 23, less than a month after he and his brigade had arrived in Harpers Ferry, Jackson ordered his troops to seal off each end of the thirty-two-mile-long sector that he held. The trains were

CROSSING

trapped. By the time the final tally was done, Colonel Jackson had kidnapped fifty-six locomotives and more than three hundred cars.

Another hostage was kidnapped during this raid—a nondescript, rather small reddish mare with soft brown eyes and a coltish gait. Colonel Jackson determined to give her as a gift to Anna, but he grew so fond of her that he kept her for his own mount, conscientously paying the quartermaster for her value. Little Sorrel she was called, and somehow Colonel Jackson sensed she would be with him to the very end of the road.

CHAPTER SIXTEEN

Colonel Thomas Jackson's "kidnapping" of a railroad resounded throughout the South, and he enjoyed some good publicity. However, a few days after this famous exploit was completed, Jackson was abruptly replaced. Brigadier General Joseph E. Johnston arrived at Harpers Ferry to take command. Jackson quietly stepped aside. General Johnston did give him command over the 1st Virginia Brigade that he had formed and had so carefully and ceaselessly trained.

In the middle of June, Federal troops began amassing on the Maryland side of the river, a force of about eighteen thousand under United States General Robert Patterson, a rather elderly and slow-moving, cautious officer. Still, General Johnston felt threatened that the superior force might outflank his 6,500 troops, so he withdrew to Winchester, about thirty miles southwest of Harpers Ferry. Jackson and his 1st Brigade were dispatched to Martinsburg, about twenty miles north. Colonel Jeb Stuart and his cavalry were ordered to observe the Federals and immediately give word if they showed any signs of crossing the Potomac.

In his position, Jackson saw nothing of the enemy and no activity was reported to him. But one thing did happen that reduced the difficulty of being relieved of his command. . .and of his boredom in Martinsburg. On June 17, he received his commission as brigadier general in the army of the Confederate States of America.

As it happened, Chuckins Satterfield was in Jackson's camp tent transcribing some of Jackson's dictation when the courier from Richmond arrived with the orders for Jackson's promotion. He witnessed the courier deliver the papers and swear Jackson in. After the courier left, Chuckins jumped to attention and said, "Sir! May I be the first to congratulate you, sir, on your commission, General Jackson, sir!"

"You may. Thank you," he answered succinctly. "Sit down, Sergeant Satterfield, and continue your work."

"Yes, sir!" Chuckins sat back down to his dreary paperwork.

Surreptitiously he watched the brand-new general, but Jackson showed no outward signs of excitement or elation at his promotion. He sat calmly at his desk, his pen endlessly scratching across paper.

Finally Chuckins could stand it no longer. "Sir? General Jackson? Would it be all right if I took a short break to have a cup of coffee, sir?"

Jackson didn't look up; his pen scratched and scritched. "Dismissed."

Chuckins ran out, grabbed the first soldier he saw, and told the news.

Soon everyone in the 1st Brigade had heard that they were now commanded by a brigadier general. And they were proud. Though Jackson had none of the glad-handing, backslapping ways of many powerful men, he carried with him an unmistakable air of authority, of sure and certain knowledge and understanding, and of honor and integrity. To a man and to the utmost they respected him and trusted him. It may even be said that they loved him.

When Jackson heard Colonel Jeb Stuart was riding into the camp, just outside of Martinsburg, with the usual drama, he came hurrying out of his tent to greet his friend.

Stuart galloped full speed through the camp, coming to a stop by abruptly reining in his magnificent mount, who skidded to a stop, threw his head up, reared and pawed the air, and came to a furious stamping halt. Jeb Stuart jumped off, throwing the reins to one of his escorts. As usual, he was greeted by the soldier's whoops and calls.

Stuart stopped before Jackson, came to a parade attention, and then saluted beautifully. "May I congratulate you, General Jackson, on your well-deserved promotion. It is an honor to serve under you, sir."

Jackson returned his salute and said quietly, "You serve with me, Colonel Stuart. We serve God and the Confederacy."

They went into Jackson's tent where they stayed for about an hour. Then Colonel Stuart and his escorts left, as dashing and daring as they had arrived.

Jackson then called in Yancy and Peyton. "You two men go to all the commanders of the regiments and tell them we'll be marching within the hour. Light field packs. Sergeant Stevens, tell General Pendleton to get the guns ready to move into Martinsburg."

They saluted and ran off to alert the command that they were moving to battle, the first fighting that they had seen.

Tethered by his tent was Midnight, and when Yancy ran to saddle him up, he saw that a private from Lexington named Henry Birdwell was visiting Midnight, stroking his nose and feeding him some dried corn.

When he saw Yancy, he snapped to attention and saluted.

"At ease, Birdie," Yancy said, returning a careless salute.

Henry Birdwell had joined Captain Reese Gilmer's Raphine Company, of the 33rd Virginia Regiment, the unit that Yancy had trained in Richmond. Now they were part of the 1st Brigade.

Captain Reese Gilmer was the ultimate Southern gentleman. He owned a cotton plantation, about thirty slaves, and his family could be traced back to the Mayflower. He was a good soldier and a good leader, and he had managed to recruit about one hundred men from his small central village of Raphine and the farms and plantations beyond. Henry Birdwell had been employed as a stable boy at Raphine Plantation, and he had immediately signed up for Reese Gilmer's company.

Henry Birdwell was one year older than Yancy, but he seemed much younger, with his open face, mild brown eyes, and short brown hair with a pronounced cowlick. He loved horses, though his family had always been too poor to buy saddle horses. He especially loved Midnight, for the high-bred stallion responded to him with a friendliness and glad whinny that was rare, except for Yancy and his family.

"Go get ready, Birdie," Yancy told him. "We're going to march out soon."

Birdwell blinked in the bright morning sunlight. "Are we going to fight, Sergeant Tremayne?"

"General Jackson doesn't confide in the likes of me," Yancy replied lightly. "All I know is that we're marching out. Here, you want to help me saddle him up?"

"Yes, sir." Quickly the private gave Midnight's back a brush-down then laid one of Yancy's fine soft Indian blankets on his back.

As they were saddling Midnight, Yancy asked, "Why are you here, Birdie? Why are you fighting?"

"They called us. And I wanted to fight for Captain Reese and General Jackson," he answered simply. "We all knew General Jackson in Lexington. We all wanted to fight with him."

Yancy nodded. "I know what you mean."

Birdie continued, "I still want to fight, but. . .I sure hope the war's over soon, like the newspapers say. I've got a girlfriend, Ellen Mae Simpkins. She's a maid at Raphine Plantation. When I get home we're going to get married."

"That's good, Birdie," Yancy said quietly. "I know you'll be happy. Now, go on. Go get ready to march."

He saluted. "Yes, sir!" he said snappily and turned and ran off like a boy on his way to his favorite fishing hole.

Within an hour, the brigade was ready to march. General Jackson rode forward and, without a word, led the way out of camp. They pushed hard all morning long. It was late in the afternoon before Jackson ordered the brigade to halt. He called all his aides and commanding officers together.

"You see that church over there?" he asked, pointing. "That is the church in Falling Waters. The Federals are just on the other side of it. They are advancing. Now, we are going to move just past the treeline of that glade over there and we're going to wait for them to advance into this open field. And then we'll take them. Position your men in three stances: first volley, from a prone position; second volley, kneeling position; and third volley, standing. Then, gentlemen, we will charge and give them the bayonet. Ride out."

Yancy caught up to him and said, "General, sir? Permission to join Raphine Company?"

Jackson frowned. "Is that the company you've been training and drilling, Sergeant Tremayne?"

"Yes, sir. I'd very much like to be with them in their first battle, sir."

"Permission granted."

Yancy saluted and turned to ride away.

Jackson called after him, "Sergeant Tremayne?"

"Yes, sir?"

"Fight hard, Sergeant Tremayne. This is for Virginia, for our homes, for our families. No matter what they think about this war, this is for them."

"Yes, sir!" Yancy said, wheeling Midnight and hurrying to the front.

As Jackson planned, the enemy came marching across open fields, and they met deadly musket fire. Jackson and his three regiments charged them.

Captain Reese Gilmer drew his sword, thrust it forward, and yelled, "Charge!"

Yancy, on Midnight, charged right behind him, sword drawn.

From then on, all was a confusion of harsh glaring light—for it was a blistering July afternoon—hot gulping breaths, the smell of blood and gunpowder, and the echoing screams of men fighting and firing and dying. Yancy saw, as if in magnification, a man fall just beside him. The soldier was on his back and the lower part of his jaw had been shot away and he clutched at the wound, his heels kicking into the ground.

A tall soldier named Ed Tompkins was beside Yancy, and he yelled and drove his bayonet into the chest of the wounded soldier. "Here's one Yankee who won't give us no trouble, Lieutenant!" he screamed. He then raced forward, yelling at the top of his lungs.

Yancy carried his rifle. Midnight carried him, directed by the pressure of his knees, and he never wavered. Yancy shot three men that he saw aiming a rifle at him, but he didn't stop to see the results. He kept riding, reloading, and shooting at the Federals in blue.

"We've got them!" Jackson shouted. "Drive them with the bayonet!"

The battle turned into a foot race. The Union soldiers turned and fled away from the advancing Confederates, but before they had gone very far, a Union artillery of hidden guns fired and shells began exploding around the Confederates. One of them hit so close it rocked Yancy and he almost lost his balance. His eyes were full of dirt, so he pulled Midnight to a halt so he could clean out his eyes.

When he finally could see, Yancy started to signal Midnight forward, but he looked up and saw a single blue-clad soldier that had a rifle aimed right at him. Yancy threw up his pistol and fired. The shot struck the Federal soldier and drove him backward. His finger was still on the trigger and he shot at the blue sky above. Yancy slowly eased Midnight forward then stopped to peer down at the soldier.

Around them was still the chaos and thunder and maddening yells of a battlefield, but for a moment Yancy was encased in quiet as he saw the first man he had ever killed. He was an older man with a russet beard, and his eyes were open. His uniform was dyed scarlet with his blood. His final expression was one of surprise as if to say, *What? This can't be happening to me!*

Yancy stared at him for a moment, but the blood of battle was still thrumming in his veins, and Midnight was spoiling to run. He reloaded his rifle, took it in his right hand and his pistol in his left, and spurred Midnight forward, yelling like fury.

But Jackson called them back.

The Reverend Colonel Pendleton then activated his big guns across the road, decimating the column moving along it. He raised his head and cried, "Lord, have mercy on their souls."

The Battle of Fallen Waters was over. As Yancy withdrew with Captain Gilmer's company, he saw a Confederate body lying in a crumpled way as if it had fallen from a great height. He dismounted and turned the body over and saw it was Private Birdwell. "Birdie," he whispered, "you'll never get back to marry Ellen Mae now." Yancy thought of how she would cry when she learned of her lover's death. *And his mother and father will weep, and his friends—all will suffer an awful loss.*

For the first time Yancy realized just what a sacrifice war was—not just for the men fighting, but for their families, their loved ones, their friends, their countrymen. *General Jackson said it,* he thought sadly: *"War is the sum of all evil."*

He hurried to report back to Jackson's headquarters, and General Jackson greeted him immediately. "Sergeant Tremayne, are you and your horse fresh or are you battle weary, sir?" he asked sternly.

"We are ready and waiting for our duty, sir," Yancy answered.

"Good, good. I have dispatches for Richmond, so you can ride?"

"Yes, sir."

"And Sergeant Tremayne—"

"Sir?"

"The sooner Richmond knows of all of our movements, the better they can direct this war and give us timely orders. Your horse is fastest in the Confederate Army, I imagine, except for maybe Colonel Stuart's. Ride hard. Don't stop."

Yancy and Midnight headed for Richmond.

Abraham Lincoln stared at the men of his cabinet gathered in the room with him. He had listened to their arguments, but basically what was being said was summed up by the blunt secretary of war, Edwin Stanton. "Mr. President, we must give the people something to see. We need a military victory."

CROSSING

Lincoln had been opposed to bringing on action, but finally he was convinced. "Very well, then, we shall have it."

The commander chosen to lead the army in this first campaign was General Irvin McDowell, a well-regarded graduate and instructor at West Point. Until the war, he had served in the adjutant general's office in Washington.

As the days of preparation took place, there was no secret about what was going to happen. It seemed that every man on the street knew the army was preparing to do battle, and most of them knew where the first field of battle was to be. It was near a creek called Bull Run, which was adjacent to a small town called Manassas.

There was almost a holiday air as the army was sent to war with marshal music, stirring tunes by marching bands, cakes and doughnuts by the thousands baked by the ladies of the land. In fact, the North was so certain of an easy victory that many families in their carriages went to the site of the impending battle and had picnics and visited with each other on a hillside overlooking the picturesque creek of Bull Run and the Manassas Crossroads.

As the Army of the Potomac marched out of Washington headed southwest, Lincoln's face grew sad, and he whispered, "Some of those young men will die. How can I bear it?"

General McDowell listened to the cries of "Forward to Richmond!" fill the air, but he moved his army slowly. He was an experienced soldier but not a brilliant strategist; nor was he the man to inspire troops.

The Confederates were well aware of both the strategic and tactical moves of the Federals, because there were spies in Washington that kept close tabs on the movement of the Union army. Commanding generals Joe Johnston and P. G. T. Beauregard knew the movements of the Federals almost as well as they themselves did.

On Friday, July 19, the 1st Brigade, led by General Jackson, arrived at Manassas Junction. He had given few orders, and Yancy had stuck close to his side acting as a courier. Now the men were placed in a line along Bull Run Creek and were ordered to stay in reserve. At this time there were arguments among the top-ranking

Confederate generals of where the Union charge would be made.

On a blistering Sunday, July 21, it was obvious that the Federals were advancing. Yancy was by his commander's side during the whole time, except when he was assigned to dispatch messages. Midnight was the fastest horse on the Confederate side, and he never seemed to tire.

Finally, the attack came, as McDowell threw his army forward. The Confederates stiffened and General Jackson took his stand on a small rise. Still ordered to hold in reserve, he watched calmly as the battle raged on back and forth. Jackson was clearly outlined against the sky on the knoll; though, of course, it was doubtful that anyone would take him for a general from his nondescript uniform and awkward, small Little Sorrel. Still, he carried a certain authority as he watched, occasionally through his field glasses, the battle raging just below. Shrapnel from Union shells sometimes showered about him. He never even flinched. At one point it seemed a sharpshooter targeted him. A bullet came so close between him and Yancy that Yancy could feel the hot air as it whined by. Then another, so close to Yancy's hair that it stirred it a bit, and convulsively Yancy ducked. Jackson didn't blink.

Uncertainly Yancy said, "Sir? Don't you think you might take cover from that sharpshooter that's firing at you?"

Jackson turned to him. His face was grim, his mouth a tight, hard line. His eyes were like the very core of blue flame, sparking dangerously. At that moment Yancy realized that General Thomas Jackson was, indeed, a dangerous man. "How do you know he's not aiming for you?" Jackson said drily and turned back to view the field through his glasses.

One more bullet came close, but not as close as the other two, whistling a few feet alongside Yancy's knees. With a self-control he had no idea he possessed, he managed not to jerk away and sat tall and straight in the saddle. It seemed that Jackson could bring out this quality of bravery in men.

The Federals advanced and were driven back by fierce Confederate forces, but the Union troops seemed to be coming from all sides. The Confederates were hard pressed all along the front.

CROSSING

Jackson pointed and stated, "Look, General Bee is being pushed back. They've been shot to pieces."

Yancy saw General Bee turn, the agony of defeat on his face. He had lost his hat and his sword was bent. Then General Bee saw Jackson, and he called out so all could hear him, "Look, men, there stands Jackson like a stone wall! Rally behind the Virginians!"

Jackson could stand it no longer; though he had been given no orders, he shouted the command, "Charge, brigade! Drive them from the field!" He spurred forward, and Yancy stayed by his side.

The rest of the day was a time of thunder and confusion, a time of blood and fear. More battle, more death, and after a while Yancy's mind rebelled against seeing the faces of the men, the horrors inflicted on both sides, the carnage.

Slowly, almost imperceptibly, the battle began to turn against the North. A charge by Jackson's 33rd Virginia regiment and by Stuart's cavalry were pivotal points in the battle that made the Northern troops retreat, and then that retreat became an insane rout. Soldiers threw down their arms and ran on foot; teamsters driving carts stampeded the crowds; the road was packed with retreating cavalry, sutlers, civilians, companies, even whole regiments of men running back toward Washington. They left their arms, their supplies, their carts and horses, their wounded, and their dead.

As the Union army fled, Jackson tried to convince his superior officers that this was the time to strike Washington, but no one would listen. He turned to Yancy in despair and said, "Now is the time to win this war, but no one sees it."

Yancy said, "Our men are pretty tired, sir."

"We'll never be in a better position to strike Washington than we are now. Go find General Johnston; I've written this note. But you tell him that the 1st Virginia Brigade will attack Washington alone if we have to!"

Yancy said, "Yes, sir!" He wheeled Midnight around and took off across the broken battlefield.

He delivered the message to General Johnston who said, "No, we're too weak and they'll be behind the barricades. Tell Jackson we have won the victory."

Dispiritedly Yancy rode back and gave Jackson the message.

Jackson just replied, "Very well. Here, Sergeant. I have written a report for the president. Take it to Richmond. Remain there until you get an audience with him."

Yancy rode Midnight south toward Richmond, believing that the battle was over and he was safe, paralleling the Confederate lines to the east. But he had not ridden more than a mile when he suddenly saw that part of the battle was still raging. A small group of Federals were engaged in a desperate fight with a force of Confederates. The Confederates appeared to be winning because they outnumbered the opposing force, but Yancy was a soldier, and he had to fight.

He tied Midnight to a scrub oak then ran forward, loading his rifle as he ran. But by the time he reached the line of battle, the men in blue had fled with the Confederates in full pursuit. Yancy considered them and realized that the Federals were sure to be taken prisoner.

He remembered his first duty was to carry out General Jackson's orders. He turned back. . .then suddenly stopped dead still.

Not ten feet away was a wounded Union officer, a lieutenant, sitting with his back against a tree. His hat was on the ground. Locks of his sandy brown hair, fine and caked with sweat and battle grime, had fallen down over his forehead. His tunic was covered with blood. He had a pistol in his hand that was aimed directly at Yancy. The lieutenant's eyes were clear enough, and the pistol in his hand was steady.

Yancy stopped dead still then threw up his rifle, but he knew that he had not finished loading it. There was no charge in the barrel, so helplessly he lowered it again.

At that moment, as he saw the officer's finger tighten on the trigger, Yancy Tremayne understood with a shock that he was only a few seconds from death. He would be facing a God whom he had never served. Strangely enough, he felt little fear, only regret that he'd never found God. A cry leaped unbidden from his lips: "God, forgive me!"

He then waited for the shot that would send him to eternity.

CHAPTER SEVENTEEN

As Yancy stared into the barrel of the pistol aimed directly at his heart, he was very aware of all of his surroundings. He could still hear the faint cries of the Confederates, chasing the company that this Union lieutenant belonged to, or so he supposed. The chilling Rebel yell carried on the still air. He could feel each great drop of sweat that rolled off his forehead and down his nose and cheeks. He could smell burning gunpowder in his nostrils.

Yancy's hands were trembling. He was intensely aware of the details of the wounded lieutenant, even noticing that he had a gold ring on his finger on his right hand, the hand that held the pistol that was aimed at his heart.

But now, even as he took these inconsequential details into his mind, he was very aware of his overall state of mind. Since he had cried out to God, he was amazed to find that the fear that had burned in him was gone. Calmly he waited for the lieutenant to fire, even standing up straight and turning slightly to face him full front. As the seconds ticked off, he couldn't understand why the end didn't come.

He shifted his gaze from the round muzzle of the pistol upward until he focused on the face of the officer. Oddly, he thought, *He looks like a good man.* He didn't expect to find goodness in a man trying to kill him, and he was unsure of what quality in the man's face made him think such a thing.

The gray eyes of the soldier stared at him steadily.

Yancy stared back, expressionlessly, and then he leaned forward, unconsciously anticipating the force of the bullet that would kill him. But no shot came.

Abruptly the officer dropped the gun into his lap. A deadly weariness washed over his face. He was pale and his lips were moving unsteadily as he spoke. "I'll be in the presence of God soon, and I don't want the blood of a helpless man on my hands." He slumped forward, his chin falling on his chest.

With somewhat of a shock Yancy realized that he was still alive and that he wasn't going to die, in the next few minutes anyway. He fell to his knees, bowed his head, and cried, "Oh, God, I believe that Jesus is the Son of the living God, and I believe He died for my sins. I put my faith in Him and I ask You, God, to save me from my sins and make me into the man You want me to be!"

He knelt there for only a few moments, and a strange peace descended upon him. Slowly he got to his feet and found that his hands were now steady.

Yancy went to the wounded man, knelt down beside him, and took the pistol that lay on the man's lap. As he did, he saw that there was a wound in his leg that was bleeding. But it was just a graze, on the outside of his thigh. He opened the officer's tunic and saw an entry wound just down and on the left of his chest. He thought that probably the ball had missed the lung, but when he eased him forward, he realized that the bullet hadn't come out.

Gently he propped the man back against the tree. Running to where Midnight waited, he grabbed an old muslin shirt out of his saddlebag. After he returned to the wounded man, he ripped the shirt into shreds and removed the man's coat. He tied the strips of the shirt together and took a larger piece and placed it over the wound that was bleeding. He used the strips to tie the rough bandage in place. Then he cut the man's trousers off and bandaged the wound in his thigh.

Yancy was just finishing up bandaging his leg when the man's dull gray eyes opened and he murmured, "Do you have any water?"

"Yes, I'll get my canteen." He once again rose and went to Midnight and got his canteen. He took the cap off and held it to the man's lips.

The soldier grabbed the canteen and looked as if he was going to gulp it down.

Yancy pulled it away and said, "Don't drink too much right now, because of your wound. Just sip it. After we get you fixed up you can have more."

The soldier's eyes were steady now, and he was lucid. He nodded and took only three small sips. "Thanks for the water."

Yancy, kneeling beside him, asked, "Why didn't you kill me?"

The lieutenant managed to smile. "For the same reason you're not killing me. We didn't want blood on our hands. Blood of unarmed men, anyway."

"What's your name, Lieutenant?"

"Leslie, Leslie Hayden." The young man closed his eyes and Yancy thought he was losing consciousness. But he opened them again to regard Yancy gravely. His voice was faint, but Yancy could clearly hear him. "I'm going to ask you a favor, Sergeant. I think I've lost too much blood. Would you carry a message to my family?"

Yancy answered, "I don't think you're going to die, but I'll do what you ask."

"My father lives just outside of Richmond, just south of the Episcopalian church. His name is Dr. Jesse Hayden. If I don't make it, will you go and tell him and my mother that I died trusting in the Lord? And tell them that I'm not afraid. I'm not afraid at all anymore."

Suddenly Yancy knew what he had to do. This man in one sense was the enemy, and Yancy had sworn to defend his homeland from men like this soldier; but now he was no longer a soldier. He was now a noncombatant, and he had shown Yancy mercy.

Yancy made a hard decision. "I'll take you to your family, Lieutenant Hayden, and your father can treat your wounds."

Surprise washed over Hayden's bloodless face. "But if we get caught, you could be executed for giving aid and comfort to the enemy."

"Then we won't get caught. I'll be back. You just hang on."

The roadside was littered with field packs and even weapons that the Federals had thrown away in their disorganized rout. Yancy had passed a wagon about a quarter of a mile back, a supply wagon with blankets and tents. Someone had taken the horse and run. Yancy rode Midnight to it, hitched him up, and hurried back to Lieutenant Hayden. He jumped out of the wagon and said, "This should get us back to Richmond with you as comfortable as can be, under the circumstances."

"My uniform. . ." Hayden said weakly.

"I've got some work clothes in my pack. We're about the same size." He pulled his extra shirt and a pair of work pants that he wore sometimes in camp when doing rough work. Being as careful as he could, he took off Hayden's tunic and redressed him. He had fine officer's boots, so Yancy took those and, wrapping the uniform and boots together, threw them to the side of the road. He had seen some dead soldiers in the field where they had been skirmishing, but somehow Yancy didn't think he could stoop to stripping them of their shoes. He had one pair of extra socks, and he put those on the wounded man and thought that would have to do.

"All right, Lieutenant Hayden, it's going to hurt, but I've got to get you in that wagon." Leaning down, Yancy put his arm around Hayden and pulled him to his feet. He heard the man sigh heavily, but he didn't cry out. They staggered over to the back of the wagon. Hayden was almost dead weight, and for a few moments Yancy wondered if he would be able to bodily lift him into it, but somehow Hayden managed to summon some strength and drew himself up to get up onto the tailgate. He then fell heavily on the bed of blankets.

Yancy jumped up into the bed and managed to pull him into a more comfortable position. "If anybody stops us, let me do the talking."

Hayden was lying flat on his back, staring up at him. "Why are you doing this?"

Yancy thought for a moment, then he smiled slightly. "Lieutenant, I think that God is telling me to help you." His own words surprised him. He hesitated then went on, "This is the first time I've ever heard from God, so I guess I'd better do what He says."

He jumped to the ground and put the tailgate up on the wagon. Quickly he climbed into the seat, snapped the reins, and muttered, "Come on, Midnight, we have long miles to go."

It was a smoky, sultry night in Richmond. Thinking hard, Yancy remembered having seen the Episcopal church just south of the heart of town. He skirted around the city. There were few people stirring, but he suspected that downtown and around the capitol would be one great buzzing hive of activity. But it was quiet, with very few home lights glowing, in this gracious residential section.

The moonlight was brilliant; its silver light bathed the street in argent beams. Before they had ridden out, he had asked Lieutenant Hayden what his father's house looked like, and the Lieutenant had described it as "a large two-story house with four gables in the front and framed by two enormous walnut trees."

The description was accurate enough, and Yancy pulled Midnight to a halt. Quickly, he tied the lines off and jumped into the back of the wagon. He hadn't wanted to waste time stopping to check on his passenger. Hayden had been very quiet, and by the time Yancy found his family home, he was afraid he might have died. He checked him and saw that he still had a faint pulse and his breathing was very shallow; he was unconscious, but he lived.

Yancy jumped out of the wagon and looked up and down the street. It was an elegant street, with two-story family homes, great live oak trees, magnolias, elms, and walnut and pecan trees. Few of the windows were lit. Yancy didn't know what time it was, but it was late.

At the Hayden residence there was only one small light in an upstairs window, and the home had a private, reserved air that made Yancy wonder exactly how he would approach this family of Union sympathizers. He still wore his Confederate gray uniform and forage cap. Undoubtedly this family would not exactly welcome him with open arms. Still, he knew he had to get Hayden to his father.

He went up the steps onto the wooden veranda, and his boots

seemed to make a lot of noise. He knocked on the door, quietly and softly. There was no answer. Sighing, he turned to go back to check on Hayden.

Then suddenly behind him was a sharp wedge of light, a quiet tread on the porch, abrupt darkness, and then a woman's voice. "Stop right where you are, Johnny Reb. Be very still, or I'll shoot you. Put your hands up over your head."

Yancy froze, put his hands up over his head, and said in a voice as calm as he could manage, "I'm looking for Dr. Hayden."

"What for? What do you want with him?"

"I'm going to turn around now. Please don't shoot me." He turned around with his hands lifted high.

There in the shimmery moonlight, he saw a young woman who was indeed holding a pistol in each hand. Both of them were cocked and both of them were pointed at his chest. She had slipped out of the front door and stood in the shadows in the corner of the entryway.

Yancy swallowed hard. "I have the doctor's son in that wagon. He's been shot and he'll die if he doesn't get medical attention."

The pistols wavered just a bit. "You wouldn't have Leslie in that wagon. He's a lieutenant in the 2nd Division, United States Army."

"Yes, ma'am, I know."

"And you're a Confederate soldier."

"Yes, ma'am."

She stared at him. She was wearing nightclothes, with a thick robe. Her eyes were great dark pools in a white, heart-shaped face. Her hair cascaded over one shoulder and reached almost to her waist. Moonlight made everything look colorless, only gradations of white and black, but he had the idea that her hair was light-colored, though not blond. She was tiny, her shoulders narrow, her hands small. In them the pistols looked gigantic, but with a sort of oddball humor, Yancy reflected that from this end they would probably look huge to anyone, no matter who held them.

"Ma'am—" Yancy began.

That moment the front door opened and Yancy saw it was an older man, tall but stoop-shouldered, wearing a robe. "What is it, Lorena?"

"I don't know, Father. Some soldier that says he wants you," she answered disdainfully. The pistols, once again, were steady.

"Are you Dr. Hayden?" Yancy asked.

"I am. And you are?"

"My name is Yancy Tremayne, doctor."

"He's a Confederate soldier," the woman said harshly.

"So I see," the older man said quietly. "How can I help you, Sergeant Tremayne?"

"Dr. Hayden, I found your son on the battlefield at Manassas Crossroads. He told me where you live and I brought him to you."

Dr. Hayden started and asked alertly, "What? Where is he?"

"He's in the wagon."

"Lorena, go get that lantern," Dr. Hayden said, pulling his night robe closer about him.

Still the woman pointed the pistols at Yancy, staring at him unblinkingly.

"Please lower those pistols, miss. They could go off."

"They will go off if you're lying," she said fiercely.

"Nonsense, Lorena, what do you think? That this man has come to lure me outside and assassinate me? Go back in and get that lantern, girl, and put those things away before someone gets shot," Dr. Hayden insisted.

She lowered the pistols, but slowly and reluctantly. Her look at Yancy was still hard, cold, and suspicious.

"Ma'am, here's my pistol, in the holster at my side. You can take it if you wish."

"Give it to me."

Wordlessly he unsnapped the flap, took his service pistol out, and handed it to her. Silently she took all three guns inside. Immediately she came back out with a lantern.

The three of them now hurried to the wagon and looked over the side. The woman held the lantern high, and in the lurid light they could clearly see the paper white face of the wounded man.

She whispered, "Leslie. . . Oh no, it *is* Leslie. . . ."

With a swift movement, she shoved the lantern into Yancy's hands, lowered the endgate, and jumped into the wagon. She laid two fingers by his throat. "He's alive, Father. Breathing shallow, pulse shallow, but he's alive."

"We must get him inside," Dr. Hayden said. "I'll get Elijah to help us carry him in." He moved quickly to the house, night robe flapping behind him.

Gently she touched Leslie's face then looked up. "Who did you say you were?"

"My name is Yancy Tremayne. My family lives outside of Lexington. Who are you, miss?"

"I'm Lorena Hayden, Leslie's sister. You're a Confederate soldier. . . . My brother is a Union officer. . . ."

"Yes, ma'am," Yancy said patiently. "I took off his uniform and put some of my clothes on him."

"Why are you helping him?"

Yancy had no time to answer for the doctor was back, and beside him was a black man, perhaps six-five and massive. "Elijah, we need to get Leslie in. Do you think you can carry him?"

"I 'spect I can, sir."

"Here, I'll help." Yancy leaped up into the wagon and lifted Hayden's shoulders while Elijah lifted his legs. Together they eased him to the back of the wagon. Then Elijah picked him up as easily as he would a child.

"Put him in his room, Elijah," Dr. Hayden ordered.

"Yes, sir."

They followed him into the house, Yancy behind Lorena Hayden. A pretty black woman with huge dark eyes was lighting candles and lanterns. As they entered the now well-lit foyer, Yancy saw that his hunch was right. Lorena had light brown hair with lighter golden streaks in it. She was small—she might only come up to his chest—but she held herself ruler-straight, and she walked proudly. The stiff, uncompromising line of her spine showed him that she still was not happy to turn her back on him.

Yancy was sitting in the Haydens' kitchen. The maid servant, Missy, had fixed him what would normally be called a breakfast, though it was about ten o'clock at night. But it was fresh and hot and delicious, and Yancy ate heartily. Seated at Missy's work counter by the stove, she had put before him ham and eggs and biscuits and grits.

Oddly, Elijah and Missy stood by the stove, silently watching him eat. Missy's hands were clasped in front of her apron, while Elijah stood silently, his hands clasped behind his back. Yancy wondered if they were slaves, but then he thought that surely they must not be, since it appeared that the Haydens were obviously Northern sympathizers. Of course, not all Southerners held slaves. Anna Jackson's maid, Hetty, was a free woman, a paid servant.

Yancy realized that they probably wouldn't speak unless spoken to, so he said, "This is mighty fine cooking, Missy. Thank you."

"Why, you're welcome, Mr. Tremayne. Maybe you want some molasses and some butter to put on them biscuits?"

"I would appreciate that, Missy."

As she was fetching it for him, Lorena and her father came in.

Yancy got to his feet at once, almost standing at attention. "How is he?"

"Sleeping, but very weak," Dr. Hayden said. "Luckily the bullet was lodged very close under the skin in his back, and I was able to remove it fairly easily. I think he has a broken rib, but at least the bullet didn't hit any vital organs. Elijah, please go sit with him and call me if he stirs in the slightest. Missy, my wife is with Leslie right now, but she's exhausted. Please see if you can get her to go back to bed."

"Yes, sir," they murmured and slipped out.

Dr. Hayden turned back to Yancy, who studied the man. He was tall, as Leslie Hayden was, over six feet, though he had a slight stoop. They were slender men, with classic features, and Dr. Hayden had bequeathed to both his son and daughter his fine light brown hair with golden streaks. Dr. Hayden had a thick sweeping mustache. "Please, Sergeant Tremayne. Sit down and finish your meal."

Missy had made a pot of coffee. Lorena fixed cups for herself and her father, and then they sat on two of the high stools in the kitchen.

Yancy felt somewhat awkward, but he was still hungry. He sat down and finished his last biscuit and the final bites of eggs and grits. Carefully he wiped his mouth with a fine linen napkin that, somehow, he found incongruous in the circumstances. Finally he said, "I know you're wondering about all of this."

"I know it was a good thing that you got Leslie here when you did, Sergeant Tremayne. Much longer, and my son likely wouldn't have survived without you."

Lorena's eyes narrowed. Now he could see that she had very dark blue eyes, almost black. Her mouth was well-shaped, her lips rather full but not vulgarly so. She asked in an even voice, "Can you tell us exactly why you brought him here? What could possibly have happened between you, who are obviously sworn enemies?"

Yancy murmured, "It's a strange story and I don't understand some of it myself yet."

Lorena and Dr. Hayden watched him intently.

He was silent for long moments. Narrowing his eyes, he lifted his head and stared into space, trying desperately to think what to tell these people, how little or how much. Regardless of the fact that he had given aid to Leslie Hayden, he had no intention of telling these Union sympathizers anything that could be construed as information about the war. He knew very well that the newspapers would all have accounts about the battle in the morning, but still he felt it wouldn't be right for him to tell them. And he certainly wasn't going to tell them that he was a courier for General Jackson. Jackson was secretive to the point of paranoia anyway, and besides that, it wouldn't be right to let them know of his position and his mission.

His mission. . .

Though he had been, for the past several hours, concerned about Leslie Hayden, he now realized that he was on a mission. He was in possession of important—and secret—dispatches to the president of the Confederate States of America from one of his top commanders. Suddenly his heart beat faster and unevenly, a raw and uncomfortable feeling. Those dispatches were still out in his saddlebag in the wagon, unguarded. . .and almost forgotten.

Yancy jumped up so quickly that he knocked over his stool. "I—I'm sorry, but I have to go."

"What?" Dr. Hayden said in astonishment. "But—but surely

you can stay and at least tell us who you are and explain to us how it came about that we should be in such great debt to you!"

"No, no, sir, I'm very sorry but I really must leave now," Yancy said, striding to the foyer to retrieve his forage cap. "Ma'am, may I please have my pistol back?" Dr. Hayden and Lorena had followed him.

Her eyes narrowed and her face grew dark with suspicion. "And why is it that you should have to leave in such a hurry, sir? Who are you going to report to, and to whom are you going to tell of my brother, and—"

"No, Lorena, no," Dr. Hayden said with sudden understanding. "Sergeant Tremayne surely has his own way to make. He would never betray us after he has gone to such trouble, and he has without doubt saved your brother's life. Leave him be, and let him go."

After hesitating a few moments, with obvious reluctance Lorena pulled Yancy's pistol out of a drawer in a side table in the foyer. She handed it to him without meeting his eyes.

"I'm sorry, Dr. Hayden, Miss Hayden. But I know that in the next few days you'll know—more—about this day, and what has happened between us. Between the North and the South. With your permission I would like to return and see Leslie, and then perhaps I may be able to speak more freely."

Dr. Hayden gave him his hand. "You will always be welcome in my home, Sergeant Tremayne, regardless of what happens out there in the fields of battle. Please do come back as soon as you possibly can."

"Thank you, sir. I will." Yancy turned to Lorena and searched her face, but there was nothing there except doubt and suspicion. As Yancy hurried to Midnight, Lorena and Dr. Hayden followed him to their porch. Their conversation carried to his ears, obviously unknown to the pair.

Lorena turned to her father. "I don't trust him. It just doesn't make sense."

"We will need to hear his story before we decide if it makes sense or not, Lorena," Dr. Hayden said mildly. He turned and gently put his hand on his daughter's shoulder to walk with him toward the stairs. "I think it's a miracle. This young man, I believe, has a good heart, honorable and true. I don't know how I know it, and I don't know why, but I believe the Lord touched him, and then he saved your brother. I know you're suspicious of all men, Lorena, but I think you can trust this one."

Without any reaction to their words as to give away that he had heard, Yancy mounted and rode away.

As was to be expected, Richmond was like a boiling cauldron after the victory at Manassas. In particular, the capitol had great swirling crowds of men at all hours, running in and out, shouting to each other, disappearing into offices and then coming back out on other urgent war business.

Of course the Department of War offices were insanely busy. That night, on July 22, Yancy reported there at about ten o'clock. He was seated in an anteroom and watched men come and go, their faces by turn fiercely delighted or grievously worried, until about seven a.m. the next morning.

Yancy recognized one of the secretaries, a dry, threadbare little man with a bald pate, thick glasses, and ink-stained fingers, when he came out of one of the offices. All night long Yancy had seen the secretary call one man in, escort another man out, take papers from that one, deliver them to another. "Dispatches!" he called, as the secretaries did when they were ready to take the messages the couriers brought in. "Dispatches from the 1st Virginia Brigade— the Stonewall Brigade!" Wild cheers and calls sounded throughout the hall. General Jackson's new nickname was already famous.

Grinning like an idiot, Yancy stood and held up his hand. "Here, sir! Dispatches from the—the Stonewall Brigade!"

Men gathered around him, clapping him on the back and shaking his hand, until he was almost dizzy. "There he stood, like a stone wall!" they kept repeating. Yancy duly delivered his dispatches, and the secretary told him to wait. He was besieged by the men who demanded detailed accounts not only of the action, but of every gesture, every word, every expression of Brigadier General "Stonewall" Jackson's. Yancy talked until he was hoarse.

But eventually the men got back to their own peculiar business, and Yancy was left to sit on the hard bench again, waiting. It was a long, grueling day, sitting on a hard bench. Yancy once went out to water Midnight and retrieve his own canteen, but he was worried he might miss his summons so he hurried back inside. From time to time he dozed, even though he was uncomfortable. He was exhausted.

At about seven o'clock that night a report circulated from the war office. In the Battle of Manassas, the Federals had 3,000 dead and wounded, and they lost more than 1,400 as prisoners. These were paraded through the streets of Richmond where crowds yelled, "Live Yankees! Live Yankees!" The Confederates had lost 2,000 men of which 1,500 were wounded; only a scant dozen had been taken prisoner. Yancy did learn that General Beauregard had taken treasures also, including six thousand small arms, fifty-four field guns and five hundred rounds of ammunition.

Poignantly Yancy thought, *And one supply cart that brought a wounded Yankee home.* He had been thinking a lot about Leslie Hayden. He didn't regret his actions. Even though some might regard his sheltering the enemy as traitorous, Yancy knew, without a doubt, that the Lord had told him to be a good Samaritan to the wounded man who had so mercifully spared his life.

Eventually the secretary returned and told Yancy, "Sir, we will have messages to return with you, but they won't be ready until tomorrow. Do you have a place to stay? I'm certain we can find room for one of Stonewall's boys!"

Yancy stood and shook his hand for the third time. "Thank you, sir, but I have some friends in town. I'll go visit them."

Yancy was glad to leave behind the roiling and boiling at the capitol. He rode slowly on Midnight, savoring the quiet after he got out of the center of town. It was a mild night, for July, with a light breeze that sometimes, as he came into the residential sections, carried on it the sweet, fresh scent of jasmine. After the stench of blood and guns and death, it was like a sweet shower to Yancy. His clothes and hair still stank of gunpowder.

He reached the Hayden home and was glad to see that there

were still warm lights on both upstairs and downstairs. Although it was only about eight o'clock, he had realized that Dr. Hayden seemed frail, and he had been afraid that the household regularly retired early. Gently he tapped the front door knocker twice. He saw the curtains move in the parlor, and then Lorena Hayden opened the door.

"Hello, Sergeant Tremayne," she said. "Won't you come in?" She turned and led him into the sitting room. Although she was polite, Lorena's tone had a chilly quality about it, and her entire demeanor was distant.

Yancy wondered what had hardened this woman so, or if she simply still didn't trust him. He supposed if that was it, it would just take time to gain her trust, and Yancy was vaguely surprised at how important that suddenly seemed to be to him.

Dr. Hayden rose to greet him. Beside him was a small woman with chestnut hair who was modestly pretty, watching him with warm brown eyes.

"This is Sergeant Yancy Tremayne. He brought Leslie home, my dear. Sergeant, this is my wife, Lily."

The woman came forward at once and held out both her hands. Yancy was surprised, but he took them in his, noticing that her bones were almost birdlike in their fragility. Suddenly her kind eyes filled with tears and she said softly, "We can never thank you enough, Sergeant Tremayne, for bringing our son home."

"I—I had to do it, ma'am. It was the right—the only thing to do."

She nodded with complete understanding. "Please, sit down. If you'll excuse me, I'll go have Missy make tea. Or perhaps you prefer coffee, Sergeant?"

"Actually I do, if it's not too much trouble, ma'am," Yancy answered, taking his seat in a wing chair across from the sofa where Dr. and Mrs. Hayden had been seated. "Especially Missy's coffee. It was very good."

She nodded and left the room. Lorena sat in a matching chair next to him, her back perfectly straight, her hands folded in her lap. He saw that she was wearing a blue dress with a white lace collar. She would have looked beautiful if she were more poised, but the set of her head was so defiant and her posture so stiff that it detracted from her china doll looks.

"So how is Lieutenant Hayden?" Yancy asked Dr. Hayden.

"He's doing fairly well," he answered. "Thankfully neither bullet hit any vital organs, though he did lose a lot of blood. Actually, the wound in his leg may give him the most trouble. It tore some muscles and ligaments, and it's possible he may have a slight limp, or at least may have to walk with a cane. But he's resting comfortably, and Leslie is strong. I believe he'll recover quickly."

"Thank the Lord," Lily said, coming back in and sitting down by her husband.

"Amen," Yancy said quietly. "And that is, by the way, the message that Leslie wanted me to give you, in case. . .in case. He said he wanted you to know that he was trusting in the Lord, and that he wasn't afraid."

"The Lord has mightily blessed us, Sergeant Tremayne," Lily said, "by sparing Leslie and sending you to him."

Dr. Hayden said gravely, "We understand, Sergeant Tremayne, the position you so willingly put yourself in, and because of that I would like to explain something about our family. We—Lily, Lorena, and I—are actually what might be called neutrals in this war, although that is somewhat unrealistic under the circumstances. We love Virginia. Richmond is our home. But we could not bring ourselves to agree with secession, and we think this war is tragically, utterly wrong on both sides. I will let Leslie explain his decision to join the Union army, if he chooses to. But I wish you to know that, as a doctor, I am attending injured soldiers from the North and the South, without discrimination, and I pray every day for the end of this war and blessings and peace for all of the men who are in it."

Yancy sighed. "Thank you, sir. That does help me to understand a little. You've been caught between two forces that seem to be inescapable, just as Leslie and I were in the battle. I assume you've heard the news?" he asked hesitantly.

"Yes, we understand that the Confederate forces had a great victory," Dr. Hayden answered. "There were many, many wounded."

"Chimborazo Hospital is filled to overflowing," Lorena said sadly. "Father has worked very hard to help."

"As you said, Sergeant Tremayne, I have to. It's the right thing to do," Dr. Hayden said with a small smile.

Missy came in then with tea and coffee service, and they took a few minutes in the homey, comfortable ritual of taking refreshment.

After Missy left, Dr. Hayden continued, "And so, now that we have given you some idea of our views on the war, I hope you will see that we would never ask you to betray any confidential or sensitive information to us. But we would very much like to hear how it happened that you found Leslie and brought him home to us."

Yancy told them the story, although he didn't say what his mission was, and he downplayed the horribly tense moments when Leslie was pointing his pistol at him and Yancy was sure he was going to kill him.

"So there I was, looking down the barrel of a Yankee lieutenant's pistol, and at the time all I remember thinking is, *I don't know the Lord. I may be facing Him in the next few minutes, and I don't know Him.* So I asked God to forgive me, and I waited. But Leslie laid the pistol down in his lap and just sort of sighed. And then I prayed, hard, and asked the Lord to save me and lead me, and then I knew. I had to help Leslie," he finished.

Lily smiled and her voice was soft and glad. "I'm so glad you found the Lord, Sergeant Tremayne. Even when we are facing death, to know Him is to know life."

"My grandmother has told me that and many other things about the Lord," Yancy said. "And they're only just now starting to make sense." He smiled. "And I can tell you that I think I have a pretty good understanding of the situation you are in, about the war and struggling to stay neutral. You see, my people are Amish."

"Are they?" Lorena asked with an abrupt interest that surprised Yancy.

"Yes, they are. At least, my father and stepmother and grandmother are. My mother, my father's first wife, was half Cheyenne Indian. She died, and we came back here, to my father's family."

"Cheyenne Indian," Lorena repeated in a half whisper, her eyes wide and dark as she looked at him. "So that's it. . . . They must be handsome people. . . ."

"I beg your pardon?" Yancy said blankly. He thought he had misunderstood her.

CROSSING

A quick, amused smile came over Lily Hayden's gentle features, and she said, "Your countenance shows your heritage, Sergeant Tremayne, and you should be proud."

"Yes, I learned their ways and I know them," he said simply. "My mother was a wonderful woman, and I am proud of her. So my father and I returned to Lexington, to his home, and he rejoined the Amish community. He married a fine woman. She's been as good to me as my own mother. They have two children now, and my grandmother lives with them."

With some difficulty Lorena asked, "So—so you, you obviously aren't—don't completely agree with their beliefs."

"Not all of them," he said. "They are fine Christian people, but they're extremely strict, you know."

"I admire their willingness to pay a high price for their beliefs," Dr. Hayden said. "But I understand that living that way of life is just not possible for everyone."

Missy came back in and said, "Dr. Hayden? Leslie's awake now, and I told him the sergeant was here. He'd like to see him."

"Please, by all means, Sergeant Tremayne, let Missy take you up to his room," Dr. Hayden said. "I know he has been wanting to see you and talk to you."

Missy led him upstairs to Leslie's bedroom, a rather spartan room with a big four-poster bed and armoire. With something of a start, Yancy saw that the armoire was partially open, and he saw four blue uniforms with gold braid hanging inside.

Leslie Hayden was slightly propped up, his face still almost as pale as the white bed linens. But his voice was much stronger and steady. He held out his hand, and Yancy shook it. "I'm glad you came back, Sergeant Tremayne."

"Good to see you looking so well, Lieutenant Hayden," Yancy answered. "You sure look much better than the last time I saw you."

"Since I was near dead, I hope I do look some better," Leslie said drily. "And that's thanks to you."

Yancy grinned. "And thanks to you that I'm not all the way dead."

Suddenly Leslie grew grave. "You took an enormous chance, bringing me here. I still don't understand how you expected to get by with it."

Yancy met his gaze soberly. "I've told your parents, and I want you to know, too. There are three things that happened on that bloody field that I'm sure of. I found the Lord because I thought I was going to die, and because of that my soul has been saved. Another is that I believe the Lord directed you to spare me. And lastly and most certainly, I know that the Lord told me to bring you here. I may not have heard a voice, but I knew then and I know now that it was His will that we met at that moment and in that way."

Leslie nodded thoughtfully. "I was in pain, and the battle—you know how you kind of go crazy in battle? How it's awful and horrible but all you can think of is to keep going, never to stop, to keep fighting?"

"I know that," Yancy said. "I've felt it."

"That's still how my mind was fixed when I saw you. But then—but then, after a few minutes, it's like my vision cleared, and my mind grew quiet. I knew the Lord had given me peace, and that no matter what happened, I could not and would not shoot you."

"And so it seems that this isn't a one-sided deal," Yancy said quietly. "You spared my life, and I thank you."

"And you saved mine, and I thank you," Leslie said. "And may God deliver us from ever facing each other over a battlefield again."

Yancy shifted. "About that. I'm afraid I have some fairly bad news, Lieutenant Hayden, about your outfit. I found out that those men of your company that were with you in that last little skirmish were taken prisoner. There were nine of them, right? Part of Walcott Company of the 8th Battalion?"

"How did you know that?" Leslie demanded. Then his face fell. "No, no, don't answer that. Of course I know you can't tell me. If the roles were reversed, I wouldn't tell you."

Uncomfortably Yancy shifted again. He had seen the detailed lists of the dead, wounded, missing, and those taken prisoner. "But I do have to tell you this. You're listed as missing."

Leslie lifted his head. "Missing. Guess I'd better lay low."

"I don't know how you'll be able to rejoin your unit, Lieutenant Hayden," Yancy said.

"I'll worry about that when the time comes. By the way, it's Leslie."

"Yancy."

"There's just one more thing I'd like to tell you, Yancy," Leslie said quietly. "I love Virginia; it's been my father's home and my home our whole lives. I can't imagine living anywhere else, and that's why I took the chance of staying here when I decided to join the Union. I couldn't face moving somewhere in the North, and I know that my family would have insisted on coming with me."

"I believe they would," Yancy agreed. "You have a good, strong family."

"But I love the United States of America, too," Leslie went on steadily. "I hate the thought of this country divided, torn apart. I want Virginia to always be a part of the United States of America. It's just that simple."

"I understand," Yancy said. "Believe me, I understand."

Lorena slipped in then and came to her brother's bedside. He reached out and took her hand. "Don't fuss. I feel fine."

She scoffed. "I didn't come up here to fuss at you like some nanny. I just wanted to tell Sergeant Tremayne that Missy has laid out a cold supper for him. After witnessing him devouring one meal, I think it's safe to think that he may be hungry." She gave Yancy a sidelong glance.

"Isn't it annoying when people talk about you like you're not in the room?" Leslie asked, his gray eyes twinkling.

"It is," Yancy answered him. "But I do have to admit that I'm hungry. I'm not surprised that Miss Hayden noticed that."

"Silly boys," Lorena grumbled, turning and marching out of the room.

Yancy watched her leave then turned back to Leslie and sighed. "She hates me."

Leslie managed a weak laugh. "She likes you. If she didn't, she wouldn't tease you."

"Really?" Yancy asked. "You think so?"

"I know so," Leslie answered. "It's when she starts getting all frosty polite that you have to watch out."

"Mmm. I'll remember that," Yancy said thoughtfully.

"See that you do," Leslie warned him. "For your own good."

Yancy moved toward the door. "You do look tired, and I'm

going to leave before your sister comes back and bodily throws me out. Good night, Leslie."

"We'll see you again, right?"

"Hope so, my friend. Hope so."

Yancy made his way back downstairs to the parlor, where Dr. Hayden and Lorena waited for him. Dr. Hayden said, "My wife has gone on to bed; she's not well. But she made me soundly promise to invite you to stay the night, Sergeant Tremayne, if you haven't made other arrangements."

"That's very kind of you, sir, but I wouldn't want to impose."

"Nonsense," Dr. Hayden said briskly, rising. "After what you have done for this family, it's as I said before, you will always be welcome in my home. Now I'm tired and I'm going to go to bed, but Missy will see to your late supper and then show you to your room."

"I'll take care of it, Father," Lorena said, rising to stand on very tiptoe to give her father a kiss on his cheek. "And I'll check on Leslie before I retire. Please don't worry. Just get some rest."

He did look tired; his shoulders were a little more stooped, and his gait was slow as he left the parlor. "I think I will be able to rest tonight. Good night, daughter. Good night, Sergeant Tremayne."

"Good night, sir."

Lorena turned to Yancy and said, "Missy's got your supper all laid out." She led him to the kitchen, where there was a fine spread of ham, potato salad, bread, and sliced apples.

Yancy bowed his head and said a short blessing in silence, in the traditional Amish way, and then ate ravenously. He hadn't had anything to eat since he had sat in this kitchen before. Even though Lorena was watching him, he was so hungry he didn't mind. Too much.

She poured him coffee and refilled his plate when he got low. When he showed signs of having enough, she said slowly, "Sergeant Tremayne, I know that I was very harsh to you when you first arrived. I'm sorry that I doubted you, but surely you can understand my feelings now that you know our story."

"I do," Yancy agreed. "It was a strange thing, what happened to me and your brother. I could hardly expect you to jump right into it and know how things were, with me being a Johnny Reb and all."

She didn't blush, but she did look slightly amused. "Well, you are, you know."

"Yes, I know," he agreed.

"Are you going to accept my apology or not?" she demanded.

"Begging your pardon, ma'am, but I don't believe I heard an apology anywhere in there."

"There wasn't?" She seemed genuinely surprised, so surprised that Yancy laughed. At first Lorena glowered at him, but then she smiled, too. "Perhaps there wasn't. So I apologize."

"Accepted."

She began to gather up the dishes and cover them with linens.

Yancy helped her. As they finished up, she showed the first sign of true discomfort with him that he had seen yet, and it secretly amused him.

"So, Sergeant Tremayne, would you like me to show you to your room now?" she asked with artificial brightness.

"That would be nice, ma'am. I have to admit that I'm tired, and I have a long ride tomorrow."

She led him toward his room and said, "Oh? Where are you— oh, no, no, never mind. Here's your room."

It was a bedroom next to Leslie's, with a bed fully long enough to accommodate Yancy's six-plus feet. It had clean linens, and the fresh smell floated in the room. On a washstand was a pitcher of water, a basin, soap, hand towels, and a razor and soapbrush. Yancy smiled a little; he still didn't have to shave—his Indian legacy. "This looks wonderful, Miss Hayden," he said, and in a grateful gesture he reached out and took her hand.

She stared up at him for a few moments, still and silent, her hand warm in his. Then abruptly she pulled free and said hurriedly, "Good night, Sergeant Tremayne," and almost ran down the hall.

Softly he called after her, "Good night, Miss Hayden."

He washed, and slept, and for six hours heard no echoes of battle and knew no fear or pain.

CHAPTER EIGHTEEN

At dawn the next morning, Yancy went to the capitol. His dispatches were waiting for him, so he rode out. It was ninety miles back to the camp at Manassas Junction; since both Yancy and Midnight had been rested, they were able to make it in less than twenty-four hours, with only brief stops for rest and food and water.

On the outskirts of the camp, Yancy saw General Jackson sitting on a split-rail fence, nodding a little in the early sunlight. Beside him, Little Sorrel grazed, her reins trailing in the verdant high grass. Yancy came to a stop, and Midnight stamped and whinnied a little, as he was accustomed to do, but the general didn't stir.

Yancy watched him affectionately. No one would ever take him for a general, much less for the mighty Stonewall Jackson. Still he wore his old, dusty, threadbare major's tunic, grimy and wrinkled. As always, his beat-up forage cap sat with the bill right down to his nose. Although he sat ruler straight, as he always did even in his five-minute naps, he still looked rumpled and awkward, like a nondescript meager clerk.

So different on the battlefield, Yancy thought in wonder. He remembered his cool courage when the sharpshooter had targeted them at the Battle of Manassas. He recalled that when Jackson rode up and down the battle lines, shouting to his 1st Brigade, it stirred the blood and gave the men courage and a sense of fierce honor and grim determination to fight for Virginia and the Confederacy—and for Stonewall Jackson.

The object of Yancy Tremayne's admiring reverie jerked a little, stirred, muttered something under his breath, then looked around. "Good morning, Sergeant Tremayne."

"Good morning, sir." Yancy saluted sharply.

Slowly, with deliberation, Jackson took a lemon out of one pocket, a small paring knife out of another, cut the top off the lemon, lifted it to his lips, and began to suck out the juice. "You have my dispatches?"

"Yes, sir."

Jackson motioned to him with a peremptory wave. "Bring them here."

Yancy dismounted and handed him the courier's bag.

"Wait," he ordered.

Yancy tied Midnight to the fence then stood at parade attention.

Jackson took out his spectacles that he needed for reading. But his eyes were not weak. He could see a battlefield well enough. As he sucked on the lemon and perused his orders, the frown on his face grew darker and darker. "If they would just give me ten thousand men, I would be in Washington tomorrow," he growled. "What a waste, what a criminal waste of time and opportunity."

Yancy knew that he spoke to himself, as he often did when they were alone. Around other officers and men Jackson spoke succinctly and without giving away any indication of his feelings. Certainly he never spoke aloud to himself. But Yancy knew that because of his prior relationship with Jackson when he was just a servant, basically, and because of Anna Jackson's closeness to Yancy, General Jackson somehow trusted Yancy more and was able to let his iron guard down. Somewhat and sometimes, at least.

After another guttural grumble of exasperation, Jackson took off his glasses, tucked them away, and looked back up at Yancy. "At ease, at ease, Sergeant. Don't stand there posing like a popinjay. Sit down and tell me about Richmond."

Yancy sat on a fence rail, took off his cap, and mopped his forehead. The July sun was climbing higher in the sky. It was going to be another scorching day. "I brought the papers, sir. They're in my saddlebag. They're full of the battle, of course—and of you."

"Me?" Jackson grunted.

"Yes, sir." Yancy grinned. "They're all raving about the famous General 'Stonewall' Jackson."

"Stonewall," Jackson mused. "What General Bee said. . ."

"Yes, sir. That's your new name, sir. And they're calling us the Stonewall Brigade."

"Good, good," he murmured. "The credit should go to the noble men who fought and to God. Not to me. All that nonsense aside, Sergeant, what is the mood in Richmond? And at the capitol?"

Yancy told him about the tumult at the capitol, centered mostly around the Department of War. He described the crowds in the streets, excitedly talking and milling about, apparently only to go over and over any small detail or gossip about the battle, and related the sight of the Federal prisoners with the crowds jeering at them. And he told Jackson of Chimborazo Hospital, which Yancy had briefly toured on his way into town to get the dispatches. "Of ours, almost 1,600 wounded, sir," he finished in a low voice.

Jackson nodded. "Brave and courageous men, God will they be healed to return to stand with us once more." He jumped off the fence and mounted Little Sorrel, still working on his lemon. "Back to my headquarters, Sergeant Tremayne. I want you to brief my aides, then you can eat and rest. Rode all day and night, did you?"

Yancy untied Midnight and mounted up. "Twenty-two hours, sir, with only two short breaks for food and water," he said proudly.

Jackson reached over and patted Midnight's sleek neck approvingly. "Fastest horse in the Confederacy, I guess, and never seems to tire. No wonder Colonel Stuart keeps trying to buy him from you. And if I know that rascal, you might better keep him on a tight rein when Stuart's around. Rogue cavalrymen been known to steal what they can't buy." Jackson spurred ahead and Yancy followed, grinning.

Anna Jackson came north by train to the camp in Manassas. On the last lap of the journey, the train was absolutely packed with soldiers. They were boisterous, exuberant. Anna sat quiet and still in her seat, her gaze downcast, but it was to no avail. She noted in her writing, *"A lady seemed to be a great curiosity to the soldiers, scores of whom filed through the car to take a look."*

Finally she arrived at Manassas Junction, where an awkward young corporal with his right arm in a sling met her and told her he was to take her to a hospital to wait for the general. She sat in a tiny, dusty, deserted office beside the front entrance.

Across the street, squads of soldiers were making coffins for their fallen companions. The sight made her deeply sad. She remembered the rowdy young boys on the train and wondered how many of them would die in the battles that must surely come. She wondered if her husband would join them. And as the thought crept into her mind for perhaps the thousandth time, she turned her eyes away from the bitter sight, bowed her head and whispered, " 'But they that wait upon the Lord shall renew their strength; they shall mount up with wings as eagles; they shall run, and not be weary; and they shall walk, and not faint.' Only in You, Lord, do I find strength."

Peace settled on her like soft satin, and she waited calmly until Jackson came driving up in an ambulance to rescue her. He jumped out and the corporal led him in.

When Jackson saw Anna, his eyes brightened, he ran to her, enveloped her in his arms, kissed her sweetly, and held her to him. He whispered, "Esposita, my darling wife, how I have missed you! How grateful I am to the Lord for bringing you to me!" As always, Jackson was oblivious to others when he was with Anna. With her, no matter who stood by or overheard or observed, he was the tender and boyishly adoring husband.

"I've missed you, my darling Thomas," she said, clinging to him. "Every day, every hour."

"Here's the buggy the Kyles have been kind enough to loan me. We're going to go to my headquarters," he said, entwining her arm with his. "Such a grand name for a tent in the Kyles' yard." He smiled down at her, for she was so tiny that she barely reached his chest. He smiled often with Anna. . .but almost never without her.

She squeezed his arm and said, "It doesn't matter, Thomas. You are my home, and wherever and whatever it is, it is a joyous home indeed to me."

❧

Jackson, disdaining a driver, drove the buggy himself. Theodorus Kyle's farm was about two miles from the Manassas railroad junction, and the brigade had encamped around the farm.

Theodorus and Deidre Kyle had a large boisterous family. Their own four daughters lived with them—for their husbands were serving in the 1ˢᵗ Brigade—and between them they had nine children. The Kyle farmhouse was large and spacious, of two floors, with two wings that had been added over time as sleeping porches. The Kyles had begged Jackson to stay with them, but with his customary humility—in some matters—he declined, insisting that he would be much more comfortable in a command tent, with his long hours and men constantly coming and going. He never realized what an honor and a boost of reputation it would have been for the Kyles to have him as a houseguest, for his fame had spread throughout the South. Without doubt he was the the most revered and admired commander in the Confederate Army.

Anna confided her discomfort on the train to her husband, though softening the effect to a mild embarrassment.

On later trips Jackson promised to send her an escort. However, he knew, even this soon after Manassas, if the soldiers would have known Anna to be Stonewall Jackson's wife, she would never have suffered the slightest disquiet. Indeed, the 1ˢᵗ Brigade regarded her with true reverence, believing she was a saint walking on earth. It wouldn't be long before the entire army believed it, too.

They passed the first camp tents, with two men sitting outside playing cards. As the buggy went by, one of them jumped up and called out the now-famous Rebel yell, and men flooded out of the tents and to the roadside. They hoorahed and called and whistled and cheered. The Stonewall Brigade did this every single time Jackson rode through the camp, even if they were in drill formation. The officers, grinning, allowed it.

For his part, Jackson gave no sign of recognition at all, driving and looking straight ahead. It had become his habit when he was on horseback to ride around the camp for precisely this reason, but in the buggy he had to take the farm road right down the middle of the brigade's tents. As they passed, the wild chorus went on and on, with men crowding to the very sides of the buggy, waving their hats and grinning.

Anna pinched his arm lightly. "Impressive, Stonewall."

"Don't tease, my darling," he said awkwardly. "They're a bunch of holloing fools, is all."

Finally they went up the private lane to the Kyle farmhouse, and there in the shady side yard was Jackson's spacious command tent. Lined up in precise rows outside were his staff officers and aides. Slightly to the side were Yancy, Chuckins Satterfield, Peyton Stevens, and Sandy Owens. Every single man in attendance was grinning like the village idiot. There was very little time for levity on Stonewall Jackson's staff, but he had been so excited about Anna's arrival that they all were in a lighthearted mood.

Jackson helped Anna down from the buggy, and to the colonel's and major's bemusement, the first person he introduced her to was his manservant Jim, who had come to take the buggy to the farm's stables. He was a tall handsome mulatto with a flashing toothy smile, and he bowed as deeply as any courtier when Jackson said, "My dear, this is Jim, who came to me after the Battle of Falling Waters. Jim, I have the pleasure and honor to introduce you to my wife, Mrs. Jackson."

Anna smiled at him and inclined her head, as ladies do when introduced to gentlemen.

A smile of pleasure lit Jim's face. "It's a right honor to meet you, ma'am. And I want you to know that I takes good care of the general, I surely do."

"I'm so glad," Anna said kindly. "I shall rest better now, knowing that he is in such capable hands."

Now Jackson escorted her to meet his staff, and she greeted each one of them, from colonel to waterboy, with the same warmth and grace. When she came to Yancy, she held out both her hands for him to hold. Then, to the envy of every man present, she said with obvious delight, "Oh Yancy, how good it is to see you again! Hetty and I have missed you so much. You were always so very helpful to us. And especially this summer I have missed you in the garden. I believe you have a gift for gardening, for everything you did for me has prospered amazingly."

Still holding her hands in his, Yancy said somewhat shyly, "Thank you, ma'am, but it's not me that the plants and flowers love. It's you and your tender care."

"Perhaps, but I must share the glory of the daisy-mums with you and your grandmother," she said lightly. "Tell me, how is your family?"

"Very well, ma'am. We write regularly, and it seems they are having a peaceful and prosperous year," he answered somewhat wistfully.

"I'm glad," Anna said. Finally she withdrew her hands from his and finished, "I hope while I am here that you may take me to see Midnight. I should like to see him again, such a glorious horse."

"I hope so, too, ma'am," Yancy said gratefully.

She moved on to Chuckins Satterfield, and the general introduced him. Despite Anna's best efforts at making him feel at ease, Chuckins's round chubby face turned scarlet, and he could only bow and gulp and mumble.

Next was the sophisticated, aristocratic Peyton Stevens. Jackson introduced him, and he swept off his dashing hat, a wide-brimmed gray felt with one side pinned up with a gold pin and sporting two small red feathers. He bent one knee, crossed one arm over, and bowed deeply, an old-fashioned court obeisance. "Mrs. Jackson, if I may say, I thought this day to be beautiful, but it is nothing compared to you."

General Jackson growled, "Impertinent young pup."

Anna gave him a mischievous sidelong glance. "Why, Thomas, I did not know that you had such chivalrous young gentlemen on your staff. I am very pleased to meet you, Sergeant Stevens."

Next she met Sandy Owens, who also was something of a ladies' man but who didn't have the panache of Peyton Stevens. "Mrs. Jackson, all I can say is that now I can see that indeed our general is a fortunate man," he said with obvious sincerity.

"Thomas and I are both blessed that the Lord led us to each other," she said.

CROSSING

And this began a brief holiday for General Jackson.

Anna had a sweet voice, both in speech and song. Jackson enjoyed when she read aloud, but he especially loved for her to sing to him. She sang "Dixie" for him; it was the first time he had heard it. He loved the song and made her sing the lively ditty over and over until they were both giggling like children.

Anna met the officers of the army and seemed especially impressed by General Joe Johnston, the commanding officer of what had come to be called the Army of the Valley. He spoke highly of Jackson, which, though Thomas was characteristically a modest man, was certainly gratifying to him.

Nearly every officer spoke of his valor and steadfastness at the Battle of Manassas. One officer commented, "If it hadn't been for your husband, I think we might have lost the battle."

Jackson said, with a reply that was to become characteristic, "No, Major, you must give credit to God and to the noble men who did the fighting."

It was a wonderful visit for Anna and Jackson, but of course it had to come to an end. He took her back to the train station at Manassas Crossing, this time with an escort of two slightly wounded men—one of them the shy corporal, who was almost beside himself with the sense of honor—who would accompany her all the way to their home in Lexington. She found herself struggling not to cry, for it upset Thomas very much when she wept.

He clasped her to him. "Sometimes I think the hardest thing about this war is being separated from you. I'll have you come again when I can, esposita."

"Soon, God willing, Thomas, my dear. I pray that it will be soon."

The sweltering July melted into a sizzling August. Oddly, as if the seasons were to be separated by the stroke of a sharp knife, the first week of September 1861 suddenly turned into autumn, with cool dewy mornings, fine freshening breezes in the afternoon, and evenings just chilly enough to really enjoy sitting around a fire, one of the few pleasures of camp life. These two months passed idyllically, with only a few very minor skirmishes, usually caused by Federals lurking around the lines, getting lost, and blundering into Confederate territory. The casualties were light and the skies were clear of the smoke of cannons and thousands of rounds of musket fire.

But idleness in a soldier's camp can become very monotonous and boring. Yancy and Peyton were glad that they were couriers, because at least they kept busy, mostly riding back and forth to the different commands of the Army of the Shenandoah that were still ranged up and down northern Virginia.

Yancy only went to Richmond once in August and twice in September, when he got to visit the Haydens. Leslie had been on a steady mend, and though he and Yancy didn't directly speak of it, Yancy knew he was planning on rejoining the Army of the Potomac soon.

As September wore on, the weather got steadily colder, and in the first week of October, the camp at Manassas had their first hard frost. The Kyle family had donated an unused cast-iron stove to General Jackson. On Monday, October 7, Jim and Yancy were struggling to install the stove in Jackson's tent. Yancy often still did chores like this for General Jackson, much as he did when he worked at the Jackson home in Lexington.

The struggle to install the stove was because General Jackson was supervising them. Inactivity irritated Yancy, but it made Thomas Jackson as grouchy and touchy as a wounded bear. Now he barked, "No, I don't want it that close to my cot. I'll be too hot trying to sleep! And not too close to my prayer bench, either. If that should get scorched I'd have the hide of both of you. Go on, put it over there by the aide's desk."

At this desk sat Chuckins, scribbling fanatically. He didn't dare look up or make a sound.

"But, sir," Jim said placatingly, "that there desk is right by the tent flap. Sure enough all the heat would go out that hole every time there's all the comin's and the goin's."

"Then put it—" Jackson began.

But he was interrupted when a voice from outside the said tent flap called, "Sir? Orders from Secretary Benjamin, General Jackson."

"What? Come in, come in," Jackson ordered quickly.

The courier came in, a young bespectacled captain in the uniform of the War Department Army Staff.

Yancy recognized him; in fact, he had handed over a couple of dispatch bags to this man.

The captain came to strict attention and saluted. "Captain Monroe Hillyard, sir, of Secretary of War Benjamin's staff."

Jackson returned the salute and bid him, "Come here, come here." He took the courier's knapsack and took out a bundle of four thick envelopes. Opening the first one, he frowned, took out his spectacles, read it again, then looked up. "You men are dismissed," he said, now calmly and quietly, to Jim, Yancy, and Chuckins.

They fled. But Yancy loitered around outside the tent with Chuckins, for he was almost certain he had seen a glance of recognition from Captain Hillyard. Couriers, of course, rarely knew the contents of their dispatches, but for a captain on Secretary Judah Benjamin's staff to act as a courier meant that likely he knew very well the messages he was carrying. The chances of his telling Yancy or anyone else about them was extremely remote, but Yancy was so feverishly curious that he wanted to take the chance. He and Chuckins manifestly had nothing to do outside the tent, but they drew away a discreet distance and paced up and down anyway.

Jim fetched a pail of water and went to the captain's horse to give him a drink. Then, as if he had strictly been assigned the job, he began brushing the horse down, whistling softly between his teeth.

It was about an hour before Captain Hillyard came out, pausing at the tent opening to pull on his gloves and replace his hat.

Boldly Yancy came to stand next to him. Yancy stopped, came to attention, gave him a snappy salute, and stared straight ahead without saying a word.

Languidly Captain Hillyard returned his salute. "You're one of his couriers, aren't you?" he asked, speaking in low tones so that, inside the tent, General Jackson couldn't hear.

"Yes, sir," Yancy answered in the same quiet voice.

"Thought I recognized you." Captain Hillyard finished pulling on his fine white leather gauntlets, pulled his wide-brimmed hat from under his arm, flicked an imaginary speck off of it, and settled it firmly on his head. Taking a firm grasp on the scabbard of his sword, he murmured, "Major General." Then he walked briskly to his horse, took the reins from Jim with a nod of thanks, and galloped briskly off.

Yancy kept his stance until the man was out of sight, watched curiously by Chuckins and Jim, who came to stand close to him. Then Yancy, with Jim following, ran over to Chuckins, gave him a friendly punch to the shoulder that almost knocked him down, and whispered to them, "Major General."

"Yep," Jim said with satisfaction, crossing his arms over his broad chest.

Incautiously Chuckins began to whoop, but he quickly clasped his hand over his mouth and stifled himself. Without another word, he turned and lumbered off for the nearest tent.

Yancy opened his mouth to say something, but at that moment the tent flap whipped open and Jackson leaned out. "Sergeant! Jim! What about this infernal stove?" But now he sounded almost jaunty instead of testy. As they hurried into the tent, Jackson asked, "Where did Satterfield go?"

Yancy started then stuttered, "Well, sir, he—he—I think there was something—maybe he forgot—" Then he swallowed and pointed. "He went that way."

Jackson looked at him, his bright blue eyes fired with intelligence. "He did, did he? If he's not back in fifteen minutes, he's going to work all night tonight and all day tomorrow and maybe tomorrow night, too, if I'm of a mind."

"Yes, sir," Yancy said.

It was an hour before Chuckins came back. But Major General Stonewall Jackson said nothing.

After the enforced inactivity of the previous two months, the month of October took on feverish activity. Jackson ordered full and complete rolls of each company of each regiment, with status of wounded included. Complete inventories of arms and material were taken and retaken; every week new orders went to Richmond.

Yancy and Peyton took turns on the Richmond run, for often Jackson had new dispatches as soon as one of them returned from a run. On these trips Yancy did pay very short visits to the Haydens. Often Jackson's orders required no reply, but still Yancy and Midnight required some rest before beginning the trip back.

The Haydens knew better than to urge him to stay, so they fell into a comfortable routine. Elijah tended to Midnight and Missy would fix Yancy a meal and usually some food to take back with him. Lorena would put clean linens on the guest room bed while Yancy visited with Leslie for a few minutes. Then he would nap for two hours, when Lorena would quietly awaken him. He and Midnight would ride hard back to the camp.

In the middle of the month, Yancy was, to his surprise, given dispatches to Winchester, the town in the northern Shenandoah Valley that was only lightly invested. As usual, none of General Jackson's staff or even officers knew anything about Jackson's plans, no matter how hard they tried to discern them. Jackson made no comment whatsoever about the contents of the courier's bag.

Yancy arrived in Winchester two days later, and it took three days for the aged, rheumatic colonel in command to prepare his answering dispatches. Finally Yancy returned to Manassas and delivered them to Jackson, who took them without a word.

It was the last week of October before Yancy learned that General Jackson had been assigned to command the army in western Virginia. He would be returning to the Shenandoah Valley that he so deeply loved.

Monday, October 28, was a fine, crisp, biting day. At noon a pale white sun glowed faintly in the sky. To the north was a bank of faint gray clouds, moving slowly south, and Yancy thought they may have an early first snow in them. He knocked on the now-familiar door of the Hayden home.

Light footsteps sounded, and Lorena threw open the door, her face alight. "Yancy! Mother and I were just talking about you. Come in, please."

Yancy came in and companionably she threaded her arm through his as she led him into the parlor. Lily was there, sewing, and Yancy saw Lorena's sewing basket beside her familiar wing chair next to the fireplace. After greeting Lily, he took what was now considered his chair, next to Lorena.

"We've missed you, Yancy dear," Lily said, for now he was on such familiar terms with Dr. and Mrs. Hayden. "It's so difficult because we never know when we are to see you again. Of course, there are thousands and thousands of families all over the States that are in the same predicament."

Her words warmed him, both because she included him as if he were family and because she so tactfully said "States" instead of "United States." The family was always careful not to draw any lines between them and him.

"I surely never know when I'm going to be here, either," he said good-naturedly, "which, as you say, is exactly the same predicament of everyone in my command."

After the Battle of Falling Waters, Yancy had come to trust the Haydens enough to tell them that he was in the Stonewall Brigade. Of course he had not told them his capacity, but they weren't fools, and he was sure they knew exactly why he popped up in Richmond so often, considering the different camps the Stonewall Brigade had occupied. He also knew that they would never question him about it and would never say anything to anyone about him.

"How's Leslie?" Yancy asked.

"He's doing very well indeed," Lily answered. "As a matter of fact, he's out marching around the garden. He's grown so weary of being inside that he spends hours, sometimes, walking in circles. But the exercise and fresh air have done him a world of good. Lorena? Why don't you go tell Missy to make coffee for Yancy and go tell Leslie that he's here. I know he'll want to come in to visit with him." The Haydens' back garden was a generous square of almost a quarter of an acre, and it was walled in, so prying eyes couldn't see the Haydens' Union soldier son.

"Yes, he will," Lorena agreed, already on her way out.

Lily rose to pull the drapes at the front windows and continued, "Jesse is at Chimborazo, although, thank the Lord, there are only a few men left. His duties are very light now. They closed the emergency field hospital at the old Shockoe railroad station, you know."

"Yes, ma'am, I heard that."

They talked desultorily about the lack of wartime activity for the last three months until Lorena and Leslie returned.

Yancy stood to shake his hand. "You look better every time I'm here. That's good. And barely a limp, I see."

"Only now when I'm very tired. Of course, it's hard to get tired out there trotting around the garden like some demented fairy," Leslie grumbled. "I'll be so glad to get back on a horse, to ride, to be of use, to work again."

"I know you feel better because you're so ill-tempered," Lorena said, taking up her sewing. "You were much sweeter when you were weak and in pain."

"Didn't have the energy to complain, Rena," Leslie said good-naturedly. He turned to Yancy. "So how long can you stay? Can you stay the night?"

"Yes, I have to leave early in the morning, but I can stay the night."

"Good," Lorena said happily then tempered it with, "Father said he may be late, and he would hate to miss you."

"Oh, yes, *Father* really wants to see you, Yancy. *Father* really misses you a lot," Leslie teased, winking broadly at Lorena, who made a face at him.

But these niceties were lost on Yancy. When he was younger he had always been very aware of feminine attentions and had been sensitive to the signals they sent him. Now he had grown to be a man so handsome, so striking, that women he met or even passed in the street would stare wide-eyed at him until they caught themselves and, blushing, dropped their gazes.

He was now six feet, three inches tall. His shoulders were broad, his arms and legs muscular from his eternal horseback riding. His thick night black hair had grown somewhat, brushing his collar, the errant lock always falling rakishly over his forehead. In the outdoors his skin had deepened to a rich burnished bronze. As he had grown into a man, he had lost all traces of childhood in his face. His forehead was broad and fine, and with his dark, slightly slanted eyes and his high chiseled cheekbones, he looked exotic and mysterious.

But for the last two years he had been at VMI and then in the army and had been much bereft of female company. He had lost that instinctive insight into women that he had formerly had. Now he was slightly puzzled at Leslie's sally but shrugged it off. Lorena and Leslie often had exchanges he didn't understand, and he assumed it usually was some private family joke.

Missy came in with coffee then, and they talked and laughed, the lively conversation never wavering. Yancy amused them with Chuckins's antics and with stories of odd, often funny things that happened in camp. Leslie had stories, too. Both of them kept the details of when and where very vague, and the characters were unnamed but always vivid.

At about four o'clock, the late editions of the newspapers came out, and the Haydens had every newspaper within a thirty-mile radius of Richmond delivered to them. Yancy, Lily, Lorena, and Leslie all spent a companionable two hours reading in silence, sipping more tea and coffee. Occasionally Elijah came in with more firewood and stoked the fire. The room was warm and comfortable and inviting, and Yancy reflected that he felt more at home here than anywhere, except at Grandmother's.

Dr. Hayden came home about six o'clock, and at seven Missy served them a wonderful meal, as usual.

When they finished, they were all getting ready to go back to the parlor and their newspapers, but Yancy stood, handed Lorena out of her chair, and asked very formally, "Miss Hayden, would you care to come sit in the garden with me for a while? I need some fresh air, and I would appreciate the company."

Hesitantly Lorena glanced at her father, who smiled and nodded slightly. "I'll go get my cloak," she said.

Yancy pulled on his caped greatcoat and Lorena returned with a beautiful dark blue wool mantle trimmed with black piping. She pulled up the hood, and the color made her eyes look like the deepest midnight. They went out the kitchen door to the back garden.

The Haydens' garden was not so manicured as some, for Lily Hayden preferred a more natural woodland look. Cobbled paths wandered here and there, screened by large shrubs and small sculpted pear and dogwood trees. In the center was an enormous live oak tree, and underneath it was a stone garden bench that had been put there in Jesse Hayden's father's time.

Arm in arm, Yancy and Lorena strolled slowly and sat down there. Most of the leaves had fallen, but occasionally, carried on the lightest air, a leaf fluttered down, dancing its final dance in the cold moonlight.

They sat in silence for a while, looking up at the hard, brilliant stars. In a restless movement, Yancy took Lorena's hand in his. He rarely touched her, although they had lately come to give each other very brief, tightly controlled hugs when he left. Now he felt Lorena stiffen slightly, but she left her hand in his.

He turned to her. "I—I may not be seeing you for a while. I can't tell how long it may be, but I expect it will be some time."

"You're leaving Manassas, aren't you?" she asked slowly, looking up as if she were speaking to the uncaring moon. It was common knowledge that the army was in the north. "General Jackson is moving, and you can't tell me where."

"I'll miss you so much, Lorena," he said in a low tone. "I know we haven't known each other for very long, but somehow that doesn't matter to me. I think about you all the time, and the more time that goes by between my visits, the harder it is to be away from you."

She turned to him. Her white, perfectly shaped face and the great pools of dark eyes made her look unworldly, like a creature of secret streams and soft mists. "I have to tell you something. It's— very difficult for me, a cruel memory of a bitter time in my life. But perhaps you may understand me a little better. . ."

To Yancy's surprise she took both of his hands in hers and turned so that she was very close to him. In an even voice she said, "When I was seventeen, I met a man, a gentleman from a good Richmond family. I was so much in love with him, and I thought he was the most wonderful man in the world. We decided to marry when I turned eighteen. My birthday is in January, so we decided to marry that very month. I ordered my dress. My mother and father and I planned a wonderful wedding in that very Episcopal church right over there. I was so happy. I thought that my life was, and always would be, perfect." She stopped and dropped her gaze, and her hands grew unrestful.

Yancy stroked them and said quietly, "He left you, didn't he?"

She nodded, and when she spoke her voice was slightly choked. "Yes, he left me. The weekend before the wedding he said he wanted to visit some family in New Orleans. As it turned out, he had found out about a woman he had known for several years, and she had just become widowed. He stayed in New Orleans, and within two months he had married her."

She looked back up at him, and her lips trembled. Tears stood in her eyes. "He didn't even send me word. After he had been gone for four days, my father made inquiries with some friends he has in New Orleans. They found out about it. And that's the only way I knew that my engagement, my trust, and my heart had been broken." Now a single silver tear rolled down her smooth cheek.

Gently Yancy brushed it away and then drew her to him, holding her close. He pulled the hood down so he could kiss her hair. It was soft and warm and smelled of flowers.

She clung to him, and he could tell that she wept, but it was a gentle thing, not at all convulsive or wracking. For a long time they stayed that way, with Lorena's face buried in his shoulder, him murmuring soothing things against her hair.

After a while she moved slightly away and pulled a handkerchief from her pocket. "I've cried all over you," she said in a slightly shaken voice as she wiped her eyes.

"I'm glad," he said.

She took a deep, trembling breath. "Now you see that I have a very hard time trusting men."

He nodded. "With good reason. But Lorena, I must know. Do you trust me?"

She looked at him for a very long time, studying his face. He met her gaze squarely. Finally she answered him. "Yes. Yes, I do trust you, Yancy."

He put his arms around her and pulled her to him again. This time she looked up at him. He kissed her, gently, her lips warm and vulnerable on his. She slipped her hands behind his neck and caressed him. It was a long, sweet, poignant kiss.

CROSSING

They stayed in each other's arms, contentedly. Then Yancy said, "You know what I'm telling you, Lorena. I'm falling in love with you."

"I know," she whispered. "And right now I don't quite know how I feel. I've been afraid for so long, and I've smothered my emotions for so long that I feel a little dazed. Like—like when your arm goes to sleep, and when it wakes up, it prickles and feels like it doesn't belong to your body, quite."

"I understand," Yancy said. "And I don't mind. But please, Lorena, can you tell me this?" He pulled back to look at her face. "Will you wait for me? Will you wait long enough to give me a chance?"

She smiled. "I will, Yancy. Gladly, I will."

Yancy could only pray that she would wait for him and that she would remain the same sweet girl he had come to love in the meantime. He knew that only time would tell. . . .

Part Five: The Battles 1861—1862

CHAPTER NINETEEN

The next morning Yancy collected his dispatches to General Jackson from the War Department and hurried out of Richmond. On the entire journey back to the camp at Manassas, Yancy could scarcely think of anything but Lorena Hayden. She had allowed him to give her a modest good-bye kiss that morning, and it had elated him.

I think she does care for me. She's just afraid, he thought, *after what that dog did to her—no, that's an insult to dogs. I'd like to meet that joker sometime, like in a dark alley so he couldn't see me coming. Leaving a girl at eighteen—*

Suddenly Yancy laughed to himself. *She must be. . .let's see. . .she said two years ago, and her birthday is in January. . . She must be twenty now and turning twenty-one in a couple of months! She's so proper sometimes—she's going to have one hissy fit!* Yancy, in the previous September, had just turned eighteen years old.

Yancy didn't mark birthdays, because the Cheyenne Indians didn't mark birthdays. They observed and judged people according to where they stood in their journeys from childhood to adulthood. No numbering system figured in their assessment and acceptance of either boys or girls; they were simply recognized when they reached different stages of life. Of course the Cheyenne marked the passage of time, but no single day or even month was recognized as a landmark in a person's life.

Yancy, like his father, was very mature for his age. At sixteen years old, Daniel Tremayne had struck out on his own, hunting and trapping, and along the way he had met many coarse and hard-bitten men. And he had earned their respect. Yancy was the same. He had reflected a man's sense of duty and responsibility by the time he had reached sixteen and had gone to work for Thomas Jackson. He was, indeed, older than his years.

I'm going to tease her about being an older woman, he reflected with amusement. *The next time I see her. . .*

He hoped against hope that it would be soon.

Major General Jackson had actually received his orders in the middle of October. United States Commanding General George McClellan was massing his sixty thousand men across the Potomac, intending to overtake Richmond. The plan was for General Irvin McDowell, with his forty thousand troops stationed north of McClellan, to join him at Richmond. This would mean the death of the Confederacy.

General Robert E. Lee saw that only too well. His only hope, and it was a slim one, was Stonewall Jackson. If Jackson could defeat and chase the Federals out of the valley, and perhaps even draw some of McDowell's forces across the Potomac to reinforce them, then Lee thought that he might be able to outfight McClellan. Lee's were delicately worded orders, for naturally Lee could not state the case so baldly and place such a burden upon one single general.

But Robert E. Lee and Stonewall Jackson had a most peculiar understanding. Lee took special care of his temperamental and eccentric general and had immediately recognized him as one of the most capable men, so obviously born to command, that he had ever known. And Stonewall Jackson understood Lee's aristocratic, gracious orders, always worded with the greatest courtesy and generally ending in some rather vague suggestions that left Jackson to interpret what Lee wanted, not what he said. And so he did; and so he readied himself to fight, and fight hard, in the Shenandoah Valley.

On November 4, 1861, General Jackson gave a stirring good-bye speech to his beloved Stonewall Brigade. But as it turned out, all the high emotion and regret was wasted, because by November 12, they had joined him in Winchester. Jackson had been appalled at the troops stationed in the Shenandoah Valley.

There were three little brigades numbering about 1,600, and they were dotted around the northern part of the valley. There were four hundred and eighty-five wild cavalrymen under the doubtful command of old Colonel Angus McDonald, a sixty-year-old Southern gentleman with rheumatism who had absolutely no control over the undisciplined boys that galloped around the valley at will.

All this to fight General N. P. Banks, who was holding western Maryland directly across the Potomac with 18,000 men, and they were moving east. In addition, more than 22,000 Yankees were just across the Alleghenies in western Virginia, under General William S. Rosecrans. And worst of all, on Jackson's western flank, General Benjamin F. Kelley and his 5,000 men had captured the village of Romney. It was only forty miles away from Jackson's headquarters.

As soon as Jackson understood his position, he had sent Yancy on a wild trip to Richmond demanding reinforcements. "Tell them," he growled at Yancy, "that the Shenandoah Valley has almost no defenses."

Even before Yancy arrived, Secretary of War Benjamin had decided to send Jackson's old brigade to the valley. He greeted Yancy with this happy news and promptly turned him right around to ride to Manassas with his orders.

Yancy was happy to be reunited with the Stonewall Brigade, but he regretted that he didn't have time to see Lorena.

The Army of the Valley wintered in Winchester. Anna joined Jackson in December in his pleasant headquarters, the Tilghman home. She stayed December, January, and February, and wrote about that winter being one of the happiest times of their lives. All through those short winter days and long nights, Jackson made his plans and drilled his troops, ever the vigilant and disciplined general. At home with Anna he was, as always, happy and even jolly.

In March, the general turned back to war, and he sent Anna home. On March 22, he began what was known as the Valley Campaign. And this campaign—it was understood in the Army of Northern Virginia and throughout the South—saved Richmond. Stonewall Jackson had understood General Lee's orders, and like the extraordinary soldier that he was, he had followed them to the utmost.

Basically, the Valley Campaign was a complicated series of maneuvers orchestrated by Stonewall Jackson, and by him alone. His staff never knew his plans. His officers never knew who they were attacking. His men never knew where they were marching to. Of course, this meant that the enemy never knew anything about the elusive Stonewall, either—until the day came that they, thunderstruck, were looking at the Army of the Valley—who were themselves often bemused, they had traveled so fast and so victoriously—from the field of defeat. Before they could decide which direction to run, forward or backward, the army, and Stonewall, was gone, and again they knew not where. In the Valley Campaign this was to happen to armies in places that were forever attached to Stonewall Jackson's laurels—Front Royal, First Winchester, Cross Keys, and Port Republic.

With 17,000 men, Stonewall Jackson had, from start to finish, faced about 62,000 Federals. The Federal defeats in the valley had so stunned Washington that they had frozen McDowell's forces so he couldn't join McClellan in the Peninsular Campaign against Richmond. So it may even be said that just the fear of Stonewall Jackson had stopped a force of 40,000 men.

When it ended on June 9, 1862, there had been forty-eight marching days. The Army of the Shenandoah Valley had marched a total of 676 miles, an average of 14 miles a day. After this they were known as Jackson's Foot Cavalry. They had fought six formal skirmishing actions and five pitched battles. They had taken 3,500 prisoners, and 3,500 Federals lay dead or were wounded in the valley. Considering the relative numbers of the armies, Confederate losses were low indeed—2,500 dead or wounded and 600 prisoners.

Jackson had also added precious supplies and arms to the needy Confederate armies. He had captured over 10,000 muskets and rifles and nine cannons. He had burned or destroyed countless tons of Federal supplies.

The Valley Campaign had succeeded without costly battles. Outnumbered by more than three to one, Jackson's superb tactics had soundly beaten a far superior force, although they were much more poorly led. In addition, his Army of the Shenandoah Valley had paralyzed McDowell's forces. Stonewall Jackson's name was now worth an army.

Senator Blake Stevens of Virginia, Peyton Stevens's father, was so proud of his son being in the famous Stonewall Brigade that he regularly sent special couriers with gifts for him. When the brigade had gone into winter quarters at Winchester, a wagon had arrived with a tent almost as large as General Jackson's, a camp stove, a padded cot, six new uniforms, two pairs of boots, six pairs of wool socks, four blankets, and two crates crammed with tins of food.

Peyton asked his old VMI roommates, Yancy and Chuckins and Sandy Owens, to share his tent with him. Yancy and Chuckins gladly did, though Sandy had to tent with the artillery. Still, whenever he got a chance he came and stayed with them.

But on Monday, June 16, 1862, all of that finery had been packed away on the brigade wagon train, and the four of them were as humbly bivouacked as though they weren't Stonewall's Boys, which they called themselves though they kept it a supreme secret. They had built a campfire and were lying in a circle around it. On the ground was an oilcloth. They lay on that and covered themselves with one blanket and an oilcloth on top of that to guard against the dew.

Sandy and Chuckins were asleep, but both Peyton and Yancy lay awake, hands behind their heads, staring up at the night sky. Yancy was thinking forlornly that he hadn't seen Lorena for almost eight months. He was surprised at how deeply he missed her.

"Can't believe we're marching tomorrow," Peyton said, interrupting Yancy's melancholy musings. "After the last few months we've had. And the battle in Port Republic was just what—yesterday?"

"Feels like it," Yancy answered, "but it was a week ago. And no wonder we don't know what day it is or what month it is or what time it is. You and I both have made two runs to Richmond in the last week, haven't we?"

"Guess so," Peyton said. "Yancy? Do you know where we're going and what we're gonna do?"

As usual, Jackson had kept his orders and plans a strict secret from everyone, even the field commanders, which drove them utterly insane. Yancy was quiet for a while. He generally did know more than almost anyone else in the command, except for maybe Jim. It was because Jackson relaxed a little more with Yancy and even held conversations with him, which was unusual for the taciturn general. Yancy knew him and understood him, and so it gave him some advantage in reading him. He had never said anything else to anyone, and he hesitated now, though he knew Peyton would never let on.

"You do know, don't you?" Peyton asked quietly.

"Well, I don't *know*. It's not like he tells me anything."

"But you know. Can't you just tell me if it's north, south, east, or west?"

Finally Yancy lifted his arm and pointed. "That way." He pointed southeast, toward Richmond.

General Lee was planning a counterattack on the Army of the Potomac, led by General McClellan, and he needed Stonewall Jackson's Army of the Valley desperately. Jackson planned to march them double-quick to Lee's aid.

They left at dawn, a bleak foggy morning that made it difficult to even see the man, or the horse, in front of them. Yancy, Peyton, and Chuckins rode in the general's train, behind the general staff. Even Midnight and Peyton's great stallion, Senator, seemed sluggish and bleary. Only Chuckins's plump mare, Brownie, seemed to plod along cheerfully as she usually did. But then, Brownie was not a Stonewall Jackson courier's horse, and in the Valley Campaign she had not ridden many reckless miles, day after day.

Midmorning the fog lifted and the day became pleasant. Some of the staff officers ranged up and down the lines of marching men, checking with the regimental officers and trying to discourage the men from straggling, for they were riding through orchard country. Yancy, Peyton, and Chuckins found themselves just behind General Jackson and had the good fortune to witness a delightful little scene.

General Jackson had given strict orders that no soldier was to say, in any manner whatsoever, anything about the plans of the army. This afforded the army a lot of mirth, for they had no clue about the plans of the army anyway, but it amused them when General Jackson showed his penchant for mystery.

Now they came upon a soldier that had stepped off the side of the road, for a cherry tree was temptingly close to it. He had climbed the tree, where he was sitting contentedly, gobbling.

Jackson stopped and stared up at him. "Where are you going, soldier?" he asked.

"I don't know."

"What command are you in?"

"I don't know."

"Well, what state are you from?"

"I don't know."

With some exasperation, Jackson demanded, "What's the meaning of this?"

He answered, chewing thoughtfully, "Well, Old Jack and Old Hood passed orders yesterday that we didn't know a thing till after the next fight, and we're keeping our mouths shut."

Jackson threw back his head and laughed, a rare sight indeed, and rode on.

Jackson marched them a roundabout way, instead of the straightaway that the couriers took, for he and General Lee hoped to deceive McClellan into thinking that Jackson was still in the valley. In fact, General Lee had even sent General Winder and his 10,000 men, ostensibly, to Jackson in Winchester. General Winder had made it there, camped a couple of nights, then had turned around and was now following Jackson back.

But this deception was hard, for the country was not made for brigades of men walking through. There were enemy pickets, skirmishes, impenetrable thickets, and creeks sometimes six feet deep to be forded. Moving the cannons was like a nightmare for man and beast alike. No trails were marked, of course, and their maps were very poor indeed. Jackson had two new guides he didn't know.

On Tuesday the twenty-fourth it rained, long and heavily. They had been passing through one of the thick woods with almost impossible thickets, and now they found that the enemy had cut so many new roads in the tangle that one of the new guides lost his way and led them astray.

But finally on the twenty-sixth the exhausted army had reached their goal, a small crossroads call Old Cold Harbor, just above Gaines' Mill, where Lee planned to concentrate his forces and attack the Federals massed there. On the twenty-seventh they moved in. Jackson was on the Confederate left, Longstreet's army on the Confederate right. There were 88,000 Confederates in the field.

Yancy had asked General Jackson to fight with his old unit from his days of training in Richmond when he was still a VMI cadet, Raphine Company.

Jackson had shaken his head wearily. "We've got more than two dozen outfits out there, with three Army headquarters—me, Longstreet, and General Lee. I'm going to need every courier I've got. I especially need you and Sergeant Stevens, for you two have the best horses. You two stick close by me."

"Yes, sir," Yancy said.

And so they followed him, from the swampy bog below Old Cold Harbor to the little hills and wooded fields around Gaines' Mill. Lee had opened fire at daybreak, but it was afternoon before Jackson reached his command post, a knoll just northeast of the Confederate center. The fighting was, and already had been, savage. General A. P. Hill in the center had attacked too soon, before he could be reinforced, and the Confederates had taken heavy casualties. The Confederates charged and would gain ground; then the Federals would countercharge, and the Confederates were forced back again. The lines stubbornly stayed stagnant, with very little ground gained nor lost for either side, but with both sides losing dozens of men by the hour.

Almost as soon as they arrived at Jackson's command post, he called for Peyton. "Ride to General D. H. Hill's command and instruct him to send in Rodes, Anderson, and Garland, and to keep Ripley and Colquitt in reserve," he ordered brusquely. Stonewall Jackson wasted no words in battle.

General A. P. Hill was badly beaten down, but the brigades that had arrived with Jackson's command were fully engaged. Finally, at about four thirty that afternoon, three of his trailing brigades under General Richard Ewell topped the hill at Old Cold Harbor. Jackson sighted them immediately and sent orders to them by Peyton.

He then turned to Yancy. "You've got to go down to General A. P. Hill, down on the battle line. He must be made aware that General Ewell is on the way to support him with three brigades. And then ride to General Lee's headquarters and assure him that we can relieve General Hill."

"Yes, sir!" Yancy said then started to turn away.

But Jackson pulled Little Sorrel up close to Midnight and Yancy stopped. Jackson said in a low voice, "You're the fastest. It's going to be hot and heavy down there, Sergeant. Ride hard, as fast as you can, and no need to linger on the line. It's just as important for you to notify General Lee as it is for you to notify General Hill. Understood?"

"Understood, sir."

"Good, good." Jackson turned away, and Yancy galloped off at Midnight's top speed, which was fast indeed.

Midnight had been around battles, of course, and had been in the line of fire before, but neither he nor Yancy had seen the savagery at the line of the Battle of Gaines' Mill. General A. P. Hill, a redheaded, brave, hot-tempered, experienced soldier was on his third horse of the day only about fifty yards back from the front lines. He wore his bright red flannel shirt, as he always did in battle, thumbing his nose to enemy sharpshooters. As Yancy approached, even over the thunderous din of battle, he could hear General Hill's scratchy voice screeching orders at the top of his lungs, liberally laced with curses.

Midnight was in tearing high spirits, foaming at the mouth,

eyes wild. He wasn't spooked; he was battle ready. As Yancy tore up to the general, Midnight lowered his backside and skidded to a stop on his back legs, reared, threw his head up, and screamed.

Even General Hill turned to see this magnificent spectacle, and he recognized Midnight and Yancy. "Ho, you, boy! Looks like that crazy beast is ready to down a few Yankees himself!" he shouted.

Yancy grinned and Midnight skittered up to the general. "He would, sir, but General Jackson gave Midnight his orders along with mine."

"Orders from Stonewall, huh? What? Attack the North Pole?"

Even with bullets whistling by him and shells exploding all around him, Yancy was feeling the irrational exuberance of battle, and he laughed. "Better news than that, sir. General Jackson sends his compliments and wants to make you aware that General Ewell is on his way to support you with three brigades."

General Hill let loose with a string of happy profanity. He finished with, "Good news from Stonewall, good news. Now you and your big black monster better be running along, little boy."

Yancy saluted. "Yes, sir, I am ordered to General Lee. Not the North Pole."

He pulled Midnight's reins to the left and felt a curious thumping blow on his right arm. Puzzled, he looked down. There was a slowly spreading red stain on his gray sleeve. He looked back up at General Hill, who was looking down at Yancy's arm. "Sir. . . ?" Yancy began.

He felt his head whip to the side, as if he had been struck sharply on his right forehead. And then, curiously, slowly, his vision faded to black, and he knew no more.

CHAPTER TWENTY

"Matthews, give him more chloroform. He's stirring a bit and I need about two more minutes to close this up," Dr. Jesse Hayden ordered the steward assisting him. Dr. Hayden waited for Matthews to apply another two drops of chloroform to the cloth covering the patient's face then resumed stitching up the stump of the man's right leg. As he bent over, his back and shoulders burned with an ache that felt like it went right down to his bones. It was the nineteenth amputation Dr. Hayden had done that day.

He finished stitching and slowly straightened up. His whole back felt like it was on fire. "Done." He looked at the tag on the soldier's clothes that were neatly folded at the foot of the operating table. "He's Thirteenth Virginia. Check with Matron to see which building we're putting them in," he told the two orderlies who were transporting men to the buildings where they would receive nursing care. Chimborazo Hospital had forty buildings. Even when receiving patients in a steady stream after a battle, the efficient and compassionate administrator, Dr. James McCaw, stipulated that every effort be made to keep the soldiers together with others in their units.

In this, one of two buildings set up to receive the soldiers coming in from the battles raging just to the east of them, ten operating tables had been set up, with a team of anesthetist and surgical assistant assigned to each table, though they had only eighteen doctors in all, rotating as they could. In both buildings, doctors performed surgery after surgery. In the building next to them was the non-emergency care receiving, and the orderlies were steadily stitching, medicating, and treating wounds—and sicknesses—as quickly as possible.

Two ambulance attendants brought a stretcher up to Dr. Hayden's operating table, a groaning man with severe shrapnel injuries on the right side of his body. He was groaning, his eyes wide and frightened and unseeing, his left hand clenching and unclenching spasmodically. Wearily Dr. Hayden saw that most likely both his right arm and right leg would require amputation.

Just then Dr. McCaw came up to Dr. Hayden and laid his hand on his arm. Dr. McCaw was a man of medium stature, with light brown hair and a mustache that was turning prematurely gray. His features were nondescript, except for the warmth and kindness of his expression. Now he said firmly, "Dr. Hayden, I believe I must insist that you stop and rest for a bit. You have been working steadily for hours on end, and I know that last month you were unwell. I don't want you to fall ill, please. We need you too much."

"But—" Dr. Hayden gestured toward the moaning soldier on his table.

Dr. McCaw shook his head. "I insist, Jesse. I'll take this table myself. You go rest, get something to eat, have some coffee, and don't come back for an hour."

"Very well," Hayden said. "I must admit that sounds very inviting. Thank you, Dr. McCaw."

"Of course." He turned to Matthews and started giving instructions for anesthesia.

Dr. Hayden went outside, stopped just outside the double entry doors, closed his eyes, and took several deep breaths. Inside, the emergency ward smelled like blood and sweat and fear, and over it all hung the distinct acrid fumes of chloroform. Outside it was warm and humid, but high up on "Hospital Hill" no stench of battle drifted on the heavy night air. He opened his eyes and sighed when he saw the ambulances coming from the east, lined up along Thirty-fourth Street.

The attendants returned to the ambulance that sat in front of the building. The driver snapped the traces, and the horses started trotting to the west, returning to the field of battle to reap another grim harvest.

Behind it another ambulance pulled up. The orderlies jumped down, climbed in the back, and brought the first man out on a stretcher. He was unconscious, mercifully, Dr. Hayden thought, for his right side and the right side of his head and face were blood-soaked. Bandages had been wrapped around the man's right arm and forehead, but if they had once been the standard white bandages, they were now the deep crimson of blood. Dr. Hayden glanced at his face as the orderlies hustled to the doors then did a sharp double-take. "Wait!" he ordered, striding quickly to the stretcher. Surprised, the orderlies halted at this unmistakable authoritative command.

Lanterns were lit outside but the light was uncertain. Dr. Hayden bent over the unconscious man and smoothed his dark hair back from his forehead. Quickly he straightened and said, "Follow me."

He hurried inside, followed by the medics. Dr. McCaw was still at the table that Dr. Hayden had occupied, but the one right next to it was empty, and it still had an anesthetist and assistant standing by. Dr. Hayden directed the men to put the stretcher there. Dr. McCaw was right in the middle of amputating his patient's right arm, but these surgeons had so much experience with that type of surgery lately that now they could do amputations with hardly a second thought. Dr. Hayden stepped close to him and said, "Elijah, this young man is a friend of my family's. He saved my son's life. I want to treat him."

Dr. McCaw nodded without looking up. "All right then, go ahead, Jesse."

Dr. Hayden turned back to the assistants. "Get those bandages off, and get his clothes off. I'll be right back."

He hurried back outside. There were always boys loitering around the hospital, begging for errands to run for a penny. He collared a promising-looking boy of about twelve that was fairly clean and neat, took a pencil and notepaper out of his pocket, and talked as he wrote. "I want you to run to the Richmond Episcopal Church on Myrtle Street. Do you know it? Excellent. Next to it is a two-story house with two big walnut trees in front. Give this note to them, and a man named Elijah is going to be coming back to the hospital with a wagon. You may ride back with him, and when you return I'll give you two pennies. A nickel if you hurry as fast as you can."

"Yes, sir," he said over his shoulder, already taking off at a dead run.

Dr. Hayden hurried back inside to his patient.

Almost a year before, Elijah had picked up a pale and limp Leslie Hayden from Yancy's wagon and carried him upstairs as if he were a young child. Now Elijah picked up Yancy Tremayne from the wagon and gently carried him upstairs to the guest room. Yancy was wrapped in a sheet from the waist down. His face and right side were still covered in dried blood, and his thick hair was caked with it. With his dark complexion, Yancy could not be said to be pale, but his face was a rather sickly tan. His right eye was swollen and blue beneath the thick bandage on his forehead. His upper right arm was bandaged from shoulder to elbow, and it was secured in a sling.

Her face as pale as the moon, her eyes as wide and dark as drowning pools, Lorena followed.

Elijah laid him down on Leslie's bed.

Lily appeared at the door, almost as pale as Lorena. "How is he? Is he badly hurt?" she asked anxiously.

Lorena went to her and took her arm. "I'm sure he isn't critical, or Father would have come home with him. Please, Mother, try not to worry. Go on to bed. I'll bring you a cup of chamomile tea."

Lily said, "I think I will sit up in bed and try to read my Bible. And thank you, my dear, but Missy has already made chamomile tea for me. Please come let me know how he is. I don't think I'll be able to sleep until we know he will be all right."

"Of course, Mother," Lorena said and went back to Yancy's bedside.

Elijah pulled some papers from his pocket. "Miss Lorena, Dr. Hayden tole me to give these to you. It'll tell us how to take care of Mr. Yancy. Why don't you go on down to the kitchen where it's good light and read it while I tend to him."

Lorena started to object—she didn't want to leave Yancy, not for a moment—but then she realized that of course Elijah would be attending to Yancy's personal needs. Just then Missy came in with a steaming copper water pot, thick tendrils of vapor rising and filling the room with the soothing scent of rosemary. Lorena inhaled gratefully. Some of the confused panic retreated, and she felt her mind cleared somewhat. "Missy, do you know where Leslie's nightshirts are?"

"Yes ma'am, when the boy comes with the news that Mr. Yancy was hurt, I took one of 'em out and steamed it to freshen it up. It's hanging in the cupboard," she said kindly.

Missy does the laundry and ironing. Of course she knows where all of our clothes are. She must feel that sometimes the gentry thinks these things get done by magic. "Yes, of course, of course," Lorena said, turning to the door. "Please let me know when you've finished."

Lorena went down to the kitchen and sat down at the oak counter where she and Yancy had sat so many times before. Pulling a lamp close, she read her father's notes.

Lorena,

First of all, please do not be too distressed. Yancy has two injuries, but at this juncture I don't believe either of them are life threatening. Clear your mind and be calm. It won't help Yancy if you are troubled.

First, his head wound: He has a scalp laceration, I believe a graze from a bullet. He sustained a simple linear skull fracture (it's just a thin line about three inches long), and the skull is not splintered or depressed or in any way distorted. This is good news; but all skull fractures are serious injuries, and he will require constant monitoring for the next twenty-four hours. The scalp laceration required eleven stitches, but the wound and the edges were clean.

For care: Wrap ice chips in a clean white towel and apply to his forehead and eye every hour for about fifteen minutes. Head wounds bleed profusely, and even with the stitches he may bleed through the bandage. Rebandage as necessary, gently cleaning any dried blood at the laceration site if necessary.

As for his mental condition, I do not believe he is in a coma. I think he is unconscious, but in a very light state as he goes back and forth into a deep sleep. He drifted into consciousness as I was stitching his arm, and he seemed to be lucid. He knew his name and could see me very well. But he was in pain, so I gave him some morphia and he slept again. Don't attempt to rouse him, but if he does wake up just ask him some simple questions: his name, if he knows where he is, if his vision is clear, if he is in pain. You may give him twenty drops of laudanum as often as every four hours if needed.

Head injury patients generally have a sensitivity to bright light and noise, so keep the room dimly lit (I suggest with candles only, and keep the drapes drawn) and speak and move as softly as possible. Also, it is best that he be propped up to a half-sitting position; he will be much more comfortable than lying flat.

I must caution you, daughter, that when people receive the shock of head wounds, they usually evidence some distressing symptoms, but in actuality they are the norm. He will likely be confused as to time; he won't know what day it is, and it will mean nothing to him when you tell him. He will have lost the instinctive sense we have of knowing whether it is day or night, and this usually results in increased anxiety. I'm sure this will be magnified for Yancy, as he does seem to have sharper senses than most men. Perhaps it is the Indian in him. At any rate, if he wakes up and seems to be alert enough to want to talk, first gently let him know where he is, what day it is, and what time it is, for he very well may not know where he is.

It is common for victims of skull fractures to have

amnesia to one degree or another. They rarely remember the incident that caused the injury, and the amnesia may evidence itself in many ways. He will almost certainly have holes in his memory, both short-term and long-term. Do not be alarmed, for it's natural that he will have trouble with his memory for a while.

As I said, I don't believe the head injury is too severe, but there are a few symptoms that would indicate a graver prognosis, and I wish you would send for me immediately should they occur. They are: convulsions, slurred speech, stiff neck, visual disturbances, or clear fluid leaking from his ears or nose.

As for his right arm, he was shot and the bullet lodged just at the edge of the humerus. I removed the bullet without trouble, but the bone is slightly chipped and it sustained a hairline crack, which is not even considered a break. We will need to keep it bandaged tightly and tied securely into the sling to keep it immobilized for a few days, but I think he will regain full use soon. He may suffer pain at the incision site, and you can administer laudanum for that, too.

The hospital is extremely busy. Men are pouring in from Gaines' Mill just east of town, where the battle was today. Dr. McCaw kindly let me take an hour's break, and I ate and even napped a little, and so I feel refreshed enough to keep working on. I am going to try to stay tonight as there are so very many emergency surgeries to perform. And you may take that as a measure of what I would term only moderate concern for Yancy. Certainly if I was worried to a great degree I would have come home with him, for as you well know in the last year, your mother and I have come to regard him almost as a son.

Keep hope in your mind, Lorena. Trust my judgment and trust yourself. You're an excellent nurse, and as you know, Missy and Elijah are wonderful with sick or injured people. Yancy could not have better care. And of course, we will all "pray without ceasing" for Yancy.

With my great love,
Father

CROSSING

Lorena read it all again, slowly. But she felt a tremendous burden and fear both for Yancy and herself. She was frightened that Yancy might actually be much more severely injured than even her father, who had practiced medicine for almost thirty years, could know. And she was frightened that she might make some horrible mistake with his care; with misjudging his state, either physical or mental; some stupid mistake with his medication. . . An ugly picture of Yancy in bone-jarring convulsions grew large in her mind. Tears welled up in her eyes, and she buried her face in her hands. She was on the verge of panic.

But Lorena knew she was a strong woman who knew where her true strength came from, and with a supreme effort, she suppressed the paralyzing dread and banished the desolate visions in her mind. She bowed her head and quoted softly, " 'Come unto me, all ye that labour and are heavy laden, and I will give you rest. Take my yoke upon you, and learn of me; for I am meek and lowly in heart: and ye shall find rest unto your souls. For my yoke is easy, and my burden is light.' " She felt a great calm and clarity of mind and strength of will flow over her and through her, and she thanked the Lord for it.

Gathering her father's notes, she went upstairs to reassure her mother that Yancy was going to be just fine. She had every confidence that she could take care of him.

Lorena stayed by Yancy's side all night, except when Elijah came to attend to him. He stirred lightly when she applied the ice chips to his forehead and eye, but he didn't seem to be in distress. Once he opened his eye—his left eye, for his right was swollen shut—and looked at her. Even with one eye, she could see that his gaze was direct and clear. But his lids were heavy, and after just a few seconds he slept again.

Her father came home at dawn, his shoulders heavily stooped, his eyes shadowed. "Hello, my dear. How is our patient?" he asked, laying his hands on Lorena's shoulders.

"He just seems to be resting quietly," she answered. "He opened his eyes once, but he slipped right back to sleep."

"You know, dear, Elijah and Missy are perfectly capable of watching him. They would let us know if there was any change at all."

"I know," Lorena agreed. "But I don't want to leave him. I want to be here if—when he wakes up."

"I understand," he said, moving to Yancy's bedside. He bent over, gently lifted his left eyelid, and nodded with satisfaction. "But you should have Elijah bring up your favorite chair from the parlor. You could rest easier in it."

She had been sitting in a side chair with a padded seat. It wasn't uncomfortable, but neither could one lounge in it. "Wonderful idea, Father," Lorena said appreciatively. "As always, your prescriptives are just perfect."

He smiled. "Also, as your physician, I'm going to insist that you rest later today. I'm going to sleep for a while. Later this afternoon, before I go back to the hospital, I'll stay with Yancy. I need to do an overall assessment of him and cleanse the arm incision and scalp laceration anyway. While I'm doing that, you can have something to eat and sleep for an hour or two. Oh no, young lady, don't you make that face at me. I insist. If Yancy wakes up, I promise I will come and get you."

"Very well," she said reluctantly. "I suppose I will need it, for I intend to sit up with him tonight."

"Good," he said and yawned. "I'm off to bed. I'll see you later, daughter." He bent and kissed her cheek and left.

Elijah brought up her chair and she sank gratefully into it. It enveloped her with comfort and a thousand happy memories of her family all together in the parlor.

She missed Leslie. He had returned to Washington in November of last year, shortly after Yancy's last visit. He had written, with vast relief, to tell them that he had joined the 8th Maryland, which was assigned to North Carolina.

It's extremely unlikely I'll ever see Yancy on a battlefield again. Tell him for me, and thank him again. And tell him that I hope we may meet as friends again soon, in a time of blessed peace.

CROSSING

She read the Bible for a while by the single candle in the room, but candlelight was too dim for reading at very long stretches. She settled back in her chair and laid her head back, closing her eyes to rest them. Without really realizing it, she fell into a light sleep.

She didn't exactly dream, but she did have a vague feeling of deep comfort and knew she was in her favorite chair. Airy images floated through her subconscious—her mother, smiling; a warm fire in the parlor; Yancy sleeping.

This faraway picture roused her a little. She stirred and slowly opened her eyes.

Yancy's eyes were open. The swelling in his right eye had gone down considerably with Lorena's faithful applications of the ice packs. In his half-sitting position he leaned back against the mound of pillows propping him up. He looked relaxed and comfortable, but his eyes were bright and sharp. His expression was not apprehensive and certainly not fearful, but as her father had predicted, he appeared to be slightly confused. "Hello," he said.

"He—hello," Lorena stuttered. She was startled, and the faraway feeling of her dreamy slumber had not yet faded.

He continued to look at her with his fathomless dark eyes.

She sat up straight, smoothed her hair back, and looked at the pendant watch pinned to her shoulder. It was 3:30 in the afternoon, and mindful of what her father had told her about Yancy's probable lack of time perception, sharply she made herself recall that it was Saturday, June 28, 1862.

Calm now, she looked back at him and asked, "Do you know your name?"

He frowned. "Yes, of course. I'm Yancy Tremayne."

"Can you see me clearly?"

"Yes, my vision is clear, but my right eye. . . ." He moved his right arm, but it was immobile in the sling. He looked down at it with some surprise. "What happened to me?" he asked.

"You were hurt. Injured. Do you remember anything at all?"

Long seconds elapsed as he stared into space blankly. "I. . .I remember a big black horse, riding a big black horse. . . ." His vision focused sharply on her face. "I'm a soldier. In Stonewall Jackson's outfit. My horse's name is Midnight, and I'm—I'm a courier for Major Jackson."

"General Jackson," Lorena corrected him gently.

He looked bemused. "That's all I can remember. Riding Midnight. Carrying dispatches for Maj—General Jackson."

"It's all right," she said soothingly. "You've had a head injury, and that's why your right eye is swollen, and that's why you're a little confused right now. It's very common with this type of injury, but it will pass."

He nodded, seemingly satisfied at the moment. His gaze wandered around the room. "What time is it?"

"It's 3:30 in the afternoon. Today is Saturday. It's June—June 28."

"Oh," he said blankly. Then he looked down and touched his bound right arm with his left. "What happened to me?" he asked again.

Lorena hesitated. She was uncertain whether she should give him the bald, frightening facts that he had been shot in battle. But he seemed steady enough and she knew that Yancy was a strong man. She replied, "You're right, Yancy, you are a soldier. You fought in a battle. A bullet grazed your head, and you have a slight fracture, and the wound required stitches. You were also shot in the arm, but the bullet was removed without any problems. The only reason that your right arm is immobilized is because the bullet lodged against your humerus—that's the big bone in your upper arm—and chipped it just a bit. Your arm isn't broken, but it'll be best to keep it still for a few days."

He listened carefully, and still he was expressionless. Lorena really couldn't tell how much he comprehended, but he was not at all distressed. His respiration, she noted, was full and steady, and his eyes stayed clear and focused. "Ma'am, could I please have a drink of water?" he asked at last.

"Of course," she said. She rose and went to the washstand, a solid chest with a marble top and a cabinet and drawers underneath. There was a large bowl and pitcher for wash water, and now Lorena had kept a pitcher of water on ice. She poured him a glass and noted with satisfaction that it was cool but not too cold, as her father had instructed. She brought it to him and hesitated, not really knowing if he was so weak that she needed to hold it for him.

But with no apparent problem he reached up with his left hand and took the glass and drank thirstily.

"More?" she asked as he emptied the glass.

"Please, ma'am."

Lorena was a little troubled by his formality, but she dismissed it as Yancy's natural courtesy. She filled the glass again.

He drank about half of it and then set it on the bedside table. She was glad to see that he apparently moved with relative ease, for the table was on the right side of the bed, by her chair, and he had made the awkward crossover of his body to set the glass down securely. He settled back into the pillows, but they had come disarrayed.

She bent over and pulled up on one slightly. "Can you lean forward a bit, Yancy? If you are able to, I think I can arrange your pillows a little better." It was a test, to see if he could sit up straighter without her help. He did. *He's very strong,* she reflected with a sort of furtive feminine admiration. *He should heal quickly.*

She finished and Yancy settled back. "Thank you, ma'am," he said.

"You're welcome." She studied him for a few moments and he met her gaze with no apparent discomfort. Lorena took a deep breath and her eyes dropped to her hands, folded in her lap. She had become nervous, twisting the fabric of her skirt into little knots. With a conscious effort she stilled her hands then looked up. "Yancy," she said, and her voice had deepened with tension, "do you know me?"

His gaze didn't waver. "I know that you're a beautiful lady and very kind. Like this room, you seem familiar, but it's a very faraway feeling, like you're not really connected to me. It's like—it's sort of like I've seen pictures of you, and this room, a long time ago, in some book."

Numbly she nodded and ducked her head again to hide her distress. It shocked her to realize just how desolate his matter-of-fact answer made her feel.

"Do I—have I offended you, ma'am?" he asked with the first sign of anxiety. "Am I supposed to—are you—have I—"

Quickly she arranged her features to hide the turmoil of emotion she felt and looked back up. "No, Yancy, of course you haven't offended me in any way. As I said, you may have some trouble with your memory for a day or two; you were injured only yesterday, you know. You are in Richmond, in the Hayden home. My father, Jesse Hayden, is your physician, but not only that, you are a close friend of our family's."

He relaxed. "That's good then," he said vaguely. He reached up with his left hand and barely touched the bandage on his head, wincing slightly.

"Are you in pain?" Lorena asked quickly.

"Well, yes, I'm getting the beginnings of a headache. And my arm is starting to hurt some."

Lorena took a brown bottle from the bedside table and carefully measured the light brown liquid into a spoon. "Here. This will ease your pain and help you to sleep."

Obediently he opened his mouth and took the dose. He made a face and Lorena handed him the glass of water. He washed down the bitter medicine with a long drink.

"Do you think you could drink some broth, Yancy?" Lorena asked him.

"I don't really want anything else right now, ma'am," he answered. His eyes were already dulling somewhat, his eyelids dropping. Laudanum was a mixture of the tincture of opium and brandy. Dr. Hayden added sugar to his prescriptive, but it did little to mask the unpleasant taste. Yancy was already feeling the effects of the powerful drug. He blinked slowly, twice.

"When you wake up again perhaps you'll feel more like eating a small meal," Lorena managed to say lightly. "For now, just go back to sleep."

He closed his eyes and breathed deeply.

Lorena now let the anguish show on her face; she pressed shaky fingers to her forehead. Feeling helpless tears rising, she got up and tiptoed to the door. She certainly wasn't going to sit by Yancy's bed and sob like a hurt child.

She had only gone a few steps, when behind her Yancy murmured, "Ma'am? What is your name, please?"

"Lorena," she said, her voice raw. She couldn't help it. "Lorena Hayden."

He blinked, then his eyes closed again.

Lorena fled, running into her bedroom across the hall. It was long minutes before she could stop crying.

" '. . . and so after seven bloody days of battle, once again our heroic Army of Northern Virginia has triumphed over the Yankee invader. The cowardly McClellan with his rabble cowers on the far bank of the James River, his plan to overtake Richmond thwarted by our brave commander, General Robert E. Lee. With a force of barely eighty-eight thousand, General Lee and his fighting commanders General James Longstreet and General Stonewall Jackson pushed the one hundred thousand Federals a full twenty miles from our beloved capital. Even though our army was so vastly outnumbered, they were so overpowering in battle that the well-bloodied Yanks could not run fast enough. In tremendous triumph, General Lee and the Army of Northern Virginia have taken close to ten thousand prisoners and have inflicted nearly sixteen thousand casualties (killed, wounded, and missing) on the enemy. In addition, General Lee has seized fifty cannons and ten thousand muskets for the blessed Confederacy.

President Davis has declared a day of thanksgiving, and rightly so. United, we loyal and grateful citizens of the Confederate States of America thank Almighty God for protecting and defending us and our courageous army, and we acknowledge that the praise for not only this, these Battles of Seven Days, but all victories in this life come only from His sovereign hand. Amen.' "

Lorena finished reading the article from the July 6 edition of the *Richmond Report* and looked up at Yancy.

He seemed troubled.

"What's the matter, Yancy?" Lorena asked.

He shrugged a little, with his uninjured left shoulder only, the way that he would probably have to make the gesture for the remainder of his life. "I dunno, exactly. I'm sure no military genius, like General Lee and General Longstreet and Stonewall. But. . ."

"Yes?" Lorena prodded him curiously. In spite of his words, Lorena had found that he had an insight into the strategic implications of the battles that was very unusual for a mere sergeant who was only one small stitch in the vast complex tapestry of war.

"It's just that I think General Lee would have planned to destroy McClellan's army, and I think he could have, in spite of being outnumbered. We're always outnumbered," he said with an endearing earnestness. "Somehow I just think that this campaign wasn't as successful as the papers make it out to be. We inflicted heavy casualties on the Army of the Potomac, yes, but it didn't say anything about our casualties."

Lorena sighed deeply. "No, the *Richmond Report* is always limited to our triumphs, it seems. But the *Dispatch* reports the casualty numbers daily. They're not good, Yancy."

"Tell me," he insisted.

She picked up the *Richmond Dispatch* and turned to the "Battle Reports" page. "So far, 3,286 killed, 946 missing, and about 15,000 wounded."

"What? Oh no." Yancy groaned and lay back heavily on the pillows. "Fifteen thousand. . . Richmond must be overrun. No wonder I never see Dr. Hayden. He's not working too hard, is he?"

"Yes, and no one on this earth can stop him," Lorena said with exasperation. "Day and night he's at Chimborazo. Sometimes he comes home to sleep for a few hours, but more often he's been staying at the hospital, sleeping in a building they've set up especially for the doctors and assistants. They have matrons attending twenty-four hours, providing meals and laundering the cot linens and cleaning the quarters. Still, he can't possibly be resting for any great amount of time. It's driving us all crazy, even Elijah and Missy."

A small half smile played on Yancy's face. "Sounds like you," he said lightly. "You've been nursing me around the clock for a week now. Not much you can say to your father, Rena."

A surge of joy ran through Lorena as, for the first time, Yancy said her nickname. Only Leslie and Yancy had ever called her Rena.

In the last week, Yancy's confusion and disorientation had cleared up amazingly. He still couldn't recall being shot, and there were still holes in his memory, of times and places. As Dr. Hayden had predicted, he had difficulty sensing the passage of time. Every time he woke up he asked what time it was and if it was day or night. And he had a nagging memory of a short, grizzled man in a red flannel shirt, sitting on a runty chestnut horse, but no matter how he tried, Yancy couldn't put the man into a setting, and he couldn't fathom why he seemed so important. The Haydens couldn't know that he was seeing General A. P. Hill at the Battle of Gaines' Mill when he was shot.

Thankfully, two days ago, Yancy had finally remembered the Haydens, including Leslie, which was a big breakthrough since they hadn't mentioned Leslie to him. Yancy remembered that he was a Union soldier and how Yancy had saved his life.

However, to Lorena's bitter disappointment, Yancy seemed to have no recollection of his declaration of love to her eight months ago. It was obvious that he liked her and enjoyed her company. His manner toward her was warm, but there was no sign of the passionate romantic man that Lorena had known last October.

Until Yancy was wounded, Lorena had held her emotions strictly at bay, in effect forcing them into a far dark corner of her heart, seldom visited. The night that Elijah had brought Yancy home, bloodied and battered, Lorena had suffered anguish she hadn't known since Leslie had been injured. She felt as if someone had taken a dagger to her heart and laid bare the love she had for Yancy with brutal strokes.

It had only grown worse in the last two days, since Yancy had finally remembered her and he had so naturally and carelessly placed her in the platonic position of a sister. She had been overcome with a scalding regret that she had so stubbornly fought her love for Yancy. Indeed, she had triumphed for a time. But now she was afraid that this so-called triumph was, in truth, a grievous defeat inflicted on her only by herself. *What if he never remembers he loves me? What if the memory of that love has been completely erased? What if that part of his heart that belongd to me is gone forever?*

Breaking in on her agonized thoughts, Yancy said, "You're

making faces. Leslie said that one day you'll get stuck that way, and then you can be a sideshow at the circus. 'The Angry Woman— Look upon Her Dreadful Countenance if You Dare!' "

"I'm not angry," she said indignantly, instantly forgetting her dreadful worries at the sight of Yancy's inviting grin. He did have such lovely straight, very white teeth. "I'm just—thoughtful."

"Yeah? Then do you suppose you could think up some food for me? I'm kinda hungry."

"Always and forever," Lorena grumbled, rising.

"How 'bout some real grub this time, instead of watery soup?" Yancy wheedled.

"It's not watery soup; it's broth. And your physician has ordered that you stay on a light diet," Lorena said, hands on hips. "In spite of the fact that he knows very well that Missy and Elijah have been sneaking you eggs and bacon and grits and kidney pie."

"Busted again," Yancy said cheerfully. "So how's about you sneak me some of that roast beef? I can smell it, you know. I have a very keen sense of smell, and it's starving me right to death."

Lorena turned and went to the door, her spine set in a stubborn ruler-straight line.

Yancy called after her, "Rena?"

In spite of herself, a swift secret smile played on her lips and she turned. "Yes?"

"Thanks. For everything. I'm pretty sure that you're my best friend," he said innocently.

Now she smiled happily at him. "I'm pretty sure, too, Yancy. And I'm very glad. One day, perhaps, you may know just how glad I am to be your friend."

CHAPTER TWENTY-ONE

"Yancy, there's a telegram for you," Lorena said, holding it out to him. He read it quickly then looked up with a glad smile. "My dad and Becky are coming. They left Lexington early this morning, so they'll probably be here tomorrow—if the trains are running as scheduled."

"I'm so glad," Lorena said. "When we wrote to invite them to come stay with us, I honestly didn't think they'd come. I mean, travel these days, especially into Richmond, is so complicated, with all the soldiers and supplies traveling everywhere. I had the idea that the Amish are so unworldly that they wouldn't get in the middle of it."

"You're right about that," Yancy said, pulling himself up straighter in bed. "I can't see anyone in the community attempting it right now, except for my father. He's different from the Amish that have always lived in that world."

Automatically Lorena bent over and fixed Yancy's pillows as he talked. They had done this so many times that Yancy had learned just how to lean forward so she could easily rearrange the three fat pillows behind his back, and Lorena knew exactly how to fix them the way Yancy liked them.

It was July 9, 1862. Lorena had been taking care of Yancy for two weeks now, and they had slowly evolved into a familiar routine where Lorena anticipated Yancy's needs, and he was sensitive to when she was tired, when she wanted to talk, when she wanted to be quiet, and when she wanted to read to him or write letters for him. They fit together very well.

Becky and Daniel did arrive early the next morning. The hospital was not quite so urgent now, so Dr. Hayden had stayed home to meet them. He and Lily waited in the parlor. As always, for every minute she was awake, Lorena was with Yancy.

The knocker sounded, and shooing away Missy, Lily and Dr. Hayden rushed to open the door. They eagerly greeted Daniel and Becky as if they were old friends and brought them into the parlor. "We're so happy that you're here. The trains must be running fairly well," Lily said. "Richmond is like a beehive filled with angry bees these days, with lots of buzzing around and in and out."

Daniel replied, "It sure is. But the trains were running, all right, transporting soldiers and lots of foodstuffs and material from the valley. So the trains, it seemed to me, were traveling as fast as they could steam."

"Seemed like about two hundred miles an hour to me," Becky said drily. "It's the first time I've been on a train, and after I get back home I hope it's my last. They're like great black, growling, smoky dragons. I may have nightmares."

Daniel said affectionately, "My wife exaggerates. She's got more backbone than I do."

Becky looked up at him. "Thank you, husband. . .I think."

She certainly didn't look as rugged as Daniel Tremayne, but then, no woman would. The Haydens saw in him a man that had experienced a hard life, and it had toughened him considerably. His reddish blond hair was bleached almost white by the sun. He was handsome in a leathery, rough way, with a chiseled jaw, straight nose, and sharp blue eyes. The scars by his mouth and on his jawbone were pronounced and added to the aura of sinewy strength.

Yancy looked nothing like him, except that he was built like his father. Over six feet, with long, muscular legs, wide shoulders, thick chest, brawny biceps—in this frame they were almost identical.

Even their hands looked alike.

Rebecca Tremayne was no fainting flower certainly. Tall and slim, Becky always stood and sat very erect, with a severe grace. With her thick jet black hair, penetrating dark blue eyes and wide, firm mouth, she was the picture of a woman of vitality and fortitude. She was not beautiful, but she was attractive in a magnetic way, even dressed in the sober Amish garments and her modest prayer cap.

Now Dr. Hayden asked, "Would you like some refreshment?"

Daniel answered, "Thank you, but we are very anxious to see Yancy, you know."

Dr. Hayden nodded and rose, motioning them to follow him up the stairs. "Certainly. I'll take you to his room, but it's time for his morning coffee anyway, so I'll have Missy bring up a pot. Would that suit you, or would you care for something else? Tea, or fresh juice?"

"We would dearly love coffee," Becky said gratefully. "Daniel and I are so glad that the Amish don't regard the love of coffee as a sin. I'm afraid we would be tempted to break that commandment if they did."

Dr. Hayden brought them to Yancy's room. He could sit up now, for Elijah had brought the wing chair that matched Lorena's up to his room, and he was comfortable in it for long periods of time.

Now he tried to stand up, but Becky rushed to him and threw her arms around him before he could rise. "Oh, Yancy, Yancy, how we've missed you! How frightened we were when we heard you'd been injured!" She released him and stepped back.

Daniel came and gave him a hug. "I'm so glad you're all right, son," he said huskily. "Hearing about you and not being there was the hardest time I've ever had."

"I'm really all right, you know. Good nursing." He winked at Lorena then said, "Becky, Father, this is Lorena. Lorena, meet my father and second mother."

Lorena held out her hand to Daniel, who took it and held it warmly for a minute, and she and Becky nodded politely, as gentlewomen did upon introductions. Lorena said, "Please, won't you make yourselves comfortable sitting on the bed? Yancy just got up a few minutes ago, and I have no intention of letting him laze around back in bed yet."

Daniel and Becky laughed as they seated themselves on the bed. Becky said, "I see you must be a good nurse for Yancy. Don't take any of his nonsense."

"She doesn't," Yancy sighed. "Reminds me a lot of you, Becky."

"I regard that as a compliment," Lorena said primly.

"It is," Yancy agreed.

Becky and Daniel looked Yancy up and down, Becky with narrowed critical eyes. "You look terrible," she said severely.

Yancy rolled his eyes. "Don't waste words or flatter me, Becky. Just go ahead and say what you mean."

"I like a lady that speaks her mind plainly, Mrs. Tremayne. I think that is a sign of honesty and therefore is a virtue," Lorena said.

"Then you and Becky are the most virtuous women I've ever met," Yancy said with exasperation.

"Thank you," Becky and Lorena said in unison, in the same sarcastic tone. They stared at each other in surprise, then both of them giggled like young girls.

"They are a lot alike, aren't they?" Daniel observed, bemused.

Missy brought coffee and served everyone. Becky eyed Yancy again with doubt. "Yancy, I really am concerned about you. Please, how do you feel? How are you progressing?" Lorena had written to them, explaining his injuries in detail.

"I'm doing well, considering," he answered thoughtfully. He still had not regained his robust color, and naturally he had lost weight. He hadn't required a bandage around his head for a few days now, as the incision was healing nicely. But it was still an angry red streak across his right temple, and the stitches weren't out yet, so the site was thick and still swollen, with the tie ends of the lurid black catgut sticking out.

He continued, "I'm having some headaches, but not so often and the pain gets less every day. And my arm is good. I've been using it a little, but Dr. Hayden says that I need to keep it pretty still for another few days. I just started getting up two days ago." He grinned. "That first time was a real corker. I thought, sure, I can just pop up out of this bed and walk around the room a few times. I stood up and then sat right back down, thank you very much, with the room spinning around me like a top and my eyes crossing with dizziness."

Lorena added, "You can joke, Yancy, but that scared me to death. If Elijah hadn't been here you would've crumpled right down to that floor."

"Maybe," he said carelessly. "Anyway, I took it real slow the next time, and got up a few times, just for a few minutes, day before yesterday. Yesterday I got up and even went downstairs," he said proudly.

"Really? Kinda soon, isn't it? Don't rush it, son," Daniel cautioned him.

Lorena sniffed. "Believe me, he won't do that again for a while. It took him about half an hour to get down the stairs, and then, of course, he was too weak to climb back up. Elijah had to carry him like a big baby."

"He did, too," Yancy agreed good-naturedly. "Embarrassing, that was. But I was so sure I could do it."

"Oh yes, you were so sure, Mr. Smarty-britches, and could anyone talk you out of it? No, sir, not Sergeant Yancy Tremayne, one of Stonewall's Boys," Lorena said disdainfully.

"Yeah, she's a whole lot like you, Beck. Good thing, too," Daniel observed cryptically.

"It is," Yancy agreed, grinning. "I'm really glad."

They talked for a while but it was true that Yancy did still tire easily. Becky and Daniel left him alone, meeting Elijah on the way out, as he was coming to help Yancy back to bed. They thanked him profusely for taking such good care of their son.

They settled in the guest bedroom and then had a very good lunch with Lily and Dr. Hayden. He explained Yancy's mental state more clearly to them. "I'm sure Lorena wrote you that memory loss is a very common result of a skull fracture. Yancy's appears to be fairly slight, but I've found that he has a natural reticence and won't talk much about his feelings, what he's worried about, if he's anxious. It's hard to tell the extent of his amnesia, but he does seem to recall all the most important people in his life—you, his family;

us, his close friends; General Jackson; his friends in the Stonewall Brigade. He's very lucid and insightful about the events in the war, so he seems to have retained all of his knowledge of being a soldier and of tactical and even strategic wartime moves."

Becky asked rather anxiously, "So it's clear what he remembers. But what about what he's lost? What memories?"

Dr. Hayden shook his head. "As I said, he's a reserved young man. He doesn't like to confide in me. He and Lorena have grown close, naturally, but she says he won't tell her anything about how his memory has been affected. I was hoping, Mr. Tremayne, that he might confide in you. It's obvious that he respects you, looks up to you, trusts you, and loves you deeply. I believe there's a better chance of his talking to you than to anyone."

Daniel nodded. "I'll talk to him alone this afternoon. And I hope you're right, Dr. Hayden. No one needs to go through something like this alone."

∾

Later that afternoon—after he and Becky rested for a time in their room—Daniel went to Yancy's bedroom and saw that he was awake, sitting up in bed, talking to Lorena.

Lorena shrewdly said, "Mr. Tremayne, if you're going to visit with Yancy awhile, I think I'll go take a nap. Certainly, though, come get me or my father if you should need us."

Daniel sat down by Yancy's bedside and they talked, mostly about home and Callie Jo, who was four years old now, and David, who was a precocious two-year-old. Yancy wanted to know all the news about everyone in the community, and so Daniel told him all the gossip he could possibly think of.

"Hannah Lapp is getting married in November," Daniel told him, watching him shrewdly. Yancy had been very enamored of Hannah when he was fifteen.

"Is she? Who's she marrying?" he asked with no sign of regret, only curiosity.

With relief Daniel replied, "Nate Raber. You remember him, Sol's middle son. Big beefy boy like Sol, but seems like a gentle and kind man."

"I do remember him, and he was a nice fellow," Yancy agreed. "He'll suit Hannah well. I'm glad for them."

Daniel studied him for a few moments then said quietly, "It's good that you remember people like Nate, that you barely knew. Dr. Hayden's told us that memory loss just goes along with your head injury. So how are you doing with that, son?"

Yancy frowned and stared into space. He was silent for long moments.

Daniel waited patiently and quietly.

Finally Yancy said in a voice that was somehow faraway, "For one thing, I have holes in my memory. They're usually connected to something I do remember. Like Leslie. I remember him, I remember what he looks like, I remember when I brought him here, home, from Manassas, but I can't remember *him*, exactly. I can't remember what he's like, his personality, his expressions. He's not really real to me. I remember him, but not all of him." He looked at Daniel anxiously. "Does that make sense?"

"Perfect sense," Daniel encouraged him. "Go on."

"And then sometimes I have mixed-up memories. I think I remember something, but somehow I don't feel like I'm recalling it right. It's fuzzy or something."

"So, what kind of things do you think have gotten mixed up in your memories like that?" Daniel asked.

For the first time Yancy dropped his gaze and fidgeted with the sheet. "Oh, just little things," he said vaguely. "Just—some things about some people."

Daniel believed one of those "people" was Lorena, but he didn't push him; he knew it wouldn't do any good.

Finally Yancy went on, "And then there's pictures that pop into my head that I know I should remember, but I can't get a grasp on them. One of these pictures I keep seeing is this man, with red hair and a mustache and a beard and a bright red flannel shirt, sitting on a kinda runty swaybacked mare. He's so familiar. But for the life of me I can't place the man."

Thoughtfully Daniel said, "Well, one thing I do know is that your mind is working right; your thought processes are obviously working well. You know, Yancy, Dr. Hayden is fairly sure that you're going to regain most, if not all, of your memories at some point. If you could tell him what you just told me, it would help him to understand where you are in terms of recovery, and then he'd be better able to help you. Do you think you could talk to him like you've just talked to me?"

"Guess so. I just don't like—complaining and fretting to people. You're different. You have to put up with me," he said with a mischievous grin, but then he sobered. "I see what you're saying, though, Father. I will talk to Dr. Hayden. I'll talk to him today."

Two days later, Becky and Lorena were sitting in the parlor with the Haydens' usual afternoon tea. Daniel and Dr. Hayden were with Yancy, and Lily had gone to the market with Elijah and Missy.

Becky and Lorena had hit it off instantly. They had already felt a kinship, because Yancy had told his family much about the Haydens, and likewise the Haydens felt they knew Yancy's family through him. Also, in the last two weeks since Yancy had been hurt, they had exchanged letters. It could be said that though they had actually been together for only two days, Becky and Lorena were already fast friends.

Lorena said, "Becky, I've decided that I'd like to give you a gift. Will you come up to my room with me?"

"Of course," she answered.

They went upstairs to Lorena's room, a cozy space with a white embroidered coverlet on the bed, a fine Persian rug, and paintings of lovely Victorian ladies on the walls. A small secretary was placed in front of the window, with a desk chair and two side chairs on either side.

Lorena sat down at the small desk and motioned for Becky to take a chair next to it. Lorena opened the middle drawer and pulled out a top-bound sketchpad. She skimmed lightly through the pages, stopped at one, and opened the sketchpad to that page. Handing it to Becky, she said, "I thought you might like to have this."

Becky took it and stared down at the drawing with amazement. The likeness of Yancy was astounding. Lorena had drawn him sitting up in bed, smiling. The scar on his forehead was clear, and she had faithfully represented that his face was somewhat drawn, his cheeks more hollow than usual. But still, she had captured that elusive boyishness Yancy had when he grinned, the sparkle in his eyes, the way they slightly wrinkled at the corners, the way his mouth stretched wide to reveal fine white teeth. She had gotten his proportions exactly correct, his shoulders still broad, and she had even captured his hands, the capable and masculine set of them. Until now Becky hadn't realized that Yancy had Daniel's hands. She loved Daniel's hands.

She looked up. "Lorena, this is simply wonderful. You've captured him, his spirit, his playfulness, even his masculinity. It's sheer genius."

"You know, I never seriously drew anything until the last two weeks," she mused. "I used to doodle, make very quick throwaway sketches of flowers or some child I had seen or a beautiful tree outlined in the evening sun, things like that.

"But when Yancy came and he was so terribly injured, he had to be monitored around the clock for two days. In those first days he was so sensitive to light that he couldn't bear anything but a single candle. I sat with him day and night, and it was too dark to sew, at all, or to read for very long. So in those long hours when Yancy was sleeping so deeply, I started just making line sketches. As the days went by and he could tolerate more light, I started doing these. And I found I was good at it," she finished simply.

"Yes, my dear, you are," Becky agreed. Curiously she looked down at the sketchbook. It was about half full. Lorena had turned several pages back to open to this sketch.

Now she watched Becky and finally said, "You're welcome to look at the others if you like. It's just that some of them are— difficult to see."

"Thank you," Becky said. She turned to the beginning and looked at the first sketch. It was, indeed, brutal. It had been done the first night he had been brought to the Haydens'. The shadows of his sunken cheeks were stark; his cheekbones looked so sharp they were skeletal. His right eye was an enormous dark swelling, and there was a bloodstain on the bandage around his forehead.

His other eye was closed. His mouth was tight and twisted slightly, as if he were in pain. "Ohh," Becky said, a half moan, half sigh.

Lorena said nothing.

Becky held the sketchbook up closer, letting the strong afternoon sunlight fall on it. She could see small round spots where the paper was slightly rippled. Teardrops.

Becky turned to the next one. A few days later, it seemed, for Yancy looked better, his eyes open, looking strangely vulnerable. Then there were several drawings of him sleeping, and his face was peaceful, each showing his injuries improving slightly. Then there were several studies of him sitting up, alert. In one of them he had an intent look on his face, obviously listening to something. Becky looked up. "Were you reading to him?"

"Yes."

With satisfaction Becky said, "I could tell. He always looked like that when I read aloud to the family at night. You've captured it perfectly. And I know very well that Yancy didn't sit for these. You did them from memory, didn't you?"

"Except for the ones when he slept," Lorena answered softly.

"Amazing," Becky murmured. She turned to the next one, the last one. It was a full page. Yancy was sitting in the big wing chair next to his bed. His body was completely relaxed. Gentle morning light shone through the window behind and to the side, lighting his face. His head had fallen slightly to the side, as he was sleeping. The lock of hair fell over his forehead. Though he still had the scar, his face in repose was, in fact, beautiful.

Abruptly Becky looked up at Lorena, her eyes wide. "You're in love with him," she blurted out.

Lorena pressed her eyes closed and whispered, "Yes. Terribly."

"You—you hide it so well. I didn't know until now, seeing these, your drawings of him. I never would have known, except for this."

"No one knows," Lorena said in a choked voice. "I've been very careful to hide it."

"Even from Yancy?" Becky demanded.

"Especially from Yancy. You see, Becky, last October Yancy was here for a whole day and night, which for him is a long visit. That night he told me that he was falling in love with me. He was so certain and sure of his feelings. I—I wasn't. I wasn't cold to him, but I held myself back from him. Purposefully. Because of some things in my past, I just didn't want to feel anything for another man, and I thought I could keep myself from falling in love.

"But the very night he came here, so terribly hurt, and I was so frightened, and he seemed so faraway, it stripped me of all that stupid pride and stubbornness. I realized how very, very much I love him."

"But then why don't you tell him? I can understand that you wouldn't want to complicate things at first, when he was so ill, but now—?"

Lorena shook her head. "I can't. Because he's forgotten me."

Instantly Becky understood. "Oh no. He doesn't remember."

"No. I think that now he feels for me much like he does his sister, Callie Jo." A crooked smile came across her full lips. "Once he even told me that he was pretty sure I was his best friend. And I am. But that's not all it is. . .was. It was so much more. Yancy is not the only one that has lost something here. I lost the best and perhaps the only chance for happiness I'll ever have." Suddenly tears rolled down her cheeks. She bent her head and sobbed, a heart-wrenching sound.

Quickly Becky came to her, bent down, and wrapped her arms around Lorena's trembling shoulders. "Don't, don't, darling, don't. Your hope is not in Yancy. You must have hope in the Lord. The Proverbs promise, 'The hope of the righteous shall be gladness.' So be glad, dear Lorena. Yancy's heart will bring back the remembrance of love."

July simmered on. In the aftermath of the Battle of Seven Days, Lee and the Army of Northern Virginia remained camped close to Richmond. Eagerly Yancy read every single newspaper he could get his hands on, starving for information about the army and particularly about the Army of the Shenandoah Valley. As always, Jackson managed to keep his movements secret. Journalists could only speculate, and generally their speculations were wrong.

President Lincoln and Secretary of War Steward, frustrated with General McClellan's stubborn reluctance to make any offensive moves with the Army of the Potomac without shrill and unreasonable demands for anywhere from 50,000 to 100,000 reinforcements, finally decided to meet him halfway. They formed the new "Army of Virginia" and put General John Pope in charge of it. All of the Richmond newspapers reported Pope's pompous and blustery speech to his men upon accession to command.

Yancy read as much as he could, but he was subject to violent headaches, so Lorena still often read to him. One hot stuffy afternoon Yancy had given up sitting in his chair, his headache was so severe. He lay in bed in his darkened room with a cool cloth on his forehead, his eyes closed.

Lorena skimmed the newspapers and picked out light, amusing things to read to him. "Listen to this," she said. "The *Richmond Report* reads, 'General Pope bombastically told his men: "My headquarters are in the saddle." When our valiant General Stonewall Jackson heard this, he shouted, "I can whip any man who doesn't know his headquarters from his hindquarters." ' Isn't that hilarious?"

Yancy scoffed, "General Jackson never said that. He wouldn't say anything like that." His voice was weak, with that slight petulant note that came to people in severe pain. His eyes were closed and restlessly he fidgeted with the cold compress.

Lorena rose, took the cloth from his forehead, and dipped it into the icy water in the bowl on the washstand. Folding it securely, she placed it back on Yancy's forehead. "Why do you say that General Jackson wouldn't say that?" she asked curiously. "I had the impression that he's a man with little use for such theatrics."

"He is," Yancy answered shortly. "But that reply is boastful. General Jackson is never boastful. Never."

Wistfully Lorena thought, *He knows and remembers everything about Stonewall Jackson, down to the last detail of his uniform and every facet of his personality. Oh, how I wish he remembered me that well!*

"Yancy, I can see you're in pain," she said quietly. "I know you're trying very hard to get better as fast as you can, but you simply cannot speed up the healing process by sheer force of will. You never ask for laudanum anymore, but today I think you should take just maybe ten drops and see if you can nap a little."

He shifted restlessly. "What time is it?"

"It's only one thirty."

"In—in the afternoon?" he asked.

Lorena was somber when she heard this. Yancy hadn't been confused about the time for a couple of weeks now. This was a definite setback. "Yes, it's early enough in the afternoon that a short nap shouldn't keep you from sleeping tonight."

After a short hesitation he said, "Okay. I do feel kinda tired."

Lorena gave him ten drops of laudanum. "I'll come back and check on you in about an hour," she told him. "But if you need anything, just call. I'll be in my room right across the hall."

He nodded, already drifting off to sleep.

She left and went to her bedroom. Since Yancy had been better, he didn't require constant bedside monitoring, so Lorena left him for naps and at night. But since he seemed somewhat worse today, she pulled up one of her desk chairs right by the door so she could hear him if he called. And then she sketched.

Still, Yancy continued to improve, in spite of occasional setbacks such as the one he'd had that day.

General Pope's Army of Virginia moved northwest of Richmond, arrayed along the foot of the Blue Ridge Mountains. McClellan's Army of the Potomac stayed at Harrison's Landing on the James River, where they had retreated to after the Seven Days battle. It was obvious that the two armies were going to try to overtake Richmond in a pincer movement.

General Lee sent Stonewall Jackson to the north to deal with Pope. This news made Yancy so restless he was miserable, knowing that his Army of the Valley would soon be in battle.

The last week of July he announced that he was going to rejoin the army on August 1.

Dr. Hayden said calmly, "Oh? And what, exactly, are you going to do when you rejoin?"

"I'm on General Jackson's staff. I'm a courier, you know that. They're in the north, and they need me," he answered with a touch of impatience.

"Mmm-hmm. And so, are you planning on riding Midnight to perform these courier duties?"

"Of course. I'm feeling much better and stronger. I'm going to ride for about an hour this afternoon, and then slowly increase the time each day until the end of the month. Then I should be fit to rejoin my unit."

"I advise against it, Yancy," Dr. Hayden warned him. "There is a world of difference between riding a high-spirited horse like Midnight and taking long walks and climbing up and down stairs."

"I've ridden horses since I was five years old, sir. I appreciate your concern, but I'm not at all worried."

But he should have been. He rode Midnight for an hour that afternoon. He returned home with a headache so excruciating that it literally left him bedridden for two days. And his arm, though the hairline crack was fully healed, had not been exercised and was pitifully weak. Trying to control Midnight, which Yancy had taken so much for granted before, made his arm hurt. It throbbed so deeply and incessantly that he finally asked Lorena to bind it up and immobilize it again.

As he lay in bed, fighting the pain but knowing that he would have to ask for laudanum to be able to rest at all, he came to the bitter realization that he had been insidiously weakened by his wounds. He knew then that it would be some time before he could join General Jackson again.

Dr. Hayden improvised a cautious regimen of exercise, progressing very slowly for Yancy, and he followed it faithfully. But August of 1862 proved to be the most maddening, frustrating month he had ever endured in his life

On August 9, General N. P. Banks, Pope's commander of II Corps, attacked Jackson at Cedar Mountain. A relatively small but bloody battle ensued; in fact, it would have been called a skirmish except for the high number of casualties on both sides. The Army of the Valley sustained about 1,350 casualties—killed, wounded, or missing—while Pope's Army of Virginia lost almost

CROSSING

2,400 men. But General Jackson was once again victorious. Pope's army retreated, and the weary, dispirited troops made the miserable retreat northward to Culpeper.

On August 10, Yancy had another headache, though it was not so painful as those he had endured before. They had been diminishing both in number and severity.

Lorena had noticed that any stress or worry tended to cause them, as happened when Yancy exercised too vigorously, and mentioned this to him.

He was coming downstairs regularly now, and this morning they sat together in the kitchen while Missy made breakfast. Yancy closely perused each newspaper, frowning. "Where are the casualty lists?" he muttered.

Sitting with him, Lorena said soothingly, "Yancy, you know that it takes a couple of days for those to be published. Be patient."

"It's so hard," he murmured distractedly. "They're my men. They're my friends."

"I know," Lorena said sympathetically. "Every single day of war is hard." She reached over to cover his hand with hers.

He grasped it hard—as if it were a lifeline—for long moments, his shoulders and head bowed. Lorena stayed very still. Then with a sigh he released her and sat up. "It is. I don't for the life of me understand why I miss it. Something must be wrong with me."

"You don't miss war, Yancy," Lorena said gently. "You miss your friends, and you feel a responsibility toward them and to General Jackson. That is an honorable and just motive to wish to return to the war. And I believe you will. . .soon."

For Yancy it would not be soon enough.

On August 17, the Richmond papers were afire with the news that General McClellan and his Army of the Potomac had embarked for northeastern Virginia, to join forces with General Pope's Army of Virginia. It was clear that they now planned to drive toward Richmond from the north.

In the next few days, Lee made his plans and began the brilliant countermoves of the two Federal armies. These maneuvers culminated in not only a victory over them but, in the end, with both Pope and McClellan suffering devastating defeats. These last terrible days of August were referred to as the Manassas Campaign. Once again the humble crossroads was to become the center of a raging war.

To Yancy's vast relief, the newspaper coverage was good, though it dealt with the campaign in generalities. General Lee's movements could not be hidden or kept secret, and so word of the events in the campaign were generally only delayed by one day.

General Lee sent Jackson to sweep around Pope's right and flank him. This movement of the Army of the Shenandoah Valley was kept a tight secret, and ultimately it trapped Pope into thinking that Jackson was retreating from northern Virginia. Jackson's first triumph was the capture of the Federal stores at Manassas Junction, a truly welcome gift for his always hungry and ragged troops.

On August 29, Pope attacked Jackson in force, thoroughly believing in a quick and easy victory. He was wrong. Jackson's army fought ferociously, and Pope flinched. The next day Longstreet arrived. In the Battle of Second Manassas, the Confederates shattered Pope's army, both physically and mentally. McClellan didn't arrive in time to save him. With this humiliating defeat, both armies fell back in ignominy, harried and driven and tortured by Jackson's pursuit, until they finally managed to flee in disarray back over the Potomac River.

On the last day of August, Yancy read of the Confederate's triumph and that they were camped at Chantilly, in northeastern Virginia. It was only twenty-five miles from Washington DC. When he read this, Yancy got chills. He had no way of knowing, but somehow he thought that this might be the critical time for General Lee to invade. Yancy knew that General Jackson, since the days of his Valley Campaign, had continuously called for an offensive action into the North. Now, after the glorious victory at Second Manassas, Yancy just had an instinct that maybe this time General Lee and President Davis might listen to him.

He went to Dr. Hayden, who was sitting in the garden, also reading the newspapers. As Yancy approached, Dr. Hayden looked up, and for an instant a shadow crossed his kind face. He knew.

"Sir, I believe that I have recovered enough to rejoin General Jackson," Yancy said bluntly, coming to stand before him, his arms crossed stubbornly. "I may not be exactly as well as I was before I was hurt, but I feel good and strong."

Dr. Hayden nodded. "You have improved almost miraculously this last month, Yancy. I'm proud of you, for you have shown courage and true determination in your recovery. I am very sorry to see you go, but I have to agree with you. I believe it is time."

Yancy was so eager that he left the very next day. He felt a deep urgency, for he sensed that General Lee would move very soon. At dawn the family was up to see him off, assembled in the foyer. He kissed Missy and Lily and Lorena and shook hands with Elijah and Dr. Hayden.

"I can never thank you enough," he said in a deep voice. "I am so blessed by the Lord to have a second family such as you. Pray for me, and I'll pray for you all to have peace, undisturbed. I—I love you all." A little embarrassed, he hurried outside.

Lorena followed him. Great luminous tears shimmered in her dark eyes, and impulsively she threw herself into his arms, whispering, "Oh, I will miss you so terribly, Yancy."

Surprised, he drew her close to him. For a short moment some shadow, perhaps of recognition, perhaps of remembrance, passed through his mind. But it was like a vapor, a mist that disappears once the light touches it.

Again he kissed her lightly on the cheek. "Don't cry, Rena. I'd rather remember you saying good-bye with a smile."

She drew back from him, scrubbed her eyes with her apron, and then determinedly gave him a smile. "Ride fast, fight hard, and hurry back. I'll wait for you."

Again Yancy had that odd flash of almost-recognition. But this was a hard day, and he had a hard ride ahead of him to enter back into a grim and harsh war. Returning her smile, he gave her a mock bow, turned, and hurried down the walk.

Lorena watched until he mounted Midnight, spurred him, and galloped up the quiet street.

In his heart, he knew she was crying and told himself it was just because she was worried about his returning to the war, but something he couldn't quite latch on to whispered that it was much more.

CHAPTER TWENTY-TWO

Yancy left Richmond at dawn on September 2. On September 3, just before dawn, he stood at the entrance to General Stonewall Jackson's headquarters tent. He had ridden about one hundred ten miles in twenty-four hours.

The tent flap was open, and Yancy could see the general inside, sitting at his camp desk, reading the Bible by the light of a single guttering candle. He looked exactly as Yancy had pictured him so often in the past two months—dusty, wrinkled, shabby, but still with that indefinable aura of strength and authority that Jackson emanated without effort.

"Sir?" Yancy called softly. "Permission to enter?"

Jackson looked up, squinting slightly, then rose and came forward without hesitation. Yancy stood at strict attention, but Jackson held out his hand and Yancy gladly shook it. "So, Sergeant Tremayne, I see you're still alive. Glad to see it."

"Thank you, sir. I am, too."

Jackson turned and motioned for Yancy to follow him and sit on the camp stool opposite his desk. "I'll have to write Anna; she's been after me for news of you. I did hear at Chimborazo that Dr. Hayden took you home to care for you. Sounded like good news to me, though I never had the pleasure of meeting Dr. Hayden.

Friends of yours, the Haydens?"

"Yes, sir. Very good friends."

"Good, good. Looks like they took fine care of you."

"They did, sir. I'm ready to rejoin. I'm sorry I was away for so long. I wanted to come back as soon as I could."

Jackson's startling blue eyes twinkled slightly. "Missed us, did you?"

"I did, sir. It's hard to explain. I just know I belong here."

"That's explanation enough for me, Sergeant. We're glad you're back, and I'm especially glad Midnight is back. He runs circles around even General Lee's couriers," Jackson said with evident relish. "I would have conscripted him while you were out, but it wouldn't have done any good since he won't let anyone but you ride him."

"Sir?" Yancy said, puzzled.

"You didn't know?" Jackson asked in surprise. "Contrary horse threw half of my aides before we figured out that he wasn't having any rider fumbling around on his back except for you. Even Sergeant Stevens couldn't ride him."

Yancy's eyes grew wide. "Midnight threw Peyton?" he blurted out; then, recovering himself somewhat, he added, "Sir?"

"Sure did. Tossed him onto a caisson and bruised his collarbone. Stevens came back to headquarters riding his own horse with Midnight tethered behind him. Said it made him nervous, that stubborn horse behind him. Felt like Midnight was planning to attack him again, from the rear, at any time. So we went ahead and sent him on to you."

Yancy was amazed at this speech coming from the terse Stonewall Jackson. He didn't think he'd ever heard the general say so many sentences in a row. And then he astonished Yancy again, for he threw his head back and laughed aloud in a creaky, rusty manner. Yancy couldn't help but grin.

Stonewall seemed to have amused himself mightily, for he laughed on and on, and finally Yancy started laughing, since it was contagious. Yancy thought, *This is crazy, me and the great Stonewall Jackson sitting here laughing like the village idiot. Maybe I really did lose my mind when I got shot in the head.*

Finally, though, the madness came to an end, and with a final chuckle, Stonewall rose. Yancy snapped to attention as Jackson said, "You look tired, Sergeant. I happen to know that Stevens's tent is the second one down the lane there, on the right, though I don't know how anyone could mistake it. It's bigger than mine and usually sounds like there's a rowdy party going on there. Go get some rest."

"Yes, sir!" Yancy saluted then turned to leave.

But behind him he heard General Jackson say softly, "Sergeant Tremayne?"

Yancy turned back. "Yes, sir?"

"You are feeling well, are you not?"

"Yes, sir. Very well, sir. I'm ready."

"Good, good," he murmured his familiar refrain. He resumed his seat and put on his spectacles. "You're going to need to be. We're all going to need to be. Dismissed."

Yancy gave Midnight to one of the "cubs," very young soldiers of thirteen and fourteen that General Jackson had adamantly refused to put in the line of battle. He always had three or four of them ostensibly on his staff as "assistants." Mostly they helped Jim with fetching and carrying and took care of the staff's horses.

One of Yancy's favorites, Willy Harper, was feeding apple quarters to Midnight, caressing his nose and murmuring nonsense to him. Willy reminded Yancy of Seth Glick, the young boy who had tailed after Yancy so much when he had first arrived in the community. Like Seth, Willy had red hair and freckles and a friendly grin. He was short and had a small frame. He looked even younger than his thirteen years.

As Yancy approached, Willy came to attention and saluted, and he looked like a little boy playing dress-up in a soldier's costume. Yancy had to stifle a grin, because in Willy's saluting hand was the last quarter of the apple. "At ease there, Private Harper."

"Thank you, sir. I'm glad you're back, Sergeant Tremayne. Did you get hurt bad?"

"Naw, just addled my brains a little bit," Yancy answered, brushing one finger against the scar on his forehead. "I think they're all back in order now. You going to take care of Midnight for me? We've had a long, hard ride. He needs to be brushed good, and then I'd appreciate it if you'd wash him down, Willy. We both got pretty muddy on the road." Yancy looked down at his new thigh-high cavalry boots regretfully. They were splattered with gloppy red mud up to the knees.

"I'll take really good care of Midnight," Willy promised. "And—and then, if you want me to, I'll report to your tent and clean your boots, sir."

Yancy started to say a stern no—after all, Willy wasn't his body servant—but then he realized, perhaps with a wisdom beyond his years, that the boy sort of hero-worshipped him, and probably Peyton Stevens, too, and this was Willy's way of being included with them. So Yancy answered, "That's nice of you, Private. I am tired and I would appreciate it if you'd take care of that chore for me. And bring me an apple, too, if you've got an extra one."

"Yes, sir!" Willy said, saluting.

"Carry on," Yancy ordered.

Like the young boy that he was, Willy led Midnight off, talking a mile a minute to the horse and grinning his goofy smile.

Yancy hurried to Peyton's tent, which indeed was unmistakable. The tent flap was open. Inside Chuckins was stirring a big pot on the camp stove; a delicious scent of stewed beef floated out of the tent. Peyton lazed on his padded cot, reading a novel with a lurid cover. Sandy Owens dozed on another cot.

"Smells good, Chuckins," Yancy said, strolling into the tent. "Daddy come through again, Peyton?"

They all hurried to him and clapped him on the back so many times that Yancy thought he'd be sore tomorrow. After their greetings they settled down to catch up on the last two months.

"First we heard that you got shot in the head," Chuckins said soberly. "We were sure you were dead. But then General Jackson got word about one of the doctors at Chimborazo taking you to his house to take care of you and that you'd been shot twice but not mortally."

Yancy nodded. "True. Bullet grazed my head"—he lifted up the heavy locks of his hair to show them the scar—"and fractured my skull. Another bullet got me in the arm, but it wasn't too bad. I'm friends with the Hayden family, and Dr. Hayden was one of the doctors working at the hospital after the battle. He decided to take me home. I must've been real lucky. I heard there were about fifteen thousand wounded after the Seven Days battle."

This launched a highly detailed, technical description of the battles Yancy had missed. After several minutes of Peyton and Sandy trying to describe the fields and order of battle, the four of them sat down on the floor of the tent and began to draw in the dirt. Chuckins produced some dried beans, and they were arranged to show the different units and their placement in the battles. They started talking about the top-secret march of the Army of the Valley to flank Pope as the Army of Northern Virginia began to march north to meet him.

Peyton told Yancy, "You missed the fireworks then, boyo. Stonewall kept the march so secret he wouldn't even tell the division chiefs where we were going. I was given one fat envelope in my courier's bag and told to go three miles north to the first crossroads I came to and wait there. Didn't know how long, didn't know what for. I found out later that Stonewall told the commanders, 'March up this road. You'll come to a crossroads and there'll be a courier there with orders telling you which way to go. At the next crossroads, the same.' "

Peyton grinned mischievously. "So there I sat, me and Senator, in the middle of nowhere at these unnamed crossroads. Finally, after about six hours, I heard marching and saw a cloud of red dust, and out of it came Colonel B. W. Ripley of the 35th South Carolina, riding like thunder and fury. I mounted up in a hurry to meet him in the dead center of the crossroads. He came up, horse snorting and stamping, and him glaring at me with an evil eye. I handed him the dispatch. He tore it open, looked up at me, and commenced to cussing fit to turn the air blue. His command finally drew up, and he turned in the saddle and yelled, 'That way!' and pointed to the left-hand road. They started marching that way. The whole time they passed by he sat there and cussed me up, down, sideways, and back again."

Through his laughter Yancy asked, "What did you do? Weren't you mad?"

"Not really," Peyton carelessly replied. "It was, you know,

impersonal. Like watching a force of nature. I was kinda fascinated, to tell the truth. He ended it when the last troops turned up the road. It was like capping a boiling pot. *Thump.* Silence. He rode off. Kinda hated to see him go."

Another one of the couriers, Smithson "Smitty" Gaines, suddenly stuck his head in the tent. "Oh, hi, Yancy. Glad you're back. Y'all won't ever guess."

Yancy sighed. "We're marching."

Smitty nodded. "Yep. Cook up three days' rations, strike the tents, and pack up tonight. We're leaving at dawn tomorrow." He popped out of view as abruptly as he had appeared.

"I knew it," Yancy muttered.

"You always do, but I didn't think even you could read Stonewall's mind from Richmond," Peyton said with no inkling of how close to the truth his words seemed to Yancy. "You know what, Yance? You're looking pretty rough. Why don't you eat some of that stew and take a rest."

"Sounds good," Yancy admitted. He stood up, took off his boots, and plopped down on his cot. "Except I think I'll eat when I wake up. I'm pretty tired."

The other three tiptoed out and pulled the tent flap shut, but Yancy could still hear his friends talking.

"I'm glad he's back," Sandy Owens said quietly, and Peyton agreed.

Chuckins said happily, "Me, too. I think it's a good sign. Stonewall's Boys are back again."

Yancy grinned as he closed his eyes, and in just a few moments he was asleep.

If he could have, General Thomas "Stonewall" Jackson would have kept their destination secret from everyone in the Army of Northern Virginia except for himself and General Lee and General Longstreet, and he had his doubts about Longstreet. But of course this was not possible. It was known to everyone in the South that on September 4, 1862, General Lee led his 40,000 battle-hardened men toward Maryland.

The first leg of the march was from the army's headquarters in Chantilly to a small Virginia town on the Potomac, Leesburg. Yancy and Peyton were, as usual, riding with the other couriers just behind Jackson's staff, who followed him. The staff officers kept a very loose formation behind the general. Yancy and Peyton had become favorites of the staff, as they were also obviously favorites of their general, so they often let them slowly ride up until they, too, were just behind Jackson.

As they passed through the small village, a woman standing in a doorway suddenly stiffened with recognition when she saw Jackson, her eyes wide. She ran fast, dashed into the road, and threw her scarf down in front of Jackson's horse.

General Jackson halted and stared at the woman on the sidewalk, obviously mystified.

One of the staff officers rode up close to him and murmured, "She means you to ride over it, General."

Now he smiled at the lady, who smiled back as if her face were suddenly lit by heavenly beams. Jackson doffed his cap and slowly rode over the scarf.

Behind him, the staff and aides exchanged delighted grins. Jackson was famous now, perhaps second only to Robert E. Lee. His face was well known from portraits in the newspapers. Ever since his triumphs at Cedar Mountain and Second Manassas, the people along the marches had recognized him. They often crowded Little Sorrel, hugging her; others touching the general's boots; mothers holding up babies for him to lay his hand on their heads; ladies thrusting handkerchiefs up to him to touch; still others handing him flowers and small flags and often, since his oddities had become known, lemons. No matter how often it happened, no matter if it was one lady or a crowd, General Jackson was obviously baffled by the attention, and it made him embarrassed and awkward. His staff loved it.

They marched and marched. On the ninth, General Lee ordered Jackson to his old command and the scene of such drama, Harpers Ferry. The strategic village was once again in the hands of the Federals, and it was vital for Lee to take it to protect the rear of the army, who were to march to Hagerstown, Maryland, and then farther north to engage the enemy.

After arranging his artillery in a careful sweep surrounding the town, Stonewall stood with his staff on a crag of Bolivar's Heights, looking down at the Federals ensconced in Harpers Ferry. The town was surrounded by hills, which made it easy to attack and impossible to defend.

One of Jackson's officers said, "It sure is down in a bowl, isn't it?"

Jackson said succinctly, "I'd rather take the place forty times than undertake to defend it once."

And so, almost before the first rolling artillery volley was finished, the Federals sent up the white flag, and 12,000 men surrendered. Jackson again had captured a rich unspoiled treasure—13,000 small arms, seventy-three cannons, and countless foodstuffs, supplies, and other stores.

It was September 15, 8:00 a.m. Even before he went down into the town, Jackson called Yancy to him. "Dispatch to General Lee. Double-quick, Sergeant Tremayne."

"Yes, sir." Yancy saluted and Midnight took off in a flurry of dust and smoke that lingered on the air. It was sixteen hard miles, on the old Shepherdstown Road and crossing the Potomac at Boteler's Ford, to Lee's headquarters just west of Sharpsburg, Maryland.

At three o'clock, Yancy returned. He was covered in dust, his boots wet to the knee. Midnight was lathering, his legs covered with mud up to his hocks. Still he pranced and stamped.

Yancy jumped off and hurried to Jackson, who was still in the village making arrangements to parole the prisoners. "Sir," he said breathlessly, "I have a return from General Lee."

Eyeing him shrewdly, Jackson took the note. He looked up at Yancy and asked, "Did you see the ground?"

"Yes, sir."

"And?"

"General Lee is hard-pressed, sir. Vast numbers of the enemy have massed east of Sharpsburg."

Jackson nodded. Lee's dispatch had said that if Jackson had not overcome Harpers Ferry that day, Lee was contemplating a retreat. He urged Jackson to come to Sharpsburg with all speed.

They marched all night, quite a feat after the last two weeks of marching and maneuvering and skirmishing. But they were Jackson's foot cavalry, and they were relentless. They reached Sharpsburg early on the morning of September 16. Two armies faced each other, intent on destruction, across a winding, cheerful little creek called Antietam.

It was September 17, 1862. Johnny Rebs called it the Battle of Sharpsburg; Yankees called it the Battle of Antietam. Each of the places on that horrendous battlefield carried its own too-clear imprint.

Dunker Church, where the bloodletting began at six o'clock that morning. And where Stonewall Jackson, calm and imperturbable in the midst of screaming bullets and murderous artillery, directed his men in his final counterattack, saving the Confederate left from complete destruction.

The North Woods, where General Joe Hooker's Union troops harassed the Confederate left all the day, visions of blue coats weaving in and out of the soft-wooded shadows, and sometimes storming out in waves, men in gray falling before them.

The East and West Woods, where both blue and gray fought and died, the sweet glades scarred by rifle fire and artillery explosions and men lying on the ground, coloring it scarlet.

The Cornfield, twenty acres of what had been well-ordered rows of sweet corn, with men of both the North and the South lying as they fell, just as the cornstalks lay from the onslaught. On that day the lines surged back and forth over the Cornfield no less than eight times. In the end neither army possessed it, only the dead.

The Sunken Road, which came to be known as Bloody Lane, because it was filled in some places six deep with Confederate dead.

Burnside's Bridge, surrounded in some places six deep with Federal dead.

General John B. McClellan was timid. He imagined General

CROSSING

Robert E. Lee as all-powerful, and in his head he always was certain that the Army of Northern Virginia was half again, or sometimes twice as numerous as it was. "Little Mac," as he was affectionately known in the army, hated to risk his men. He could map out grand strategies, but when it came to completely committing his army to an aggressive offense, as General Lee always did, Little Mac would procrastinate, always asserting that the job could not be done unless he had more reinforcements, more cannons, more rifles, more ammunition, more aides, more couriers, more food, more tents, more blankets, more shoes, and more intelligence. Even his defensive moves were halfhearted and ineffective because of his reluctance to fight.

At Sharpsburg he outnumbered General Lee's army almost two to one, with a force of 75,000 facing Lee's army of 40,000. All that day McClellan attacked and defended in a piecemeal fashion. The Confederates cut up those Yankee pieces even more, and in pieces they retreated.

The Army of Northern Virginia lost over 10,000 men, killed, wounded, and missing. Federal casualties were close to 12,500. When the final awful numbers were tabulated, 22,546 men had fallen on that Bloodiest Day.

One thing happened to Yancy that day that should have made him glad. But because it happened at such a grim and critical moment during the Battle of Sharpsburg, he recalled it with wonder, mixed with the pall of dread that overlaid his every image of that battle.

When Jackson had withdrawn from Harpers Ferry, he had left General A. P. Hill's division behind to deal with the parole of their 12,000 prisoners and to inventory and transport the captured guns and material to Sharpsburg. Consequently, he was late arriving on the field; in fact, he arrived just at the moment that the Confederate right was about to crumble, and thus the Federals could easily have flanked them and then utterly destroyed them.

When General Jackson sighted the first of Hill's troops as they appeared on the Shepherdstown Road, Jackson sharply called out for Yancy. He rode up and the general grabbed Midnight's bridle.

"General Hill is just arriving on the road, there, to the south. No time to write a dispatch; ride to him as fast as you can and ascertain if he is still at his strength and numbers or if he has lost stragglers along the road. And hurry back to me."

"Yes, sir," Yancy said and hurried off toward the south.

General A. P. Hill was already at the line of battle and was directing the first brigades marching into their positions.

Yancy rode at a blinding gallop to the front, through confusion of soldiers hurrying to get placed along the line. He drew up to the head of the brigade. Then he reined in Midnight so abruptly that he reared and screamed. General Hill turned, and in a single blinding instant, Yancy's mind was filled with images imprinted as surely as if he were seeing them with his eyes instead of his brain:

General A. P. Hill, in his blazing red flannel shirt, shouting orders and cursing at the top of his lungs on the bloody center of the Battle of Gaines' Mill.

Grinning at Yancy. "Orders from Stonewall, huh? What? Attack the North Pole?"

Looking down at his right arm, watching the dark stain spread.

Stunning blow to his head. . .gray. . .then black.

Yancy remembered it all—the noise, the screams, the guns, the smell, the fear, the pain. It filled his mind for a moment, and he had to shake his head to clear it. Then he rode up to General Hill and shouted, "General Hill! Message from General Jackson!"

And so he thought no more about it. He knew he would not have time until much later that night.

As night fell, the few guns firing here and there spluttered out. Lee's officers were expecting an order to retreat. In spite of the fact that the Confederates had undoubtedly driven the Federals from the field in a shamefaced retreat, the Army of Northern Virginia had been mauled badly, and withdrawal would have been understandable and perfectly honorable.

But Robert E. Lee stood his ground.

The Army of Northern Virginia camped that night. Fatalistically they ate confiscated supplies more plentiful than they had since

Second Manassas, anticipating another cruel fight the next day. Faithfully they believed in Robert E. Lee and with certainty believed, in spite of their cruelly reduced numbers, that they would drive the hordes of men in blue from the field once again.

Yancy and Peyton Stevens found a grassy swath under a bullet-scarred oak tree in the West Woods, where General Jackson had set up his overnight headquarters. Both of them were deadly tired, though they only felt a peculiar numbness, and they were ravenously hungry. They built a fire, neither of them speaking, only gathering up wood and hollowing out a shallow hole and going through the business of lighting the wood in a light breeze.

Peyton Stevens was pale and drawn and looked twice his age. Yancy was pasty-faced, the hollows of his jaw deep, his cheekbones sharp, his eyes red. They had fat peaches from one of the orchards they had passed on their march from Harpers Ferry. As always, Peyton had plenty of stores of tinned beef, peas, salmon, and even lobster. Yancy had brought a loaf of fresh bread from the prison bakery at Harpers Ferry that had, miraculously, survived in his haversack, along with some confiscated beef jerky.

As they ate, they slowly began talking, just a little, about the day, telling each other of the dispatches they had taken to which commander, and of the situation at the time. Both of them had been to General Lee's headquarters twice that day, and they compared notes on the beloved "Marse Robert" as his army called him.

"It's too bad that Chuckins can't do courier duty sometimes, as he loves General Lee so much." Yancy stopped, sat up, and looked around blankly. "Where is Chuckins, anyway?"

Peyton answered, "General Jackson called all his clerks together. He's taking them to tour the field hospital to get the information about the dead and wounded."

"Oh," Yancy said unhappily. "I'd rather ride through a hail of bullets than do that."

Peyton didn't answer.

Knowing that General Jackson could call them to duty at any time, after they ate they spread their blankets and went to sleep.

Long after midnight, Yancy was roused from feverish, hateful dreams of blood and gore by a small, pitiful sound. He sat up.

Charles Satterfield sat against the trunk of the oak tree, his knees drawn up, his arms hugging them, and his head resting on them. His shoulders shook. The little noises that Yancy heard was Chuckins sobbing quietly.

Yancy went to him, sat down by him, and put his arms around him. Chuckins buried his face in Yancy's shoulder. Chuckins cried for a long time, but finally the sobs subsided and he drifted off to sleep, leaning against Yancy's side, Yancy's arm still around him. They slept until dawn.

CHAPTER TWENTY-THREE

In October 1862, General Lee reorganized and streamlined his army. Major General James Longstreet was promoted to Lieutenant General and named commander of the newly-created First Corps. Major General Thomas "Stonewall" Jackson was also promoted to Lieutenant General and named commander of Second Corps. The Army of Northern Virginia was now not only in spirit, but also in letter, a cohesive unified whole.

Jackson called Yancy and Peyton into his headquarters tent. "I've just received a promotion, by the grace of God," he said humbly. "And for your outstanding service, your courage, your valor, and your dedication to the army, General Lee and I have agreed to give you field promotions to Second Lieutenant."

He rose, raised his right hand, and, stunned, Yancy and Peyton did the same. Jackson swore them in with the Confederate Officers Notice of Commission, and then they took the Loyalty Oath. It was some time before Peyton and Yancy could actually believe that they were now lieutenants.

A few days after his own illustrious promotion, Jackson received a letter from Anna suggesting that she take steps to publicize his career. His reply was ever that of the devout Christian that he was:

Don't trouble yourself about representations that are made
of your husband. These things are earthly and transitory. There
are real and glorious blessings, I trust, in reserve for us beyond
this life. It is best for us to keep our eyes fixed upon the throne
of God and the realities of a more glorious existence. . . . It is
gratifying to be beloved and to have our conduct approved by
our fellow men, but this is not worthy to be compared with the
glory that is in reservation for us in the presence of our glorified
Redeemer. . . . I appreciate the loving interest that prompted
such a desire in my precious darling.

The Battle of Antietam almost claimed another casualty—President Abraham Lincoln. News of the horrendous bloodshed so anguished him that he came very near to physical prostration, and his grief was so great that his advisors, for a day or two, feared that he might suffer a mental breakdown. However, being the keen and stalwart leader that he was, he quickly overcame his desolation and turned again to leading his country in war.

In the aftermath of the shambles at Sharpsburg, Lincoln knew very well that it was the perfect opportunity to destroy the Army of Northern Virginia and shorten the war. He could clearly see that the Army of the Potomac, again fortified to 110,000 men, should pursue Lee's weakened and exhausted army into Virginia and crush them. But Lincoln could also clearly see that General George B. McClellan had no such plans in mind. After Antietam he had trumpeted his great triumph and settled down there to winter, safely and comfortably back across the Potomac and near to the 73,000 troops guarding Washington.

Determined to prod him, Lincoln made a surprise visit to him and the army on October 1. He stayed for three days, much of it spent pressing "Little Mac" to move the army forward. Yet he could sense it was to no avail.

Early one morning the president invited his close friend, Ozias Hatch, to go for a walk. On a hillside, Lincoln gestured with exasperation to the expanse of white tents spread out below. He asked, "Hatch, Hatch, what is all this?"

"Why, Mr. Lincoln," Hatch replied, "this is the Army of the Potomac."

"No, Hatch, no," Lincoln retorted. "This is McClellan's bodyguard."

After this fruitless visit, Lincoln tried peremptorily ordering McClellan to cross the Potomac and engage Lee.

McClellan flatly refused and engaged in a long series of shrill telegraphic demands for more reinforcements and more supplies.

Lincoln reached the end of his considerable patience. On November 5, 1862, he relieved McClellan of duty, directing him to return immediately to his home in Trenton, New Jersey, where he was to await "further orders," which he had no intentions of ever sending.

When he learned of his dismissal, McClellan wrote his wife that night:

> *They have made a great mistake. Alas for my poor country!*
> *I know in my inmost heart she never had a truer servant.*

But that November, McClellan saw war for the last time.

For the third time, President Lincoln asked General Ambrose Burnside to take command of the Army of the Potomac. For the third time he refused, again insisting that he was not competent to handle so large a force. But when he learned that if he did not accept, the command would go to an officer that Burnside had long detested—General Joseph Hooker—he reversed his decision.

General Robert E. Lee was uncertain of what this change of command would take. He lamented McClellan's departure. "We always understood each other so well," he remarked to Longstreet with his characteristic modesty. What he really meant was that McClellan was transparent to him. General Lee, from the beginning of his adversary's command, had understood that McClellan dawdled, he was reluctant to seize the offensive, he was an incredibly poor strategist, and that most of his reputation as a military genius was due to adroit political posturing. Lee rarely spoke so harshly aloud of anyone, however, so he merely continued, "I fear they may continue to make these changes till they find someone whom I don't understand."

It was, indeed, a while before General Lee came to understand Ambrose Burnside. It was not because Burnside was clever, however. It was because he was so incredibly incompetent that Lee viewed him with disbelief. . .until he proved it.

However, when Burnside took command, Lee had good reason to be wary, because his army was split in two. This was because at the beginning of November, in the last days of McClellan's command, "Little Mac" had perhaps deep down begun to sense his own downfall. He had begun to slowly deploy the Army of the Potomac into Virginia, creeping down to Warrenton, Virginia, on the east side of the Blue Ridge Mountains. His strategy, as Lincoln had been pressing for months, was to stay astride Lee's lines of supply from the Shenandoah Valley and then to press south toward Richmond, engaging Lee from the north.

The problem, as always, was that McClellan dawdled along so slowly that Lee had been given time to position his army in what would most likely mean another Confederate victory and another Federal rout. Lee sent Jackson and Second Corps to the valley, threatening McClellan's western flank. He sent Longstreet and First Corps to Culpeper, twenty miles to the southwest, directly in McClellan's path.

Still, Lee was no fool, and he understood the peril that his army was in. It was divided in half, which in military terms equaled a weakening of the whole. As always, Lee was terrifically outnumbered—at this time the Army of the Potomac numbered about 116,000 men; the Army of Northern Virginia, 72,000. Again, as always, the Federal army was much better equipped than Lee's men. Lee knew very well that if the Federal army could be led by a daring and courageous commander instead of Little Mac, the odds of a victory for the Confederates would be diminished indeed.

And so, when Lee finally did see the new strategy of Burnside's Army of the Potomac, he was puzzled. On November 19, he learned that Burnside was moving the entire army south, along the east side of the Rappahanock River. Burnside was abandoning a promising opportunity to strike the two separated wings of the Army of Northern Virginia. Also, he was skirting around the Confederates again, a move very reminiscent of McClellan. Lee couldn't understand how Burnside could hope to gain a better position, but that was because Robert E. Lee was a military genius, and it was difficult, if not impossible, for him to comprehend utter military ignorance.

Abraham Lincoln and the War Department did not view General Burnside as ignorant. They had approved his grand new strategy. He proposed to position the army on the east side of the Rappahanock, just across from Fredericksburg, which was a picturesque village that stood squarely midway between Richmond and Washington. Burnside planned to build floating bridges across the Rappahanock River, send across the army quickly and in force, take Fredericksburg before Lee could block him, then move south and seize Richmond.

The plan depended on speed. General Burnside did succeed in marching his forces quickly, a stunning change from the days of "Little Mac." The army began their march on November 15, and by November 19, they were in position, a long, heavy blue line from Falmouth, north of Fredericksburg, some miles south of Fredericksburg at a possible alternate crossing called Skinker's Neck. From Stafford Heights, a series of hills on the west side of the river, Federal cannons brooded menacingly, aimed directly at the eastern shore.

And there and then the Army of the Potomac stopped and stayed, immovable and unmovable. Once again, incomprehensible Union hesitation gave Robert E. Lee ample time to deploy his army and position them on the most favorable ground. Fredericksburg was down in a little valley, with a line of gentle hills just behind it. Longstreet's First Corps was on the right, arrayed along a ridge called Marye's Heights. Jackson's Second Corps was on the left, along a crest of hills that looked down on wide, flat fields that stretched from the river all the way to the steep banks of the hills.

And so the two mighty engines of destruction faced each other across the gentle river and the forlorn little town. And still Burnside waited.

❧

General Thomas "Stonewall" Jackson was not, in war, a man who could tolerate inaction very well. Every day he rode or walked the heights behind Fredericksburg restlessly, eyeing the army across the river with flaming blue eyes, envisioning scene after scene of vicious attacks. He was as cross as a fishwife, so irascible that his staff and aides—though they always accompanied him—stayed at a discreet, safe distance.

But in the last week of November, suddenly General Jackson's temperament sweetened tremendously. He was cheerful, making his clumsy little attempts at wit, smiling more often than anyone had ever witnessed. None of them knew what had caused this sea change in their general, for as always, he was intensely private and secretive.

Jackson had been expecting news from Anna, and finally he received a letter. It read:

My Own Dear Father—

I know that you are rejoiced to hear of my coming, and I hope that God has sent me to radiate your pathway through life. I am a very tiny little thing. I weigh only eight and a half pounds, and Aunt Harriet says I am the express image of my darling papa. . .and this greatly delights my mother. My aunts both say that I am a little beauty. My hair is dark and long, my eyes are blue, my nose straight just like Papa's, and my complexion not at all red like most young ladies of my age, but a beautiful blending of the lily and the rose. . . .

I was born on Sunday, just after the morning services at your church. . . .

Your dear little wee daughter

On December 10, Yancy was reading a letter with much pleasure:

. . .and so I hope you like the sketches, and that they may cheer you. I believe that my favorite is the one of Missy in the

kitchen, it's such a comforting and homey scene. Remember
how many hours we spent in there, reading the newspapers
and watching her cook, our mouths watering? Or yours, at
least, as always. While you were here I came to believe that
Missy is right, your stomach goes all the way down both your
long legs to your ankles.

We are going to try to send you some Christmas presents.
I find it a miracle that the mail still runs smoothly, by all
appearances. I know you'll be glad to know that we get letters
regularly from Leslie. He is doing very well and always
mentions you and writes of the hope of better days when we
may all be together as a family again. (Your second family, of
course!)

We pray for you daily, and we miss you very much. I miss
you very much. I understand that since you are camped at
Fredericksburg along with General Lee, naturally he would
send all of the army's messages to Richmond. But we do miss
the days when General Jackson's dashing courier would ride
in all hours of any day for a visit. Should any opportunity at
all present itself for you to come to us, we should be so very
glad to see you. Blessed Lord grant that it may be soon!

From your best friend (probably),
Lorena

Yancy perused Lorena's sketches for long minutes, a smile
playing on his lips. Mrs. Hayden, smiling down at the artist as she
mounted the stairs, candle in hand; Dr. Hayden, putting on his
ancient slouch hat and holding his beat-up medical bag, going out
the door to Chimborazo; Missy, frowning down at a steaming pot
on the stove as she stirred it—these three were all obviously done
from memory. But Elijah's picture was blatantly posed. He stood
looking straight at the artist, his bulky arms crossed in front of his
chest. On his face was a smile so wide it seemed it would split his
face. In her letter Lorena had said that he had stood as still as if it
were a glass-negative photograph, even when she had told him to
relax. He didn't stop posing until she had finished all but the fine
shading.

Yancy chuckled to himself. *She's so talented, I had no idea.* He looked over the sketches again and thought, *It'd be great if she'd do some of herself and send them to me. I bet she never draws herself, she's so modest. . .but I'm going to write her and beg her. Bet she'll do it for me. . . .*

He got up and went to the little folding desk in their tent, sitting down with pencil and paper, and began:

Dear Best Friend (I'm pretty sure),

But that was as far as he got. Peyton, who was on courier duty that morning, came into the tent. "Hope you enjoyed your morning off, Yance," he said, going to his storage trunk, taking out a cigar, and lighting it with pleasure. General Jackson disapproved the use of tobacco, so the aides and even the staff officers basically hid and smoked. "We've got an assignment."

Yancy rose, threw on his tunic, and began buckling on his saber. "Are we riding?"

"No. That is, no courier duty. General Lee found out that there are still some holdouts in Fredericksburg, mostly old people and ladies with small children, and it's upset him. He's ordered all of the couriers that aren't riding today and all of the wagons that can be spared to go into town and help them evacuate."

When General Lee had arrived on November 20, he had been greeted with delight and relief from the inhabitants of Fredericksburg, believing that he would save their town from the Federals massing across the river. Regretfully General Lee had explained to the mayor and the city council that it was impossible to defend the little town. Federal artillery was aimed straight down at it from Stafford's Heights, and no number of charges by any thousands of infantry would be able to dislodge such well-placed guns. It was, Lee explained, a basic tenet of warfare that even privates knew. Infantry assailing well-placed defenders on high ground was simple suicide. Sorrowfully the city leaders came to understand this and ordered an evacuation of the town.

Twenty-two couriers and aides went down into town, followed by eight sturdy supply wagons that had been emptied. Peyton and

Yancy, perhaps because their horses were the showiest—or maybe because they naturally tended to assume leadership positions—led them in.

Many of the people were already standing outside in heavy traveling clothes, some with trunks, some with their possessions simply knotted up in sheets. On Main Street through the center of town, just down from the Episcopal church, was a boardinghouse—a clean, simple three-story building painted white with neat black shutters.

As they neared it, Yancy could see that there were about a dozen people standing outside, with their trunks and cases on the walk. He reflected that he would start loading these people up first, and he rode to that side of the street.

He guided Midnight up to the hitching post directly in front of the building and scanned the little crowd. Suddenly he drew in a painfully quick sharp breath. His head and hands felt too warm. His vision narrowed until all peripherals disappeared. He stiffened and froze so suddenly that Midnight, sensing the intensity of Yancy's agitation, grew stock-still.

She stood just to the right of the door of the boardinghouse. Her hands were in front of her, holding the handle of a small portmanteau. Her face was upturned as she watched Yancy. It was heart-shaped and she was pale and sad, and her eyes were dark and filled with tears. She was wearing a royal blue mantle, and the cape was drawn up, and soft tendrils of her light brown hair damp in the dismal mist escaped, curling around her face.

Yancy did not see this girl. He saw Lorena. She looked up at him, her soft voice catching in her throat as she told him of her sorrow, the blue mantle framing her perfect face, her eyes shimmering with tears.

I loved her. . .I love her! I—I've loved her for so long! How—how could I have forgotten my darling Lorena? How could I have seen her every day, laughed with her, talked to her, listened to her sweet voice, and not feel this great longing? How, how. . . What have I done? What can I do?

"Yancy," Peyton said softly, touching his arm, "are you all right? You look like you've been struck by lightning."

"What?" Yancy said vaguely. His gaze was still locked on the girl, though in his mind he still saw Lorena.

"Yancy," Peyton said more insistently, "you're almost as pale as a white man. Are you sick?"

With an effort, Yancy tore his gaze away from the girl, took a deep breath, and managed to focus on Peyton's face. In spite of his joking words, Peyton looked concerned. Yancy passed a hand over his brow, realizing that one of his headaches, very rare now, was starting to threaten him with a vague ache behind his eyes. "No. No, I'm not sick. I'm—fine. I just. . ."

He couldn't possibly articulate what had happened to him. Yancy, private man that he was, had never told his friends about his memory loss after he was wounded. He stole a look back at the girl. Now he could see that she didn't really look like Lorena; this girl was tall and curvy and her features were nothing like Lorena's. There was a very old man standing next to her, holding her arm, and Yancy realized that he must be her grandfather, perhaps, and likely he was the reason she had not attempted to evacuate.

Yancy forced himself to say firmly, "It's okay, Peyton. Don't worry about me. How about we start with these people here? I'll go back and bring up one of the wagons if you'll start organizing them."

He turned and rode back to the line of wagons behind the mounted couriers, taking the few minutes to calm himself and to bring his chaotic thoughts to order. He had a job to do, and it was important. These people needed him to be kind and attentive and reassuring. He would have to put his shocking revelation about Lorena aside for now. Later, perhaps, he would figure out what to do.

The next night, December 11, at 2:00 a.m., Federal engineers started building bridges. The night was smothered in a heavy, wet fog, and it was bitterly cold. Though the sounds were completely recognizable, the clanks of tools and crash of timbers sounded oddly muffled on the thick air. Still, they were enough for the sharpshooters Lee had stationed along the Confederate side of the riverbank.

CROSSING

They fought off the bridge builders all night and all the next day. Supremely frustrated, Burnside fired 5,000 shells into Fredericksburg, reducing it to rubble. Still the sharpshooters picked off the engineers every time they showed their faces.

Burnside ordered the army to cross in pontoon boats, which they did successfully, though with some losses. The Confederate skirmishers fell back slowly, grinding the first line of Yankees down, giving every yard grudgingly. But finally they were threatened to be overwhelmed, and they withdrew to the safety of the heights.

That day, the Union soldiers had literally sacked the entire town, dragging furniture, pianos, paintings, dishes, linens, clothing, books—anything they could get their hands on—out into the streets and destroyed them. They stole every valuable they could find and every scrap of food and drink. Fires raged all over the city from the Federal shelling, and the soldiers often took torches from the houses that burned and set others on fire.

From the grim heights behind the benighted town, Robert E. Lee watched Burnside's army. More and more of them swarmed across the Rappahanock, the pontoon boats crossing again and again, each time full, coming from the east side. Surely, Lee thought, Burnside would not do the unthinkable—attack these unassailable hills. Lee's army was ordered in what was as close to perfect position as could ever be in war. He had the high ground, with almost no cover below in the approaches to the foot of the hills, his artillery arranged so as to inflict sure death over carefully laid zones of fire. No sane opponent would dare attack him.

Yet Burnside did just that. He was not insane, though throughout the Battle of Fredericksburg, Lee and his generals had very good cause to wonder.

On December 13, in the cold gray dawn, Burnside ordered the attack to begin. They attacked Jackson, on the Confederate right, and were beaten back with heavy casualties. They attacked Longstreet, arrayed on the invulnerable reaches of Marye's Heights.

The Federals were routed, with heavy casualties. Again and again, brigade after brigade charged First Corps' guns and massed musketry. The slaughter was horrendous.

Burnside ordered a final assault on the center at dusk. They fell in their hundreds crossing the open ground to those impossible heights. At dark, at last, the guns were silenced.

In one day of massacre, the Union army had sustained 12,653 casualties in killed, wounded, or missing; the Confederate army, 5,309.

On the next day, a truce was declared and the armies recovered their dead and wounded. The truce ended that afternoon, and the Federals resumed their battle formation on the field. Lee, Longstreet, and Jackson readied themselves for another attack. It did not come.

That night a violent rainstorm assaulted the area. The next morning, Lee and his lieutenants looked out over a deserted battlefield.

In the storm, the Federals had crept back across the Rappahanock River. The Battle of Fredericksburg was over.

CHAPTER TWENTY-FOUR

"Yancy, what are you doing?" Peyton asked lazily. He was sprawled on his cot, smoking a cigar, blowing smoke rings into the air.

"I don't know," Yancy answered distractedly. He was pacing, though not in a fast back-and-forth manner. He would sit at the camp desk, stare down at the papers spread out on it, then jump up and stride to the tent opening. He'd open the flap and stand there, staring outside for long moments. Then dropping it, he would go to stand by the camp stove, open it, jab irritably at the coals, slam it shut, and then walk a few paces back and forth. Again he would sit down at the desk and moodily peruse the papers. He had been doing variations of this routine for almost an hour.

"I don't know either," Peyton retorted. "But I do know that you're annoying me to distraction. If you don't stop twitching I'm going to have to kill you."

"At least I'd be out of my misery," Yancy muttered. He put his head in his hands.

Peyton sat up and regarded his friend with concern. "C'mon, Yance. You've been a train wreck ever since Fredericksburg. It was bad, I know, but it sure wasn't as bad for us as Sharpsburg, and you came through that like a trooper. Is it—is it just getting to you? All of it?"

"No, no, it's not the war," Yancy answered bleakly. "It's—it's—I can't explain it."

"Look, you're my friend," Peyton said evenly. "I know you're not much for talking about yourself and your troubles. But just tell me this much—is there anything at all I can do to help?"

"No. . .no."

"Is there anyone that can help you?"

"Not really, no."

Peyton gave up. He lay back down and blew another perfect smoke ring. "Okay, then," he said resignedly. "But don't forget. If you don't calm down, I *am* going to kill you."

Yancy's trouble was Lorena, of course.

After Fredericksburg, the army had camped about twelve miles south of the town, in a serene wooded area alongside the Rappahannock. Jackson's headquarters were at Moss Neck Manor, a gracious plantation mansion with long columned porches. As always, Jackson had refused to stay in the house; he firmly held that soldiers, even if they were lieutenant generals, should quarter in tents. About a week later, however, he developed an earache, a condition that had been cropping up throughout the fall and winter. He bowed to his physician and then consented to use a three-room outbuilding that served as an office, a study, and a library for the master of the plantation, as his office.

The staff had camped nearby on the manor grounds. Peyton, Yancy, and Chuckins were again living comfortably in Peyton's tent. It was January 1, the first day of the year 1863, and they had been at leisure ever since December 18, when the last Union halfhearted rearguard action had finally allowed the last of the demoralized Federal army to cross the Rappahannock.

And Yancy had been in turmoil since December 18, when his entire being was no longer taken up with battle. On that day, as they had retrieved their belongings from the wagon train and had set up their tent, Yancy had found the letter he had started before the war's events had provided a so-welcome distraction.

"Dear Best Friend (I'm pretty sure)," it read.

Yancy had stared at the innocuous words for a long time. Finally, numbly, he had written a peculiar, disjointed letter, clumsily telling her that he missed her and her family, and he hoped to see them soon. He loved the sketches. Then he begged her to do some drawings of herself and send them to him. In this request he tried to mimic the notes he had hit when he had wheedled her for something—a second portion of roast beef, for her to read to him, for her to fix him bacon and eggs late at night. But the tone was false. It read like begging, and he thought that glimpses of his desperation showed through. He tried and tried to figure out how to rephrase it, but Yancy was not a very subtle man, and he finally gave up, signed the letter, "Your friend, Yancy," sealed it up, and sent it to the mail tent by Willy before he could change his mind.

And then the mental torture began. Every day, all day. *She is my best friend, I'm sure. But is that all she feels? It must be. All that time, she was warm and friendly and kind and even loving—but like a sister. Was she relieved that I forgot October? That night, she was so unsure; she wasn't distant but she was so very cautious. Maybe she finally came to realize that she doesn't love me, can't love me. . . .*

But what if. . .what if. . .she does have feelings for me? I was so oblivious, so ready to just be friends, she couldn't possibly have forced herself on me, blind fool that I am. Maybe she thinks that I'm gone forever, that I lost my love for her completely.

The problem was that Yancy had no idea which scenario was the truth. Was he her best friend, or was he her lost love? He didn't know, and it gnawed at him constantly. And he simply could not figure out how to find out the truth. He thought it would be foolish to write her and blurt out that, yes, he'd forgotten he loved her but now he remembered. And by the way, had she fallen in love with him yet?

For the same reason, he didn't ask for leave to go see her. What would he say? What *could* he say? Like running in an eternal, endless, maddening circle, Yancy went over and over these thoughts.

On this day, Yancy had received his Christmas gifts from the Haydens. Dr. Hayden had commissioned Leslie's tailor to make Yancy two brand-new uniforms for his promotion. As an officer he wore a mid-thigh frock coat, double-breasted, with heavy embroidered gold braid on the cuffs and polished brass buttons. On the trousers, a gold stripe gleamed down the breeches. They also had four fine lawn dress shirts made for him. They had sent him a brand-new pair of leather boots, thigh-high, in the cavalry style. They had even sent him a new kepi cap, with a gold braid.

But the best gift was from Lorena. Yancy had received three letters from her since he had written her that awkward letter from her "friend," but she had never sent any self-portrait, nor had she mentioned it. Yancy was not really surprised. She was modest, and he thought that her beauty sometimes made her feel uncomfortable. It would be hard for her, he knew, to honestly present herself as the very lovely woman that he knew she was.

But for Christmas, for him, she had done it. She had done two drawings of herself. One was full-length. She was standing in front of a window. Yancy knew it well. It was the window in the guest bedroom, where he had spent two months recovering from his wounds. In the picture she held the drapes slightly open, and golden sunlight fell on her face as she looked down at the quiet street. Yancy had seen her like this a hundred times.

The other picture was three-quarter face. She was looking off to her right, smiling a little. It was an uncanny likeness that captured the warmth in her eyes, the long dark lashes, the mysterious half smile on her full lips when Yancy knew she was secretly amused.

When he first saw them, his heart leaped; surely these pictures of her were so personal, even intimate—a gift from a woman that could be made only for her love.

Then his heart sank. Perhaps, in his consuming love for her, he was transferring his feelings to the pictures, giving them a meaning that Lorena had never intended.

And so Yancy had again spun off into his maddening universe whose center was the riddle that was Lorena, staring again and again at the pictures on the camp desk, prowling around the tent like some caged animal, until Peyton had brought him back to a semblance of his senses.

Now, as he watched Peyton peacefully blowing smoke rings, he realized that it was true—not only was he driving himself crazy, he was driving his friends crazy. He determined that he would find the strength to control himself and his riotous emotions. And he would find a way, somehow, to find out about Lorena and her feelings for him. He had no choice. He had to, or he thought that he would, quite possibly, truly go mad.

Chuckins came in, stamping the snow from his boots, shrugging off his overcoat, humming happily. "Hullo," he greeted them. "Stonewall gave me the afternoon off." He warmed his hands at the stove for a few moments. Then, looking at Yancy's strained face curiously, he walked over and innocently looked at the pictures of Lorena on the desk. He whistled with appreciation. "What a pretty lady. Is she your girl?"

Yancy looked down at the sketches for the hundredth time. "I don't know," he said blankly.

Peyton said with exasperation, "Chuckins, don't ask anybody any questions. Yancy doesn't know anything. I don't know anything. And neither do you. If we don't leave it at that, I'm going to have to kill Yancy. And we don't want that, now, do we?"

"No, Peyton," Chuckins obediently agreed.

"No, we don't. So, Chuckins, whatcha gonna cook us for supper?"

Never was there such a splendor of Confederate generals and colonels as at the dinner that Lieutenant General Thomas "Stonewall" Jackson gave for his favorite tormentor, Major General Jeb Stuart, and his commanding officer, General Robert E. Lee. The dining room at Moss Neck was luxurious. The costly china, crystal, and silverware glowed; and the long, gleaming table was the height of elegance.

But neither the magnificence of the dining room nor the dashing uniforms of the officers—even Jeb Stuart's flamboyant swashbuckling garments—outshone General Jackson. Stuart had sent him a dazzling officer's frock coat, with the traditonal grouping of four sets of three gleaming buttons arrayed down the double-breasted tunic, which was trimmed with gold lace. Even the gilded buttons were ornate, stamped with "C.S.A." The three stars embroidered on the collar and the complex embroidery on the sleeves were of the finest close-woven work. Admirers had given him a gold sash, a new saber and scabbard, and even gleaming knee-high boots.

Of course Jeb Stuart couldn't resist taunting him. Raising his glass, he said, "General Jackson, I must compliment you on your finery. I see that I am outshone, and I resent it extremely. Tomorrow I will endeavor to renew my entire wardrobe."

As always when Stuart teased him, Jackson blushed like a girl. "Couldn't outshine you, General Stuart. You are the biggest and finest peacock of us all."

In the ease of the moment, one of Jackson's colonels added, "At Fredericksburg, when our general first rode through the troops in his new fancy dress, one of the men had said, aghast, 'Old Jack's drawed his bounty money and bought new clothes!' Another grumbled something like, 'He don't look right, like some struttin' lieutenant. I'm afraid he'll not get down to work.' "

Jackson's servant Jim was a wonderful cook, but for this special occasion he had outdone himself. Some of the lesser officers had not seen such bounty since the war began. They feasted on turkeys, hams, a bucket of Rappahannock oysters, fresh-baked white bread and biscuits, pickles, and other sumptuous delicacies. Most of the food was gifts to Jackson from admirers. Ladies from Staunton had even sent him a bottle of wine, which Jackson readily served and which Jeb Stuart badgered him about.

Even General Lee joined in with gentle teasing of his own, smiling at Jackson. "You people are only playing soldier," he said. "You must come to my quarters and see how soldiers ought to live." General Lee's headquarters were, as always, a plain tent near Hamilton's Crossing on the Rappahannock.

There were other—perhaps more modest—dinners that General Jackson gave. Undoubtedly he enjoyed wintering at Moss Neck. Though it was not a time of battles, neither was it strictly a time of leisure for Jackson. One of his main priorities had always been drill. He drilled his men constantly, and often he directed the drills himself, always demanding and exacting and seeking to better the men.

Another onerous task that he was obligated to do during this relative cessation of hostilities was reports. His last report had been of Kernstown, one of the parts of the Seven Days Campaign back in July of 1862. Since then he had been engaged in fourteen battles in eight months, and as the commander of first the Army of the Shenandoah Valley and then Commander of Second Corps, he always had much administrative work.

During this tedious time, he had found Sergeant Charles Satterfield's help invaluable. Not only was Chuckins a fine clerk, but he also was able to phrase Jackson's reports professionally, succinctly, and with perfect clarity.

One definite pleasure that Jackson had during the long winter months was the friendship of Janie Corbin. She was the five-year-old daughter of his hostess at Moss Neck. She was welcome at his office at any time, and she played for hours on the hearth while Jackson droned his dictation on and on to Chuckins and his other clerks. More than once he paused in his work to watch her, his grim warrior's expression softened to gentleness. Sometimes he would take her on his knee, and then they would do Janie's favorite pastime—he would cut out paper dolls for her, folding paper to fashion figures holding hands.

Every time, she would pull the long line of figures apart and ask, "And who are these, Gen'ral Jackson?"

"Those, ma'am, are the men of the Stonewall Brigade," was always Jackson's solemn reply.

As the winter drew on, Yancy could sense that Jackson grew more and more homesick. Often after work he would take a ride on his favorite mount, Little Sorrel, and wander along the riverbank.

Once he met Yancy, who, needing the fresh biting air of February to clear his mind, was by the banks of the quiet river. He was walking along, leading Midnight, when Jackson came up on him. Yancy came to attention and saluted, but Jackson made a careless gesture and said, "At ease, at ease, Lieutenant. May I join you?"

"Of course, sir, it would be my pleasure."

They walked along in silence for a while. Jackson stopped and stared across the river. "They're still over there," he said grimly. "They've got a new commanding officer, did you know?"

"Yes, sir," Yancy answered. "My friends in Richmond send me the papers when there is important news in them. General Hooker was appointed just a few weeks ago, was he not?"

"Mmm," Jackson assented. "Our intelligence has a lot on him. Acquitted himself admirably during the Seven Days and Second Manassas. Reported to be courageous and a military professional. He floundered at Fredericksburg, as they all did. It's said, and I believe, that it was probably due to deficiencies in his commanding officer, General Burnside. Hooker replaced him."

" 'Fighting Joe Hooker' he's called," Yancy said.

"Yes, and that's why I think that soon there is going to be a fight," Jackson said, narrowing his eyes as if he could see Hooker's thousands arrayed across the river.

Both of them searched that forbidding west bank for long moments, then by mutual assent they turned and started walking again.

At length Jackson said, "Did you know, Yancy, that I haven't seen my home in Lexington for almost two years? And it's been nearly a year since I've seen Anna. . .and I have yet to see my baby daughter."

Yancy was astonished, both that Jackson was confiding in him in this manner and that he had used his given name. It was the first time, he realized, that the formal and reticent man had ever called him 'Yancy.' *He must be horribly homesick,* Yancy thought with great sympathy.

As he reflected on General Jackson's plight, he realized that his own troubles were small compared to his commanding officer's. During the last two years, he had seen his family several times, and he had seen the Haydens and Lorena fairly often. General Jackson's daughter was almost three months old now, and he had never set eyes on her. Yancy imagined that the longing he felt for Lorena was not to be compared with Jackson's yearning for his daughter, especially after he had lost two babies, one with his first wife, Elinor; and then he and Anna had lost their daughter in 1858.

Quietly Yancy said, "Sir, I pray for you all the time, but now I will pray fervently that you may see Mrs. Jackson and your daughter very soon."

"Thank you, Lieutenant Tremayne," he said, returning to his usual cool reserve. They walked on and then he added, "Her name

CROSSING

is Julia. Julia Laura. And yes, may the merciful and bountiful Lord grant that I see her soon."

As the winter melted into Virginia's warm and welcoming spring, General Jackson grew restless. At his headquarters at Moss Neck he had too many visitors, both soldiers and civilian admirers. He was entirely too accessible there. Perhaps, too, echoes of General Lee's gentle teasing at Jackson's dinner still faintly hung on in his mind; Jackson knew very well that General Lee always headquartered in a plain soldier's tent, with only his camping equipment, a camp stove, a military desk, and a cot. His only accessory was a hen that stayed under his cot and laid an egg for him every morning.

The fact that Jackson's health had deteriorated during the winter—and his physician's strict orders that he must not camp outdoors—faded from his disciplined mind. He determined to move to a tent headquarters at Hamilton's Crossing, very near to General Lee, and he set the move for March 15. General Jackson demanded promptness at all times and in all endeavors, and so by the evening of the fifteenth he was well established, his headquarters already organized, and his staff fully bivouacked, too. They began their routine again, that of drill and Jackson's endless reports and the mountain of administrative tasks of running an army corps.

On the eighteenth, the weather was particularly inviting. A balmy breeze stirred the air that was filled with spring butterflies and dandelion fluffs. The sun was kind, a pleasant warmth on the shoulders, and a benevolent lemon yellow glow.

Jackson, in an unusually good mood, dismissed his clerks and determined to go outside and sit in the sun for a while and read the Bible. Jim spread a blanket for him under a little dogwood tree just by his tent. It was in full flower, the simple white blossoms dazzling.

Around Jackson, soldiers worked gathering firewood, helping Jim arrange the general's stores, policing the area just around the general's headquarters. His staff and aides were also outside enjoying the day, some quietly reading; some gathered in groups talking about battles, horses, sabers, rifles, ammunition—all the things that all soldiers were interested in.

For once Sandy Owens had been able to join Yancy, Peyton, and Chuckins. Peyton had managed to bribe the supply wagon team that was setting up their tents, and they had put up Peyton's tent in a favored spot, just behind and to the right of General Jackson's tent. Today they had set up a friendly horseshoe competition. Naturally, with his artilleryman's eye, Sandy Owens was beating the tar out of the other three.

They saw Dr. Hunter McGuire, chief medical officer of the First Corps, and also General Jackson's personal physician, by his request. McGuire was young, with handsome, sensitive features. When the staff and soldiers saw the stricken look on the doctor's face, they stopped what they were doing and watched him as he slowly walked, shoulders bowed, to Jackson.

Jackson looked up, and seeing McGuire's face, scrambled to his feet.

McGuire came close to him and murmured something to him that no one could hear.

Jackson reacted with shock, his eyes widening and his jaw convulsively clenching. Then, to everyone's astonishment and dismay, he walked—almost stumbled—to a tall stump of a sweetgum tree that had been cut to accommodate the campsite. Jackson sank down on it, bowed his head, and began to sob. This, from the man that had stared dry-eyed at thousands of his beloved men lying on the bloody field at Sharpsburg, was the most heart-wrenching sight that Yancy had ever seen.

Even before they knew what had happened, tears began to roll down Chuckins's face.

The news spread fast among the still, silent men. Little Janie Corbin had died of scarlet fever.

Jackson mourned for her. His men mourned for their beloved general.

❧

Soon, however, General Jackson and his men had cause for rejoicing.

On a dreary Monday, April 20, at noon, Jackson and his escort rode to Guiney Railroad Station. Before the train had come to a complete stop, he jumped up and pushed his way into the coach. There he saw his daughter for the first time.

She was fat, pink, and sleepy. Anna recalled that he would not take her in his arms because of his dripping coat, but he stared at her and made funny little baby coos to her. Jackson had arranged for them to stay at the Yerby home, which was near his headquarters. Once they arrived and were in the privacy of their room, Anna wrote:

> *He caressed her with the tenderest affection and held her long and lovingly. During the whole of this short visit, when he was with us, he rarely had her out of his arms, walking her, and amusing her in every way he could think of—sometimes holding her up before a mirror and saying, admiringly, "Now, Miss Jackson, look at yourself!"*
>
> *Then he would turn to an old lady of the [Yerby] family and say: "Isn't she a little gem?" He was frequently told that she resembled him, but he would say: "No, she is too pretty to look like me!"*

On April 23, when Julia was five months old, Anna and General Jackson decided to have her baptized at the Yerby home. The ceremony was to be done by Reverend B. Tucker Lacy, a minister who had long been with the valley troops and who Jackson had named the unofficial chaplain general for the Second Corps.

When the staff and aides heard of the baptism, Yancy went to Reverend Lacy's tent. "Sir, many of the aides would like to attend the baptism. May we have permission?"

The chaplain refused, though not in an unkindly manner: "I'm sorry, Lieutenant Tremayne, but it is to be a private service."

"Yes, sir," Yancy said, crestfallen. But then, gathering his courage, he went to General Jackson's tent.

Even with Anna and Laura there, Jackson still attended to all of his military duties. Jackson sat at his desk and called Yancy in at his request.

"General Jackson, sir. I've just been to see Reverend Lacy to ask permission to attend Miss Julia Jackson's baptism. But he refused, saying that it was to be a private service. Several of us aides hoped to attend, so may we at least assemble outside and perhaps see Miss Julia and you and Mrs. Jackson after the ceremony?"

Expansively happily, Jackson waved his hand. "Mrs. Jackson and I would be glad for you and the other aides to attend. I request that you give Mrs. Yerby a list, so that she might know how many people we have to accommodate. But you and the rest of my staff are welcome."

Yancy dashed off to tell the others.

The Yerby parlor, though it was a generous room of large proportions, was crowded that spring afternoon. Yancy and many of the other young men had never witnessed the Presbyterian baptismal rite. He was awed at the solemnity of the occasion and the resounding, profound, eternal words of the ceremony from the *Book of Common Prayer*. Yancy noticed the beatific look on Stonewall Jackson's war-hardened features and thought he had never seen such pure happiness on a man's face.

The Yerbys' hospitality was such that they had prepared light refreshments on the lawn for the soldiers that attended. Two long tables, set with creamy white tablecloths, held a big bowl of fruit punch, gallons of iced tea with fresh mint, fresh-squeezed lemonade, and pitchers of thick, cool buttermilk. On the other table were oatmeal cookies, slices of still-warm nut bread, a tall frothy sponge cake, peach slices, apple slices, fat cherries, nectarines, and, in an amusing bow to General Jackson, a bowl of cheery yellow lemons.

After a pleasant half hour, Anna and the baby came out to sit on the veranda. General Jackson sat by them, motioning the nearest soldier to come up, by which they understood that they might come see the baby. Jackson beamed, his eyes glowing with inner warmth, his glances at Anna and Julia so tender that most of his soldiers could hardly believe he was the same grim warrior they saw on the battlefield. Discreetly, they filed by one by one, no one lingering except to bow to Mrs. Jackson and thank her.

When Yancy came up to them, Anna smiled up at him and said quietly, "Yancy, my dear, how you have grown! I would wish to see you, so that we may catch up on our news, and so that you can tell me everything that the general has done that I must scold him for."

Even at this gibe, Jackson smiled at her then told Yancy, "Unless something untoward happens, I believe you may take an hour or two tomorrow to visit my wife. But that is only if you stay discreet and give her no cause to scold."

"No, sir, I wouldn't ever do that," Yancy said hastily. Bowing, he said, "Then I shall be happy to call upon you tomorrow, Mrs. Jackson. Thank you kindly for the invitation."

"I look forward to your call," she responded graciously.

At two o'clock the next afternoon, Yancy sat at that same table on the Yerbys' veranda with Anna Jackson. Next to her was her maid, Hetty, holding Julia. The plump, good-natured baby looked around her with interest, and at Hetty's low nonsense talk, would sometimes smile.

"She is much like him," Yancy observed. "It's not so much that she looks like him, but she has so many of his features. It's so distinctive, to see black hair and blue eyes. It's quite striking in men or women. And she has his straight nose and the same lips."

Anna said, "Many people have told him that she resembles him, but he always says that she is much too pretty to look like him."

"Well," Yancy said, "maybe it could be said that she looks like the general, only prettified."

Anna giggled, a pleasantly youthful sound coming from a mature woman. "Oh! So true. I must tell Thomas that."

"Don't tell him I said it," Yancy said hastily. "He's not gentle with anyone but you, ma'am."

"I know," she said softly. "No one would ever believe what a loving and tender husband he is. And how jolly and happy he is at home."

"I would never have believed it if I hadn't seen a little of it when I was working for you," Yancy agreed. "And I've never tried to tell anyone about him at home. They'd laugh me to scorn and call me a liar."

Julia started fussing a little and Anna said, "I believe she is ready for her nap, Hetty. You may take her on up and put her to bed."

"Yes, Miss Anna," she said and went inside with the baby.

Yancy said, "It was so kind of you and General Jackson to share Julia's baptism with us. I had never seen a service like that. It was wonderful. I could feel the presence of the Lord the whole time, and it made me remember again how wonderful it is to be saved."

"It is, of all things, most to be cherished," Anna agreed. "And I'm so very glad, Yancy, to see how you've grown, not only to manhood, but to a fine Christian man. I know how hard it was for you to find your own way to Christ, but I rejoice that you did."

Yancy smiled a curious half smile. "For one of the worst days of my life, it was the best day of my life. But you know, yesterday also brought it home to me like never before that I've never been baptized. And it makes me kinda sad, because of course I want my family to be with me when I am. But no Amish bishop would ever baptize me; in fact, I guess I'm still being shunned," he finished sadly.

Anna reached over and patted his hand, her tiny white hand in stark contrast to Yancy's muscular dark bronze hand. "The next time you come home, I will introduce you to our minister, Reverend White. I'm confident that even if you don't choose to join the Episcopalian church, he would be glad to baptize you. After all, no matter which church we attend, we are all God's beloved children, and sisters and brothers in Christ Jesus. And I know that Reverend White will be glad to arrange a baptism in any way that will be acceptable to your family."

"Thank you so much, Mrs. Jackson. Already I feel much better," Yancy said.

Anna nodded, then a mischievous look came into her dark eyes. "You were always a good-looking boy, Yancy, but now you are a very handsome man. Tell me, surely there is a lady somewhere? Or maybe even two, or three?"

Yancy would never dream of answering Anna Jackson with anything less than the truth. "There is one lady," he answered somewhat shyly. "But we—I'm not sure exactly how we stand. It's so hard, being apart. You and General Jackson know that better than anyone."

Anna studied his face thoughtfully. Yancy knew she could tell that there was much he wasn't telling her. "It is so trying for families and people who love each other to be torn apart by this awful war. But as always, the best and most hopeful comfort we have is in the Lord. I will pray for you and your lady, Yancy. I will pray that you will find each other in these days of turmoil, and that you will learn of each other, and if it is God's will, you may find happiness together."

"Thank you, Mrs. Jackson," Yancy said in a somewhat choked voice. "That is my prayer, too."

"And now," she said briskly, "what is all this that you say you will not tell me of the general. Because you see, Yancy, that I must depend on my friends, like you, to keep me aware of his misdeeds and misbehavior."

Yancy laughed, his discomfort eased. "Mrs. Jackson, you are the only person on this earth that would dare use those two words in connection with General Stonewall Jackson. I can assure you that he has no familiarity with misdeeds and misbehavior. And even if he did," he added slyly, "though I'm glad you call me your friend, I would be scared out of my wits to report anything to you that might cause you to scold him. No, no. I'm afraid, Mrs. Jackson, you're going to have to find another informant. One more courageous than me."

General Jackson spent every single minute that he could spare from his duties with Anna and Julia, mostly in the privacy of their room at the Yerby mansion, where they could concentrate solely on each other and the baby. Jackson could not watch Julia enough; he often knelt by her cradle for as long as an hour, simply watching her sleep. Together he and Anna prayed, and Anna told him she had never known such deep spiritual meaning as Thomas's prayers for her and Julia.

General Lee did call, and Anna obviously was a little nervous to meet this exalted, walking legend. But his courtly, fatherly manners soon put her at ease, and she came to admire him as most people did upon meeting him.

On Sunday she and Jackson attended Sunday service with Reverend Lacy presiding. Jackson was pleased as General Lee greeted

Anna with his customary courtly charm; the old bachelor General Early paid endearing homage to her; and many of the other officers were introduced to her and paid her the highest compliments.

For his part, this may have been the best Sunday service that Jackson had ever attended. All that long winter he had seen the other generals' wives with their husbands at Sabbath services, and it had made him long all the more for Anna. Now, with her at his side, he thought his happiness on this earth could not be more complete.

The days passed all too swiftly. It was dawn on April 29. Jackson and Anna slept deeply. The baby had not stirred. Abruptly the coarse noise of boots sounded on the stairs, and then a peremptory knock came at the door.

"General Early's adjutant wishes to speak to General Jackson," an urgent young voice called.

Jackson got out of bed and immediately began to dress. "That looks as if Hooker were crossing the river," he said. He hurried downstairs to hear what the courier had to say then came running back up to their room. "I was right," he told Anna grimly. "Federals are crossing the river as we speak. There is going to be a battle, and you and Julia must hurry south. I'll arrange a transport and send it to you." He went to stare at the still-sleeping Julia for long moments then gave Anna a hasty kiss and left.

Jackson hurried to the front and saw that generals Early and Rodes were already making proper plans to receive the enemy. Jackson quickly went to his headquarters, where intelligence reports were already starting to come in. It appeared that the movement at his front was a feint and that the main force of the Federal army was crossing the Rappahannock in force to the north of him.

In the next two days, Lee and Jackson were to decide where he must concentrate his forces. He must lead them to a hostile track of impenetrable underbrush and stinking marshy ground known as the Spotsylvania Wilderness, for the Federals were mired in it. Two miles from the eastern edge was a rise and a crossroads with an old public house called Wilderness Tavern. Nearby was a farm owned by a family named Chancellor. This lonely crossroads had come to be called by the exalted name of Chancellorsville.

CHAPTER TWENTY-FIVE

In January 1863, Lee had dispatched General Longstreet to southeast Virginia, in the area of Suffolk, where the Federals were investing a nominal force. But it could have turned into a major movement that threatened Richmond, so Lee had sent all but three brigades of First Corps. On April 29, Jackson and Lee had to face the fact that the Federal incursion over the Rappahannock was in force, and they were facing about 130,000 Union soldiers with a force of about 60,000 effectives. The remainder of the Army of Northern Virginia was over 150 miles away, and Hooker was moving fast. He was landing forces both to Lee's north, at Kelly's Ford, and to the south, in Lee's rear, at Fredericksburg.

General Jackson spent all day and most of the night of the twenty-ninth reconnoitering the Federal dispositions, observing the developments of the rapidly changing situation. Reporting back to General Lee, they came to the conclusion that the movement to the south was a feint and the much larger body of the Union army that was crossing at Kelly's Ford was the main attack. On this day they had started slowly making their way through the Spotsylvania Wilderness.

Since both Lee and Jackson were valiant and daring men and leaders of men, they decided to attack. Lee gave the responsibility for planning and executing the attack to his trusted lieutenant,

General Jackson. Immediately he sent out engineers, mapmakers, and scouts to reconnoiter the area and give him an accurate, detailed picture of the ground and the Union army's position.

By the thirtieth, Hooker's III, XI, and XII Corps were concentrated at Chancellorsville, in number almost 75,000 men in the little oasis in the middle of the miserable wilderness. He readied them, set them in battle order, and on May 1, he advanced eastward, deploying his three corps into strong positions on high ground along the Plank Road and the River Road.

Jackson moved in, attacking on both the Federal flanks. Stonewall rode back and forth among his troops, always ordering, "Press them, men. Press them." Jackson's hardened veterans did just that. The firefights that erupted on both flanks were fast and vicious.

Then, suddenly, the Federals began to retreat. Hooker had ordered the Federal advance halted, to abandon the ridges, and fall back to the positions they had held around Chancellorsville. Hooker seemed to lose his nerve in this, his first encounter with Robert E. Lee. And so this mighty Union army that outnumbered Jackson's men by more than two to one, fell back to a defensive positon.

That night, Lee and Jackson again met to review the events of the day and discuss their plans. Lee could not help but believe that Hooker wanted him to attack him where he was, and Lee was determined to do so. After more reconnoitering, Jackson found a way to march across the Federal front unseen and circle around to Hooker's right flank. Jeb Stuart had reported that it was "up in the air," which meant it was completely exposed, with no reserves.

Together Lee and Jackson sat on cracker boxes before a small campfire. The conversation that followed was typical of two men who understood each other perfectly.

"General Jackson, what do you propose to do?" Lee inquired.

"Go around here," Jackson answered, indicating his route on a map.

"What do you propose to make this movement with?" Lee asked.

"With my whole corps," Jackson answered without hesitation.

"And what will you leave me?" Lee asked evenly.

"The divisions of Anderson and McLaws."

"Well, go on."

This short laconic exchange had enormous portent. Jackson was proposing one of the most daring moves ever done in war, against all military tenets and wisdom. He would split their already outnumbered forces, leaving Lee with only 14,000 men as he faced Hooker's 75,000. Jackson would take 26,000 men through the woods to Hooker's right flank, believing that he could roll back that flank, attack their rear, and force the entire enormous army to retreat.

Lee began to write out orders. Jackson left to prepare for the road.

On May 2, just after 8:00 a.m., the head of the column began their march. At a crossroads Lee waited, watching. Jackson, on his faithful Little Sorrel, rode to him. They exchanged a few words no one could hear. Then Jackson gave a familiar gesture. He pointed down the road and glanced at Lee from beneath his cap. Then he rode down that road. Lee watched until he disappeared from sight. He found himself wondering if he would ever see Stonewall Jackson again.

Yancy, as he always did, rode as near behind General Jackson as he could possibly get. Jackson rode in the vanguard, an old oilskin raincoat wrapped about him, hiding his splendid uniform. As always, even with his new cap, he wore it with the brim right down on his nose. But even these eccentricities did not mask the power and the warrior's burning will in the man. Though staff officers sometimes shuffled him aside, Yancy felt the overwhelming magnetism that they all felt toward Jackson when he led them into battle. Stubbornly he stayed close.

It took all day for Jackson's corps to flank the six-mile front of the Union army. Yancy received reports that in spite of the fact that Jackson moved his ten-mile-long train on a track unknown to either side until the previous night, Stonewall was still spotted at least three times, and his moves were reported to Hooker.

Hooker had received the reports, including an assault General Sickles had made on the Confederate rear. From the number of ambulances and wagons in the train, Hooker jumped to the conclusion that the entire Confederate Army was retreating. His staff officers believed it, too, and they relaxed at their headquarters at Wilderness Tavern, sitting on the porch drinking toddies, ignoring all further reports of Jackson's movement.

Jackson got his troops into position on Hooker's unguarded right in the late afternoon. The Federals who were in plain sight of Jackson's column were cooking supper. Jackson looked at his watch, and automatically Yancy checked his. It was 5:15 p.m. Major Eugene Blackford rode up, coming from the front.

"The lines are ready, sir," he reported.

Jackson turned to General Rodes, whom he had selected to lead the attack. "Are you ready, General Rodes?"

"Yes, sir."

Jackson's voice was low and slow. "You can go forward then."

Bugles sounded, men started running, regimental flags flew, and the savage Rebel yell on the air was like a series of explosions.

The enemy, obviously terrified by the sudden onslaught, turned and ran. Hooker's right flank rolled like a tidal wave before them. Jackson's troops had smashed the first line and held the high ground. The army was as panicked as they were at First Manassas. Like wild animals they fled. Plunging, panting, pushing, trampling, they ran into the deep thickets of the wilderness.

The victorious Confederates ruthlessly pursued them. But darkness came, and in the vast entangled forest, Jackson's attack lost its momentum. Battle lines came apart, officers were lost, men got scattered, communications broke down. The Confederates had no choice but to stop and regroup.

Jackson was impatient. As always he wanted to press forward, to pursue his prey and destroy them. He halted on the Plank Road, where he had observed the main body of the enemy retreating. "Lieutenant Tremayne," he called in a low voice.

Yancy hurried to him.

"Go to General Hill; I don't have time to write out orders. You tell him to move forward, relieve General Rodes's men, and prepare for a night attack. Bring me back his answer with all speed."

"Yes, sir." Yancy turned and galloped back toward the edge of the wilderness to General Hill's command.

He found him, having anticipated Jackson's orders, already forming his men up to march. He was wearing his red flannel battle shirt, which always brought strong memories of Gaines' Mill, when he was wounded, to Yancy's mind. He related Jackson's orders, and Hill answered, "Ride back to General Jackson and relieve his mind. My men are already on the move, and I expect them to reach General Rodes within the hour. I'm going to ride forward shortly to join General Jackson in scouting the enemy lines."

Yancy hurried back to the Plank Road.

General Jackson had gone slowly ahead along the unfamiliar ground in the strong moonlight. With them rode Lieutenant Joe Morrison—Anna's brother—Lieutenant Wynn of Jackson's staff, and his signal officer, Captain Wilbourn. Softly they moved, quieting their mounts, whispering, for they didn't know how close they were to enemy lines. Silently, cautiously, they crept forward. It was about nine o'clock, and the full moon rode high. Then, in the near distance, they heard axes ringing and trees being felled. The enemy was strengthening his breastworks.

They were crossing right in front of the Eighteenth North Carolina, who were lined parallel to the road. Earlier that evening they had heard rumors that a Union cavalry attack was forming along their front. As they stared through the thick brush, they saw men—officers, mounted officers in fine uniforms. A quiet order was given, "Fire, and repeat fire."

Musket fire barked along the quiet road.

Little Sorrel reared and twisted right, then carried Stonewall Jackson into the depths of the wilderness.

"Cease firing, men!" General A. P. Hill, who had just that instant caught up with Jackson and Yancy and the others, thundered out through the woods.

Joe Morrison shouted, "Cease firing, cease firing! You're firing at your own men!"

"That's a lie! Pour it on 'em, boys!" It was never recorded who the officer that gave the firing orders was.

Another volley rang out. Jackson reeled in pain and lost Little Sorrel's reins. She plunged into the brush, and Jackson was hit soundly on the forehead by a low-hanging branch. His right hand had been shot. With his left he picked up Little Sorrel's reins and guided her back to the Plank Road, where his frantic escort still was. When he reached them he was slumped over the saddle, bent almost double.

Yancy and Lieutenant Wynn hurried to him and pulled him down, gently setting him on his feet. Then, slowly, supporting him, they took him to a small tree by the road and made him lie down beneath it for safety's sake.

Captain Wilbourn hurried, unafraid, toward the Confederate line of muskets that had shot at them, seeking their commanding officer. Lieutenant Wynn went to try to find an ambulance.

Yancy took off his frock coat and was rolling it up to make a pillow for the general's head, when General A. P. Hill rode up and threw himself off his horse. He hurried to Jackson and said painfully, "Oh, I tried to stop their firing. General, are you in much pain?"

"It's very painful," Jackson answered. "I think my arm is broken. I think all my wounds came from my own men." In the wash of sterile moonlight, Jackson's long face was deadly pale, the gash on the broad forehead colored a gory black.

Major General A. P. Hill threw himself down by Jackson and drew his head onto his lap.

Yancy reflected that it might be said that General Hill was Jackson's bitterest enemy in the army. Through the last two years, they had argued rancorously. Jackson had put Hill under arrest. Hill had made a list of charges against Jackson and submitted them to General Lee. Jackson had accused Hill no less than three times of neglect of duty. Even a few days before they had enjoined this battle with Hooker, Jackson and Hill were still squabbling.

Yancy, of course, knew all this. All of Second Corps did. Now he watched in wonder as the hotheaded and acrimonious Hill ever so gently drew off Jackson's gauntlets, the right one filled with blood, and then removed his sword and belt.

Captain Wilbourn returned, evidently unable to find any officer, and the enlisted men refused to leave the battle line to carry a litter for, as Captain Wilbourn had discreetly said, "a friend of mine that is wounded." Above all they didn't want the men to know that it was Stonewall Jackson, or morale would likely hit solid rock bottom.

Lieutenant Wynn returned and reported that though he couldn't find an ambulance nearby, he had gotten word to the nearest brigade, which was General Pender's, to send their surgeon. "I was afraid to go all the way back to Chancellorsville to get Dr. McGuire," he said anxiously. "I knew Dr. Barr could make it here much faster."

Jackson murmured, "Very good." Then, looking up at Hill, who still cradled his head, he whispered, "Is he a skillful surgeon, Hill?"

"He stands high in his brigade," Hill assured him. "We will have him see to you until Dr. McGuire can come."

Jackson seemed satisfied. Vaguely he looked up at the glowing night sky and murmured, "My own men."

Dr. Barr arrived and examined Jackson. He had been wounded three times—one bullet in the left shoulder, another in the left forearm, and one in the right palm. Captain Wilbourn had tied a handkerchief above the wound in his forearm as a tourniquet and had torn up a shirt to fashion a sling. He had also put strips of cloth around Jackson's right hand. "The wounds are already beginning to clot," Dr. Barr said, "so I don't believe any additional bandaging is needed right now. But he must be taken to a field hospital as quickly as possible."

Hill, who as a major general was the senior officer, ordered Barr back to his brigade. Sounds of firing and shouts of, "Halt, surrender!" sounded in the woods. The booming of artillery sounded closer, and the shells began to light up the woods very near to them. Hill tenderly slipped Jackson's head aside then stood. Now that General Jackson was wounded, he was next in command. General Hill was the only other major general in the field that night. "I'm going to go form the troops and meet the attack, General Jackson. And I will do my utmost to keep the men from knowing that you are wounded."

"Thank you," Jackson said faintly.

Hill left one of his staff officers, Captain Benjamin Leigh, to help, and another officer, Lieutenant James Smith, had joined them. It took six to carry a litter, so Lieutenant Morrison finally collared two soldiers and made them help. They had four rearing, stamping, spooked horses, so it was decided that Captain Wilbourn and Yancy must lead them, for no one could control Midnight but Yancy.

Once one of the litter bearers dropped his side because he had been shot through both arms. Joe Morrison managed to keep the litter from dropping. Then shells started sailing over their heads, screaming their death song, and by the roadside broken branches and young saplings were crashing to the ground. The other soldier simply lay his side of the litter down and fled. As gently as they could, Morrison, Wynn, Leigh, and Smith laid the litter down as the tornado of fire—canister, grape, and minié balls—continued.

Leigh ventured into the fiery woods and asked every man that he encountered for help, but they either ignored him and kept firing toward the enemy lines or they would melt back into the shadows. Finally, frustrated, Leigh went to a firing line and yelled, "General Jackson is wounded! We must have help getting him to safety!" Instantly he was surrounded by men, already fighting for the honor. Leigh chose the two stoutest, and they returned to the litter. Under heavy fire but without flinching, they and Yancy and Wilbourn went through the wilderness.

Finally they found an ambulance to transport the general to Reverend Melzi Chancellor's house, where Dr. McGuire waited. He joined Jackson in the ambulance and knelt by the litter. "I hope you are not badly hurt, General," he said in his customary kindly tone.

Jackson answered clearly, with no sign of fear, "I am badly injured, doctor. I fear I'm dying. I'm glad you've come. I think the place in my shoulder is still bleeding."

McGuire attended him as best he could in the jolting ambulance. It was close to eleven o'clock before they reached the Second Corps field hospital. Dr. Harvey Black, the chief surgeon, had heard the grievous news of Jackson's injury, and he had arranged for a special tent to be set up for him and had it warmed. They carried Jackson in and settled him on a comfortable cot, covered with warm blankets. Slowly he regained some color, and his short, painful breaths eased. Two other doctors were in attendance.

Dr. McGuire told him, "We must examine you, General."

Jackson nodded stiffly. It was obvious that he was controlling the pain with his iron will, though Dr. McGuire had given him whiskey and morphia.

McGuire continued, "We will give you chloroform so that you will have no pain. These gentlemen will help me. We might find bones badly broken, General, so that the only course might be amputation." McGuire paused then asked quietly, "If that is our conclusion, do you want us to go on with the operation?"

Jackson's voice was weak, but the answer was firm. "Certainly, McGuire. Do for me whatever you think best."

One of the doctors spread a soothing salve over Jackson's face to protect his skin from the acrid chemical. Then he folded a cloth into a cone over his face and dropped chloroform onto it, the heavy, bitter odor permeating the room. The general breathed deeply several times and murmured, "What an infinite blessing. Blessing. Blessing. . . Bless. . ."

The minié ball was just under the skin of his right hand, and McGuire removed it. He rolled it in his palm and sighed. "A smooth-bore Springfield. Our troops."

It was indeed necessary to amputate Jackson's left arm. The skilled surgeons, each of whom had performed this operation hundreds of times in the past two years of war, accomplished it in record time.

The general woke up a couple of times but slept the rest of the night peacefully.

The next day was Sunday, May 3. It was a pleasant, sweetly clear day. All of the fruit trees were blooming—apple, pear, cherry, and peach. Their delicate scents floated on the still air.

General Jackson's faithful chaplain, Reverend B. T. Lacy, led a small funeral procession of a few of Jackson's aides and staff officers to his family estate nearby, Ellwood. Yancy trailed behind, exhausted because he had not been able to sleep for worry about the general.

The solemn procession went to the Lacy family burial plot, where a very small grave had been dug. Reverend Lacy and the men said the Lord's Prayer. And then they reverently interred Stonewall Jackson's crushed arm.

The Sabbath was always a good day for the general. He awoke and ate a light breakfast and was cheerful. He sent Yancy with a dispatch for General Lee, just a few lines about his wound and the victorious attack the previous night. He visited with Reverend Lacy and told him that he had thought he was on the point of death when he had fallen on the litter, had prayed, and had immediately felt the peace of the Lord enter him, and he still knew that peace. Lieutenant Smith, another of Jackson's young aides, came in with some reports of the ongoing battle, and Jackson received them intelligently.

Yancy rode as if he were being chased to General Lee's headquarters. He didn't want to be away from General Jackson for even a minute. General Lee read Jackson's few scrawled lines, his handsome face grave. Then he quickly wrote a note and gave it to Yancy to take back to the general. Again Yancy pushed Midnight to his fastest gallop, a ride so smooth it was almost dreamy when he stretched out so elegantly.

Yancy brushed by the aides and officers gathered outside the tent and went in to Jackson. After all, he was the general's courier, and he had the right to deliver his dispatches to him. "General Lee sent this, sir," he said.

Jackson said, "Please read it to me, Lieutenant Tremayne."

Yancy read:

General,

 I have just received your note telling me that you were wounded. I cannot express my regret at this occurrence. Could I have directed events, I should have chosen for the good of the country to be disabled in your stead. I congratulate you on your victory, which is due to your skill and energy.

      Very respectfully, your obedient servant,

        R. E. Lee, General

Jackson looked embarrassed. Turning slightly away, he said in a choked voice, "General Lee is very kind. But he should give the praise to God."

That night Jackson slept peacefully without waking up and awoke Monday morning feeling well, and he ate well.

Early on, Dr. McGuire had a note from General Lee advising him to move the general to the rear. The Federals were threatening to cross the Rappahannock at a ford nearby, and they might drive in the direction of the field hospital.

Jackson blithely said, "If the enemy does come, I will not fear them. I have always been kind to their wounded, and I'm sure they would be kind to me."

The doctors were still discussing whether it would do more harm than good to move Jackson, when they received another note from General Lee that evening. It was peremptory in tone, which was unusual for the courteous general. He *ordered* them to move Jackson.

The next day they put General Jackson in an ambulance, and Yancy packed up his bedroll in preparation for leaving. Captain Wilbourn was returning to the front, and he came to speak to Yancy as he was saddling Midnight. Yancy came to attention and saluted.

"I know that you and Mrs. Jackson are friends, and General Jackson does seem to have a closer relationship to you than to the other aides," Captain Wilbourn said. "But, Lieutenant Tremayne, do you not feel that you should return to duty?"

"Sir, I am on duty," Yancy answered, staring straight ahead. "I am General Stonewall Jackson's courier."

Captain Wilbourn stared at him for a moment, and then his stern face softened. "I see. Carry on, Lieutenant."

"Yes, sir."

Engineers went ahead of the general's train, grubbing up roots, removing logs and branches, digging up jutting rocks, and filling in sinkholes and ruts to make the ride in the spartan ambulance as smooth as possible. Reverend Lacy, Dr. McGuire, and Lieutenant Smith rode with him. Yancy rode behind, with Jim driving a cart that had General Jackson's belongings in it.

The rule of the road was that the heavier vehicles had the right of way. When the ambulance driver tried to make teamsters pull aside, all he got for his trouble were harsh refusals. But when they were told that it was Stonewall Jackson being transported, they ran their wagons into the ditch, hopped out, and stood bareheaded, some of them in tears as the ambulance passed. From them the word passed quickly up the road that "Old Jack" was coming.

They also passed many men, veterans of Second Corps who were very lightly wounded and were walking to the field hospital. They shouted friendly messages to him, and many of them cried out that they wished they had been wounded instead of the general.

All along the road now hundreds of people gathered. Yancy searched their faces and saw in them the same reverence and sorrow that those who knew him well felt. Men stood with hats in hand; women bowed their heads and wept. Many people now came with gifts, whatever delicacies their meager farms could offer. Yancy and Jim collected pails of milk, cakes, pies, honey, dried fruits, bags of fried chicken, and fresh biscuits until the wagon was filled to overflowing. Jackson was endearingly surprised and grateful at the attention.

He was cheerful and bright most of the day, but in the afternoon he grew weak and nauseated. They stopped for a time and opened the ambulance doors for the general to get fresh air. And Dr. McGuire good-naturedly honored Jackson's old favorite remedy for nausea—cold towels on the stomach. People stood by watching them but remained at a respectful distance. All Dr. McGuire had to do was to ask the nearest man, "Is there a well near here with cold water?"

Half a dozen men and women took off running. The first man that made it back, panting, his face red, had a bucket of icy cold water. When the others came back, they were so crestfallen that Yancy and Jim told them that they were a godsend, too, because all of the attendants were very thirsty and so were the horses. This seemed to cheer them up; it made them feel as if they, too, were helping their revered general.

It was twenty-seven miles to the Chandler farm, a family that Jackson knew slightly. They arrived at about eight o'clock that evening. The Chandlers had taken in many other wounded soldiers, including two that had the highly contagious disease erysipelas, so the Chandlers offered General Jackson their study. It was an outbuilding much like Jackson's headquarters at Moss Neck Manor. It was a small plain building, cool and shady, nestled beneath three huge oak trees.

After they settled in, Jackson said he was very comfortable. He had tea and bread for supper. A spring thunderstorm broke, with the drowsy rhythm of rain on the roof, and Jackson slept.

Wednesday morning dawned a cool and freshly-washed morning. To Yancy's surprise, Peyton rode up and greeted Yancy before he went in to deliver his dispatches. After their hellos, he asked, "How is he?"

Yancy answered, "Pretty good, I think. He seems to be in good spirits. And Jim told me that he's talking about staying here just a few days, then moving to Ashland and resting there for a couple of days, and then home to Lexington to recover. Jim told him, 'And then you can come back and beat them Yankees better with one arm than they can do with two!' "

Peyton grinned, relaxing somewhat. "As he himself says, 'Good, good.' So listen, Yance, these dispatches I've got from General Stuart. He told me that I ought to give them to Dr. McGuire and that it would be best if the general didn't hear. Do you want to go inside and fetch him?"

"Sure. In fact I know General Jackson is sleeping right now. Jim can stay with him while I get the doctor." He went inside and came out with Dr. McGuire.

Reverend Lacy and Lieutenant Smith were seated outside the general's bedroom when Yancy told the doctor that there were confidential dispatches for him, and Dr. McGuire had motioned them to come. Peyton handed him the envelope, and Dr. McGuire read it quickly then looked up. He didn't dismiss Yancy and Peyton; he was not so strict as the officers, and he understood their particular friendship with Jackson.

"General Stuart says that he has received some reports that raiding Union cavalry may be in this district," Dr. McGuire told them gravely. "He advises us that he can't send a guard this far from the front."

"I'll ride around and do some reconnaisance," Yancy instantly volunteered. "I'll watch this afternoon and tonight."

"If there's a Yank around, Yancy will sniff him out," Peyton said. "Indian, you know."

Dr. McGuire grew thoughtful. "If by chance General Jackson is taken prisoner, I am determined to stay with him, to take care of him."

Reverend Lacy said, "I, too, will stay."

"And I," Lieutenant Smith said.

Yancy said, "I go where Stonewall goes. I'm his courier, and it's my duty to stay by his side."

Peyton sighed. "How I wish I could stay with him, too. But without him, the commanders are sending dispatches all over this mess of a battlefield every five minutes it seems. I have to get back. Dr. McGuire, the men are starving for news of General Jackson. Yancy says he seems to be doing well. May I give them a report?"

"Certainly. General Jackson is recovering—"

Peyton interrupted, "Sir, excuse me, but this is so important to the men that I would prefer to write it down just as you say it." From the courier's bag he took out pencil and paper.

Dr. McGuire continued, pausing to let Peyton write. "General Jackson's recovery is very satisfactory. His wounds are healing cleanly. His spirits are good. He is eating very well considering the trauma of his injuries and the surgery. He sleeps peacefully. He is keenly interested in the progress of the battle and is always glad for news of his men. We expect Mrs. Jackson and baby Julia to join us, perhaps tomorrow."

"Thank you, sir," Peyton said gracefully. "I'll return as fast as I can with this good news." He mounted Senator, gave them a jaunty salute, and dashed off.

General Jackson seemed to be doing so well that Dr. McGuire decided to let Jim watch him while he got a much-needed night of sleep.

Yancy scouted all over the district that day and night and saw no sign of Union soldiers, cavalry or otherwise. He returned at about midnight and was about to bed down when a shadowy figure slipped outside. Jim came to Yancy's campfire. "I'm watching the

gen'ral tonight. I was thinkin' mebbe you might like to help me."
Yancy was one of Jim's favorites, mainly because he was one of
Jackson's favorites.

Yancy jumped up eagerly, and they tiptoed back into the house.
Without speaking they took chairs by the general's bed. On the far
side of the room, Dr. McGuire slept on a sofa, his face tranquil, his
breaths deep and restful.

And so the two kept watch, Jim with uncomplicated affection,
Yancy with somewhat more complex emotions. He esteemed
Jackson personally, but he also had the sense of separation from
him, the chasm between a mere soldier and the great man that is
his leader in the bloody business of war.

Neither Jim nor Yancy slept, though both of them got up to
stretch and move around a bit, careful to be quiet so as not to wake
either the doctor or the general.

Jackson seemed to be sleeping quietly, but around two thirty
he started getting restless. Then at about three he came awake all
at once, his mouth drawn into a tight line, his face grimacing with
pain. His eyes quickly roved around the room, and he whispered,
"H–hello, Jim. Hello, Yancy. I don't feel well at all, Jim. Would you
get me some cold wet towels for my abdomen?"

"Sure, sir," he said, and left to fetch icy water.

Yancy said hesitantly, "Sir, are you in pain?"

"I am," he admitted with difficulty. "My right side. . ."

"Sir, shouldn't I wake Dr. McGuire to check on you?"

"No," Jackson said harshly. "The man hasn't slept in three
nights. Leave him be. The cold towels will do the trick."

But they didn't. Jackson steadily worsened, the vague pain in his
side gradually turning into paroxysms of agony with every breath
that he took. Still he refused to allow Jim or Yancy to awaken the
doctor. He managed to hold out until the first chilly gray light of
dawn, and finally he asked Yancy to get Dr. McGuire.

The doctor sprang awake and hurried to Jackson. After
listening to his heart and his chest, Dr. McGuire knew what
was wrong. Jackson had developed pneumonia in his right lung.
Immediately he gave Jackson morphia for the paralyzing pain he
was experiencing.

It eased his breathing and obviously lessened his pain. But in his weakened state, the powerful drug affected his mind, and all day he wandered in and out of consciousness, sometimes talking to himself, sometimes talking to people who weren't there.

Anna arrived that afternoon with Julia and Hetty. One of the doctor's staff attendants had been dispatched to meet the train. As soon as Anna got into the buggy, she sensed that things had gone wrong. Immediately she asked the young attendant how her husband was.

"The general is doing pretty well," he answered with some hesitation.

Anna asked no more. She had to wait on the porch until the doctors finished dressing Jackson's wounds. Finally Dr. McGuire came to fetch her. As soon as she saw her husband, she knew that he would never return to Lexington. He was well on the way to his final home.

She knew of his wounds and the surgery, of course, but there was no way to prepare herself for the sight of his missing arm, the stump thickly bandaged, and his swollen, misshapen right hand. His face looked sunken and skeletal. He slept, but there seemed no repose in it, for his breaths were short and ragged.

Gently Dr. McGuire awakened him.

He looked up, and the old familiar light came into his dull eyes when he saw Anna. "My esposa, my love, how glad I am you have come," he said. When he saw Anna's distress he said, "I know you would give your life for me. But I'm perfectly resigned. Don't be sad. I hope I am going to recover. Pray for me, but always remember in your prayers the old petition, 'Thy will be done.' "

Then he sank into a stupor, mumbling incoherently. After a time he barely opened his eyes and murmured, "My darling, you must cheer up and not wear such a long face in the sickroom."

She asked him several times that afternoon when he roused if he wanted to see the baby.

He always replied, "Not yet. Wait until I feel better."

Anna sat all that long afternoon and evening with him. Dr.

CROSSING

McGuire only interrupted when Jackson began to show pain, to give him more morphine.

Occasionally Jackson would rouse and speak endearments to Anna. Once he said, "My darling, you are very much loved." Another time he whispered, "You're the most precious little wife in the world."

On Friday, he seemed to rally a bit, though he admitted he was exhausted, and throughout the day he grew noticeably weaker. Again he wandered in and out of consciousness.

On Saturday, he wanted to see Julia, and Anna brought her to him. Jackson beamed at her, obviously completely lucid. His splinted right hand was huge and clumsy, but Julia seemed to have no fear of it as he caressed her. She smiled at him and he murmured, "Little comforter. . .little comforter."

That afternoon Jackson wanted to send Yancy to get Reverend Lacy.

McGuire frowned. Upon his examination he had found that both of Jackson's lungs were filled with fluid. His respiration was shallow and fast, like a hoarse panting. "I beg you, General, I don't think it would do you good to converse with the reverend just now," Dr. McGuire said.

But Jackson insisted, and Yancy fetched Reverend Lacy. Jackson's first concern was to learn if Reverend Lacy was continuing to work on an armywide observance of the Sabbath. Lacy assured him that he was. Then Jackson spoke for a while of his favorite topic in this world—spiritual matters. In spite of his determination to see the chaplain, Jackson was utterly exhausted when he left.

His condition steadily worsened. That night, as Anna sat with him, she asked gently, "Thomas, might I read some Psalms of consolation to you?"

Vaguely he shook his head and mumbled, "Too much pain. . .to be able to listen." But in a few minutes he roused somewhat and said apologetically, "But yes, Anna, please do. We must never refuse that."

She read in her soft voice.

After a bit Jackson said, "Sing to me."

Anna, who had managed to remain calm and steady as she read, knew that she couldn't sing Thomas's favorite hymns without crying. She went and got her brother, Lieutenant Joe Morrison, who after he had helped Jackson that awful night had stayed on to attend to him. Together brother and sister sang.

As the night wore on, Jackson's breathing became short, wheezing gasps. But after they had sung several hymns, Anna said, "The singing had a quieting effect, and he seemed to rest in perfect peace."

In the morning, Dr. McGuire had a somber meeting with Anna and gave her his tragic prognosis. "I believe he will die today, Mrs. Jackson. I do not think he will see another night."

Calmly Anna nodded and went back to her husband's bedside. Long before, Jackson had told her that he had no fear of dying, but he hoped that when that time came he would "have a few hours' preparation before entering into the presence of my Maker and Redeemer."

She steeled herself for this last and most difficult service for her husband. She roused him from his stupor and said quietly, "Do you know the doctors say that you must very soon be in heaven?"

His eyes were open, and he looked at her but said nothing.

Anna repeated it and added, "Do you not feel willing to acquiesce in God's allotment, if He wills you to go today?"

He stirred a little but apparently didn't comprehend what she was saying, and so she repeated it, softly and clearly. This time he focused on her face and said, "I prefer it." His words came out slurred, just a little, so he repeated, more firmly, "I prefer it."

They talked a little while longer, and then the surgeons came in to examine him, though they did not redress his wounds. They disturbed him as little as possible. He sank into a stupor when they left.

Later he roused again to see Anna kneeling by his bed. Again she told him that before the sun went down he would be in heaven.

He thought for a moment then asked, "Will you call Dr. McGuire?"

Instantly his faithful physician was at his bedside.

"Doctor," Jackson said, clearly and alertly, "Anna informs me that you have told her that I am to die today. Is it so?"

Always gentle, always warm, Dr. McGuire replied, "General,

the medicine has done its utmost."

Jackson pondered this for a bit, staring up at the ceiling. Now, instead of his habitual "Good, good," he already seemed to be seeing a higher plane, and he said, "Very good, very good. It is all right." And then he comforted Anna, who at last was weeping.

She stayed, and they talked from time to time. Jackson seemed to have recovered his full senses. Later he said, "It is the Lord's Day. . .my wish is fulfilled. I have always desired to die on Sunday."

In the warm, bright afternoon, he again wandered. He gave orders, spoke to his favorites on his staff. He mentioned Yancy once, murmuring that he should ride hard and return quickly. He fought battles, was at home in Lexington with Anna and Julia, was praying. He fell silent.

Only Anna was at his bedside, holding his bandaged hand, crying silently.

The clock struck three sonorous notes.

His breathing grew shallower; his chest barely rose.

At 3:15, his eyes closed. Clearly and gladly he said, "Let us cross over the river and rest under the shade of the trees."

And so he did.

CHAPTER TWENTY-SIX

The once-splendid uniform that Jeb Stuart had given Stonewall Jackson was bloodstained and slashed to shreds. Jim had found a suit of civilian clothes to fit, but then he was so distraught that for the first time he could not attend his general.

Yancy, Lieutenant Smith, Dr. McGuire, and Reverend Lacy dressed General Jackson in the clothes then wrapped him in a military cloak. They covered the coffin in spring flowers and banked lily of the valley at the head.

Anna stayed with him most of the night. He showed no trace of the suffering he had endured in his last days.

The next day, Monday, May 11, 1863, the funeral party left for Richmond.

Yancy didn't want to leave Midnight behind, so he wrangled an empty cattle car and settled the skittish stallion in it. Midnight didn't do too well on trains, so Yancy planned on staying with him.

To his surprise, riding as if a bandit was on their heels, Peyton, Chuckins, and Sandy came flying up. They spotted Yancy and without prelude started loading their horses into the boxcar with Midnight. Their faces were grim, and Chuckins had traces of tears on his face.

As they settled in the car, Yancy asked, "How did you get leave?

CROSSING

General Lee wouldn't let the Stonewall Brigade take leave. He wouldn't even leave the field himself." The Battle of Chancellorsville was still raging.

"Most of the staff and aides got leave," Peyton answered. "Since General Stuart took over command of Second Corps, he's used some of us, but he has his own staff and couriers aplenty, you know."

"But what about you, Sandy?" Yancy asked curiously. Sandy was a pivotal part of General Pendleton's battery. He had consistently gotten praise for his bravery and daring in every battle they fought, and he was the number one gun captain. Many men asked to be on his gun crew.

Sandy shrugged carelessly. "I went to General Pendleton and requested leave. He refused, telling me about General Lee's stand on furloughs right now. So I said that I was giving him notice that I was deserting, and since the penalty was either getting arrested or getting shot, I told him I'd appreciate it if he'd take the next few days to decide which it would be. I would report back after General Jackson's funeral and he could do whatever he wanted. So he gave me leave."

For most of the trip the four friends stared into space, remembering. Every once in a while one of them would say, "Remember First Manassas? He stood there, the bullets whizzing by him, as calm as a summer's day. . . ." And another memory, and another. "Do you remember. . .remember. . .?"

When they neared Richmond, they got up and groomed the horses until their coats shone like polished glass in sunlight. Then they worked on their uniforms, polishing buttons, arranging their sashes just so, making certain that their sabers hung just right, the scabbards spotless, polishing and repolishing their boots, flicking every single speck of dust off of their tunics. The four looked splendid together. Peyton's and Yancy's long tunics, with collars and cuffs of infantry blue, had gold lieutenant's flashes on the collar and elaborate gold embroidery on the cuffs. They wore dark red sashes, the regimental color of the Stonewall Brigade. Chuckins and Sandy were still sergeants, so their sleeves had the distinctive three chevrons. Chuckins's sash was the regimental dark red, but Sandy's insignia and sash were the bright scarlet of the artillery. Motionless and silent they stood for the last few miles, not wanting to sit down again on their blankets and get dusty. They were determined to show nothing but perfection for General Jackson.

Black-draped carriages had been sent for Mrs. Jackson, Hetty and the baby, and two ladies that accompanied her, and for the staff officers escorting the general.

One of them, an older man who had purchased a commission as a captain, was an Episcopalian minister—for Jackson had several ministers on his staff—and was a notorious stickler for rules and protocol. As the officers helped the ladies into their carriage, he muttered to a lieutenant, "What are those impudent boys doing? We had not planned for a mounted escort. Go tell them to fall back and follow at a discreet distance."

Anna followed his critical gaze, and her weary, reddened eyes softened. "No, sir," she said with uncharacteristic curtness. "Leave them alone."

The captain looked vaguely disapproving but said no more.

In truth, Anna felt it was very fitting that they should escort General Jackson. Yancy, Peyton, and Chuckins were the only members of the Stonewall Brigade there, and Sandy was one of the few VMI cadets that had left the institute to follow Jackson into war. For a fleeting moment, the sight of them made Anna forget her overwhelming sorrow. They looked so noble, so dignified, and they were all such handsome young men.

Leading this group were Yancy on Midnight and Peyton on his gorgeous gold palomino, Senator. To each side were the smaller horses, Chuckins's pinto, Brownie, and Sandy's elegant buckskin mare, Jasmine. Even the simple Brownie seemed to sense the solemnity of the day, for she held her head high and tossed her glossy mane and stepped proudly.

Slowly the procession made its way the two miles to the executive mansion. Throngs of people crowded the streets in uncanny silence, merely watching the funeral cart with its flower-draped casket go by. They stood still, their grief-stricken faces imprinted in Yancy's memory. Most of the women, and many of the men, were weeping.

When they reached the mansion, Governor Letcher met Anna, and Mrs. Letcher took her to the governor's private rooms, where mourning clothes and a veil were waiting for her. The staff officers knotted in little groups, planning where they would stay the night.

Yancy told his friends, "I'm going to the Haydens. Right now. I just won't wait any longer. I just can't."

Chuckins and Sandy had no idea why he spoke that way. But Peyton, for all his lackadaisical ways, had come to understand that Yancy was in love with Lorena Hayden—the lovely woman in the drawings—and that there was some problem, insurmountable it would seem, between them. He nodded encouragingly to Yancy. "Go. Chuckins and Sandy are staying with me." Senator Stevens had an enormous mansion on the James River.

Without another word Yancy turned and rode off.

Chuckins turned to Peyton, his honest face puzzled. "What was all that about?"

Peyton answered with his old litany, soberly this time. "Yancy doesn't know anything. I don't know anything. Sandy doesn't know anything. And neither do you."

Recklessly Yancy rode Midnight hard through Richmond's streets. Although the way from the railroad station to the executive mansion had been congested with people, the side streets were all but deserted.

He clattered up to the Hayden home, as he had done so many times before—but this time was different. He jumped off Midnight and started to run to the door but then paused. Again he wiped off his dusty boots, straightened his tunic, swiped the buttons to make them glow, checked his sash and saber, then smoothed back his hair. The errant forelock promptly fell down over his forehead again, but he scarcely noticed. Taking a deep breath, he went to the door and knocked.

Missy answered it. Without a word to him, she took him in her arms and hugged him. "I'm so sorry you lost him, Yancy. It's a sad day for everyone in the South."

"Thank you, Missy," he said. "It is a very sad time."

"They's in the parlor. Go on in," she said, wiping her eyes with her apron. "You're family. Ain't no need for me to announce you."

Yancy went to the parlor and hesitated, standing almost at attention in the doorway. Ever since General Jackson had died, he had not felt at all like himself. His mind, for one thing, seemed to have come to a screeching halt, stopped in that warm room where Stonewall took his last breaths. He felt like one of Stonewall's Boys, bereft and lost, stuck in time as Yancy the soldier, stiff and unyielding.

The only other thing he felt was a tremendous desire to see Lorena. He had no plan of what he would say to her; he couldn't picture it in his half-blank mind. He just knew he had to see her.

At the sound of his footsteps and the slight metallic sound of his scabbard, Dr. and Mrs. Hayden looked up.

Yancy, frozen in the doorway, could only manage to say, "Hello. I—I came with—with—escorting General Jackson."

Lily Hayden hurried to him and hugged him much as Missy did. "Oh, Yancy dear, we are so very glad to see you, but so very sorry it is in these tragic circumstances. Are you all right?"

"Yes, ma'am."

She held him at arm's length, and she and Dr. Hayden looked him up and down. They both seemed puzzled at Yancy's obvious distance.

He couldn't frame the words to say to reassure them. Finally he blurted out, "Where's Lorena?"

"Why, she's in the garden, dear," Lily answered after a slight hesitation and a glance at her husband. "Why don't you go on out to see her?"

Without another word, Yancy turned and marched out to the garden.

She was there, cutting flowers. Her dress was a cheerful spring muslin, with tiny sprigs of peach-colored roses entwined with little tendrils of ivy. She wore a wide-brimmed hat with a peach ribbon tied under her chin. The setting sun barely touched her face, lighting it with a soft golden glow. Lorena didn't look up, as she was humming to herself and obviously didn't hear his approach.

As Yancy hesitated just outside the kitchen door, watching her, she began to sing. It was a song he had never heard before. Her sweet, clear, high soprano voice, and the hymn itself, rent his heart, a confused torrent of great joy mingled with inconsolable sorrow.

Hark! Hark my soul! angelic songs are swelling,
O'er earth's green fields and ocean's wave-beat shore:
How sweet the truth those blessed strains are telling
Of that new life when sin shall be no more.

Angels of Jesus, angels of light,
Singing to welcome the pilgrims of the night!

Onward we go, for still we hear them singing,
'Come, weary souls, for Jesus bids you come';
And through the dark, its echoes sweetly ringing,
The music of the Gospel leads us home.

Angels of Jesus, angels of light,
Singing to welcome the pilgrims of the night!

Angels, sing on, your faithful watches keeping;
Sing us sweet fragments of the songs above,
Till morning's joy shall end the night of weeping,
And life's long shadows break in cloudless love.

She began to hum the refrain again, but something unseeing touched her, and she looked up, right into Yancy's eyes. Much like him, she froze.

Long moments passed.

Yancy, in a choked voice, said, "Lorena. . . ? Lorena. . ."

She dropped her basket, dropped her shears, dropped the red, red rose she had just clipped. She ran to him so fast that her hat tumbled over her back, held by the ribbons. When she reached him she threw herself into his arms, and even though she was such a tiny woman, she moved so fast and hard that he almost staggered as he embraced her.

"Oh, Yancy, Yancy, you've remembered, haven't you?" she cried against his chest.

"Yes. Finally. . .I've come back to you," he murmured. "Lorena. . ."

"I love you! Desperately!" she said, pulling back and putting her hands on his face. "I've loved you for—forever!" Then she pulled him down to her and kissed him long and passionately.

He lifted his head and stared down at her. "Are you sure? You love me?"

"Oh, yes, yes."

He sagged a little, his shoulders bowed, and he dropped his head. He still held her in the circle of his arms.

She waited.

In a voice so low she could barely hear him, he said, "That's—that's good, Lorena. Because I not only love you, I—I need you. Much, much more than when I was hurt and sick. I need you now, so much, because—because—"

"You grieve for him," she said softly. "You've lost him. I know, all too well, what it is to lose someone you love."

"I do grieve, and I did love him," Yancy said with difficulty. "And all I've been able to think of to comfort me—is you."

"I will do that," she said. "From now on, forever, I will guard your heart as if it is my own."

He pulled her to him with a low groan. Yancy had not shed a tear in all this horrid war and did not cry when Stonewall Jackson died. And now, as if he were a lost child, he held her close and sobbed.

Yancy and Lorena went to speak to Dr. Hayden and Lily, returning from the garden where they had, both literally and figuratively, found each other. They went into the parlor, hand in hand.

Lorena's parents looked up as they entered. Dr. Hayden looked mystified, but after seeing their glowing faces, Lily smiled.

"We—we have something to tell you, sir, ma'am," Yancy stuttered. He shifted from one foot to the other awkwardly. "We—I mean, Lorena and I—"

"Just say it, Yancy. It's quite all right, you know," Lorena said with her old exasperation.

Yancy blew out a long whistling breath. "Okay. Okay. See, Dr. Hayden and Mrs. Hayden, we—I mean, Lorena has said—I asked her—"

"We're in love," Lorena blurted out. "And we're engaged."

"What?" Dr. Hayden asked, bewildered.

"Finally," Lily muttered. She rose, went to them, and kissed each on the cheek. "Come, come, Yancy, I'll bet you didn't look nearly so terrified when you were riding into one of those famous battles we keep hearing about."

"Yes, ma'am. I mean, no, ma'am." He and Lorena sat in their old chairs, but they reached across to hold hands.

"This is wonderful, perfectly wonderful," Lily said happily, taking her seat by her husband. "Although for a long time now we've looked at you as a son, now you truly will be, Yancy. I couldn't be happier, both for you and for my Lorena."

"Thank you, ma'am," Yancy mumbled. He seemed almost—but not quite—as stunned as Dr. Hayden.

Lily asked eagerly, "Have you made any plans yet? Set a date?"

Now a shadow crossed over Yancy's face, and he focused and became intent. "No, ma'am. I thought, somehow, that Lorena might want to wait until the war is over before we got married—"

"No," Lorena said firmly. "No, I don't want to wait."

"I don't either, once I thought about it," Yancy agreed. "I've thought about a lot of things since General Jackson died. One thing I realized, since I knew him and Mrs. Jackson before, they didn't waste time. They took every possible minute that they had together and treasured it, no matter what the circumstances. I know that if you had told Mrs. Jackson before she married him that he would die so soon, so young, after they'd been married less than six years and when their only daughter was only four months old, she would say that she wouldn't hesitate, she would marry him anyway, as soon as she could. And that's the way we feel," he finished firmly.

"Exactly. I'm just sorry that we can't get married today," Lorena grumbled.

"What?" Dr. Hayden said again.

"General Jackson is going to Lexington, to lie in state one day. And then on Friday he's to be buried. With your permission, sir, ma'am, I'd like for Lorena to come to Lexington, to be with me these next few hard days. It would be such a comfort to me," Yancy said, now confident. "And then I would like for us to visit my family on Saturday. I will bring her back on Sunday. And then I have to return to Chancellorsville."

"Of course," Lily agreed instantly. "That will be perfectly fine. Missy can go as your chaperone, dear. I only wish that Jesse and I were well enough to travel to Lexington for General Jackson's funeral and then to go visit Becky and Daniel. But I think it would be too much of a strain, don't you, dear?"

"Hmm? Oh. Oh yes. A strain," Dr. Hayden repeated.

Lily patted his knee. "Poor dear, he hadn't a clue. Of course, I knew all along."

Lorena put her head to the side, like a small bird. "You did? However did you know, Mother?"

Lily smiled, a sweet expression that was often on her face. "I hope you find out, my darling Lorena, because only then will you understand. Mothers know. Mothers always know."

"I want to know," Lorena said softly, looking at Yancy. "And I dare to hope it may be soon."

On that night they embalmed him.

The famous artist, Frederick Volck, and his assistant, Pietro Zamboggi, made his death mask. Oddly enough, Volck had visted Stonewall Jackson's camp in December of 1862, at Fredericksburg, when Lee, Jackson, and Longstreet were camped on the heights above the town and faced Burnside's doomed troops below. Volck had even done some sketches of Stonewall after his staff persuaded him to pose on a stool. As he was prone to do, Jackson fell asleep, and the staff roared with laughter, which woke him up. He was embarrassed but good-natured about it. The work which the artist did this night was very different from that cheerful scene.

He lay in state the next morning at the executive mansion, in the Reception Room. The public was not allowed in there, but any person who could scrape up any connection to the Confederate government and came to the mansion that night was allowed to view the shadowed features. Many lingered for long moments, and many more tears were shed.

Without being asked, and without consulting anyone, Yancy, Peyton, Chuckins, and Sandy came to the executive mansion at dawn that Tuesday. They were greeted at the door by a disdainful butler. "And you are. . . ?" he asked snootily.

"We are General Jackson's honor guard," Yancy answered firmly.

"I have no knowledge of this," the butler said suspiciously.

Yancy stepped up to stand very close—too close—to the butler. He looked down at him; the man was at least a foot shorter than Yancy. In a soft tone that brooked no nonsense and may even have had a bit of menace in it, he said, "Then you may go wake up Mrs. Jackson and ask her about us. She has given us permission to escort her husband all the way to his resting place." This, of course, was not strictly true. But Yancy knew Anna Jackson, and he knew that she would, and did, wish it.

The butler took a hasty step back, almost stumbling. "No, no, of course I wouldn't dream of disturbing Mrs. Jackson. Please come in and follow me to the Reception Room."

Yancy took his place at the head of the general's coffin with Peyton at the foot. They stood unmoving at strict parade attention, staring straight ahead. After four hours, Chuckins and Sandy relieved them. They took these shifts until the afternoon, when General Jackson's pallbearers and funeral procession arrived, and Jackson was taken to the House of Representatives.

His coffin was placed in the hall and put on a white-draped altar before the speaker's bench, with the Confederate flag draped over it. The assembled crowd to witness the placing of General Jackson in state included President Jefferson Davis and his aides, several generals and other high-ranking officers and their staffs, the governor, the cabinet, Richmond city officials, and a number of Virginia and Richmond politicians. They had a long prayer.

After it was over, Yancy pushed people aside and the four friends marched to the general's casket. The crowd seemed stunned, but before anyone could say anything, Anna went to Yancy and put her hand out. He took it in both of his.

"Thank you, Yancy," she said softly, but it echoed throughout the silent room. "He was very proud of you, all of you. He would be glad that you are here." She turned and swept out, her long black skirts whispering on the polished floor. Immediately the crowd broke up and followed her. Yancy and Peyton took their stations guarding the general.

More than twenty thousand people filed through the hall that day and evening. They piled so many flowers about the bier that some had to be taken away to make room for people to pass by the coffin. As it grew later, officials made several attempts to close the doors, but they were soundly shouted down by the hundreds and hundreds of people who had waited in the line of mourners so long and so patiently. Taking pity on them, Governor Letcher ordered the doors left open until everyone who wanted to see the general had filed by and said their good-byes.

Yancy, Peyton, Chuckins, and Sandy guarded him all day until midnight. They never showed any weariness at all. They never wavered. They stayed at his side until the last mourner left the hall of the House of Representatives.

The next day, Stonewall returned to the institute for the last time. By train he went to Gordonsville and then Lynchburg. At each stop the station was crowded with hundreds of people. They pressed close to Anna's special car, crying out to her. Many times they called out, pleading to see Julia. Anna took pity on them, and Hetty held Julia up to the window dozens of times to be kissed. Julia bore it well, never crying, never fussy, often smiling.

From Lynchburg they took a canal barge to Lexington. The four friends insisted this time on leading the funeral procession to the institute. There VMI cadets took over the escort, marching with their arms reversed. Jackson's big gray horse that had been a gift from an admirer was the riderless horse. He was led by a VMI cadet, empty boots in the stirrups turned backward.

They took Stonewall to his old lecture room, which had not been used since he left. There he lay the entire day, and another long procession of grieving men and women passed by the window. Roses were piled high beneath it. All day the slow, mournful firing of the institute's cannon sounded, mourning the loss of their most revered and valiant soldier.

Daniel, Becky, Lorena, and Missy stood at the front of the crowd that lined the way to Virginia Military Institute. Yancy, Peyton, Chuckins, and Sandy led the funeral procession with great somber grace. When the cadets met them, the four friends returned the cadets' salutes, turned and rode to the rear of the procession, then turned to the side and dismounted. Yancy hurried to join his family.

After Stonewall Jackson had been placed in state at the institute, they all returned to the farm. Daniel had brought the buggy, so Becky and Missy rode with them, while Yancy rode Midnight.

The Shenandoah Valley was breathtaking in spring. Every scene was richly colored in a hundred shades of green, every field had riotous wildflowers blooming, every house they passed had luxurious gardens surrounding them. Lorena couldn't see well enough out of the buggy's back window, so, being the outspoken lady that she was, she demanded that Daniel let her sit with him on the driver's bench. Of course, Becky was just as demanding, and so she climbed up with them, and the three of them sat crowded together, shoulder-to-shoulder.

Yancy laughed at them. Since he had at last found his comfort in Lorena, his mind and soul and even his body felt lighter, more alive. He could smile and laugh now.

As she had done countless times before, Zemira came out onto the porch to meet them. Behind her scooted Callie Jo, now five years old, and David, who was three. They weren't shy children at all.

Callie Jo ran to Yancy, supremely unmindful of Midnight's prancing hooves, while David waddled to the side of the buggy, held his arms up, and lisped, "Hold 'im."

Yancy jumped down and swooped Callie Jo up high in the air. "Hello, Jo-Jo. Missed me?"

"Yes, Nance," she answered in her little-girl voice. "Now, ride me on Minnight."

"Not now. Later. Right now I want you to meet my friend Miss Lorena. You'll like her."

Zemira came straight up to Lorena when she climbed down from the buggy, threw her arms around her, and hugged her soundly. Then she stood back and looked at her with dancing eyes. "Well, if you aren't just the tiniest little bitty thing I ever saw in my life. And Becky says you can boss Yancy just fine. Big trouble in a little package, I'll bet."

Holding Callie Jo, Yancy came up to them and said, "You know it, Grandmother. But she's pretty nice. Most of the time."

They all went into the house, talking. As usual, Zemira had cooked an enormous meal for them—ham, fried chicken, new potatoes, sauerkraut, green beans, creamed corn, and, of course, Yancy's favorite, Amish Friendship Bread. They found their seats, Callie next to David, in his homemade high chair, and Lorena sitting by Yancy. Without a word, Daniel, Becky, Zemira, and even Callie Jo and David bowed their heads. Lorena glanced at Yancy, and he bowed his, too. Silence ensued. Yancy looked back up as he realized Lorena might be puzzled at their silent praying as he was when he first came here. After a few moments, he pinched her arm, and she looked up to see everyone starting to help themselves to the delicious food.

They kept the conversation light during the meal, mostly talking about the farm, the crops, the doings in the community. No talk of war or death shadowed this family time together.

After they finished and cleared away, Becky and Zemira put the children to bed and they all gathered in the parlor. It was a cool night, and Yancy and Daniel built a small, cozy fire.

Yancy and Lorena sat close together on the settee, and across from them Daniel, Becky, and Zemira sat on the sofa. Yancy reached over and took Lorena's hand. "I have two very important things to tell you," he said. "The first is that I spoke to Reverend White, the pastor of the First Presbyterian Church in Lexington. Mrs. Jackson had been kind enough to write to him and tell him of my situation. You know that I've been a Christian for almost two years now, but I've never been baptized. I want you to be with me when I am, of course. But I know that no bishop in the Amish church will baptize me. Mrs. Jackson explained this to Reverend White, and he's agreed to come out and baptize me here, so that you can all be present."

"Thank the Lord!" Zemira exclaimed, beaming. "That will be a day of rejoicing, for sure and certain, grandson!"

"It will," Daniel agreed. "I had thought about this, you know, Yancy. But I didn't know how to solve it. Many ministers would be wary of baptizing someone that is not in their congregation."

Yancy nodded. "I can understand that. Mrs. Jackson understood immediately. I had the opportunity to be there when she and General Jackson had their baby baptized, and I visited with Mrs. Jackson the next day. She told me of Dr. White, and she must have written to him that very day. Pretty soon I got a kind letter from him, welcoming me into the service of God and assuring me that he would be honored to baptize me at any place I chose."

"I will write to Mrs. Jackson and to Reverend White to thank them," Daniel promised. "It's good to have faithful and caring brothers and sisters in the Lord."

"Even if they're not in the community?" Zemira, the lifelong Amish woman, asked suspiciously.

"Well?" Daniel countered, grinning. "Even if they're not?"

"Hmm. Even if they are those English, I suppose," Zemira agreed. Somewhat.

"Which sorta brings me to the next thing I want to tell you," Yancy said. "I'm sorry to say, Grandmother, that I have asked this English to marry me. And she's been fool enough to say yes."

With glad cries, Zemira and Becky jumped up, pulled Lorena to her feet, and hugged her so many times that she felt bruised. Daniel and Yancy stood and solemnly shook hands as men do.

Finally they all regained their seats, Yancy and Lorena glancing at each other and exchanging beaming smiles. Happily Becky asked, "When? When, Yancy?"

He sobered, though he didn't wear the same desolate face that had so marked him a few days before. "I have to go back, you know. After the funeral. The Yankees at Chancellorsville are still making noise, and General Lee says that we have to stay and be vigilant, for no one knows when the next battle will be."

Zemira sighed. "Very true. All we know is that there will be another, and another, in this wicked old world. But"—she brightened—"you children look so happy. I know that you will have a good life together. And won't you have some pretty babies!" Both Lorena and Yancy blushed, and Zemira laughed at them.

"Anyway," Yancy continued, "just as soon as I can, when we may see a few days of peace ahead, I'm going to ask for a furlough. Then I'll come home and bless Reverend White again. He said he'll marry us anytime, even if it's only with an hour's notice. But you know that I'll try very hard to make it a time when you all and Dr. and Mrs. Hayden can be there. Neither Lorena nor I can imagine getting married without our families."

"Then we'll pray for days of peace ahead," Daniel said. "Many of them."

They talked long into the night before Daniel, Becky, and Zemira finally headed off to bed.

Yancy and Lorena sat out on the porch for a few minutes before they retired. They stood close together at the porch steps, looking at the vast tapestry of stars blanketing the blessed valley. "New moon," Yancy murmured. "New love. New life." He turned to her and took her in his arms.

Lorena said, "I knew I had already found true friends in Becky and your father, but now I know that they and your grandmother have already begun including me in the family. I don't think I've ever been happier. I will never forget this day."

"And I will never forget you again, Lorena," he promised. "And I will never leave you again. No matter what happens. No matter where I am. I'll be with you always."

"And I with you," she whispered. "For always. . .beginning now."

EPILOGUE

On the next day—another innocent, pretty Virginia spring day—General Stonewall Jackson took his last journey. Reverend White conducted a short service. Then the procession went to the Lexington Cemetery. In the shadow of the hills he knew so well, in the valley that he loved so much, Stonewall Jackson was finally at rest.

After the earthly good-byes were said, Anna Jackson, crying softly beneath her veil, turned and walked away from her husband's coffin. She didn't look back. The attendees followed her out of the cemetery. . . .

Except for four boys, whom Stonewall Jackson had taught to be men. They came to stand by his coffin, with their beloved flag draped over it. Mounds of flowers surrounded them, the air heavy with their heavenly-sweet scent.

"Atten–tion!" Yancy ordered in a low voice.

Together, very slowly, they raised their hands to give one last salute. They held it for long moments then together snapped back to attention. In silence they stood.

"I will always believe we were closer to him than the others," Peyton said quietly. "Guess no one else would believe it."

"I do," Chuckins said staunchly.

"I do," Sandy agreed.

Yancy said, "It's the truth. We were Stonewall's Boys."

the SWORD

PART ONE: FLORA & JEB 1855—1861

CHAPTER ONE

Flora Cooke glared at her full-length reflection in the cheval mirror. So far, in the endless preparations for a young lady of good family to ready herself for a ball, she had put on her chemise, knickers, and stockings and then had pulled on the great bell-shaped crinoline. She pushed it to one side, and it swung airily back and forth, never touching her legs. "Ding, dong," she said whimsically.

The nineteen-year-old girl in the mirror was plain, Flora knew very well. But she was so lively, so quick and intelligent, and of such willing wit that she was well known as a "charmer." She did have some good physical attributes, too; her chestnut-brown hair was shiny and thick and took a curl very well, and she had that very unusual combination, for brunettes, of having royal-blue eyes. Her brows were perfect arches, and her long, thick lashes were the envy of many women. Her complexion was like the most delicate magnolia blossom. Though she was not conventionally pretty, Flora had always had her share of male admirers.

And another reason for that, Flora knew, was because of her figure. From a skinny, awkward thirteen-year-old with blemishes covering her face, she had bloomed into a delicate, small woman with a tiny waist and hands and feet, sweetly rounded shoulders, a long graceful neck, and a perfect bosom. She had the classic hourglass figure, while being as dainty as a porcelain figurine.

She was still contemplating her reflection with some satisfaction when her maid, Ruby, came in holding her new ball dress, a peach-colored taffeta confection. The neckline was low, the sleeves off the shoulder, as was fashionable for evening wear, and Ruby had just finished starching and ironing the eight cotton, lace-trimmed ruffles in the wide skirt. Carefully she laid the dress out on Flora's bed then turned to her, hands on hips. "Miss Flora Cooke, am I standin' here looking at you with no corset on?" Ruby snapped, her eyes flashing. She was a shapely girl, an ebony black with wide, liquid, dark eyes, only two years older than Flora herself.

"You are," Flora answered absently. "Mm, the dress looks heavenly, Ruby!" She picked up a ruffle and rubbed it between her fingers, savoring the crisp feel of the thick taffeta and the still-warm stiffness of the cotton ruffle underneath.

"Don't you be gettin' around no subject with me," Ruby sniffed. "Why am I standin' here looking at you with no corset on? You know you ain't going to no ball without no corset on like a Christian woman."

"I am a Christian woman, and I am going to the ball with no corset, and you know I don't need one, so help me get my dress on," Flora said. "We need to hurry and do my flowers and my hair. You know it just won't do for me to be late. Father would probably order a squad up here to drag me downstairs."

Ruby proceeded to help Flora put on the dress, which was quite a process. The skirt itself was fifteen yards of taffeta and six yards of cotton ruffle. It was heavy, it was stiff, and putting it over Flora's head practically amounted to throwing a canvas tent over her.

As Flora struggled to find the neck opening and the sleeves, through the crackling of the fabric she could hear Ruby muttering, "They is Christian women with corsets, and they is Christian women with no corsets. . . . Leastenways she got bloomers on. Mebbe they go next. . .liken as if Colonel Cooke would allow a dragoon. . .ten-foot pole near you. . . ."

Finally the dress was in place, and Ruby buttoned up the twenty-three buttons in the back. Though of course Ruby would never admit it, Flora did not need a corset to pull in her waist. A man's hands could span it easily.

Flora carefully spread her skirts so she could sit at the dressing table for Ruby to do her hair. Sitting while wearing a crinoline was tricky. They were cages, in effect, wide cotton petticoats with whalebone or sometimes even very light steel sewn into slowly widening circles. The sewn-in ribs were stiff to hold out the circular shape of the very wide skirts but still thin enough to bend so the wearer could sit down, and they had enough tensile strength to regain their shape when standing. However, when sitting down, if a lady did not learn how to spread her heavy overskirts out—in a graceful manner, of course—to distribute the weight correctly, the entire hoop could simply balloon in a great circle up over her head. At boarding school, Flora and her friends had often played this game, laughing like pure fools at the sight but still fervently learning how to do it correctly so that this abomination would never happen to them, especially, heaven forbid, in public.

Early that morning, Ruby had rolled the ends of Flora's hair tightly around little rags. Now she began to carefully remove them, leaving little ringlets. Then she parted her hair in the middle, pulled it back, and began to secure it at the base of her neck, with the springy curls falling down her back. On the grounds of Fort Leavenworth, Kansas, many of the officers' little houses had gardens, and Flora had found a friend who had a camellia bush with peach-colored flowers. She had gathered enough that morning to arrange in her hair and have a small bouquet at her breast. With their shiny, dark-green leaves, they adorned Flora's hair and complexion perfectly.

As Ruby began to arrange them in her hair, Flora watched her carefully in the tri-mirror mounted on the dressing table. Her eyes narrowed. "Don't just poke them in there any old way, Ruby. Arrange them elegantly," she chided her. "I want to look just perfect tonight."

"Mm-hmm," Ruby said knowingly. "Just gonna aggravate them soldiers, ain't you? Knowing that Colonel Cooke—"

"I know, I know," Flora interrupted her, "wouldn't let 'em get a ten-foot pole near me. You're wrong, you know, Ruby. Father is perfectly fine with me socializing with soldiers. After all, he's been one his whole life, and I've been around them my whole life. And besides, I don't want to aggravate them, whatever that means."

"You'm knows right well what it means, Miss Flora. Don't I see you right here right now in that there mirror, smiling and practicin' taking 'em with your eyelashes?"

Ruby had a habit of quoting Scripture, usually incorrectly, and Flora was fairly certain that this reference had something to do with a proverb about women and their eyelids, but already Ruby had moved on. She was now more carefully arranging the flowers in Flora's hair, and she talked constantly. "Miz Lieutenant Blanton's flowers sure are pretty with your dress, Miss Flora, if I do say so, and I was talking to her girl Lizzie, and you know what? Lizzie says that she heard Miz Blanton talkin' about her brother Leslie Spengler marryin' their cousin! Their own cousin! And him from a good family, as good as yourn is!"

"It's only his fourth cousin, Ruby. It's hardly—"

"I don't keer. It ain't right. What about that handsome Finch boy, prancin' around in his showy uniform? Is he gonna marry up wif Miss Leona? That man what always wears those big tall hats—stovepipes, they call 'em, and don't they look just like that and silly besides. What's been chasin' after her ain't as good-looking, but he's got money, Miss Leona's maid, Perla, says. I think Miss Leona Pruitt better look ahead, 'cause without no money, the mare don't go. Leastenways you ain't gonna have to worry about that, Miss Flora. Some rich man in Phillydelphia is gonna snatch you right up soon as you go to capturvatin' them—"

"I think you mean 'captivating' them, and I do no such thing," Flora said haughtily.

"—captivatin' 'em, and you do do such a thing, begging your pardon, miss," Ruby said sassily.

Flora's brow lowered, and she started to argue with Ruby, but something stopped her.

Flora had been brought up in a world of men. She had been born in Jefferson Barracks, in Fort St. Louis, and had lived in one army fort or barracks or encampment since then. Her father, a career army officer, had been at posts all over the United States, including Indian fighting in the far West. Now he was colonel of the Second U.S. Dragoons, the commanding officer of Fort Leavenworth, Kansas.

Her mother had died when she was young, and her father had brought her up as a young lady, sending her to a prestigious boarding school in Detroit. Flora had graduated that spring of 1855, an accomplished and elegant young lady, and had come to visit her father for a couple of months before going to stay with her St. George relatives in Philadelphia to make her social debut.

Still, for most of her life, she had been surrounded by men, and she knew they liked her. They were attracted to her, but it was none of her doing. She didn't encourage them or flirt with them.

Or did she?

"Well," she now said good-humoredly to Ruby, "maybe I do."

When she was finished dressing, Flora went downstairs to the parlor.

Her father sat in a straight-back rocking chair by the window, reading the *U.S. Army Ordnance Manual*. All he ever read were the Bible and military manuals. He looked up and smiled, a mere quick softening of his thin lips. "You look very lovely, my dear."

"Thank you, Papa," Flora said, pleased. She seated herself on the sofa. "Thank you for the new dress. Thank you for all of them. And especially for the riding habits." Flora was an avid horsewoman.

"You're welcome, my dear, and seeing you tonight makes all that money that I've spent on those fripperies worthwhile." Although the words were light, he had reverted to his stern manner.

Colonel Philip St. George Cooke was every inch a soldier, a cavalryman. A handsome man, he had thick silver hair, intense, dark eyes, and a dashing, neatly trimmed mustache and short beard. He had a military bearing, always holding himself erect and always precise in his movements and speech. He was a rather humorless man, though not ill-tempered. He was simply austere.

Now he said in his somber manner, "Flora, there is something I must tell you before we go to the ball. This morning Gerald Small came to see me."

Surprised, Flora asked, "Mr. Small was here this morning?"

"No. He came to my office. He said he had to see the quartermaster, so he thought he would just stop by on his way. Rather unorthodox, I think. . .considering the topic."

Flora rolled her eyes. "Please don't tell me I was the topic. Oh Papa. . .I was? Oh, how like him! To just 'stop by on his way' to a business meeting to make a romantic gesture!"

"Flora, perhaps he is not the most romantic of men, as you say, but he does come from a good family, and he is a fine, upstanding young man. The Smalls are very good people of business, and he is going to be a very wealthy man."

With exasperation Flora said, "Papa, we are not talking about investing money with him. Please do not tell me that he asked for my hand. Even though he's been calling for the last month, he's never made any sort of overture such as that. He's usually too busy talking about his silly sawmill."

"No, Flora, it was not that he was asking my permission before he even asked you," Colonel Cooke replied. "He was just, in the most gentleman-like manner, inquiring if his attentions toward you were viewed favorably by me."

She stared at him. "I was wrong. This is a business deal. What did he do next, suggest that you discuss prices?"

Cooke frowned, and that was a stern thing indeed. "Flora, I'm surprised at you. That is crude, not at all something that I would expect a daughter of mine to say."

She was defiant for a moment, but then she dropped her head. "I'm sorry, Papa," she said quietly. "You're right, of course. I beg your pardon, and I will attempt never to be crude again. It's just that Mr. Small is so—so businesslike. He is not romantic at all. He rarely does speak of anything but business matters. And besides, you do want me to go to Philadelphia, don't you? To enter society? I thought you didn't want me to be stuck here with a penniless soldier or some *nouveau riche* merchant settler."

Cooke's eyes softened slightly. "I don't know why we're arguing about him anyway. I knew you wouldn't have him. And Flora, believe me when I tell you that I want what's best for you. And I want you to have the kind of life and man and marriage that you want, whether it is here or in Philadelphia society. But Flora, do you know exactly what it is that you want?"

"Maybe." Flora shrugged. "But Father, I don't—I want—that is—" She stopped awkwardly. Her father had been a good parent, in his way. He loved her dearly, Flora knew that. But there were some things that she could never explain to him, could never make him understand.

Flora, in her secret heart, wanted a man to love her with a heat and a passion that would match her own. Though she was still an innocent, she knew that she could have deep and intense love— emotional, spiritual, and physical—for the man of her dreams. He would be dashing and careless and courageous, and she would start falling in love with him as soon as she met him. She had no face in her mind. Truth to tell, she didn't care what he looked like. She just had a vague sense of a man with a commanding presence, with spirit and daring. But how could she tell her father—the stolid, unimaginative soldier—of her dreams?

Suddenly she smiled affectionately at him. "Papa, I will tell you what I don't want. I don't want to spend the rest of my life talking about sawmills. Now, sir, you look very smart and officer-like in your uniform. Will you consent to escort me to the Independence Ball?"

Fort Leavenworth, Kansas, Flora reflected on the way to the ball, was not nearly so bleak as many of the army outposts were. It was finely situated on the gentle bluffs overlooking the Missouri River, in the easternmost part of the territory. The endless plains and prairies were only a few miles away, but Fort Leavenworth was still in fertile country, with the Missouri River to the east, the Little Platte River just to the south, and countless streams and tributaries crossing the green unsettled lands in between.

A small town had sprung up, mainly because Fort Leavenworth was the eastern terminus for the Santa Fe Trail and the Oregon Trail, and so the fort had assumed great importance. The town—appropriately called Leavenworth—had been born to support the settlers moving west and the fort itself. Although it had only formally incorporated in 1854, it was already thriving and growing quickly.

Accordingly, the fort had more and better accommodations and appointments than most. One of these was the Rookery, a fine two-story home with a wide veranda where the commanding officer lived. Another was the meetinghouse, a large hall where town meetings were held, where the troops assembled for instructions or visiting lecturers, and where festivals were held. One of these was the July 4th Independence Ball; this was the second annual one, she had learned, and the entire army post and most of the town's citizens were expected to attend.

Escorted by her father, Flora entered the ballroom and hungrily ran her eyes over the floor, delighted as always with the kaleidoscope of color created by the women's dresses. Scarlet, emerald green, pink, and purple, all shades and hues, blended wonderfully as the couples danced a waltz. It was exactly the sort of thing that Flora delighted in, for she loved color, excitement, crowds, dancing, and music.

As soon as they came in, Gerald Small rushed to Flora's side. With a stiff smile, she offered him her gloved hand and he bent over it, a sort of deep dip as if he were bobbing for apples. As the thought occurred to Flora, her smile widened and her eyes sparkled. Gerald Small obviously mistook this for gladness to see him, and with some surprise, he returned her smile. It was an automatic, spare sort of smile, as if it was practiced. Flora suspected that it might be.

Formal greetings were exchanged, then Colonel Cooke went to speak to a group of the older officers in a corner of the room, while Gerald began to shepherd Flora to the chairs lining the walls. With an inner sigh, she allowed him to lead her.

Gerald Small was, like his name, a short, compact man, with ash-blond hair and mild blue eyes. His features, too, were small, with a thin, straight nose and short lips in a rather sharp-boned face. He always dressed stylishly, and tonight he wore a fawn-colored pair of trousers and a dark brown coat with a bowtie drooping fashionably down from around his neck.

They reached the chairs and sat down. Gerald pulled his chair close to Flora, looked deep into her eyes, and said in a low voice, "I thought I was going to be late, for I have been literally in despair trying to find a skilled saw filer. I had heard that a man coming in the latest wagon train from Chicago was such a man. I questioned the wagon master and several of the trail hands and thought that perhaps this might have been one of the settlers named Odom, but when I finally located Mr. Odom, what do you think I found?"

Already Flora was having trouble concentrating on this deadly boring conversation, but she managed to reply, "I don't know, Mr. Small. What did you find?"

"He was nothing but a common cutler," Gerald groaned dramatically. "A knife sharpener, for goodness' sake! And so I have yet to find a saw filer, and it's possible I may have to hire one from Kansas City! Can you imagine the cost of paying a skilled saw filer to move out here and begin work in a brand-new sawmill?"

"No, I can hardly imagine it," Flora said wearily. "Mr. Small, I know this is very forward of me, but they are beginning the polka, and I should love to dance. It is one of my particular favorites."

He looked bemused at Flora's peculiar request—women simply did not ask men to dance—but gamely he took her arm. "Of course. I declare, I have been so worried about my saw filer that I quite forgot my manners. May I have this dance, Miss Cooke?"

He was not a bad dancer, but he was mechanical, and his conversation during the dance was very much like his previous one—indeed, much like all his previous ones, Flora reflected. He led her around the floor, the oddly automatic movements seeming peculiar in the spirited dance, still lamenting about his saw filer and, also, if Flora was hearing him correctly, about something called a "pitman arm."

When the polka ended, he led her back to her chair, holding her arm. As they reached their seats, he said in her ear, "I shall fetch you some punch, as it is rather warm in here and I should like you to be refreshed. There is a matter of some importance I want to discuss with you when I return."

She took her seat, suddenly wishing she was going to hear more about the saw filer and Mr. Pitman's arm.

However, as usual, Flora was not alone for long. She had made three particular friends, two girls whose families were at the fort and one girl from town. They crowded around her, bringing their gentleman escorts at hand, and some other of the troops from the fort joined them. Flora found herself at the center of a crowd, and as always, she was entertaining them. Someone had complimented her on her hair, and she was telling the story of Ruby poking the flowers into it. "It was like she was sticking them into a vase, all every which way. I think if I hadn't made her do it all over, I'd be looking like I was wearing an urn on my head," she said drolly.

Miss Leona Pruitt—who would have incurred Ruby's wrath had she known it—had the "handsome Finch boy" on her arm and said warmly to Flora, "Oh, that's nonsense, Flora. You always look so lovely, especially with all of your new clothes for your debut! And that new dress. . . Please, stand up and turn around. Let us see it!"

Choruses of agreements followed, so Flora stood, held her skirts gracefully, and turned slowly.

"Oh, it's just beautiful," Leona Pruitt sighed, a little enviously. She had six sisters, she was the fourth one, and she very rarely got a new ball dress.

Flora had completed her turn and started to reply, but suddenly a man standing in a group rather far down the room caught her attention. He was tall with reddish hair and a fierce mustache and thick, long beard. He was barrel-chested and strong-looking, and Flora could have sworn that even at this distance she could sense an immense physical strength.

Abruptly, midlaugh, he turned to look directly at her, and their eyes met. The smile faded from his face, and Flora's eyes widened. To Flora, it seemed as if they stared at each other for a long time, but she knew it must only have been seconds.

When she collected herself to turn back to the group, they were still saying admiring things about her new dress. She felt odd, answering them automatically, still sensing some sort of vague physical connection to the man. It was as if he were standing too close to her, and she felt uncomfortable. But of course he was not; she stole another quick glance, and he, too, had turned back to his acquaintances and was laughing again.

Now she noticed Gerald at the fringe of the group, holding two cups of punch, and saying rather ineffectually to two dragoons who were crowded close, "Mm, excuse me? That is. . .if you would excuse me, please, um, sir? Private?"

Admittedly the group was rather loud and merry, and for an instant, Flora felt sorry for Gerald. He never seemed to actually have any fun. She started to say something, to beckon him to her side.

"Good evening, ladies, gentlemen," a booming voice said. He was looking directly at Flora, and she froze. He was not quite six feet, but his sheer physical size made him seem like a big man. His dark blue dress uniform was of a 2nd lieutenant of the 1st U.S. Cavalry and was immaculate and pressed to perfection, his thigh-high cavalry boots shined to dark mirrors.

She looked into his eyes and suddenly felt much too warm and knew her cheeks were flushing. He had blue eyes, hot blue like the July noon sky, and he looked at her as if he already knew her, all about her—too much about her.

He stepped into the circle around her—people automatically moved aside for him—and stood looking down at her. He smiled at her, and the smile was gentle, but his eyes danced with devilment. "Hello, ma'am. I'm very new here, so I don't know many people yet. But I would like to dance with you. The very next dance."

With a supreme effort, Flora collected herself. What was wrong with her anyway? She'd met at least a hundred soldiers in her life, many of them strong, handsome, dashing men. Here was another. And a very forward one at that.

"Sir, I hope you feel welcome here at Fort Leavenworth, but I'm afraid we have not been properly introduced," she said, much more stiffly than she intended. She sounded like her father, she reflected with exasperation.

He turned around and looked at the people around Flora. They all stood close, waiting eagerly for the progression of the interesting scene. Except Gerald, who looked utterly taken aback.

Finally the man pointed to a soldier, a private in a 1st Cavalry uniform. "You! You're Eccleston, aren't you? Private Eccleston? Jerry Eccleston, is it?"

"Sir, no sir," he said, stepping forward and standing at painful attention. "I'm Private George Cary Eggleston, sir."

"Do you know this lady, Private Eggleston?" he demanded, gesturing to Flora.

"Yes, sir. No, sir. I've been introduced to her, sir," he answered, his boyish face turning deep crimson.

"Then introduce us," the lieutenant ordered.

"Yes, sir," Eggleston said and then, still at attention, stepped to stand by the lieutenant's and Flora's side. "Lieutenant Stuart, I have the pleasure of introducing you to Miss Flora Cooke, the daughter of our commanding officer, Colonel Philip St. George Cooke. Miss Cooke, it is my honor to present to you Second Lieutenant James Ewell Brown Stuart of the 1st Cavalry. He has just arrived here from a posting at Jefferson Barracks, near St. Louis."

Lieutenant Stuart took Flora's hand, and even through her glove she could feel the heat from his lips as he pressed a kiss to her hand.

Private Eggleston, with ill-disguised relief, stepped back, quickly grabbed a girl's arm, and rushed off to the punch table.

James Ewell Brown Stuart took Flora in his arms and swept her off right in the middle of a waltz. Already Flora could tell he was a wonderful dancer, both powerful and graceful. "My friends call me Jeb," he said.

Flora still felt a little breathless, but she was a resourceful woman, and the little charade of the introductions had given her time to calm down. "Do they, sir?" she replied lightly. "What do first acquaintances call you when they've only known you for about thirty seconds?"

"Lieutenant Stuart. But I want you to call me Jeb."

"I will not, sir. We may have been properly introduced—of a sort—but I would never take such a liberty with a man I've just met."

"Hm. And so I suppose I may not call you Miss Flora?"

"Certainly not."

"Guess I'd better behave"—he sighed theatrically—"since you, Miss Cooke, are the daughter of my commanding officer. But you can still call me Jeb whenever you want to."

"I'm afraid at this time I don't want to, Lieutenant," Flora said, teasing him. She sensed the high spirits of her dancing partner and was quite sure he sensed hers as well.

"You will," he said airily. "Won't be long, either. You will."

Flora rolled her eyes. "You're very sure of yourself, aren't you?"

"Pretty much," he answered airily. "Aren't you?"

She was taken aback at his words.

The dance ended, and Lieutenant Stuart took her back to her seat.

Gerald, who was sitting alone waiting for her, rose, his finely modeled face rather sulky. "There you are, Flora. I thought you were supposed to wait for me to bring you some punch."

"I'm sorry, Gerald, but the waltz is my favorite, you know," she said carelessly.

"Thought it was the polka," he muttered darkly.

"No, not at all. The waltz," she said brightly. Then she introduced the two men.

Gerald looked up at the powerful bulk of Jeb Stuart and his penetrating eyes and fierce beard. To Flora, his face registered something close to contempt, as if he were a nobleman being introduced to a commoner. "How do you do, Lieutenant?" Gerald asked frigidly.

"Much better, now that I've been introduced to Miss Cooke and have had the great pleasure of dancing with her." He turned back to Flora, bowed slightly, and said, "Since you love to waltz, Miss Cooke, I'd like to claim the next one. Until then. . ." He moved to return to his group of friends, and Flora couldn't help but watch him walk away. He knew it. When he reached them, he turned and winked at her.

"Arrogant," she breathed to herself, turning quickly back to Gerald.

"I thought that I was to get you some punch, and then we were going to talk," he said accusingly as they sat down. "The punch grew warm."

"I didn't realize that we were on a timetable," she said, a little sharply. "I understand those were your plans, but this is a *dance*, Mr. Small. People *dance* here."

"Yes, yes, dancing. But I have something very important I want to speak to you about, Miss Cooke."

"But—but surely we don't have to have such a serious discussion right now, do we?" she pleaded. In spite of herself, her eyes kept searching out Lieutenant Stuart.

"It is, as I said, very important," Gerald insisted. He reached over and took her hands, and Flora was so startled she didn't draw them back. "Miss Cooke—that is, may I call you Flora?"

"No," she said absently. The musicians were playing an allemande now, and Lieutenant Stuart, Flora saw, was dancing with her friend Leona Pruitt. Leona had a brilliant smile that lit up her face, and she was definitely bestowing that smile on the lieutenant. It distracted Flora much more than it should have.

"What?" Gerald said, shocked. "But—why ever not? I've been calling on you for almost a month now."

With an effort, Flora turned her attention back to him. "Yes, I know, Mr. Small. You've been very attentive, and I enjoy your company. But just think, we have only known each other for less than a month. In fact, we hardly know each other at all, do we?"

He blinked several times. "I thought we knew each other. We do know each other."

She sighed. "What is my favorite color?"

He looked utterly blank.

"Do I play any musical instruments?"

Still the same uncomprehending stare.

"And where, Mr. Small," she continued, now gravely, "am I moving to, in just a little over one month, to make my social debut?"

"I know this one," he said desperately. "Philadelphia. You're— oh, I see. You are leaving in a month, then."

"Yes."

He shook his head and took her hand again, though this time Flora resisted slightly. She didn't want to vulgarly yank it away, however, so he held it and looked at her, his mild blue eyes suddenly filled with determination. Flora thought that it must be how he looked when he was about to close a business deal. "No, Fl—Miss Cooke. I think—I know that before then you will find that you want to stay here, with me."

"Please, Mr. Small, you are mistaken. I do appreciate your attentions, but I'm afraid you may have misunderstood mine." Flora went on as reasonably as she could to try to convey that she was not at all interested in him, but the look on his face merely grew more closed and stubborn. "And so, you see that I am trying to make certain that you make no mistake concerning our—our—"

"Miss Cooke," Lieutenant Stuart said jovially, "finally! It is our waltz." He held out his hand. Flora pulled away from Gerald, but he stood with her, looking up at Jeb Stuart.

"I think you should know, Lieutenant," he said with a definite snobbish timbre to his voice, "that I have spoken to Colonel Cooke."

"Me, too," Jeb said mildly. "He's my commanding officer."

"No, I mean—what I mean is, I've spoken to him about Fl—Miss Cooke," Gerald insisted.

"Have you?" Jeb asked with interest. "I don't blame you. I'd like to talk to people about Miss Cooke, too. But mostly I'd like to talk to her. So if you'll excuse us, Mr. Small. . ."

Again they left Gerald standing helplessly alone, confused and irritated.

Jeb grinned down at her. His grin, and his laugh, were completely infectious. "Is he a lawyer or something?"

Flora found herself smiling like a girlish idiot the entire time she talked with him. "No, he's a businessman. Right now he's opening a sawmill. He and his family already own a hotel and a flour mill."

"Is he rich?" Jeb asked.

"I don't know," Flora answered carelessly. "It's really no business of mine."

"That's good," Jeb said beaming. "So you're not going to marry him then?"

"What! Marry him? No, no, no. No, that's just not possible," Flora fumed.

"No, it's not," Jeb agreed. "It's not meant to be. That much is obvious."

"What are you talking about? You don't know him. What am I saying? You don't know me, either."

"But you just told me you're not going to marry him."

"But that doesn't mean it's not meant to be," Flora shot back.

Jeb threw back his head and laughed. All around them people watched him, and they couldn't help it; they grinned.

Finally Flora saw the absurdity of the conversation and giggled a little in spite of herself. "I think—no, I know that was the silliest argument I've ever had with a person."

"Let's hope all our arguments turn out to be silly, and then we'll laugh at them afterward," Jeb said. He squeezed her hand the tiniest bit. Men, of course, did not wear gloves during dancing or dining. She was very aware of the heat of his hand, of how it swallowed hers, of the way he very gently touched her back, but she could still sense the power, the vitality of him.

"All of them?" she asked. "So we are to have arguments, then?"

"It was meant to be," he said, now quietly. "All of it. You, me, this night, this dance was meant to be."

She searched his face and found none of the usual frivolity there. He looked thoughtful. "What do you mean, Lieutenant?" she asked softly. "How can that be?"

He searched her face for long moments. "I have always believed that God prepares a man for one certain woman. And He prepares that woman for him."

"That is a very deep theological concept, Lieutenant Stuart," she said, trying to restore some lightness to the curious turn the conversation had taken. "So how would this woman know which man was fated to be her husband?"

Sensing her slight withdrawal, Jeb answered, "All you have to do is take a look at Eve. There she was. There he was. She knew right away that God had made them to be together."

"Your logic is flawed, sir. She had no other choice to make."

He made a slight shrug, although it didn't affect the grace of his dancing. "You're probably right, ma'am. Logic isn't my strong point. Dancing, however, is. And may I say that you are one of the finest dancers of any lady I've ever seen."

"Thank you, Lieutenant. You are a very skilled dancer yourself."

"Thank you, ma'am! I love music, and I love dancing," he said enthusiastically. "I'm afraid I have no skill in music, except for a keen enjoyment of it. Do you play an instrument or perhaps sing, Miss Cooke?"

"I play the piano, and even some guitar, and I enjoy both very much. I do sing, although not as well as some. But like you, sir, I do enjoy all good music."

"And waltzing," he added. "By any chance, may I claim the rest of your waltzes tonight, Miss Cooke?"

SWORD

"It would be considered very impolite for us to monopolize each other, you a newly arrived single gentleman, and an officer, and me, the daughter of the commander of the post," she considered. "But I don't think either of us shall be ostracized too much. Yes, Lieutenant Stuart, you may have the waltz for the rest of the night."

"How about all of the dances for the rest of the night?" he asked impishly.

"That would be entirely too scandalous. The waltzes are enough. And you, sir, do not tell me how 'it is meant to be.' I've already pointed out the flaw in that theorem."

There were several more waltzes during the ball. In general, Flora felt neither Lieutenant Stuart nor she was considered to be acting in a rude manner—except by Gerald Small, who continued to try to monopolize her—but the fact that she and the lieutenant danced together so much was certainly noted. She was certain Jeb Stuart commanded attention wherever he went and with whatever he did. And of course, as Flora was the commanding officer's daughter, her actions were of interest to the entire fort and the little town.

Toward the end of the evening, Gerald Small began dancing with a pretty blond girl whom Flora did not know, and he kept casting triumphant, slightly mean glances at Flora. She barely noticed and was sure she missed some.

As it happened, the last dance of the night was a waltz. At the end, Lieutenant Stuart escorted Flora back to her father. They exchanged greetings, and Jeb said, "Sir, I have found out that Miss Cooke has quite a reputation as an expert equestrian, so I have asked her to go for a ride with me tomorrow afternoon. She has agreed. Will that be acceptable to you, sir?"

"Of course, if Flora wants to go," Colonel Cooke said.

Jeb said in a most courtly manner, "I count it a great privilege, and I will be very careful to see that your daughter is safe. Thank you, sir." He turned to Flora. "Miss Cooke, I cannot adequately express my appreciation for your company tonight. It has been a delightful evening, and I owe my enjoyment of it expressly to you.

Thank you, and until tomorrow, Miss Cooke." He bowed gallantly.

"Until tomorrow, Lieutenant," she replied as she curtsied prettily.

Colonel Cooke studied his daughter's glowing face. "You just met him tonight, and you've already agreed to go riding with him, Flora?"

"Yes, Father. Surely you have no qualms? Already I have ascertained that he is a Southern gentleman of the first quality, from a noted Virginia family, and a Christian man. I'm sure no one would think ill of me or of him."

"No, of course not. That's not what I meant," Cooke said as they walked slowly toward the door, arm in arm. "He's a fine man and a truly excellent soldier. It's just that I suppose I've never seen you take to anyone quite so quickly."

She laughed, just a little, and squeezed his arm. "Papa," she said lightly, "perhaps it was just meant to be."

CHAPTER TWO

Laughing with delight, Flora looked over her shoulder and called, "Is the 1st Cavalry always so slow?" Easily her mare jumped a broken-down snake fence and reached the border of the pecan orchard half a minute before Jeb Stuart caught up to her, his big white stallion easily clearing the fence.

He jumped down, grinning as always, his blue eyes dazzling in the blinding summer sun.

"Begging your pardon, ma'am, it's not that the 1st Cav is so slow. It's that you're fast. You beat me fair and square, Miss Cooke." He reached up to hold her hand as she dismounted. "I thought I would let you win, you know. Turns out I should have asked you to spare my manly feelings and let me win."

Affectionately Flora patted her mare's heaving sides. She was a pretty gray palfrey, a gift from her father upon her graduation. "Her name is Juliet, a noble and delicate name, but she runs like a hardworking quarter horse."

"This is Ace," Jeb said, slapping the big horse's haunch. "And we always won until we met you two. Let's walk them out, shall we?"

"Yes, let's walk back to that little creek where we started. It's very warm, and I think that the water may be much cooler than what we have in our canteens."

Jeb had shown up at exactly two o'clock, as promised, resplendent in his cavalry uniform with the dark blue coat and sky-blue trousers, both with golden trim and insignia. He wore a wide-brimmed black hat with a golden band.

Flora had been so excited about seeing him again that she could barely get dressed, alternately berating Ruby for being so slow and urging her to hurry up. Finally, however, she had dressed in her very best new riding habit, emerald green of heavy cotton with a snappy jacket with a tight waist and peplum. The skirt was ground-length and had a small train, as it must for women to be able to cover their legs and feet appropriately while riding. She wore a dashing brimmed hat, pinned up on one side with a gold brooch that had belonged to her mother.

Jeb had made appropriate greetings to her father, but Flora was so anxious to ride that she had almost immediately demanded that they go. They had cantered outside the fort and come to one of the countless streams that crisscrossed the rolling hills above the river. On the other side was a wide field filled with black-eyed Susans growing riotously and the graceful lines of a pecan orchard on the far side. Flora had immediately challenged Jeb to a race.

Now they walked slowly back across the field. Jeb looked at Flora's sidesaddle, mystified. "I've never understood how ladies can even sit on a horse on those contraptions. And especially I've never thought a lady could beat me in a race riding one. What I've heard is certainly true, Miss Cooke. You are one fine rider."

"I've been riding since I was four years old," Flora said. "And I do love to ride. I even like to shoot." She glanced up at him slyly.

With his dress uniform, he wore his cavalry saber and his pistol in a black leather holster. "No, no, ma'am!" he blustered. "You've already beaten me soundly at riding. I'm not going to let you shame me right down to the ground by outshooting me."

"Maybe some other time," she said.

"I hope there are many other times," he said quietly. Then, as he was wont to do after a sober moment with her, he reverted back to jollity. "Now I know you can ride and sing and play the guitar and piano. I know you can dance better than any lady I've ever seen. Tell me everything else about you."

"Everything?"

"Everything. I want to know it all."

"Oh, but no lady would ever tell all about herself. We must remain mysterious, so as to keep men intrigued," Flora teased. "Besides, you already know a lot about me, and I know very little about you, Lieutenant. Tell me about your home and family."

Jeb told her about his family in Virginia, about his father, Archibald Stuart, who had long represented Patrick County in the Virginia Assembly and then was a congressman. He mentioned some of their connections to other prominent Virginia families, such as the Prices and the Pannills and the Letchers. "But it was through one of my father's political connections that I got my commission to West Point," he said with some pride.

"A fine institution," Flora said. "My father says West Point cadets make the very best soldiers in the world."

"I'm a better soldier than I was a West Point cadet," Jeb told her, eyes dancing merrily. "I graduated with 129 demerits. I think they just graduated me because I was so rowdy and raucous they didn't want me to corrupt any more cadets. I had a nickname there, you know."

"What was it?"

"They called me Beauty. It was because I was so homely, I guess. Like you call a tall man 'Shorty.' "

"I don't think you're homely, Lieutenant," Flora said casually. "Not at all."

He looked pleased, like a young boy. "Really? Anyway, that's why I grew the beard. . .to cover up my homely aspects."

As they walked, Jeb bent and picked about six of the black-eyed Susans, then presented them to her with a bow. "Now you, Miss Cooke, have nothing at all homely about you. You're like these flowers, bright and glowing in the sunshine. And I must say that your riding outfit there is about the prettiest concoction I've ever seen. You truly are a 'beauty' in it."

"Thank you, kind sir," she said, accepting the wild bouquet with a queenly gesture. Flora was rather accustomed to compliments from men, but deep down she knew that Jeb Stuart's admiration pleased her more than any other.

They reached the cool deep shade of the cottonwoods that bordered the little singing stream, and Jeb filled their canteens with the cold, fresh water.

Flora watched him, bemused. In truth he was just a little above average height, but he was a big man, with broad shoulders, giant hands, and long legs. For being so brawny, he was curiously graceful, with a rolling stride, but on horseback he had a power and grace that she had never seen before.

And whoever in the world could say he was homely? He's one of the most handsome men I've ever met! Men are blind to male beauty, I suppose. . .but women certainly are not. They crowd around him like honeybees to the comb! He's just so imposing, so. . .commanding. . .so. . .

The end of the thought made her blush, and at that moment he stood and turned back to her. A knowing, amused look crossed his face as he stepped up to hand her the canteen. She dropped her eyes and took a long drink of the refreshing water.

Jeb drank then led the horses up to the stream so they could drink. "Would your mare wander, do you think?" he asked her.

"I don't think so, but even if she does, she always comes to me easily," Flora answered.

"I've got a trick to get Ace to come to me if he's off foraging," Jeb said, looping the horses' reins around the pommels. "Let's take a little walk along this stream."

They walked in the shade of the trees along the grassy bank. The stream was really just a little bubbling trace only a couple of feet across at its widest part, but in places it was waist-deep.

"I love this little stream. I ride here often," Flora said. "I don't even think it has a name."

"Then let's name it," Jeb said. "How about Beauty's Stream?

Meaning you, of course, Miss Cooke."

"And you, Lieutenant Stuart. After all, if West Point says it, then it must be so."

They came to a great fallen hickory tree just at the edge of the water. Flora sat down on it. Still holding her little bouquet, she threw one of the bright yellow flowers into the stream, and they watched it bob merrily away.

Jeb cocked one booted foot up on the log and leaned over her, not too close but near enough for her to again feel the sense of his physical presence so strongly that he might have been touching her. "I hear, ma'am, that you are planning to go to Philadelphia soon, to make your social debut."

Her face still averted, watching the peaceful stream wander by, she answered quietly, "That is true, Lieutenant. That has been my plan. I mean, it is my plan."

"I see." He was quiet for a moment, his piercing blue eyes gazing into the distance. "How soon?"

"Next month. Around the fifteenth."

He roused a little. "Oh? Oh well, that gives me plenty of time." He was teasing her again.

She looked up at him and made a prim face. "Plenty of time for what, sir?"

"Plenty of time for my plan."

"And what, exactly, is this plan?"

"Just because you told me your plan," he said jauntily, "doesn't mean I'm going to tell you mine. Not yet, anyway."

"Not yet? Then when?"

"Maybe. . .mm. . .maybe when you start calling me Jeb."

She sniffed and tossed another flower into the water. "It will be some time then. I only met you yesterday."

"Was it?" he asked intently. "Seems like I know you already. Seems like I've known you for a long time, Flora."

She was so enthralled with his words, and his nearness, that she never even noticed he called her by her given name. Nervously she stood, brushing her skirt, and somehow stumbled just a little.

He took her arm, presumably to steady her, but somehow she took a step, and he took a step and then they were standing close, facing each other. She stared up at him, directly into his piercing eyes, as he slowly searched her face almost hungrily. Very slowly he put his hands on her waist, and his fingers met in the tiny span. Flora felt the warmth from his hands spread through her, an oddly heavy sensation that made her catch her breath. He made a very slight move, lowering his face closer to hers, but then she saw a clear reluctance cloud his eyes and tighten his mouth. And suddenly she knew, as women sometimes did, that he was afraid to embrace her, afraid to make such advances too soon, afraid he would offend her, afraid he would frighten her away.

But Flora was not frightened, not at all; and she did not want him to be either. "May I. . . ," she said softly, almost imperceptibly moving closer to him.

"What?" he asked in a deep voice.

"May I. . .touch your beard, sir?" she asked, smiling a little.

"Yes," he answered abruptly. His hands tightened on her waist until he almost hurt her.

Slowly she reached up and buried her fingers in his thick cinnamon-colored beard. "It's very soft," she said.

He stared at her, his eyes suddenly dark and brooding.

With one finger, she traced the outline of his beard up to the thick mustache, smoothing it a little, and then touched his lips. "So warm. . . ," she murmured.

He kissed her then. She could tell how difficult it was for him to restrain himself, because his hands on her waist were urgent, but his kiss was light, a mere brushing of his mouth against hers.

Then he lifted his head, and with an obvious effort dropped his hands and moved away from her. "I'm—I'm sorry," he said in a guttural tone.

"I'm not," Flora said lightly. To give him a few moments to recover himself, she bent to pick up the remaining flowers, still lying on the fallen log. She herself was deeply stirred and realized that already this man had a power over her that she had never imagined could exist. She took a deep, shuddering breath as she commanded her mind, her emotions, and even her body back under control. With careful movements, she rearranged the flowers back into a tight little bouquet and turned back to him.

He had recovered, all right. He was watching her, again with the joyful merriment that seemed to emanate like an aura from him. "I've never known a woman like you. I've sure never known a lady like you, Flora."

"You may call me Flora," she said primly. "But for my part, I shall still address you as Lieutenant Stuart."

"You won't know my plan until you call me Jeb, remember?" he teased, taking her arm, lightly now but with a slight air of possession.

"I may already suspect more of your plan than you realize, Lieutenant Stuart," she said airily. "But it may be that now you don't know mine."

"That's probably all too true," Jeb agreed. "What man was ever such a fool to imagine he knows what a woman's thinking? Not me."

They slowly walked back to the field, where the horses were well in sight, grazing. Flora and Jeb walked right up to Juliet, who stood obediently and let Flora take the reins.

Curiously she watched as Jeb reached in his pocket then called out in a clear ringing voice, "Ace! C'mere, boy!" He whistled, a clean, loud, boyish sound on the still hot air. Alertly the horse lifted his great head then set out at a gallop straight for Jeb, coming to a sliding stop just in front of him. Jeb chuckled and pulled a little packet tied with string out of his pocket. Quickly he untied the string and emptied the white granules into his hand. "Sugar," he told Flora. "Works every time."

"Yes, I can see that it does work very well for you, Lieutenant Stuart," she said sweetly. "Every time. We had better be getting back. In spite of what you may think, sir, I have not utterly lost my sense of propriety. We've been gone for almost two hours, and that is quite long enough, considering."

Jeb stepped up to her, again put his hands around her waist, and bodily lifted her up to set her on her saddle before she could protest. "You could never lose any sense of propriety, Miss Cooke. In fact, as far as I'm concerned, you're just about perfect. And so, since tomorrow will be our second ride, perhaps it may be for three hours?"

"You truly are very sure of yourself, aren't you?" she demanded, a little flustered.

"Am now," he said, swinging up into his saddle. "Tomorrow, then?"

"Yes—yes. Tomorrow."

CHAPTER THREE

Flora dipped her hand into the milk-glass jar, got three full fingers of the rich cream, and started applying it to her face.

Ruby came to the dressing table, snatched up the jar, and set a corked bottle down in its place. "Here, you needs to put this on yo' face, Miss Flora."

Suspiciously Flora picked up the bottle. It was colored a dark purple, and she could barely see a thick substance coating the sides as she turned it back and forth. "It looks like bacon skimmings. What is it?"

"It's Mam Dowd's Anti-Freckle Skin Lotion. You know, Mam Dowd, down to town, that makes all the herbs and potions and cosmeticals for white ladies?"

Flora uncorked it and held it up to her nose, then yanked it away. "Good heavens, it smells like rancid bacon skimmings, too!"

Stubbornly Ruby crossed her arms. "Now you just put that on your face, Miss Flora. You out riding in the summer sun all day ever day, with that pretty white skin. You got to cover it with some pertection."

"I'm not going to get freckles. Give me back my Essence of

Gardenia cream, Ruby. It's protection enough."

"Hit says in Levitican that if youse got spots youse has to go outside the camp," Ruby said with an air of triumph. "And that was for sure talkin' about freckled white ladies."

"It's Leviticus, and it was talking about—Oh, never mind what it was talking about! Give me back my cream, Ruby. If I put that grease on me, I'll likely slide off my horse. And after one whiff of that, Jeb would turn and run away at a gallop."

With a dire frown, Ruby put the jar of cream back on the dressing table and quickly whisked the bottle into the bosom of her shirt. "Listen at you, callin' him by his give name already! And you barely knowing him a month!"

"It's been a little over a month and a half," Flora retorted.

"Mm-hmm. And you ridin' out all over the countryside with him most every day. What does that tell me, Miss Flora? You lettin' him take some liberties?"

Flora stopped rubbing the cream into her skin, and her gaze went to a far-off distance.

Since that very first time they had ridden out together, and Flora had dared to touch Jeb and invite him as she had, they had both known the powerful attraction they had for each other —and they had both been wary ever since. For Flora, even though she had not quite realized it at the time, it had been a test for her. She already knew that she was attracted to Jeb Stuart—to his jovial personality, his humor, his ready laugh, his avid attentions to her— but she had not really understood what it was like to feel passion for a man. And in those few moments, and in that brief kiss, she had come to know passion, deep passion, and had comprehended in some way that this tremendous rush of feeling was what men found so very difficult to control. But women could. And Jeb did.

From then on they had held hands sometimes, and Jeb often took her arm. One twilit night on the veranda he had kissed her very lightly again, to say good night. But they had been very careful to keep a certain distance from each other. Flora did admit to herself that she reveled in Jeb's touch, and sometimes she deliberately took off her gloves—that perennial, eternal must for a well-brought-up young woman—just so she could feel his rough, heated hand. Jeb knew when she felt this way, she could tell, and she could just as certainly sense his reining himself in, holding himself back, only giving her as much as she asked for, as much as she was ready for.

She smiled dreamily. "Maybe I'm taking some liberties with him," she whispered to herself.

"Whut'd you say?" Ruby said suspiciously. She was behind Flora, putting a final polish on her riding boots.

"Nothing."

"Well, the scriptures say dat a woman what lets a man take liberties is gonna end up in the pit!" With righteous vigor she polished away.

Flora laughed. "I don't think so, but neither Jeb nor I are going to end up in the pit. And yes, I call him Jeb and he calls me Flora because we've given permission for each other to use our given names."

"Right out of the pit," Ruby said grimly. "With you knowin' him less'n a month."

"I believe this is what is termed 'a circular conversation.' All right, Ruby, I'm ready. Please help me with my boots."

With a final defiant rub, Ruby knelt down to help pull on Flora's boots. They were fine, black knee-high leather boots, handmade by a boot maker in Baltimore especially for Flora, and the fit was so close that Flora could neither get them on nor pull them off by herself.

"For—such little—feet as—you got—these boots sure is— hard to git on." Ruby grunted as she pulled up on the uppers to get Flora's foot into the boot. Finally she got the right one on and went to work on the left one. "But—hit's a mighty—good thing— that you got—such little feet—'cause white ladies—don't s'pose to have—big feet." She stood up and looked Flora up and down with satisfaction. "You is such a tiny lady, no wonder Mr. Lieutenant Jeb throws you around like a little kitten."

Ruby had caught them once, when Jeb had come to fetch her for a ride. Her father had been at headquarters, and Jeb had picked her up, swung her around, and then tossed her onto the saddle. He did this often when they were alone, but this time Ruby had seen them, and she had been holding it over Flora's head ever since. "I'm of a mind that the colonel might not like to think that Mr. Lieutenant Jeb is jugglin' his daughter around like some clown in a travelin' fair."

"You're not going to tell him, Ruby. . . ," Flora said, her cheeks reddening. "Please don't tell him."

"Well. . ."

"You can have that magenta silk petticoat you like so much, Ruby," Flora said with inspiration. "I don't like that color much for me, but it would be wonderful on you."

Ruby's eyes lit up. She had longed for the petticoat ever since Flora had received it along with some dresses she had ordered. "Well, I'm not one to be carryin' no tales; in the Proverbs it says talebearers will be backbit. So thank you for the petticoat, Miss Flora." Hurriedly she disappeared into Flora's dressing room to find the treasured article.

Flora was wearing her navy blue riding habit, trimmed in light blue. As it looked so much like the cavalry uniforms, Flora had bought a wide-brimmed felt hat and had trimmed it with some of her father's gold military braid and a tassel. Now she crammed the hat on her head, cocked it to a jaunty angle, pinned it securely, and hurried downstairs. It was almost three o'clock, and Jeb was never late.

Her father was in the parlor, gravely pacing before the empty fireplace. He looked up as she came in. She hurried to kiss him. "Hello, Papa. You were so quiet I thought you were taking your afternoon nap."

Colonel Cooke didn't smile much, but he did when Flora kissed him. "No, actually I was waiting so that I might speak with you, Flora. I assume Lieutenant Stuart is on his way?"

"Yes, sir. He should be here at three."

"I see. That does give us a few minutes." He led her to the sofa, and they sat down. "I've had another letter from Mrs. St. George.

She says that although you have delayed your visit, you've still given them no reason for the delay nor a date when they may expect you."

"Yes, I know, Father," she said quietly.

"You haven't confided in me either, Flora. But I think I understand. It's Lieutenant Stuart, isn't it?"

She looked up at him and met his gaze directly. "Yes, sir."

He studied her for long moments. "You don't want to leave because of him. Flora, you first met this man on the Fourth of July. How can you make such a momentous decision, to put off such an important event as your social debut, on the basis of such a short acquaintance?"

"I—I can hardly explain it to you, Father. But I can promise you that I know I am not making a mistake. I know what I'm doing." He looked doubtful, and she went on eagerly. "Papa, I know how very much you love the Lord, and how you've taught us to trust in Him in all things. And I do. I trust in the Lord, especially in this. I trust in the Lord, and I trust Jeb Stuart."

He listened to her closely then nodded. "Flora, ever since you were a child, you've been strong in the Lord, and you've been sure of yourself and your place in this world. You were a good child, and you've grown to be a good Christian woman. I don't know Lieutenant Stuart very well, and so I can't say that I trust him, but I do know you, and I do trust you. He does make you happy, doesn't he?"

"Oh yes, Papa! So very happy!"

"Then I'm glad for you, my dear. I hear him thundering up now. I declare that man can sound like an entire squad when he's galloping around on that great thumping stallion. Go on, Flora. After about thirty times I suppose he doesn't have to come in and make any obeisance to me anymore," he finished gruffly.

"Thank you, Papa, and I won't be too late!" She rushed out, her face glowing.

Jeb had found a way to ride down to the Missouri River. Just south of the fort the high bluffs lowered a bit, and he had found a place that was not at such a steep incline. Ace had managed it easily. Jeb told her he had waited until he was certain of her expertise on a horse, and then he had taken her there.

Today was only the second time they had come, for it took over an hour from the fort, riding at a businesslike trot. But on this day they rode slowly, talking and enjoying the cheerful summer day, the cool breezes that found their way up the banks from the river to sweep across the deserted fields, the smell of wild honeysuckle and green grass and thick rich dirt.

When they reached the path down to the river, with a smile Jeb went in front of Flora, assuring her that if Juliet were following Ace she would be less likely to let herself get in a dangerous slide down the still-steep hill. Ace picked his way carefully, and so did Juliet. When they got to the riverbank, Jeb tied up their reins and let them loose.

"Do you have your old trick, your sugar?" Flora teased.

"Of course." He looked at her face expectantly, and in unison they said, "Works every time!"

They began to walk along, arm in arm. "You and your tricks," Flora muttered, now with ill humor. "All sugar, all the time, with the ladies especially."

"Are you jealous?" he asked slyly.

"No."

"You sure?"

"Yes, I am sure. It's just such a spectacle sometimes. Some of them, like my friend Leona Pruitt and those two blond sisters, the Aldridge girls, practically swoon every time you talk to them. For shame, Jeb Stuart. You shouldn't flirt so much."

"I can't help it," he said with an ingenuous, bemused air. "Ladies are just so pretty, so little and soft and sweet."

"You can't keep a bunch of ladies as pets, Jeb," Flora said darkly.

"You are jealous," he said with delight. "It's so cute."

"I am not cute. And I am not jealous."

He patted her arm. "You sure don't have a reason to be."

The shores of the Missouri River were sometimes thick yellow mud in the rainy season, but now, in August, they were dry and cracked. The river was still strong, its flow sure and steady, the clear water twinkling like stars in the late red sunlight.

"Did you know that the Missouri River is the longest on the continent?" Jeb asked.

"Longer than the Mississippi?" Flora asked with surprise.

"Yes ma'am." They looked up at the buff-colored bluffs high above them. "It is one of God's wonders of creation."

"I'm so very glad that you think such things," Flora said quietly. "So often you're so rollicking and rowdy that one would think you never had a serious thought in your head."

He glanced at her. "But you know different, don't you, Flora?"

"Oh yes. I may not know everything about you, Jeb, but I know you. I know you very well. I know that you are a loving, giving Christian man."

He stopped and turned her to him. "But Flora, do you really know me? Can you know my heart? I feel that you do. I've felt that ever since the first night we met."

She stared up at him; she was so tiny, and he loomed over her. But that fact had nothing to do with her sense of the power she felt from him. It was, she knew, because he had spoken the truth that night, and she had known it in her mind, in her body, and in her spirit. "You said that God made each man for a certain woman, and that that woman was made for that man," she said softly. "I remember. I'll never forget it. I can't forget it."

Suddenly he dropped to one knee, took her hand, yanked off her glove, and pressed his lips to her fingers. He looked up at her, and his blue eyes blazed as the hottest part of the fire. "Flora, you are the woman for me. I've known it all along. There's never been any other woman, and never will be, that God has made for me. Only you. Please, Flora dearest, would you do me the greatest honor, bestow upon me the greatest joy a man could ever have, and consent to be my wife?"

Breathlessly she replied, "Yes, Jeb. I was meant for you. I always was and forever will be."

He leaped to his feet and kissed her, deeply, a long kiss full of joy and passion and giving. For the first time, Flora surrendered herself. She gave in completely to all of the love and longing that she had for him and matched his desire with her own.

It was Jeb who finally pulled away from her. He swallowed hard and was breathing a little heavily. But the old Jeb could not be held down for long. He threw his hat up in the air and shouted, "Did you hear that? Miss Flora Cooke is mine! Finally! Whoo hoo!" Then he grabbed her around the waist, hoisted her up, and whirled around and around.

Flora laughed with sheer delight, throwing her head back and her arms in the air.

Jeb set her down and then, grinning like a fool, went to fetch his hat.

Flora was trying to straighten her own hat, as it had fallen to her back, held on by the gold braided straps. "I'm dizzy," she told Jeb, "and I don't think it's only from turning in circles. I can hardly believe it, even though—even though—"

"You've always known it, that you would marry me, ever since the Independence Ball," he said smugly, helping her settle her hat and pulling the bolo tie up under her chin.

"I didn't even think I'd be calling you Jeb by this time," she replied smartly. "Much less that I'd be calling you my fiancé. Oh! My fiancé!"

"Sounds good, doesn't it? But I can't wait till it's 'my husband.' That sounds even better. Can we get married now?"

"Silly bear," she said, playfully pinching him. It was like pinching a concrete pillar. "I do think we should at least have a decent engagement, considering we've hardly had what's considered a decent time for a courtship."

Impatiently Jeb took her left hand, removed her glove, and tucked it into his waistband along with the other. "You are now my fiancée, and I am going to hold your ungloved hand, no matter how scandalous it is. And what do you mean by a 'decent engagement'?

There's nothing at all indecent in us, and I'll fight any man who says there is."

"I just meant that we should plan a wedding far enough in the future so that we could make arrangements for our families to be there," Flora said soothingly.

"Your family and my family are scattered all over about a dozen states," Jeb argued. "It would take too long to try to herd them all together. I want to get married now."

"Jeb, stop saying that. You know perfectly well that we can't get married now."

"I know not now, like today. But soon. It already seems like I've been waiting for you forever, Flora. I mean it."

She looked up at him and saw that he was perfectly serious. *And why not?* she thought. *By the standards of time, we haven't been together long enough to be this much in love. . .but Jeb is right. It does seem as if we've been waiting our whole lives for each other. . .and I suppose we have. We know it's the right thing in God's eyes. What do we care what men think?*

"What about November, Jeb?" she asked finally. "I would like to have a nice church wedding and for at least some of my family to be able to come. The St. Georges and the Virginia Cookes. And surely in that time your father and some of your sisters and brothers may be able to make arrangements to be here."

"Still too long," he grumbled, "but if that's what you want, my heart, then that's what we'll do. We'll marry in November." Then he added, "Do you know what day it is?"

"Thursday?" Flora guessed, mystified.

"Actually it's Wednesday, but that's not what I meant. Today is August 15th."

"Oh, August 15th," Flora repeated with wonder. "I was going to leave today."

"Oh no you weren't, not unless me and Ace hopped on that train with you. That was my plan, you see. I can tell you all about it now. I planned that you would not leave on August 15th or any other day. I planned that you'd be with me, on this day and every day from now on."

She smiled at him. "I won't pretend anymore, Jeb. I knew. Maybe not at the ball, but the very next day, I knew. And I was happy."

"Are you, Flora? Can you really be as happy with me as I am with you?" he asked, putting his arm around her and pulling her close.

"Yes, because I believe in the Lord, and I believe you are my gift from Him," Flora answered. "Even better than us, Jeb, He knew. God always knew."

Flora was happier than she had ever known, had ever known that a woman could be, as she prepared for her wedding. Her friends—and also now Jeb's friends, who included just about every man he met—teased her about moving from the grand Rookery to "one room and a kitchen." The officer's quarters were little more than that—though they did, of course, have a bedroom—but Flora and Ruby had hours of fun fixing it up.

As always, Jeb was the dashing, careless cavalryman. He would find Flora at the Rookery or at their new little house, come rushing in dusty and smelling of horses, and grab Flora to kiss her and hug her as if he hadn't seen her for months.

He teased Ruby unmercifully, and she adored him. She was fully as determined to make the house nice for "Miss Flora and Mr. Lieutenant Jeb" as Flora was, but sometimes Flora suspected she was so enamored of Jeb that she worked twice as long and twice as hard, sewing new bed linens, polishing the hardwood floors, and scrubbing the kitchen until it shone. Ruby even papered the dreary wooden walls with fine wallpaper Colonel Cooke ordered for them from New York, a small rose print that Ruby spent hours upon end matching up as she hung the thick strips. Jeb's family sent them a fine woolen carpet for the bedroom, and Ruby would barely let Flora walk on it.

In the middle of September, the 1st Cavalry was sent on a

raid, a hard raid hunting wild Cheyenne, and Jeb didn't return until November 4th. Sorrowfully Flora had to break the news to him of the death of his father. Jeb couldn't possibly go to Virginia. The 1st Virginia was a brand-new regiment and leaves were hard to come by, and besides that, Jeb's father had actually died on September 20th.

And then the snows came hard in November, so Jeb and Flora had a small wedding at the Rookery, with only fifteen in attendance and Flora's father. Flora wore her white graduation dress, and she glowed.

For once Jeb Stuart was serious, his voice deep and sure as he promised to love, honor, and cherish Flora until death parted them. In her heart, Flora knew he spoke truth, and she knew that she would cherish this man for all of her life.

He kissed her, his new bride, and they walked out of the parlor, for there was to be no reception. Jeb and Flora just wanted to go home. As they left, Jeb said, "Flora, I knew of God's goodness, but I never knew He would be so good to me. You are my life, Flora. I loved you when I met you, and I promise I will love you until the day I die."

"You are my heart and my life, Jeb," she said simply. "I can't believe God has blessed me with you."

"It was meant to be," he said, smiling. "I always knew it was meant to be."

Two weeks before, Jeb had written a cousin. In telling him of Flora, he had repeated Julius Caesar's famous quote, somewhat altered:
Veni, vidi, victus sum.
I came, I saw, I was conquered.
And so, for the only time in his life, he was.

CHAPTER FOUR

The room was cold even though the fireplace held a roaring, lusty fire. Flora huddled in one of the big overstuffed horsehair armchairs by it, covered with a woolen lap robe, reading the Bible by a kerosene lamp. The cabin was rough, but Flora and Ruby had made it, on the inside at least, into a snug little cottage, with pictures on the walls and rag rugs on the floor and nice heavy black velveteen drapes for keeping out the Kansas winter.

With affection Flora looked at the twin chair next to hers. It was Jeb's, and it had the imprint of his bulky frame in it. For many nights they had sat close together, reading or talking, holding hands, staring dreamily at the fire, contented and happy.

She looked up, and the calendar on the wall caught her eye. It was one she'd gotten with a picture of an angel watching over two children who were making their way down a dangerous pathway. *December 23, 1856. I can't believe we've been married for over a year. It seems like no time at all. . .or it seems like always.*

Ruby came in the kitchen door.

Flora could hear her stamping the snow off her boots and muttering to herself. Wrapping the robe around her, she went into the tiny kitchen. "Ruby, dear, what are you doing here this time of night?"

Ruby was still Flora's maid, but she had moved in with a man named Turley. The circumstances of their relationship were a little vague, but Flora never pressed her. Ruby was certainly not a slave; she was a paid servant, and Flora believed that Ruby's personal life was none of her business.

"Tomorrow's Christmas Eve, ain't it? And looky here, not a sign of a fire in this here stove! What you gwine to feed Mr. Jeb when he gets home, I ask you? Snow?"

"I don't think he'll be able to make it home for Christmas, Ruby," Flora said dispiritedly. "No one's heard from the 1st Cavalry in two weeks."

"He'll be here," Ruby said solidly, shedding several layers of outer clothes, scattering snow as she went. "And you with no Christmas dinner fixed for him. Good thing I brung over this here turkey to cook tonight, with Mr. Jeb comin' home with no fire in the stove and jes' icicles to eat."

"He's a soldier, Ruby. He can't always do what he wants," Flora argued.

"He said he'd be here, an' he'll be here. If'n you don't know Jeb Stuart, I do. When dat man sets his head on something, he gets it done." Finally down to her skirt and blouse, she started tying on an apron and stared at Flora. "Am I standin' here lookin' at you with your bare feet?"

"I—I was just reading—"

"Miss Flora, you git back to that sittin' room right now and set down and wrap up, and I mean it," she scolded. "Otherwisen, your toes'll likely freeze off, and then what? Then you'll just have little hooves like a little tiny pony, and they won't be cloven hooves, neither. So that means the Bible says they'd be dirty."

"I think you mean unclean, Ruby," Flora said with amusement over her shoulder.

Ruby disappeared into the bedroom muttering, "Like I got time to go huntin' wool socks for silly white ladies dat would let their own feet freeze off and can't even cook their own supper." She fetched Flora two pairs of wool socks, still muttering. "You is a good woman, Miss Flora, but you better make sure you be a good wife to Mr. Jeb. Freezing your feet off is one thing, but not havin' a man his dinner when he gets home is 'nother can of worms altogether."

Ruby had cheered her up; she had been depressed, missing Jeb. She always missed Jeb terribly when he was on a patrol. She felt alone, lonely, and somehow bereft, as if a part of her were missing. *And I suppose it is. I am bone of his bone and flesh of his flesh*, she reflected. She had been reading Genesis, and she turned back a few pages to read again of the union of Adam and Eve and how God had ordained this miracle for all married people.

And in spite of what Ruby thinks, I am a good wife to Jeb. And oh, I'm so glad! I was so afraid I wouldn't be, that I wouldn't know how to be, that I wouldn't be good enough for a man like him. But it hadn't worked out that way. She smiled, thinking about her honeymoon and how wonderful it had been. Jeb had been very gentle, and she had quickly learned to please him. A memory floated to her mind of how she had awakened the morning after her wedding and how for a moment she'd been terrified to find a man in her bed. But since then, every night she slept with him and every morning she woke up to him, she had been filled with joy. She'd learned that the intimacies of marriage were part of the wonder of being a wife, married to a man she loved passionately. She was so grateful that she and Jeb suited each other in that way.

From the kitchen, Ruby called, "I got this here fire going good now, no thanks to some folks. And I got that lazy Turley to scrounge around and get you a turkey. It's a little scrawny, but I'll roast it up good. And he got some sweet taters, too, and I knows how much Mr. Jeb loves sweet tater pie."

Suddenly Flora was hungry; she had been listless all day, missing Jeb so much that she didn't really want to eat. But she felt much better now, and so she got up, fetched her warm wool robe and slippers, and joined Ruby in the kitchen. "Where in the world did

Turley get that turkey, Ruby?"

"Hit's a wild turkey, but he dressed it out so nice it almost looks like one boughten at a market. Turley, he's a right good hunter. And he does what I says, 'cause then he knows I'll be nice to him."

Flora reached out and touched the bird. "He is a good size." A thought came to her, and she glanced up at Ruby. "What do you mean 'be nice to him'?"

"Jes' whut it say."

"Why, Ruby, surely you don't mean you'd be letting Turley take some liberties?" Flora teased.

Ruby smiled, and the new gold in one of her front teeth gleamed. She had just gotten it from the new dentist in Leavenworth, and it was her pride and joy, so she smiled most of the time. "I knows what I be doin', Miss Flora, and ain't no call for you to be tellin' me about no liberties. Me and your poor papa thought you and Mr. Jeb would scandal the place up to heaven till we got you two married. Good thing we did, too, jest in the devil's nick of time."

"Yes, thank you so much for that, Ruby. Jeb and I are grateful."

"Orter be. What are you doing in here, anyways?"

"I'm hungry."

"Oh, so now Miss Flora's hungry, is she? Droopin' too much over Mr. Jeb to even put on socks like a Christian woman, but now youse hungry?"

"Yes," Flora said meekly. "But I'll just fix myself some ham and beans real quick, and then I'll help you."

"Oh, jest sit down at the table there. I can fix them ham and beans faster'n you can find the pot to cook 'em in."

"But I want to help," Flora insisted. "Jeb should have a good Christmas dinner, and I really am very grateful to you and Mr. Turley for providing us with this feast."

"Thought you said Mr. Jeb wasn't coming home for Christmas," Ruby said smartly.

"Well, perhaps he will," Flora said, with much less doubt now.

"He said he would, and he don't tell no stories, not dat man. Men like Jeb Stuart don't grow on no trees. You jest better hang onter him, Miss I'm-Too-Pouty-to-Make-Supper."

"I intend to do that, Ruby. So you just step aside and tend to that turkey. I can fix my ham and beans, and then I'll help you with those sweet potatoes for Jeb's pie."

The day dawned with a bright sun, and the snow began melting. The bitter cold of the Kansas winters had not been pleasant, but Flora was used to them. She'd gotten up early, and she and Ruby had spent all day cooking. Ruby knew how to make corn bread dressing, so the two of them had gone to the commissary and had gotten cornmeal and fresh milk so Ruby could teach her how to make it. They were busy all day, and the time went quickly. They finished cooking in the late afternoon.

As evening fell, Flora had again almost lost hope of Jeb returning in time for Christmas.

"You might as well quit looking out dat window. He'll come when he come," Ruby said. "Now you set down here and behave. I'm gwine ter knit Mr. Jeb a pair of new wool socks. They'll be too late for Christmas, but I knows his birthday is in February. I'll be finished long afore then."

"I should learn to knit," Flora said aimlessly, her gaze wandering again toward the window. Though night was falling, she still hadn't closed the curtains. She hoped Jeb would see the welcoming light— if he came home.

"He'll be here," Ruby repeated with emphasis. "You got dat present wrapped you got for him?"

"Yes, it's under the bed."

"What about me? You gots mine wrapped?"

Flora smiled. "Yes, I have. Do you want it now?"

"No, I don't want it now. It ain't Christmas. I'll take it tomorrow 'fore we eat all dis turkey and dressing."

Ruby went to bed early that night. The small house had a room in the attic that had been fixed up by the previous tenant, and she often stayed up there when she worked late. It was actually warmer,

Ruby said, than the downstairs.

Flora waited and listened to every sound. The night was quiet, and a soft gentle snow had begun to fall. She finally rose and murmured sadly to herself, "I might as well go to bed. He's not coming."

She turned to go to the bedroom, when suddenly she heard the sound of horses. She quickly ran to the door, and despite the cold she threw it open.

Bordering their tiny yard were the parade grounds, and a troop was coming in—and then she saw Jeb! He swung out of his saddle, gave some orders, tossed the reins of his horse to one of the men, then hurried toward the house. Flora could see his blue eyes sparkling yards away. He bounded to her, swept her up, and swung her around. "How's my very favorite girl? I've missed you so much! I bet you didn't think I'd make it in time."

"I wasn't sure, but Ruby was positive." She took his heavy overcoat.

Jeb kissed her lovingly and said, "I'm going to thaw out a little." He went to the fireplace, holding his hands out to warm them.

"Did you see any Indians?" she asked as she hung his coat on the back of a cane-back chair to thaw out and dry.

"Not a one. I think they're all hunkered down for the winter, which shows that they're smarter than the 1st Cav. What's been happening around here?"

"Nothing much. We're going to have a good dinner tomorrow."

"That sounds fine! I'm tired of eating stringy antelope."

Flora scrunched her nose and made a sour face, thinking about eating stringy antelope. "That man Turley, the one so sweet on Ruby, brought her a turkey, so we're going to have turkey and dressing with sweet potato pie."

"My favorite!"

As he stood there warming his hands by the stove, Flora was aware of the strange feeling she had. She called it an expansion, but that didn't adequately describe it. She just felt more alive, more energetic, so much happier with Jeb. When he came into the room or when she touched him, the love she felt for him seemed to grow larger and larger. She went to him and took his rugged hands and held them to her cheeks. "You're so cold."

"My hands are grubby and dirty. Flora, you're going to freeze yourself."

"I don't care."

"One of the men asked me what it was like to be married. One of the younger fellows. He must have marriage on his mind."

"What did you tell him, Jeb?"

"I told him it was like going to heaven here on earth."

Flora laughed and lightly pulled his beard, something she often did. "Well, your supper may not exactly be heaven on earth. Ham and beans."

"Better than antelope. Oh, I'm so glad to be home for Christmas with you, my best love! I got you a present, but you can't have it until tomorrow morning."

"I have presents for you, too, Jeb. So yes, let's wait until tomorrow."

He picked her up and squeezed her and said, "I'll go clean up, and then I'll eat. But I'll hurry, because I'm ready to go to bed," he added mischievously. "I haven't slept with you for two weeks. In fact, I may skip supper."

"You'll do no such thing! Ruby tells me that if I don't feed you a good supper when you get home, I'm headed straight for the pit. Or you are. Or someone is, anyway. No, I want you to eat, my darling. I'll wait." She smiled at him. "After all, I haven't slept with my very own stove for two weeks, either, and I want you to be nice and full and happy when we go to bed."

The next morning, Flora arose early. As she dressed, she could smell the sweet scent of burning oak. Jeb never seemed to get tired. Even after long patrols, he came back with boundless energy. Quickly she finished dressing and did her hair. She went in to find that he already had big hot fires made in the fireplace and also in the cooking stove.

"Can't have too much fire after those snowy prairies," he said.

He came over and kissed her. "When do I get my present?"

"Anytime you want it."

"I want it now, then," he said boyishly.

"I want mine first," Flora said.

"All right." He walked over to where he'd thrown his camp bag. He sorted through it and pulled out two packages, one larger than the other, wrapped in brown paper. "This one first."

Flora took the larger of the two packages and tore it open. Inside she found a bolt of beautiful emerald green muslin with tiny white flowers.

"You look so pretty in that color. I know Ruby can make you a dress fine enough for a queen."

"Oh Jeb, it's perfect! Thank you so much, my darling."

"Here's the other present." He handed her a small velvet box.

She opened it and found a necklace with a gold chain and a tiny cross of emeralds that matched the fabric perfectly. "Oh my goodness, Jeb, it's absolutely beautiful! But however did you pay for this? It must have been a dear price, indeed."

"No, you are the pearl of great price," Jeb said, fastening the necklace around her neck. "And its beauty cannot compare to you, Flora, my dearest." He kissed her tenderly.

Then she said excitedly, "I have two presents for you, Jeb." She went back into the bedroom, came out with a box, and handed it to him. "I think you'll like it. She watched as he opened the box and then laughed as his blue eyes lit up. "You didn't expect that, did you?"

Jeb pulled out the golden spurs. One of the other officers had ordered them for Flora, so she had been able to keep them a secret from Jeb. "Now you can be the most dashing cavalier of all, riding around with your golden spurs. But promise when you wear them you'll always think of me."

"Flora, my girl, these are something!" Jeb rubbed the gold admiringly and said, "No one else can beat this finery. I'll be strutting for sure." He looked up at her with his ever-present boyish grin. "And who else would I think of but you? I think of you always, my dear."

"I knew you'd like them, and they suit you, Jeb."

"Thank you, thank you, Flora. So. . .where's my other present?"

She rose and came to sit on his lap. "Well, I'm afraid that you can't actually have that one until around August."

Jeb stared at her for a moment. "What? What does that—in August? Are we going to have a baby? In August?"

"Yes, we are. Merry Christmas!" She watched him as he absorbed this, and she saw the intense pleasure come over his face. Flora had been a little worried about this, because though she and Jeb had always agreed that they wanted children, it was different when it became a reality.

But now Jeb's blue eyes positively sparked, and he hugged her, hard. "Just what I wanted! You couldn't have given me anything better! Think I'll be a good papa?"

"You'll be a wonderful father, just like you're a wonderful husband," she answered, rising to seat herself back in her own armchair.

Jeb, radiating energy as always, started walking the floor. He couldn't hide his excitement, nor did he want to. He wasn't a man who hid things like that. "The dragoons have a good carpenter. I'll have him make us up a cradle and a crib and. . .and. . .some little tiny chairs and a table. . ."

Flora laughed. "It might be awhile before we'll be needing all that, Jeb."

Then Ruby came down the ladder that led up to the attic, yawning.

Jeb said in his booming voice, "Ruby, guess what? Me and Miss Flora are going to have a baby around August."

"Well, ain't dat fine." Ruby grinned. "You wants it to be a boy or a girl?"

"Either. Or both would be just fine with me." He winked and laughed. "I don't care as long as it's healthy and strong. You ought to get married and have a bunch of babies, Ruby."

"I ain't studyin' about any of that foolishness now. I'll be busy helpin' Miss Flora to take care of your baby, Mr. Jeb."

"That's real good, Ruby. Miss Flora and I need you. That reminds me. I have a present for you, Ruby," Jeb said. "It's a surprise." He went back to his bag and pulled out another package and said, "I'll bet you'll like this one."

Ruby opened the package, stared up at Jeb openmouthed, and said, "Dis is the finest bonnet I ever saw in my livin' life, Mr. Jeb." It was a black silk hat trimmed with dangling jet beads and an enormous bunch of cherries.

"I've got something for you, too, Ruby," Flora said. She went to a small table with a drawer and pulled out a package. She handed it to Ruby.

She opened it with obvious anticipation. "It's a ring! Ain't it pretty? And it's gold just like my tooth."

Jeb slid an arm around Flora's waist. "I hope you like your presents, Ruby."

"Why, a woman would have to be crazy to not like dis bonnet and dis here ring. Jest wait till Miss Alma Strong sees me. I'll put one in her eye, I will. Now you two set back and lemme get dis turkey going. We're going to have the bestest meal you ever had, Mr. Jeb Stuart, and you, too, Miss Flora, to go with the bestest Christmas I ever had."

"Me, too," Jeb said to Flora. "The best I ever had."

That winter passed happily for the Stuarts. As Jeb had said, there were no reports of troublesome Indians at all. They had indeed gone into winter quarters.

Flora, as tiny as she was, began very soon to show. By early spring she had already gained so much baby weight she had to be very careful about doing any energetic housework or even taking long walks. She encouraged Jeb, however, to get out and ride around and visit with his men as often as possible.

He was not a homey kind of man. After he found out Flora was pregnant, he hung around the house most of the time, but Flora was reminded of a caged lion. He paced, he fidgeted, he made unneeded repairs on the cottage just so he could hammer something and make noise.

Finally she persuaded him that he needed to ride the horses to keep them in good condition, he needed exercise, and he needed to be with the new 1st Cavalry as they were still a regiment in training. With ill-disguised relief, he started riding, some for pleasure and some patrolling, scouting around the countryside, learning the ground and the territory.

And soon he was called to his grim duty again. The 1st Cavalry got news from the frontier that the Cheyenne were raiding wagon trains, and in May they rode out to hunt them down.

It was a fine spring morning, even on the dreary plains of the border of Kansas Territory. The 1st Cavalry had been following a number of Cheyenne for nine days, their scouts finding clear tracks but always days old.

Jeb rode with two of his longtime friends who had joined the 1st Cavalry, along with Jeb, back in St. Louis: Pat Stanley and Lunsford Lomax. Their commanding officer was Colonel Edmund Sumner, and the men respected him as a good soldier and officer. Still, the men were restless, for they had thought they would find the renegade Indians before now.

"We'll find 'em," Jeb said confidently.

"How do you know?" Stanley asked.

"Because if we don't chase them down, if they've got any grit at all, I'd imagine they'll find us," he answered.

Two days later his words proved prophetic. They had come into a small bowl of the prairie surrounded on three sides by small, smooth hills. That afternoon they stared into the west and saw three hundred Cheyenne warriors lined along one of them.

Colonel Sumner immediately shouted orders for battle formation, and the straggling column quickly formed up as the Cheyenne, screaming bloodily, started riding down the little hill. Jeb fully expected Colonel Sumner to order a carbine volley—Jeb had already started pulling his rifle out of the sheath—when the commander thundered, "1st Cavalry! Draw sabers! Charge!"

The men, sabers glinting like steely death in the dying red sun, charged, screaming and yelling furiously. The line of Cheyenne riding toward them wavered, slowed. . .and then they turned and fled.

Jeb spurred Ace so furiously that he got ahead of the battle line and rushed into the scattered Indians, yelling like fury. Only a few of the officers had barely kept up with him, including Stanley and Lomax. Close by him, Stuart saw an Indian turn and point a rifle right at Lunsford Lomax, and Jeb thrust at him but landed only a thin slash on the Indian's side and rode past him, then turned back. The Indian now had his rifle pointed at Jeb.

Close by Jeb heard, "Wait, Jeb! I'll fetch him!" He saw Pat Stanley, unhorsed, kneeling and pointing a carbine at the Indian. He pulled the trigger, but the rifle misfired, and Stanley was out of ammunition. Quickly the Cheyenne rode toward Stanley, who watched helplessly as the warrior raised his rifle to point directly at Stanley's head.

Jeb shot forward, and this time landed a killing blow to the Indian's head. But as he fell he fired, and Jeb felt the shot hit him high on the breast.

Stanley jumped up and ran to him. "Jeb, you're shot! Stay here. I'll get my horse and get you to the rear." He disappeared and soon came back riding his horse, which had managed to unseat Stanley in the middle of the fray but then had only moved a few feet off to unconcernedly graze a little.

"I don't think it's too bad," Jeb said cheerfully. "But I guess I had better go get it seen to. No sense bounding around on Ace, here, until the bullet plows around and finally blunders into my heart." Blithely he rode to the rear.

. . .I rejoice to inform you that the wound is not regarded as dangerous, though I may be confined to my bed for weeks. I am now enjoying health in every other respect. . .

Flora kept reading those two lines over and over and weeping harder each time the words burned into her heart.

Her father had been an Indian fighter for many years, and she and her sisters had always worried about him when he was on patrols. Flora had seen injured men, had even seen men killed and brought home to weeping wives and families.

She'd thought she knew and understood the dangers of a soldier's life. But this was different. This was her husband, her beloved Jeb. And though his letter was so obviously cheerful, with the energetic note of his demeanor clearly coming through, Flora sobbed helplessly with the sudden harsh reality she was now facing. Jeb was a soldier, he was in constant mortal danger, he could be injured—he could even be killed. Thinking of it, she felt as if she herself might simply pass out into a cold, lonely darkness and oblivion.

How long she remained in this desolation, she really didn't know. But finally she rose and washed her tearstained, swollen face and smoothed her hand over her swollen belly. She couldn't do this to herself. She couldn't do it to the baby. And most certainly she could not do it to Jeb. If she were a weeping, wailing wreck of a woman all the time, Jeb would go mad with grief, she knew. He was happy with her, he found joy and pleasure in his life with her, and she was determined that she would keep it that way.

She would find the strength in the Lord, to live with His comfort, to live under His care. She would learn to live her life with Jeb—no matter what the circumstances, no matter what the hardships or the grief—to the fullest, every day, to be grateful to God every day for him, and never to forget all of the countless treasured moments they had. She would be strong, and she would be full of joy, always, for Jeb.

She would do this. No matter what the cost.

The wounded of the 1st Cavalry were not able to get back to Fort Leavenworth until August 17th.

Flora saw them come into the parade grounds, and she saw Jeb's big body lying on a travois. Though she was so big now she couldn't possibly run, she hurried as fast as she could to his side. He looked up at her, and with an almost stunned relief, Flora saw that his eyes were clear and dancing as merrily as ever. She knelt by him, awkwardly.

"The baby's not here yet," Jeb murmured. "Oh, I'm glad."

"I am, too. He waited until he could see his father."

"Flora, my best girl, you can't know how I've missed you." He joked, "I would have hurried back much sooner, but these lazy fellows wouldn't come along with me."

She ran her fingers down his face and entangled them in his soft beard. "You're pale, my darling. Your letters. . . You seem not to be hurt too badly."

"I'm not," he grunted then pulled himself up to a sitting position. "And I'm as tired of this infernal machine as a man can be. I can walk into that infirmary myself. There're no men big enough to carry an ox like me, and somehow I don't think they'd welcome Ace pulling me in."

"No Jeb, don't. You're scaring me," Flora begged even as he stubbornly pushed himself to his feet.

He took her hand, brought it to his lips, and kissed it, as he had so many times before. Flora never tired of it. "Please don't be frightened, Flora. I never want you to be frightened of anything in this world. I am fine, really. I'm so much better, thank the Lord, and I feel very well, if only a little weak."

Flora nodded. "All right, then. I do have to agree that perhaps I might walk you into the infirmary, instead of Ace." She put her arm through his.

He hesitated and said uncertainly, "Flora, I know this must be so hard for you, but you're really all right, aren't you? I mean, you grew up in a soldier's house and you married a soldier. You always knew, didn't you? You always knew what it would mean?"

She could see the fear in him, as she knew she would. And she steeled her thoughts and cried out to God and then smiled up at him. "Of course, Jeb. Just know that I love you, I will always love you, and I will always be waiting for you when you come home. Now come on, silly bear, and let the doctor see you."

No matter the cost.

CHAPTER FIVE

Flora entered the room and paused abruptly at the scene that was taking place before her. Her lips curved upward in a smile, and she felt a rush of love mixed with pride.

She had been confident, almost from when she met him, that Jeb Stuart would make a good husband. He was always considerate, even gallant to her, a man who was faithful to everything that marriage stood for. But many men who had these qualities didn't necessarily take well to infants. She'd been relieved, however, as Little Flora had come through the first year and a half utterly adored by her father.

Flora remained silent, watching as Jeb, who was lying flat on his back, set Little Flora down upon his chest. She leaned forward, making little yelps of joy. Grabbing Jeb's luxurious beard, she tugged at it and yelled, "Paaah! Paaah!"

"Well, be careful there, little darling. You're going to pull my beard out, and you would see what an ugly fellow I am. Did you know I grew this beard just to hide my ugly face?" He suddenly reached out and grabbed her and held her high in the air. She chortled with joy, and he lowered her until their noses touched.

"Jeb, what in the world are you doing? You always have to play on the floor," Flora demanded, coming to stand over them.

"I'm just too big. There's not enough room anywhere else," Jeb said, lifting Little Flora high again as she squealed.

"You're supposed to be rocking her to sleep."

"I tried to, but she talked me out of it." Jeb grinned. His eyes sparkled with merriment, and his red lips, almost hidden beneath his thick mustache, revealed a smile, exposing his excellent teeth. "I miss out on so much time with our little princess here, I have to make up for it."

"You've been playing with her for over an hour. We have to feed her and put her to bed."

Jeb got to his feet reluctantly.

Flora reached out and took their daughter.

"I'll just watch and you feed," Jeb said. "I think it'll be better that way."

Flora was still nursing Little Flora, so she opened the front of her dress and the baby began to nurse noisily.

"No sweeter sight on earth than that to me," Jeb said. "Everyone I know says children take in their mother's character when they nurse, so she's going to be sweet and beautiful like you."

Flora couldn't help but smile. "You must want something, Jeb. You never say those sweet things to me unless you want something."

"You hurt my feelings, darling."

"I couldn't hurt your feelings with a sledgehammer. What is it you want?"

Jeb pulled a straight chair close beside her. A thoughtful expression replaced his wide smile. "I've been giving a lot of thinking of what I am to the Lord."

"I don't know what you mean."

"I've never been a very deep thinker. I'm a lot better at action," Jeb said, stroking his beard. "But a man has to think about his spiritual life, too, and I've been doing a lot of that."

Flora felt thrilled, for she had often wondered about the depth of Jeb's spiritual life. He had an experience with the Lord years ago, but Flora wasn't certain it was a conversion as she thought of it. She thought of being "converted" as she was. This included repenting of her sins at the preaching of a traveling Methodist evangelist, confessing Jesus and following Him in baptism, and taking the Lord's Supper. Her life had been tied up with church and such devotions, but Jeb had never seemed pressed to do such service to the Lord.

Jeb leaned back, teetering on the back legs of his chair, as he often did. He kept his hands on his heavy thighs. He was wearing only trousers and an undershirt, for May had come, bringing hot weather with it. He teetered back and forth. "I've been a believer in Jesus for a long time, Flora. You know that. There's never been a doubt in my mind that He is who He says He is and He came to do what He said He did. But since we've been married, I've been watching you, and I can't help but think that I've let the Lord down."

"And what is it you want to do, Jeb?"

Stuart spread his arms out in gesture and his eyes opened wide. He had piercing eyes that could see farther than any man in the company, and when he turned them on people, they were riveted, as they were on Flora now. "Why, Flora, I need to do what you've done. I need to join a church and start living as a Christian."

"I think that would be wonderful, Jeb. You've always been a good man, I know."

"I try to be, but from what I read in the scripture, that's not enough. I wrote this letter to my mother. Let me read you just a bit of it." He pulled a paper from his pocket and began to read in a low, serious tone:

"I wish to devote one hundred dollars to the purchase of a comfortable log church near your place, because in all my observation I believe one is more needed in that neighborhood than any other I know of; and besides, 'charity begins at home.' Seventy-five of this one hundred dollars I have in trust for that purpose, and the remainder is my own contribution."

Flora exclaimed, "Why, Jeb, I know your mother will be so

pleased. The church is so far she can't go very often."

"She mentioned that a few times to me."

Flora stroked Little Flora's silky hair. "And what church were you thinking about joining?"

Surprise washed across Jeb's face. "Why, Flora, I want to belong to the same church as you and my mother. The Episcopal church."

Joy flooded through Flora, for she'd spoken to Jeb's mother, and they had written each other, both praying that Jeb would make a step just as this. "I have to write your mother and tell her." Then she shook her head. "No, you put it in that letter that you're going to join the Episcopal church. I know she will be so glad."

"It wasn't a hard decision. You know, I promised my mother when I was very young that I'd never touch a drop of liquor, and I never have and I never will. But I think there's more to being a Christian than just not doing things that are evil. When I ride into battle, I'd like to know that if I get put down I'd be in the presence of the Lord."

Flora held out her hand, and Jeb took it. "What a wonderful surprise you've given me, Jeb." She hesitated then added, "And I have a surprise for you, too."

"You do? What is it?"

"It's about your son." Flora laughed when she saw Jeb's expression. This sentence seemed to amaze him completely.

Then he cried with delight, "You mean we're going to have another child?"

"Yes we are, and I'm praying that God gives us a little Jeb to go along with Little Flora."

Jeb came off of his chair and began pacing the floor. "Well, thank God above! Nothing could've pleased me better." He leaned over and kissed her cheek. "You're a perfect mother, and I'm working hard to be a good father."

Flora reached up and put her arm around his neck to pull him closer to her. His beard was scratchy, but she didn't care. "I'm so happy, Jeb. You're the best husband any woman could ever have. And you already are better than a good father. You're a wonderful father."

Jeb straightened up and said, "You know, it's even more important now that I try to make some extra money. I think I'm going to go to the War Department."

Jeb had been working on a simple mechanism that would allow a soldier to remove his saber from his belt instantly and replace it exactly the same way. At the present time, the removal of the saber was awkward and unwieldy.

He went on, "If I can get them to adopt this, we'll make some money off of it. It'll be good for the army, too."

"Jeb, I think that's wonderful. When will you take it to them?"

"I'm going to write up the proposal and draw diagrams. Then I'll be ready to present it to them."

"I bet they'll buy it, too. You're a resourceful man, Jeb Stuart."

Summer had passed, but in October it seemed that it was almost as sweltering in Washington as it had been in August.

Jeb sat waiting in a large anteroom at the War Department. It had been with some trepidation that he'd asked the sergeant at the desk to deliver his message to General Stratton. That had been over an hour ago.

As Jeb waited, he noticed an odd escalation of activity in the War Department offices. Men hurried up and down the corridors, clutching papers, doors opened and slammed, and soldiers went into General Stratton's office and then came back out, barely glancing at the bearded young officer from the 1st U.S. Cavalry waiting in his outer room.

And then General Stratton opened his door himself. Stratton was a lean, hungry-looking individual with hawklike features. He had the red eyes of a drinker. He was known to be a good officer, however. He called to Jeb, "Lieutenant Stuart, please come in."

"Yes, General." Springing to his feet, he went into the office. It wasn't as ornate as he expected, although Jeb admitted to himself that he'd had little enough to do with generals.

Before he could say a word about his invention, Stratton said,

"I've got a duty for you, Lieutenant. I know you came here of your own doing, but there's something you must do for me."

"Certainly, General, you just name it."

"I need for you to take a message personally to Robert E. Lee. You're acquainted with Colonel Lee, if I'm not mistaken?"

"Yes, sir, he was the commander at West Point when I was there."

"A very serious matter has occurred. There's been a rebellion led by a man named John Brown. Have you heard of him, Stuart?"

"Yes, sir. I even met him once. Old Osawatomie Brown. He was causing trouble in Kansas. He is always causing trouble."

"That's the man, all right. I've written this letter to order Colonel Lee to take charge of a force. Brown and his men have taken the arsenal at Harpers Ferry. They are trapped in the engine house, and they have hostages. We have sent ninety U.S. Marines ahead, because we have no army units close, only local militia. You might as well know what the orders are. Colonel Lee is to take command of all forces in Harpers Ferry and arrest John Brown and the other mutineers. The War Department has authorized him to use any means necessary to do so. Please hurry, Lieutenant."

"Yes, General, I'll leave immediately."

Lieutenant Stuart arrived at Arlington, the Lees' gracious white-columned mansion, just a few hours later. They visited only briefly, for Stuart's message, and the orders he carried, were urgent. No train was available, but the War Department sent a locomotive to take Colonel Lee to Harpers Ferry. Jeb asked to go along as his aide, and Lee agreed. Just before they left, he telegraphed ahead for all action to stop until he was there.

The two men talked of old times at West Point. Lee was interested in Jeb's career, news about the Indians, the Stuart family, every detail of Stuart's life. Stuart remembered that Commander Lee had always been this way with the cadets.

The train arrived at Harpers Ferry, and they immediately left the car. Lee was in civilian dress, a black suit, well-tailored and neatly pressed. He looked like a prosperous merchant on holiday. But he was a soldier and a leader, and he took charge immediately.

"What is the situation, Lieutenant Green?" he asked as soon as they arrived.

Lieutenant John Green, head of the militia, summed up the action briefly. He was a short young man, well built, with a thick, solid neck and a pair of steady gray eyes.

"Brown has raised a rebellion, and there are at least a dozen men dead, including the mayor of Harpers Ferry. We are pretty sure he has about thirty hostages. And sir, one of them is Colonel Lewis Washington." He was George Washington's great-grandnephew.

"Indeed?" Lee asked. "Do we know of the well-being of the hostages?"

"Sir, we don't know, but we think that none of them have been harmed. Old John Brown has been communicating, somewhat, with us. He doesn't seem to intend to harm his hostages. Not now, anyway."

"Where are the mutineers now?"

"They're in the engine house, Colonel."

"Take us there, sir."

"Yes, Colonel, this way." Green led them to a solid brick structure about thirty feet by thirty feet.

The doors were stoutly battened. Lee considered it, then asked, "How many do you think are inside now?"

"Not too many, Colonel. Half a dozen, maybe."

Lee nodded then turned away, his eyes sharp, his face intent. He looked up behind them, he looked around, and he studied the engine house itself for a long time. Then decisively he said, "Lieutenant Stuart, I want you to carry to the engine house a written demand for surrender. If the raiders refuse, a party of marines will rush the doors. We want to avoid killing them, so we'll use bayonets only."

Lee found a place where he could write and took some time to compose the message to Brown. He handed it to Stuart and said,

"Can you read this, Stuart?"

The dawn was breaking, but the light was still weak. Jeb narrowed his eyes, scanned the paper, and said, "Yes, sir."

"Very well. Lieutenant Stuart, you will go to the engine house and relay the terms to John Brown. If he refuses to surrender, wave your hat. That will be the signal for attack. Lieutenant Green, please pick twelve marines to make the attack and twelve marines to be held in reserve."

The marines ran to the engine house and lined the walls in the front.

Jeb simply walked up to the door, banged on it, and called, "John Brown! Lieutenant Jeb Stuart here. Please come to the door."

It cracked slightly, and a carbine, cocked, was shoved through and pointed right at Jeb's belly. Behind it in the half-light, Jeb saw Old Osawatomie Brown.

Unconcernedly Jeb read:

"Colonel Lee, United States Army, commanding the troops sent by the president of the United States to suppress the insurrection at this place, demands the surrender of the persons in the Armory buildings.

If they will peaceably surrender themselves and restore the pillaged property, they shall be kept in safety to await the orders of the president. Colonel Lee represents to them, in all frankness, that it is impossible for them to escape; that the armory is surrounded on all sides by troops; and that if he is compelled to take them by force, he cannot answer for their safety."

Brown was silent as Jeb read the note, but as soon as Stuart finished, he began to talk. He made demands, he argued, he wanted this, and he demanded that.

From inside someone called, "Ask for Colonel Lee to amend his terms."

And another voice shouted, "Never mind us! Fire!"

Robert E. Lee was standing at least forty feet away, by a masonry pillar, but even at that distance he recognized the voice of Colonel Lewis Washington. "The old revolutionary blood does tell," he said.

Finally Brown shouted, "Well, Lieutenant, I see we can't agree. You have the numbers on me, but you know that we soldiers aren't afraid of death. I would as leave die by bullet than on the gallows."

"Is this your final answer, Mr. Brown?"

"Yes."

Stuart stepped back and waved his hat.

The marines looked up at Colonel Lee, who raised his hand. The marines battered in the door and rushed in with Lieutenant Green.

Colonel Washington stepped up and said coolly, "Hello, Green." The two men shook hands, and Washington pulled on a pair of green gloves. The sight of such finery was in odd contrast to his disheveled appearance.

Firing began, lasting for no more than three minutes. When it ended, a marine lay at the entrance of the engine house, clutching his abdomen. Old John Brown lay on the floor, unconscious from blows from the broad side of a marine's sword.

Lieutenant Stuart went in just as the firing stopped and the raiders were captured. He reached down and snatched Old Brown's bowie knife to keep as a souvenir.

During the night, some congressmen and several reporters had come to Harpers Ferry. The leading men of Virginia quizzed Brown, who refused to incriminate others. He was perfectly calm and made no attempt to try to defend himself.

Finally one reporter asked, "What brought you here, Brown?"

"Duty, sir."

"Is it then your idea of duty to shoot down men upon their own hearthstones for defending their rights?"

"I did my duty as I saw it."

Colonel Lee and Lieutenant Stuart, having accomplished their task, were obviously finished. They remained in the town for another day, mostly to rest from their sleepless night. The next day they took the train back to Washington as casually as if Harpers

Ferry were just an interesting interlude, no more.

But Old John Brown's raid was big news, all over the North in particular. Good and responsible men cried for his release and defended his actions as that of a righteous, godly man. And when they executed John Brown, he was lionized as a saint.

His death was possibly the first small tendril of the clouds of war that would soon gather over America.

Revolution had for years merely been a political topic. But in November 1859, when Abraham Lincoln was elected president of the United States, the rhetoric was over, at last bursting into flames. The Southern states began to secede from the United States to form their own sovereign country, the Confederate States of America.

The beginning of the war took place in a fort just off the coast of Charleston. The man who lit the first spark was white-haired Edmond Ruffin, an editor and ardent secessionist at sixty-seven years of age. At 4:30 a.m., on April 12, 1861, he pulled a lanyard, and the first shot of the Civil War drew a red parabola against the sky and burst with a glare, outlining the dark pentagon of Fort Sumter.

Fort Sumter was a United States Army post, but it had no real military value. In April Major Robert Anderson, commander of the post, had few supplies, and the Confederates had turned away his supply boat. Fort Sumter was built to accommodate a garrison of 650 men, but for years it had only had a nominal military presence. On that day in April there were 125 men there. Forty of them were workmen.

The fall of Sumter was simply a matter of time. The people of Charleston stood on the balconies and the roofs of houses to watch the blazing of the guns and the firing of the shells. Major Anderson surrendered the fort the next day.

Thus the war began. Five bloody, terrible years lay ahead for America.

SWORD

If ever men found themselves in a terrible position, the soldiers of the United States Army in the spring and summer of 1861 were well and truly caught in the worst. Many of the finest soldiers and officers were Southerners. Jeb Stuart knew each man would have to make the wrenching decision of whether to remain with the Union and fight against his home state or resign from the Federal Army and take up arms with the newly formed Confederate States of America.

However, for Stuart, whose undying loyalty was to Virginia, the decision was easy. As soon as President Lincoln called for seventy-five thousand volunteers to fight the war against the South, with Virginia's quota of eight thousand men, Stuart's mind was settled. He began packing as soon as he received notice he'd been appointed a captain in the 1st United States Calvary. On May 3rd, he wrote the Adjutant General of the U.S. Army:

> Colonel: for a sense of duty to my native state (Va.),
> I hereby resign my position as an officer of the Army of the
> United States.

That very same day, he sent a letter to General Samuel Cooper, Adjutant General of the Confederate Army:

> General: having resigned my position (Captain 1st Cavalry)
> in the U.S. Army, and being now on my way to unite my
> destinies to Virginia, my native state, I write to apprize you of
> the fact in order that you may assign me such a position in the
> Army of the South as will accord with that lately held by me in
> the Federal Army.
> My preference is Cavalry—light artillery—Light
> Infantry in the order named. My address will be: Care of
> Governor Letcher, Richmond.

Jeb Stuart and his family reached Richmond on May 6th and found a commission waiting for him as Lieutenant Colonel of Virginia Infantry. The city was filled with men spoiling for a fight. The Army of the Confederate States of America was quickly coming to life.

CHAPTER SIX

To Flora, Richmond was dirty, noisy, and crowded. Men from all over Virginia were hurrying to the capital to enlist in the hundreds of companies that were putting out the call. The streets teemed with rough men, and the shops were always crowded and couldn't keep stocked.

Flora didn't have any friends in the city. The Stuarts had been in Richmond for only three days when she fell ill.

Their son, Philip St. George Cooke Stuart, had been born the previous June and was almost a year old. Little Flora was not quite four.

Flora bent over Philip's crib, and a wave of dizziness and nausea washed over her. Black spots danced in front of her eyes. She felt her way to the sofa and fell on it. For a moment, she tried to properly sit up, but she felt so weak that she finally just lay down on it.

Philip fussed for a few minutes, but then he grew silent again and Flora was glad he had gone back to sleep. Little Flora was on her bed in the single bedroom, napping. Wearily Flora closed her eyes to rest, though she could never fall asleep during the day when she was alone with both of the children.

Ruby had refused to leave Fort Leavenworth, for she had a new man and she had sworn that they were to be married. Flora missed her terribly.

She fought the feelings of bitterness that she felt because of the war that had brought her husband to this place. She was cooped up in a tiny house in a strange city with two small children, and she had barely seen Jeb since they had arrived. Drawing a deep shaking breath, Flora thought, *And this is only the beginning. He'll leave any day, and I won't know when he'll ever come back. I won't know if he's well or if he. . .*

She left the thought unfinished. But Flora was quite sure she would feel this same dread, for the war's duration, as a burden on her heart. She knew this, but she fought hard not to dwell on it.

After a while, the dizziness subsided and Flora got up and went to Philip's crib. He was still asleep, and no sound came from Little Flora in the bedroom. She thought of Jeb, of how God had been so good to her in her marriage. She was to this day still desperately in love with Jeb Stuart. She knew every angle and bone of his body. She knew every inflection of his voice. Her eyes knew in detail every inch of that cherished face. With the single-mindedness only found in women so desperately in love did she think of him.

As she made her slow way into the kitchen, she prayed. *Lord Jesus, I need Your strength, and I need Your help. Please send someone to help me, Lord, someone who can help me with the children. . .someone who can be my friend.*

And Lord, watch over Jeb, always.

Jeb dismounted and went into the house. He called out, "Flora!" and heard her answer faintly from the bedroom.

He found her lying on the bed, covered with two thick quilts in spite of the heat. She was pale and had purple shadows under her eyes.

"Flora, my darling, what's wrong?"

"I'm—I guess I'm just tired," she replied weakly.

SWORD

He laid his big hand on her forehead, his touch as delicate as a woman's. "No, you're ill. You're feverish. How long have you been sick?" Jeb had been gone for a day and a night, working with his new recruits, doing the mounds of paperwork required for a unit commander, meeting with his new officers.

Flora relented and said, "I started feeling a little unwell yesterday. I got up early and took care of the children, but I thought that I would just lie down and rest for a little while."

Jeb said grimly, "This won't do, Flora. I'm going to find someone to stay with you."

"Who?" Flora asked. "And however can you find a woman, just like that? You're so busy you don't have time for such things."

Jeb was stricken. The melancholy in his wife's voice and her words wounded him as surely as if he had been stabbed. He had a tender heart as far as his wife and children were concerned. He stroked her hair and said quietly, "I'm going to leave you just for a little while. I promise you that the Lord will help me find someone to help you and take care of you."

Flora managed to smile.

Jeb leaned over and kissed her and looked over at Little Flora, who lay beside her. She was asleep sucking her thumb. "There's my princess," he whispered and touched her silky hair. He straightened up and said, "I won't be long, my dearest."

"All right, Jeb. You're right. I know that the Lord will help us."

Stuart left the house, his mind racing and sorting through ideas. The problem was even more severe and immediate than he had let on to Flora. He had just received word that it was time for his regiment to report to Harpers Ferry, where he would be second-in-command to Colonel Thomas J. Jackson, and he couldn't think of a single person who could help him. He had to leave at dawn.

Finally he headed toward the fairgrounds. Many men from Richmond had enlisted in his command, and perhaps one of them would know of a suitable woman whom Jeb could hire as a maid and companion. Riding onto the fairgrounds, crowded with tents, he went straight to his headquarters.

One of his newest officers, Lieutenant Clay Tremayne, was on his magnificent black stallion, drilling six mounted men on maneuvering commands. Jeb watched them for a while with satisfaction. Though his command was infantry, many of the men had fine horses, and it was perfectly acceptable to their commander. He would have mounted all of them if he could, for he had wanted a cavalry command above all things.

When they finished, Jeb called Tremayne to him and said, "You cut a fine figure on a horse, Lieutenant. And you've learned the orders very well. You drill them like an old hand."

"Thank you, sir," he said with pleasure. He was a fine-looking man, six feet tall with broad shoulders. His face was strong with a hard jaw and dark, intense eyes.

Jeb frowned and shifted on his feet. "By any chance, Lieutenant, do you recall that man who was talking about having such a large family? He's from here, and his family has been here for a long time."

Clay thought and finally answered, "I'm sorry, sir. I know many of the men are from Richmond, but I can't recall exactly the one you're speaking of. Colonel Stuart, is something wrong? Do you need me to find this man?"

"No, it's a personal matter, nothing to do in particular with the man I'm thinking of," he replied, worried. "It's just that my wife is ill, and we have two small children. I really need to find a woman to come in and help her. It's very important that I find one quickly, since we have to move out in the morning."

Clay gave him a crooked smile. "Sir, I just happen to know of a woman—or a girl—who is an excellent nurse. I can personally assure you of that. And she is here."

"Here?" Jeb repeated. "What do you mean? Here, at the fairgrounds?"

"Well, yes sir, she is. She's. . .rather unorthodox. But as I said, I can personally vouch for her character. I'm sure she would be happy to help you and your wife."

"Tell me more about her," Jeb said, his eyes piercing as they drilled into Clay.

"She is with her grandfather, and they are peddlers. Their wagon is here, and they've been selling goods to the men. She's young, only seventeen. And she wears, uh, breeches."

"Breeches?" Jeb repeated blankly. "You mean men's trousers?"

"Yes, sir. She's from Louisiana, and—oh, I think you'll understand better if you meet her, sir."

"Take me to her," Jeb ordered.

Clay led him to the north side of the crowded field, where a big wagon stood. Outside it a small man sat on a camp stool by a small campfire. The figure that knelt close to him, feeding small logs onto the fire, looked like a young boy. As Clay and Stuart drew near, she looked up, and then Jeb could clearly see the delicate features of a girl.

Clay bowed, rather formally. "Sir, I'd like for you to meet two good friends of mine. This is Jacob Steiner, and this is Miss Chantel Fortier. This is Colonel Stuart, my commanding officer."

"I'm very happy to meet you," Jacob Steiner said, bowing his head. He was a small elderly man, rather stooped.

"You've just arrived in Richmond, Mr. Steiner?"

"Yes, although we've been here several times before. I've been a peddler for many years, and I've been all over. But I am beginning to believe that in these coming perilous days, the Lord has led us here, to the South, for a purpose."

"You're a Christian man?"

Jacob Steiner smiled. "You've noticed I am Jewish, but yes, I am one of those rare converted Jews."

Clay spoke up, "I have to tell you, Colonel, that Miss Chantel saved both of us."

"Saved you in what way?" Stuart asked with interest. He studied the young woman dressed in a man's trousers and shirt, with a floppy hat that covered most of her black hair. She had the strangest violet eyes. But in her gaze Jeb found kindness.

Jacob Steiner answered, "She found me sick on the side of the road and nursed me back to health. The same thing happened with Mr.—I mean, Lieutenant Tremayne. We found him wounded. My granddaughter is such a good nurse that he recovered very quickly."

"She's the best nurse I've ever known or heard of," Clay said vehemently.

Jeb Stuart was a man who could assess a situation and make quick decisions. "Miss Chantel, I have a problem, and I need some help."

Chantel asked him, "What sort of a problem, Colonel?"

"My wife has fallen ill. We have two small children, and she's simply not able to take care of them by herself right now. I need someone to come in and help with cleaning and cooking, but mostly to take care of my wife and children. Would you be interested in helping me, ma'am?"

Chantel glanced at Jacob. "If *Grandpere* agrees, I'll be happy to do what I can."

"Why, of course, Colonel," Jacob said readily. "Chantel is a good person and has a healing touch, I believe. If you need her to stay at your home, I will go and check on her and your family each day to see to their needs."

"Thank you, sir," Jeb said with great relief. "And thank you, Miss Chantel. I will be glad to pay you a fair wage."

"I don't need money, me," she said carelessly. "Grandpere gives me all the money I need."

"I'm glad of that," Jeb said, "but still I insist on paying you. I know this is very sudden, but I'm afraid that my command is ordered to move out in the morning. Would it be possible for you to come with me now, Miss Chantel, to meet my wife?"

"I will come," she answered. "Just let me get a few things."

She turned, but Jeb said, "Ma'am?"

"Yes?" she asked, turning back to him.

"I just wanted to tell you that you're an answer to a prayer. I'm very worried about my wife, but now I feel that you're going to be a very big help to her."

Chantel said warmly, "I will help her, and I will take care of your little ones, Colonel Stuart. And may the good God bless you and your men as you go to fight." Her gaze slid to Clay Tremayne.

Jeb noted that Clay smiled at her, but she merely turned and disappeared into the wagon.

❧

Jeb opened the door to his home and motioned for Chantel to enter, following closely on her heels.

Flora was stretched out on the couch with Philip lying beside her. Little Flora was sitting on the floor, playing with a rag doll.

Jeb hurried to kneel by the sofa. He took Flora's hand and kissed it. "Dear Flora, the Lord has blessed us. This is Miss Chantel Fortier. Miss Chantel, this is my wife, Flora."

Flora said weakly, "I'm very glad to meet you, Chantel. I'm— I'm sorry I can't get up to meet you properly."

"No," Chantel said firmly. "You're sick, Miss Flora. That's why I'm here. And for these two darlings, too."

"This is Little Flora. She's a little grubby right now, but she's my angel. And this is our son, Philip."

Chantel took off her hat, laid her pack down by the sofa, and said in a businesslike manner, "First, I give Little Flora a bath, and Philip a bath. And then I give you a bath, Miss Flora."

Jeb laughed as he stood. "The best thing in the world for them. I'm already very glad that you're here, Miss Chantel."

"Oh, I am, too," Flora agreed. "I haven't felt like bathing the children. I haven't even felt like cleaning up myself."

Expertly Chantel picked Philip up and pressed her hand to his fat bottom. "First his cloths need changing, then baths. After that, I fix you something good to eat, Miss Flora, so you can get strong again."

"That would be wonderful," Flora said. "Jeb, are you going to be here tonight?"

"I am," he said slowly. "But there's something I have to talk to you about."

Chantel held out her hand to Little Flora, who immediately grinned up at her and took it. Carrying Philip, she led the little girl into the bedroom and quietly closed the door.

Flora searched Jeb's face, and then she sighed. "You've been called out, haven't you? When must you leave?"

"At dawn."

"Then," Flora said quietly, "it is very good that the Lord has sent Chantel to us."

Jeb knelt by her again and took her hand. "The Lord is good," he said. "He will never forsake us. Not you, Flora, and not me. I know that, wherever I go now, He is with me."

"Yes, He is," Flora whispered, pressing his hand to her cheek. "And wherever you go, I will always be here, waiting for you to come home."

PART TWO: CHANTEL & JACOB 1859—1861

CHAPTER SEVEN

Chantel Fortier came out of a deep sleep as a sudden and blinding fear shot through her. Hands were touching her body. When her eyes flew open, she looked into the face of her stepfather, Rufus Bragg. Bragg had a brutal face, and he was leering at her and running his hands over her body. Chantel cried out, "You leave me alone!"

"You need a man, girl," Bragg said, grinning like a sly snake. He grabbed the top of the lightweight shirt that Chantel wore.

She had been sitting up late with her mother and was exhausted, so she had simply gotten into bed without undressing.

"I know how to make women feel good," Bragg snickered. He gripped the top of the thin shirt and tore it.

Chantel struck out with both hands, fingers extended like claws, and raked Bragg's face. He cursed and lost his grip on her. As he did, Chantel rolled to the other side of the bed and jumped up into the corner. She was trapped in the room, and Bragg was laughing at her.

"I like a woman with spirit," he growled, moving slowly around the bed.

Chantel whirled and picked up the sawed-off shotgun that was leaning on the wall beside her bed. She had put it there for just a time like this, for this wasn't the first time her stepfather had put his hands on her. She drew back the twin hammers, and the deadly metallic clicking stopped Bragg in his tracks.

He stared at her, his eyes narrowing, "You wouldn't have the nerve to shoot me, little girl."

"Get out of here or I'll give you both barrels!" She was deathly afraid but determined. "You leave me alone, or I swear I'll kill you, Bragg."

For a moment, he looked uncertain, but then he laughed in his ugly hyena bray. "You got some spit, Chantel. As soon as your ma dies, I'm gonna marry up with you."

"I would never marry you! Never!"

"You ain't but fifteen, and the law says you got to do what I say when your momma dies. Everything she has will be mine—and that means you, too. So you will marry me, too, little girl." He crossed his arms and nodded as if she had agreed with him. "I'm gonna have you, Chantel. You just make up your mind to that." With one last leer, he turned abruptly and left the room.

Chantel was so shaken she thought that her legs wouldn't support her. She sat down on the bed, trembling in every nerve. Bragg had been after her for over a year, since her mother had been sick. He found excuses to touch her, and he made crude remarks. The fear that had driven Chantel to fight him off turned into a sick emptiness deep inside her. Still she trembled, but now with a treacherous, nauseous weakness. With an effort, she leaned the shotgun back against the wall; then she fell on the bed and began to weep. Her body shook, but she muffled her sobs, for her mother was in the next room.

Finally the storm of weeping ceased. Chantel took a deep shuddering breath. She stood up and retrieved the shotgun. The weight of the gun gave her some courage.

He'll get me. . . He'll never stop coming at me, no!

Moving to the window, she gazed out at the bayou. The moon

cast its silver image on the still dark waters, and the hoarse grunt of a bull gator broke the silence.

Chantel leaned over and put one hand against the wall and began to pray. *I can't leave* ma mere, *good God. So You keep him from me, yes!*

Chantel's spirit was crying out for her mother, who was dying. She knew that her stepfather was evil and would never leave her alone. She'd never understood why her mother had married Bragg after her first husband, Chantel's father, had died. The thick hatred she bore for her stepfather was like a sickening sour taste in her mouth.

Chantel knew nothing about the law, but she suspected that Bragg might be right. *When ma mere dies, he'll take me.* The thought caused a wave of fear, as sharp as the knife she always carried. She lay on the bed, grasping her knife in its leather sheaf in one sweaty hand and holding the shotgun with the other. Chantel waited for the dawn.

At daybreak, just as the sun was coming up, Chantel heard the sound of Bragg riding away and felt a welcome relief. She rose quickly, still fully dressed, for she had been wakeful all night, expecting Bragg to come back into her bedroom at any moment. Hurriedly she went into the kitchen and fixed a broth of turtle soup for her mother.

Carefully she set a tray with the broth and some hot ginger tea. After staring at it for a moment, she turned and ran outside, then returned with a piece of honeysuckle vine and laid it across the plain tray to make it look as pretty as she could. She then took the tray into her mother's room.

Even though her mother had been very ill for more than a year, still Chantel received a small shock when she saw her for the first time every day. She was so pale and thin! Her eyes were sunken, and her color was pale. Chantel forced herself to smile. "I have something good for you, Mere. You'll like it."

"I'm not very hungry, child."

"You've got to eat to keep your strength up, yes."

"Maybe just a little bit."

Chantel set the bowl down and helped her mother sit up. Her mother's bones felt as fragile as those of a bird, and there was practically no flesh on them. The doctors had said that it was "the wasting disease" and they could do nothing for her. In the last two months it had seemed that the life was draining out of her moment by moment.

Chantel fed her mother, but she could eat only a few spoonfuls of the broth. Wearily she then said, "I can't eat no more, me."

"Maybe you eat some later."

"Chantel, sit down. There is something I must say."

Chantel put the tray aside and drew a chair close to the bed. "What is it, Mere?"

Her mother reached out and took her hand. "The good God has told me that it's time for me to go."

"No, Mere, you mustn't say that!"

"It is the good God who has told me this in my spirit. You must not grieve for me. I'll be glad to go home, I'm so tired and I hurt so bad."

"Maybe you get better."

"No, Chantel, you know I won't, and I'm ready. I want you to listen carefully."

"Yes, Mere, what is it?"

"I've been praying for you to find the Lord Jesus, and you will. But when I'm gone, you must leave this place. You must go to my sister Lorraine in Mississippi."

Chantel didn't question her mother, for she knew that her mother was aware of Bragg's evil ways, and this was her attempt to protect her. "It will be safe for you there. Promise me, *cherie!*"

"I promise," Chantel said, "but my heart is breaking for you."

Her mother pressed her hand. "God has appointed us a time to go, and it will be good for me. Now I pray that God will watch over you." She bowed her head and began to pray.

As she did, Chantel felt the tears begin to run down her cheeks. She wiped her eyes on her sleeve, and after her mother ended her prayer, she said, "It will be well, ma mere. God will take good care of me."

Chantel left the room, carrying the tray, her heart as heavy as it had ever been. She knew that her mother couldn't live long. She also knew that as soon as she was gone, Bragg would be after her, and there was not a soul in the world who could help.

Chantel had helped her father make the boat called a pirogue before he died. She remembered as she pushed it out into the dark waters of the bayou how they had worked on it together. He hadn't lived long after this, but he'd taught Chantel how to get through the waters of the bayou and the swamp in the frail craft.

Taking up a pole, she pushed off from the shore, and the *pirogue* seemed to glide across the water. The smell of humus was thick in her nostrils. She glanced up as a flight of brown pelicans in a V formation made their way across the sky. The sun was as yellow as an egg yolk. Despite the heaviness of her heart, Chantel admired the beautiful wild orchids that carpeted the still waters. Then she made her way through large pools, green with lily pads that clustered along the bayou's banks. They were bursting with flowers. She quickly went into the heart of the bayou, where she watched a flight of egrets, then a blue heron lifting its spindly legs carefully, its needlelike beak darting down on a fish. He tossed the fish up in the air, caught it, and swallowed it. Chantel smiled as it went down his long thin neck. "You have a good breakfast, you," she said.

The air was moist and cool, but it wouldn't remain so long. She reached the enormous cypress, where she had tied one end of a trotline. She started to pull up the line, and she felt it trembling. "I got me a big fish," she said with satisfaction. Even as she spoke, a flash of white caught the corner of her eye. She whirled around quickly and saw a cottonmouth that was thicker than her leg. The white in the mouth was exposed, giving it the name. She smelled the stench that these snakes give off, and it made her shudder. Quickly, Chantel reached down and picked up the shotgun. In one smooth motion, she loaded it and pulled one of the triggers. It tore the monster's head off, and Chantel nodded with satisfaction. "You ain't gonna bite nobody no more, you!"

She looked around to be sure that there were no alligators. She saw none, so she began to run the trot line. She pulled up the line, and on the third baited hook, she found a large catfish that weighed over six pounds she assumed. Carefully she pulled it off, avoiding the spines, which were poison. When it was free, she kept her thumb in its mouth, holding it carefully. She picked up a pair of clippers and clipped off the spines, then tossed the fish into a sack that she had brought.

Picking up the line, she continued to check for more fish. Many of the baits had been lost, but finally the line resisted her. "I got me something down there," she said. She tugged at the main line, and finally the head of a huge snapping turtle appeared. He'd swallowed the bait and was now snapping at her and hissing. "You go on and hiss, old turtle. You're gonna make a nice soup, I tell you." She heaved the turtle into the boat, and with the hatchet she always carried, she chopped off its head. The mouth kept snapping as it lay in the boat. She picked it up with her thumb and forefinger and threw it into the swamp. "I gonna eat you tonight, me."

She continued until she'd run the trotline; then she reversed the boat and headed back. As she reached the shore, she saw Ansel Vernier, a good friend. "Ansel, I got plenty of fish. I give you some."

Ansel helped her pull the pirogue to the bank. She pulled a large catfish out and handed it to him. He spoke in French saying, "Thank you, Chantel. You have good luck today."

"See this big turtle? He'll make a good soup. Come over tomorrow. I give you some of it."

"Maybe I will."

Ansel was a small dark man with a mouth as big as the catfish he held in his hand. He now said, "How is your good mother?"

"Not good at all, Ansel, very weak."

"I will pray for her and light a candle when I go to church." He shot an unhappy glance toward the house then turned to her. "Is Rufus at home?"

"No, he's gone to get drunk in town. I wish he'd just stay there."

Ansel nodded. He knew that Bragg was an evil man, and he feared for Chantel. "What will you do when your mother goes to God?"

"I will stay here, me. This was ma pere's place."

Ansel was troubled. "Thanks for the fish. Let me know if you have trouble, little one."

Two days passed and Chantel knew that her mother couldn't live much longer. She had no family, but the Cajuns who lived close in the bayou came by. They tried to comfort her, and they brought food, which her mother was too sick to eat. Chantel was just too grieved.

Eventually Bragg came home drunk. As he entered the house, he grabbed at Chantel.

She whipped her knife out of the sheath.

"That's all right, Chantel. I'll have you soon."

"You'll never have me!"

"Yes I will. You'll see."

That night Chantel sat up with her mother, who was in a terminal sleep. Her breathing was barely discernible. She finally woke up sometime in the early hours. "I go to meet—Him. May the good God take care of you."

Her mother didn't move again, and Chantel was unable to tell the moment when she left this life. She folded her mother's hands across her breast as the hot tears rolled down her cheeks.

She was only fifteen, and she was more alone in the world than any fifteen-year-old ever should be. She knew that she would have to leave, but she knew that no matter what Rufus Bragg did, she had to see her beloved mere buried like the Christian woman that she had been.

Chantel was surprised at how many people came to the funeral. The priest was there, and the neighbors, young and old. Most of them had known Chantel's mother for many years. They all came by, some of them embracing her, all of them expressing their grief.

Ansel came by and took her hands and kissed them. "Why you not come and stay with me and my family? You be safe there, cherie."

"I'll be all right, me," she said dully.

Chantel noticed that none of them said much to Bragg. He seemed to expect it. His eyes rested on her often. Every time she caught him looking at her, fear grasped her.

Father Billaud was one of the last to leave. "What will you do now, Chantel?"

"I will stay here. This was ma mere's house, ma pere's house."

The priest was obviously upset by this. "It may not be the best thing for you."

Chantel shrugged.

"Do you have no other relatives?"

"My mother has a sister who's in Mississippi. Maybe I go there."

"I think that would be the best. Come to me if you need help, child."

"Yes, Father."

As Billaud turned and left, Chantel followed him out. They saw Bragg outside waiting, it seemed, for Father Billaud to leave.

He was a small man, this priest, and there was a light of anger in his eyes. "I will warn you, Rufus Bragg, that if anything happens to that girl, you'll pay for it."

"You would make me pay, priest?" Bragg was laughing at him. "Nothing will happen to her. After all, I'm her family."

"You're an evil man, Bragg. You mind what I say. I will have the law on you."

"There ain't no law in the bayou. Now get off my land, priest!"

Father Billaud had no choice. He turned and walked away.

Chantel heard Bragg laughing at him as he left.

Four days after the funeral, Chantel was alone in the house. Rufus had gone out again to get drunk. She had been afraid, and she fastened her door with a bar that she used each night. She also kept her shotgun and knife beside her. She didn't see Bragg that day, but still she lay awake for a long time. Finally, she drifted off to sleep.

She awoke to the sound of a crash and saw the door, battered and hanging on its hinges. Bragg came in, his eyes red with drink and lust written on his face. "I'm gonna have you, girl, just like I said."

"You leave me alone!"

"No, I won't. Not ever." He reached out and grabbed her. Chantel ran to the door. He was drunk and clumsy, but fast for a big man. He grabbed at her gown, which tore off one shoulder. He laughed. "You ain't gonna have no place to run, you!"

Chantel dodged as he made another grab for her. She ran to the fireplace and grabbed the iron poker. Moving faster than she ever knew she could, she turned, swung with all her strength, and hit him in his head.

He staggered back and put both hands to his forehead. Then he held them up in front of his eyes, and they ran with blood. "I'll get you for this, Chantel!" he growled. He moved toward her again, reaching out to grab the poker.

But Chantel took a quick step back, then hit him again, a solid blow.

This time his eyes rolled up. He went to his knees and fell forward.

Chantel could hardly breathe. "I have killed him," she whispered. She then saw that he was breathing.

She ran back to her room and dressed quickly. Earlier that day, she'd already decided to leave, for she knew this would come sooner or later. She grabbed the sack filled with her mother's jewelry that she'd kept hidden from Bragg. She had the money from her father that they'd never told Bragg about. She left the room and went into her mother's room. She took the fine pistol that was her father's and the Bible that was her mother's. She went into the kitchen and began stuffing bacon, flour, and coffee into a bag. She then she added a frying pan, a saucepan, and a coffeepot.

She went back into the front parlor to see if Bragg was still breathing. She saw that he was, so she ran back to her room in a hurry. She grabbed two blankets and the sawed-off shotgun and went outside. She wrapped everything in two blanket rolls. She grabbed some grain for the horse, Rosie. She saddled Rosie, put the blanket rolls on, and then mounted the mare. "Go, Rosie," she said and kicked with her heels. The big horse moved ahead at a trot. She wasn't a fast horse, but she was a strong one and had stamina.

Chantel didn't look back at the house, but she stopped by the small graveyard where her father and now her mother lay. She bowed her head and tried to pray. All she could think to say was, "I'll be fine, ma mere. The good God will take care of me."

As she left their land she was thinking, *Bragg will come after me. I must leave the bayou.* With one last look behind her at the house and the dark waters just beyond, Chantel rode away from the only life she'd ever known.

CHAPTER EIGHT

Chantel kept Rosie at a steady pace all night long, pausing only once to let her rest. Finally she stopped and wrapped herself in a blanket, and despite her fear of Rufus Bragg finding her, she fell asleep. Dreams came to her, and she woke once to find herself whimpering, drawn up in as small a space as she could.

The sun finally touched her face and awakened her. She rose quickly, her eyes going to Rosie, whom she'd tied out in a patch of grass that bordered the swamp. Rosie was still dozing.

Quickly Chantel gathered enough sticks to make a nice, hot cooking fire. She filled a pan with water, then spooned in the coffee and balanced the pot on two stones. As soon as the coffee was bubbling and wafting a delicious smell to her nostrils, she broke out the pan and fried up some bacon. When the grease had melted, she poured it out then tossed two slices of bread in to let them toast. She ate nervously, and from time to time she glanced back to the south, wondering if Rufus had gained consciousness and was already after her.

When she finished, she cleaned up the pots and utensils, packed them, and then fed Rosie some grain and watered her. After Rosie was finished, she saddled her and put the blanket rolls in place, tying them down with strips of rawhide. Mounting up, she said with a confidence she did not feel, "Come on, Rosie. We got places to go."

Rosie seemed tireless as Chantel rode all day, only pausing once to rest. She was still in bayou country. The air smelled of the soaked earth. Once, far away, she saw a blue heron rising from the reeds and knew that it must surely be the bayou's edge.

She knew roughly where her aunt Lorraine lived. She'd been there once on a visit when she was only seven years old. She had made so few trips in her life that it was burned in her memory.

She rode until sunset and slept lightly. At dawn she rose, and she and Rosie continued on their lonely journey.

Chantel slept well that night. Already the hard riding and even the solitude seemed to be making her feel more peaceful and less afraid.

The next day she came to a crossroads that she remembered. More by shrewd instinct than remembrance, she took the right-hand road, due east. There were a few travelers on the road, but they were the first people she had seen since she'd left her home days before.

Eventually around midday, she came to the small town—really just a settlement of a dozen houses, a general store, and a blacksmith's shop. She remembered it distinctly and guided Rosie to the house where her aunt Lorraine lived. She saw that the huge walnut tree was still out in the yard behind the house. She remembered her mother gathering walnuts and breaking them with a hammer.

Dismounting in front of the house, she tied Rosie to a small tree. Then she went up to the door and knocked. No one came, and she grew discouraged.

She was about to go around the house to see if perhaps they may have outbuildings when suddenly the door opened and an elderly woman stood before her. "What you do here?" she demanded.

"I'm looking for my aunt. Her name is Lorraine Calvert."

"She no live here no more." She peered suspiciously at Chantel. "This is my place now, me."

"Where did she go?"

"She find a man, and they move away. Someone say they go up north to find work. Go away now. This is my house."

A bleak depression settled over Chantel. She was barely able to mutter a slight thank-you to the lady. She went back and mounted Rosie. She turned her head almost instinctively to the west to make sure Bragg wasn't there. Not knowing what else to do, she rode east the rest of the day, keeping a steady pace.

She stopped at an inviting little clearing by the side of a small river. Chantel filled her canteen with fresh water then let Rosie drink and graze a little as Chantel rested in the cool shade. But still Chantel felt closed in, and in spite of herself, pictures rose up in her mind of Rufus Bragg coming around the bend of the road at any moment.

They rode on. It seemed like a long, dreary day.

Finally the sun dropped beneath the horizon and darkness overtook them. Along with the darkness a fear closed in on Chantel Fortier. As she made her camp and cooked her evening meal, she felt more alone than she'd ever felt in her life. In some way, she felt more desolate than she had when her mother had died. She supposed that even then some hope for her aunt Lorraine had comforted her. But now that faint shred of hope was gone.

She lay down and put her hands behind her head, remaining wakeful and worried. After a time, she began to pray aloud, for it seemed to give her some comfort. "God, do You know I got nowhere to go? I got no people and nobody to look after me except You. I've lost ma mere, and now You are all that I have. Help me to find a place, me. Please, keep me safe from all harm."

She began to think. *I better keep going northeast. I'd do better in a big town. Maybe I could find some work, me. I can cook and sew and read and write and take care of horses. I can fish and hunt. Maybe I find someone to help me. . .someone to be with, to be friends with. Maybe I'll even find a home. . .*

Chantel had thought that she was too burdened and worried to sleep, but she was very young. She pulled her blanket closer around her and fell into a deep dreamless sleep.

The sun was high in the sky. Chantel had ridden steadily northeast after rising at dawn. She began to pass more travelers and realized she was coming to a settlement. She thought about cutting across the country to bypass it, but she did need more supplies.

It was a small but busy little town, with several houses, several shacks, and even a hotel. Businesses lined the main dirt road through the settlement: a tailor's, blacksmith, livery, mercantile, and two saloons. The biggest and finest of these had a sign: LAUREL GENERAL STORE.

Nudging Rosie ahead, she dismounted and tied her to the hitching post just outside it. In front of the saloon just down the road were two rough-looking men sitting on straight-backed chairs, with an upturned crate for a table that held checkers. As she went into the store, one of them whistled at her and said, "Hey, sweetheart, get your grub; then you can have a drink with Leon and me."

Paying no attention to them, Chantel went into the store and found no customers, but a heavyset, whiskered man was there working. He had pale skin and dark eyes with a droopy mustache that hid most of his mouth. "Good day, miss. What can I get you?"

"I need coffee, bacon, and a loaf of that sourdough bread." Chantel waited in front of the counter as the man found what she asked for.

"Thirty-three cents, ma'am," he said. As she counted out the money, he cocked his head to the side and asked, "Where's a young lady like you heading all by yourself?"

"South. To Lafayette," she answered shortly, not looking him in the eye. Quickly she grabbed the bag of her goods and hurried out of the store.

She tied her sack to the pommel. She was anxious to get out of this dirty little town, and she would sort out the supplies later.

Out of the corner of her eye, she saw the two checker-playing men sauntering toward her. One of them was tall and had a slight limp. The other was a small man, odd-looking because his hat was much too big for him. He looked like a little boy wearing his father's headgear.

"Hello there. My name's Charlie, and this is Leon. What's your name, pretty lady?" the tall one asked her.

Chantel didn't answer. She grabbed the saddle horn and started to raise her foot to the stirrup.

The smaller man—Leon—said, "Wait a minute, there. Why don't we talk for a while? Make acquaintance, like? You'd like me and Charlie. We're nice fellows."

"That's it," Charlie agreed, sucking on a shred of a toothpick. "Come on. We'll buy you a drink."

"No," Chantel said evenly.

With her left hand she reached up again for the pommel, but the one called Charlie grabbed her arm and pulled at her, muttering, "Now just wait a minute here—"

Instantly Chantel drew the knife from the sheath at her side and held it up so that the sun glinted on the sharp blade. "Let me alone, you!"

Charlie laughed and put both his hands up in a gesture of surrender. "You don't need no knife. We just gonna have a little fun."

"No, we're not gonna have fun," Chantel said between gritted teeth. "I'm not going to tell you my name, I don't care what your names are, and I don't want to drink with you. And if you don't leave me alone, I'll cut you. I swear I will, me."

"She's a little spitfire, ain't she?" Charlie said with admiration.

"Uh—yep, she is," Leon agreed, but not with quite so much admiration. He was very slowly backing away.

With one last disgusted look at them, Chantel mounted, still holding the knife in her right hand. Without another word, she turned and headed out of town. Though she wanted to look back, she made herself stare straight ahead. Though no one could have seen it, Chantel was very scared, her heart skipping along like a wary little rabbit's. She whispered, "Thank You, good God, for taking care of me."

She was at least two miles past the settlement, riding again in silence and solitude, before she could calm herself down, and then a weary sort of numbness settled on her. Blindly, not knowing what new fears may lie ahead, she rode east with the sun warm on her back, but she had a coldness in her heart.

❧

Ten days after her encounter with the two men, Chantel was still traveling steadily northeast. She was getting low on supplies because she was avoiding towns.

She had tried to stop once more, but the same thing had happened. A group of toughs were lounging around outside the saloon, and they called out and whistled to her as she passed. One young man with a knife scar on his face ran up to Rosie and grabbed her reins, grinning and calling Chantel "a pretty piece." Chantel had kicked his face then spurred Rosie to her fastest lumbering gallop, bypassing the general store without regret.

Right then she knew that, as young as she was and with the way she looked and traveling alone, it was bound to happen no matter where she went. Once again she stiffened her resolve and decided that if she had to she'd drink water and eat fish and small game.

She had traveled far from the bayou now, but it was pretty country. There were a lot of farms with cotton fields, and the few homes she saw were usually whitewashed two-story homes with painted shutters and deep verandas. The woods were deep and secret-looking, and sometimes Chantel thought she might like to just disappear into them and live there, like a wild thing that would not be tamed. But something kept her on the road, and something kept her going northeast. She was past questioning why. She just rode.

Not far off the road, she saw a nice farmhouse. A young lady sat on the porch holding a baby. On impulse Chantel went up the path to the house. "Hello, ma'am," she said uncertainly.

The woman was in her middle twenties and pleasant-looking. "Hello. Are you traveling alone?"

"Yes, ma'am, to my family in Tennessee, ma'am," Chantel said her polite lie.

"About a mile up this road there's a fork. The left one will take you to Jackson. The right one continues northeast, just a mule track, really, and it's a long way to the next settlement that way, all the way to Baxley. Would you like some lemonade?"

"No thank you, ma'am, I'd better be going on, me." Chantel left, with the woman staring after her. She came to the crossroads and followed the right-hand fork, which led in a more northerly direction than Chantel had been riding. The woman hadn't lied, for the road was no wider than the width of a wagon. She could even see the ruts that wagon wheels made.

She traveled on in her dogged way for two days.

That morning she awoke to a dirt-gray dawn and ugly dark clouds in the east. After two hours a light rain started and then turned into a downpour. Rosie was soaked, and Chantel was soaked, but she was lucky because she had a good piece of canvas that she could arrange over the saddle to cover the saddlebags that held her supplies. Still, she made a miserable sodden camp and wished she were back in her nice house on the peaceful bayou. Without Rufus Bragg, of course.

The next day the rain kept on, and she gave up and found a deserted barn. Half the roof was falling down, but the other half seemed solid enough. She pulled Rosie in and unsaddled her. She found enough dry wood in the barn to get a fire started. She took off her clothes and wrung them out and hung them on a few sticks and branches close to the fire. She fed Rosie and rubbed her down good. The barn still had some sweet-smelling hay, and Rosie munched happily on it.

Chantel was hungry and ate four eggs, all that she had left, a big greasy chunk of fried salt pork, and her last piece of bread. She huddled by the fire, glad to be out of the rain, savoring the warmth and comfort of the fire. She had managed to keep her blanket rolls dry, and after she ate she was sleepy. That night she slept sounder than she had in days.

She slept a little later than usual because the day was still gray. Though the rain hadn't completely stopped, it wasn't the mad torrent it had been the day before. At first she was tempted to stay in the barn, but whatever it was that seemed to be driving her made her decide to ride on that day. It rained off and on, and the twilight fell early, for the sun had never come out that miserable day.

Suddenly something caught her eye up in the road, and she pulled Rosie over. "Whoa, girl," she whispered. "There's something up ahead." It was just a big shadow, looming up right in the middle of the road. Cautiously she rode closer until she could make out that it was a wagon, stopped right on the track. She stopped Rosie again to watch. For long moments she listened, but she heard no sound and saw no movement.

She pulled the shotgun from the sheath and rode slowly past the wagon, giving it a wide berth. As she passed it, she saw a horse, still in the traces, lying in the road. It was obviously dead. Again she pulled Rosie to a stop, turned her, and called out softly, "Hello, is anyone here?"

The crickets had begun singing, but just barely louder than their shrill calls she heard a voice coming from the wagon. Dismounting, Chantel tied Rosie to the seat upright, still holding the shotgun. She went to the rear of the wagon, stopping once again to listen but hearing nothing. Finally she came to the opening at the back and lifted the canvas cover. No lamp was lit inside, but she could make out the form of a man lying on the floor. "Are you sick?" she asked hesitantly.

A man's weak voice answered. "Yes, I'm afraid I am. Very sick."

Chantel stood irresolutely, afraid of being out there in the wilderness, alone, and maybe trying to help a man who was not good, a man who might be like Rufus Bragg or the men in towns who looked at her so greedily and licked their lips. She shuddered a little but then closed her eyes and took a deep breath. Chantel knew herself. She couldn't ride on and just forget. She had to help this man. Whoever or whatever he was, she would not leave him here, like her, alone and frightened in the wilderness.

CHAPTER NINE

With determination Chantel tucked up the canvas flap and climbed up into the wagon. She drew close and looked down at the man.

He was elderly, she could tell, lying flat on his back, and as her eyes grew accustomed to the dim starlight, she could even see the lines in his face. His hair and his beard were as white as snow. He didn't speak, and she could see that his cheeks were sunken in and his eyes were dull with pain. Even as he stared at her, his eyes began to close and his head lolled to the side.

She glanced around and saw that, although the wagon was huge, most of the space was taken up with shelves filled with goods of all kind. There were canned goods, fresh vegetables and fruits, bolts of cloth, hardware, tack, tools, and many small unlabeled boxes. The man lay stretched in the space between the shelves in the middle of the wagon, and there was barely enough room for her to kneel beside him. She spotted a lantern hanging just by the canvas flap for the opening, with a box of matches on a neat little shelf just underneath it. Quickly she lit the lantern and squeezed by so that she could kneel down by the sick man.

"You are very sick," she observed. Now that she could see him more clearly, she could make out the pallor of the old man's face, the skin that looked stretched too thinly over the bones. It was a death's-head look, they called it, and she had seen it on her mother.

The old man coughed weakly. "Yes, I've been very ill indeed. How did you find me?"

"I was just traveling along the road, and I saw your wagon. Your horse is dead, no?"

"Yes, that was the problem." Another coughing fit seized him and racked his small frame. When it passed he continued in a weak whisper, "My horse died, and I tried to dig a hole to bury him. But I was so tired, and then the rain caught me. I got wet and there wasn't any way to dry off."

"You're still wet," Chantel said, feeling the dampness of his clothes. "You need to get warm and put on dry clothes."

"Yes, but first some water, please? I had my canteen here, but I drank it all." Bewildered, he looked around.

Chantel knew he had a fever. When she had been feeling his clothes, she had touched his neck, and it was hot. She jumped up. "Never mind, you. I'll get water."

Chantel hurried to get her canteen and the tin cup she used for coffee. She filled it half full and gave it to him. She had to pull him up and hold him in a half-sitting position, but he drank thirstily.

"Could I have some more?"

"Maybe you drink just a little bit at a time, yes?"

"Maybe that would be better."

Chantel nodded. "It's still wet outside, but I'll build a fire and get you dried off."

"There are two tents stored under the wagon. One of them is much too large, but the other is small, maybe small enough for you to put up. There's also a small stove stored right behind the seat. In the cold weather, I heat the tent up with the stove."

"I can do this," Chantel said sturdily. She got her blankets and hurried back up into the wagon. She put one of them over him and rolled up another to rest against his back so he could stay in a half-seated position. Once again she refilled the cup and warned,

"Little sips only, yes?"

"Yes, I'll do that," he agreed.

"I'll be taking the lantern. I'll need it to find everything," she told him.

He merely nodded, obviously exhausted, and his eyes closed again.

Chantel headed for the wagon opening and for the first time saw the fold-down steps that made it so much easier to come in and out of the wagon. Without hesitation she flattened herself in the mud beside the wagon and looked at the frame underneath.

Sure enough, there was a great roll of canvas that must have been a huge tent and another much smaller roll, both tied with sturdy rope and simple knots to the undercarriage. Quickly she untied the smaller tent and pulled it out. She had never had a tent, had never even been in one. But she had seen them before, and Chantel had a quick mind, so it took her little time to figure it out. She found the stakes and tent poles and immediately could picture how to stake out the tent and then raise it. This she did, quickly and efficiently. It was a small tent, but it was high enough for one to stand upright.

Secured right behind the driver's seat was a stove, and beside it was a box that held rich pine, which would burn almost instantly and was the best and quickest way to start a fire. The stove was small indeed, but large enough to warm the little tent and cook a little bit on the top. She set it down near the tent opening and laid the pine knots along the bottom.

Running now, she hunted, almost despairing of finding any dry wood, but not far off the road she found an enormous oak tree with many fallen branches, some of them as thick as her arm. The thick greenery of the leaves above seemed to have sheltered them from much of the rain.

Soon the stove was throwing out a cheery heat, and Chantel was heartened. But she looked around at the muddy ground and knew that she couldn't lay the old man on the ground.

She went back into the wagon and saw that the man was still sleeping, his head fallen to the side, his mouth slightly open. His breathing had a funny, rattling, wet sound. She sighed and held the lantern high to look around.

Soon she spotted them, cleverly stored, as all the many items in this wagon seemed to be. Folding cots were attached to brackets above the shelves, and they had thin but soft canvas mattresses. On a shelf underneath the neatly piled bolts of fabric were several blankets folded into uniform squares. Chantel hurried to make him up a bed in the tent, which was now pleasantly warm.

Returning to the back of the wagon, she climbed in and said, "I have the tent up, and the stove is making it warm. If I help you, can you go there?"

"I think so." The old man struggled, and Chantel went to his side and put her arm around him to lift him up. He coughed then smiled faintly and said, "I'm sorry for being such a bother."

"No bother to me," she said awkwardly.

She helped him as he took tentative steps. He was weak indeed, and she practically had to carry him. It took them a long time to reach the tent. Immediately he collapsed onto the cot gratefully.

"Mister, you need to get outta those wet clothes."

"Yes, I'm—so—very cold."

Chantel went back to the wagon and found some dry clothes for him. She returned and saw that he had been able to sit up on the edge of the cot and remove his shirt. "Here, put this warm shirt on." She helped him put his arm through the sleeve and buttoned it up. "You lie down. I take your pants." The old man didn't argue. He lay back, and Chantel lifted his feet and legs onto the cot. She removed his sodden shoes and wet socks, and she put on a pair of thick socks she found with the rest of his clothing. He was very thin, and his skin was sodden, but he still burned with fever. She looked up and she saw that he had passed out again. It took a little struggle, but she finally was able to put the dry pants on him. She then put the blankets around him. "You be warm soon, you," she said quietly.

The old man didn't answer. By the dim lantern light she studied him. He was thin-boned, his cheekbones pronounced, his cheeks hollowed. His mouth was short and full, and he had a pronounced nose. She knew that he was old, but at fifteen years of age, she couldn't tell the difference between thirty and sixty. He seemed to be resting quietly now, so Chantel decided to take care of Rosie and investigate the wagon more. She was hungry, and she knew that when the old man woke up she should try to get him to eat.

First she went and untied Rosie and led her to the great oak tree. Although the rain had stopped, it was still the driest, most comfortable place she could think of for her sweet, hardworking horse. Chantel unsaddled her, rubbed her down, and gave her the last of the grain. There was grass growing underneath the tree, though, and soon Rosie was grazing contentedly.

For perhaps the dozenth time that night, she climbed back in the wagon. She rummaged around in the foodstuffs, and to her surprise she found something she had never seen before: chicken broth in a can. She set about trying to figure out how to open it; it seemed like it would be a dangerous business with her hunting knife. It took her a little while before she figured out the tool she needed to open it, and then triumphantly she found a can opener. She took a couple of carrots and stalks of celery and with satisfaction used her opener on the can of broth. Soon she had a thin but nourishing soup bubbling on the stove.

"It smells good."

Startled, Chantel turned to see that the old man was awake. "Hello," she said a little shyly. "You sit up and eat. It's good for you when you're sick." Again she had to help him sit up and propped him with some rolled-up blankets from the store in the wagon.

When he was comfortable, he asked, "What is your name, child?"

"Chantel Fortier," she answered, spooning up soup into the ever-useful tin cup.

"That's a French name."

"Yes, ma mere gave it to me. *Chantel* means song."

"Yes, I know. It's a very pretty name. It's very nice to meet you,

Miss Fortier. My name is Jacob Steiner."

"How long since you ate, Mr. Steiner?"

"Two days, I think." He passed a trembling hand over his forehead.

Chantel said firmly, "I better feed you." She dipped the spoon in the broth, tasted it first, and then blew on it. "Ver' hot, too hot. I blow it for you, me." She blew on the spoon, tasted it again, and then fed it to him.

He opened his mouth immediately, swallowed it, and whispered, "That's very good, child."

"We feed you a little bit at a time." She fed him half the cupful of broth, but that was all he could manage. Again he asked for water, and Chantel gave him a small amount, again cautioning him to take small sips. "You're so sick, Mr. Steiner, you'll just eat a little, drink a little, then more when you're better."

He took several small sips then sighed tremulously. "I think you saved my life, Miss Fortier."

"You call me Chantel. Everybody does." She knelt down beside him and put the broth down. "You want to lie down and sleep?"

"No, I want to sit for a while. The heat feels so good."

"You talk so funny—why is that?"

"Because I grew up in another country, Germany."

"Where's that?"

"Far across the sea. I've been here many years, but I know I still have an accent. You have an accent, too, Chantel."

"I talk like Cajun. That's what I am."

Steiner seemed to be revived by the warmth of the tent and by the warm food. He smiled a little, a gentle smile so genuine that Chantel could clearly see the kindness and warmth in him. The very few remaining wisps of doubt she had about him disappeared.

"Cajun," he repeated. "Creoles from the southern parts of Louisiana, I believe. Is that where your people are?"

"I have no family."

"You're all alone?"

"Yes, all alone."

"How did you end up on this abandoned road?"

She stared at him, bemused, and finally answered slowly, "I don't know. I just rode and rode and came here. It's a good thing for you I did, me."

Steiner smiled, "Yes, indeed very good. I owe you my life, child. I could feel myself getting ready to go meet God."

Chantel was silent for a moment. "My mother went to meet with the good God not long ago."

"And your father?"

"Him, too, but longer ago. And my stepfather—" Abruptly she broke off.

Steiner shot a quick glance at her. "You were afraid of him?"

"He—he wasn't a good man. He wouldn't leave me alone, so I have to run away."

Jacob nodded sadly. "And so where were you running?"

"My mother had a sister. But when I got there, she'd gone, so now I have no one."

Jacob said quietly, "Well, that isn't exactly true. You have God and you have me. You've saved me, and now I'll be your friend."

Suddenly tears came to Chantel's eyes. She'd felt so alone so many nights under the canopy of stars. Even when the sun was shining and the world was bright around her, she had an emptiness in her that was almost like a physical ache. "That—that would be good, Mr. Steiner."

"Call me Jacob. Friends call each other by their given names."

"Is Jacob a German name?"

"No, Jacob is a Bible name."

"You named from a man in the Bible?"

"Yes, in the book of Genesis."

"You're a Christian man then?"

"I'm a Jew, Chantel. Do you know what a Jew is?"

"No, I never knew any Jews."

"It would take a long time to tell you. Let me say this: I was born into a Jewish family, and we were taught that one day a Savior would come, a Messiah. All Jews are waiting for that."

"And who is he? Do you mean Jesus?"

"Yes, it is Jesus. Most Jews don't believe that. They're still waiting for a Messiah. I found Jesus as my Messiah, so now I'm a Christian Jew. That's very hard for some people to understand, but I love the Lord Jesus."

"Ma mere loved Jesus. She talked to me about Him sometimes."

"Do you have Jesus in your heart?"

"No, I'm alone, me." She hesitated then added, "I go sometimes to church, but I don't know what it means."

"Well, perhaps later we can talk about that."

She saw that his eyes were drooping, so she said, "You sleep for a little. When you wake up, I give you more broth."

As she helped him to lie back down, he asked, "Chantel, shall I tell you something?"

"Yes, what is it?"

"I knew you were coming."

Chantel stared at him. "How did you know that?"

"When I was so very sick, it seemed as if I were awake, and I had a dream. Do you ever dream, Chantel?"

"Sometimes, but not when I'm awake."

"I still don't know if I was awake or asleep, but I dreamed that I wasn't going to die. I just knew someone was coming to help me, and so I rested better. Then I woke up and saw you, and I knew that God had sent you."

"The good God? I talk to Him sometimes, but He don't answer me. He didn't tell me to come. He doesn't know where I go."

"God knows you and has known you since before you were born. And He chose you to help a poor old man that was dying." He put out his hand.

Chantel instinctively took it. "I don't know about all that. I just know I find you."

"We'll talk later. I'm very sleepy." He lay back.

Chantel covered him with the blankets. She checked the stove and then walked outside. She was fascinated with Jacob Steiner. She hadn't ever met anyone like him. His appearance, his speech, and everything about him was strange to her. She studied the stars for a while and then decided that she might sleep in the wagon. Making up a nice bed with one of the cot mattresses under her and a clean blanket, she thought about Jacob Steiner, about his dream, and about his insistence that God had sent her to save him. She thought that was just the old man's mind wandering in his sickness and settled down to sleep.

As she drifted off, it fleetingly occurred to her that maybe Jacob Steiner had been sent to save her.

The next day Jacob had improved considerably. Chantel fed him eggs, for he had a large supply. He ate three of them for breakfast. "You're a good cook, Chantel," he said.

"Anybody can cook eggs."

"People who can cook eggs always say that. But the people who can't cook eggs know better."

The sun had come out and the earth had warmed up. The smell of the earth and the woods was strong in Chantel's nostrils, and she sniffed appreciatively. Then she turned to him and said, "You rest some more, Jacob. I think you'll need to rest a few days. I'll cook for you, and you'll get better and stronger. Right now I'll get Rosie, me, and we'll move your poor old horse far away. Not good to be so near dead animals."

"You're a very resourceful child, Chantel," he said, settling back down on the cot.

"I don't know what that means, me," she said uncertainly.

"It means that I'm glad God sent me such a smart and strong girl to help me," he said then closed his eyes.

For three days Jacob rested. Chantel cooked for him and helped him get up and walk around for a while on the third day. Even she realized that, as sick as he had been when she found him, it was amazing that he recovered so quickly.

He talked to her, and she found it easy to converse with him. Surprising even herself, she told him all about her mother, the tragic death of her father, and her evil stepfather. She told him all about her journey, how frightened and lonely she had been. Finally she was able to admit how glad she was that she had found him.

"It was a miracle of God, my dear," he told her over and over. "A miracle for me and a miracle for you."

He read the Bible to her, and even though she didn't understand much of it, it gave her the same warm, secure feeling that she used to have when her mother was alive. Her mere would read to her on the long, velvet nights on the bayou, her voice quiet and soothing, and Chantel felt as if the world was a good place, and her life was rich and would always be happy.

Oddly, in the hours Jacob Steiner read to her, sometimes this same peace would steal over her, an almost forgotten dream. She still thought of the good God as a very great Being, off somewhere up in the sky, who talked to a few lucky people like her mother and Jacob Steiner and Father Billaud. It was a worship of Him, of a sort, and in Chantel's childlike way, she loved Him. Considering the hardships of the past month, that in itself was a miracle.

The wagon lurched in the deeply rutted road. Chantel and Jacob were tossed from side to side. But now Jacob knew he was strong enough to ride most of a day, with two or perhaps three rests.

The wagon lurched again, sticking a little in the old timeworn tracks. But Rosie was a strong animal, so she pulled the wagon easily.

Jacob commented, "That's a good horse you have."

"She's not fast but ver' strong."

Jacob didn't say anything for a while, thinking on an idea that had been forming over the last couple of days. Finally he turned to her and said, "You're running away from this evil man, your stepfather."

"It wouldn't be good if he finds me."

Jacob nodded. "You do well to be afraid of men like that. I've been praying, and I believe that God wants us to travel together."

"Together, you and me?"

"Yes, and we'll help each other."

"How will we do that?"

"Well, you see, you, Chantel, have a horse. And here I am with a wagon."

Chantel laughed, something she had been doing more often lately. "They go together, they do."

"Yes, they do. Let me tell you what I do. I am a peddler. I buy materials and food cheaply, then I go through the country and I stop at houses. I stay in the country mostly, for people there can't get to stores as often. I sell the goods, and when I run low, I go buy more goods. I have a good business. And I would like for you to be my partner."

"A partner?"

"Yes, we'll work together. I'm getting old now. Have you wondered how old?"

"Yes, me, I am fifteen."

"And I am sixty-one, and I cannot do what I could when I was young. You're young and strong. You can do the things I can't do." He could see that she was considering it, her eyes alight. "Would you like to do that?"

"Yes, I would like to, me. I'll go with you, Jacob."

"I'm very pleased." He smiled as his eyes rested on her. "The Bible says that two are better than one."

"That is true," Chantel agreed with a deep sigh. "I've been one. I don't want to be one, me."

"You and I are partners. We will help each other. The good God will look after us."

Chantel sat back, relaxed,

Jacob watched her. He could see a peace come over her face. He recognized that much of the hurt and the fear she carried with her was in the process of healing.

God, You must help me to be good to this young woman. Keep that evil man far away from her, and help us that together we can find a way to serve You. I pray this in the name of Jesus. And he whispered, "Amen, and Amen."

CHAPTER TEN

I guess you know what you're doing, Morgan, but if I was you, then I'd let Clay simmer down in there for a week or two."

Morgan Tremayne shrugged and said, "Well, Mac, if I thought it would do Clay any good, I'd do that. But it doesn't seem to matter if he's in jail or out. Clay is just Clay."

Mac Rogers, the jailer in charge of the Richmond jail, scratched his face. His fingernails rasped across his unshaven cheek. "How many times is this you've bailed him out?"

"Too many."

"Why don't you quit doing it then?" Rogers asked. "It's just throwing money down the drain."

"He's my brother, Mac. Family, you know. You're just stuck with them."

"Well, it's your money, Morgan. I'll fetch him for you." He took the twenty dollars that Morgan handed him, jammed it into his pocket, and went through the back door leading to the cells.

Left alone in the office, Morgan stood with his feet planted firmly, staring into space. He waited without moving until the door opened again and his brother, Clay Tremayne, came in. As always, Morgan couldn't keep himself from comparing himself to his brother and feeling he came up lacking in many ways.

Morgan was six feet tall, but he was not a large man. He was slim and lithe, with smooth muscles. He took after his mother, with dark auburn hair and dark blue eyes. His face was finely modeled, with a thin nose and wide mouth.

Clay Tremayne was as tall as Morgan but was more strongly built. His hair was dark brown, almost black, and he had brown eyes with thick curly eyelashes. His face was more masculine than Morgan's fine features, with a strong jaw and high cheekbones. He was a fine-looking man, well-built and athletic. There was a rashness and devilment in his smile that seemed typical of everything that Clay Tremayne was.

"I knew you'd be here to rescue me sooner or later," Clay said with that familiar smile on his handsome face.

"Why do you have to make such a fool of yourself, Clay?" Morgan asked.

"Because everything I'm not supposed to do is what I like to do."

"Don't you ever feel bad about the way you're treating your family?"

"Once in a while"—Clay shrugged—"my conscience hurts me a little bit. Maybe I'll straighten up one of these days."

"Clay, you've been getting into these scrapes ever since we were kids. You're not happy; you know you're not. You need to let God into your life."

Clay stared at Morgan and the smile disappeared as if an unpleasant thought had come to him. "Why don't you give up on me, Morgan? God has."

"That's not true."

"It is true, and I don't blame Him. I tried God, but it never worked out."

"No, you've never tried God. You've done what you wanted to your whole life, and most of those things are not good."

"I know," Clay retorted shortly. "But they sure can be fun. In any case, I appreciate you bailing me out, Morgan. You're a good fellow."

They went outside. Morgan's horse was hitched there, and just down the street—perhaps luckily for Clay—was the Planter's Hotel, where Clay kept a permanent apartment. Morgan mounted up then said, "Clay, I've got to warn you about something."

"What is it this time?"

"Stay away from Belle Howard. And stop your gambling."

"Why should I stay away from Belle? She's one of the best-looking women I've ever seen. And as for the gambling, I win more than I lose."

"Well, I guess maybe your gambling is your business, but with Belle you're playing with fire. Don't you realize the Howard family is as proud as Lucifer?'

"I'm not running around with Belle's family, just her."

Morgan's eyes narrowed, and then his lips grew tight. "Clay, you know her brothers are fire-eaters. They almost killed Shelby Stevens. He wasn't doing much more than looking at her."

"Ah, those fellows have an overdeveloped sense of honor." Suddenly Clay grinned. "Belle doesn't, though."

Morgan grimaced. "Why is it, Clay, that you always want what you can't have? There are plenty of loose women for you to chase after, but Belle Howard is a different story. She's from a respected family, she's supposed to be a lady, and if you mess with her, it can get you killed."

"Not if they don't catch me," he said, grinning.

That same night Clay went to the Silver Slipper with only five dollars in his pocket. He boosted it up to fifty playing blackjack. He didn't like blackjack all that much, so he soon found a poker game. For over two hours he played, losing some but winning more.

His chief opponent at the table was Lester Goodnight. Clay told him carelessly as he shuffled, "You need to find another hobby besides poker, Les."

"I'm a good poker player, but somehow when you play I never win." He sat up straight on his chair. He was a thin man with stubborn features and a ready temper. "Nobody wins as much as you do on luck alone."

Clay's eyes narrowed and darkened to a smoldering black. "You want to explain what you mean by that, Goodnight?"

Goodnight had lost a great deal of money. He leaned forward, and as he did, the gun at his side was clearly visible. "I'm saying a man that wins like you do isn't a straight player."

Kyle Tolliver had been in the game, and now he leaned forward and said, "Clay, let's get out of here." He was Clay's best friend, and he saw that Goodnight had been drinking and was known to pull a gun on other men.

Clay turned and grinned at Kyle. "My family must pay you a fee to follow me around and make sure I do the right thing."

"Let's go. You've won enough."

"He ain't leaving until he gives me a chance to win back my money," Goodnight muttered.

Clay considered him, his gaze still fiery, but then he suddenly appeared utterly bored. "How about tomorrow night, then? I'm tired. I didn't get much rest in that jail, Les."

"All right, you be here tomorrow or I'll come looking for you."

"I wouldn't do that if I were you," Clay said casually, rising and straightening his cuffs, flicking off an imaginary speck. "You don't know what kind of mood you might find me in. I'm in a pretty good mood tonight, or I might have taken offense at some of those fool things you said, Les. I'll be right here tomorrow night. You just be here and bring your money."

Kyle and Clay left the Silver Slipper and headed back toward the hotel. Kyle grumbled, "You could've been shot back there. What's even worse, I could have been shot back there."

"Oh, Goodnight ain't gonna do that. He's just sore from losing. He needs to learn how to lose gracefully, don't you think?'

"I think I don't want to go through any more duels over your dumb honor again," Kyle retorted. "Poor old Manny Clarkson bled like a slaughtered pig."

"Squealed like one, too. Aw, c'mon, I never meant to kill him. You know that, Kyle," Clay said good-humoredly. "He's just like Lester Goodnight. Needed a lesson in manners."

"Right, just like I said. I don't want you to feel like you have to teach some manners to Lester Goodnight, even if you do just shoot him in the shoulder. Maybe going to the Silver Slipper tomorrow night isn't such a good idea."

"You sound like Morgan. He gave me a sermon this morning about gambling. And about leaving Belle Howard alone."

"Morgan has sense. You should listen to him."

"I do listen to him. I've always listened to him. It's just that I don't necessarily do all that stuff he says."

Kyle insisted, "Morgan's a good man, a smart man, Clay, and you know it. He's a man to listen to."

"All he did was tell me to leave Belle Howard alone."

"That's good advice. Those brothers of hers will kill you if they catch you fooling with her."

"Aw, everyone's getting their knickers in a twist over Belle Howard. Truth to tell, Kyle, I've no plans to see her. I haven't called on her."

"Then why are you worrying Morgan and me so much by talking about her all the time?" Kyle demanded.

Clay shrugged. "Sorry, buddy. It's just too much fun."

Belle Howard and her sister Virginia had come into town from the family plantation outside Richmond. They were doing some shopping and made plans to attend a production of *Hamlet*, which was to be performed by a traveling group of actors at the Drury Theater.

The two women were in their hotel room, and Belle was trying to pick out a dress to wear. She finally chose a pink satin with white satin braiding trimming the many ruffles, held it up to herself, and turned to her sister. "What about this one, Virginia?"

Virginia was sitting down by a side table that held a silver tea set, reading a book. She looked up to answer her sister. "It looks very well, but it's cut too low in the front."

Belle Howard smiled and came over and patted her sister on the shoulder. "We're here to have fun, remember?" Belle said. "I know, Virginia, why don't you wear my pearls tonight? They would look so well with your new dress. And my pearl comb, too."

Belle Howard was two years younger than her sister Virginia. She knew she had a spectacular figure that men often desired. Her sister was a thin woman with mousy brown hair and brown eyes that often reflected dissatisfaction with Belle. In truth, Belle knew Virginia was jealous of her, which was natural enough. She couldn't possibly voice a complaint such as Belle had been given all the good looks and she'd been given none. Virginia was in fact smarter than Belle, but of course this didn't matter to the men who were only interested in Belle's beautiful features and buxom figure.

Belle patted Virginia again and said, "We'll have a good time tonight. Don't worry." She turned to the mirror, held up the dress again, and studied herself. She liked what she saw in the mirror, which was a woman with rich dark hair and velvety blue eyes that were shadowed by thick lashes. Her complexion was perfect, and her features were bold. She had a mouth that seemed to be made for kissing. She was full-figured; her waist was not as small as she would have liked, but tied into a strong corset she had an hourglass figure. Belle sighed as she glanced back at her sister. She was well aware of Virginia's resentment, but there was nothing she could do about it.

A knock on the door sounded. Virginia rose and said, "I'll get it." She opened the door and found Amy Cousins waiting. "Come in, Amy."

Amy and Virginia were the same age and the best of friends. Amy was pretty enough but didn't possess Belle's startling beauty.

"I'm glad you were able to come," Virginia said, obviously pleased. "Are you looking forward to going to the theater?"

"*Hamlet* is such a gloomy play," Amy answered. "I don't know why we want to sit through it and see everyone die."

"Oh, don't be so grouchy," Belle said. "It'll be fun. You're looking so nice, Amy."

"Thank you, Belle. Are you wearing that pink? You'll look gorgeous in it, as you always do." She turned back to Virginia. "Anyway, Virginia, I want to ask you to stay the night with me, at our house."

"That's very nice of you, Amy, but as you see, Belle and I have this wonderful room."

"My cousin, Vincent Young, is visiting us," Amy said eagerly. "You know how fond he is of you."

Virginia paused. Belle knew her sister liked Vincent Young. He was twenty and rather bookish, studying to be a lawyer, but Belle had heard Virginia say that in the times they had met at parties and balls and dinners they had done very well together.

"I think Vincent is in love with you," Amy prodded her. "If you stay the night, you can spend some time with him."

"Papa would never agree to have Vince as a son-in-law," Belle said carelessly.

"Yes, he would. His family is doing well in their business. Vincent will be a successful lawyer one day. He is respectable enough to suit Father," Virginia retorted.

"I heard Vince tell my mama that he'd be a good match for you," Amy said.

"Did you really?"

"Yes, I did, but you've got to put your foot forward because he's shy. Won't you come stay with me? And then, of course, we would all go to the theater together."

Belle smiled, for she saw the interest that her sister had shown. "I think you should go, Virginia. I like Vince, and I think he is interested in you."

"Do you really think so, Belle?"

"I do."

"You come, too, Belle," Amy urged her. "You know we have lots of room."

"No, you two go along. I'll be all right." Secretly Belle was pleased, for she knew that as long as her sister was around her fun would be severely curtailed.

"If you think it's all right, Belle," Virginia said.

"I'll be just fine, and you two will have such fun. Now run along. I'll see you at the play."

Belle made her way to the theater, just down and across the main street of Richmond. It was scandalous, her going alone, but she knew that she was such a favorite of her father's that even if word got to him, nothing would be done about it.

She had been to the Drury Theater several times before, and she saw people of Richmond society whom she knew. She took her seat, which would be next to the Cousins family, but then changed her mind. *I'll have to stay away from Vince. I never told Virginia, but he was interested in me at one time. He may be Virginia's last chance to get married.*

She got up and moved to a seat well toward the back of the theater. The play began, and she watched intently. Truthfully, however, she found Shakespeare hard to follow, so her mind roamed elsewhere. It was a very long play, too, and when it was over, she saw Virginia, escorted by Vincent Young, leaving the theater with the Cousins family.

Belle had no desire to see them. She found that she was tired and bored with the evening and decided just to go back to her room and make an early night of it. A couple of her gentleman acquaintances spotted her and begged her to let them escort her back to the hotel, take her to supper, come back to their homes for after-theater parties. . . . But rather shortly Belle disentangled herself from them. They were boring, actually, and represented no interesting new conquests.

When she reached the Planter's Hotel, to her surprise she saw Clay Tremayne lounging outside, smoking a cigar. When he saw her, he grinned and threw the cigar away, as men never smoked in the presence of a lady. It was just that usually ladies were not out on the street at this time of night.

"Belle! How wonderful to see you," he said, coming forward to take her hand and kiss it.

"Hello, Clay," she answered coolly. "How are you? Did you go to see *Hamlet*?"

"No, I was in the card room, but it got so close and stuffy. And I am heartily sick of hearing talk about politics and secession. So I decided to come outside for some fresh air," he answered. "And to wait for you, of course."

"You lie, sir." Belle studied Clay carefully. She liked his manly good looks, and he was fine company. On two occasions he had halfheartedly tried to take liberties with her, but she simply laughed at him and shoved him away. It had irked her that he had given up so easily. She added, smiling invitingly at him, "You had no idea I was even in town."

"I'm caught. I certainly didn't know you were staying here at the hotel. May I invite you up to my room for an after-theater sip of brandy, perhaps?" he asked innocently.

"I'd just be another notch on your belt," she said drily. "You have enough of those already. Your belt is so notched there's barely room left on it for another."

"Either you're complimenting me, ma'am, or insulting me," Clay said mischievously. "I choose to take your consideration as a compliment. Now, please allow me to return the compliment and take you to supper."

"I don't know, Clay. I'm tired. I was just going to go to my room and go to bed early tonight," she said.

"It's just supper, Miss Belle," he said, grinning. He had a most attractive smile, full of devilment. . .and promise. "I heard a rumor that Wickham's Restaurant got in a shipment of fresh oysters today, particularly for the theater-goers. I do recall, do I not, that fresh oysters are a particular favorite of yours?" Wickham's was one of the few restaurants in Richmond that stayed open late on theater nights for the attendees to have a late supper.

Belle did love fresh oysters, and they were a rare treat. Still she hesitated. Going to the theater alone was just on the edge of respectability, but dining alone with a man in a public restaurant went over that edge. Still. . .she was suddenly hungry, and Clay did look particularly handsome that night in a black suit coat and tie and a silver satin waistcoat. "All right, Clay. You remember correctly, sir, fresh oysters are my favorite, and I suddenly find that I am overcome with hunger," she said, her smile dazzling.

Clay bribed the maître d' so that they would have a curtained booth to themselves. Clay encouraged Belle to order whatever she liked, and they frivolously ordered two dozen fresh oysters. Clay also ordered champagne.

Belle had only drunk champagne a couple of times before, but she loved it dearly. "What have you been doing with yourself, Clay, besides being in jail?" she asked playfully between oysters and continual small sips of the cool, fizzy champagne.

"You heard about that, did you?"

"Everybody's heard about it. I don't see why your family puts up with you."

"They have to. Key word is *family*, you see. They're sort of stuck with me." He quickly ate one of the oysters while staring at Belle. "And that's not necessarily a bad thing. I think, if you'd give me a chance, you might even like to get stuck with me."

"Oh? And whatever makes you think such an impertinent thing?"

"I don't know. But you really should give it a try, just to see, you know. I could start out by coming and calling on your father and sitting on your porch and courting you like the other young gentlemen do."

"I doubt you'd ever find a seat on my porch, Clay Tremayne," she said primly. "I would guess all you'd see is it flying by when my father booted you out of the house."

"He doesn't like me? That's hard to believe, isn't it?"

Belle laughed, a small ladylike tinkling laugh that she knew men liked. "I'm sure you think so. He wouldn't think about it for a minute."

They finished all of the oysters and the entire bottle of champagne. Belle hadn't noticed, but she had drunk most of it while Clay had merely sipped on two glasses. As they left, she felt light-headed, giddy—and reckless.

When they reached the hotel, Clay said, "You must let me escort you to your room, Miss Belle. A gentleman would never leave a lady on the steps of a hotel."

"That is very true," Belle agreed happily. "I am on the second floor."

"Are you? What a very great coincidence. So am I," Clay said. They reached her room, which was several doors down from Clay's apartments. "Why don't I go to my room and fetch a nice bottle of old brandy that I've been keeping for a special occasion? I can come back, and we'll have a toast. To *Hamlet* and to oysters."

A small voice in the back of Belle's mind insisted that this was a very bad idea, but she felt so happy and careless that she ignored the little nag in her head. "Oh, that sounds wonderful. Brandy is a fine spirit to top off a wonderful meal."

He bowed deeply. "I shall join you shortly then, ma'am."

Belle hurried into her room, took off her hat, gloves, and cape, and quickly patted her hair into place. She saw that the color in her cheeks was high, and her eyes were sparkling like stars. She reflected with satisfaction that she was in particularly good looks this evening. Perhaps it had something to do with the very welcome attentions of Clay Tremayne.

He returned with a bottle and two heavy crystal brandy snifters. She started to just drink from her snifter, but with a smile, Clay stopped her. "Fine brandy is much like a fine woman. You have to warm it up gently, savor its scent, breathe it in, before you finally partake of it."

Vaguely Belle knew that in another time and another place she might have taken some offense at this, but she couldn't quite work it out. Giggling, she rolled the brandy in the snifter, holding the crystal in the palm of her hand as Clay instructed, breathing in the intoxicating scent, and finally sipping the liquid.

The next drink, and the next, were not quite so polite and poetic.

She never knew afterward when it got out of hand, but she found herself falling more and more under his spell. When he put his arms around her and kissed her, she seemed unable to resist. *You don't want him to stop,* were the final whispers of that little warning voice in her mind.

Things were going exactly as Clay had hoped. He had Belle right where he wanted her and continued to press his advances.

"Clay. . .we shouldn't," she whispered weakly.

"We should," Clay answered in a deep voice, caressing her cheek and her neck. "Belle, I want you. I need you. You're so very beautiful—"

It was exactly at that point that the door burst open. Barton Howard, Belle's eldest brother, was standing there. His face was flushed with rage, and his eyes were glittering.

Before Clay could say a word, Barton drew a gun and fired. The bullet struck Clay in the side, and it turned him half around.

Even slightly drunk, Clay was quick. His own pistol was hanging from his belt, draped over the back of a satin chair by the bed. He pulled the pistol and fired in the general direction of Barton Howard, who stumbled, reeled backward, and fell facedown.

Belle stood and cried, "You've got to get out of here, Clay! They'll hang you if my other brothers don't kill you first."

Clay hesitated, staring down at Barton Howard. He was an excellent shot, and he surely never would have shot to kill Barton if he'd been sober. In fact, he had aimed just in the man's general direction, more to scare him than shoot him. But he had been drinking too much, and his shot was wild. Had he killed this man?

Belle knelt by her brother. She looked up at Clay, her eyes wide and horror-stricken, her face deadly pale. "He's still alive, Clay, but that won't matter to either of my brothers, Charlie or Ed. Don't you see? Even if you haven't killed Barton, you'll have to kill them—or let them kill you!"

Barton Howard, even now, was muttering and scrabbling vaguely at the floor.

Clay was still frozen, rooted to the floor, staring down at him.

Belle hissed, "Clay, don't be a fool. Run!"

Clay looked at her, and then his mouth tightened into a thin line. He knew she was right. He grabbed his pistol belt and his coat and shot outside her room. He could hear heavy footsteps pounding up the west stairwell and suspected that it was probably Belle's other brothers.

He hurried to his room and gathered up all his money. His side was red with blood, but he knew that the bullet barely grazed him. Cautiously opening the door, he could hear Charlie Howard's angry roar from the direction of Belle's room.

Feeling completely like a coward and a heel, Clay silently ran down the east stairwell and to the livery stables. Quickly he saddled his horse and mounted up. His one thought was to get away. He spurred Lightning into a run and headed away from the city of Richmond.

Entering his own sitting room, Dr. Ritchie said, "Barton's not going to die." The doctor was young for his profession, but he had a successful practice in Richmond. An earnest-looking man, he polished his glasses as he gave the news to Belle Howard and her other brothers. "The bullet hit him in the chest, but it bounced off a rib and missed all the vital organs. The surgery to remove it was tough, though, so he'll need to stay in bed, probably for several weeks."

Ed and Charles stood tensely by the fireplace, while Belle sat in a straight chair, bent over, her face buried in her hands. She looked up as Ed said, "Thank you, doctor." He then stared hard at her.

The doctor glanced at Belle, then at her two angry brothers, and returned to his examination room, where Barton Howard lay, still unconscious.

Ed muttered, "You've disgraced yourself, Belle."

Belle looked up at him beseechingly. It had been a horrifically long night. Her brother's surgery had taken hours. It was still an hour till dawn, one of the bleakest hours. Her eyes were so swollen from weeping that they were barely open. "I—I—I just drank too much, Ed. It got out of control."

Ed Howard shook his head, a jerky, furious movement. "You know what kind of man he is. I'm ashamed of you, Belle. Tremayne is a no-good piece of trash. What I want to know is where he was going."

"I don't know. How should I know? We—we weren't exactly discussing future plans," she said, burying her face in her hands again.

With a last disgusted look at his sister, Charlie turned to Ed. "His people live in Lexington. If he's hurt, he'll probably head there. Belle did say that Barton got off a shot. Even if it didn't knock Tremayne off his feet, Barton couldn't have missed at that range."

"He was bleeding," Belle moaned.

Neither of them seemed to pay any attention to her.

"He won't go home. He's the bad seed in the family, but he does keep them out of his affairs," Ed said reluctantly. "What about Atlanta? He's got Tremayne cousins there, I know."

"Why can't you just leave him alone?" Belle said, looking up and feeling a spark of life for the first time. Her very first inclination had been to blame everything on Clay, but Belle Howard was a strong woman, and she had her own sense of honor, in spite of the way she had behaved. "It's not like he blindfolded me and kidnapped me, you know. It's not all his fault."

Ed glared at her. "You're not going to be a tramp, Belle, if we have to keep you locked up, so you just stop that kind of talk right now. Tremayne is the one who has to pay for this. I'm not going to think any more about shooting him than I would about shooting a rabid dog."

❧

Clay rode through the night, hard. He stopped once to check his wound. The bullet had hit him in the upper abdomen on the right side, had slid along a rib, and then had ricocheted out. He had a gash six inches long on his side, and he could see bare bone. Gritting his teeth, he poured brandy on it from a flask he always carried, thinking grimly, *And this is the last time I'm touching this stuff!* Then he tore up one of his white cotton shirts into strips and bound it up. It was extremely painful, but still he kept riding. He planned on riding straight through to Petersburg, where he could take a train to Charlotte, North Carolina. He had friends there, and some business connections. It never entered his mind to involve his family in this sordid affair.

Just before dawn, Lightning started limping, and Clay knew he had pulled a tendon. This was not too uncommon for hard-ridden horses, and not really serious, but the only way for the horse to recover was to rest. He knew of a settlement called Lucky Way about a half mile off the main road to Petersburg. After he turned off on the rough trail that led to the little town, he dismounted to walk Lightning so as not to stress his foreleg any more. "Let's just hope this really is a Lucky Way for us, boy," he managed to joke.

His plan was to stay out of sight, which he did. Ordinarily he would've gone to the saloon and gotten into a poker game, but he stayed in his own room in a dirty five-room boardinghouse. The only time he went out of his room was to stop at the general store, buy some horse liniment, and tend to Lightning.

He slipped around the town at dusk. It was a small town, which made it difficult to keep from calling attention to himself, but he spoke to no one except the stable hand and the surly woman who ran the boardinghouse.

After three days, Lightning had lost all signs of soreness in his foreleg. Clay decided to ride on to Petersburg. It was a hard ride, a day and a night straight through, and Clay knew that he shouldn't put much stress on Lightning, but he realized that once they had gotten on the train, Lightning could rest up again. He left Lucky Way in a sad, blurry dawn that promised rain later.

Clay thought of little else but of what had taken place in Richmond. He cursed himself for a fool, and a stupid one at that.

He knew he had acted like the worst kind of scrub with Belle. *I should've stayed away from her. She didn't deserve all this. I hope Barton doesn't die. That'll get me hanged for sure.*

Once he got on the main road, he kept Lightning at a steady fast trot that would eat up the miles. During the day, he passed several wagons and other riders, but the traffic waned as night fell. The whole day had been overcast, but it had never rained. Now, dark ominous clouds scudded over the half-moon brooding above him.

About three hours after sunset, he heard riders behind him. Clay was not the type of man to always be looking over his shoulder with fear, so he had wasted very little time worrying about the Howards. If anything, he thought they might search Richmond for him and maybe contact Morgan in Lexington, but it simply had not occurred to him that they might hunt him down. So, since the unknown riders were moving at a fast pace behind him, and the night was so dark, he cautiously pulled Lightning over to one side to let them pass.

They drew nearer, two men, riding hard. They were still at least forty feet away from him when the black clouds cleared the moon. Even in the dimness, Clay recognized the bulk of big Ed Howard. At the same time Ed shouted, "That's him, Charlie! Standing right there! Ride!"

Clay spurred Lightning, and like his name, he bounded into a gallop so fast that the men fell farther behind. Still they rode, yelling like hounds baying.

Clay barely heard the gunshot before it seemed as if a giant had simply kicked him in the back. He flew through the air and landed in the mud. He felt himself losing consciousness, and his last thought before the blackness set in was, *I'm dead, God. You've finally killed me. . .*

The two brothers rode slowly to the side of the road and looked down at Clay Tremayne, sprawled facedown, unmoving. Ed lowered his shotgun then slowly dismounted. He kicked Clay, not very hard, in the side. "He's dead, Charlie," he muttered. "Miserable dog."

Charlie didn't speak. He dismounted his horse and stood beside Clay, then knelt down by him. He grabbed his hair and yanked up his face. Clay's eyes remained closed. Charlie took his pistol then started working on taking a diamond signet ring off Clay's finger.

"Stop it, Charlie," Ed ordered him in a harsh voice. "He's dead. We had to kill him for what he did to Belle, but we're no thieving trash. Just leave him."

Charlie grunted then stood and threw Clay's pistol down to the ground. "You're right, Ed. I'm not going to sink as low as he is. Was. Let the buzzards have him."

They mounted up and rode back north without looking back.

But each knew Clay Tremayne lay in the mud without moving.

CHAPTER ELEVEN

I think we need to celebrate, child."

Chantel sat loosely on the wagon seat holding the lines. Spring in the Southern states was lovelier than anything she had ever known. Sweet-scented breezes blew the trees back and forth so that they swayed like dancers. All along the back roads were foxes, rabbits, squirrels, and multitudes of butterflies. She turned to smile at Jacob, who was watching her intently. "What do we have to celebrate?"

"You don't know?"

"Well, I know things are going ver' well. We've sold lots of goods, and I think, Grandpere, that we've made a lot of money, you and me. Is that what we want to celebrate?"

"The Lord has blessed us exceedingly," Jacob agreed placidly, "and that is always something to celebrate. But what I meant was, we should celebrate the two years we've been together. If I'm not mistaken, it was as the month of March was ending, two years ago, that you saved me."

A surprised look came to Chantel's face. "Has it been that long? It has, yes? I'm seventeen now. I was fifteen, me, when I found you, Grandpere."

Jacob nodded. "Every day I thank God for bringing us together. I know I would have died if you hadn't saved me, daughter, and these last two years of life would not have been nearly so good as they have been. . .if they would have even been. I could never have continued in this work without you, Chantel. I can never thank God—or you—enough."

"Never you mind that, Grandpere," she said quickly.

Jacob still thanked her, often, and expressed his affection to her. It embarrassed her, for though her mother and father had been loving people, they were not outwardly affectionate. "I've been so happy. My life has been so good, yes, so much better than I ever dreamed it would be." She reached over with her right hand and patted his shoulder a little awkwardly, aware of the thinness of his frame and the fragility of his bone structure. "We make a good pair, don't we, you and me?"

Indeed the two were very happy together, if they were something of an odd couple: the elderly Jew in the sunset of life and the exotic-looking young woman that Chantel had become. She had come into full bloom, and she had a dream of a figure, for she was strong and lithe and worked hard every single day. Her skin was an attractive golden hue, as Cajuns sometimes had, and her violet-blue eyes, wide-set and perfect almond shapes, were of startling beauty. She was in perfect health and always felt energetic and strong and eager for each new day.

Still, she had an abhorrence of male attention, so she stubbornly wore loose men's breeches and men's cotton shirts that were too big for her. She kept her trousers up with a wide leather belt that had her knife sheath fitted to it, for she still carried it, always. She crammed her blue-black hair up into a felt hat with a big floppy brim that half hid her face. Jacob had bought her two pairs of fine leather boots, one brown pair and one black pair, but no matter how he pleaded, Chantel would not let him buy her any women's clothes, even modest skirts and plain blouses, much less pretty dresses.

As they rode along, Chantel thought back over the last two

years. They had indeed been good for her. Her fear of being caught by her stepfather had long faded, like a vague remembrance of a bad dream. They always traveled the South, crisscrossing the roads across Alabama, Georgia, the Carolinas, Tennessee, and Virginia.

"Pah," Jacob had grunted to her one time. "Business isn't nearly so good in the North. Too many cities, too many big towns, too many people all huddled together, and too many mercantile stores. Here the farmers are glad to see us because they need us. They are hospitable, and there aren't nearly as many ruffians riding the roads."

It was true. People received them everywhere they went. They were lonely on the homesteads, they were anxious to talk, and they definitely had need of Jacob's goods. Sometimes it could be three days' journey from a farm to a nearby town to get supplies.

Today it was an easy ride, for they were going north to Richmond, and it was a good road. For the last two months they had been lazily roaming around southern Virginia, cotton and cash-farming country, and business had been good. Most of the great plantations in the South were close to the big towns, like Charleston and Savannah and Atlanta and Richmond. It was the smaller farmers, farther from the cities, who welcomed the peddlers so happily.

Chantel glanced affectionately at Jacob. She had made a fine feather cushion for the wagon seat and had fashioned two pillows to fit in the corner of the seat, leaning against the back and the side upright. He had plumped them up and settled back in them, and Chantel thought he was falling asleep.

Before he dropped off, he murmured, "Virginia. . .I think it is my favorite. . .the Shenandoah Valley."

In silence she drove, enjoying the freshening day. The night before it had rained off and on, so Chantel had set up the little tent and stove for Jacob. Even in the warmth of spring he still was chilled at night. Last night Chantel had slept in the tent, but on clear nights she usually slept out under the stars, by a small, comforting campfire.

Now all traces of yesterday's lowering skies were gone. The air was fresh and smelled of wet dirt and new grass. Clouds of spring's first yellow butterflies floated in front of the wagon sometimes, and once a fat honeybee made a lazy dizzy flight alongside it for a while. Chantel watched it with amusement.

"What's this?" she asked herself. Just ahead, on the left side of the road, was a big black stallion. He was fully saddled, his reins hanging down to the ground. He seemed to be grazing, but as they drew closer, Chantel could see a lump on the ground. The horse was nuzzling it, it seemed, with some agitation.

"Grandpere," she said softly, so as not to startle him.

"Hm! Hmm?" he said, pushing his hat back and looking around sleepily.

"Just up here. Do you see him? A fine horse, he is, with no rider."

Jacob straightened up and stared. "What's that at his feet? Better stop the wagon, daughter."

By the time they drew up to the horse, they could see the man.

Chantel pulled Rosie to a stop and leaped down to the ground, her boots making a squishing sound in the deep mud as she ran. Sliding to a stop, she came to her knees right beside him. In the bright innocent sunshine, she could clearly see the matted blood in his dark hair and the dried blood on his back. One or two places were still oozing. She touched her finger to it and held it up to Jacob, who had reached her side. "Fresh," she said. "He's still alive."

Ignoring the wet ground, he creakily got to his knees beside the wounded man. "He's been shot in the back. It looks like with a shotgun."

"We'll have to get him to a doctor, Grandpere," Chantel said in a low urgent voice.

Jacob shook his head. "It's still at least three days to Richmond. I don't know of any settlements around here, and if we start getting off the road hunting one, this man will probably die on us. We have to do what we can here, now."

Chantel bit her lower lip. "I can nurse sick people, me. But I don't know anything about gunshot wounds."

With some difficulty, Jacob got to his feet. "Neither do I, daughter. But I don't think the Lord has given us a choice about it, so that means He will guide us. You'll have to put up the tent. Thank goodness you were smart enough to start hauling stove wood in the wagon. It'll take us both to get him into the tent, but I know that we can help this man. Can you do all that, daughter?"

"Yes, I can, me. You watch what I do."

Jacob wasn't able to do much physical work. While Chantel put up the tent, he started gathering supplies he knew he would need. Before he was finished, she had put up the tent, made up the cot, and started a fire in the tent stove.

"What do I do now?" she asked breathlessly, popping up in the wagon's opening at the back.

"We'll have to get him inside. I'll help. Not much, maybe, but it will take both of us."

They went back to the man. The horse still stood close to him, though he shied a little every time Chantel and Jacob drew near.

"I'm strong, Grandpere. I can probably drag him to the tent. I'm afraid I'm going to hurt him though."

"Better hurt him than let him die."

Chantel rolled the man over and reached under his arms. He was a big man and strongly built. She began to back up to the tent that she had set up in a shady stand of three big oak trees, not far off the road. Although she was indeed a strong young woman, the man's heavy weight was hard to handle, and she had to stop twice. She was breathing hard and grunting by the time she got to the tent.

When she finally dragged him inside and up to the cot, she looked down doubtfully. "Do you think we can get him up on the cot, me and you?"

"I can do that much," Jacob said with determination. "I'll get under his legs, and you get him under his arms again. You count to three, and we'll heave him up."

"This is too much for you," Chantel fretted. "Maybe I can do it, me."

"Not this, not by yourself." Jacob leaned over and grabbed the man by the legs and nodded. "Do it, daughter."

Chantel took a deep breath, got as firm a grip on him as she could manage, and murmured, *"Un, deux, trois!"*

To Chantel's surprise, they lifted the man easily and quickly onto the cot.

Jacob said, "We have to take his clothes off and wash him up as best as we possibly can, and hurry. Then we have to turn him over so I can get those shotgun pellets out."

Chantel fetched a cracker box for Jacob to sit on, then knelt by the cot to help clean up the man.

"He has nice clothes, this poor man," Chantel said as they undressed him. Even though the garments were caked with mud and dried blood, she could tell the quality of the fabric and the tailoring.

"And nice jewelry and lots of money and a very expensive pistol, too," Jacob said speculatively. "He was grazed once, in the side, some days ago, I think. It's bandaged and healing. But whoever shot him with the shotgun and left him for dead didn't rob him, and they didn't steal his fine horse."

The big kettle of water was hot, and Jacob instructed her to pour half of it into a washbasin and the rest of it into a big clean pot. "Let the water in the pot boil," he said, "while we wash him off. Quickly, quickly, Chantel."

They sponged him clean then turned him and carefully dabbed off the dirt and blood from his wounds. Once they got him cleaned up into a recognizable human, they could see that he was still breathing. His respiration was deep and slow.

"That's good, I think," Jacob said. "Now, you see that bag I've brought? Get all of those implements out of it and throw them into the pot. And set the big tongs in so the teeth are in the water but the handle is out of it, leaning to the side."

"This pot of boiling water?" Chantel asked hesitantly.

"Yes. While they boil, I'll finish cleaning out these wounds. You'd better go and move the wagon up here, out of the road, and unhitch Rosie. And see if you can catch this man's horse."

At that moment, they heard a soft thump, and the big black horse stuck his nose inside the tent and made a snuffling sound. In spite of the man's grave condition, Jacob and Chantel laughed softly. "I don't think I'll have trouble catching this horse, me," Chantel said. "I'll hurry, Grandpere, so I can help you."

She moved the wagon up by the tent then unhitched Rosie. The black horse watched her solemnly, staying close to the tent. She let Rosie graze, not tethered, for Chantel had found that the gentle horse rarely wandered more than a few feet from their camp.

She walked up to the black horse. He shied just a little and tossed his head but stayed still as she reached up to pat his nose. She rubbed his neck for a while, murmuring little endearments in broken French. He seemed to be completely relaxed, so she unsaddled him and stored the fine-tooled saddle and the man's saddlebags and blanket roll in the wagon.

The stallion's skin twitched with relief, and he pawed the ground. Then he began to graze, all the while staying close to the tent.

"You're not going anywhere, are you, boy? I don't think I'll tie you up either. You stay. Rosie never had such a fine gentleman to keep her company."

She went back inside the tent. Jacob had taken all of the tools out of the water with the tongs: two sets of tweezers, one large and one small; a tiny, very sharp knife; and a small pair of pliers. Chantel watched as he took the knife and made a very small cut. Then with the tweezers, he pulled out a steel shotgun pellet and dropped it into an empty basin, where four others rolled around making a loud tinny noise.

"Most of these wounds are not very deep. He must've been some distance away from whoever shot him."

Chantel watched as he continued to pull the pellets out of the man's back.

"See if you can see any more," Jacob finally said, standing up for a few minutes to stretch. "My eyes are getting tired."

"It's getting dark. I'll light some lanterns," Chantel said. She took a lantern and carefully searched all over the man's back then looked back up at Jacob. "You got them all, I think, Grandpere. But what about his head? His hair, it's thick, yes?"

"I may have to shave it to be able to find them," he said wearily. "I can't see as well as I could when I was younger."

"No, I think he wouldn't like that," Chantel said with a vehemence that surprised her.

"Oh? Why would you think that, daughter?" Jacob asked curiously.

"He just wouldn't. He has such pretty hair, so nice and thick. He doesn't want to be bald, him," Chantel answered firmly. "But, Grandpere, I watch you. I see, I know. I'll take the little balls out of his head. You rest then maybe cook us some nice stew."

Jacob watched her with some amusement then said, "All right, daughter. You generally can do exactly what you put your mind to do. But before you touch him or the tools, you must wash your hands, wash them good, with the carbolic soap. Scrub under your fingernails with the brush."

Chantel cocked her head to the side. "How you know all this, Grandpere? I thought you didn't know gunshots."

"I don't," he admitted. "But you know I've been praying for this man ever since we found him. And the Lord keeps bringing Leviticus to my mind. It's filled with many rules for keeping clean, for cleansing, and so I felt that He was teaching me how to take care of this man."

"It's in the Bible to take care of gunshots?" Chantel repeated, astonished.

"No, no, dear daughter. I'll read some of Leviticus to you sometime and explain," he said. "But for now you go ahead and wash up in that hot water, but be careful not to burn yourself. I'll rest for a while, and then I'll get us some supper together."

It took Chantel almost three hours to make sure she had removed all of the shotgun pellets from the man's head. The experience had felt very odd to her. She had hung two lanterns close over his head and had bent over him. Time and time again she had run her fingers through his hair to feel the small bumps where the pellets were buried. They had sponged the man's hair, but of course they had not thoroughly washed it. Still, Chantel could catch a drift of a fragrance, a very slight scent. It was not a heavy or strong smell like hair pomade, but a clean scent, something like lemons.

During the entire time she tended him, she was very aware of the peculiarity of the situation, doing something that under other circumstances would be so intimate, running her hands through his hair and caressing it. Except for when she had tended Jacob, it was the only time she could recall ever touching a man in such a manner.

Jacob fixed them a hearty stew, and they ate it slowly with soda crackers, watching the still-unconscious man.

They had left him lying on his stomach, and Chantel had fixed a small pillow to cradle his head, with his face turned to the side. "Do you think he will wake up?" she asked Jacob hesitantly. "Do you think he can?"

"He can if the Lord wills it. And I know the Lord has willed it. So we will pray that He will do the real healing for him."

"How do you know, Grandpere? Has the good God been talking to you again?"

"No, the good God didn't have to tell me that this man will live."

"He didn't? Then how can you be so sure, to know?" Chantel demanded.

"Because once, about two years ago, an angel was sent to find a dead horse and a live man," he said. "Today an angel found a live horse. . .and what we thought was a dead man. But he wasn't. If we had been sent here to give him a Christian burial, Chantel, we would have found him dead. Haven't you thought, haven't you wondered? We had passed several riders and wagons on the road today, coming and going. How was it that no one found this man, that only you found him?"

She considered this, her fine brow slightly wrinkled. "Maybe this horse, he runs away and is afraid when the people came. And then they couldn't see the man down in the ditch."

"Maybe. But this horse didn't run away when we came, did he? Not even when we stopped and walked up to the man."

Suddenly Chantel smiled, and it lit up her face. "So, Grandpere, now the good God, He is talking to the horse?"

It gave Jacob such pleasure to see Chantel smile. Although he knew that she was happy, she rarely smiled so freely, so openly. Seeing her glowing face, he couldn't help but smile back at her. "All creatures serve God, Chantel, even that horse out there. It's by the Lord's will that we all live and breathe. I don't know this man, but I know one thing: it was not God's will for him to die. Not today."

The next day the stranger woke up.

It was early afternoon. Jacob had put a cot out under the tree, and he was napping peacefully in the kind March sun.

Chantel was in the tent, cutting strips of clean white linen to make more bandages. From time to time she glanced up at the man, who was still in the same position, lying on his stomach with his face turned toward her, eyes closed.

She was looking down, folding the strips into neat squares, when she heard a rustling sound. The man had managed to prop himself up on his elbows, and he was watching her.

Chantel flew to the cot. "You're awake! Be careful, don't move around too much. You've been shot. In the back."

"Mm—uh," he groaned softly. "Shot. . .it hurts."

"I know," she said soothingly. "That's why you have to lie on your stomach."

His head dropped, mainly from weakness. He licked his lips. "So. . .thirsty."

"Water, I'll get it, me," she said and hurried to pour water from the canteen into a cup. She held it to his lips, and he took small sips, the only way he could manage in his awkward position. Then he allowed himself to sink back onto the cot.

"Thank—thank—"

"It's all right," Chantel said. "Just rest."

"Stay. . . ," he whispered, and then his eyes closed again.

He was much the same for two more days, only waking up for minutes at a time, sipping water, talking very little.

Chantel stayed close, for she had found that the moment his eyes opened he would immediately search for her. She washed his clothes and hung them in the sun to dry, but wryly she reflected that there was no way to mend all the little holes that the shotgun blast had made. She cleaned his boots and polished them until they shone, then stood them up in the wagon, stuffed with brown paper to keep their shape. She made him a new shirt out of the same bolt of soft linen that they were using to make the bandages.

She read her mother's Bible, and Jacob would often sit with her and read aloud. Several times a day Jacob prayed for the injured man, and Chantel was, as always, amazed at the fervency, the sense of realness, of her grandfather's prayers.

And the man got better. Early in the morning of the third day, he woke up, focused on Chantel, and then pulled himself up. "Good—morning, isn't it?"

"Yes, morning. You look better," she said, filling the water cup.

"That's good. Because I still feel like a train ran over me," he said. He drank thirstily, and this time he took the cup for himself. "I—I think I'd like to sit up. Can you please help me, ma'am?"

"I drag you in here like a dray horse," she said, her eyes alight. "I think I can help you sit up, me."

It really was hard, though, getting him turned over and turned around, and then pulling him up to sit on the edge of the cot. When they finished, he was out of breath. "I'm as—weak as a newborn little kitten," he gasped. "What—what day is it?"

"I don't know," Chantel said with endearing sincerity, "for I haven't looked at Grandpere's calendar today. But I think you want to know this. We found you five days ago, all shot, you. We thought you were dead."

"Five days," Clay repeated with shock. "I've been out for five days?"

"Only four," Chantel said. "Today is five days, and here you are now."

He nodded. "I hate to trouble you, ma'am, but I'm not quite ready to crawl over to that canteen. May I have more water?"

As she poured his cup full, she studied him from the corner of her eyes. It was the first time she had really seen him. He was very handsome, she thought. His eyes were dark brown, wide-set, and fringed by thick, dark lashes. His nose was a straight English nose with a thin bridge, his cheekbones high and pronounced, his jawline firm. Though he was still pale, he looked tough, not pretty, very masculine.

She handed him the cup, and he drank slowly, not gulping. She sat down on the upturned cracker barrel and watched him.

"Thank you, ma'am," he finally said. "May I ask your name?"

"My name is Chantel Fortier. What is yours?"

"Clay Tremayne. I'm so happy to make your acquaintance, Miss Fortier. I have a feeling that I owe you a very great debt. I haven't been aware of too much these last days, but I do know that you have been an angel, taking care of me as you have. And—isn't there an older gentleman?"

"Oh yes, ma grandpere. He naps in the sun, like an old lizard, he says. He'll wake soon. He'll be glad to see you sitting up and talking."

"I wouldn't be if it weren't for you two, I believe," Clay said gravely. "I don't remember being shot. All I remember is lying in the mud, thinking that I was dying. I guess I would have if you hadn't found me."

"Do you know who shot you?" Chantel asked curiously.

Jacob had told her that when he woke up he might not remember much, might not even know who he was. Sometimes that happened to people who had head wounds.

"Oh yes, I remember that," Clay answered drily. "But begging your pardon, Miss Fortier, I really don't want to talk about it."

"No, no, it's not my business, me," she said hastily.

"It's not that. It's just that—let's say it's better if you and your grandfather don't get involved," Clay said quietly. "At least, no more than you already are."

Jacob came in then, blinking in the half-light of the tent. "So sir! It's a blessing to see you sitting up and looking so well. Thank God for His tender mercies." He sat down on the other cot, for Chantel had set up one so Jacob could sleep in the tent as well.

"Let me introduce you, Grandpere," Chantel said quickly. Clay's courtly manners had impressed her, and she had learned much of polite social convention from Jacob. She introduced them, merely naming Clay as "the gentleman that has been staying with us."

Jacob asked, "How are you feeling? How are your back and your head?"

"My back is sore, and it burns," Clay admitted. "And my head aches. But my mind is so much clearer. I feel as if I've been wandering in a nightmare. Except when I woke up to see Miss Fortier, here. You have done me a great service, sir. I can only say thank you right now."

"You are welcome, sir, and do not forget to thank the Lord, who showed great mercy to you by sending us along to find you. Is there anyone that we should send word to that you're all right?"

"I don't think so, Mr. Steiner."

"What about your family?"

Clay swallowed hard. He faltered at Mr. Steiner's query about his family. What should he say? What could he say?

He felt that he ought to lie to these people, simply to protect them. He had been left for dead, but what if it was known that he was still alive? For all he knew, he had murdered Barton Howard, and they might very well try him and hang him for that.

But looking at Jacob Steiner's kind face and Chantel's innocent eyes, he knew he could not lie. "Sir, I have not been a good man, and it's possible that I may have committed a serious crime. To tell you the truth, until I can find out—some things—I believe it would be better for my family not to be notified of my. . .difficult circumstances."

"But surely, no matter what you have done, your family should not think that you may be dead!" Jacob exclaimed.

Clay shook his head and was shocked at the excruciating pain it caused. "N–no, sir. I have thought about it, and it's almost certain that my family thinks I have traveled to the Carolinas to visit friends."

This made perfect sense to Clay. After all, one of the Howards had shot him in the back and left him for dead in the ditch on a lonely road.

Although in the South a man might defend his sister's honor even to the death, that was not the gentlemanly—or legal—way to do so. Clay was sure that the brothers would have told no one that they had done this. There had been such a ruckus at the hotel, Clay knew that it had caused a scandal for Belle, and it was indeed very likely that his family would think he had just left town for a few days. He had done so before.

"Very well, Mr. Tremayne, you must do as you see fit," Jacob finally agreed.

"Thank you, sir. And I would like to assure you—that is, I'm not the kind of man—I wouldn't—"

Jacob rose slowly. "I don't believe you would ever do any harm to me or to Chantel," he said evenly. "I don't know what you have done or think that you might have done. It's none of my business. That kind of thing is between a man and God. He alone has the right to judge you, Mr. Tremayne, not I. And I can already see that you are not the kind of man to steal from us," he added with some amusement. "Such a man with such a horse. . . Even though I don't know horses, I can see that one must have cost you a pretty penny."

Actually, Clay had won Lightning on a bet, but somehow he was extremely reluctant to admit this to Jacob Steiner. And he was surprised. "Lightning? I figured he was long gone, either bolted or stolen."

"No, he stays with you," Chantel said. "Always. He's the reason

I found you. His name is Lightning? That a good name for that horse."

"The reason you found me?" Clay repeated. "But what—how—?"

Jacob said firmly, "Mr. Tremayne, you may feel better, but I can assure you that you're still in a very weak condition, and you are starting to look exhausted again. Rest now. Chantel and I will be here when you wake up."

"You're right, sir," Clay murmured. "I do still feel very unwell." He struggled to lie back on the cot, and Chantel helped him. "Thank you, Miss. . ."

"Chantel," she said. "Everyone calls me Chantel."

But he was already slipping into sleep.

CHAPTER TWELVE

Clay opened his eyes to stare up at the top of the tent. He had come to know that stretch of canvas very well, even when it was dark. He knew every crease, every spot, every loose thread. He had been staring up at it for a week now. But even as he monotonously traced the familiar folds, he was grateful, at least, that he could lie on his back to look up at it.

He still had not remembered anything of those first four days after Chantel and Jacob had saved him, lying on his stomach, his back in shreds, his head banging as if a strongman were hammering on it. The only thing he had known in that dark time had been Chantel's lovely face, her quiet voice, her soft hands. Idly he wondered how she kept her hands so soft. She worked like a man every day.

Earlier she had had to saddle Lightning for him. He had been determined to try riding, though Chantel and Jacob had warned him that he was still weak. Stubbornly he had led Lightning out to the wagon, hauled his saddle out of it—and promptly dropped it.

Without a single word, but with a dire I-told-you-so look, Chantel had picked it up and saddled Lightning.

Clay had managed to mount by himself, but after ten minutes of riding Lightning even at a slow walk, his head was pounding so hard he could hardly see through the red veil of pain. His back felt as if it were on fire. He had given up, retreated to his cot, and collapsed.

Suddenly his mouth started watering. He remembered he had eaten nothing since breakfast, and he was ravenously hungry. It might have had something to do with the fact that a thick, rich aroma of stew floated into the tent. With an effort, he rose, steeling himself against the dizziness he still felt when he stood up quickly, and went outside.

Chantel looked up from the campfire. "Going for a ride?"

"Very funny, ma'am," Clay grumbled.

"Come over here and sit down, you."

In the past two weeks, Chantel and Jacob had made their campsite into a homey, comfortable place under the stand of the oak trees. The trees were very old, their trunks enormous, their branches spreading and joining to make a thick roof of spring-green leaves. The cot mattresses were thin enough to bend, and they made nice comfortable seats leaned up against the trees.

Chantel had cleared a space right in the middle of the three trees for a good campfire, with a place to roast eggs and potatoes in the hot ashes and a tripod over the center. Now she bent back over, stirring the big iron pot full of beef stew. Jacob had had one roast of smoked beef that was about to ruin, so she had decided not to let it go to waste.

Clay moved one of the empty cracker boxes close to the fire, where Chantel had already placed hers. He watched her. He had never known a young woman like her before. She was the most curious combination of tomboy, toughness, sweetness, and world-weary innocence. At seventeen she was still coltish, with only hints of the grace that would surely be hers in full womanhood. He reflected how tender and gentle she had been when he was helpless, but as soon as he had come to his full senses and regained some of his strength, she had immediately withdrawn from him. She had been polite, but she didn't stay in the tent when he was resting or seek out his company in any way.

She glanced at him, and he could see that his scrutiny was making her uncomfortable. "Did you tell me you just turned seventeen, Chantel?" he asked casually, dropping his gaze.

"Last month I'm seventeen years. And you, Mr. Tremayne, how many years are you?"

"It's a coincidence, I believe. My birthday is in February, too, so last month I turned twenty-five."

"And you don't have a wife," she said with elaborate casualness.

"No, no wife."

"Why not?" she asked, coming to sit by him. "Don't you like women?"

Clay laughed shortly. "Oh yes, Chantel, I like women. I like them a lot. It's just that I never found a woman who could put up with my wicked ways."

Her mouth tightened. "So. You are a wicked man?"

"Guess I am."

"Why? How are you so wicked?" she demanded.

"I don't know," he answered with a wry half smile. "Just too lazy to be good, I guess. I'm the black sheep in all of my family, so I can't blame my heritage or my upbringing. What about you, Chantel? You've never said anything about your family."

"Ma mere and ma pere are dead. Now Jacob is ma grandpere," she answered shortly then jumped up. "The stew, it is done. Are you hungry?"

"The smell of that stew has been making me hungry since I opened my eyes."

She brought him a bowl of steaming stew and a big wedge of corn bread. "I make corn bread. Grandpere loves it. Do you like it?"

"Yes, ma'am, I surely do. Thank you."

Jacob came into the little campsite. He usually took a walk at twilight to be alone and pray. "If this were a restaurant, the aroma of that stew would bring in a full house," he announced, seating himself on one of the cot mattresses against a tree.

Chantel hurried to plump the mattress behind him so he could settle in comfortably. "You're hungry, Grandpere? You want me to bring you some stew?"

"You take such wonderful care of me, daughter," he said. Jacob found another box and sat down.

Chantel brought him stew and corn bread then fixed her own bowl of soup. Clay noted that she sat down near Jacob, cross-legged on the ground, instead of returning to her seat on the cracker box by him.

Sighing, Clay got up and moved his box closer to them. He took another bite of stew then said tentatively, "Even though I've been utterly at your mercy for two weeks, I know we don't know each other very well. But may I ask you two a personal question?"

"Of course," Jacob answered.

"What—would you please explain about your family? I mean, how did a German Jew get to be the grandfather of a Louisiana Cajun?"

Jacob smiled. Chantel looked amused but didn't smile. "We are not related by blood, Mr. Tremayne," Jacob answered. "But the Lord has done a wonderful thing in uniting us in affection. And the story of how we met is going to sound oddly familiar to you."

Jacob told Clay all about how Chantel had found him, so deathly ill, and had nursed him back to health. Chantel kept her eyes downcast, steadily taking a bite of stew then a bite of corn bread. He finished by saying, "And so you see, Mr. Tremayne, she has not only been your savior; she also saved me."

"You saved Mr. Tremayne, Grandpere," Chantel said.

"No, Chantel," he said gently, "you saved him and me. God sent you to save us. It's just that simple."

"That's an amazing story," Clay said. "We both have amazing stories, Mr. Steiner, of our guardian angel."

"I am no angel, me," Chantel said impatiently. "And I keep telling you, Grandpere, the good God never told me to go look for you or for Mr. Tremayne. He doesn't tell me things like He tells you."

"Me neither," Clay agreed.

"Pah, He talks to both of you all the time," Jacob argued. "You just don't listen. Both of you are running away from God. I don't know why. Maybe I'm too old, and I've forgotten what it's like to be so young and full of yourself that you don't have time for God. But you will. One day He will catch up with you, Chantel, and you, too, Mr. Tremayne."

Clay and Chantel exchanged glances as if to say, He's very old, after all. At least that was what Clay's meant.

Jacob noticed and first frowned darkly, but then he was amused. He was generally a very good-humored man. "Anyway, speaking of catching up to you, Mr. Tremayne, I would like to ask you a question. No, don't look so disturbed. I quite understand that you don't wish to talk about your recent experience. It's just that I was curious about your future plans."

Clay looked troubled. "I don't have any. I did, but somehow, since I was. . .injured, and I've been here with you and Miss Fortier, I just haven't felt like following through with what I had originally intended to do. You've both been so good to me, and I find that I am rather reluctant to—to—"

"To leave us?" Jacob suggested. "That is good, Mr. Tremayne, because you see, that is God talking to you. I know, I know, you don't hear a great booming voice from the heavens or a whisper in your ear, but it is God leading you all the same. So please, Mr. Tremayne, we would like to invite you to stay with us for as long as you would like."

Clay's eyes rested on Chantel. She nodded, and again Clay was reminded of the contradictions in this mercurial girl. "Please stay with us, Mr. Tremayne, if you would like to."

"I would," he said with relief. "For a little while. But there is one problem."

"What is that?" Jacob asked.

"Where were you planning on going?" Clay asked. "This is the main north-south road out of Richmond. Were you traveling north or south?"

"We were on our way to Richmond," Jacob replied. Seeing Clay's face darken, he went on casually, "But there is one wonderful thing you will find about being a peddler. You can go wherever you wish whenever you wish. Perhaps we may go south instead."

"But I thought we were going to buy supplies in Richmond, Grandpere," Chantel said, mystified.

"I don't think Mr. Tremayne wishes to go to Richmond," Jacob told her gently.

"Ohh," Chantel said solemnly, studying Clay's face.

"It might be awkward for me at this time," he said reluctantly. "If possible, I would like to find out something before I return. I was thinking that perhaps I could find the last two weeks' Richmond newspapers in Petersburg. They would tell me what I need to know."

Jacob nodded. "We passed through Petersburg two days before we found you. I can stock up there just as well as I can in Richmond. With the railroad junctions there are many warehouses where I can buy supplies wholesale. We'll go to Petersburg then."

"Thank you, sir," Clay said with relief. "And thank you, Chantel, for saving my life and now for inviting me into yours."

Even by the dim light he could tell that she blushed as she dropped her gaze. "You're welcome, Mr. Tremayne."

"You've allowed me to call you Chantel," he said lightly, "and I feel that you know me well enough now. Won't you please call me Clay?"

She hesitated, then a trace of a smile moved her mobile mouth and her eyes lit up. "All right then. You're welcome—Clay."

Chantel drove the wagon very slowly, because even though they had waited for two more days, Clay couldn't ride Lightning for long periods at a time. Sometimes he would lie down in the wagon, and sometimes he would sit up in the driver's seat with her while Jacob took a turn resting in the wagon. During one of these times, out of the corner of her eye, she saw Clay running his hand over the back of his head, over and over again.

"Does it hurt, your head?" she asked.

"It's better. I get better every day. It's just that I can feel a lot of little places back there, especially when I wash my hair. They're starting to itch."

"Don't scratch them, They're where the little pellets were," Chantel warned him.

"I can't believe Jacob didn't shave my head to get to them," he murmured. "But I'm glad he didn't. Ruining my manly beauty and all."

Chantel smiled to herself but said nothing.

They traveled until late afternoon. Clay was riding Lightning while Jacob took a turn driving, and Chantel sat beside him. Clay said, "It's getting late. We'd better start looking for a place to camp."

"I see a house up there with lights in the windows," Jacob said. "It looks very welcoming. Perhaps the Lord is giving us a sign."

"It's a little late to be calling on people, isn't it?" Clay asked.

"We're peddlers, not rich cotton planters," Jacob said complacently. "We don't have to go by such rules."

"Ah yes. I forgot," Clay said with an odd look on his face. It was, after all, the first time he'd been a peddler.

They pulled up into the yard and saw a man and a woman peering out of the curtained windows. Jacob got down while Chantel and Clay stayed near the wagon, watching.

Jacob knocked on the door and was met by a tall, lanky man with blue eyes and red hair. He looked suspicious until he saw Chantel, the peddler's wagon, and Clay holding the horses. Then he asked in a pleasant tone, "Good evening, sir. Are you having some trouble?"

"No, no, thank you, sir. I am Jacob Steiner, a peddler. Although it is late, I saw the lights, so warm and welcoming, of your lovely home and thought perhaps you and your wife would like to see some of my goods. I have hard-to-get spices, dress goods, canned foods, tools and knives, pots and pans, kitchen utensils, and many other things you may find of interest."

"I see," he said, considering. "Well, Mr. Steiner, my name is

Everett Sloane, and you are welcome in my home. And. . . ?" he made an inquiring wave to Chantel and Clay.

Jacob motioned them over and made proper introductions. "Please, come in, come in, all of you," Sloane said. As they came in, a thin woman just a little shorter than her husband entered. She had brown hair and kind brown eyes. "This is my wife. Anna, I'd like you to meet Mr. Jacob Steiner, his granddaughter, Chantel Fortier, and their good friend, Mr. Clay Tremayne."

"Please come in," Anna said. "As soon as we saw you drive up into the yard, I knew we would have good company for a pot of hot coffee, and I put the kettle right on."

"Her coffee's terrible," Sloane said, his blue eyes dancing. "But at least it'll be hot."

She was already returning to the kitchen, and she threw back over her shoulder, "You won't have to worry about it, since you won't be having any, Everett Sloane."

They settled in the Sloanes' sitting room, a comfortable room with overstuffed chairs, two rocking chairs set by a pleasant fire, a horsehair sofa, and two side tables. One held an open Bible, the other had a stack of books, including *The Farmer's Almanac*, *Virginia Crop Reports 1850–1855*, *Common Diseases of Cattle*, and surprisingly, *Great Expectations* by Charles Dickens and *Sense and Sensibility* by Jane Austen.

Jacob nodded approvingly as he took his seat on the sofa. "I see the Word is well read in your house, Mr. Sloane. That is a good thing, a blessing upon a house."

"Yes, my wife and I are Christians, Mr. Steiner. Er. . .you aren't from these parts, are you?"

"No, I am Jewish. I come from Germany originally. But God blessed me exceedingly, and I have come to know the Lord Jesus as my Savior. In my travels it is always heartening to meet others of His flock."

Anna came in with a large tray with a coffeepot, plain stoneware cups, and cream and sugar. She set it on a side table and said, "I'm not much of a one for standing on formalities. I'd feel better if you all came and fixed it the way you like it."

"Anna, Mr. Steiner here is one of God's chosen people," Sloane announced. To Jacob he said, "Pardon us, Mr. Steiner, but we've never actually met a Jew. And I wasn't aware that there were any that were Christians, too."

"They are few and far between," Jacob said.

Seating herself beside Jacob on the sofa, Anna said with interest, "A Jew? A Christian Jew? Why, that is very interesting. There are so many things I'd like to know about Jews."

"You're welcome to ask me anything you like, Mrs. Sloane," Jacob said placidly.

"Well, then, the first thing I'll ask is if you would all do us a great honor and stay the night with us," she said, beaming. "And the next thing I'd ask is—Mr. Stein, could you, as a Jew, eat ham for breakfast?"

Jacob laughed, an old man's creaking, wheezy laugh that still was delightful to hear. The rest of them grinned along with him. "Why, Mrs. Sloane, when the Lord Jesus died for me, He set me free from burdensome rites and rituals. And I have to tell you that eating a thick slab of fried ham for breakfast is one of the greatest freedoms I've known!"

Jacob told them of growing up in the synagogue, of living in a Jewish family, of the richness of his heritage, of how their lives revolved around their history and their beliefs. He brought Judaism alive to his listeners.

Even Chantel, who had often heard Jacob speak of these things, got much more of a sense of what it meant to be Jewish than she ever had before.

"Although it is true my kinsmen don't know the Lord Jesus," he finished, "we, as Jews, learn much more of the great Jehovah, or Yahweh, than is usually taught Christians."

"Do you speak Hebrew, sir?" Clay asked with curiosity.

"Oh yes, we are all taught Hebrew," Jacob answered, his eyes alight. "It is my second language. English is only my third."

Apparently he had forgotten that he had hosts, for Clay

requested, "And do you have a Hebrew Bible?"

"Oh, I would love to hear the Word read in Hebrew," Anna said. "I've always been curious as to how it sounds."

"Chantel, would you fetch my Hebrew Bible?" Jacob asked.

She slipped out of the room and soon returned with a big leather-worn book. She had always been fascinated by the book, wondering at the words written in a language she did not understand.

Jacob read the first five verses of Genesis to them.

Clay murmured, "So that's what it sounds like. It's rich and very beautiful."

They were silent for long moments, the Old Testament sounds echoing in their thoughts.

Finally Everett Sloane roused and said, "And so, Mr. Steiner, I understand that you may have a few items I'm in need of out there in your wagon. I'd surely like to have a new whetstone. If Anna would be nice to me and make me some tea every once in a while, I might be persuaded to buy her some cloth for a new dress."

"We've been out of tea for months, and you know it," Anna retorted. "But I'll take the material for a new dress anyway, particularly if you have any sprigged muslin."

"Oh, we do," Chantel said, jumping to her feet. "A pretty light green with little pink flowers, it is, Mrs. Sloane, and it will look so pretty on you, yes."

Clay and Chantel went to the wagon to fetch bolts of fabric, some tools, a selection of whetstones, and some newly sharpened glittering knives, both kitchen knives and hunting knives. Jacob had taught Chantel how to sharpen knives, and she was an expert cutler.

They talked and looked at much of Jacob's goods and finery. Everett Sloane did buy a whetstone and the green sprigged muslin for Anna. As a gift, Jacob gave Anna a slim, white leather lady's New Testament, and he gave Everett a new hunting knife. "And so that peace may rest upon this house," he said solemnly, "I give you both a tin of Earl Grey tea."

❧

Clay traveled better the next day, staying on horseback for most of the time. Still, it was early evening when they had reached the outskirts of Petersburg. They decided to camp and go into the city early in the morning.

"What do you want for supper, Grandpere?" Chantel asked as she considered the supplies they had.

"Mm. . .how about ham and eggs?" he asked mischievously.

True to her word, Anna Sloane had prepared them an enormous breakfast of smoked ham slices, fluffy scrambled eggs, griddle cakes, bacon, little boiled potatoes, biscuits, redeye gravy, white gravy, and a delicious apple conserve, her own recipe. Jacob had eaten three slices of fried ham and a big pile of eggs. Anna had sent with them an enormous smoked ham and a dozen fresh eggs.

"Again? You really do love that ham, don't you, Grandpere?" Chantel said, giggling. Clay watched her curiously, for he could honestly say that he had never seen such a light, girlish expression from Chantel.

They feasted—again—on ham and eggs and biscuits slathered with butter and Anna's apple conserve.

After they ate, Jacob said he was tired and was going to bed early, and he retired to the little tent. In the field where they had camped, the grass was so thick and deep that Chantel and Clay had simply laid down a couple of horse blankets by the campfire to sit on.

The night was cool. A thousand fireflies lit up their campsite. Their ethereal lights delighted Chantel. "I've never seen so many," she said softly. "It's like being in the stars, they twinkle and shine so."

"I haven't camped out since I was a young boy," Clay said. "I'd forgotten how very beautiful spring nights can be. So much better than smoky card rooms and stinking saloons. You always feel kind of. . .soiled, I guess you'd say, afterward. This is clean and fresh and makes you feel healthy and strong. No wonder I've recovered so quickly."

He watched Chantel. She was sitting gracefully, her face upturned, her legs tucked trimly under her. Her face was dimly lit, and her profile was stunning, with her wide dark eyes and straight nose and generous mouth.

She turned to him, her expression curious but with a trace of pity there that pierced Clay's heart. "Is that your life, Clay? Is that what it's been, gambling and saloons?"

He dropped his eyes. "Guess so. Told you I was wicked." He was uncomfortable, so he asked quickly, "So what about your life, Chantel, before you saved Jacob and he became your grandpere?"

She picked at her breeches. "When I was little, life was good, with ma mere and ma pere. But then he died, and ma mere"—she swallowed hard—"she married a man. A very bad man."

"Your stepfather," Clay murmured. "So he was not good to you."

"Not good at all, him," she said vehemently, and then she drooped a little and said so quietly that Clay could barely hear her, "And then ma mere died. And I had to run away."

"Oh Chantel," Clay sighed. "No one should have to go through what you've been through. Especially a wonderful, lovely, giving woman like you."

"Do—do you really think I am lovely?" she asked shyly. "I think I look like an ugly boy, me."

"No, no," he said. On impulse he put his arm around her, and she moved closer to him. "You try to look like an ugly boy, Chantel, and now I think I understand why. But you aren't, and you never could be. I think that you may be one of the most beautiful women I've ever known. Inside and outside."

She listened to him, so closely, her eyes burning on his face, so eager she was to hear this reassurance. A slight breeze stirred her heavy, glossy hair, and Clay smoothed it back then caressed her cheek. Her skin was soft and warm. He leaned closer, and then his lips were on hers. The kiss was soft, not at all demanding. He merely touched his mouth to hers gently, as if he were tasting her.

Chantel closed her eyes and breathed deeply, and she touched his face. Before he even realized what he was doing, he pulled her to him and kissed her again, with more urgency. For long moments she surrendered to him, her body soft and pliant beneath his hands.

But suddenly she stiffened, her eyelids flew open, and she pushed him away. "What—what are you doing, Clay?" she said with abrupt shock. "Stop it!"

"Chantel, please," he said gutturally, trying to pull her close again, so deeply was he filled with her sweet scent, the warmth and softness of her lips, the passion but yet the innocence of her kiss.

She slapped at his hands, her distressed expression turning to one of outrage. "Get your hands off me!"

He jerked back, suddenly appalled at what he had done. "No—Chantel, I'm sorry—"

"No, you're not," she said, grimacing. She jumped to her feet and gave him a last glance, one of disgust. "You warned me, you. You told me you were a wicked man. And you are."

She ran and jumped into the wagon and yanked the canvas flap closed behind her.

Clay pressed one hand to his now-aching head. *She's right. I am a wicked man. What's happened to me? How did I turn into this—this—worthless weasel, to treat women like this? With Belle, at least she did know what she was getting into, even if she was drunk. But Chantel? A pure, innocent girl like that, and she saved my life, and this is how I repay her? By pawing her like some sweaty, greasy piece of trash?*

Clay had never felt so badly in his life, even after the sordid situation with Belle. He thought that he should saddle Lightning and just disappear. But then he realized how cowardly that would be. He owed Chantel more than an apology. He had to face her and confess to her and beg her forgiveness. And he had to face Jacob Steiner, too, and ask his forgiveness as well, for betraying his trust.

He stayed up most of the night, feeding the fire, berating himself and rehearsing the speeches he would give Chantel and Jacob in the morning. Several times he tried to lie down, but he was so miserable he knew he couldn't sleep. The self-recriminations going around and around in his head seemed so loud that his head ached almost as badly as when he had first been injured. So he jumped up and paced more. Finally he fell into an uneasy doze just before dawn and slept for about an hour, stretched out on the horse blanket with no pillow and no blanket. When the first cheerful rays of the rising sun caught his face, he woke up with a groan.

He would have made coffee and breakfast for Chantel and Jacob, but all of the supplies were in the wagon. They had camped just beside a small stream, so he went and hurriedly bathed in the cold water. After he dressed, he began saddling Lightning.

Chantel came out of the wagon and warily looked around for him. A question came into her eyes as she saw that he was already saddling up, but she merely said, "I'll fix breakfast, me. Jacob will be up soon."

"I'll help you," Clay said. "Since you've taught me how to cook so well."

"No," she said curtly. "I'll do it myself."

She had just gotten the pans and utensils and food out of the wagon when Jacob came out of the tent, blinking and yawning. He observed Clay saddling up Lightning and arranging his packed saddlebags and bedroll. He saw Chantel's grim face and the shadows under her eyes. "It's a beautiful morning for such mournful faces," he observed, taking a seat on one of the cracker boxes Chantel had brought out of the wagon.

With the air of a man going to a flogging, Clay came to stand by him and Chantel, who was sitting by the fire, heating up the frying pan. "Chantel, I cannot express to you how very sorry I am for my behavior last night. You have been nothing but polite and kind to me, and I was very wrong in what I thought and what I did last night. All I can do is ask you to forgive me. Can you do that, Chantel?"

She had slowly risen as he spoke, watching him warily. For long moments, her face was hard and suspicious. Then the darkness in her eyes faded, though she still looked distant. "Ma grandpere has taught me this, that we can't carry around bad things in our hearts, like being angry and upset at people for the things they do," she said evenly. "I forgive you."

"Th—thank you, Chantel," he said awkwardly. He had been ready for her to berate him, to accuse him, to shout how terrible he had been to her. With a grieved sigh, he turned to Jacob. "I have betrayed your trust, Mr. Steiner," he said simply. "And this is so much worse, so much more treacherous of me, because you and Chantel literally saved my life. Please forgive me."

"I forgive you, my son," he said gently. "It takes a very good man, a very strong man, to face the wrongs he has done and to honestly express his sorrow for them. It would be a sin indeed not to forgive you."

A humorless grin twitched Clay's mouth. "I'm the only sinner here," he muttered.

"No," Jacob said firmly. "We are all sinners. Our sins differ, that is all." His eyes went to Chantel, who at first looked defiant but then dropped her eyes. His eyes went to Lightning, who stood saddled and already tossing his head, ready to go.

Clay saw his gaze and said, "I'll be leaving you now."

"Where are you going?" Chantel asked abruptly.

"I—I don't know," Clay said wearily. "I just think it's for the best."

"Why would you think that is best?" Jacob asked. "You have made a mistake, you have admitted it and asked forgiveness and received it. Whatever it is, it is over and forgotten. Stay with us, Mr. Tremayne, for I believe the Lord will tell you where you need to go and what you need to do. Don't you think that's right, Chantel?" he asked her gently.

"Yes, Mr. Tremayne, if Grandpere feels it is right, it is right," she said quietly. "It would be fine with me if you will stay."

He studied her, and she met his inquiring gaze directly. He saw cool courtesy, a distant gaze, with no hint of either welcome or censure. He noted, of course, the formal use of Mr. Tremayne. Resignedly he said, "Thank you, Miss Chantel, Mr. Steiner. That is more than I expected and certainly much better than I deserve. I would be glad to stay with you, at least until I find out what my situation is in Richmond."

Chantel fixed breakfast while Clay and Jacob sat talking, mostly about the town of Petersburg. It was a central terminus for the railroads, and though it was not a large city, it was always busy. They ate, and Clay felt the awkward silence between him and Chantel so acutely that it was a relief to him when they finally were packed up and pulling back out onto the busy road. Clay rode ahead a bit, attempting to put some space between him and these people he had treated so badly. These people whose treatment of him left him wondering about many, many things.

Jacob and Chantel rode in silence for a while. Chantel was driving, and she stared straight ahead, her eyes searching the far distance. Finally Jacob said, "He's just human, you know. He's just like all of us. He needs the Lord in his heart and spirit so that he can learn to be a better man."

"I didn't say he was a bad man," Chantel said tightly. "I've known much worse, me. I don't hate him, but I'm still angry at him. I know, I know, Grandpere. I will try to stop the anger in me. But one thing won't change. I'll never trust him."

"I understand, daughter," Jacob said sadly. "That is the thing about sin. It is a betrayal of God and a betrayal of others. Sometimes even of those we love most."

Chantel shot him a strange look but said nothing more. She stayed silent until they reached the city.

CHAPTER THIRTEEN

As soon as they started down the main road of Petersburg, they knew something momentous had happened. Men rushed up and down the street, clutching newspapers, calling out to acquaintances. Boys ran, too, from sheer excitement, ducking among the crowds, yelling. Prosperous-looking men smoking fat cigars stood in groups of three or four, talking animatedly. Southern gentlewomen were never known to stand out on the street for any reason, but here and there were groups of them, dressed in their graceful wide skirts, poring over newspapers and talking among themselves with animation. Riders galloped recklessly up and down; the road was choked with wagons and buggies.

"I wanted to go to the newspaper office first thing," Clay told Jacob and Chantel.

Jacob nodded. "We'll drive on up to the edge of town and wait. Will you come and let us know what's going on?"

"Yes, sir, I'll find you," Clay replied. Dismounting, he tied Lightning to a hitching post and began to thread his way through the throngs.

He found the newspaper office, but there was such a crowd that he couldn't even get outside the building.

A tall rawboned man who was dressed in a farmer's rough clothing was standing beside him.

Clay said, "Good day, sir. Would you mind telling me what's going on?"

"Waiting for the next edition," he answered succinctly.

"But—you mean the paper is putting out more editions than just the morning one?"

"Oh yes, as soon as they get more information by the telegraph they print it up," he answered then looked at Clay curiously. "Haven't you heard the news?"

"I guess not, sir. I've been—er—in the country for three weeks. We didn't hear much news."

The man's pale blue eyes lit up. "U.S. Army tried to resupply Fort Sumter in South Carolina. Confederate forces fired on the supply ship, turned them away. Virginia seceded from the Union, and now the Confederacy is gearing up. There's going to be a war, all right."

Clay was shocked. Of course he had been aware of the political tensions ever since Abraham Lincoln had been elected, and seven Southern states had seceded in January and February. But other Southern states were hesitant, distancing themselves somewhat from the most voluble "fire-eating" states like South Carolina and Mississippi.

Though he had not closely followed all of the political maneuverings, Clay had thought, somewhat vaguely, that a compromise would be found. In particular, he had believed that Virginia, with her close ties to Washington just across the Potomac River, would not make such a momentous decision, even though she definitely depended on the cotton economy and had many slaves.

As he stood there brooding, a man came out with his arms stacked with newspapers up to his chin. The crowd started shouting and waving coins in the air. Clay pushed forward, paid his nickel, and grabbed the paper. Two-inch-high headlines read: LOYAL SONS OF VIRGINIA! ANSWER THE CALL! There were two small articles about some appointments to the Confederate States of America War Department, but most of the two pages were covered with advertisements of different units forming as volunteer companies, with prominent Petersburg men organizing them.

After the crowd had dispersed, Clay went into the busy office. A small, bespectacled man looked up from a littered desk and asked, "May I help you, sir?"

"I hope so," Clay answered. "By any chance do you carry copies of any Richmond newspapers?"

"Oh yes, sir, we do. But they've been as hard to keep on hand as our own *Petersburg Sentinel* has been. Were you looking for any specific date, sir?"

"I'm not exactly sure. Do you have editions for the last two weeks?"

The man shook his head. "Oh no, I'm afraid those would be long gone. Or—perhaps we might have one or two, in the storeroom."

"Would you mind just checking, sir?" Clay asked courteously. "It would be a very great help to me."

"I don't mind," the man said. "Wait here just a moment and I'll see what I can find." He went to the back of the offices and through a door.

In only a few minutes, he returned. "As I said, it's not as if there are stacks to go through. We've had a difficult time keeping any editions on hand. I'm afraid all I could find were two editions of the *Richmond Dispatch*, from just two and three days ago."

"Thank you, sir, you've been most helpful," Clay said. After paying him for the newspapers, he left. But he was so anxious to see if he could find some news about Barton Howard that he stopped on the plank sidewalk just outside the newspaper office and started to search through them. A small whisper went through his mind, *Not an obituary, please, God, no notice of a funeral. . .*

But on the second page of the newspaper from three days ago, he found what he was looking for. A sizable advertisement read:

MOUNTED RIFLES—The undersigned are engaged in

raising a company of Mounted Rifles, the services
of which to be offered to the State as soon as the
organization is effected. Such persons in the country
who are used to the rifle who wish to join will apply to
us, at the office of the Virginia Life Insurance Company.
Uniforms free.

> Barton C. Howard
> Charles Howard
> Edward Howard

Clay threw his head back and closed his eyes with relief. "He's alive," he murmured to himself. "Alive."

Passersby stared at him curiously, but he stood unmoving, muttering to himself for a few moments. Then he tucked the newspapers under his arm and walked slowly down the street to where he had hitched Lightning. As he walked, he collected himself, and his mind began to churn.

He patted the horse's silky black nose then opened the newspaper again. Notices such as the one the Howards had placed were numerous. Also, there were a lot of articles about the organizations of the hospitals and the ladies of Richmond meeting to assemble small sewing kits for the men, to roll bandages, and to collect funds to buy pencils and paper for each soldier.

But two of the notices in particular caught Clay's attention.

VOLUNTEER COMPANIES, now in Richmond, or men
who intend to volunteer, will proceed at once to the
Camp of Instruction, at the Hermitage Fair Grounds. All
Captains and volunteers will report in person to Lieut.
Cunningham, Acting Assistant Adjutant General.

And:

RESIGNATION OF A U.S. ARMY OFFICER—Capt. J. E. B.
Stuart, late of the U.S. Cavalry, has resigned his

commission, rather than head the minions of Lincoln in their piratical quest after "booty and beauty" in the South. The officer in question arrived yesterday, and tendered his services to Virginia.

Clay had read of Captain—then Lieutenant—J. E. B. Stuart and Colonel Robert E. Lee in their involvement with John Brown at Harpers Ferry. The newspapers had been fulsome in praise of Lieutenant Stuart and Colonel Lee's decisive and quick action in apprehending the raiders. For days they had written articles about John Brown, of course, but usually they included more praise of the two officers, and there had been much about Lieutenant Stuart's exploits in the West, fighting Indians.

Staring at Lightning thoughtfully, he said, "Well, old boy, I think we're bound for the cavalry. Captain J. E. B. Stuart sounds like the kind of man I'd like to serve with. And I'll bet you can beat his horse."

Mounting up, he made his slow way through the crowded streets until he reached the warehouse district north of town, close to the railroad junction.

Jacob and Chantel waited for him there, under some shade trees by a tin dispatcher's shack.

"I brought some newspapers," Clay said. "The South is going to war."

Jacob nodded sadly. "Those dark clouds have been gathering for some time now."

"And I found out what I needed to know," Clay said, dismounting and coming to stand by the wagon. They were sitting in the back. He hesitated for long moments, slowly tying Lightning to the wagon, his head down. "I thought I might have killed a man. But I didn't."

Jacob and Chantel glanced at each other. "Why did you try to kill this man?" Chantel asked.

Clay stared off into the distance. "It's a long story, and it's not a story that I want to tell anyone if I don't have to. He did take a shot at me first. But in a way he had good reason to."

Jacob said, "Clay, Chantel and I already know you are a sinner. We know this because all men are sinners. We have no right to judge you and no right to demand that you confess to us. Leave your sin behind, and ask forgiveness from God, and He will save you from all of your sins. Simple."

Clay smiled, a twisting of his mouth with no humor in it. "It's not always that simple, Mr. Steiner. Not for a man like me anyway."

Jacob started to reply, but then he stopped and grew silent. As a wise man, he knew that arguing with men in Clay's position did little good.

Chantel stared gravely at Clay, her violet eyes wide and dark. Her face was unreadable. All that Clay saw was disgust and dislike when she looked at him, but his perception was colored by guilt.

He dropped his eyes.

Finally she asked quietly, "So, what will you do, Mr. Tremayne?"

Again it pained Clay that all warm familiarity was gone from her voice, and they were back to the formalities of relative strangers. "I'm going to join the army, of course, Miss Chantel."

"But why?" Chantel asked with a quickness that surprised him.

For the first time that day he was able to look her squarely in the eye and speak pure truth. "Virginia is my home. I may be a wastrel, but I love my home. If Virginia fights, then I fight."

"One thing I have learned, in all my time in the South," Jacob said, "is that these people love this country. And, in some ways, they already consider themselves set apart from the North. Many men will fight, Chantel. It will be a terrible war."

Clay asked curiously, "And what will you do, Mr. Steiner? Where will you go?"

"I've been praying for God to give me some direction," he answered, frowning. "But sometimes He demands that we walk in faith, without clearly seeing the path laid out for us. I do feel, though, that I will stay here, in Virginia. If, of course, my granddaughter will stay with me," he said, patting her shoulder affectionately.

"I will stay with you always, Grandpere," Chantel said in a low voice. "You're my family, you."

Jacob smiled at her then turned to Clay. "And so, Clay, you are going to join the army. Do you go to Richmond then?"

"Yes, sir."

"All right. Would you be so kind to escort two peddlers there?"

❧

Sheriff Asa Butler appeared shocked to see Clay walk into his office. He was leaning back in a wooden chair on wheels but shot bolt upright when he saw him. "Clay Tremayne! I figured you were halfway to Atlanta by now."

"No, Sheriff. I've been—in Petersburg," Clay said. "I came back to town to join the army. But first I wanted to come here to see if I have any charges against me."

He leaned back again, the chair creaking noisily with his considerable bulk. "No, as a matter of fact, you don't. And that would be because of Miss Belle Howard. Those brothers of hers tried to send her back home before I could talk to her, but she just came sashaying in here by herself and told me what happened. Or most of it anyway. Enough for me to know that Barton Howard came busting in on you two, guns blazing. Miss Howard said that you weren't even really trying to shoot him. You were just returning fire, and then you took off."

Clay said, "It's true I didn't shoot first, Sheriff."

Butler nodded; then his eyes narrowed as he looked Clay up and down. "So where'd you go, Clay? Ed and Charles disappeared for a couple of days after all the ruckus. Thought maybe they might have gone looking for you."

"Yes, they did."

"Did they find you?" Butler asked alertly. "You're looking kind of whipped, Clay. You're skinnier and pale."

Clay shifted on his feet uncomfortably. "They found me, all right. But Sheriff, I want to forget all that now. If I'm not going to jail, I'm going to war. Somehow that makes all this seem kind of. . .unimportant, if you understand me."

"No, I don't think I do," Butler said grimly. "If there's a crime committed in my territory, I need to know it, and I need to do something about it."

"I've committed a crime. I shot a man, and even if it was self-defense, in other days you would have arrested me and made me stand trial for it. But those old days are gone now, aren't they? We're getting ready to go to war, and the Howard brothers and I are on the same side, fighting for Virginia. I want stupid arguments like the one we had to be forgotten. There are much more important things at stake now."

Butler continued to stare hard at Clay. "If I know those boys—and I do—I think they might have been so red-eyed mad about Belle that they might've chased you down. I think they might've chased you down like a stray dog. And when they found you, they might not have worried about who shot first or any niceties like self-defense."

Clay was surprised at how close Butler had come to the truth. But it was true—the Howard brothers were all notorious for their tempers. Butler had dealt with them before. Clay merely shrugged and said, "Like I said, Sheriff, I want to forget all that now. So, unless you need me for anything more, I'm headed over to the fairgrounds."

The sheriff finally nodded. "All right, Clay. Maybe you're right. It's time to fight some Yankees instead of each other. Me and my boy are joining up, too. I expect you'll run into the Howards. If you have any more trouble with them, you just let me know. War or no war, I'll slap them behind bars so fast their eyes will cross."

"Thank you, Sheriff. But I don't think I'll have any more trouble with them."

"Better not," he said.

The Hermitage Fair Grounds, a wide field just northwest of the city, had in October of 1860 been renamed "Camp Lee," after Colonel

SWÖRD

Henry Lee, or as he was better known, "Light-Horse Harry Lee," the best cavalryman in the Revolutionary War and a proud son of Virginia. Even before Lincoln's election, soldiers—in particular, cavalrymen, for Virginia men loved their horses—had gathered as volunteer companies in Richmond. By November, sixteen companies, about eight hundred men, were camped there and gave weekly parades and reviews. An article in the *Richmond Dispatch* praising the encampment said, "The land is now overshadowed with ominous clouds, and none of us can tell how soon the services of the troops may be needed."

Now that the time had come, the fairgrounds—as people continued to call it—was a mass of men, with hundreds of tents large and small.

As Clay rode onto the grounds, he saw that there were probably as many horses as there were men. Even poor men in Virginia usually had at least one fine saddle horse.

There was much shouting:

"Here! Henrico Light Dragoons here!"

"Hey you, Private What's-your-name! What do you think you're doing, riding a mule? Get down off that horse!"

"Officers of Company B Chesterfield! Meeting at two o'clock this afternoon!"

Such was the confusion that Clay had no idea where to go to enlist. A big two-story home was on a small rise overlooking the fairgrounds, and he guessed that would be the headquarters, so he carefully moved Lightning along in that general direction.

He paused before a large tent, obviously a field headquarters. Two men on powerful horses were standing at the ready behind a line drawn in the dirt. Ahead of them a path had been cleared to the far side of the grounds. Obviously a race was in the making, and Clay stopped to watch. The signal was given, and the snorting horses thundered off. Men lining the path cheered and whistled and yelled catcalls. When the race ended, the smaller horse, a graceful bay, had won over a much larger and more powerful gray. The two men turned and trotted back, grinning.

Someone slapped Lightning on the neck, and Clay looked down. A man stood there, broad-shouldered and barrel-chested, wearing a wide-brimmed U.S. Cavalry hat. He was wearing a U.S. Army frock coat, but the insignia had been removed. As he looked up, eyes narrowing in the bright sunlight, Clay saw that he had blue eyes so bright they looked as if they projected their own light. His cinnamon-colored mustache and beard were thick and bushy.

"Hello, sir," he said, "that is a fine-looking mount you have there."

"Thank you, sir," Clay said, dismounting to shake the man's hand. "I'm Clay Tremayne, from Lexington."

"I'm Jeb Stuart," he said, "of the great state of Virginia. I've just been commissioned as a Lieutenant Colonel of Virginia infantry. Are you here to enlist, Mr. Tremayne?"

"Yes, sir, I am," Clay replied. "I was just on my way up to head-quarters to see the adjutant."

Stuart stroked Lightning's neck then in the expert manner of a true horseman, ran his hands down his chest and forelegs. "Very fine animal." Standing upright again, he looked at Clay, and again Clay was impressed by his piercing blue eyes. Just now they were dancing with joviality. "I'd like to invite you to join me, Mr. Tremayne. I've already assembled a very fine group of men, and I think you'd be a valuable addition."

"Me or my horse, sir?" Clay asked, stolid.

Stuart laughed, a rolling, booming laugh from deep in his chest. The men surrounding him couldn't help but grin, including Clay.

"Both," Stuart said. "In fact, if you think you might want to join up with some other outfit, I may ask your horse to volunteer."

"But sir, didn't I understand that you're a colonel commanding infantry?" Clay asked in confusion.

"So they tell me," Stuart said with some regret. "But somehow, it seems, most of the men who have volunteered for my command have very fine horses. It looks like we may be mounted infantry. Until we're cavalry, that is," he finished with a devilish grin.

Clay thrust out his hand. "Sir, my horse's name is Lightning, and he wishes to volunteer. And sometimes I think this horse is smarter than I am, so I generally do whatever he wants to do."

Jeb Stuart said, "My kind of man."

It was nine o'clock before Clay returned to Jacob's wagon.

He and Chantel had stopped under a stand of trees just north of the fairgrounds, and they had been doing a brisk business all day. Although the government was provisioning the soldiers effectively, their numbers had grown to around eight thousand men in the city of Richmond, and so the food was spare and plain. Men flocked to the peddler's wagon, buying candy and dried beef and canned foods.

Even at nine o'clock at night, there were still a bunch of them there, gathered around Jacob's campfire, laughing and talking and trying to flirt with Chantel. Clay noticed that she smiled at them and was polite to them, but she took no part in any private conversation with any of them.

After a while they drifted away, and Clay rode in.

Jacob called, "Clay! Come in, come in. Share our fire. And I think that we have something left for supper, though I must say that we've almost been cleaned out of foodstuffs. I'll have to get busy tomorrow and go to the warehouse district. I know I'll be able to find wholesalers there. Anyway, we want to hear about your day."

Clay dismounted and hurried to help Chantel, who was setting up a tripod over the fire. Soon they had it done, and she brought out a big iron pot. "I've been soaking these potatoes and carrots in beef broth all day, me," she told Clay. "I put back one big slab of beef. I had to hide it or Grandpere would have sold it." She gave him a very small smile.

Chantel had laid out the cot mattresses under the trees, and they went to sit by Jacob. Clay told them about Jeb Stuart. "And so Lightning volunteered to fight for the Glorious Cause, and Colonel Stuart is allowing me to come along with him. I hope you get to meet Colonel Stuart. He's a very interesting man."

Jacob looked out over the field, a sea of tents lit by hundreds of lanterns. "So many men," he murmured. "And they've come so quickly to go to war."

"All over the South there are camps like this," Clay said. "And we're spoiling for a fight. In fact, Colonel Stuart already has his orders. In a few days, we're going to Harpers Ferry. The commanding officer there is a Colonel Thomas Jackson. He's already invaded," he told them, grinning. "Colonel Stuart told me he crossed the Potomac and seized Maryland Heights. Sounds like a good start to me."

"It sounds as if you and your colonel spent some time talking," Jacob observed. "That's unusual, isn't it?"

"Yes, but then he's not like any officer I ever heard of," Clay answered. "He's not at all standoffish. We started out talking about horseflesh and went to see some of the horses that his men have. Then we just started talking about the forces and some of the plans the War Department has already formed. And then he did something else I've never heard of."

"What's that?" Chantel asked curiously.

"He gave me a note to take to the adjutant when I enlisted," he said. "I thought it was something to do with the regiment. But when I went in to enroll, the clerk looked up at me and asked, 'Have you attended West Point, sir?' Of course I said that I hadn't, and then he told me that Colonel Stuart had recommended me as an officer. Second Lieutenant," he finished with pride.

"Is—is that a good thing?" Chantel asked uncertainly.

"Sure is. I mean, this is a whole new way of forming an army, so a lot of the companies that form elect their officers. It's not as if you have to have a commission from the War Department, unless it's a promotion to a colonel or above. But still, I can't imagine why Colonel Stuart just decided like that to make me one of his second lieutenants. Maybe it was because it's so obvious that Lightning is a gentleman of quality."

"Maybe," Jacob said lightly. "But then again, maybe he saw the same thing in you."

"Doubt that," Clay said, smiling a little at Chantel. She didn't return it, but he thought that maybe her expression was not quite as remote as it had been.

"I wonder," Jacob went on, "just how many men will join this new army in the South. It will take many, many men to form an army that could defeat the United States Army in the North."

Carelessly Clay said, "Who are they, anyway? They're businessmen and merchants and farmers. In the South we grow up with rifles in our hands from the time we can walk. I believe with leaders like Colonel Stuart we will outfight them every time."

"Maybe," Jacob said softly. "I only pray God will shorten the time, and it will be over quickly."

"It will be," Clay said confidently. "I think that we'll whip them, Jacob. And I think that they'll turn and run right back across that river and leave us alone."

Jacob nodded, but his thoughts were nowhere in agreement with Clay's. He had lived in the North, traveled around it for years. He had seen the enormous bustling cities and gotten a sense of the hundreds of thousands of men who were of age to be in an army. He had seen the great factories, the commerce, the prosperity of the northern parts of America.

All of these were in stark contrast to the South. It was sparsely populated, its economy was based on cotton, and almost all of the industries that existed were based on cotton, too. There were no great munitions factories in the South, and as far as he knew, it had not developed an import-export trade to the extent that they could easily import arms.

But he said nothing of this to Clay, who was so obviously excited. Since he had known him, Clay had seemed to be a beaten man, aimless, unhappy. At least now he had a sense of purpose.

Chantel was saying, "But you said you'll be leaving in a few days?"

"Yes, ma'am, that's the word."

"You mean, you're going to go, and there will be fighting?"

"The war has started," Clay said. "Not here in Richmond. But yes, Miss Chantel, I am going to leave, and I am going to war."

She started to say something and then seemed to change her mind. Finally she said, "May the good God watch over you always, Clay."

PART THREE: CLAY & THE GENERAL 1861—1862

CHAPTER FOURTEEN

"Go to sleep, little baby.
Go to sleep, little baby.
Four angels around your bed.
To calm your sleepy little head."

Chantel was singing softly to Little Flora, or *La Petite*, as Jeb and Flora had begun to call her sometimes, who had gone to sleep on her lap. Looking across the room, she saw that Flora was watching her with a smile on her lips.

Flora was holding Philip, and they were playing with some wooden blocks.

"Why are you laughing at me, Miss Flora?" Chantel asked.

Flora said, "I was just thinking what a good mother you would make."

"Me? I don't have a man. I don't have any plans to get one, me."

"You'll get a man. I'm sure of that, and a good one, too."

Chantel continued to rock, studying the face of the child in her lap. "She is such a pretty girl," she whispered softly.

"We think she's going to look like her father. She has his eyes."

"I think no. I think she's going to be pretty like you. It's hard to tell what your husband looks like with that bushy beard. Why don't you make him shave?"

"I gave up on that a long time ago," Flora smiled. "He's proud of his beard. Besides, he says it hides his ugly face, but I don't think he's ugly. I think he just hates to shave."

From the open window, the sounds of birds singing drifted in. Chantel listened, and memories came to her of the different birds she had known in the bayou. She missed the large herons and the brown pelicans and the other birds that she knew so well.

The door opened, and Jeb stepped inside. He always looked as if he was in a hurry, and he never seemed to be tired, which always amazed Chantel. "Don't be so loud. You'll wake La Petite," Chantel warned.

"She'll be glad to see me." Jeb smiled. He kissed Flora and Philip, then came over, put his hand on Little Flora's head, and stroked the soft hair. "Well, you won't have to be taking care of us any longer, Chantel."

Chantel stood up. "You found someone?"

"Yes. She's a widow woman about thirty-five, I guess. Her husband was one of my men killed at Harpers Ferry. I had to go tell her of her husband's death and found her all alone. She truly needs the money. I think she'll do well."

Chantel felt a sudden pang and said, "I will miss your family. I will even miss you, too, sir. I will. Even if you are a general."

Suddenly Jeb laughed. His laugh, like the man, was big and rollicking and seemed too large for the room. La Petite stirred and opened her eyes. Jeb picked her up and swung her around, as he still did Flora sometimes. She squealed with delight.

His command had indeed been changed to the cavalry, and he had received promotion first to full colonel and then to brigadier general. Now he was commanding the 1st Virginia Cavalry. Ever since this had happened, Jeb had been happier and jollier than ever before.

"Jeb, you are going to make that child dizzy and give her a sick stomach," Flora said with mock sternness. "Just because you're the best officer in the Confederate Army doesn't mean you can mistreat the children."

Jeb walked over and put his hands on Flora's shoulders. "You always think I'm the best soldier in the world."

"Because you are," Flora said firmly. "Everyone knows it."

"All of this 'everyone' you're talking about doesn't include my men. They think I'm a slave driver."

"I think you are the best cavalryman and the best officer, Jeb," Flora said. "You never get tired. You're so strong and active. Most men wear out at the pace you drive yourself."

"Well, when they decided to join the cavalry, that's what they signed on for." He moved toward Chantel, fishing in his pocket. "Miss Chantel, I don't know what we would have done without you." He pulled an envelope from his pocket and held it out to her. "Here. I added a little extra to your wages."

"You don't have to do that, General Stuart," Chantel said. "I like your family, and Miss Flora has been a good friend to me."

"You're worth every penny of it. Now, you be sure and come back and see us all. Especially the children. They've grown very attached to you."

"Please do visit me, Chantel," Flora said sincerely. "You've been a good friend to me, too."

"I will do that," Chantel promised. She had only stayed with the Stuarts that first week, while Flora recovered from her illness. After that she had come every other day, bringing supplies and food, cooking staples, taking care of the children, and giving Flora a rest. She had no belongings at the Stuart home, so she said her good-byes and left.

She reached the main street of Richmond, which was, as usual, swarming with all sorts of activity. The streets were clogged with wagons being brought in and others that were outward bound, filled with supplies to be carried to various points of the Confederacy. The air echoed with the noise of people shouting and talking, and even the curses of the mule skinners came to her loud and clear.

She had often wondered why mule skinners spoke in such rough language but had given up trying to figure it out.

Suddenly a man stepped in front of her and stopped her. "Well, I know who you are. You're the woman that took up with Clay Tremayne."

"Let me pass."

"Just a minute, missy. You're a right pretty girl. You may have been Tremayne's woman, but you need a real man like me. I'm Ed Howard."

Suddenly things came together. "You are one of the men who shot Clay."

"Sure am. I'll do it again, too, if I get a chance. Come along. You and me will go have something to drink."

"Leave me alone!" Chantel tried to pull her arm out of Ed Howard's grasp, but he held it tightly and laughed at her efforts. She slapped at him, and her hand made a red outline on Howard's face.

"Why, you little cat!" he snarled and started to shake her.

But then his wrist was grasped so tightly he grunted involuntarily. He turned and saw that Morgan Tremayne was holding him. Morgan was not a big man, but he had a wiry strength, and his mild blue eyes were now hot with anger.

"Let go of me, Tremayne," Ed said, grunting, writhing a little in the awkward postion. "What do you care about this little bit of sauce?"

"Apologize to the lady," Morgan said, and twitched his hand just a bit.

Ed Howard cried out as the pressure on his hand grew intense. "Leave it, Morgan. You're breaking my fingers."

"You need to learn some manners," Morgan said. "I said, apologize."

Charles Howard came up behind Morgan. He had a cane in his hand, and Chantel saw him swing it and cried, "Look out!" But it was too late. The cane struck Morgan in the back of the neck, and he fell forward.

Both men laughed, and Charles said, "So, this is Clay's little piece. That's right, little lady, I want to have a word with you, too." Both brothers started toward her.

From down the street, Sheriff Asa Butler had seen Charles knock Morgan down, and he had hurried to stand in front of the brothers like a big wall. He put his hands—they were wide and powerful—on both brothers' chests and shoved them so hard they staggered. "Back off, you two."

They both started yelling at Butler, but he made a quick cutting motion with his hand, and they shut up. "So, lemme get this straight. Morgan hurt your dainty little hand, Ed. And you, Charles, you're kinda getting in the habit of sneaking up on people and hitting them from behind, aren't you?"

Charles's face turned a deep crimson, but then he said rather sulkily, "C'mon, Ed. Waste of our time anyway." They went strutting down the street.

Chantel said, "Thank you, Sheriff."

"You be careful, Miss Chantel. If these two bother you anymore, you just let me know. You look kind of shook up, Morgan. You all right?"

Morgan had gotten to his feet during this exchange. He rubbed the back of his neck where Charles Howard's cane had hit him with the force of a hammer. "Aw, guess I'm all right, Sheriff. Probably have a good headache tonight though."

Butler considered him. "You know, Morgan, I could arrest Charles Howard for assault. If you want to press charges."

"I think our two families have tangled enough," Morgan said drily. "Thanks, though, Sheriff."

The two men shook hands, and the sheriff walked back down the street.

Chantel said to Morgan, "You tried to help me. Thank you very much."

"I wasn't enough help," Morgan said. "I sure am sorry that I couldn't keep those swine from insulting you."

"Well, you tried, and that's what counts. You're a much better man than them, you," she said disdainfully.

Morgan made a little bow. "I'm Morgan Tremayne, ma'am."

"Yes, I heard the sheriff. You're Clay's brother?"

"I am. He's told you about me?"

"Not really," Chantel said. "Mr. Tremayne, he doesn't talk much about his family or his past."

"But he's told me about you," Morgan said. "When I was walking by, I heard what Ed Howard said. I knew you must be Chantel, the angel that saved my brother's life."

Chantel shrugged. "I must go back to camp now. Ma grandpere will be waiting for me."

"There's going to be a celebration at the fairgrounds tonight. There'll be some food and music and fireworks and speeches. I don't like the speeches much, but the food will probably be pretty good. Would you go with me?"

Chantel considered it then said carelessly. "Yes, I'll go with you, Mr. Tremayne. But only if ma grandpere comes with me."

Morgan grinned. "Your grandfather is welcome to come, too, Miss Fortier."

"Our wagon is at the camp. You'll ask for me there. Any of the soldiers will know."

"I'll come about five o'clock. That'll give us plenty of time to get there for the food."

"All right, Mr. Tremayne." She was interested in Morgan Tremayne. He didn't look like Clay, except maybe in their stances and the way they walked. But she had been impressed by the way he had so quickly defended her from Ed Howard's unwelcome attentions.

Making her way back to the wagon, Chantel found Jacob sitting on a box staring out into space. "Hello, daughter. How were Miss Flora and the children today?"

"Ver' well. Colonel Stuart came home. He found a woman to help take care of his wife and baby, a live-in. What are you doing, Grandpere? You look funny when I come up, like you're wondering about something."

Jacob shook his head and chewed his lower lip. "I can't figure God out."

Chantel laughed. "I don't think anyone can figure God out. If you could figure Him out, He wouldn't be God. No?"

"No, He would not be," Jacob agreed, "but it doesn't stop silly men like me from trying to figure Him out. Anyway, what would you like for supper? What about we go see if the butcher on Front Street has barbecue today?"

"We don't have to. There'll be a lot of barbecue at the celebration, I think."

"What celebration?"

"The celebration at the fairgrounds tonight. I met Clay Tremayne's brother. Morgan is his name. He asked me to come, and I told him I would only come with him if I could bring you. Will you come, Grandpere? Because I won't go if you won't. And there will be fireworks," Chantel said, her eyes sparkling. She had never seen fireworks until they had come to Richmond.

"Fireworks," Jacob considered, "and barbecue. Of course I will come."

"Good. So, Grandpere, what is it you are worried about? About the great God?"

Jacob frowned. "You know, Chantel, in the Bible there are so many cases of men, and women, too, that God told exactly what to do. You take Moses, when he saw that burning bush. God said, 'Moses, you go to Egypt. You're going to deliver My people.' No question about it. Moses argued a little bit, but he knew what God wanted."

"You still worried about what we're going to do?"

"Well, I'm too old to fight. I'm no good with mechanical things. I couldn't work in a factory; I'm too old for that even. But you know, Chantel, I'm still certain that God has brought us here. You and me."

Chantel said sturdily, "Then we wait. That Scripture you read to me from the book of Revelation last night. . .it was what God said to one of the churches there. He said, 'I have set before you an open door and no man can close it.' When God opens a door, we will go through it. Yes?"

"You have turned into a very smart and sensible young woman," Jacob said. "Yes, indeed, we will wait, and a door will open. I'm so glad you're with me, daughter. You're such a blessing to me."

"Thank you, Grandpere," Chantel said, a little embarrassed, as she always was with any expression of affection. But she knew, deep in her heart, that she loved Jacob Steiner as much as any granddaughter ever loved her grandfather.

"Hello, Clay," Morgan said, coming up to pat Lightning's nose.

Clay looked up from his grooming. "Well, hello, Morgan. What are you doing here?"

"I wanted to come and talk to you. I've been worried about you, Clay."

Clay put down the currying brush and gave Lightning one last rub. "I've got some coffee over here."

The two men went over to the stove inside the stables. Clay picked up a battered coffeepot, found two mugs, and filled both of them up. "So what is it that's worrying you now, Morgan?"

"Clay, you know I don't like to interfere in your personal life, right?"

Clay simply nodded in response.

With some hesitation, Morgan finally said, "I just met Miss Chantel Fortier."

"Did you? And what did you think?"

"Well, she looks strange in that men's garb, but she seems like a lady anyway, and a nice one."

"So how did you meet Chantel?"

Morgan told him about the run-in he'd had with the two Howard brothers. "I didn't even see Charles until he knocked me down with his cane. I think they might've commenced with a beating, but Sheriff Butler showed up just in time."

Clay grimaced. "I guess I'll have the Howard brothers on my

back for the rest of my life. Sorry, Morgan."

Morgan shrugged. "I didn't do it for you, Clay. I did it for Chantel. And by the way, I asked her to go to the celebration with me tonight."

"And she agreed?" Clay said with surprise.

"Yes, she did. Why are you so shocked? Some people think I'm the brother with the looks in the family," Morgan said, punching his shoulder.

"Not at you, you handsome devil," Clay said, grinning. "At her. I didn't think Chantel was much for letting men escort her around."

"Well, she did say she wouldn't come unless her grandfather did," Morgan admitted. "So I kinda doubt she's smitten with me."

Clay shook his head. "I kinda doubt she's smitten with men much at all. And maybe especially Tremayne men."

Morgan gave him a sharp look. "Is there some reason for that, Clay? Something I should know about?"

"No, Morgan," Clay said with a hint of sadness. "It's over and forgotten."

❧

Morgan showed up at exactly five o'clock, and Chantel introduced him to Jacob.

"I'm glad to know you, young man," Jacob said and put out his hand. "It's nice to meet Clay's family."

Morgan shook his hand. "I'm happy to know you, sir."

Jacob looked mischievous as he said, "Thank you for inviting me to go with you two young people. I wouldn't go, but Chantel promised me that there would be barbecue."

"Oh yes, sir, I'm sure there will. There always is at a Southern feast," Morgan said. "Lots of eating and drinking and making merry."

"And fireworks, yes," Chantel said happily.

Traveling through the growing throngs of people in wagons and on horses, Chantel, Morgan, and Jacob soon arrived at the fairgrounds. As Morgan escorted her toward the attractions, Chantel quickly became aware of people staring at her, as they always did. It was beginning to make her uncomfortable, and she began to think that perhaps her breeches and men's shirts were reflecting on her much more scandalously than simple skirts and blouses might. After all, her hunting and fishing days in the bayou were long gone—as were the days when breeches could hide her figure.

But soon she forgot her worries. There were lanterns strung all along the fairgrounds, and many torches on long poles stuck into the ground. And indeed the fireworks were splendid. The cadets from the Virginia Military Institute, who were there training the volunteer companies as they formed, fired off their cannons. The artillery show made a delightful rolling roar, with spectacular flames spitting from the cannon mouths.

Also, there were not one, but three barbecues—a steer, a pig, and a goat. Jacob gleefully ate some of all three, along with tastes of many of the side dishes supplied by the merchants of Richmond. "If only they could find a way to put this potato salad in a can," he mourned. "I could sell hundreds of cans of this."

A band played marching music, and patriotic songs were sung, and there were speeches from various politicians. President Jefferson Davis was there, and Chantel was fascinated by him. He was the most dignified man she had ever seen. His face was hawklike, his cheeks sunken in, and one of his eyes seemed to have a film over it. He was not an inspiring speaker, but people listened respectfully and cheered loudly when he finished.

Finally the speeches were over, and the band started playing dance music. Morgan asked her to dance.

"No, thank you," she said firmly. "I don't dance."

"But why not?" he asked.

"I never learned those fancy dances, me. All I know is a *zydeco*."

"What's a zydeco?"

"A Cajun dance."

"Well, we don't have to dance. We can listen to the music."

Jacob said, "Now that I've eaten, I think I'm going to go on back to the wagon and get a good night's sleep. You'll bring my granddaughter home, Mr. Tremayne?"

"Yes, sir, I will. I will see she gets home safely."

As soon as Jacob left, Morgan said, "He seems like a fine man. Strange, isn't it? I mean, your grandfather being a Jew and a Christian."

"Ma grandpere, he is wonderful," Chantel said softly. "I don't care if he is Jewish and Christian."

A group of cavalrymen walked by, splendid in their new Hussar jackets and cavalry sabers. All of them wore brogues, with their pants tucked into their socks, except for one—Clay Tremayne. He grinned when he caught sight of them and came over. "Hello, Morgan, Chantel," he said. "You're staring at my boots." Clay had new cavalry boots, thigh-high, polished to a sheen.

"Trust you to turn out like a dandy, even in uniform," Morgan said.

"I think they look nice, me," Chantel said. "General Stuart wears these boots."

"Chantel to my rescue again," Clay said. "Are you having a good time, Chantel?"

"Oh yes, I love fireworks. And Grandpere ate so much barbecue and potato salad it made him sleepy."

"For such a small man, he sure can put away the food," Clay said. "It's a good thing you're such a fine cook, Chantel. Morgan, I've been thinking. Since Mother and Father are here in town, don't you think they'd like to meet Chantel and Mr. Steiner?"

"I think that's a very good idea, Clay," Morgan agreed. He turned to Chantel. "Clay's told the family—finally—about what happened with the Howards and how you and Mr. Steiner saved his life. How about having supper with our family tomorrow night?"

"I was asking her, Morgan," Clay objected.

"What difference does it make?" Morgan argued. "Either one of us—"

"Never mind, you," Chantel said, amused. "If ma grandpere will come, I will come."

"He'll come," Clay said firmly. "I'll tell him that we're having supper at Wickham's."

❧

Clay had not told the whole story to his family until they had come to Richmond, as almost all of the prominent citizens of Virginia had, to find out about the organization and plans for the coming war. Although he had not mentioned names—out of consideration for Belle—of course his parents had already heard of the scandal. Clay had told them of how sorry he was that he had behaved so badly and had even excused the Howard brothers. "You know, once I thought about it, I'd probably do the same thing if some lousy dog had treated the Bluebells that way."

Clay took after his father—muscular, with thick brown hair and intense brown eyes. Morgan took after his mother—slim and tall, with auburn hair and dark blue eyes. And then, of course, were the Tremaynes' surprises—late-in-life twins, Belinda and Brenda, now seven years old. They were like foundlings, with strawberry-blond hair, angelic little heart-shaped faces, and big, round sky-blue eyes. There was such a difference in the ages between the twins and the brothers that usually Clay and Morgan just called them the Bluebells.

Clay had reserved a small private dining room at Wickham's, and the Tremaynes, Chantel, and Jacob Steiner all settled in.

"I recommend the fresh oysters," Morgan announced.

Clay looked pained, while Chantel made a horrible face. "I don't like raw oysters, me. They're cold. Food should be hot and drink should be cold."

"Very well, then, no oysters," Caleb Tremayne said. "Clay tells us you are such a good cook, Miss Fortier, that even Wickham's can't outdo your meals. Does anything sound good to you?"

"Everyone calls me Chantel, me," she said rather shyly. "I like steak, Mr. Tremayne."

"As do I," Jacob said. "One grows weary of preserved meat. As peddlers, so often that is all we have."

They all settled on steaks, even Belinda and Brenda. As they were eating the first remove, lettuce and tomato with mayonnaise, they kept glancing out of the corner of their eyes at Chantel. Clay had warned them about Chantel's masculine clothing, and his mother had impressed upon them how rude it would be to mention it.

Still, Chantel could see the little girls' wide-eyed amazement, and she asked kindly, "Have you ever seen a girl wear men's breeches?"

"Oh no, Chantel," Belinda answered.

"Mother said we were not to say anything. It would not be polite," Brenda said.

"But you didn't say anything, did you? I did. You see, back in Louisiana I live in the swamp, me. I go fishing there for fish and for turtles and alligators, and a dress is no good for fishing."

"Alligators?" Belinda and Belle repeated in unison. They did this often.

"Did you ever catch one?" Belinda asked.

"Oh, all the time. Once I got one on as tall as you. Big enough to bite my head off."

"How did you catch him?"

"Well, ma pere did most of it," Chantel admitted. "But I helped ma mere cook him, me. He was good eating, that fat alligator."

Caleb and Bethany Tremayne looked vastly amused, and Bethany said, "I've never had alligator. I doubt anyone in Virginia would know how to cook one."

Chantel ducked her head. "No, I don't fish and hunt much now, me. But these breeches, I wear them since I was a little girl. It's all I have."

Clay watched her with some surprise. He had not been aware that Chantel had become embarrassed about her clothing until now.

"Well, skirts and blouses are easy to make," Bethany said lightly. "Clay tells me that, along with cooking, you are an excellent seamstress, Chantel. You know, there is a dressmaker here in Richmond that has nice working clothes for sale at a very reasonable price. If you required alterations, we could make them together, for I love to sew."

"No, I—that would cost so much money, wouldn't it?" Chantel asked.

"Not too much for my granddaughter," Jacob said firmly. "Mrs. Tremayne, if you would be so kind as to tell us about this dressmaker, I will certainly see to it that Chantel gets some clothes."

"I would like to visit her myself," Bethany said. "I'm going to order new dresses for me and the girls, in Confederate gray with gold trim. It's going to be all the rage now, you know. I would be happy if Chantel would accompany us."

"That would be nice," Chantel said awkwardly. "Thank you, Mrs. Tremayne."

Chantel was fascinated by Clay's family. Instinctively she had realized that Clay, in spite of his rakishness, was a quality Southern gentleman. But she had never met any of the Virginia aristocracy, the old moneyed families. She had a feeling that perhaps the Tremaynes gave her and Jacob a much better reception than others of their class would. But then she recalled how kind and uncritical Jeb and Flora Stuart had been, and they were of very good family, too, Clay had told her. She wondered that people so far above her station would be so kind to her.

Caleb turned to Jacob and said, "Clay's told us about how you two saved his life. I'd like to hear your story, Mr. Steiner."

Jacob smiled. "Let me tell you, sir. I became a Christian many years ago. Very hard for a Jewish man. The synagogues will not have you because you are not holding up the traditions of Judaism, and some Christians are suspicious of you. But I did the best I could to study the Bible and find out how to follow the Lord Jesus."

"I think that's very admirable, sir," Caleb said. "How did you meet Miss Fortier? Chantel, I mean," he added with a courtly bow in her direction.

"Almost the same way your son met her. I grew sick. I was all alone. I could hardly move. As a matter of fact, I was dying, and this young woman"—he turned to her and smiled beatifically—"she nursed me back to health. And she decided to stay with me. We were coming here, to Richmond, and on the way we found your son badly hurt, and it was Chantel who nursed him back to health. She makes a fine nurse."

Chantel thoroughly enjoyed the meal and visiting with Clay's family. She hated to see the evening coming to an end. Before leaving, she and Bethany confirmed plans to visit the dressmaker's the very next day.

Clay and Morgan walked Chantel and Jacob out to the carriage they had hired to bring their guests to the restaurant. Jacob began questioning Morgan about the best warehouses in Richmond for foodstuffs.

Clay took the opportunity to lead Chantel a few feet away for a bit of privacy. "My family is very grateful to you."

Chantel replied earnestly, "You have a good family, Clay. You are a lucky man, you."

"I am, though I sure don't deserve it."

Chantel sighed. "I'm jealous. All I have is Grandpere." She looked toward Jacob with love in her eyes. "He's wonderful, but it's good to have a big family."

"Well, I think my family would take you in a moment. They've asked me a thousand questions about you, and I can tell even the Bluebells love you. They pester you with questions, but that shows they like you."

"I like them, too."

Clay sighed. "I've been a bad son, Chantel. Very bad."

Chantel stared at him. "Why have you been a bad son, Clay? Nobody makes you do these bad things." As Clay lifted his eyes, Chantel saw they were filled with misery.

"I don't know. Everybody seems to know where they are going except me. I was raised in a Christian family, as you can see. They make it seem so easy to live for God and do what is right."

"That's what Grandpere always says, that it is easy."

Clay looked at her. "What about you, Chantel? Are you a Christian?"

"Well, no. I'm not like Grandpere or your family," she said with some difficulty. "The good God doesn't talk to me. I don't understand Him."

"Not as easy as they make it out to be, is it?" Clay said wryly. "In any case, it's been a good visit. Maybe you and Jacob could go back to the valley with my parents. He's told me how much you like the Shenandoah Valley. You know, Chantel, the war is going to be here, in Virginia, especially around Richmond since it's the capital. You and Jacob would do better to be out of it."

"No, I don't think Grandpere is going to leave," she said thoughtfully. "He hasn't told me anything, me. But I know him. The good God is telling him something, and I think it will be here for us."

Clay frowned. "Well, at least the city should be safe. For a time, anyway."

Jacob and Morgan joined them at that moment. After thanking them again, Jacob climbed into the carriage.

"Good-bye, Chantel, Jacob," Morgan said.

Clay added, "I expect I'll be seeing you soon."

"Good-bye, Clay, Morgan," Chantel said. She joined Jacob in the carriage then turned to see the Tremaynes all had come out. They were calling their farewells and waving, all of them smiling. She smiled back at them and waved. "They are good people, Grandpere."

"Yes. Very fine. Even Clay, for all his faults."

"I wish he were different."

"I think he wishes that, too," Jacob said, "and we'll pray that he will find Jesus."

CHAPTER FIFTEEN

With a sigh of relief, Clay sat down at the base of a huge chestnut tree. The patrol had been out for four days now, riding hard and far, and although the men were mostly drained of energy, General Jeb Stuart never slowed down. Clay closed his eyes wearily and leaned back against the tree.

The man's unbelievable. Never tires, rides into enemy fire like a fiend, comes back laughing, then comes back to camp to have music and dancing.

They had eaten a good meal, for somehow Major Dabney Ball, the chaplain of the regiment, had rounded up some chickens. Clay had gotten his share and finished up one last fat chicken leg as the sun slid ponderously down behind the rim of a ridge to the west. He heard a nightjar whining, and over to his left a nightingale began its sweet song.

He opened his eyes in slits and watched for a time as the dark purpling into the night went on, and slowly the dying light fell across the grove of trees where they had camped. Each tree in the woods stood out singly and purely against the sky and then turned green-gold by some magic mixture of the disappearing sun and the drifting clouds far overhead. July had brought blistering heat, but with evening came a blessed coolness. Clay simply let the weariness drain from his body as the night came on.

The campfires were burning, and as usual, the music had started up. A slight smile creased Clay's broad lips as he thought of the strange incongruity of Stuart, the fierce fighting general and Stuart the music lover.

Stuart must have music! He had practically kidnapped Sam Sweeney, a tall, good-looking fellow in his early thirties who was a magician, of sorts, on a banjo. He was the younger brother of Joe Sweeney, who was probably the most famous of the traveling minstrels and was said by some to be the inventor of the banjo. He had once played for Queen Victoria. But Joe had died, and now it was his younger brother, Sam Sweeney, who carried on the tradition in Brigadier General Jeb Stuart's camp.

Clay had noticed that as soon as music of any kind would start, Stuart's feet would begin to tap and shuffle, and it was not unusual to see him dancing around to the music when they played rousing fast songs. "He sure does love music," Clay murmured. He opened his eyes more fully and watched the men who had gathered, Sweeney on the banjo, Mulatto Bob on the bones, two fiddlers, and the Negro singers and dancers. They were singing "Her Bright Smile Haunts Me Still," a plaintive sad song, but then they played the "Corn Top's Ripe," and finally one that seemed to have been written especially for General Jeb Stuart: "Jine the Cavalry."

A movement caught his eye, and Clay looked up to see Major Dabney Ball leaving the campfire. The chaplain came over, plopped himself down beside Clay, and exhaled his breath. "That's good music, Lieutenant."

"Yes, it is, Major. Of course, General Stuart would get rid of them if they weren't good musicians, and go 'volunteer' some more," he told the parson.

Dabney Ball was a tall, lanky man with long arms and legs. Even his feet were long, and his face, also. He was unlike any chaplain Clay had ever seen or heard of. Ball was called the "foraging parson," for he was a self-appointed commissary officer. No chicken was safe in a territory covered by Preacher Ball. No, nor pigs or even yearling calves. He not only foraged meat, but occasionally he would set up bakeries for the unit. He was one of Stuart's myriad kinfolk, a thirty-nine-year-old minister who had left a Washington pastorate after eighteen years in the pulpit and now served as the most colorful chaplain in the Confederate Army.

Clay said, "I heard you had a little trouble with a Yankee, Chaplain, as you were helping these chickens contribute to the Glorious Cause."

"Oh, that didn't amount to a thing. I met a Yankee plunderer on the highway. He had got a bunch of chickens, hams, and ducks that were obviously Southern property. So I shot him and took his feet out of the stirrups and dropped him on the ground. And then his horse volunteered for the Confederacy."

"You think that was the Christian thing to do?" Clay asked, his dark eyes alight. The men often teased the chaplain about his warlike attitude.

"We're in a holy war, Lieutenant Tremayne," Ball said. "We've got to wipe the Yankees out so that God can rule over this land."

"Amen," Clay said but could not cover his grin. "That was a fine prayer you prayed at our service last Sabbath day, Chaplain. Usually I have a tendency to doze in services, but I remember that fine prayer."

Ball turned and said, "Are you a believer in the Lord God Jehovah, Lieutenant?"

Clay answered with surprise, "Well, of course I believe in God, sir. Only a fool wouldn't."

"It's not enough just to believe," Ball said. He leaned closer to Clay and looked deep into his eyes. "The Bible says you must be born again. Have you ever been born again, sir?"

"No, I haven't, I'm sorry to say."

"Sorry to say!" Ball snorted. "What a feeble excuse of a reason for not trusting in God. You're sorry to say. Do you have any plans for letting God have your life as He demands, Lieutenant Tremayne?"

Clay was accustomed to Major Ball's outspoken evangelism, but somehow it still intimidated him. "I don't have any plans right now, Major Ball," he said in a low voice. "Except to live out the night."

"God's going to catch up with you, Clay Tremayne," Ball said, echoing Jacob Steiner's words. "One of these days you'll be just like the apostle Paul. He was just on the road, commencing to his sin, and God simply knocked him out of the saddle."

"If that happened to me, God would sure get my attention," Clay said lamely.

"Don't wait for it! Don't wait for it! You've got to find God, boy. You're here tonight in good health. As you said, tomorrow you may be facing God in judgment."

"I sure hope not, sir."

Ball leaned over and put his bony hand on Clay's shoulder and squeezed it hard. "I don't want that to happen to you, my boy. Jesus died for you. He loves you. Keep that on your mind. It's not enough to be afraid of hell as you ought to be, but you need to find the Friend of all friends. When your father and mother forsake you, when your friends betray you, Jesus will still be your friend. You think about that, Lieutenant."

Using Clay as a fulcrum, Ball shoved himself up. "I'm going to talk to Private Finch. He's right close to the kingdom. I'm hoping he'll come in tonight."

As Ball walked off into the growing darkness, Clay shook his head. *He's a funny fellow*, he observed to himself. *Shoot a Yankee down and then come back to camp and preach to all of us lost men. The next day he goes out and steals a bunch of chickens for all of us. I guess he fits in real well with Jeb Stuart's cavalry.*

Chantel had been into town, and when she returned, she saw that Jacob was excited.

His dark eyes were flashing, and he was pacing back and forth. It was most unlike him.

"What's the matter, Grandpere?" Chantel demanded. "Is something wrong?"

"Wrong? Oh, no, no, no. As a matter of fact, daughter, I'm telling you that the greatest thing has happened."

"What is it? Tell me, tell me!"

"All right, I will. Come here and sit down, daughter. This will take some telling." Jacob led her to the two camp chairs he had set up.

Since they had been camped in Richmond for three months, Jacob had finally bought six fine wooden straight-back chairs, and Chantel had fixed racks on the outside of the wagons so they could be conveniently hung there.

Chantel sat down, and at once Jacob said, "You know, daughter, for months now we have been praying that God would give us an answer. Isn't that right?"

"Yes, Grandpere."

"Well, I'm here to tell you"—Jacob grinned broadly—"I have had a revelation."

"And so the good God has been talking to you again?"

"No, not His voice, of course, Chantel. I've tried to explain that to you, but it's difficult. I was just sitting here peeling an apple and watching that big squirrel that comes every day for a bite to eat. I hope no hungry private shoots him. He's gotten quite fat and sassy since I've been feeding him. Anyway, I wasn't even praying or anything like that, and all of a sudden something began to make itself known. I don't know how to say it any different."

Chantel nodded, though she, of course, didn't and couldn't understand.

Jacob continued. "We've been wondering how we could best serve God, and I had never thought of such a thing before, but this is what God told me we would be doing. We're going to serve the Lord by serving our men. These fine fellows in uniform."

"Serve them?" Chantel asked in surprise. "But how? We're

peddlers. We travel. We sell our goods."

"Oh, we will still travel, yes. We are going to be sutlers, and we are going to serve the officers and soldiers of the Confederate Army. And you are going to have a new title."

"What is this, a title?" Chantel asked, mystified.

"Here, look at this. It was in a newspaper from New York, and I clipped it out. I had read about a woman serving, but it was with the U.S. Army. She had a special uniform. I'd seen it in a paper and clipped it out."

Jacob handed her the clipping. It was faded and not very clear, but Chantel could make it out clearly enough. The woman was young, apparently, and facing the camera. She wore clothes with a distinct military style. It was a dark skirt, a white blouse with a string tie, and a short black jacket, with the conspicuous Hussar stripes that many military units sported, including the Confederate cavalry. On her head she wore a campaign cap, and around her shoulder was a strap that suspended what appeared to be a canteen.

"Read what it says, daughter."

"All right:

"Mary Tippee is one of those ladies who is serving as a sutler, or as the French have it, a *vivandiere*. Miss Tippee serves in the one hundred and fourteenth Pennsylvania regiment otherwise known as Collis's Zouaves. Miss Tippee follows the troops as they cover the ground headed toward a battle and passes out tracts and small copies of the Gospel. She also carries canteens and a supply of water so that she can supply the troops when they are thirsty."

"There. . .you see?" Jacob cried. "That's what you are. I'm a sutler, and you are a vivandiere."

"Pretty French word," Chantel said. "I like her clothes. Much more than these boring skirts and blouses I've been wearing." True to her word, Bethany Tremayne had taken her to a dressmaker's, and Jacob had encouraged her to buy five skirts and five blouses. Chantel had chosen two black skirts and three gray skirts, and plain white blouses. She still wanted to stay in the background, not to be noticed, but she was young, and she secretly yearned for pretty clothes sometimes.

"We will go to the dressmaker's," Jacob decided. "You will have bonnie blue skirts, a shiny white blouse, and a red sash around your waist. And your jackets, we will tell her to make them of Confederate gray, with the black stripes for facings, like General Stuart's men wear. And I know that Clay Tremayne will help us find you a campaign cap. You will look lovely, dear daughter, and when the men see you they will know you are their vivandiere."

"But, Grandpere, there are hardly any sutlers in the South. They know they can't run the blockades to get supplies. We can't get them here—that is what I was going to tell you. Everything that comes in goes to the army. Even the merchants aren't getting their regular shipments," Chantel said worriedly. "How will we get supplies? How will we have anything to sell to the men?"

"God will provide, oh yes, Chantel," Jacob said happily. "Now that He has finally let me know what I am to do, He has also shown me how to do it. And you and I, we will carry the Gospel to these young men before they go out to risk their lives in battle. And when they return, we will give them comfort and hope in the Lord Jesus."

The excitement of a battle to come was in the air. As Chantel and Jacob made their way to General Thomas Jackson's headquarters, many of the men, on catching sight of Chantel, stopped and stared blatantly. She was self-conscious in her new demi-uniform, her vivandiere clothes. But, she told herself sturdily, it was no worse than when she was wearing her trousers or even her modest skirts and blouses. Chantel was the type of woman whom men stared at. She looked straight ahead.

Jacob stopped a short rotund lieutenant with rosy cheeks and mild blue eyes. "Lieutenant, could you direct me to the tent of General Jackson, the commanding officer?"

"I certainly can, sir. You head on right as you are going, and within a hundred yards you will see a tent with a flag in front of it. That will be General Jackson's. Shall I take you there?"

"No, that won't be necessary, Lieutenant. We can find our way. Thank you very much."

Jacob moved steadily, and Chantel followed him.

Some of the men were singing, and others were cleaning their equipment. None of them seemed at all concerned that very soon they might very well be lying dead on a battlefield.

"Why aren't they afraid, Grandpere?"

"They've never seen a battle. They have ideas about what war is like, glorious and noble. I'm afraid they'll soon find out that it's nothing like that."

General Jackson's tent was indeed marked by a flag. A tall, skinny corporal stood outside at attention. He studied Jacob and Chantel and then asked evenly, "Can I help you?"

"We would like to see General Jackson, if that's possible, young man," Jacob said pleasantly.

"Sir, General Jackson is very busy at the moment with military matters. I'm sure you understand."

"Please, sir. Could you at least ask him? It's very important to us." Jacob's sincerity was so obvious, the corporal relented.

"All right, sir. I'll ask if he might have a moment." The soldier turned and went into the tent. He was so tall he had to duck his head. Almost at once he returned and said with some surprise, "Come in, sir, ma'am. The general will see you."

Chantel stepped inside followed by Jacob.

From behind a camp desk a tall soldier with a full dark beard stood to his feet at once. He was not a handsome man, but he had penetrating light blue eyes. He was dressed in a shabby old army coat with major's stripes, faded and peeling, still visible on the collar. He bowed slightly to his visitors saying, "I'm General Thomas Jackson, at your service."

"My name is Jacob Steiner, General, and this is my granddaughter, Chantel Fortier. We thank you for seeing us."

"How can I help you, Mr. Steiner?" He was not rude, but he was businesslike.

"We want a permit to follow the troops. I am a sutler, sir, but I have no permit. I've been told that's necessary. Miss Fortier is a vivandiere."

"I don't believe I know that term."

"It really means a female sutler, General. We'll be taking our wares to the troops so that they can buy foodstuffs and supplies of all kinds, except alcohol."

"You don't serve alcohol, Mr. Steiner? I would have thought that sutlers would, in an army camp."

"No sir, I do not. I have seen too many lives wrecked and ruined by alcohol to have any part in that vicious trade."

"I congratulate you." Jackson's eyes then lit up warmly, and he smiled, giving his stern face a more welcome look. He waved to two backless canvas stools in front of his desk. "Please, sit down, Mr. Steiner, Miss Fortier."

Jacob continued, "We also intend to pass out Gospel tracts and small pamphlets containing the Gospel of John. I'm hopeful that we will be able to witness to the men about the Lord Jesus Christ."

Jackson looked curiously at Jacob. "I see, sir. So you are a Christian?"

Chantel saw that Jacob was smiling. "Ah, you see that I am Jewish, General Jackson. But I am a born-again believer. I like to call myself a completed Jew. I'm an old man now and can do little for the war effort, but I can bear witness to the glory of God in the Gospel of Jesus Christ."

"Excellent! Excellent!" Jackson said. "I am happy to hear it. I wish we had five hundred more just like you, Mr. Steiner. But I am afraid sutlers in the South are going to be few and far between."

"You will give us the permit then, sir?"

"Certainly I will. Here. I will make it out now." Jackson moved around to his desk, sat down, took a sheet of paper, scribbled on it, and then said, "You will be given a formal permit, a printed one, but this will do if anyone challenges you." He turned to Chantel. "Miss Fortier, I would hope that most of the Southern men in the army are gentlemen. Sadly, that is not always true. It is possible that you might hear things that would offend you."

Chantel smiled. "General Jackson, these men don't bother me, no. I am happy to be with ma grandpere and to help in this way."

"Well, if any of them become troublesome, you come to me, and I will see that they are taught better manners," he said, and there was no doubt that this intense man meant exactly what he said. "I'm glad that you will be here for my men, Mr. Steiner, Miss Fortier. Men always need God, but in war, they need Him more than ever, for His strength, His courage, and His comfort."

"So true, General," Jacob said, folding the paper up and sticking it in his inner pocket. "And the Lord has shown me that that is exactly why Chantel and I have been called to serve Him in this way. To minister to your men."

"Good. If I may be of any help to you, let me know."

Jacob bowed slightly and said, "Thank you, sir,"

As they left and walked back toward their wagon, Chantel said, "He is a stern man, him. But not so much when he talks about the good God."

"I had heard that Thomas Jackson was a Christian man," Jacob said. "And he will need God for the heavy burdens he must bear."

The morning air was clear, and the men were fresh, as were their mounts as they galloped along the road. Jeb led them, and Clay rode alongside him. He saw that Jeb's face was aglow, and he called out, "Sir, you don't expect we're going to have any action, do you?" It was just a routine patrol, three days north of Richmond. They had heard that the Yankees sometimes sent small troops, just probing really, to test the lines on the south side of the Potomac.

"You never can tell, Lieutenant," Jeb said airily. "We might get lucky."

No sooner had Jeb spoken than he stood up in his stirrups and said, "Speak of the devil; there's some bluebellies."

Clay looked down the road and saw a troop of Union soldiers. They had come to a halt, having spotted the cavalry.

"Let's get 'em, boys!" Jeb yelled. "Draw sabers! Charge!"

Following orders, Clay drew his saber and spurred Lightning.

The entire troop rode their horses at full speed in a charge, yelling like wild men.

Clay saw at once that the Federals had no hope. They were unseasoned troops, and the sight of the cavalry rushing with sabers flashing was too much for them. Most of them threw their weapons down and ran. Clay thought that they would pursue them and take prisoners, but Stuart ordered, "Don't let them escape! Cut them down!"

They rode, hard and fast, catching up quickly with the fleeing soldiers, and Clay saw the men in blue cut down easily, too easily. He took no pleasure in the action, for it was a slaughter.

The entire action took less than five minutes. The bodies were scattered about half a mile along the small back road, mostly men in Union blue. But Clay saw also that three of their own troops were lying on the ground.

He quickly guided Lightning to them and saw that two of them were obviously dead, but one man was alive. He stepped out of the saddle quickly and knelt beside the soldier who was on his face. When he rolled him over, he saw that it was Sam Benton, a young man in his company who always had a ready smile, an expert fisherman who often caught fish for his company when they were out in the deep woods. He could coax fish out of the smallest and most unlikely stream, and he always shared with as many men as his catch allowed. Now Clay saw that there was a terrible wound in Sam's chest, and there was no hope for him.

As he knelt over the dying soldier, Clay remembered how Sam had told them a couple of nights ago that he was engaged to marry a girl named Johanna Redmond. The young man had been very excited and was hoping that he could persuade her to marry him soon, before the army had to move out, as they surely would. Now the blood bubbled up from his lips, and he whispered something. Clay put his ear down close to his face.

"Guess. . .they got me good, Lieutenant Tremayne." He shuddered for breath and said, "Sir, when you get back to Richmond, would you. . .go to Johanna?"

"I remember Miss Johanna Redmond," Clay said, picking up his hand and squeezing it. It was already dead-cold. "I'll find her."

"Tell. . .Johanna not to grieve long. Tell her I want her to find a good man, have his children—be—be—happy. You tell her that, sir, and that I loved. . .her. . .dearly."

Those were his last words. A compassion that he had not known he was capable of suddenly welled up inside Clay, and he felt as if his heart was bruised. In Sam Benton's death something precious was lost, and he knew that this was a symbol of the thousands of young men who would redden the soil with their blood before the war was over.

Chantel stepped out of the wagon, blinking in the early morning sunlight. She and Jacob had been taking inventory, listing all of the supplies—and there were many—that they needed to restock. She was carrying a big box of buttons. The box was cleverly slotted for each type of button to be sorted—black, blue, and white bone, brass and copper—but somehow they had gotten all mixed up, and she was going to sit down, have a second cup of coffee, and sort them again.

To her surprise, she saw Clay riding slowly across the fairgrounds toward the wagon. His uniform was soiled, and his back was bent wearily. He dismounted and said, "Hello, Chantel. It's been awhile, hasn't it?"

"Hello, Clay. Yes, I believe it's been nine or ten days since we've seen you. You don't look well, you."

He nodded grimly. "I've been better." Rousing a little, he asked, "What's that uniform? You look very pretty."

"We're sutlers. We're staying with the army," she said proudly. "And this"—she held out her skirt—"is my uniform. I'm a vivandiere now, me."

Clay frowned darkly. "So Mr. Steiner has decided to stay? Here, with the South?"

"Yes, the good God has told him this. What's wrong, Clay?"

He pulled off his hat, pulled two chairs off of the rack on the wagon, and courteously held one for Chantel before seating himself. Leaning forward, he rested his elbows on his knees, clasped his hands, and stared off into the distance. "Don't stay here, Chantel. You and Mr. Steiner should leave. You should go far away from here, someplace safe."

Chantel shook her head stubbornly. "The good God doesn't talk to me like he does Grandpere. He doesn't tell me this, to stay here with the army. But He told Grandpere, and so we will stay. I'm not afraid, me."

"No, you wouldn't be, would you?" Clay said, turning back to her. "You have great courage, Chantel. I know you're not afraid. It's just that it's war. It's not just the danger. It's the horrible things you see, the terrible things that men do to each other, the great sorrow of it."

"What's happened?" Chantel asked softly.

Clay sighed, a deep, grieved sound. "We've just had an action where some of our fellows didn't make it. One of them has a sweetheart here. Her name is Johanna Redmond. He died with her name on his lips, and he asked me to go to her and tell her. The bad thing about it is I didn't really know him that well. That's what's so bad about it, in a way. That he died with only me there to comfort him. But I promised, and I must find her and tell her."

"Yes, if you promised, then you must do it," Chantel said. "But you see, Clay, that when the time comes for some of these soldiers, we will be there. Grandpere and I will be there, and Grandpere will tell them of the Lord Jesus, and He will comfort them."

"I wish you and Mr. Steiner had been there to be with Sam. I know he was a Christian, but I—I didn't know what to say to him.

And I don't know how I'm going to comfort his sweetheart, either."

An impulse came to Chantel, and she said, "I will go with you, Clay. I will help you."

Clay said with surprise, "You will? You would do that for me?"

"I will do it for the dead soldier and for his lady," Chantel answered. Seeing Clay's crestfallen look, she softly added, "And to help you, Clay. Wait just a moment; I will tell Grandpere."

She went to the wagon, where Jacob was still listing supplies, and spoke to him.

She returned to Clay, who was tying Lightning to the wagon. "The Redmond house is just off the town square. We can walk."

They began walking. She waited for him to tell about the action, but he said nothing. Finally she asked, "Were there many men killed?"

"Only three of ours, but quite a few of theirs. I really don't want to talk about it, if you'll pardon me." Bitterness tinged his tone, and his head was bowed as they walked along the street.

One of the other young men in Clay's company knew Sam Benton and the Redmond family, and he had told Clay where the Redmonds' home was.

The two of them mounted the steps and knocked on the door, and after a few moments a young woman timidly cracked the door.

"Miss Johanna Redmond?" Clay asked, quickly removing his hat. "I'm Lieutenant Clay Tremayne, of the Richmond 2nd Horse. This is my good friend, Miss Chantel Fortier."

Her eyes searched his face and saw the sorrow there. With some sort of a plea, she looked at Chantel and saw the compassion there, on the face of a stranger. She closed her eyes for a moment then opened the door wider.

"Please, come in." She led them into a small parlor and sat down on the sofa. "It's Sam, isn't it?" she said, the fear making her voice hoarse.

"I'm afraid so, Miss Redmond," Clay said with difficulty. "There was an action, two days ago, and—and—"

"Is he going to be all right?" The tone was hopeful, but the look on Johanna Redmond's face was already knowing and agonized. "He's all right, isn't he? He's in the hospital?"

Clay tried to speak, but he simply could not find the words. He looked down and fiddled with his hat.

Chantel sat down by the woman and took her hand. "I'm so sorry, Miss Redmond. Your fiancé was shot, and he died. Lieutenant Tremayne was with him."

Johanna Redmond stood for a moment, and her face slowly dissolved into a rictus of grief. She turned away from them, went to a wall, and leaned against it, racked with great sobs. "Oh, Sam! My Sam!" she cried out.

Clay stood helplessly, his head down.

Chantel went over and put an arm around the woman and comforted her in a low voice. Finally Johanna allowed Chantel to lead her back to the sofa, and she sat down, her head buried in her hands.

Clay swallowed hard and said, "Miss Redmond? I was there, with Sam, when he— I was there, and he asked me to give you a message. I think I know it word for word. He said, 'Tell Johanna not to grieve long. Tell her I want her to find a good man, have his children, and be happy. Tell her that I loved her dearly.' He died with your name on his lips, and he was a good man. A fine soldier." Clay could not think of another word to say.

Chantel asked, "Do you have anyone here with you, Miss Redmond?"

"My mother—she is upstairs napping. I'll go up to her. . . ."

Chantel looked at Clay, and he nodded. "May the good God be with you, Miss Redmond," she said, rising.

Clay said, "General Stuart sends his regrets and asked me to tell you that you have his prayers."

When they got outside in the clear sunlight, Clay murmured sadly, "He was a good man, Chantel. He had a whole wonderful life ahead of him, with her. And now he's dead."

Chantel had had trouble forgetting her resentment toward Clay ever since he had attempted to kiss her back in those first days, but now she saw something else in him. He had a bad reputation and he had done evil things, but she saw now that he was a man of great compassion, and this counted for much.

She entwined her arm with his, the first time she had touched him with any familiar gesture since that night. "Come with me, Clay. We will go talk to Grandpere. He will comfort us. He and the good God will comfort us."

CHAPTER SIXTEEN

Abraham Lincoln sat in his office in Washington, and Jefferson Davis, one hundred miles away, occupied the office of the presidency of the Confederate States of America. The two men were in precarious positions politically, for both the South and the North were clamoring for battle to settle the question of slavery. Both the North and the South had visions that the war would be short. The South expected that the North would be beaten decisively and would allow them to go their own way, with the Confederacy a permanent political entity. The North, on the other hand, was equally convinced that they must crush the Confederacy and maintain the Union.

Abraham Lincoln had been chosen to lead the people of the North, but he was by no means a unanimous choice. Now as he sat in his office and looked around his cabinet, he saw doubt and even disdain on the faces of some of the men he had chosen to help him lead the Union in the battle that was to come. His face was drawn, already lined, even though his presidency was in its infancy. He listened quietly to these men who were entrusted with the union of the United States of America.

SWORD

Lincoln kept his eye on the ranking general of the North, the hero of the Mexican War, General Winfield Scott. Scott was old and overweight and exhausted from a lifetime of serving his country, but Lincoln could see that he was stirred and determined. Scott had already proposed his plan of crushing the Southern forces. It was called the Anaconda Plan, and it was simple. Winfield said it would be necessary to throw a ring around the Confederacy and crush it slowly, as a boa constrictor crushes its prey.

Lincoln's glance went around the room, and he listened as man after man insisted that Scott's plan was too slow. Most of them saw Scott as being outdated and not a fit man to lead the nation in this tremendous endeavor. They were all in favor of immediate action and continued arguing with the old general.

Finally, Secretary of State William Seward, who felt himself more able to govern than Lincoln, said, "Mr. President, we must take the quick road. We have a fine army, and we must use it at once. Our armies are more numerous, our equipment is better, and they have nothing but a group of individuals."

"They have Robert E. Lee," General Scott said loudly. "He is the South's greatest military asset, and he can out-general any man we put against him."

Immediately the rest of the cabinet took exception to Scott's statement, and finally Lincoln, sensing which way the wind was blowing, broke in saying, "Gentlemen, I see great value in General Scott's plan, and I feel we must pursue it. . .in the long run. In the meanwhile, the people are protesting that we are doing nothing. They forget that our army is composed mostly of volunteers for the term of three months. That is not time to train an army, as we all well know."

"The very reason why we shouldn't fight right now," Scott spoke up.

"I wish that it were possible to wait, General. I know you are right and our men are green, but the men of the South are fighting forces that are green, also. I've made the decision that we will throw the Army of the Potomac into action against the South."

"Who will be the commander?" Seward demanded at once.

Lincoln knew that everyone in the room expected him to name George McClellan, who had experienced some success in minor actions. Lincoln, however, felt differently. He said plainly, "I am appointing Irvin McDowell as the commander of the Union armies." He saw the arguments rising and cut them off short. "General McDowell will be the commanding officer. My mind is made up. I will instruct him to attack the Southern forces at once."

Doubt was as thick as a night fog in the room, but there was no arguing with Abraham Lincoln when he spoke this firmly. So the cabinet began to make plans for an immediate attack on the South.

General Irvin McDowell was a large man, six feet tall and heavyset, with dark brown hair and a grizzled beard. His manner was modest, and only from time to time was he dogmatic in his conversations. He had a strong will along certain lines, for instance, in his belief that alcohol was an evil. Once he had suffered an accident in a fall from a horse that had rendered him unconscious. The surgeon who tried to administer some brandy found General McDowell's teeth so tightly clenched together that he could not administer it. McDowell was determined—apparently even when unconscious— not to take liquor.

Now he was prodded into motion by a civilian president who could only identify the seriousness of the battle to come by saying that both armies were equally green and untrained. McDowell saw clearly that Lincoln did not take into consideration that the Northern army would be on the attack while the Southerners would defend. McDowell was not a military genius, but he knew that defense was simpler than attack.

But orders were orders, and he set out at once to put the army into motion. He reissued ammunition and saw to it that food for the entire campaign was ordered and would be in place when the men needed it and made certain that his supply line was well established. Then he gave orders for the army to move toward

Virginia. He knew that the South was already thrown into a battle line around a small town called Manassas. A creek called Bull Run flowed by that town, and it was there McDowell knew that the action would take place.

～

Lincoln's counterpart, Jefferson Davis, had been chosen over fire-eaters in the South with the hope that he might be able to obtain a peaceful solution. Davis had been a military hero during the Mexican War and a powerful member of Congress for years. The Southern people were charmed by the music of his oratory, the handsomeness of his clear-cut features, and the dignity of his manner.

As he sat in his office preparing for the battle that he was being forced to order, Davis was troubled by the superior forces that the North would assuredly throw against the Confederacy. Davis had taken what steps he could to provide for defense.

The main line of advance from Washington was blocked at Manassas Junction, and Davis had chosen General P. G. T. Beauregard, the hero of Fort Sumter, with twenty-two thousand men and a smaller army of twelve thousand men under General Joe Johnston, to meet McDowell. Davis was well aware of the greenness of the Confederate troops, and he was also aware that the men of the South would be outnumbered by the Northern troops. He had done all he humanly could, and then he prayed.

This was the setting for the first battle of the war, called Bull Run by the South and Manassas by the North. It was fought on Sunday, July 21, 1861. As that day approached, the two armies left their homes and prepared for the largest battle thus far in the Civil War.

～

"This is not what I thought war would be like, no," Chantel said as she and Jacob made their way down the crowded streets of town. They were following all of the companies stationed in Richmond as they marched to Manassas. Townspeople crowded the streets, tossing flowers to them and cheering them.

Jacob glanced around and shook his head. "It won't be like this after the battle."

"What do you mean, Grandpere?"

"You see these men? These soldiers that are laughing now, and drinking and singing? Many of them will be dead. Others will have lost arms or legs or been wounded terribly. But they haven't seen war yet. They don't realize. God give them strength, for they will."

Indeed, there was a carnival-like atmosphere throughout the South. The saying had become commonplace: one Confederate could beat three Union soldiers. Sometimes that was even amended to say that one Confederate could beat ten Union soldiers. No one knew exactly why or how this equation had been decided, but the men of the South believed it firmly.

Chantel heard her name called and turned to see Armand-Pierre Latane shouldering his way through the crowd, smiling as he approached. A captain in Major Roberdeau Wheat's Louisiana Tigers, he had come to Jacob's wagon one day to purchase some new handkerchiefs, for he was something of a dandy, from New Orleans. He had been delighted to find Chantel, a beautiful young Cajun girl, in the camp. He stopped by the wagon often, ostensibly to buy buttons or tinned oysters or bootblack, but mostly to talk to Chantel.

He came to walk beside them. He looked trim and neat in his dress uniform, a gray frock coat with gold trim, light blue breeches with the navy blue infantry stripe down the side, and a long, gold-handled sword in a silver sheath. "Good day, Mr. Steiner. Hello, cherie," he said. "So you've come to join the fun."

Chantel said, "I didn't think it would be like this, Armand. You're going to fight in a battle, not on your way to a party. Aren't you afraid, you?"

"Afraid? No, not me. Somebody else may get shot but not Armand Latane."

Jacob saw that the man was being deliberately obtuse and asked gently, "I trust your heart is right with God, Captain. You should know that there is a chance that you may be wounded or even die."

Armand's face grew more serious, but he shrugged carelessly. He was a handsome man with well-shaped features and jet-black hair. "Even if we were afraid, no man would show it. We each try to outdo the other in audacity, you may say."

"Where are we going, exactly?" Chantel asked. "And when will the battle start?"

"It's not far to Bull Run. We have word that troops have already left Washington and are headed this way. Our men are ready for them. Perhaps tomorrow, perhaps the day after, we will fight."

The soldiers were not keeping very good parade line; they mingled with the crowds, stopped for drinks at the saloons, wandered here and there to say good-bye to friends. Now a company of cavalry, trotting in close order, shouldered the crowds aside. Chantel saw that Clay was leading the column. He looked toward the wagon, obviously seeing if it was Jacob's, then pulled Lightning out of the formation with a muttered order to the corporal riding beside him.

He saluted Latane smartly, and Armand gave him a crisp salute back. "Lieutenant Tremayne, you and your men look like you're ready for a fight."

Clay smiled briefly. "General Stuart's always ready for a fight. And I know that Major Wheat and you Tigers will give a good account of yourselves, too, Armand."

"*C'est ca*," Armand said, shrugging carelessly. "The Tigers will taste blood tonight, Clay."

Clay said, "Good morning, Chantel, Mr. Steiner. So, you're following us to Bull Run?"

"Oh yes," Jacob said eagerly. "I've never been so sure of God's will for me. And I am blessed to have Chantel with me. She is so courageous and strong, she follows this hard path with me."

"Yes," Clay agreed, smiling at Chantel, "we are all blessed to have you both. Chantel, soon you won't just be my angel and your grandfather's angel. I know you'll be an angel of the battlefield."

Chantel blushed a little then asked, "Can you ride with us, Clay?"

"I'm afraid I can't. But you have a true gentlemanly escort here in Captain Latane. I have to go. I'm on an errand for Colonel Stuart. Look after them, Armand," he finished.

"It will be my honor," Armand said formally.

Clay spurred Lightning, and he trotted ahead, but after a few steps, he turned and looked at Jacob, his eyes dark and brooding. "Pray for me," he said, then turned and galloped away.

General Irvin McDowell was unhappy. His blunt features twisted into a scowl as he said to Colonel James South, "Look at them, South. They act like they're going to a picnic."

South turned his gaze upon the marching columns of soldiers, and indeed they were in a strange mood. Many of them had plucked flowers and had shoved them down in their muskets. Even as he watched, a group left the line of march and went over to pick berries beside the road.

"Look at them picking berries! How are we supposed to win a battle with berry pickers, South?"

"They'll be all right once the firing starts."

"I'm not sure at all about that. In any case, do the best you can to sober them up. They won't be thinking about picking berries tomorrow. Many of them won't be thinking anything, for they'll be dead."

South said steadily, "I think we have a sound battle plan for whipping the Rebels, sir."

"I think we'd better have. We'll be fighting on their grounds. So we'll hit them in the middle, South, as we decided. Then you will take your troops around to our right and close in on their left flank. They won't be expecting that."

"No, and we'll succeed, General. You'll see."

Senator Monroe Collins and his wife left Washington in a buggy.

The senator told his wife, "We'll enjoy watching the Rebels take a pounding."

"But won't it be dangerous?" Minnie Collins asked. She was a rather shy woman, and the very thought of getting close to a battle frightened her.

"It'll be all right, Minnie. Our boys will run over them. They'll be running like rabbits!"

"How can you be sure, Monroe?"

"Why, our army is the best. The Rebels are just a bunch of ragtag farmers and lazy slave owners. Our men are real soldiers. We'll get to see the Rebels turn and run. It'll be something to tell our grandchildren about."

Judith Henry lay dying in her bed. She was an eighty-year-old woman who had been sick for a considerable time. Her daughter hovered over her asking, "How do you feel, Mother?"

"Not well, daughter."

"You'll be better soon. We've sent for the doctor."

Judith Henry listened then asked weakly, "What is the noise?"

"Oh, there are some soldiers, but they won't come near us."

The Henry house was not important in itself. It was a small whitewashed house not far from Young's Branch, a small creek only a few miles away from the Centerville Turnpike. It had been a peaceful valley, but on this day an air of doom hung over it.

The dying woman lay as still as if she had already passed, but she still breathed. Suddenly a terrific explosion struck the house, and a shell killed Judith Henry. A moment later her body was riddled with bullets as the house burst into flames.

Henry Settle was proud of his new uniform. He was a young farmer from Pennsylvania who had enlisted for three months against the advice and begging of his mother. Now he was a part of the Union Army that advanced toward Bull Run Creek.

Suddenly ahead there was a tremendous explosion as a cannon went off and muskets began to crackle like firecrackers. Settle looked around and saw that he was not the only one in shock. Many of his friends in the company had slowed down; some had stopped, staring ahead blankly. They had sung songs all the way, marching to Manassas, and had laughed about how they would throw the Rebels back and take over Richmond. Then the war would be over.

On both sides of Settle, men began to drop, and there were cries of agony and screams of fear as the officers pressed the men forward. For the first time, Henry Settle knew that he was in a deadly position. He tried to swallow, but his throat was dry. Just ahead of him he saw his best friend, Arnie Hunter, shot to bits by musket fire and fall facedown into the new spring grass.

"I can't get killed," Settle whispered. "I've got to go back and take care of Ma." But even as he uttered this, a cannonball hit him and killed him instantly. He fell, and no one even stopped.

Across Bull Run Creek, the Confederates were holding fast, but there were many casualties. Major Roberdeau Wheat, the tough commander of the Louisiana Tigers, had been shot down. He was carried to a field hospital, and the doctor had said, "I'm sorry, Major Wheat. You have been shot through both lungs. There's no way you can live."

Wheat grunted, "I don't feel like dying yet."

"No one's ever lived shot like this."

"Then I will be the first," Wheat said. And so it was. Roberdeau Wheat lived. Even as he argued with the doctor, he saw Jeb Stuart's cavalry riding through the field hospital. Finally, General Beauregard had called them in to hit wherever the firing was hottest.

Clay had gotten into the habit of bringing his company up as close behind Colonel Stuart as he could. He had ridden until he was beside Stuart and his aides as they advanced toward the battle.

Jeb was riding an enormous black gelding, thick in girth but fast. At full gallop they topped a little rise and faced an infantry regiment, scarlet-uniformed Zouaves.

"They may be some of the Louisiana Tigers, sir," Clay said. "Many of them wear those baggy breeches."

Jeb spurred forward almost into the midst of them, followed closely by Clay. Stuart shouted, "Don't run, boys. We're here."

At that moment a flag in the midst of the regiment unfurled and snapped in the hot breeze. It was the Stars and Stripes.

Jeb's eyes widened, but in a flash he drew his sword and yelled, "Charge!"

Clay drew his saber and slashed at the white turbans of the men in blue and scarlet.

The Yankees, a New York Zouave regiment, panicked and scattered in confusion, yelling as they ran, "The Black Horse!" Their cries echoed over the field. They left eleven guns unsupported, and a Virginia infantry regiment hurried forward to turn them back toward the Union lines.

Jeb and his men rode on, shouting madly, into the thick of battle.

The Federals watched as, time after time, the Rebel line had formed, hardened, and had run through the Union lines, capturing artillery and overrunning and capturing their supply wagons. Thomas Jackson had stood like a "stone wall," and they had smashed themselves against his infantry time and time again. The Black Horse, with the larger-than-life Jeb Stuart at the head of the column, slashed through the blue lines, here and there, wherever it seemed the Yankees stood firm.

"Where are our reserves?" the men demanded. They were wearied by thirteen hours of marching on the road, they were angry and disheartened, and finally men began to cry, "We've been sold out!" The rumor spread, and the Union troops faltered and then panicked. They turned and fled past officers on horseback, who were flailing with their sabers, urging them to stand. But the men were now afraid, and fear spread like a plague among them. They ran.

Senator Monroe Collins and his wife suddenly were surrounded by crowds of frightened men who had thrown their weapons down. "The Rebels are coming!" was the cry. "The Black Horse, they'll run us over! Save yourselves!"

Collins managed to get his buggy turned around, but on the bridge across Bull Run, it suddenly broke down and blocked the fleeing pack of soldiers. Men splashed through the creek. Behind them Rebel officers shouted orders: "Chase 'em, boys! Run 'em down!"

Jefferson Davis came to the battlefield and met General Thomas Jackson, who after this day was called "Stonewall." Jackson was covered with dust, but his blue eyes flashed like summer lightning. "Sir, give me ten thousand men, and I can be in Washington tomorrow."

Davis was ready, but his commanding officers disagreed. One said, "Sir, our men are weary. The Yankees will have a guard around Washington. We can't march that far and then fight our way through."

And so the battle ended as Jefferson Davis said, "We've come as far as we can. We've won the battle. The Yankees are whipped."

But even as he spoke, he doubted. And again he prayed.

CHAPTER SEVENTEEN

Winter had come, and the armies went into winter quarters. Both North and South planned campaigns for the spring, but during the bitter cold months, they mostly just brooded at each other across the Potomac River.

The 1st Virginia Cavalry was quartered just south of Manassas. Sitting at a desk inside the farmhouse that he had rented for himself and his family, Jeb Stuart looked out the window. The sun falling on the white blanket caused the snow to glitter like tiny diamonds, and for a while he sat, enjoying the sight, but then he sighed and turned back to the figures on a paper he had before him. He continually pestered the commissary in Richmond for more supplies and equipment for his men.

But the Confederacy was poor. Stuart also felt the pinch of inflation, for the Northern blockade of the Southern states in the East was working all too well. The salary of a brigadier was very modest, and Jeb worried, because even the necessaries of life—food, clothing, and medicine—were getting harder and harder to come by. He was pleased that his brother, William Alexander Stuart, owner of the White Sulphur and the Salt Works, among other enterprises, had voluntarily ensured Stuart's life, making Flora the beneficiary.

He heard Flora singing softly, and he left his office and went to the bedroom. He found Flora bending over Little Flora, who was lying in their bed, pale and thin. "Is she any better, my dearest?"

Flora turned to him, fear in her eyes. "No, she isn't. As a matter of fact, Jeb, I think she may be worse."

"I'll have the doctor come by and look at her again."

"I wish you would. Still, it seems that the doctors can't help her."

Moving over to Flora, Jeb put his arm around her then reached down with his free hand and touched the child's brow. "She's burning up with fever," he murmured. Although Jeb Stuart feared nothing on the field of battle, this was a fear that gnawed at him constantly.

They stood together looking down at the child who meant so much to them, and then Flora said, "I hope Jimmy won't catch anything like this."

When their son had been born, Jeb and Flora had been glad to name him after her father, Phillip St. George Cooke Stuart. But after the Confederacy had formed and Colonel Cooke had stayed with the Union, Jeb had staunchly refused to have his son bear Cooke's name. They had changed it to James Ewell Brown Stuart Jr., and they called him Jimmy.

"We'll pray, Flora. God's will be done," Jeb said, but his usually booming, jovial voice was quiet and sad.

The entire South had been jubilant over the victory at Bull Run, and the people were still living on that excitement. They had won the battle, but the cost had been high. The hospitals in Richmond were filled, and many wounded soldiers had been taken into private homes.

Jacob told Chantel, "I've been thinking, daughter, that it's time for us to do something for God."

"What is that, Grandpere? I thought we were doing something for God," Chantel replied.

"We are, and I'm very proud of you. But I think we should start making regular visits at the hospital. I can get together some things to give the poor wounded men, perhaps, and you could help me give them out and talk to them."

"They love candy, they do," Chantel said. Sweets were hard to come by these lean days.

"We'll take all we have, and this afternoon you and I will make our visits. Perhaps we could lead one of the wounded men to the Lord. Wouldn't that be wonderful?"

"Yes, it would, Grandpere."

The field hospitals, during the summer, had been mostly a series of large tents pitched just outside of Richmond. But when the winter had come, and the hospitals were full, one of the large warehouses had been taken and converted into a field hospital. Cots were lined against the walls, and every bed was filled. A large woodstove was burning, throwing off a great heat, but it reached only within a few feet of the great barn-like structure with the soaring roof. It was not enough to heat the whole building, and most of the wounded were under all the blankets that could be found for them.

"Why don't you start over there with that row of men. I'll take this one," Jacob said. He smiled. "I know they'd rather see a pretty young woman than me, but tomorrow I will see them, and you can take this side. Try to encourage them all you can, child."

Chantel, wearing her vivandiere uniform, was a little apprehensive, but her heart went out to the lines of men, many of them terribly wounded. She stopped at the first bed.

A young man looked up and asked, "Are you a soldier, miss?"

"Oh no, I'm a female sutler, a vivandiere. This is my uniform, though, for ma grandpere and I serve the army. Do you like candy?"

"Yes ma'am, I purely do."

"Good. I like candy, too, me." She reached into the paper sack, brought out a peppermint candy, and handed it to him.

Hungrily he popped it into his mouth. He was pale and

obviously had taken a severe wound in the shoulder. He sucked on the sweet and said, "I always loved sweets. Reminds me of home. My mama used to make taffy for me. Sure wish I had some taffy," he said wistfully.

"Where is your home, soldier?"

"I come from Bald Knob, Arkansas."

"That's a funny name."

"Yes. Everybody laughs at that, but that's where I'm from." He sucked on the candy thoughtfully. "Don't guess I'll ever see it again."

"Perhaps you will," Chantel said. "The good God may bless you and heal you."

"Are you a Christian, ma'am?"

At that instant Chantel fervently wished she was a believer, but she knew she had to be honest. "No—no. I don't understand this, me. I'm not like Grandpere and other people who know the Lord, so well, so easy."

"Oh," the young man murmured, obviously disheartened. "I don't understand it too good, either."

"Ma grandpere is a Christian, and I know he would like to talk to you. Would you let me get him?"

His white face and dull eyes brightened a little. "That would be good, miss. I'd like to talk to him."

Chantel turned and walked across the aisle between the two rows of beds. "Grandpere," she said, "the young man over there wants to know about the Lord. Will you come and talk to him?"

"Why, certainly I will. That's why I'm here." Jacob turned, and Chantel walked with him. "What's your name, young man?" he asked.

"Clyde Simmons, sir. I come from Arkansas. Caught this"— he grimaced and motioned to the stained bandage across his abdomen—"in a skirmish just off the river last week. It's not getting any better, and the doctors don't say much. Kinda makes me think I may not make it."

"None of us knows about that. I may go before you," Jacob said gently. "But the important thing is to be ready to go."

"I know, sir. I've heard preachers, but it never took, it seemed like. Somehow just never seemed like the time." He sighed deeply. "Seemed like I always thought there'd be more time."

"One thing about God, though, son," Jacob said firmly, "is that He always has time. It's never too late to come to Him."

Chantel brought a straight chair. "Sit down beside him, Grandpere. You'll get tired. I'll go visit some others, me, while you talk."

She continued her progress, stopping at each bedside and handing out sweets, but she kept looking back, and once she saw that her grandfather's face was lit up as he talked, he was so happy.

She turned another time and saw that her grandfather was motioning for her. She went to him, and he said, "Good news, daughter! Clyde here has confessed his sins, and he has asked Jesus to come into his heart. He's a saved man now. I'm going to give him one of the gospels of John that we brought." He took the small booklet out and handed it to Clyde Simmons, who took it and then said sadly, "I can't read, sir."

"Well, my granddaughter here will read to you, won't you, Chantel?"

"Yes. I'd be glad to, Grandpere."

"Good," Jacob said with satisfaction. "I'll go visit a few of the other men before we go."

Chantel sat down and opened the Gospel of John. She began to read. " 'In the beginning was the Word, and the Word was with God, and the Word was God. . . .' "

As Chantel left the hospital with Jacob, she said, "I'm so tired. Why am I so tired, me? I haven't done any real work."

"It is a strain, daughter," Jacob admitted. "We see all these poor boys, some of them have little hope of living, and it not only tires our spirits, it drains us physically. But God's going to bless us. Three of the young men asked Jesus into their hearts today. We'll go get a good rest, and then tomorrow we'll bring something else to them."

"You know, we have the supplies, Grandpere. I can make gingerbread."

"Yes, we have plenty of supplies," he agreed. "Tomorrow you take enough to make gingerbread for all of them, Chantel. The hospital cooks will help you."

Chantel nodded. "I would like to see Mr. Simmons again. A friend of his said he'd read to him. That's good. He looks so ill, Grandpere. Do you think he'll live?"

"I'm not sure, but I know if he dies, he'll be in the arms of Jesus. Isn't that wonderful?"

Chantel felt only sadness at the possibility of the death of the sweet young man. Again she thought, *I don't understand Grandpere, the joy he has with all this death and blood and sorrow. Sometimes it seems like the good God lets ver' bad things happen to people. But then, I'm just an ignorant girl. . . .*

The next day Chantel took the supplies for gingerbread to the hospital kitchen: flour, sugar, eggs, cinnamon, ginger, and cloves.

A very large black woman was the head cook, and she asked, "Where you come up wid all dis, little girl? I didn't think there was a speck of cinnamon to be had in the South!"

"Ma grandpere, he has it," she answered. "For him, the good God provides."

They baked great trays of the soft, mouthwatering, sweet bread, filling the whole hospital with the spicy aroma.

By early afternoon, when Jacob arrived and Chantel and the cooks brought the trays into the hospital, the men were jolly and called out to her, "Our vivandiere! Hello, Miss Chantel. We knew it was you, bringing us gingerbread."

Chantel blushed and helped hand out gingerbread to all the men. Then she went to Clyde Simmons's bedside and said, "Hello, Mr. Simmons. I thought you might like for me to read to you a little today."

"Sure would. My friend Gabe here, he read some to me. But I know we'd all like to hear you read again, Miss Chantel."

Chantel looked at his friend, a short, solid young man with an open friendly face, who was missing a leg and was on crutches. "That was good of you to read to your friend," she told him.

Someone brought her a chair, and she sat down and began to read. A small crowd of the walking wounded gathered, and other men sat on the beds close around her.

Chantel was reading Psalm 119. From time to time she looked up, and her heart felt a deep and profound sadness. They were mostly young faces, most of them filled with apprehension and fear. She well knew that the reputation of military hospitals was terrible. More men died of septic infection, or diseases that the wounded passed around, than on the field of battle. She let none of the grief show in her face, however, and she continued reading.

There was a commotion at the door, and they all looked up. A group of officers came in. The contrast they made with the sick and injured bedridden men was startling—they all seemed tall and strong, bringing in the stringent smell of the winter outdoors, shaking the snow from their coats and stamping their boots to clear the mud from them. The doctors came to speak to them, standing in a group just inside the door.

Chantel saw Clay Tremayne and Armand Latane among them.

The group broke up, and the officers began to roam among the beds, looking for their men.

Clay came to Clyde Simmons's bedside, greeted the men around her, and then said, "Hello, Chantel. I had heard that you were a hospital angel now."

"Hello, Clay," she said, a little embarrassed but pleased. "Grandpere and me, we visit the men, bring them things. I've been reading to them, me."

"She brought us a bunch of gingerbread, Lieutenant," the man in the bed next to Simmons said. His eyes were bandaged, and his body was thin, but he was animated, which pleased Chantel.

"You come to visit one of your men, Clay?" Chantel asked.

"Yes, I'm here to see Private Mitch Kearny. He's in my company."

"Oh yes, I've met Mr. Kearny, me. He's just down the row here. I'll take you to him."

She handed the Bible to one of the men and said, "Can you read, soldier?"

"Yes ma'am, I can. Real good."

"Well, you take up where I left off while we go see the lieutenant's friend." The two moved down the aisle, and three beds from the end Chantel stopped. "You have a visitor, Mr. Kearny."

The wounded man was middle-aged and looked like he had been a farmer. He had lost an arm, which was a worry, as so many amputees died after the surgery.

"You're looking good, Mitch," Clay said. "Did you get some of that gingerbread?"

"Sure did. It was good, too. Thank you again, Miss Chantel."

Clay told him some of the news of what the unit was doing and told him of some of Jeb Stuart's patrols.

Chantel saw that Kearny seemed to be cheered, sitting up straighter in the bed, his eyes brighter than before. She looked around and observed that all of the men that the officers were visiting seemed heartened.

Armand Latane came over to them, and Clay introduced him to Mitch Kearny. Kearny saluted with his left hand. "Heard about you Louisiana Tigers, Captain. Heard Major Roberdeau Wheat walked away from getting shot in the chest. Story goes that he was hit in both lungs, but he argued with the doc and was so ornery that he lived through it."

Armand laughed, his white teeth flashing. "Us Cajuns, we're too mean to die. Except for Miss Chantel, here. She's too sweet to die."

"You're a Cajun, Miss Chantel?" Kearny asked. "I wondered, with the way you talk and all. It's pretty, I mean."

"Ah yes, we're all pretty, too, Cajuns," Armand said airily. He turned to Chantel. "I find myself in dire need of some new gold buttons, ma'am. Would a vivandiere have anything like that in her sutler's wagon?"

"Of course, Armand," she said, rolling her eyes. "Only you still have money to buy gold buttons, you."

"Then with your permission, I'll stop by later and collect." Armand then added mischievously, "You can show me how to sew them on, Chantel, cherie?"

"You know I'll sew them on for you," Chantel said dismissively. "Now get along with you, and go speak to Grandpere."

With a courtly bow, he went down the line of beds to where Jacob sat talking with a man with his arm in a sling and his head bandaged.

Chantel turned back to Clay, who was watching Latane with smoldering dark eyes. "What is it, Clay? You and Armand, you don't have a falling-out, do you?"

"No," he muttered. "Not yet." He said his good-byes to Mitch Kearny, then asked Chantel in a low voice, "Would you walk me out?"

"Of course," Chantel said, and she took his arm as they walked slowly to the door.

"I thought you might want to know," he said with some difficulty, "General Stuart's La Petite is very sick."

"Oh no," Chantel said, distressed. "What is it she has, poor baby?"

"The doctors say it's typhoid."

Chantel pressed her eyes shut for a moment. "Typhoid," she repeated softly with dread. "Such a terrible sickness, yes. Is she—?"

Clay finished her unspoken question. "They don't think she's going to make it. You know, Chantel, you really helped Miss Flora when she was ill. I think you were a real comfort to her. Maybe you could stop by and talk to her. She's glad to be with General Stuart, of course, but she doesn't have any real close friends in Richmond. I think she'd be glad to see you."

"I will see her," Chantel said. "Maybe I can help with La Petite." She sighed. "I don't know about losing a child, me. But I know about losing ma mere. Sometimes friends can help when no doctors can."

Chantel went to the Stuart house, unhitching faithful Rosie and riding her the two miles to the little farmhouse. She passed through the hastily erected log huts that Stuart's men had built for the winter, and many of them called out to her as she passed. They never called out rude or suggestive things anymore. They had all come to know their vivandiere and were as proud of her as if she were a star on the stage. Sutlers, particularly beautiful vivandieres, were very scarce in the blockaded Southern army.

She reached the house, and after she knocked on the door, it was a long time before it opened.

She saw that Flora had dark shadows under eyes, and her hair had not been carefully done as it usually was. Her blue eyes were shadowed with weariness and sadness. But at the sight of Chantel, they brightened a little. "Chantel, how wonderful it is to see you. I've been thinking about you. Please come in."

Flora led her into the sitting room, seated herself on the sofa, and patted the seat next to her for Chantel to sit by her. "I've been thinking about you, because you're such a wonderful nurse. When I first came to Richmond, I was so ill. I don't know what we would have done without you, Chantel. And now. . .our La Petite is ill."

"Yes, Miss Flora, Lieutenant Tremayne tells me this. I came to see you and to see La Petite, sweet baby. How is she doing?"

Flora sighed and dropped her gaze. "She's not well at all, Chantel. She is very sick."

Jeb came in and kissed Flora then smiled rather weakly at Chantel. "How are you, Miss Chantel? It's so kind of you to come by and see my Flora. She gets lonely here in camp sometimes."

"I brought some chamomile, for tea," Chantel said. "And honey, too. Maybe La Petite, she can drink some tea. Even when you're very sick, it makes you feel better."

She and Flora made tea; then Flora took her in to see La Petite. She slept, her body wasted away to that of an infant. The little girl's eyes fluttered open once, and she smiled a little at Chantel. Chantel took her fevered hand and murmured little endearments to her. But Little Flora never stayed awake for long, and in a few minutes she had passed out again.

Chantel could see very clearly that the little girl could not live long. She offered to help Flora in any way she could and asked if there was anything that she and her grandfather could bring them.

In a distant voice, Flora answered, "Thank you, Chantel, but there's nothing in this world that you could bring to help La Petite now. But you come back, please. She was glad to see you, I think."

She left, deeply saddened. It was things like this that confused Chantel about the Lord. How could He take a sweet, innocent little child like La Petite? How could He do such a terrible thing to good Christian people like Miss Flora and Jeb Stuart? Chantel didn't know. She thought that she would never know.

Two days later little Flora Stuart died. The doctors did all they could, but typhoid was a devastating disease with a high mortality rate, especially among children.

Chantel and Jacob called on the Stuarts.

Flora was so devastated she could hardly speak, holding herself stiffly erect on the sofa in the sitting room, her eyes haunted and filled with sorrow.

Jeb stood by her, his hand on her shoulder. "God has taken our little girl, Mr. Steiner. But Flora and I know that she is with Him, and she suffers no more. And one blessed day we'll see her again in heaven."

"It is a good thing to know the Lord Jesus in these terrible times," Jacob said, his eyes glinting with unshed tears. "He alone can comfort us in this dark night of the soul. She rejoices, General Stuart, and those who are left behind must know that and rest in Him. May the peace and blessings of God be on this house, and on you both, now and forever."

When they left, Chantel found that she was almost angry. "I'll never understand God, Grandpere," she said in a low, tense voice.

"It seems that if ever He would bless someone, He would bless Miss Flora and General Stuart."

"And He has blessed them," Jacob said gently. "The Bible tells us that when someone dies, we must rejoice. I know that we cannot be happy and carefree on the outside. But when we know the Lord Jesus, our hearts have joy and peace always. Even when a child dies. Because we know that this earth, this old terrible world, is not our home. Our home is in heaven, a glorious place, where there are no more sorrows, no more tears. General Stuart and Miss Flora may be here, yes, and they will grieve. But their hearts are already at home with Little Flora and with the Lord Jesus. There they will always be, forever, and they will be at peace."

CHAPTER EIGHTEEN

The burden of office lay heavily on Abraham Lincoln, and not the least of his problems was General George McClellan. McClellan was a small man and was already called Little Napoleon by some of his admirers.

In all truth, he had more confidence in himself than any man ought to have. It was revealed in a letter to his wife in which he wrote: "The people think me all powerful, but I am becoming daily more disgusted with this administration. It is sickening in this extreme and makes me feel heavy at heart when I see the weakness and unfitness of those in charge of our military."

The president often discussed military strategy and tactics with McClellan, but he saw quickly that McClellan had little confidence in anyone's opinion except his own.

Once a secretary, who had overheard McClellan speaking arrogantly to Lincoln, said angrily, "The man is insolent! You need to get rid of him, Mr. President."

Lincoln had said merely, "I will hold McClellan's horse if he will only bring us success."

A year had passed since Bull Run, and there had been minor

battles, but only one major battle in the western theater, the Battle of Shiloh. It had been bloody, and as usual the Confederates had been outnumbered, but they had driven the Yankees back, licking their wounds.

Lincoln was anxious to move on, and he had pressed his views upon McClellan, telling him, "General, you need to follow through on the same plan we had for the first attack. We could still go right through Bull Run, and we have a powerful enough army now to overcome any resistance."

McClellan flatly refused to admit that this plan had any virtues. He stubbornly insisted that Lincoln was not a military man, and he must leave the disposition of great armies, and the military plans, to the generals. In particular, to him.

For their part, the South had been lulled into a sense of false security by their victory at Bull Run, although strategically they had accomplished little. The only grand strategy that was working at this time was the North's blockade.

The Southern economy went downhill quickly. Meat was fifty cents a pound, butter seventy-five cents, coffee a dollar fifty cents, and tea ten dollars. All in contrast to cotton, which had fallen to five cents.

The South was hemmed in, and the blockade was working all too well. Their only hope was to be recognized by England or a foreign power that would encourage the peace party in the North to declare the war over.

Jeb was sitting on the floor playing with little Jimmy. He doted on the boy, who at the age of two was definitely showing a precocious side. He was an attractive child, resembling his father in being sturdy and having the same russet-colored hair. Jeb was throwing the boy up in the air and catching him, and little Jimmy was laughing and gasping for breath.

"Jeb, you stop that! You're going to hurt that baby," Flora said sternly.

"No. He likes it, don't you, Jimmy?"

"Yes!" he said. At the age of two, he had learned a few words, and now he said, "Throw! Throw!" which was his signal for his father to toss him up into the air.

Flora came over, took little Jimmy away, and said, "You get up off the floor now, General. Dinner is on the table."

"All right, sweetheart." Jeb came to his feet in one swift motion and followed her into the dining room. He sat down at the table and said, "Mashed potatoes and fried chicken. What could be better?"

Flora put Jimmy in the improvised high chair then sat down.

Jeb at once bowed his head and prayed. "Lord, we thank Thee for this food and for every blessing. Bless us and our Glorious Cause, and we ask that You give us victory. In the name of Jesus, we ask this. Amen." Immediately he dumped a huge dollop of mashed potatoes on his plate and picked up both wings. "My favorite part. You can have the white meat, Flora."

Flora fixed a plate for little Jimmy and let him dabble in his mashed potatoes, trying to keep the mess to a minimum. Flora fixed her own plate and began to eat, but she looked up to say, "Jeb, I'm so happy that you haven't been in any more big battles."

"Well, I expected there to be more, but since Bull Run, all has been quiet, here at least. There have been some actions over to the west, but out there they taught the Yankees a lesson, too."

"I hope they never come."

Jeb's mouth was stuffed full, and he talked around it. "Oh, they're coming, Flora. McClellan's built up an enormous army, well equipped. Our spies have kept tabs on him, and the latest word is that they are already beginning to move. We know they're on their way. We just don't know exactly where they're going to cross into Virginia. Yet."

Flora took a small bite from the breast, chewed it thoughtfully, and then asked, "Jeb, do you think General Johnston is the right man to lead the army?"

President Davis had appointed General Joe Johnston as commander of the Southern army. He was a slow-thinking, slow-moving, cautious man. For a moment, Jeb hesitated, and she could see that he was troubled. "Sometimes I think he's timid, Flora, and that's not what we need. We need men like Stonewall Jackson. I wish we had a dozen like him! Look what he's done in the valley."

Indeed, Stonewall Jackson's Valley Campaign had been the only bright spot in the Confederate military picture. With one small army, Jackson had moved from place to place, traveling hundreds of miles on foot so that his men were called "Jackson's Foot Cavalry." He had singly defeated two Union armies.

Jeb went on, "General Jackson is the most popular man in the Confederate Army right now. Jackson scared Lincoln so bad that he pulled back two different armies so we won't have to fight them." When he finished, Jeb got to his feet and said, "I've got to go, sweetheart. I don't know what will happen, but you'll be all right here. We'll never let them get to Richmond." He leaned over, kissed her, and then picked up Jimmy and held him. "You be a good boy, Jimmy. Be good like your mother. Not like your wicked old father." He kissed the boy, handed him to Flora, and then left.

❧

"The Yankees are coming!"

The spies had brought word that McClellan's huge force was headed up the peninsula, and Jeb and his cavalry were in the thick of the fighting. As usual, Clay's 2nd Richmond Company stayed close behind their general.

The action was bloody and was called by some the Battle at Fair Oaks and by others Seven Pines. Both sides lost many men—dead, wounded, and captured.

But the most significant event was that General Joseph Johnston was severely wounded. Jefferson Davis, without hesitation, made the wisest move he had made since his inauguration as president.

He appointed Robert E. Lee to head the Southern forces. Lee at once took charge and renamed the army the Army of Northern Virginia.

❧

"General Stuart, I have a task for you."

Jeb had been called to General Lee's headquarters, which was nothing more than a simple soldier's tent. The two men had been good friends when Stuart studied at West Point. Jeb's eyes were fiery blue as he said, "I'm anxious for action, General Lee. Just tell me what to do."

Lee studied Jeb Stuart carefully. "I want you to make a movement in the enemy rear. Inspect their communications, take cattle and grain, burn any Federal wagon trains that you find."

"Yes, sir."

"General, the utmost vigilance on your part will be necessary. The greatest caution must be practiced to keep you from falling into the enemy hands. And let me remind you that the chief object of your expedition is to gain intelligence for the guidance of future movements. Should you find that the enemy is moving to his right or is so strongly posted as to make your expedition inopportune, you will return at once."

Jeb Stuart could not conceal his joy. He was like a small boy as he slapped his gloves against one hand and said, "General, if I find a way open, I'll ride all the way around him. My father-in-law is in charge of their cavalry, you know. I've never forgiven him for going with the North, so I'm going to show him up."

Stuart left and handpicked twelve hundred men, including Robert E. Lee's son, nicknamed Rooney. He rode at once to share the news with his men, and he made a gallant figure. His gray coat was buttoned to the chin, he carried a saber and a pistol in a black holder, and he wore his polished thigh-high cavalry boots with the golden spurs. As always, a black ostrich plume was stuck in his hat, floating above the bearded features. His eyes were brilliant, and he made the perfect picture of a dashing cavalier.

As the troop left, one officer called out, "When will you be back, Stuart?"

"It may for years. It may be forever." Stuart laughed and spurred his horse forward. The troop thundered around McClellan's men. Several times Federal horsemen appeared and tried to make a fight of it, but Stuart's yelling riders simply swallowed them up.

Clay was watering Lightning when they had stopped to rest their horses. He watched Stuart, who was contemplating the country ahead of him. "What next, General?"

"Well, we've already come eighteen miles southeast of Hanover Courthouse. The enemy is going to expect me to go back to camp, I know. I've already learned what General Lee sent me to learn. The right flank of McClellan is in the air, and there are no trenches on the ridges on the west. The enemy could be struck in the flank by an infantry assault."

Clay did not speak; he merely watched and listened. Finally he saw Jeb Stuart straighten up and order, "Move the column ahead at a trot."

"Yes, sir." The pace picked up and they soon became a group of cheerful horsemen. From time to time they had to spur their horses when pickets appeared and took after them, and they had a couple of skirmishes.

But in the end, Jeb Stuart completely encircled McClellan's enormous army, something that had never even been thought of, much less accomplished, before.

When Jeb Stuart rode in with his men, he gave his report in such colorful phrases and in rhetoric that was almost epic in praise of his officers. "Their brave men behaved with coolness and intrepidity in danger, unswerving resolution before difficulties. . . . They are horsemen and troopers beyond praise."

General Lee's order in reply reflected the pride of the command in Stuart's feat. "The general commanding announces with great satisfaction to the army the brilliant exploit of Brigadier General J. E. B. Stuart. . .in passing around the rear of the whole Federal army, taking a number of prisoners, and destroying and capturing stores to a large amount. . . . The general commanding takes great pleasure in expressing his admiration of the courage and skill so conspicuously exhibited throughout by the general and the officers and men under his command."

Word spread like wildfire across the entire Confederacy, and everywhere was heard the name of Jeb Stuart. He was a hero, and the newspapers could not find language elevated enough.

"You're going to get bigheaded, I'm afraid," Clay said, grinning at Jeb as the two of them were riding to check on the men.

"Aw, if I do, Flora will take me down a peg or two. We showed those Yankees though, didn't we, Tremayne?"

"Yes you did, sir. What do you think will happen now?"

Jeb stared to the north, where the vast Federal armies were waiting. Clay saw that he was more serious than he had ever seen him. "We're going to be hit with an army of a hundred and sixty thousand men, Lieutenant. We're outnumbered, clearly five to one. It's as I said all along, we can't match the Yankees man for man. But we will always best them in daring and courage."

At that moment, Clay Tremayne saw what it was in Jeb Stuart that made men follow him right into the mouth of guns, straight toward almost certain death. There was that quality in him that few men had. Confidence, courage, audacity—it was a mixture of all of these, plus a joy in battle that few men ever experienced.

Clay observed, "That lesson you taught them, General Stuart. You've embarrassed and humiliated McClellan, and he'll throw everything he's got at us."

"And we will stop them, Lieutenant. God will surely lead us to victory."

❧

Historians writing about what came to be called the Seven Days Battle have great difficulty. They were days of confusion, of missed or misunderstood orders, of men wandering, lost in the unmarked countryside.

McClellan's army got caught on the wrong side of the river so that he was never able to bring his full force together at once to hit the Confederates—or so he maintained afterward.

The Confederates, on the other hand, were not accustomed to the tactics, and the sometimes vague orders, of Robert E. Lee. From the first battle to the very last, some colonel or general got confused, and men who should have led failed miserably. Even the great Stonewall Jackson faltered.

In battle after battle, no one was the victor except death and the grave.

Finally the long terrible days wore both armies down. McClellan had had all he could take, and again he ordered a retreat.

Strangely enough, McClellan could have won the battle, and the Civil War could have ended at the Seven Days Battle. But McClellan, for all of his organizational ability and all of his dynamic talk, could not do one thing that a successful military commander must do: he could not send men forward into the fires of battle. This was McClellan's tragic flaw, and Lincoln had seen it before.

Time after time during this Seven Days campaign, McClellan might have defeated the South, but time after time he failed to throw enough forces in to win. He would send men in piecemeal, and they would be cut to pieces, and then he would send in another, equally small part of his army. Never once did he throw the full weight of the Army of the Potomac against the greatly outnumbered Confederates.

So, although no one could have been said to have won the battle, the war was lost for a time to the North and won for a time to the South.

McClellan was pulling his forces out, and they had gathered together on what was called Malvern Hill. Lee and the army were hot on their trail. When they came to the sight of Malvern Hill, Lee looked up and studied the ground. It was not the best place for an attack, but Lee was hungry to destroy it. He turned and said,

"Gentlemen, we will attack."

General Longstreet said, "That's a bad hill. The Yankees are well entrenched. There's no cover."

Lee had unlimited confidence in the Army of Northern Virginia, and now he made one of the two sad mistakes in his military career. "Charge the hill," he said.

There was no choice but to obey. Clay looked up at the hill and said to his corporal, "Some of our boys aren't going to come back from this ride."

"No. You're right. I don't understand General Lee."

"He's too audacious, I think. People don't know that, but he's like a Mississippi riverboat gambler."

The bugle sounded, and Clay spurred his horse. He was in the first line of attack. The guns began to boom from the Federal emplacements. Musket balls were whistling by, and men were falling. Clay rode hard ahead, following Jeb Stuart, ignoring the sights and sounds of sure death all around him, until the retreat sounded.

He was about to turn when a terrible blow struck him in his right arm. He looked down and saw that his sleeve was already covered with blood from shoulder to cuff, and he knew that the arm was shattered. In spite of the pain that almost blinded him, he wheeled Lightning around and rode back by himself.

Thirty minutes later he was in a field hospital, his uniform stripped off his upper body. The doctor was looking down at the arm, and Clay saw his face grow stern. "That arm's got to come off, Lieutenant."

"No, it doesn't."

"You'll get gangrene in it and lose it anyway. Let me do it now."

"No!" In spite of his treacherous weakness, he almost shouted at the doctor.

Then General Stuart loomed over him. "How are you, Lieutenant?" he asked.

"Don't let them take my arm, General," Clay said harshly. "Tell him. I say no."

"A man can soldier with one arm, Tremayne," Stuart said

staunchly. "You'd better let him do it."

"No! I'd rather die. . . ." That was his last word, for he began drifting away into unconsciousness.

Before the blackness closed about him, as if from faraway, he heard the doctor say, "General, we'd better take it while he's out."

"No," Stuart said with sudden decision. "It's his arm, and it's his decision. He may die, but I don't know but that I'd do the same."

All Clay knew then was the darkness.

PART FOUR: CHANTEL & CLAY 1862—1865

CHAPTER NINETEEN

Sometime during the night, Clay struggled out of the black pit of unconsciousness that held him prisoner. There was a window across from him that revealed the moon and stars as they shone brightly, peacefully in the night sky, and he stared at it blankly for a while. His mind slowly and reluctantly swam to the surface.

The room was quiet save for the moanings and mutterings of his fellow patients. He glanced to his right, and there, far down the room, a medic sat at a desk reading a book by the pale yellow light of a lantern.

As he lay there, his mind in that place where it was not yet awake and yet not fully asleep, Clay became slowly aware that something was growing in his mind. It was like a tiny light from somewhere far down a dark road, so dim that it could barely be seen. It grew larger and brighter, and it was not, Clay knew, a physical light, not a real light at all, only something deep within him. But his spirit seemed to glow—there was no other way he could think of it.

As the sensation grew, he relaxed and let his body grow limp. He had kept himself so tense waiting for the next jolt of pain in his arm that every muscle in his body ached sharply. But now a sense of quietness, almost of ease, came to him. His eyelids became heavy, so heavy he could not keep them open, and he slept again.

When he stirred again, and his mind once more started its torturous way to full consciousness, he saw through the window that the dim gray light of morning shone through. With a start, he awakened fully and looked down at his side. His right arm was still there; the doctors had obeyed Jeb Stuart's order. He lay back on his pillow with weak relief.

"How do you feel, Clay?"

Chantel was sitting by his bed. He wondered if she had been sitting there long.

"Hello, Chantel," he murmured. "I—I got shot."

"Yes, I know. Are you thirsty?"

Clay felt a raging thirst. He licked his dry lips and nodded, and she picked up a pitcher on the table beside his bed, half-filled a tumbler, then reached under his head and held it up. The water was sweeter than any drink that Clay had ever had, and when he had drained the glass, she put his head back on the pillow, and he said, "That was good. Thank you, Chantel."

Chantel replaced the glass and turned to look at him, her face grim. "Clay, I've got to talk to you, and you must listen to me."

"What is it?"

"The doctors say that your arm has to be taken. There's no other way."

"No." The word leaped to Clay's lips even before she had finished talking.

"But Clay, they say you may die if you don't. They think they see the gangrene started."

"I'd rather die than be a cripple. I know that's foolish, Chantel, but it's the way I feel."

He saw that her face was fixed in an expression of sadness, and he said, "Don't worry about me. I'm not going to die, Chantel. But even if I do, I'm going to die a whole man."

"But you may die, Clay," she pleaded. "You will leave behind so much—your family, your friends. You will leave Grandpere— and. . .you will leave me."

He stared at her, for Chantel had never expressed any endearments to him, had never shown him anything but common courtesy and politeness. His affection for her had grown much, though he worked hard to deny it, for he had always thought it was hopeless, that he had ruined any chance he might have had with her that night he had so clumsily tried to kiss her. Now she was watching him, her eyes great and dark, and suddenly he could see that she had feelings for him. But his face closed, and he said, "Chantel, I won't let them cut off my arm. You have to understand. I don't want to live like that. I won't live like that."

Chantel pleaded with him. "Many men have lost an arm, a leg, their sight, and they are still good men and happy men. That is not something an arm or an eye makes, Clay. You are a strong, handsome man, and you can be happy, even with one arm."

But Clay merely lay there, his lips drawn tightly together, until she finished. "I don't want to talk about this anymore." He closed his eyes and drifted back into sleep.

Chantel continued her silent vigil, now with a sense of hopelessness. For she had seen that Clay Tremayne would never change his mind.

She went back to the wagon and asked Jacob to talk to Clay, and Jacob agreed at once. She went to the hospital with him but left the two men alone. She talked to others down the line but kept her eye on Clay and Jacob.

She got to one young man, and he said, "You want to get this letter off for me, Miss Chantel?"

"Of course I will, Leonard."

He handed her the envelope and then said, "Maybe you better look over it to see if I spelled everything right." She read the letter quickly and was amused, for it said:

Alf sed he heard that you and hardy was a running together
all the time and he thot he wod just quit having anything

more to doo with you for he thot it was no more yuse. I think
you made a bad chois to turn off as nise a feler as alf dyer and
let that orney, theivin, drunkard, cardplaying hardy swayne
come to see you. He ain't nothing but a thef and a lopeared
pigen toed hellion. He is too ornery for the devil. I will shute
him as shore as I see him.

"Are you sure you want to say this?"

"I purely do. I hate that Hardy Swayne. He's a dead man if he don't leave my sister alone."

Chantel struggled to find something to say. Finally she offered, "Maybe your sister loves him."

"Ain't no sister of mine going to marry up with a no-account skunk like him. She can just find some other man to love."

"But Leonard, a woman can't just switch off love," she said with a passion that surprised her.

"Why can't she?"

"Well, when we love somebody, we can't just stop loving him even if he's not what he should be. What if our mothers, our fathers, stopped loving us when we do wicked things? What if God stopped loving us then?"

Leonard shook his head and said firmly, "God never told nobody to be stupid! Ain't any woman who marries up with Hardy Swayne gonna have a good life. He'll drink and steal and lie and beat her, and she'll have to raise her kids by herself. It's only a stupid woman would ask for that kind of life. Now, ain't that so, Miss Chantel?"

Painfully Chantel thought of her stepfather and wondered for the thousandth time how her mother ever could have married such a man. Resignedly she finally answered, "I—I can't answer that, me. But if you're sure, I'll mail the letter."

"Thank you kindly, Miss Chantel."

Leaving Leonard's bed, Chantel went to visit another young man. She had become very fond of him. His name was Tommy Grangerford, and he was the same age that she was, eighteen years old. He was terribly wounded, a chest wound that very few ever survived. She forced herself to smile brightly. "Hello, Tommy. How are you feeling?"

"Oh, I can't complain."

"You never do."

"Do you have time to sit down and talk to me, Miss Chantel?" he asked hopefully. "I know you're real busy and all, but I've been kind of lonesome."

"I always have time for you, Tommy," she said kindly.

She sat down and for twenty minutes talked to him. From time to time, the terrible pain that racked him would twist him almost into impossible positions, and she would dab the clammy perspiration from his face. Finally, in desperation she went to the medic and asked for more laudanum for him.

"Might not be a good thing, Miss Chantel," the medic said reluctantly. "He's had a lot of it already, and if you give a man too much, he can die."

"He's going to die anyway, he is," Chantel said sadly.

The orderly gave in. "All right, ma'am. Here it is."

She went back and gave Tommy a large dose of the strong drug, and soon he lay his head back on the pillow. His eyes fluttered, and he said softly, "I won't be here long, Miss Chantel. But I'm tired, and I'm ready to go home. You know, in the Bible it says that man will go to his long home. That sounds so good, so restful. My long home. . ."

She waited until his breathing grew deep and even. From his bedside, she could see Clay's bed and her grandfather talking earnestly to him.

After a while, she saw Jacob rise, motioning to her. She came down the ward and glanced at Clay, who was asleep. They left quietly.

When they got outside, Chantel asked anxiously, "What did he say, Grandpere?"

"The same thing he said to you, I'm afraid, daughter. He's got his mind made up that he will not lose that arm. I talked to him, because I know the doctors say he's going to die if they don't amputate, and asked him if he didn't know he must come to the Lord and ask Him for salvation. But," he continued with a sigh, "Clay Tremayne is a stubborn man. He says it would be a cowardly thing to come to God now that he's helpless. I can't make him realize that we're all helpless."

Chantel dropped her head wearily. "Then he is lost."

Jacob patted her arm. "We don't know that, daughter. The good God has His own plan for Clay Tremayne, just as He does for me and for you. We will wait upon God, and we will pray, and we will see."

Two days later, Chantel sat with Tommy Grangerford, for she knew he was dying. It was late, and there was no one with him but Chantel. All of the other patients slept.

They had been talking quietly, and sometimes Tommy drifted off. But once he roused, and his voice, which had been thin and weak and thready, grew stronger. "I never told you how I got saved, did I, Miss Chantel?"

"No, you never have, Tommy."

"Well, I heard a sermon, and it scared me. I was scared to death to face God with all my sins. The next day I was out in the field chopping cotton, and my ma and pa, they were down the row from me. My brothers and sisters were there, and I was doing my best just to think about chopping cotton. But somehow that didn't happen. I knew all of a sudden that God was telling me something, and I couldn't shut it out. I never heard any words, but God told me, *Tommy, this is your last chance. I died for you because I love you. You let Me come into your heart.*"

Tommy shook his head and smiled. "I just couldn't stand it, Miss Chantel. I knelt down right there in the dirt in the cotton field, and I cried out, 'Oh God, I'm a sinner, but I know Jesus died for me. Forgive my sins, please, and come into my heart.'"

"And what happened, Tommy?"

"Well, my ma and pa, and my brothers and my sisters, came rushing to me, but even before they got there I knew something had happened to me. I had been carrying a heavy load, and everything was so dark and miserable. But even as I knelt there in the dirt, I knew that something had happened. That I had something new. I didn't hear voices or see visions. It was all inside me, Miss Chantel. My parents were crying and holding to me, and I was crying. My poor ma and pa had been praying for me all my life."

"And what happened then?"

"Well, I was afraid I'd lose that peace that came to me in that cotton field. But I never did. I went to the Baptist church the next Sunday morning, and I told the preacher I wanted to be baptized, and I was baptized that very day. I started reading the Bible, and people helped me learn how to serve God. We all need someone to help us learn about Him, don't we?"

"Yes, we do," Chantel said thoughtfully.

"Miss Chantel, I think God has put Jacob Steiner in your life to help you find your way to Jesus." His voice grew softer and weaker, and he said, "Listen to your grandfather, Miss Chantel. Don't miss out on Jesus. I want to see you in heaven."

Tommy died an hour later while Chantel was still holding his hand. He had not spoken again, but his last words she knew she would never forget, his urging her to meet him in heaven.

Chantel was broken as she never had been. She held Tommy's still hand and wept, torn by sobs. She began to pray then, and suddenly, in the gloom of that hospital ward, she was aware of what Tommy had said. That God had told him that it was his last chance. A cold fear washed over her. *Maybe this is my last chance.* She tried to pray but could not frame the words.

After a long struggle, suddenly she whispered, "I can't even pray, Lord!" And then it came to her. She thought about her stepfather and how she had hated him—and still did. And then she suddenly knew why she couldn't pray. She remembered a part of the Bible that Jacob had read to her. The Scripture was, "If you forgive men their trespasses, your Heavenly Father will also forgive you: but if you forgive not men their trespasses, neither will your Father forgive ye your trespasses."

The verse went like a sharp knife into Chantel's spirit, and she knew that she could not hang on to that hatred and come into the kingdom of God. She finally bowed her head and whispered, "I've hated my stepfather, Lord, and You say I must forgive him. So the best I can, I forgive him."

It took some time. Chantel struggled, hard, for she had years of bitterness in her spirit. Finally, blessedly, she was able to let go of all the hatred and resentment, and then she called on Jesus, and Jesus came into her heart. She knew it as well as she knew her own name. The hot tears of grief streaming down her face changed to tears of joy, and she began to thank God. Chantel knew that nothing for her could ever be the same again.

Chantel saw Jacob's eyes open, and then he reached out and held her, hugging her with all his feeble strength. She had just awakened him and told him how she had found Jesus.

"Thank God," he kept saying. "Thank the good God."

She said, "I'm going to have to have some help."

"God will send people to help you. Me for one, and if necessary, why, the good Lord will send a mighty angel out of heaven to take care of you, for you are His daughter now and nothing will ever change that."

Chantel was still crying. "I've become a crybaby, me."

"Those are tears of joy, my sweet girl, and there will be many more of them. I thank God that He has reached down and lifted your soul out of sin and put your name in the Book of Life, and He says He will never blot it out, no never, not throughout all eternity."

Chantel listened, and the words soaked into her spirit like balm.

She hardly slept, but at dawn she didn't feel tired. She hurried to the hospital, anxious to tell Clay about her night. As soon as she came through the door she saw one of the doctors, an elderly man named Hardin, motioning to her. She went down the aisle, smiling and greeting Clay and the men, but not stopping to talk.

Dr. Hardin said, "Miss Chantel, I know that Lieutenant Tremayne is your special friend."

"Yes," Chantel said. "We've known each other a long time, you may say."

"I've talked to his family, and they've begged him. And if you're his friend, maybe you can talk some sense into him."

"I doubt it," Chantel said under her breath, but the doctor was still talking, glowering like an angry bulldog.

"The fool just will not let us take that arm off! He acts like he's the only man who ever lost a limb. I know that gangrene is setting in—by now I can tell it a mile away. What I think is we ought to dope him up, and then when he's unconscious, take the arm. He'll be angry when he wakes up, but he'll live. If we don't, then we're going to lose him."

"You can't do that," Chantel said dully. "He may be a fool, but he is a man, and he has made this decision. But I'll try, Doctor. I'll try to talk to him again, me."

Chantel went to Clay then, and he was already angry and upset.

"I saw you talking to Dr. Hardin, and I know what he said. He's already been here nagging me. Once and for all, I say no. I won't do it. Don't talk about it anymore, Chantel."

Chantel had left the hospital soon after talking to Clay, for Jacob was moving the wagon to be closer to General Stuart's headquarters, at his invitation. Chantel helped him lash down all the supplies and pack up their camp.

When they reached their new campsite, as always, Chantel unpacked the big sutler's tent and began to put it up. But by now all of the men knew her and Jacob, and she wasn't allowed to lift a finger. The soldiers put up the tent and helped Chantel and Jacob stock it.

Most of them, by now, had no money at all, but Jacob still gave them things—buttons, needles and thread, wool socks, shoes, warm undershirts. He gave away so much that for the dozenth time Chantel wondered how they ever kept a stock at all.

Then she stayed in camp, talking for hours with the soldiers and to Jacob, who was still rejoicing with her. It was late in the evening when she returned to the hospital.

The slow hours passed, and Chantel knew that it was past midnight. How far past she didn't know. She had prayed until her mind was numb. Clay had fallen into a restless sleep, and she had watched him for a couple of hours, moving restlessly and muttering, his forehead wet with perspiration. Over and over she sponged him with a cool damp cloth, but it seemed that nothing could soothe him.

Finally she leaned forward, folded her hands on his bed, and laid her head down. Her fingers barely touched his side. She began to pray aloud, though in the quietness of the ward she kept her voice to a soft whisper. She whispered, "Oh God, I ask You to help Clay." She waited, for her mind felt strangely blank. She found that it was much harder to pray aloud than in the privacy of one's own heart.

But then thoughts, and the words, came to her. "I was unfair to him. He would never have hurt me, not intentionally. I just had so much anger inside me, Lord, and I couldn't let go of it, and I blamed him for something that maybe, deep down, I wanted him to do. Because I know now that I love him, Lord. Maybe I always have. But now, here we are, we two! Finally I let You save me, and he can't find his way to You. And now he may die. Please, please, have mercy on him, Lord Jesus. Don't make this his last chance."

For a while she was quiet, merely resting, her fingers lightly touching him, and she remembered how she had touched his face that time he had kissed her. She had loved his touch then, even though she had so cruelly pushed him away and made him feel guilty. She sat up then lightly laid her hand on his arm. It felt hot and was stiff with the thick bandages.

Bowing her head, she whispered, "Lord, I don't know much about You, but I know Jacob has read to me that You will heal people. I know there's no hope for Clay in doctors and medicine. But Jacob says nothing is impossible with You, so I'm asking You to heal Clay's arm."

She went on praying for a long time, until she grew so weary she could hardly stay awake. She finally left, still not knowing any answer from God. She felt sadness, but as Jacob had always said, still she knew joy deep in her heart.

Clay had not been asleep the entire time Chantel had been there. He wandered in a dim haze, his mind coming up to half consciousness at times. He had heard some of Chantel's prayers, and they had moved him. Dimly he thought, *Lord, I don't know what to say to You. I don't know You. I don't understand anything about You. But I'm glad Chantel has found You. And about this healing business, You know I couldn't ask You for that. I've no right. But I'm so grateful that she did.*

He knew he had fever, and he was having trouble thinking clearly. *Chantel loves me*, he thought with wonder. *Or was I just dreaming? That is a wonderful, blissful dream. . .but no, I heard her. I know I did.* And he knew at that moment, as hurt as he was, and as hopeless as life seemed to be, he loved her. *And like Chantel told You, Lord. . .I think I always have.*

Clay woke up, and the first thing that he was aware of was that the excruciating pain in his arm had subsided. Then he knew that his fever had passed, for he came instantly, fully awake.

One of the medics had come to change the bandage on his arm. He was a tall, thin man with a good bushy growth of whiskers. His name was Grady Wynn, and he was one of those men who had a great compassion for sick and injured men, a naturally good caregiver.

"Good morning, Lieutenant," Wynn said. "Sorry to wake you up, but it's time to change this bandage. How about, while I'm at it, we get the doctor and let him take this thing off?" he finished brightly.

"No," Clay said automatically, watching him with a newfound alertness.

"Thought not, but it never hurts to—what? What's this?" Wynn said in a shocked voice.

Clay looked at his arm curiously, but Wynn laid the last layer of bandage back on it and said, "Don't move, and for once do what I say, Lieutenant Tremayne. I'll be back."

Wynn moved quickly, and in only a few moments came hurrying back with Dr. Hardin. "Look at that arm, Dr. Hardin," Wynn said. "Just look at it."

The doctor stared at Wynn then stepped forward and lifted the bandages. Clay was watching his face, and he saw the doctor's eyes fly open wide with astonishment.

"Will someone tell me what's going on?" Clay demanded.

"Your arm. It's healing," Dr. Hardin said in a mystified voice.

"Huh?" Clay said, lifting his head up with some effort to look at his arm.

Wynn said, "But I thought gangrene wouldn't heal."

"No. It usually doesn't." Dr. Hardin poked at Clay's forearm then pinched it hard. "You feel that?"

"Yes, it hurts."

Dr. Hardin stared at him. "I pinched you yesterday, and you didn't feel anything."

Hope began to rise in Clay Tremayne. "What are you saying, Doctor?"

Dr. Hardin was a tough man. He had to be. He dealt with death and terrible wounds constantly, every day since the war had begun. His face was a study, and finally he said, "I have no explanation for this, but your arm is healing. Unless I'm mistaken—and I don't think I am—you should be all right, Lieutenant Tremayne."

Clay felt numb, in an odd sort of way. There was a seed of hope and of joy deep inside him, but for a long time he couldn't think, couldn't speak. All he could think of was the prayer that Chantel had prayed for him.

All day he lay there, feeling alternately stunned and deliriously glad. Dr. Hardin came back by several times to lift the now-loose bandage and peer at Clay's arm. He went away shaking his head.

The men heard of it, and they talked among themselves, but they didn't bother Clay. He just stared into space, sometimes smiling, rarely speaking to the doctors and medics. Sometimes he lifted the bandages himself and stared at his arm in disbelief.

Late that afternoon Chantel came. Even before they had said hello, Clay asked, "Have you talked to Dr. Hardin?"

"Yes," she said, and her eyes were glowing. "He says your arm is healed."

"He says he doesn't know how it happened, but I know, Chantel. I was awake, sometimes, when you prayed for me last night. I know this is God's answer to your prayer."

"He really is the good God, Clay." She reached out to take his hand—his right hand, now cool and not at all swollen—and tears showed in her eyes. "I'm so happy for you."

Lifting her hand, he kissed it and said, "Thank you, Chantel, for not giving up on me."

"I wouldn't give up on you, Clay. I never could." She bowed her head slightly and asked so softly that Clay could barely hear her, "And did you hear all my prayers, so?"

"Most of them," he answered. "I think, Chantel, that you are a very wise woman. I think you know that I care for you, that I've cared for you ever since I first saw your face, my angel in that dark time. And I would beg you to have me, right now. . .but I know this—I know that now you'll only have a man of God. And I'm not a man of God. So I won't try to push you, Chantel, as I did once before. I'll never make that mistake again."

Chantel looked up, smiled, and gently smoothed his hair back from his forehead. "God has healed you. You may not know it now, but you already belong to Him. You owe Him a great debt, Clay Tremayne, and once you told me that you are a man that always pays his debts. Oh yes, you owe God now. And one day, like me, you will learn to love Him."

CHAPTER TWENTY

Flora watched her husband and son as they played. Long ago she had given up trying to tell Jeb not to toss the child around as if he were a kitten. As she thought this, she was reminded of those long-ago days, when Ruby had said exactly the same thing to her. For Jeb was like a very large friendly dog, and he played rough. But little Jimmy was like his father. He dearly loved to play "throw."

Jeb was lying flat on his back. Little Jimmy was on his stomach, and as his father held him high, he would laugh and swing his arms as if he were trying to fly. Even though Jimmy had grown, Jeb still tossed him up in the air, over and over again.

Sitting in the rocking chair, Flora watched them, a smile on her face. But then, though she tried to fight it, a nagging worry came to her, as it so often did. She thought about the vulnerability of Jeb on the battlefield. She had heard his men talk about his absolute disregard for danger. It was even in the newspapers that they reveled in stories of General Stuart's fearlessness. He seemed to court it, his horsemen said, riding to the sounds of the guns, waving his saber and laughing as if he were going to a party.

Flora's worry was as unfriendly and persistent as a wound, and there was nothing, it seemed, that she could do to stop it. She had learned to live with it, as women had, both North and South. They sat at home, waiting, hoping for the war to end and their men to return for good—and dreading and fearing the message that they were dead or wounded.

She had been the daughter of an army officer for her first twenty years, but only a few scattered battle actions against the hostile Indians had broken the peace. They had not been serious, and her father had never been wounded. Though of course she had worried about her father, it was nothing like the painful constant thoughts that she could be a widow.

Shaking off her fears, Flora said, "You know, Jeb, I was thinking of taking a walk and going over to see Mr. Steiner and Chantel. I've been hungry for a chocolate cake, and I don't think there's one bit of chocolate in any store in Richmond. But if there is any in this city, Jacob Steiner will have it."

"Throw," Jimmy sternly ordered, and Jeb tossed him high, then caught him and set him on his feet.

"We better escort your pretty mama to the sutler's, or some soldier's likely to snatch her up and keep her," he said, rising quickly. For such a bulky man, he moved swiftly and surely.

"That would never happen, Jeb," Flora said, secretly pleased.

He came to her, grabbed her around the waist, and swung her around, grinning as she protested.

"You put me down right now, Jeb."

"No, I won't do it. I guess I'm just too much in love with you to keep my hands off of you."

In spite of herself, she laughed, and she was almost dizzy when he finally put her down.

Swooping little Jimmy up, he took her arm. "I'd like to see Mr. Steiner, too, and thank him. He's been so good to my men. I don't know how he ever makes a cent. He gives away more than he ever sells, I think."

They went out into the August evening. It was still hot and sultry, but Flora found the evening air pleasant. The light scent of jasmine was carried on a light evening breeze. "I can't imagine where he's getting his supplies, either," she said. "He never seems to run out of anything. Somehow I can't imagine Mr. Steiner as a daring blockade runner."

Jeb laughed, a rich joyous sound that Flora never tired of hearing. "I think he's like Elijah, and that sutler's wagon is his cruse of oil. I think every night God just restocks it for him."

They walked through the forest of tents, the camp of Jeb's 1st Virginia Cavalry. The men stood stiffly and saluted him, and usually Jeb returned it with a joke or a question about them, their supplies, their sweethearts, their ailments.

Jeb put little Jimmy down and let him run around, for he was a favorite among the soldiers. Flora and Jeb walked slowly to let the men see their son, ruffle his thick hair, pick him up and hold him, and tease him about riding out with them on patrol.

Flora's eyes shadowed a little. "Your men—they're such good men. They'd follow you anywhere, Jeb, even to the death."

"I know," he said quietly. "They've done it, time and time again. I'm grateful to God to have such men, to have the honor of fighting alongside them." He glanced at Flora then added awkwardly, "Please don't trouble yourself too much, Flora. You know that all we can do is ask God to give us strength and courage. We're all in God's hands."

She sighed heavily. "I know, Jeb, and I do try. But I can't help worrying about you."

Flora realized Stuart was well aware of her concerns for him, he knew her as she knew him, but like other soldiers, he avoided making any promises he might not be able to keep. Despite what people said about her husband's eagerness for battle and the strange moods that seemed to strike him when the guns sounded and the bugles rang out the charge, she knew he was not unaware of the dangers. He had said once, "All I ask of life is that if I have to die, I do it in a cavalry charge." He was a simple man, no deep thinker, but an excellent officer and leader of men. And a wonderful husband and father.

Now he laughed, as he often did when trying to allay her fears. "I'm too tough to kill, Flora. And even if they did kill me, they couldn't kill me but once. Don't worry. Put it all out of your head."

She knew that her fears were a burden to her husband, and she had to be strong and not add to his cares. She managed to smile up at him. "I can do that, husband, for you. Now, you'd better go get Jimmy. I declare, I think that boy is actually going to set him up on that enormous horse."

Jeb went over to the group of men standing around a big chestnut gelding. Flora watched, and even though she knew what was going to happen, she still rolled her eyes when Jeb swung Jimmy up high and set him on the horse. All the men laughed, and the young man who had been holding Jimmy yelled, "Charge!"

When they reached the sutler's tent, a gentle twilight was cooling down the air.

Jacob and Chantel sat around a small campfire. One of the men had made Jacob a little table out of some spare lumber, and a bright lantern sat on it, bright enough so that he could read.

They greeted the Stuarts happily, and Chantel immediately scooped up little Jimmy. "You've grown, you! Soon you'll pick me up, no?"

He giggled and said, "Throw!"

"I think I'll leave that to your father," Chantel said.

Jacob asked them to stay for a while, but Jeb said, "No, thank you, sir, we won't be staying. We just came out for a short walk. My wife is on a search for chocolate, and since she mentioned it, my mouth's been watering for one of her chocolate cakes. Would you have any such thing in that tent?"

"Oh yes, I believe we do," Jacob said. "Chantel, you know where everything is. Won't you take Miss Flora and give her all the chocolate she needs?"

Chantel and Flora went into the big tent, where goods were stacked all over four long tables that Jacob had bought when they made their semi-permanent camp. "Here's the chocolate, Miss Flora. Powdered or bars."

She still held little Jimmy, whose eyes lit up when he saw some hard candy wrapped in shiny red paper. "Mine," he said, pointing a stubby little finger.

"Jimmy, no, not yours," Flora said firmly.

"Oh, can't he have just one piece, Miss Flora?" Chantel pleaded. "If it's all right with you, of course."

"Well, just one," Flora relented. "And you must add it to the bill. I'll have the bar chocolate, please, and a sack of sugar. What a pleasure, to just walk in and be able to buy them. Jeb and I were saying how hard it is to find even meat and bread these days, much less such luxuries as chocolate and sugar."

"Ma grandpere, he's a good scrounger, the soldiers say," Chantel said proudly.

Flora smiled. "Jeb says he's like Elijah. We think God just restocks your wagon every night."

"I don't know Elijah yet, me," Chantel said, her brow furrowing. "It's going to take a long time to learn all the Bible."

"I don't know of anyone that knows all of it," Flora said lightly, "except for maybe your grandfather. Other than that, how is your new life, Chantel?"

"Good, ver' good," she answered with satisfaction. "I feel so much better now in the hospital with the soldiers. I can talk to them about the Lord, instead of running like a little rabbit for Grandpere."

"It is so good, what you're doing for the men. Those poor wounded boys in the hospital, they're terribly lonesome."

"Yes, and they're afraid," Chantel said a little sadly. "They don't say so, but I can see it in their eyes. They want their mothers or their sisters."

"Yes, but from what I hear, they're always so glad to see their vivandiere. And what about that young captain who was courting you. Have you been able to see him much lately?"

"Captain Latane? Yes, he comes to visit sometimes. He's a Cajun, like me, so we have fun together."

Flora nodded. "Jeb told me about Lieutenant Tremayne, about

how his arm was miraculously healed. You know, that happens sometimes. It's always a mystery, but who can know the mind of God? But I know what good friends you are, and I know you're so happy for him. Jeb was very glad to have him back."

"Yes, it was a miracle, thank the good God. I—I see him, too, sometimes. But General Stuart has kept him busy, I think," she said hesitantly.

Seeing her reluctance, Flora merely smiled and said, "Well, I think this is all we need for now, Chantel. Now, how much do we owe you?"

Chantel shook her head as they left the tent. "Grandpere, he decides about the money. You'll have to ask him, Miss Flora."

Jacob staunchly refused to let Jeb pay him. "It's a gift, General Stuart, for your wife and your fine boy. All I ask is that you send me a piece of your chocolate cake, Miss Flora."

They gathered up little Jimmy, who was sucking on a second piece of candy that Chantel had sneaked him. Jacob and Chantel watched them walk slowly away in the evening shadows, arm in arm.

"He's a fine man, General Stuart," Jacob said. "Rarely does one see such a warrior with such a heart for God."

"She worries for him," Chantel said in a low voice. "It must be hard for your man to be a soldier."

Jacob glanced at her then patted her shoulder. "It's always hard for the ones left behind, daughter. So we must pray that much more."

Stepping out of the wagon the next morning, she found Armand waiting for her with a smile. "Good morning, cherie."

"Hello, Armand. What are you doing this fine morning?"

"I came for some of that special tea you sold me last time."

"You must have really liked it."

"Well, I did. But it's actually for my sergeant. He absolutely loved it and says he won't fight a war without it, him."

Chantel walked toward the tent, which was closed up. Jacob

was still asleep in the wagon. Since they kept it cleared out now, he and Chantel had plenty of room to set up their cots. Armand helped her fold up the tent flaps. She asked, "So. You and your sergeant, are you moving out soon?"

Armand followed her closely as she moved down the tables looking for the tea. "You know, cherie, I think maybe you are a Yankee spy out to get military secrets from me. If you don't let me have my way with you, I'll turn you over to the guard."

He had put his hand on her shoulder and tried to look fierce, but Chantel laughed and pushed him away. "I wouldn't waste my time on a captain if I were a spy. I'd find me a general. You don't know enough about what's going on, you."

"Oh, you hurt my heart," he said, placing his hand on his chest theatrically. "And you're wrong, my cruelest love. I know everything about what's going on."

"Then tell me," Chantel demanded.

"Well, I may not know everything," Armand said, putting two chairs out for them to sit down. "But everybody knows we're going to invade the North. General Lee will hit them hard. We're tired of them coming into our country. It's time to go up there and put a stop to it."

Chantel was concerned, for she really liked Armand. "You be careful, you. Don't you get yourself hurt."

"Would you miss me?"

"Oh yes, Captain. You're the only Cajun I know in this place."

He made a face and said, "I must settle for that, although—"

"I know. It hurts your heart," Chantel finished for him.

On September 13, 1862, three soldiers were crossing an open field that had been a recent Confederate campsite. They stopped long enough to take a break, and one of them noticed a long, thick envelope lying on the ground. He picked it up and found three cigars inside wrapped in a sheet of official-looking paper. One of the soldiers, a man named Mitchell, examined the documents.

"Headquarters, Army of Northern Virginia, special orders 191." The three men took it at once to the company commander, who took them to regimental headquarters. Eventually they were standing in front of the commanding general, General McClellan. He studied the paper and saw that this was Robert E. Lee's complete battle plan for the invasion of Maryland. McClellan said with excitement, "Here is a paper with which if I cannot whip Bobby Lee, I will be willing to go home!"

Indeed it seemed that McClellan had the men, the ordnance, and now the secret plans that should have enabled him to destroy the Confederates. But when the two armies lined up facing each other across Antietam Creek, a fast-running small river that ran close to the town of Sharpsburg, it seemed that none of these great advantages did him any good.

In essence, the Union general began sending his men across the bridges that spanned Antietam Creek. From the very first, his method was wrong. Again, instead of sending a huge overwhelming force, he sent his men in piecemeal. They fought bravely, but there were not enough of them in any one charge, and the Confederates entrenched across the creek shot them down by the hundreds with musket fire and artillery.

Three times McClellan renewed the strategy, and each time he again failed to send the complete force he had. If in any of these three attempts he had sent his entire command across, the Army of Northern Virginia would indeed have been destroyed. Lee and Jackson were engaged in shifting the few men they had from one spot to the next location that was attacked. In each of the three charges, the Confederates barely survived. But they did, and three times they beat the Union forces back. It was a case of nerves, and McClellan had no taste nor stomach for this kind of fighting.

It was the bloodiest day in American history; more men were killed on that day than any single day. Lee waited for McClellan to come across the creek in force, certain that he would. He knew that he had far too few men left to defend another attack. But to his amazement, the attack did not come.

SWORD

Lee gathered his wounded, bloodied army and made his way back toward Richmond. Once again he had survived along with the army, as tattered and beaten as it was. Thousands were dead, and more thousands were wounded.

Abraham Lincoln was exceedingly angry when he heard how McClellan had, once again, let the Confederate Army slip out of his grasp. He did not say so then, but he had, no doubt, made the resolution McClellan would never command the army again.

When discussing the fighting later, Jeb Stuart said sadly to Clay, "The troops we lost today were the best that General Lee had, the best that he could ever hope to have."

"What does it mean, General?"

Stuart had lost many of his own men and could barely speak, for he loved his soldiers. Finally he answered, "We will keep on fighting. God in His mercy will help us."

CHAPTER TWENTY-ONE

Chantel noticed as she moved among the throngs on the Richmond streets how threadbare and worn some of the clothing of the citizens was. In truth, the blockade had been more successful than the North had even expected. Occasionally a ship would slip through and disembark its cargo, and in every case hundreds of people would be standing there waiting to pay almost any price to get precious goods that were unobtainable anywhere in the Confederacy.

Chantel, on her way to the Stuarts', smiled to herself, for she was carrying a quarter of fresh beef. She thought that some of these genteel ladies coming empty-handed out of the shops, had they known it, might have knocked her down and stolen it.

Jacob had finally told Chantel the mystery of how he obtained his continual store of supplies. "Gold," he had said the night before as they sat by their campfire. "Pure gold. These poor people with their Confederate money, pah! A pile of it won't buy a loaf of bread. But the love of money—real money—runs strong in a man." He told her how he went to the storehouses that still received supplies and they would always sell any goods to him first because he paid them in gold. "I have a big pile of it, hidden in the floor of the wagon. I will show you where it is, Chantel, should the Lord call me home."

"But, Grandpere," she said, shocked, "you take Confederate money for the goods when you sell them at all. How can you be making any money doing that?"

"I have lots of gold, and more where that came from," he said gleefully. "God has shown me what to do with it, and God is not interested in making money. He's only interested in us being obedient to Him when we have it."

Arriving at the house the Stuarts rented, Chantel knocked on the door.

Almost at once it was opened, and Flora stood there holding little Jimmy.

"Hello, Miss Flora," Chantel said. "Ma grandpere, he sends you some beef."

"Oh, that is so wonderful! It's been so long since we had anything but dried jerky. Oh, please come in, Chantel." Flora's eyes lit up, and as she turned, little Jimmy made a grab at Chantel's sleeve and caught it. "He likes you, Chantel," Flora said as she led her to the kitchen.

"Well, I like him, too. Let me hold him." Flora put him down, and Chantel held out her arms.

The child came to her at once. He was learning to talk now and called her, "Cante," which was as close as he could come to her real name. "Cante! Cante!" he yelled.

Chantel reached into her bag, which was slung across her chest. "Here. You can have one piece. I don't want to spoil your supper." She laughed as Jimmy grabbed the morsel of candy and popped it into his mouth then looked up at her with a satisfied expression. "You're much easier to please than most men."

Flora laughed. "Yes, he is. Here, let me put that meat up."

After putting the meat under a cloth to keep the flies away, she and Chantel sat down at the sturdy oak worktable. Chantel sat with Jimmy on her lap. To amuse him, she pulled off her bag and set it on the table, and he immediately began to reach into it and pull out the contents. Chantel kept all kinds of things in her bag: paper, pencil, buttons, candy, a spoon, a small New Testament, headache powders. With delight Jimmy pulled out a sheaf of paper and a pencil and started drawing.

"I've got enough for one cup of coffee apiece," Flora said. "After that's gone, we'll be drinking acorn water."

"Acorn water? What's that?"

"Oh, people take acorns and bake them and crush them up."

"It sounds awful. What does it taste like?"

"Like burned acorns." Flora shrugged.

Chantel made a face. "I'll bring you some real coffee, me. Grandpere wouldn't like it if he knew General Stuart was drinking from acorns."

"I wasn't trying to hint, Chantel," Flora said, but she was smiling. "But I should have known. If your grandfather has it, he will share. He's worth his weight in gold."

"More than you know, Miss Flora," Chantel said, amused. "Now, tell me all about Jimmy and about General Stuart. Soldiers talk, they do, but they never know anything."

"Jeb doesn't tell me much," Flora said quietly. "I worry about him, you know. I try not to let him know it, but of course he does. I pray, all the time, that I'll just enjoy the time we have with him and not fear the future."

"Sometimes that's hard, not to be afraid, when men go to war," Chantel said, her eyes gazing into the distance. "Even for Christians, I know now, me."

Flora eyed her knowingly. "And who do you fear for, Chantel?" she asked gently.

Chantel dropped her eyes and ran her hand over Jimmy's hair. It was thick and looked wiry, but actually it was very soft. "He—he's just a friend," she said rather lamely. "But I've known him for three years now, me. So I worry about him, Lieutenant Tremayne."

"I see," Flora said. "Jeb says he is a fine man and one of his best soldiers. He's told me that even when he sets the formations for the column, he looks up and Lieutenant Tremayne is there, always close to him."

Chantel nodded. "He's loyal to General Stuart, he is. He said he wouldn't want to serve anywhere else, with any other man."

"He's not a Christian, is he?" Flora wisely guessed.

"No ma'am, he isn't. He just can't seem to find his way to the good God," Chantel answered. "And so, we both know. . . Anyway, I don't see him much, since he got out of the hospital."

Flora reached over and patted her hand. "One thing I know about being a Christian," she said, "it means that God has a wonderful plan for our lives if we'll just let Him lead us. He is faithful and true, and He will give us joy, always, no matter what happens."

Chantel said unhappily, "Grandpere has told me this. But it's hard sometimes. Especially when we want things the Lord doesn't want us to have."

"He will give you the desires of your heart," Flora said simply. "Trust Him."

In the three years Abraham Lincoln had held the office of the president, he looked as if he had aged thirty years. The war had worn him down, and now once again, he had to choose a commander for the Army of the Potomac.

He had chosen wrongly several times. McClellan was the wrong choice. He simply did not have the nerve of a fighter. Pope had been another failure, and Burnside a complete disaster when he was commanding at Fredericksburg. Finally, in desperation, Lincoln decided, "It will have to be Joe Hooker. They say he can fight. I hope he's able to get an army ready."

Indeed, General Joseph Hooker was probably the best Union general in seeing that his men were well cared for. He was able to wrangle new uniforms and new equipment for them in record time.

Hooker himself was a handsome man. He had a complexion

as delicate as a woman's, fine blond hair, and the erect bearing and demeanor of a soldier. But he was a drinking man, and a womanizer as well, so naturally he did not have the mentality about his soldier's morals as much as others did.

He was called Fighting Joe Hooker, but no one knew exactly why, for he had not been the brightest star in the army, although he had won several minor engagements. He had more confidence than was merited, and the phrases, "When I get to Richmond," or, "After we have taken Richmond," cropped up frequently in his talk. And now he had his chance to take Richmond and stop the Confederacy, for Fighting Joe Hooker was appointed as commander-in-chief of the Army of the Potomac.

CHAPTER TWENTY-TWO

I want you to bring the children and come out to the camp, Flora."

Flora looked up from Jimmy, who was sitting in a dishpan enjoying his bath as usual. He was splashing and chortling, and his eyes gleamed. "What for, dear?"

"Oh, several things. First of all, there's going to be a good meal. And there's going to be good music and good preaching. You know our chaplain?"

"You mean Major Ball?"

"Yes, Major Ball, our champion scrounger."

"What's he done now, Jeb?"

"He's gone out and liberated the awfulest bunch of food you ever saw. I don't know where he gets it. People here in Richmond are going hungry, almost, and he comes into camp with the carcasses of four of the fattest pigs you ever saw and two young steers. The men have made a big barbecue pit, and he's barbecuing them."

"But where does he get these things? Does he buy them?"

Jeb's eyes sparkled. "Buy them? Not the foraging parson! He goes out and takes them from the Yankees, somehow or other. We just hear rumors of him suddenly appearing on one of the Yankees' outlying pickets and holding 'em at gunpoint and liberating their supplies. He says the Lord provides and blames all the stuff he brings in on the Lord's doing. Maybe he's right. In any case, it's going to be a great meal."

"Why yes. Of course Jimmy and I would love to be there."

"While we're eating, I'll have all my minstrel men do some singing and dancing. We might do a little dancing ourselves." Jeb came over, put his arm around Flora, hugged her and kissed her soundly, then reached over and poked little Jimmy's fat stomach with his finger. "You want something to eat, Jimmy?"

"Eat!" he cried. "Eat, Papa!"

"You're my son, all right," Jeb said.

"He looks just like you, Jeb. Or just like I think you must have looked when you were his age."

"Not likely." Jeb grinned. "Remember, they didn't call me Beauty at the Point because I was so pretty. It was because I was so homely."

"You're not homely, as I've said a thousand times. And every woman in the South, it seems to me, thinks you're just as handsome as I do. It's a good thing I trust you, Jeb. Because I would be one miserable wife if I didn't, the way women chase after you."

"I think it's my hat," he said, his blue eyes dancing. "That fancy plume gets 'em every time."

Flora laughed. "Silly old bear."

"Anyway, after the feast, Stonewall Jackson has organized a religious service. He's the finest Christian man I ever knew and the best soldier. I've never known any man like him. Guess there aren't any men like him."

"We're all very proud of the general," Flora said. "Not just for his military successes, but for being the kind of man he is."

"Did I tell you, Flora? The other day he asked for a glass of water, and someone gave it to him. I noticed he didn't drink it right off. He just sat there, holding it for a minute. I asked him, 'General, are you going to drink that water?' He looked at me with those eyes of his that look right through a man. Then he said, 'Yes,

SWORD

General Stuart, I am, but I always give thanks for everything. Even a glass of water. I made it a habit to give thanks for the little things as well as the big things.' "

"It must be good to be that close to the Lord," Flora said. "Most of us aren't. We're not strong enough."

"He's a strong man, not just in the Lord but in war. If we had about five more Stonewall Jacksons, we'd run the Yankees back all the way to Washington screaming for help."

"Every Christian in the South prays for him every day. And for you, my love, and General Lee and all of our men."

"You keep it up, sweetheart. I'll be back later to fetch you and Jimmy." He gave her another kiss and leaned over to kiss little Jimmy's soapy face.

The child happily grabbed his beard.

"You're like your mama. She likes my beard, too." He laughed, and then he left.

❧

"Look, Clay, there's Miss Flora with Jimmy." Chantel pointed and said, "Let's go speak to her. I want to see little Jimmy, too."

"He's a pistol," Clay said, "just like his papa."

The men had set up a bandstand, a platform of rough-hewn logs covered with strips of canvas, contributed by Jacob Steiner. Out in front of it they had gathered up every bench, every camp chair, and every cot they could find so that everyone could have a seat.

General Stuart and Flora were seated in the front row, as were such dignitaries as General Stonewall Jackson, Major Roberdeau Wheat, General P. G. T. Beauregard, and most all of the other officers of the Army of Northern Virginia. Even the august commander General Lee was in attendance. He was a handsome man, with his neatly trimmed beard and thick silver hair. He was always immaculate—his uniforms pressed to crisp perfection, his boots shined, his white gauntlets spotless.

Clay and Chantel made their way over, and Flora greeted them with a smile. "Hello, Chantel. Lieutenant Tremayne, you look splendid. And you look well. I'm so glad you have so miraculously recovered from your grievous wound."

"I am well, very well, thank you, ma'am," Clay replied. "It's so good to see you, Mrs. Stuart. And who's this young man? He looks like a certain general I know."

Chantel added, "It's like the general was shrunk and his beard plucked off. A tiny little General Stuart."

"Watch him," Flora said, setting him down. Promptly he took off. "He even walks like Jeb."

"Really?" Chantel asked. "I hadn't noticed."

"As a matter of fact, Jeb has a strange walk. He's like a centaur in the saddle, with never a false move, but his walk is not graceful in the least. His upper body seems to get ahead of his feet, and he rolls along, bent somewhat from the waist."

Little Jimmy was too small to walk like anything but a toddler, but still Chantel and Clay laughed at Flora's remarks.

"I'll go get him, me," Chantel said. "He looks like he's marching to Washington."

She ran to catch him, and she swooped him up into her arms so fast he whooped with surprise. Then he turned to see who had latched onto him and said with delight, "Cante! Eat, eat, Cante!"

"As you can see, he takes after Jeb in other ways, too," Flora said as Chantel rejoined them, the wiggling little Jimmy held tightly in her arms.

"I agree with Jimmy," Clay said. "Let's eat. Shall we, ladies?"

He led the two women, Chantel still holding Jimmy, over to a long table, two of them put together and covered, somewhat oddly in the rustic setting, with two fine white linen tablecloths. Four soldiers stood carving the pork and the beef from still-steaming big cuts.

"Mrs. Stuart, we're so glad you came to be with us," the private said, a young man who had joined Jeb Stuart as soon as the 1st Cavalry was formed. "May I have the pleasure of serving you some of this fine beef?"

"That would be nice, sir," Flora said kindly. "Thank you so much."

They moved down the table. At the other end were piled mounds of fresh-baked bread and many hundreds of roasted potatoes. All they had had in camp, in quantities enough for the crowd of men, was the chaplain's kidnapped meat and flour for bread, and that was all they had planned on serving. But early the previous morning, Jacob had disappeared with the wagon, and when he returned, he had twenty cases of roasting potatoes. Chantel had teased him. "I guess you spent more of our gold on all that, hmm, partner?"

The three got their plates filled, and Clay carried his and Chantel's back to the front row of benches, for Chantel still carried little Jimmy. They got seated, and Flora handed him an enormous beef rib, which he gnawed happily on, smearing his entire face with grease.

"Like a little hungry puppy, you," Chantel said affectionately.

Major Ball came to them and bowed. "Good day, Mrs. Stuart, Miss Chantel. Hello, Lieutenant Tremayne. Mrs. Stuart, I'm so happy you and Jimmy could come be with us today and share in this feast that the gracious Lord has provided. Will you be staying for the service?"

"Of course I will, Major Ball. I'm looking forward to it," Flora replied.

"What about you, Lieutenant?" he asked, turning to Clay. "Are you ready for a good dose of Gospel preaching?"

"Looks like I'll have to be, won't I?" Clay said grinning.

He liked the chaplain a great deal. He had been shocked at their first patrol, when Major Dabney Ball had ridden to the front right alongside of Jeb. When they had met the enemy, he fought just as fiercely as all of Stuart's men did. After the battles, Clay had watched as he walked around among the wounded, even in the midst of action, as if he were in a park on a summer day.

He had asked Ball later, "Weren't you afraid you'd get hit, Major?"

"No sir, I am not afraid. The Lord is going to take care of me.

Besides, when the Lord means for me to go, then I'll go."

Major Ball saw the men taking the stage, and he said, "Well, it looks like your husband's minstrel show is about to start. General Stuart does dearly love his music."

Clay had seen and heard the musicians many times. They began to play, and Stuart joined them. Often he sang along, and the whole crowd joined in. They sang, "Her Bright Smile Haunts Me Still," "The Corn Top's Ripe," "Lorena," and finally the one that they always sang, that Jeb Stuart loved the best: "Jine the Cavalry." Even Stonewall Jackson and the grave Robert E. Lee sang.

As the music was going on, Chantel leaned over and said to Clay, "I've never seen an officer like General Stuart. He jokes and talks with the soldiers just like he was one of them."

"That's right," Clay said heartily. "That's the kind of man he is. He's the only general I've ever seen that could make a common soldier feel absolutely at ease."

"He's gotten to be such a hero, so famous," Chantel said. "It's hard to believe that he would have any humility at all."

"You know, I asked the general once," Clay said very quietly so that Flora could not hear him, "why he put himself in the front. He's so recognizable, any Yankee would give his boots to shoot him. I told him he was going to get himself killed if he didn't use a little caution."

"What did he say, Clay?"

"He said, 'Oh, I reckon not. If I am, they'll easily find someone to fill my place.' "

Suddenly a laugh went up, for the general had gotten up. Jeb Stuart, the terror of the Yankees, the master of the Black Horse, began dancing around, a great bearded warrior with his plumed hat and his golden spurs clanking at his heels. He began dancing around with one of the black men, and then the others joined in a mad frolic.

Flora sat shaking her head.

But Stonewall Jackson and even General Lee laughed.

After a while, the musicians left the platform, and Major Ball stepped up. "All right. We're going to have a service right here. We've had our party, and now we're going to hear a word from God."

Major Ball was a tall, thick-set man with a shock of black hair and a pair of strangely colored eyes, penetrating hazel eyes. His voice normally was quiet and even, but when he stood up to preach, it was like the sound of a trumpet. "I'm going to preach a very simple sermon to you today. My text is one that you all know—one that has often been called 'the Gospel in a nutshell.' I refer to John 3:16. You know the verse. It says, 'For God so loved the world, that he gave his only begotten Son, that whosoever believeth in him should not perish, but have everlasting life.' "

Chantel was fascinated as the chaplain began to speak. He had a compassion for lost men that showed clearly on his face. He spoke of how God loved the world that did not love him. "We're all of the world, and we're all sinners. It is one of the great mysteries of the Bible and of life to understand why a just and holy and perfect God could love miserable sinners such as we all are. But the Bible says He loved the world, and He gave His Son. We're going to speak now of that gift that God gave for our salvation."

As the sermon went on, Chantel had her eyes fixed on a young man who was across the way from her. It had grown dark, but there were lanterns stationed so that she could see his face clearly. She saw that he was very young and that he was somehow afraid. She could not take her eyes off of him, and she whispered to Clay, "Do you see that young man over there? The private with the yellow hair?"

Clay looked over and nodded. "I can't recall his name just now. He's in the Stonewall Brigade."

"He's so young," Chantel said. "And he looks so afraid."

Clay studied the man and nodded. "I guess he is. Most of us are, I guess. I envy men like General Jackson and the major who don't have to worry about what'll happen if they get killed."

Major Ball was saying, "There you have it, dear friends! That's who God is, a compassionate loving Father, but He still gave His only Son, His beloved Son, Jesus, and He condemned His own Son to death, so that He paid for our sins. How can we turn away from our Father God? How can we ever say to Him, 'No, I don't need Your love'? We can't. Once we realize, deep in our hearts, what He has done for us, the great and eternal and kind love that He has for us, we cannot help but ask Him humbly to take us in and to be our most beloved Father."

The silence was profound, and Chantel saw that some men wept openly. She glanced at Clay and was shocked to see his dark eyes glint with unshed tears.

The chaplain finished, now speaking quietly in the reverent silence, "I know you men. You're like all men. You've dabbled in the defilements of the world, you've shamed yourselves, perhaps you've shamed your families. Maybe you've given up and you think, 'God can't care for me. I'm not worth caring for.' But this Scripture says that He does. If you'll just come to Jesus tonight, you'll find out that He will open His arms and welcome you with a love that is everlasting."

The chaplain began to urge the men to come forward who wanted to be prayed for, and many came. It was just a few at first, but then more and more men, hats in hand, went to the chaplain and stood silently, heads bowed, as he prayed with them.

Chantel turned to Clay and saw that his face was working; he was struggling. Even as she watched, he bowed his head and closed his eyes.

Chantel knew that God was dealing with him. She slid her hand into his, and he grasped it as hard as if it were his only tenuous hold on life. Chantel bowed her head and prayed.

Finally she sensed Clay relax, and his painful grip on her hand loosened, though he still held it. She looked up at him. His face was rather pale, but he looked back at her and smiled.

She asked, "Did you ask the good God to save you, Clay?"

"I did," Clay answered steadily. "And just like you and your grandfather have told me, I feel different now. I know that He is in my heart. For the first time since this war started, I know I'm safe."

"Even unto death," she said quietly, "we know we live. Forever and ever."

❧

Clay and his corporal, a sturdy man of about forty-five named Gabriel Tyron, were riding side by side slightly behind General Stuart. Clay was aware of the jingling of the horses' harness, some of the men laughing and talking, the ever-present sounds of the night in the South. A thousand crickets called, in the distance bullfrogs sang out their throaty single notes, the nightingale trilled her lonely sonnet. This was all a familiar scene to him, and now that he had become a Christian, he was not at the mercy of his fear. He felt alive and alert and strong.

"I think this battle is going to be bad, Lieutenant," Corporal Tyron said.

"Why do you say that, Corporal?" Clay asked curiously. The man was a career soldier, and he, like Clay, had already been through terrible battles. It was unlike him to say such a thing.

Tyron shrugged. "I got me a bad feeling."

"That's just superstition, Tyron," Clay said firmly. "We're heading for a fight, for sure. But no matter what happens, it can't be much worse than what we've already seen."

"No, this is different. My mother, she had what they call second sight."

"What does that mean?"

"It means that she saw things that couldn't be."

"What kind of things, Corporal?"

Tyron frowned. "My mother saw her brother after he was killed."

"What do you mean? At his funeral?"

"No, sir," he said, shaking his head. "Her brother, my uncle, was killed in a mining accident out west. One day, Mama, she looked up and saw my uncle standing in the door. She was surprised, and she asked him when he had come back from the West. He just smiled and said nothing, and then in a minute he was gone."

"I don't understand," Clay said with some impatience.

"My uncle, he had been killed the day before. It was a full week before Mama got the letter. But she saw him that day."

"I don't believe that's true," Clay said in a more kindly manner. "Not that I doubt your mother, but she must have been mistaken."

"You think what you like, Lieutenant, sir. But I think that God speaks to us in different ways, and I think He spoke to my mother in that kind of way."

The cavalry rode on, and late that night they made camp. They had been there for a couple of hours, and Clay was seeing to the well-being of his men, going around to ensure they had something to eat, talking to them, encouraging them.

He was at the edge of their camp, and he looked into a clearing a little ways away from them where there was a small fire. With a shock, he realized that General Lee was there. He was sitting on a cracker box, and across from him, not five feet away, was General Stonewall Jackson. General Stuart was with them, and General Lee was speaking to him in a low voice.

Stuart nodded then turned and walked fast, back toward his tent. As he passed Clay, he said, "Saddle up again, Lieutenant. We've got to ride."

They rode west, and Clay, as always, stayed close behind General Stuart. Sometimes, in the night, they heard talking and laughing just on their left, and Clay realized they were riding very close to Union pickets.

Every once in a while, Jeb would throw up a hand for the column to stop, and then he would listen, his head cocked as if he were waiting for something. Then he would nod with satisfaction and move quietly on.

They were in a wilderness, with rough tracks for roads that seemed to begin out of nowhere and then end abruptly. Finally Stuart called for the column to halt, though he didn't dismount, so neither did Clay. Stuart took a map out of his jacket and called for a lantern. An aide brought him one, and Stuart studied the map, his right leg thrown over the saddle horn in a negligent gesture, one that Clay had seen many times.

"I think that Reverend Lacy lives around here somewhere," Jeb said quietly to Clay, who had lingered close to him. "If we can find him, I'll send word with him back to General Jackson and General Lee."

Finally they found the Reverend B. T. Lacy's small cabin. He was Stonewall Jackson's chief chaplain. Jeb roused him and said, "Go back to camp, just east of here, close to the old Wellford railroad yard. Tell General Lee that I have found the end of their line, in a clearing about eight miles from them, and it looks to me like they're up in the air."

In Stuart's absence, the two generals had made a momentous decision, and some audacious plans.

It was indeed a daring move, one that could have been an utter catastrophe. Robert E. Lee had asked Jackson to find a way to get at Hooker's army, and he had decided, when he got word from General Stuart, to try and flank them at the weakness in the line that Stuart had found. Stonewall had asked Lee if he could take his whole corps, leaving only two stripped-down divisions with Lee. Robert E. Lee had about 14,000 men left with him as Jackson made his flank sweep. Joe Hooker had about 100,000 men. All Hooker had to do was to drive straight at him, hard and fast, and the Army of Northern Virginia would be destroyed, and the Civil War would be over.

It never happened.

Fighting Joe Hooker talked a good game. Once he called the Army of the Potomac "the finest army on the planet." Before the battle had even begun, in his headquarters he boasted, "Robert E. Lee and the Confederate Army are now the legitimate property of the United States."

At the beginning of the battle, he was cocksure, filled with confidence, but he had never tackled the likes of Robert E. Lee and Stonewall Jackson. As events unfolded, he grew unsure, indecisive. Instead of rushing his men into the fray and taking Lee head-on and running over the inferior force, which he easily could have done, he lingered, he made excuses, he stalled.

Then Stonewall Jackson and his corps appeared, apparently out of nowhere, shielded by Jeb Stuart's fearless cavalry, and struck his flank. Hooker completely lost himself and ended up helplessly frittering away every chance he had to effectively fight back. He never had control of the battle, and finally, in the end, he met the fate of others who had run up against Robert E. Lee and Stonewall Jackson.

Jackson's corps had, in effect, cowed Joe Hooker, and as a result, the Army of the Potomac was like a loaded cannon, but one that no one would aim and shoot. Still, Stonewall Jackson was never a man to be satisfied. Even as the darkness fell, he was leading some of his officers, looking for a way to strike Hooker another blow.

They were in the deep woods, with the lines so close and entangled that from one foot to the next they couldn't tell if they were closer to Federal troops or to Confederates. An overeager, keyed-up North Carolina infantry regiment fired a volley that knocked Jackson out of the saddle, wounded in the left shoulder, the left arm, and his palm. Jackson was carried away from the battlefield. His war was finally over.

"General Stuart," the messenger said, "I have terrible news."

"What is it, Lieutenant?"

"General Jackson has been shot. He's not expected to live. General Lee orders you to take command of the army."

What could have been the proudest moment of Jeb Stuart's life turned out to be one of the most bitter. He had admired Jackson all of his military career; in fact, the two men, polar opposites though they were, had made fast friends. It was said that Jeb Stuart was the only man in the world who could make Stonewall Jackson laugh out loud.

Now his great head dropped, and he said, "I will assume command."

Jeb Stuart was a cavalryman. But he took command of an entire army, infantry, artillery, and all, and he did a fine job. He managed to send Hooker back to Washington in disgrace. But there was no joy in Stuart's heart nor in the heart of any Southerner. In losing Jackson, they had lost so much, and they had loved him well. General Lee, when he heard that Jackson's left arm was shattered, had sent word, "You're losing your left arm, but I am losing my right arm." A pall fell over the Confederacy. It seemed that the army would never be the same again.

CHAPTER TWENTY-THREE

If Jeb Stuart had expected to be promoted after serving so well and salvaging the Battle at Chancellorsville, he soon found out that this was not to be. There were mentions of his bravery, the excellence of his command during this battle, but he remained in charge of the cavalry. No doubt both General Lee and President Davis were convinced that this was his most valuable contribution. And though Stuart might have felt some twinges of regret at being passed over, in his heart he likely agreed with them. He loved the cavalry above all.

In midsummer he arranged for a review of the cavalry at Brandy Station. There had been little action, so the troops were all available, and by the time the review was set in motion, ten thousand cavalrymen sat their horses in lines almost two miles long, and Stuart galloped onto the field.

One of his gunners, George Neese, said of Stuart:

> He was superbly mounted, and his sidearms gleamed
> in the morning sun like burnished silver. A long black
> ostrich plume waved gracefully from a black slouch hat

cocked up on one side, held with a golden clasp. . . . He is the prettiest and most graceful rider I ever saw. I could not help but notice with what natural ease and comely elegance he sat his steed as it bounded over the field. . . he and his horse appeared to be one and the same machine.

In those few golden days of summer, it seemed as if the enemy was a world away.

Stuart's officers were gathered together, and he explained that there was a drive to invade the North. "Our job," he said, addressing his men, "is to cover the Union Army, to find out their dispositions, to see if we can find a weakness in their flank. They are just over that ridge." He pointed east, to the Blue Ridge Mountains. "That will be an easy enough task. We'll have no trouble."

Afterward Clay was talking with several of the other officers. Clay had noticed some difference in General Stuart's manner, and he was worried. "He doesn't seem to be as alert or as focused as he usually is."

"General Stuart knows what he's doing," a major scoffed. "He's never let the army down."

Clay could argue no more against his superior officers, and so he kept his mouth shut and followed Jeb Stuart, as always. But Clay had been right. Instead of watching the Union Army and sending reports to Lee on the western side of the Blue Ridge, Stuart led his army on side trails and in ineffective and meaningless skirmishes. Once they captured a huge wagon train.

Clay was worried, and Corporal Tyron could see it clearly. "Lieutenant, won't this train slow us down?"

Clay shrugged. "General Stuart says he's ordered to interfere with their supply lines. This is interfering."

On the other side of the mountains, Robert E. Lee worried

as the Union forces began to move against him. Without Stuart's intelligence, he was blind.

And Jeb Stuart's mistakes were going to haunt him.

"General. . .General Longstreet, please wake up!"

Longstreet came awake instantly and sat up on his bed. He pulled his fingers down through his thick beard and said, "What is it, Lieutenant?"

"Harrison's back, sir."

"The spy?"

"Yes, sir. He says he's got information and you have to hear it."

"I doubt it." Nevertheless, he got up and said, "Have him come in."

The officer departed, and Longstreet sat down at a chair behind the field desk and waited. He did not care for spies as a whole, but this one seemed to be better than most. As soon as the man entered, he pulled off his hat and said, "Hello, General. I'm back."

"What have you got, Harrison?"

Harrison grinned and said, "I came right through your lines. It's a good thing I wasn't a Union Army."

"What have you got?" Longstreet repeated.

Harrison was a slight man with a foxy face, innocent-looking enough. He was able to pass for a farmer or a workman of any kind. For this reason, he was able to move anywhere unobtrusively and get information that others could not. "I got the position of the Union Army."

Longstreet grunted. "Where are they?"

"It wasn't easy."

"I've no doubt, Harrison, and I admit you've always done us a good job. So where is the army?"

"Less than a day's ride away from this here spot."

Instantly Longstreet straightened up. "Can't be," he muttered.

Harrison was offended. "I'm telling you, General, they're less than a day's ride away, and they're going to get you if you don't do something."

"Show me." Longstreet pulled out a map, and Harrison began pointing out different locations, telling him of their dispositions. Then he added, "Oh, and I forgot to tell you. They got 'em a new general."

"Who is that? What happened to Hooker?"

"Lincoln got tired of him, I reckon, after that last dust-up at Chancellorsville. Now he's got George Meade. That's what the papers say."

Longstreet knew that a catastrophe had suddenly reared up ahead of him. He got up and said, "We'll have to tell General Lee."

The two left Longstreet's tent and made their way to Lee's tent. They found Lee seated at his desk. "Harrison here says that the Federal Army is not a day's ride away, sir."

Lee stared at the scout. "I've forgotten your name."

"Harrison, sir."

"Well, Harrison, you saw this for yourself?"

"Plain as day. I saw General Buford leading his corps." He began to name off other units, and Lee and Longstreet were both silent.

Finally Lee said, "We are in your debt, sir."

Harrison knew this was his dismissal. "I'm glad to be of service, General." He turned and left the tent.

"This changes things," Lee said. "I had no idea the Union forces were so close."

"It's Stuart's fault. You haven't heard from him, have you?"

"No, I haven't. It's the first time he ever let me down, General Longstreet."

"He ought to be broken for this." Longstreet was a slow-moving man, the exact opposite of General Jeb Stuart. He liked to think things over and come to decisions slowly, whereas Stuart would throw himself in and worry later about the results.

"Never mind that now, General. We must make some decisions."

Lee walked over to a map, looked at it for a moment, and said, "We'll keep going here. We'll come out of the mountains close to this little town."

"What town is that, General?"

Lee peered at it. "Gettysburg," he said.

The Battle of Gettysburg should never have been fought. Lee was not himself and made his worst decisions, which he himself admitted. He had a terrible case of dysentery, and the heart disease that would later kill him was giving him severe problems. He was without Stonewall Jackson, and in his place he had a man he did not fully trust.

Lieutenant General Richard Ewell was a good soldier, but he had lost a leg and apparently had lost some confidence along with it. Even before the first gray lines took the field, the Union forces had entrenched on the high ground, and the plains below were nothing but a killing field.

The battle started on July 3, 1863, and both sides incurred disastrous losses. On the second day, the next step was made by General Lee. He sent men around to his right to a place called Little Roundtop. The Confederates were unable to take it, and the following day General Lee ordered a full assault on the center of the Union line.

General Longstreet argued vehemently against the attack. He came as close to insubordination as he ever had with General Lee, for the Union army was entrenched on a ridge. They had the high ground, with full range to sweep the valley below with murderous fire. Lee listened to him, but finally he pointed at the ridge and said, "The enemy is there, and I'm going to strike him."

The Confederate division that led the strike was under the command of General Pickett. He led his men across an open field into the mouths of the artillery and muskets of a huge army. They were shot to pieces, and only a few pitiful remnants were able to stagger back to the safety of the lines.

Jeb Stuart finally rode in and went to General Lee, but Lee was angry with him and showed it. Stuart had ridden up and dismounted, and Lee had reddened at the sight of him and raised his arm as if he would strike him. "General Stuart, where have you been?"

Stuart was shocked. "I have been carrying out my assignment, sir."

"I have not heard a word from you in days, and you are the eyes and ears of my army!"

Stuart had swallowed hard and then said, "I brought you a hundred and twenty-five wagons and their teams, General."

"Yes, General Stuart, and they are an impediment to me now!"

Stuart was dismissed, and he did well for the rest of the battle, but there was no hope for the Confederate Army. At Gettysburg, Robert E. Lee, for the first time, suffered a crushing, brutal defeat.

Chantel was horrified, as was everyone who had gathered to watch the Army of Northern Virginia come back from the battle. Endless lines of wagons were full of wounded men. Blood was dripping out of the wagons, and some were crying to be killed. "Shoot me! Shoot me!" she heard one voice pleading. "Oh, my wife! My poor babies! What will happen to them after I'm dead?" Other cries like this broke her heart. She hurried to the hospital.

Hours later she looked up and saw Clay, and she ran to him. "Are you all right, Clay?"

"I'm fine, just—tired," he said dispiritedly. Then he laid his hands on her arms and said evenly, "Chantel, Armand was hit."

Instantly she cried, "Is he dead?"

"No. I just stopped to see him for a minute. He's—there are still a lot of men out there. At the fairgrounds. I came to the hospital to see if there were any doctors." He looked around, anguished at the men lying on the beds and even on thin blankets on the floor. "But I can see that they have everything they can do right here."

"I must go to him, Clay."

"Yes, go," he said. "I'm going to see to my men that are here, and then I'll follow you."

She ran to the fairgrounds. The big field was full of wounded men just lying on the ground. Finally she found Armand and knelt over him. He was feverish and thirsty. As always after a battle, she had replaced her bag with a canteen around her neck. Now she lifted his head and gave him a drink.

"Ah, that was good," he whispered. His face was pale, and his side was bloody. "Oh, it was so bad, cherie. So very bad."

"I know, I know, Armand," she said soothingly. "Here, let me see." She gently pulled open Armand's bloody tunic. She saw that his wound, though painful, was not likely to be serious. "You're going to be all right, Armand," she said with relief. "I'm going to clean this out a little and bandage it." She poured some of the cool water in her canteen over his side, and he shivered. Pulling up her skirt, she ripped her petticoat to make a bandage.

Even wounded, Armand could not resist. "I never thought I'd see your petticoat, cherie," he joked weakly. "Especially not this way."

When she finished this rough field dressing, he drank again, still shivering, and Chantel wished desperately for a blanket. "You're going to be all right, Armand. I know it hurts, but please believe me—you're going to be fine."

He nodded weakly then murmured, "It was a terrible thing. We had no chance at all, Chantel."

"So many wounded," she said sadly.

"And more dead. We had no chance," he repeated. "We could not believe that General Lee could make such terrible decisions! Men heard, when Pickett came back from that last charge, General Lee met him. He kept saying, 'It was all my fault. It's all my fault.' He was a broken man."

Chantel stayed with him and tried to decide whether to return to the hospital and see if there was some way she could get some supplies to these many wounded men. But soon Jacob arrived with the wagon filled with supplies and medicine, and three medics were with him. She and Jacob stayed at the fairgrounds and worked all day until late into the darkness by lantern light. The wounded were still coming in, and many women from Richmond and from the country around came to the hospitals and out to the surrounding fields, the last places they had to put so many wounded. Many men died that night.

Chantel kept doggedly working, giving the wounded men

water, sometimes dressing their wounds, comforting them. The medics had brought many tents, and they were organizing the wounded men and getting them all under shelter. Chantel had made sure Armand was taken care of and then had gone back to work.

She felt a soft touch on her hair as she knelt over a man who was unconscious, tucking a blanket around him. The medics had not gotten to this part of the field yet, but Chantel was bringing armloads of blankets to cover them and canteens to give them water. She looked up, and Clay was there.

He lifted her to her feet and took her arm. "I tried to get here sooner, but many of my men were taken down to the south field by the ironworks. I've been there all day. You look exhausted, Chantel. Come over to the wagon and sit down for a minute."

She allowed him to lead her to Jacob's wagon, and she sat on the back, as she had done so many times before.

Clay settled in beside her. "Did you find Armand?"

"Yes, and the medics said that he wasn't badly wounded. I thought that, me, but I was glad to hear them say it."

"I am, too," Clay said. "I count him as a friend."

Chantel sighed. "It was terrible, wasn't it, Clay?"

"The worst I've ever seen. It was General Lee's worst day. He was ill. He had no business trying to lead an army. But it really doesn't matter who is leading you or who you are. War is a cruel, senseless business."

She took his hand and held it in hers. "I'm glad you're back. I prayed for you so hard."

Clay turned to her. "When the bullets were flying and the shells were bursting, I thought of you."

He watched her hungrily, and with a little smile, Chantel put her hands on his face. "This time I really want you to kiss me, Clay."

He kissed her then, softly and gently. "You know how much I love you, Chantel. I don't have the words to tell you."

"I know. I feel the same way. I do love you, Clay. I have, ever since I first saw you, so terribly hurt. I was so young. Maybe I don't know exactly what love is then. But I do now, me."

He swallowed, hard. In a distant voice, he said, "If we weren't in this terrible war, you know what I would ask you, Chantel. But right now I can't even think of it. I don't want to say it, not right now, in this terrible time."

Chantel, as always, was a very practical girl. "We are going to marry, you and me," she said firmly. She reached up again, pulled his head down, and kissed him solidly. Then she put her head on his shoulder. "We are going to trust God to bring us out of this terrible war, and then we will be together, and we will be happy, Clay. I know this, because it is the desire of my heart."

CHAPTER TWENTY-FOUR

It is difficult to put a finger on the exact moment that a war makes a final turning. Most wars are either brief affairs wherein a huge force overruns a small one, or they are long tedious affairs that go on for years. In these long wars, much is done, but very few turning points in which the whole direction of a war is changed can be specifically cited.

The Civil War, however, presented a clear-cut and definite turning point. The South won many battles during the early part of the war, and this drove Abraham Lincoln and, indeed, all the Northern leaders, nearly to distraction. The source of the strength of the Confederacy was in General Robert E. Lee. He was the South's greatest military asset, and beside him was Stonewall Jackson, perhaps the second most potent force that kept the Confederacy alive and fighting ferociously.

Lincoln tried general after general, all of them failing to defeat Lee and Jackson. At Bull Run, Lincoln sent General McDowell, which proved to be a sad mistake, for McDowell was sadly defeated. In the Seven Days Battle, which was a short but very bloody affair, General McClellan, who was the idol of the North and one of the neatest men who ever wore the uniform, proved that he was unable to stand against these two soldiers. In the Battle of Second Manassas in August of 1862, General Pope was Lincoln's choice. He failed miserably, as had his predecessors. At Antietam, the bloodiest day of the war, Lincoln tried McClellan again. McClellan had the battle in his grasp. All he had to do was make one great charge, but he was psychologically and emotionally unable to send men to their deaths. In the Battle of Fredericksburg, Ambrose Burnside threw himself against Lee and Jackson and introduced the Army of the Potomac to a slaughter from which Burnside and the army had to turn and run. Hooker spoke well and was a fine-looking general, but in the Battle of Chancelorsville, he lost his courage.

The South won that battle, but they lost Stonewall Jackson, which was a grievous loss indeed. No one can know if Gettysburg would have been any different, if this giant among men had been there, standing sure and true "like a stone wall." He was not there, and Robert E. Lee was defeated, though the Army of Northern Virginia was not decimated. Still they fought on.

But then came the turn of the tide, a point in time that fated the South to a full and final defeat. Abraham Lincoln chose Ulysses S. Grant to be commander-in-chief of all the Union armies. This sealed the fate of the Confederate States of America. Unlike most of the commanding generals before him, Grant was very unimpressive to look at and was not much of a one for talking, nor parades. His uniform was usually scruffy, and at times he even wore the uniform of a private, with the general's stars, denoting his rank, only showing on his collar.

His choice to succeed him as commanding officer of the Military Division of Mississippi, which was the command of all the troops in the Western Theater, was a general named William Tecumseh Sherman. These two men spelled the death of the Confederacy. Grant told Lincoln, "I'm going to go for Lee, and Sherman is going to go for Joe Johnston. That's the plan."

The first battle Grant engaged in with Lee was a bloody affair called the Battle of the Wilderness. As usual, the Northern troops suffered great losses.

Always before when this had happened, the Northern generals had retreated to Washington and built up their forces again. But Grant was different. He and Sherman both were men who believed in total war, with no mercy shown, to bring a quick end to a foe. Grant was determined to wear down the South, and if he had to lose three men for every death the Southern army incurred, so be it. Behind him lay the immense numbers in the North, while the South was already sending sixteen-year-olds and fifty-year-olds into battle. Sherman was a cold-eyed realist, and his most famous statement was, "War is hell." And he set about to make it so. He set out for Georgia, and the South has never forgotten the cold-blooded and terrible devastation that followed in the wake of Sherman and his men.

With the appointment by Lincoln of Grant and Sherman, it was as if a steel door had suddenly slammed on the South and their army. For after this there really was little hope.

It was October 9, 1863, and Jeb Stuart stood beside the bed where his wife, Flora, lay. He was holding the newest Stuart, a daughter. He looked down at Flora, reached over, and put his hand on her hair. "You choose a name, dear, and I'll choose one."

Flora was exhausted from the struggles to bring the child into the world, but she answered, "I've always wanted a daughter named Virginia."

"Excellent! That's who she'll be."

"And what name will you choose?" Flora managed a weak smile.

"Of all the men I've known, my gunner Pelham was the most noble. He was indeed the gallant Pelham as everyone called him, and to this day I miss him terribly. I'd like to call this child Virginia Pelham Stuart."

"A fine name, Jeb."

Jeb walked the floor, looking into the face of his new daughter, smiling, taking her tiny hand in his strong one. Finally he gave the child back to Flora and then sat down beside her in a worn walnut rocking chair. As he rocked, he grew strangely quiet.

Flora saw that he was grieved. "What's the matter, Jeb? You look troubled."

"I guess I am, my dear Flora."

"Can you tell me what it is?"

"It's hard to say. I feel, Flora, that I let General Lee down at Gettysburg. All the papers say so, and some of my best friends in the army accused me of not being a good soldier."

Flora shook her head and extended her hand, which he took. She squeezed it and said, "You mustn't grieve, dear. You did what you thought was best. If you made a mistake, others have made theirs."

"I've told myself that many times," Jeb said in a subdued tone. "I don't know what made me act as I did. At the time it seemed as if I was following orders, doing exactly what General Lee had asked me to do. But now, looking back, I can see that I made a terrible mistake and should have come back to him days earlier."

"Jeb, you are a man of God, and you put your trust in Him," Flora said steadily. "Don't look back with useless regrets. As you said, you were doing your best, your utmost to perform your duty. That is all a man can do, even the great General Jeb Stuart. Now, let's talk about something else, something cheerful. What are we going to do when this awful war is finally over, do you think?"

Stuart looked up at her with surprise. It was as if he had never given a thought to that time. "Why, I suppose I'll stay in the army. Get a nice, comfortable command. I can sit behind a desk, and then every night I will come home to you and the children. Maybe we can have two or three more."

Flora smiled and said, "Right now I just want to hold Virginia Pelham Stuart. She is precious."

"Yes, she is. I think she's going to look like you, Flora, and I hope she does. And I hope she is loving and kind like you. You've been the best wife a man ever had."

Tears came to Flora's eyes, for Jeb was often jocular and paid her many light, sometimes silly compliments, but this, she knew, came from his heart. "Thank you, Jeb. You can't know how much that means to me."

"It's true, Flora. I thank God for you every day. With His help and your love, I know I can fight on."

Clay and Corporal Tyron dismounted, took off their hats and gauntlets, and wearily threw themselves down to lean against a big spreading oak tree. The tree was on a small rise, and because of its deep shade, it had minimal undergrowth. It stood like a sentinel, its branches sketching a graceful silhouette against a shroud-gray sky. The two men were silent for a while, taking sips from their canteens, savoring even the tepid, gritty water.

Idly Clay said, "You know, Corporal, I had some funny ideas about battle before I saw one."

"And what is that, sir?"

"Well, I'd seen pictures in books, you know, of armies out on open fields all neatly lined up with their rifles all held in the same position. Not a man was out of step, and they squared off facing each other, and then they marched right toward each other." He rubbed his eyes. "It's not like that. It's nothing like that."

Corporal Tyron said, "That may have happened in Europe, but when those lobsters came over here fighting for old King George, they found out that that nonsense won't do over here. We're not strutting fools. We're soldiers, and we fight hard. We fight any way we can, anyplace we can."

"It's especially true here in the South," Clay observed. "Too many trees, too many forests, too many rivers. It's hard to find a place to have a review, much less to put two huge armies together." He looked out over the desolate landscape.

The sky was a death-gray caul, and a layer of stinking gray smoke hovered over the ground. They had just fought for two days in what was to be called simply the Battle of the Wilderness.

Ulysses Grant had begun his relentless push toward Richmond as soon as he had taken command of the Army of the Potomac. He came straight on, 122,000 strong, crossing the Rapidan and heading due south.

Lee, with his army of 66,000, chose to meet him in the middle of nowhere, miles of empty fields and dense woods just south of Fredericksburg. He counted on the bewildering trackless forest of stunted pine, scrub oak, and sweet gum, with their impenetrable thickets of wild honeysuckle vines and briars, to keep the Yankees from bringing artillery to bear. It worked.

But still the woods caught fire from the hot shot of thousands of muskets.

Tyron said, "I have to say, Lieutenant, that I have seen some bloody Indian massacres, but this was much, much worse. No such thing as a battle line. It was just men by themselves hiding behind trees and under rocks, and the bluebellies were the same. And then"—he sighed—"the woods caught fire."

Looking out over the scorched earth, Clay remembered horrific scenes from the last two days. "Men just burned to death," he murmured painfully. "They were wounded and too weak to crawl away."

Clay and certainly Max Tyron were, by now, battle-hardened veterans. But on this dark day they were both literally exhausted. Their uniforms were filthy, as were their faces and indeed their entire bodies.

The battle had been a nightmare. After the first volley, the black powder had thrown a cloud of smoke over the thick woods, and a man could not see five feet away. He did not know at times whether he was firing at his fellow soldiers or an enemy.

Jeb's cavalry had tried to front the infantry, but scouting was impossible. In the woods, even when they could find a trail, it was merely a path, with undergrowth so thick on either side a whole division of Yankees could have been five feet away and they never would have seen them. Finally they had dismounted and joined in the killing field.

SWORD

Clay started out in good formation with his company, but in the massive tangle of men in the wilderness, he and Tyron had gotten completely separated from any recognizable command, and that morning they had found themselves alone, so they had ridden to the live oak for some welcome shelter.

Clay had thought that he might never sleep again; the scenes in his mind were so fresh and vivid that he hated to close his eyes. But then he woke up with a start and realized that both he and Tyron had fallen asleep sitting straight up. "Corporal," he said, shaking Tyron's shoulder. "Wake up."

Tyron's eyes flew open, and he was alert immediately. "I hear it."

They listened, and Clay nodded grimly. "That's 1st Cav's bugle call," he said. "Just over to our left. Not too far either."

They struggled to their feet. Lightning and Tyron's horse had remained standing under the tree, not even grazing. As they mounted up, Tyron said, "Hope there's something left of us."

"And I hope," Clay said grimly, "that we're going to ride out of this wilderness and never come back."

The two armies regrouped, leaving twenty-five thousand casualties in the Wilderness. The Federals lost almost eighteen thousand men, killed, wounded, and missing. Always before, such losses sent the Union generals scuttling back to Washington. But Grant pressed on mercilessly, and Lee had to use all of his considerable military genius to move about his numerically inferior forces to counter him. Of course, Jeb's riders were all over the country, scouting out the lines and dispositions.

On May 11, Jeb was in the saddle early, and the weary 1st Virginia Cavalry rode out, heading south. As usual, Clay managed to work himself around until he was riding with Stuart. As always, Stuart was jovial, laughing, his manner as carefree as if they were going to a ball.

They had had several run-ins with Federal cavalry, which seemed to be crawling all over the countryside. Clay remarked,

"I think this is the most fighting we've done one-on-one with bluebelly cavalry."

"Grant took the leash off Phil Sheridan," Jeb told him. "No Union general has ever used the cavalry like they should. They keep nibbling away at the commands, using them to guard supply trains, escorting prisoners, and standing pickets. General Sheridan is a little bitty spitfire, 'bout as tall as an upright musket, with a temper like a mad dog. But he's a smart man and a good officer. That's why all of a sudden they're everywhere we look. They're out ahead of the main body of the army, but not just to scout. They send out enough to form a fighting force."

"Guess we'll fight them then," Clay said.

"That's what you joined the cavalry for, Tremayne," Jeb said cheerfully.

They passed a pleasant oak arbor with a fresh spring bubbling up and running downhill in a fast-running, cold stream. Jeb called a brief halt for the men to refill their canteens and water the horses. As usual, he stayed in the saddle, right leg thrown over it, studying a map. Clay stayed mounted and idled near him. "Right here," Jeb said, mostly to himself. Then he looked up at Clay and said, "A little nothing place named Yellow Tavern should be right ahead of us. I figure that's where we'll find some Yanks to shoot."

"We're ready, sir," Clay said confidently.

Jeb took off his hat, smoothed his hair back, then settled it back on his head. The long ostrich plume waved airily in a light dusty breeze. "You know, Lieutenant, we're only about six miles north of Richmond."

"Yes, sir, I know," Clay said.

Jeb's blue eyes clouded, and he grew unusually grave. "I never expected to live through this war. But if we are conquered, I don't want to live anyway."

Clay stared at him. It was so unlike Stuart, and Clay had never suspected that his general felt that deeply about the war. Before he could think of a suitable reply, Jeb suddenly grinned and yelled at the men to hurry up. It was time to get moving again.

SWÖRD

Yellow Tavern was named after an ancient inn that was painted a sickly yellow, and what town there was didn't look much better than the inn. It was a shabby, mean little bunch of old houses and storefronts all huddled together. To the north were thick woods, clearing nearer the tavern. Fenced-in fields almost surrounded the small settlement.

They reached it about 10:00 a.m., and there was not one blue coat in sight. Stuart made dispositions of his men; because the cavalry corps had been split up to counter Sheridan's numerous units, he had only about eleven hundred men with him. Basically they just took what scant cover they could find and then waited.

At about noon they saw the first Yankees, and by about two o'clock they knew they were badly outnumbered. Stuart had sent to Richmond for reinforcements and expected them at any time. The first attack came before any reinforcements reached them.

In the blue ranks of the 5th Michigan, a trooper named John A. Huff rode along, one in a sea of blue coats. He was forty-two years old and in 1861 had joined the 2nd U.S. Sharpshooters, a crack regiment that had become famous as Berdan's Sharpshooters. He had won a prize as the regiment's best shot, an expert among hundreds of crack marksmen.

Huff had been wounded and had gone home but had returned later and reenlisted in the Michigan cavalry. He was a good soldier, though he was not spectacular. He was married and had been a carpenter before the war. Huff had mild blue eyes, brown hair, and a light complexion, and stood only five feet eight inches tall. Late in the morning of May 11, he was moving toward a battle, but he, no more than the rest of his fellows, knew whom they were to fight.

Jeb Stuart's cavalry, along with the rest of the Confederate Army, were accustomed to being outnumbered. But by four o'clock, they had taken some heavy losses, and though the Yankees had, too, it seemed the distant woods never stopped crawling with more oncoming men. Every squad, every company, had wounded men.

Blithely Jeb Stuart rode here and there, whistling a tune, encouraging them. "Stay steady, boys," he shouted. "Give it to 'em! Shoot them! Shoot them!"

Clay stubbornly followed him everywhere, and he grew more and more nervous. The fire was heavy, and he said, "General, there are men behind stumps and fences being killed, and here you are out in the open."

Stuart turned, and there was laughter in his light blue eyes. "I don't reckon there's any danger, Lieutenant," he said.

He turned and in a canter rode to a placed cannon on the near side of the road from the town. Every trooper manning it had been injured. On his big gray horse Stuart called out to them, "Steady, men! Line it up and give it to them!"

Suddenly a group of Federal cavalry that had gotten through the line of battle filed along to the left of the fence on the far side of the dusty road. They were passing within ten or fifteen feet of General Stuart. One blue-coated horseman who had been dismounted in a charge trotted along with them. Clay saw him pull his pistol, take what looked to be a casual aim on the run, and fire. The man was John Huff.

Just in front of him, Stuart reeled in his saddle.

"General, are you hit?" Clay asked.

"Yes."

"You wounded bad?"

"I'm afraid I am. But don't worry, boys. Fitz will do as well for you as I have."

Clay and several other troopers surrounded Stuart. One of them, Captain Dorsey, rode very close and steadied the general so he could stay in his saddle. They rode toward the rear.

Jeb said, "No, I don't want to leave the field!"

Captain Dorsey said gently, "We're taking you back a little, General, so as not to leave you to the enemy."

Stuart relented and said, "Take the papers from my inside

pocket. Keep them from the Yankees."

Two troopers dashed off to get an ambulance and to find General Fitzhugh Lee, Robert E. Lee's nephew, who served as divisional commander of the 1st Virginia under Stuart. Under fire, Clay, Captain Dorsey, and the other men surrounding Stuart had to keep falling back. Stuart said, "You officers need to leave me and go back and drive them."

Clay said, "No sir, just a little farther in the rear now, and we'll wait for the ambulance."

"I'm afraid they've killed me, Lieutenant. I'll be of no use. You go back and fight."

"I can't obey that order," Clay said. "I'd rather they get me, too, than leave you for them. We'll have you out of here."

Very soon the ambulance, General Fitz Lee, and Jeb's doctor, John Fontaine, arrived. As soon as Lee arrived, Stuart said, "Go ahead, Fitz, old fellow. I know you'll do what's right."

They loaded him into the ambulance, and not a single word, not a groan, crossed his lips. But just before the ambulance pulled out, he raised himself up and called out in his booming voice, "Go back! Go back! Do your duty as I've done mine. I would rather die than be whipped!"

Troopers were all around them, falling back from the still-oncoming Yankees.

Clay's mouth pressed together in a tight line. Wheeling Lightning, he turned and galloped back toward Yellow Tavern, shouting to the faltering men as he went. Stuart's words had cut into his very soul, and he knew he must obey his order and return to the battle still raging behind them.

He was afraid it would be the last order he ever received from Jeb Stuart.

❧

Although they were only six miles outside of Richmond, fighting raged all along the Brooks Turnpike, the main road into the city. The ambulance was forced to take back roads. They reached a quiet little bridge on a deserted road, and Dr. Fontaine called for a halt so he could examine Stuart.

With his final order to his men, they had returned to the fray, so with Stuart now were Lieutenant Walter Hullihen and Major Charles Venable from his staff, Dr. Fontaine, two couriers, and three men of the general's escort.

Dr. Fontaine unhooked Stuart's double-breasted jacket and unwound his gold satin sash, now crimson with blood. His face grew grave.

Stuart turned to Hullihen, one of his favorites, whom he always called "Honeybun." With weak cheer he asked, "Honeybun, how do I look in the face?"

"You're looking all right, General. You'll be all right."

"Well, I don't know how it will turn out, but if it's God's will that I shall die, I am ready."

Dr. Fontaine had observed that the bullet was very close to Stuart's liver and might kill him at any time. He poured out some whiskey into a cup. "Try some of this. It will help you," he said.

"No," Stuart said at once. "I've never tasted it in my life. I promised my mother that when I was just a baby."

They urged him to drink, and finally he relented and held up his hands. "Lift me." He took a drink of the whiskey and settled back, seeming somewhat eased.

For long hours they made their torturous, circuitous way toward Richmond. They went through small towns and passed many soldiers, and the word spread that General Stuart had been wounded.

Despairing of reaching Richmond, Dr. Fontaine finally ordered the couriers to ride ahead to Mechanicsville, a small outlying district of Richmond just to the northwest. He told them to go to the home of Dr. Charles Brewer and tell them to prepare a bed for the general.

Dr. Brewer was Jeb's brother-in-law; he was married to Flora's sister, Maria. It was very late before they reached the Brewer home. At midnight a dismal thunderstorm broke, and it began to rain.

SWÖRD

In the city the bad news spread quickly. Even before dawn crowds lined the streets and gathered outside of the Brewer home. In the throngs, women wept.

Flora Stuart was in the country, at the home of Colonel Edmund Fontaine. He was the president of the Virginia Railroad, and his gracious plantation house was about a mile and a half from the major junction at Beaver Dam. She received the telegram with the news early the next morning.

Beaver Dam was about thirty-five miles from Mechanicsville, and in peaceful times she could have reached Jeb's side in less than a day. But war was the ruler of this land, and along with bloodshed it brought all the follies and vagaries: railroad tracks were torn up, side roads were blocked by fiery skirmishes, bridges were burned. The raging storm continued on, turning even good roads into impossible quagmires. Flora did not reach her sister's home until eleven o'clock that night. She was three hours late.

Throughout the day, Stuart's condition grew steadily worse. Like Stonewall Jackson had, almost a year ago to the day, Jeb Stuart returned again and again to the battlefield, muttering orders to his men. Once he rose up and shouted, "Make haste!"

In one of his peaceful times, when he was calm and quiet and free from the terrible pain, he gave instructions about his personal effects. He gave away his two horses to two of his men; he instructed that his gold spurs be sent to his longtime friend, Lily Lee of Shepherdstown; he said that his official papers must be disposed of. "And," he said quietly, "give my sword to my son."

President Jefferson Davis had hurried to Jeb's side. He asked, "General, how do you feel?"

"Easy, but willing to die if God and my country think I have fulfilled my destiny and done my duty."

After the president left, Reverend Joshua Peterkin of Saint

James Episcopal Church came and prayed with Stuart. After the prayer, Jeb said slowly, "Sing. Let's sing 'Rock of Ages.' " The men gathered in the room sang the old stately hymn, and Stuart joined in, singing in a low voice. After the hymn was over, he was visibly weaker.

Later on in the afternoon, Stuart asked, "How long can I live, Charles? Can I last through the night?"

His brother-in-law shook his head. "I'm afraid the end is near."

Stuart nodded. "I am resigned, if it be God's will. I would like to see my wife. But God's will be done."

The day wore on, endlessly, it seemed, to Jeb's attendants. That night Dr. Brewer was standing over him, and Jeb said, "I'm going fast now. God's will be done." And then he was gone. The pulse was still. It was twenty-two minutes before eight on the evening of May 12, 1864.

As soon as Flora arrived, she knew by the gravity of the men standing aimlessly about on the veranda and in the entryway exactly what had happened. She went in to him, to be alone with him in the candlelight. Slowly grief overwhelmed her. But it did not seem strange. In her deepest heart, she had always known this would happen.

And so passed the Knight of the Golden Spurs from this world. He had gone to his long home.

Weeping, Flora's sister, Maria, snipped off a lock of Jeb's red-gold hair, tied it with a ribbon, and thrust it into an envelope. Then she slowly assembled the few things in his pockets:

An embroidered pincushion, worked on one side in gold thread: Gen. J. E. B. Stuart. On the other side was a Confederate flag bearing the legend: GLORY TO OUR IMMORTAL CAVALRY!

A copy of an order to Stuart's troops, written with his customary dash and flair:

SWORD

We now, as in all battles, mourn the loss of many brave and valued comrades. Let us avenge our fallen heroes; and at the word, move upon the enemy with the determined assurance that in victory alone is honor and safety.

A letter to Flora, telling her of his plans to bring her to his headquarters.

An original general order of congratulations to the victorious infantry he had led at Chancellorsville.

A letter from his brother, W. A. Stuart.

A letter asking Jeb to find a government job for a friend.

A poem on the death of a child, clipped from a newspaper.

A New Testament.

A handkerchief.

A lock of Little Flora's hair.

CHAPTER TWENTY-FIVE

The funeral was held on May 13th at Saint James Church, with the Reverend Peterkin officiating. There was no music in the Richmond streets, no military escort. The city was so nearly under siege that customary honors could not be performed, even for this most well-beloved son of Virginia.

President Davis was at the funeral, and all of the officers that could be spared from active duty, but none of Jeb's men were there. In the church, Flora's helpless sobs were drowned out by the cannon fire on the heights just above the city.

The coffin went into the waiting hearse. Four white horses drew it, and their headdresses were made of black feathers, so suggestive of the fancy ostrich plumes that Jeb had worn in his wide-brimmed hat. At Hollywood Cemetery the Reverend Charles Minnegerode spoke very briefly in his thick German accent. They placed the coffin in a vault, and the carriages moved away. Just as the funeral party left the cemetery, the rain began once more.

North of Richmond, in a vicious skirmish on Drewry's Bluff, Clay paused for a moment as he realized that Jeb Stuart was being buried in the city below. He felt as if his heart would break, for he, and all of Jeb's men, did not think of Stuart merely as their general. He was noble and fearless and valiant, he was their leader, and they loved him.

Clay thought, *His time was so short, Lord, too short! He and Miss Flora were so happy, and even in her grief I know that she doesn't regret a single minute. I'm a fool. I've been a fool. I need to beg Chantel to marry me, right now, war or not. Even if she were my wife for only a day and I died the next, it would be worth it!*

Then, recalling his general's last command, he turned, drew his saber, yelled, "Charge!" and galloped toward the enemy.

Again, in spite of overwhelming odds against them, the Confederates beat back the Union forces from their attempt to send gunboats up the James River to Richmond. After the battle, Clay and his company were ordered to return to the front lines, about eight miles north. The night was wild, with violent thunderstorms sweeping them with walls of rain. No lantern could shine in such a maelstrom, and so the horsemen began carefully picking their way along the road north, lit only by constant stabs of lightning.

Clay lingered behind, glancing back toward Richmond. He looked up; the troop was some distance in front of them. Suddenly he wheeled Lightning and turned back south at a breathtaking gallop.

After the Battle of the Wilderness, Jacob had contributed his enormous sutler's tent to the Glorious Cause. The wounded streamed in again by the hundreds. The hospitals, the warehouses, the barns, and the private homes that could accommodate patients were already overflowing. Surrounding Richmond, in every clearing, were field hospitals. Jacob's tent had made a good surgeon's operating room.

Jacob had rented a tidy little cottage just on the northern outskirts of town, close to the fairgrounds, where hundreds of two-man pup tents still sheltered wounded men. Chantel and Jacob traveled around to the different field hospitals every day in the wagon, which had become a medical transport and which now held bandages, liniment, rubbing alcohol, and medicines instead of sutler's goods.

It was almost three o'clock in the morning when he reached the little cottage, but Clay was beyond caring. He banged on the door and called out desperately, "Chantel! Chantel, please!"

After only a few moments, she opened the door, pulling on a dressing gown. Her long black hair was down, and her eyes were huge and luminous. "Clay—" she began, but he stepped forward and swept her into his arms, holding her so tightly she could barely breathe. He kissed her with desperation. She clung to him tightly. Behind her Clay could see Jacob peek down the hallway from his bedroom, but then he quickly disappeared and closed the door.

Clay fell to his knees as if he were praying and clutched both of her hands. "Chantel, my most precious love, I had to come. I had to come *now*. I—I don't want to be alone anymore. I want you to be my wife, because then even when I'm not here with you, I won't be alone. You'll be a part of me, and I'll be a part of you. Will you please, please marry me?"

She, too, fell to her knees and took his face in her hands. "Don't you know, Clay? Don't you know me? You'll never have to beg me for anything, ever. Especially not this. I will marry you. I would marry you right now if we could."

"Oh Chantel," he said, clutching her to him. "How I wish we could, right now! But soon, soon! As soon as I can arrange it. I don't know how I will, but I know this. You're the only woman for me. God sent you to me that awful day. Just to me, because we are supposed to be together. I know this is His will."

"I know this, too," Chantel said. "I would never love anyone but you, Clay Tremayne."

Slowly he rose and helped her up. He searched her face. "I can't stay."

"I know," she said quietly. "But you send me word, Clay. I'll be right here waiting."

SWÖRD

❧

On May 29, Chantel and Jacob sat in the sitting room, a homey small corner of the house with two comfortable rocking chairs, a sofa, and two armchairs.

Gathered around was Clay's family. Chantel and Clay's mother, Bethany, sat on the sofa, the twins squeezed between them, quietly sewing. Chantel was making a gold satin sash for Clay, and Bethany was embroidering the distinctive Hussar's facings on a new short jacket. Although the day was warm, a fitful rain dampened the air and a small but merry fire snapped in the fireplace. Morgan and Caleb Tremayne stood by it, sipping coffee and talking quietly to Jacob, who sat close in one of the rocking chairs.

"I don't understand how he's going to get leave to come," Morgan said. He spoke in a low tone, thinking Chantel would not hear.

She didn't look up from her sewing. "He'll come," she said firmly. "He'll be here."

Grant had continued in his unyielding march toward Richmond. Lee had moved the Army of Northern Virginia to Cold Harbor and planted them squarely between Grant and the city. They were arrayed in a battle formation that was seven miles long, and they were digging in. No soldier could hope for a leave. Grant and his tens of thousands were too close.

But three nights previously, a scared little boy of only thirteen, a courier, had brought the message from Clay. *In three days, dear Chantel, you and I will be married. God bless you, my darling.*

It was noon, and they had a light dinner. Afternoon brought more rain. Bethany began to teach Chantel to knit. Chantel said very little, but she looked happy and expectant, never doubtful.

The twins grew impatient. Belinda said, "Maybe Clay can't come. Maybe it's raining too much."

"Raining too much," Brenda echoed.

Chantel smiled. "You should know Lightning would bring Clay even in the rain. Clay promised, he did. He won't break his promise. He'll be here anytime now."

And at about three o'clock, he came riding up, Lightning snorting and stamping, and he had another cavalryman with him. Chantel had barely opened the door when they came in, snatching off their dripping hats and frock coats. Clay kissed her soundly and said, "Did you think I wouldn't make it?"

"No, I didn't think that, me," she said, blushing a little. "You promised."

Morgan was helping him out of his coat. "Well, I want to know how you wrangled a leave. There hasn't been a soldier inside the city for weeks."

"I asked politely the first time," Clay answered, "but that didn't work too well. So I told Captain Dorsey that I was going to desert. And the captain said that he couldn't hear me too well, and he turned his back and stalked off. And then I deserted. And this is my friend, Private Elijah Young. He's a preacher."

Young, a slight man of thirty with fine blond hair, wide blue eyes, and thin features, said mournfully, "Lieutenant Tremayne made me desert, too."

"Too bad," Clay grunted. "I needed you. I want to get married. Right now."

"What, like this?" Young blurted out. Both of them were dusty and damp and smelled like horses. Their boots and scabbards were splashed with red mud. Clay had a long streak of black powder on his cheek.

Nonchalantly, Chantel licked her fingers and reached up to scrub it off. "Right now, just like this, Pastor Young," she said. "I want to get married now, too, me."

And so Young fished a slim book from the pocket of his frock coat—*Rites and Ceremonies of the Christian Church*—and went to stand in front of the fireplace. Clay took his place in front of him. Jacob came to Chantel, entwined her arm in his, and escorted her to Clay's side.

"Who giveth this woman in marriage?" Pastor Young asked.

"I'm her grandfather," Jacob said quietly, "and gladly I give her to join in marriage with this man." He took his seat in the rocking chair.

Clay took Chantel's hand and turned her so that they were facing each other. When they repeated the timeworn, solemn vows, they spoke only to each other.

"And now, Lieutenant Tremayne, you may kiss your bride," Young said, grinning boyishly.

They had not kissed many times, because both of them had been so careful to preserve the purity of their relationship. This kiss, Chantel thought, was like a vow and a promise in itself, that she and her husband gave to each other.

The men all congratulated Clay, and Bethany and the twins hugged Chantel. But only minutes after he had finished the ceremony, Private Young said, "Lieutenant, you may have ordered me to desert, and I did. But now I'm heading back, before the provosts come looking for us. Please don't order me to stay deserted."

"Go on, and if you meet those provosts on their way here," Clay said grandly, "you tell them I said they can arrest me tomorrow. Because tonight is my honeymoon, and if I have to fight off a battalion to have it, I will!"

The Tremayne family was staying in town with friends, and they had invited Jacob to come stay with them so that Clay and Chantel could have their one night together in her little house. They didn't linger long, and soon Clay and Chantel were alone.

He kissed her again, softly and sweetly. Then he lifted his head and stared down at her, slight worry furrowing his brow. "I'm so sorry it had to be like this," he said. "I would have liked for us to have had a big wedding and at least a weeklong honeymoon."

"I would like that, too," Chantel said, "but I would rather be married to you now, like this, instead of waiting for that big wedding. But I—I—" She blushed and finished shyly, "I wish we had a longer honeymoon, too. Still, one night now is better than a week when this war is over. I just—I'm not—I don't know—"

He pulled her close and ran his hands over her thick glossy black hair. "I have another promise to make to you," he said in a deep voice "I promise that on this night, we'll learn what real love, God's pure and abiding love that He gives to a man and wife, really is. Both of us will learn."

The 1st Virginia Cavalry, under the command of Fitzhugh Lee, fought on as valiantly as they ever had under Jeb Stuart, although without the same fierce joy. Clay fought the Battle of Cold Harbor in June, and then the Army of Northern Virginia wheeled around to Petersburg. Grant had circled them and invested the old city to approach Richmond from the south, and once again Lee positioned his men between him and the capital of the Confederacy. The siege of Petersburg lasted from June 1864 through March 1865.

During the winter, when both of the armies listlessly huddled in their winter quarters, Clay managed to get leave several times to ride back to Richmond and see Chantel. But that first year of their marriage, they were together few enough times that Chantel could count them on her fingers. Though she worried, she refused to lose hope. In her heart she believed that Clay had been so grievously wounded and had been healed, and that had been God's plan to bring them together. All during that endless year, even as the Confederacy slowly disintegrated into a smoking ruin, she was certain that she and Clay would live out their days, together, in peace.

By the end of March 1865, General Lee knew that the end was near, and he could no longer guard Richmond. The army moved west to join other forces in the Shenandoah Valley. Clay sent Chantel and Jacob to his parents' home in Lexington. Grant, with nothing to stop him now, occupied Richmond and dogged Lee. The forlorn retreat of the Army of Northern Virginia lasted only a week. It ended at Appomattox Court House.

SWORD

General Grant rode up to Wilmer McLean's fine two-story home. He was shabby and dusty. He had on a single-breasted blouse made of dark blue flannel, unbuttoned in front, showing a waistcoat underneath. His trousers were tucked into muddy boots. He had no spurs, and he wore no sword. The only designation of his rank was a pair of faded shoulder straps with four dimmed stars.

The aides he had sent ahead were waiting for him, and a group of Confederates, dressed in rather worn full-dress uniforms stood around the home.

Grant dismounted. "He's already here?" he asked an aide.

"Yes, sir."

Grant nodded and hurried into the house.

Clay had found the remnants of the Louisiana Tigers, and Armand Latane was there, in his full-dress uniform. It was clean, but it was faded and patched, as was Clay's uniform. They watched as Grant and General Phil Sheridan went inside with several other officers.

"And so it's over," Armand murmured. "At last. I joined, I fought, I thought that we would win. Until the winter, in Petersburg."

Clay said quietly, "You know, when I joined, I just knew the South would win. I kept thinking that, even after Grant came after us and kept pushing us back, throwing more and more men at us. But on the day Jeb Stuart was shot, I began to think that we were going to lose. It's as if all my hopes were in him. That was wrong. No one man can win a war. But I couldn't help it. Not one day since that day did I ever think again that we would be able to beat them." The two could say nothing more.

Finally the door opened, and the two generals came out. Clay sighed deeply when he saw Robert E. Lee. He was dressed in a new uniform, spotless and crisp. A great heavy sword, the hilt bejeweled, was at his side. He stood erect, his bearing as always dignified and grave, but deep sadness was written on his face. His eyes went out over the fields and valley below, where his army waited for him to speak to them for the last time. He mounted Traveler, his beautiful, graceful gray horse, and settled his hat on his head. As he rode through the silent gray ranks, he said, "Go to your homes and resume your occupations. Obey the laws and become as good citizens as you were soldiers."

Clay stacked his musket, setting it upright alongside Armand's. "I hope I never have to raise my hand to another man again," he said wearily. "All I want is a quiet life, a simple life, with Chantel."

Armand laid his hand on Clay's shoulder. "My friend, your life might be simple, yes. But with Chantel I doubt it will be quiet. You got the prize, my friend. Never forget that."

"Never," Clay repeated firmly. "I never will."

He could see his house, up on a rise, with a small green valley below it. It was almost a mile off the main road. He rode slowly, for Lightning was weary. Clay himself had grown thin and was a much weaker man than he had been before wintering in Petersburg. But as he drew nearer to his house, he suddenly felt a surge of energy that somehow translated itself to Lightning. The horse raised his lowered head as in the old days when he had caught the scent of battle, and with the slightest touch of Clay's heels, he began to canter and then to gallop.

Chantel was sitting on the veranda, sipping tea and knitting. At the first distant sounds of hoofbeats, she looked up alertly. Then she jumped to her feet, lifted her skirts, and took off down the road at a dead run.

Clay slid off Lightning even before he stopped. Chantel threw herself into his arms. For a long time they stood there, clasped in each other's arms, saying nothing. Finally Clay put one finger under her chin, lifted her face, and kissed her. The kiss, too, lasted for a long time.

Lightning stopped for a moment, but as they stayed clasped in their embrace, he unconcernedly trotted past them and went to the shade trees on the side of the yard, where there was a watering trough.

Arm in arm Clay and Chantel walked toward the house. "It's

over," Clay said, marveling. "It's over, and I'm home. And the biggest miracle is that you're here. My wife. I love you dearly, my wife."

"I love you dearly, too, me," Chantel said, laughing. "It's good that you're home. You're too skinny, you. Maybe I catch an alligator and cook it, fatten you up."

"Even alligator sounds good right now," Clay sighed. "It's been a long time since I've eaten a good, solid meal."

They went up onto the veranda, and Clay started to go in, but Chantel pulled at his arm and said, "Sit down here for a minute with me. I should get to see my husband alone for a little while when he comes home from this war."

They sat down in two rockers, Clay pulling his so close to Chantel's that she couldn't rock. But she obviously didn't care. They held hands and looked out over the peaceful valley.

Clay said, "On the way home, I thought a lot about what I would like to do, Chantel."

"And what is that?"

"Well, first I want to be the best husband who ever lived," he said lightly. Then he sobered a little and continued, "I'm sick of fighting. I'm sick of killing and hurting men. I want to do something good, something to help people instead of hurting them. I think I'd like to be a doctor."

With delight Chantel clapped her hands. "Oh Clay, you would be such a good, such a fine doctor! And you can get rich and buy me lots of pretty dresses!"

"I surely will," he said, grinning. "All you want."

"But that's not the only reason I would be glad you'll be a doctor," she said firmly. "There is another reason. You must hurry, Clay, and start studying right now."

"What? Why?" he asked, bewildered.

"Because," she said slowly, "around about September I'm going to need a doctor."

He stared at her wide-eyed. Then his gaze fell to the knitting on the little low table by Chantel's chair. Slowly he reached down, lifted it up, and saw with shock that Chantel was knitting a pair of baby's booties.

"This—we're going to have a baby?" he breathed.

"Yes."

"In—in September?"

"Yes."

Clay jumped up, Chantel jumped up, and he put his hands on her waist and held her high in the air and whooped like a madman.

They were just like a young couple who had lived in Fort Leavenworth, Kansas, in 1855.

They could have been Flora and Jeb Stuart.

the SURRENDER

PART ONE

CHAPTER ONE

Miss Mary Anna Randolph Custis walked out onto the porch and paused, as she usually did, to look around and savor the day.

It was a hot, hard, bright morning in August of 1829. The sky was a deep blue with no cloud puffs to soften it. Below the gracious home on the hill was the lazy Potomac River and just beyond lay the city of Washington, DC. The distance mellowed the outlines of the shabby town, and heat shimmers made it appear dreamlike.

Mary lifted her head and sniffed appreciatively as she caught the elusive scent of roses, the last blooms in the luxuriant rose garden by Arlington Mansion.

She went down the steps and surveyed the pony cart waiting in the drive. A slave held the mare as Mary inspected the eight large baskets in the cart. Filled with sweet cherries, they glowed a glorious crimson in the glaring sun. For a moment Mary considered parking the cart under a nearby oak tree so she could paint it: cart, horse, slave, cherries, and all. They made a wonderful picture, and one of Mary's loves was painting. She was a gifted artist.

Finally aloud she said, "No, I suppose the hands will enjoy the cherries much more than I would enjoy painting them." She came around to pet the mare's nose and asked, "Did you get the things I wanted for Bitty, Colley?"

The slave, a small somber man, nodded. "Yes, Miss Mary. I put the mugs and the pitcher and the ice block under the seat, all packed nice in sawdust. But don't you want me to go fetch one of the boys to drive this around?"

"No, I'm taking it," Mary said firmly. "But I don't want to bounce around in the cart. I'm just going to walk." She pulled the mare's reins down and wrapped them once around her hand.

"But Miss Mary, it's hot, and it's probably a two-mile walk all around the quarters," Colley said helplessly as Mary started walking down the drive.

"I'll be fine, Colley. Stop fussing. You're as bad as Bathsheba," she said over her shoulder.

Colley returned to the house, muttering, "That Miss Mary's got a stubborn streak wide as that river! Ain't no telling her nothing!"

Mary heard his muttering, and a fleeting smile crossed her lips. She had heard such dire imprecations all her life—from the helpless entreaties of her mother and father to mutterings and grumblings from house servants like Colley, who were prone to taking more liberties than the farmhands.

Only twenty-two years of age, she was already finding that she understood some of their care for her, particularly her parents' concern. Mary Lee Fitzhugh Custis and George Washington Parke Custis had had four children, and Mary Anna was the only one to survive infancy.

She was tiny, her frame as small and delicate as a bird's, and she was fragile. She had dark brown hair, thick and curly, and her rich brown eyes were probably her best feature, wide and fringed with thick dark lashes below the smooth oval of her forehead. She was not pretty, she knew: her chin was too pointed, her nose too long, her mouth not full and pouty as was the fashion. But she was attractive, particularly to men, as they found her interesting, amusing, and vivacious. Though she was small, she had a fire within her, and it showed in her alert, quick expression and her sparkling eyes.

Walking down the path to the south slave quarters, she savored each moment. The grounds surrounding the house were a clean, solemn forest, cool even in the hottest of summers. It was quiet and peaceful. Accompanying the creaks of the cart and the mare's plodding steps were the cheerful calls of birds. Everywhere Mary looked was a shade of green, mottled only by the lichen-gray stands of boulders that were allowed to stay in the much-manicured woods.

When she reached the first cabin, she saw with dismay that the elderly slave Bitty wasn't sitting out on her porch, as she always did in fine weather. Tying the mare's reins to a porch post, she knocked on the door and called softly, "Bitty? It's me, Miss Mary. May I come in?"

"Yes, ma'am, miss." She heard faintly.

She went inside and saw the woman on her small bed, struggling to get up. Quickly she went to her side and laid her hands on the woman's shoulders. "No, no, Bitty, don't get up. I heard you weren't feeling well, so I came to see about you." She propped up a pillow so Bitty could sit up. "I brought you some things. I'll just be a minute."

From the wagon Mary got a tin pitcher and two covered mugs and then went back to get the ice block. It was sitting in a small crate filled with sawdust and covered with a linen cloth. When she had all the items on the kitchen table, she pulled a chair up to Bitty's bedside and asked, "How are you feeling, Bitty? What's wrong?"

"Touch of catarrh is all, I guess," she said tiredly. "Dunno how I got it in middling of summer, but here it is. Sneezing and coughing and sniffling like it's dead winter. Cold one minute and hot the next."

Mary nodded. "That's the fever. I brought just the thing for you, some wine whey, and it's still warm. It'll break that fever, and then maybe you'll feel like having some fresh cherry cordial. I even brought you some ice so you can have it nice and cold." Mary brought her one of the covered mugs and a spoon. "Here, this will make you feel so much better, Bitty."

"I'm just not very hungry, Miss Mary," she said wanly. She was normally a hearty woman, thickly built and sturdy, but now Mary could see that she had lost some weight and looked drawn.

"None of that," Mary argued. "Either you eat it, or I'm spoon-feeding you."

"Yes, ma'am," Bitty said resignedly.

Though Bitty had been a farmhand, Mary Anna, along with all the slaves, was aware of her strong will. After Bitty took a few cautious spoonfuls, Mary could see from the slave's reaction she liked wine whey, which was basically milk boiled with white wine.

Mary continued to watch her, hawklike, until Bitty finished.

Taking the mug and spoon, Mary efficiently washed them up and laid them by the sink to dry. "Father bought forty bushels of sweet cherries," she told Bitty as she chipped ice to make her a small cordial. "I'm taking a bushel to everyone. Would you like me to leave yours, Bitty, or would you rather that I take them back and have the kitchen put them up for you?"

"No'm, I love cherries. I'd like to have them," Bitty said, her eyes brightening. "And please tell Mr. Custis my thank-yous. And to you, too, Miss Mary."

After making sure Bitty's cabin was in order, Mary went back out to the wagon and continued her long circular walk around the Arlington property, stopping at each cabin to give the families the cherries, greeting all the children by name and asking all the women—the men were working—little details about their families and their work at Arlington. Finally her cart was empty, and it was almost a half-mile walk back up to the house. Though it irritated her, Mary admitted to herself that she was tiring, so she drove the cart back home.

As she pulled up to the gracious portico, her maidservant

Bathsheba came hurrying out of the house, scolding with every breath. "There you are, all hot and wearied. Your hair all down, and your dress smudged all 'round at the hem! Ain't a bit of sense in you going wandering all over this place like a peddler, but can a body tell you that? No, ma'am!"

"No, ma'am," Mary smartly repeated as she climbed down from the cart. "I wasn't wandering, Bathsheba. I was going around to the quarters, taking everyone some cherries. It was a very pleasant walk."

As Mary went into the house, Bathsheba followed her, making shooing motions. Bathsheba had actually been Mary's nursemaid and was now a woman of forty, round and plump, with a jolly disposition, although she was often as severe with Mary as she had been when she was a willful child. As she followed Mary up the stairs, she said, "Now you knew you was having a caller this evening, Miss Mary, and what did you do? Go traipsing off and get hot and get your dress as dirty as an urchin, and what happened to those nice curls I did this morning?"

"They melted," Mary answered shortly. "I got hot. I want a sponge bath, Bathsheba, and then I'll change clothes. I still have plenty of time."

"No, you ain't," Bathsheba argued. "How is it you're such a smart girl, and you can't tell time for nothing? You know Mr. Robert is always right on spanking time to the minute, and you always keep him shuffling his feet and fidgeting, talking to your mama and daddy."

As they went into her bedroom, Mary turned and smiled mischievously at her maid. "Oh, Mr. Robert will wait," she said. "He always waits."

❦

Robert E. Lee passed the apple orchard, the overseer's house, Arlington Spring, and the dance pavilion and turned up the wide drive to Arlington Mansion. He felt like the object of a master's painting of a soldier riding at ease. He hoped he also looked the part.

Perfectly erect in the saddle, he sat the horse so easily it was as if they were one. He wore the dress uniform of a lieutenant in the United States Army, Engineer Corps. His gauntlets were of the softest yellow kid. A simple dark blue frock coat with a single row of brass buttons, the somber grandeur of a military uniform was evoked by the high collar with a wreath encircling the single star of a lieutenant embroidered in gold thread and heavy gold epaulettes. His trousers were plain blue, and he wore spotlessly shined boots. His spurs were gold. The US Army regulation hat for officers was a low-crowned, wide-brimmed blue with gold braid trim. It was called a "slouch hat," but there was nothing at all about Robert E. Lee that might be called slouchy.

At twenty-two years of age, Lee had reached full maturity. According to many young ladies he had become an exceedingly handsome man, but he was not so sure himself. His wide brow lay beneath black hair so thick and glossy and wavy that many women desperately envied it. His eyes were well set, of a brown so dark that sometimes they looked black. He had a straight patrician nose and a wide mouth, slightly upturned at the corners, which gave him a habitual expression of goodwill, though his jaw and chin were very firm.

Passing through the farm fields, he came to the grounds of the estate, which had been left so heavily wooded that it was called "The Park" rather than the grounds. Ahead he relished the first glimpse of Arlington House, as he had each of the many times he had visited this home. Set up on a gentle hill above the river, the wide veranda with eight great Doric columns made the house look more like a Greek temple than a private dwelling. It invoked a feeling of serenity and peace.

When he reached the house, a servant appeared to take his horse, and Colley opened the door to him. "Good afternoon, Lieutenant Lee," he said, taking his hat and gauntlets. "If you'll just come with me, suh." Colley led him into the drawing room.

George Washington Parke Custis and his wife Mary, who was called "Molly," greeted him warmly, and soon Robert was installed in a comfortable armchair, sipping a cherry ice.

As with all the rooms he had seen in Arlington House, he thought the parlor was elegantly appointed, the furnishings lavish, but it was still a comfortable room. The two tall windows had white linen shades, which were opened to the east. The fireplace had a brass fire screen fashioned as a peacock, with brass andirons in a holder with the same design. A large rectangular looking glass was over the George III chimney piece. A Dutch oak bookcase, a gold velvet camelback sofa with matching armchairs, and two William IV rosewood carved round tables made a comfortable corner for visiting.

"Mary will be down soon, Robert," Molly said. She was a pretty woman, with a blue-eyed-blond English look. "George bought enough sweet cherries for the entire plantation, and Mary took them around to everyone. She returned a bit later than she intended, I'm sure. I apologize for her tardiness."

"Please, Mrs. Custis, there's no need for apologies," Robert said, his dark eyes twinkling. "To know Miss Custis is to wait for Miss Custis. I would be afraid she was unwell if she were on time."

"'S truth." George Custis harrumphed. Short, balding, tending to plumpness, and generally of an amiable temperament, he still was impatient at times. "That girl will be late, no matter what I or her mother do or say. So, Robert, you cut quite a dashing figure in your shiny new uniform. Have you received any orders yet?"

"Yes, sir, I'm ordered to the Savannah River in Georgia, to Cockspur Island," he answered eagerly. "The US Army has decided to construct a fort there."

"Georgia?" Mr. Custis repeated darkly, as if he had never heard the word. "Cockspur Island? Sounds dreary and troublesome. I don't believe we have family in Savannah, do we, Molly?"

"The Edward Carter family and the James Randolph family

live in Atlanta," she said thoughtfully. "But no, I don't believe we are connected to Savannah."

George Custis was George Washington's step-grandson and a descendant of Baron Baltimore. The Parke and the Custis families were among the original colonists of Virginia. Mary Custis's maiden name was Mary Lee Fitzhugh. She was Robert's mother's cousin. The Parkes, the Custises, the Lees, and the Fitzhughs were all Founding Families, the aristocracy of America. George Custis in particular was so proud of his step-grandfather that he had collected much of George Washington's possessions and displayed them proudly at Arlington. Northern Virginia was his birthright, Arlington was his home, and he very rarely thought about any such obscure hinterlands as Savannah, Georgia.

Mary came in, tranquil and with slow grace in spite of the fact that she had kept Robert waiting, a breach of etiquette that she often committed with no apparent regret. Robert rose as she entered wearing a white dress patterned with small pink roses and a green sash encircling her small waist above the bell-shaped crinoline. Her cheeks were delicately flushed, her eyes were glowing, and the warmth in her smile of greeting was unmistakable. She held out both her hands, and he took them and bowed. "Mr. Lee! I'm so happy you called. It's good to see you again. How long will you be here this time? Where are you staying?"

Settling back in his chair, Lee replied, "I was just telling your mother and father that I'm assigned to Savannah, Georgia, but I don't have to report until the middle of November. I'm staying at Eastern View." This property was owned by one of his Carter cousins and was just outside of Alexandria, Virginia.

"Oh, good. Then you can call every day," Mary said with a mischievous glance at her father.

George Custis said, "Don't be foolish, Mary. Lieutenant Lee doesn't have time to call here every day and sit twiddling his thumbs waiting for you."

"Perhaps he does," Mary said. "Perhaps we should ask him."

She turned to him, eyes sparkling. "Mr. Lee? How is your schedule these days?"

"I've set aside plenty of time for thumb-twiddling," he replied. "I was sure to include it on my calendar, Miss Custis."

Molly Custis looked amused, while her husband made a slight grimace.

Robert knew Mr. Custis liked him and thought him a fine-looking man with an impeccable manner and noble bearing. But while the Lees were one of the most prominent families in Virginia, they were also poor, and Robert knew it was difficult for George Washington Parke Custis to envision the heiress of Arlington as living on an army lieutenant's pay. For years now the bond between Robert and Mary had grown from childhood friendship to one of mutual affection and esteem. Now that both were in their twenties, Robert knew the master of Arlington understood very well where his daughter's wishes lay, but Robert was not sure her father could be glad for her.

They talked for a while about small things: family, mutual acquaintances, and the army. As it grew later in the afternoon, Molly suggested, "George, I'd very much like to sit out on the portico and watch the sun set. Mary, Lieutenant Lee, perhaps you would care to join me?"

Mr. Custis decided to join them, too, and as the ladies collected their fans and instructed the servants to bring tea and cakes, he began to tell Robert about a new addition he had just acquired for the conservatory, a rare orchid.

As the four went out onto the veranda, Mary took Robert's arm, and the moment there was a lull in her father's raptures, she said, "Yes, Father, the orchid is interesting, and perhaps after we watch the sun set you might show it to Mr. Lee. But I noticed this morning that the last roses have bloomed, and I know he would like to see them."

"Yes, sir," Lee said instantly to Mr. Custis. "Perhaps you would give Miss Custis permission to show me your roses? Arlington

House is, after all, quite famous for the grounds and the gardens. I haven't toured the rose garden since last spring."

"Of course, of course," he said, smiling happily after Robert mentioned Arlington. "Mary, hurry on, so Lieutenant Lee can get the full benefit of the last light."

They walked down the steps and around to the north side of the house, where the large rose garden was situated. As they got out of the view of the veranda, without any signal passing between them, Mary clasped Robert's arm tighter and drew closer to him.

Robert slowed his pace so they walked very slowly down the rows of rosebushes. Though many of the bushes were already bare of flowers, some of them still had lush blooms on them. The garden's sweet scent enveloped them.

"You must miss your mother terribly, Robert," she said in a low voice of sympathy. "Please tell me, how are you coping?"

The last time she had seen him was at his mother's funeral, about a month and a half previously. Robert had nursed his mother through years of debilitating illness. "I do miss her very much," he said. "But she was a godly woman, and she is with her heavenly Father, well and whole and joyful. I couldn't wish her back." Brightening, he pointed to a red rose in full bloom, almost as big as a dinner dish. "That indeed is a glorious rose, Mary. Now I won't worry too much that I was exaggerating about Arlington's rose garden just so we might have a few moments alone."

"You? Exaggerate or prevaricate? Nonsense! There is not a shred of vanity or guile in you," she said, squeezing his arm. "And while I do understand that your code of honor as a gentleman would never permit you to even think of any dishonesty, I don't understand how you've kept from getting vain. You're perfectly lovely, Robert."

He flushed. "Men aren't lovely, Mary. I can't imagine why you would say such a thing about me. It's ridiculous."

"I think not. My cousin, Katherine Randolph, told me that she heard that at West Point they called you the 'Marble Model.' Perhaps I should call you that instead of lovely."

His face must have reflected a curious mixture of confusion, vexation, and embarrassment, as Mary laughed. "Never mind, Robert. I don't mean to embarrass you. If I did, I would have said that in front of my parents."

"Yes, I know, and I'm very grateful to you for sparing me that at least," he said with exasperation. Then, raising his eyebrows and cocking his head, he said, "I've heard gossip about you, too, Miss Custis. I heard that you've sent away several beaus this summer, among them congressman Sam Houston. And now the word is that Mr. Lynville Fitzhugh is actively courting you."

"Pah, he doesn't do anything *actively*," she said dismissively. "I understand that ever since Beau Brummel became an *arbiter elegantiarum*, languor of manner and contrived boredom are all the fashion on the Continent these days. I couldn't conceive of marrying such a silly man. Besides, he has a cast eye. And he's my cousin."

"Everyone in northern Virginia is your cousin, Mary," Robert said. "I'm your cousin."

"That's completely different," she said stoutly.

"How? Why?"

"Because you have the elegant and polished deportment of a gentleman, you are intelligent and accomplished and cultured, you are energetic and hardworking, and you don't have a cast eye," she finished triumphantly.

"I see," he said lightly. "I had no idea I was such a paragon. But I am beginning to see that it could definitely be to my advantage."

"To me you've always had many advantages over other men I've known, Robert," she said.

He stopped, turned, and took both of her hands. His dark, intense eyes searching her face, he said quietly, "And to me you've always been the most intriguing, the most charming, the most gracious, and the most captivating woman I've ever known."

"Do you mean that?" she asked breathlessly.

"Every word," he said firmly, "and every sentiment. But you

do understand, don't you, Mary, the position I'm in right now? I only graduated West Point in June. Now, thanks to the mercy and goodness of the Lord, my mother is at rest. I'm in the army, and I haven't even performed my first duty yet. I feel that I have a new life, and it is just beginning, just now."

"I understand, Robert," she said. "I understand everything. I'll be here, you know. When you've learned your new life, I'll be right here."

He bent to kiss her then for the first time, a mere brush of his lips against hers. When he raised his head, they exchanged brief smiles. Though it was unsaid by either of them, that kiss was a promise that they would keep.

CHAPTER TWO

Lieutenant Jack Mackay adjusted his wide-brimmed slouch hat so as to channel the heavy cold rain away from his neck. Then he continued the conversation. "But Robert, I really think my sister has become extremely attached to you. Don't tell me you haven't noticed!"

Lieutenant Robert E. Lee looked up quickly in alarm. "Jack, you don't think I've been misleading Miss Eliza, do you?"

"Of course not," he said dismissively. "And neither does she. But she does find your attentions very welcome. I can tell."

"I enjoy her company very much," Lee said, "and also Miss Catherine's. Both of your sisters are amiable and pleasant ladies." He resumed walking slowly along the earthen embankment, occasionally stopping to plunge a sharp stick into the side.

In the previous month, November, a gale had destroyed part of this earthen wall, and the site for the fort had flooded. Due to illness and then rambling bureaucratic shuffling in Washington, the major commanding the site was not there. It had been up to Lieutenant Lee to supervise the repair of the breach and to strengthen the entire protective mud wall. He inspected it several times a day when it was raining, even on a dismal and cold day such as this.

" 'Amiable and pleasant,' " his friend repeated. "That could be said of every lady of our acquaintance. Robert, I don't like to intrude, but may I ask you a question of a personal nature? Rude of me, I know, but I hope that you'll excuse me because of our long friendship."

Lee and Jack Mackay had been at West Point together, and they had been at Cockspur Island now for over a year. Somewhat to Mackay's surprise, Lee grinned at him. "You're going to ask me about why I've never courted anyone."

"Well, yes. Certainly you've had ample opportunity. The ladies all adore you. Barely notice I'm in the room when you're there," he added, grumbling.

"Nonsense," Lee said crisply. "Anyway, the answer to your admittedly rude, though forgivable question is that I have been courting a lady for a long time now."

Mackay nodded. "Miss Custis, isn't it? I know that every summer you spend most of your time up around Arlington House. And I know that you write her often."

"It is Miss Custis," Lee admitted readily. "It's always been Miss Custis."

The new commanding engineer reported to Cockspur Island just after Christmas. By spring, he had made his best evaluation: the plan for the fort would not do, and it must be redesigned. In April, Second Lieutenant Robert E. Lee was reassigned to Fort Monroe in Hampton, Virginia. Although it was almost one hundred eighty miles to the gracious home on the hills above Alexandria, it was still much closer than Savannah, Georgia.

Lieutenant Lee reported to his new post on May 7, 1831. Now with certainty in his course, he secured a leave of absence and made his way again up that long slope to Arlington House.

It was a gorgeous day, balmy with occasional cool breezes that carried the sweetest scent of all, jasmine. The cherry trees and dogwoods in the park were blooming, their virginal white flowers bright against the cool green of new leaves. Northern Virginia was in her best dress, that of a sunny spring.

He was greeted happily by the family, at least by Mary Custis and Mrs. Custis. George Custis welcomed him but was perhaps a touch less effusive than his wife and daughter.

Lee, of course, noticed this, but it made no difference to him. He knew Mary Custis as well as any person on earth can truly know another, and her thoughts and desires were the only thing that mattered to him.

They sat on the veranda for a while sipping lemonade and talking mostly about Arlington, for Mr. Custis invariably brought the conversation around to his much-beloved home. As he and Lee talked, Mr. Custis soon warmed up to him, as he always did. Robert E. Lee was cordial and pleasant, and he had a quick and curious mind. He never feigned interest in any of Mr. Custis's topics, whether it was George Washington or some scheme Mr. Custis had for an agricultural enterprise or news of the economy in England. Lee was truly interested in all of these things and many more.

Robert was invited to dinner, and just after sunset, they all repaired to the dining room. As it was still cool in the evenings, a fire had been lit, but in Robert's opinion it did little to make the formal room more inviting. It was a magnificent room, grandly furnished. A very long Charles X mahogany table was centered in the room, covered with the finest French damask cloth. Intricately carved mahogany Chippendale chairs lined the walls, except for the four set at the table. An enormous George II serpentine-front sideboard was on one wall, the fireplace on the other.

A slave, dressed in a dark suit with a tailed coat, white vest, and spotless white gloves, stood behind each chair. Robert saw with an inward sigh that he was stranded at one end of the long expanse of the table. Mr. Custis said grace, and the servants began to prepare each dish for the diners from the sideboard.

Before her father could monopolize the conversation again, Mary asked, "Mr. Lee, please tell us about your new position. I've never been to Hampton Roads, though I've heard it's a most pleasant holiday spot."

"Hampton Roads may be, but I'm afraid Fort Monroe isn't quite as congenial," Robert said. "At least there is actually a fort, which is more than can be said for Cockspur Island."

"And what is to be your work there, Lieutenant Lee?" Molly asked.

"Construction on the fort itself is pretty well complete. It houses a garrison, and in fact, they have just begun artillery training there. But the outerworks still aren't finished, and it's been decided to build an adjacent fort just offshore, on a rock bank sunk in deep water. I'm rather excited about the project," he said, warming to the subject. "I do hope I'm assigned to work on the new fort, and not just finishing the outerworks on Monroe."

"Good heavens, Mr. Lee, you've practically spent the last two years chin-deep in that swamp in Georgia," Mary said spiritedly. "To this day I cannot imagine how you kept from dying, either from some noxious swamp fever or from catching a deathly chill in the winters."

"I must have a strong constitution," he said. "Do you know, I've never been ill in my life, except for the usual childhood things."

"Yes, I know," Mary said so assuredly that her father gave her a strange look. "But most mortal men do get ill at one time or another in such an environment. I'm glad that you'll be better situated at Fort Monroe. So since it sounds already well established, I assume that they have adequate housing there? You know, officer's quarters—and married officer's houses?"

George Custis choked slightly on a bite of roasted pork, Molly Custis smiled knowingly, and Mary stared at Robert, her eyes sparkling, her expression challenging.

Robert E. Lee was definitely a man to squarely meet a challenge. "Oh yes, Miss Custis. Naturally I was most interested in the housing available. I saw several homes for officers. In fact, I am very partial to one of them. It is small, but it could be made into a comfortable home, I think, with the right touch."

"A woman's touch, I'm sure you mean," Mary added mischievously.

"Of course. Could any house be called a home without the right woman's touch?" Robert said with aplomb.

At this Mr. Custis felt it was important to intervene, so the rest of the dinner conversation revolved around Arlington and tidbits of family news.

After dinner they retired to the formal drawing room, which adjoined the dining room. Mr. Custis talked to Lee for almost two hours. They found themselves talking about the Revolution, and about George Washington as a general, and of course about one of his most trusted young cavalrymen, General "Lighthorse" Harry Lee, Robert's father. As the men talked, Mrs. Custis sewed and Mary read.

At length Mr. Custis said he was going to go to his office and go over some papers and excused himself.

Mary laid aside her book, and Robert asked, "What are you reading, Miss Custis?"

"*Ivanhoe*," she answered promptly. "I like Sir Walter Scott very much. I know that you don't care much for novels, Robert, but would you please read to me? My eyes are growing a bit tired."

"It would be my pleasure," Robert answered. He had a low, melodious voice, and with his warm manner, listeners found his recitations very enjoyable.

"Chapter fourteen begins with a poem by Warton," Robert said, and quoted with feeling:

" In rough magnificence array'd
When ancient Chivalry display'd
The pomp of her heroic games

SURRENDER

And crested chiefs and the tissued dames
Assembled, at the clarion's call,
In some proud castle's high arched hall.

Prince John held his high festival in the Castle of Ashby. . . ."

After he had read for about an hour and was about to begin a new chapter, Molly Custis said, "Lieutenant Lee, it is such a great pleasure to hear you read. But I'm sure you need some refreshment. Mary, why don't you take Lieutenant Lee into the dining room and get him something from the sideboard?"

"Of course, Mother," Mary said, rising and going toward the dining room.

Robert followed her, but they had only taken a few steps when Mrs. Custis said, "Mary?"

"Yes, Mother?"

Molly Custis never looked up from her sewing. Quietly she said, "I had Colley set up refreshments in the family dining room, dear."

"Oh?" Mary said in surprise. "Oh! Of course. Come along, Robert."

Instead of going back into the formal dining room, Mary led him across the hall to a much warmer, more pleasant room. It was a large room. Two-thirds of it was taken up by a plain rectangular wooden table that held six places. At the other end of the room was a cozy family parlor. It was a much more intimate setting than the grand drawing room.

Mary led him to the sideboard, took a plate, and put a piece of fruitcake on it. "Tea? Or—"

He put his arm around her, turned her to him, and drew her close. "Mary, I don't want to wait for tea or cake or anything else. I love you, Mary, I love you so much that I can't imagine life without you. Would you do me the very great honor of marrying me?"

"Finally," she murmured and put her arms around him. They

kissed, a long, lingering, sweet kiss.

Robert E. Lee and Mary Custis both felt a rush of joy, for at last they were home.

❧

Truth to tell, George Washington Parke Custis was hiding.

His office was more like a library—a comfortable room with a mahogany barrister's desk, three walls lined with filled bookcases, and a window that looked out on the lawn and the park. By this window in summer he placed his favorite chair, perhaps the only piece of furniture in Arlington House that was shabby. It was a solid leather wing chair, overstuffed, with a matching hassock. Mr. Custis could spend hours in this chair, reading, looking out the window onto his magnificent grounds, or dozing. But on this early morning, he sat uneasily, trying to concentrate on a Dickens novel, but more often looking out the window, his brow furrowed.

A peremptory knock sounded at the door. "Father?"

"Come in, Mary," he said resignedly.

She came in, and he noted that she was looking particularly well this morning, wearing a sky-blue dress and matching ribbons in her curled hair. Her color was high, and her dark eyes were fiery. "Father, I can't believe the way you treated Robert! How could you?"

He stood slowly, laid down his book, and said in a kindly voice, "Mary, dearest one, please come sit down with me. Please?"

She looked rebellious, but then relented and followed him to the corner by the fireplace, where there was a sofa and loveseat. She took her seat on the sofa, and her father sat by her.

Taking her hand, he said quietly, "I didn't refuse Lieutenant Lee, you know."

"I know that. It wouldn't have done any good if you had. What I don't understand is your attitude of clear reluctance, Father. Robert isn't offended, because he is so kind and understanding. But I am offended for him," she said ardently.

"Mary, I like Robert. No, that's not quite correct. I hold him in very high esteem. But I do have two objections to your marrying him. One I told him of, and we spoke of it at length. The other I said nothing about, but of course he would be aware of my concerns."

"It's all that malicious gossip about his half brother, isn't it?" Mary said with disdain.

"It's not just gossip, my dear. The story happens to be true," Mr. Custis said gently.

Robert E. Lee had an older half brother, Henry Lee, the son of "Lighthorse" Harry Lee's first wife, who had died. Henry Lee had inherited the Lee family mansion, Stratford, and had married a neighbor, a young woman of means. Her sister, a seventeen-year-old girl, had come to live with them. After the death of their first child, Henry's wife became addicted to morphine, and Henry and his wife's younger sister had an affair. All of this had happened many years previously, but it had only come out that year, because President Andrew Jackson had appointed Henry Lee as consul to Algiers. He and his wife, who had recovered from her addiction and reconciled with her husband, traveled there. But all of Henry Lee's past, instead of merely being whispered about, was now soundly denounced on the floor of the Senate, and every senator who voted went against his confirmation. He had moved to Paris that summer of 1830, and the couple now lived in obscurity there.

Mary argued, "I don't care if it is true. It has nothing whatsoever to do with Robert."

"But it's his family," Mr. Custis said. "Even his father, an esteemed general and friend of my grandfather's, with so many opportunities, went to debtor's prison and left his family penniless."

"Yes, it is a terrible thing what happened to Robert and his mother and brothers and sisters," Mary said evenly. "But his mother was a strong, determined, godly, loving woman who passed on all of those qualities to Robert. And she taught him self-reliance and frugality and self-control. His other, nobler qualities, like personal courage and sense of duty and honor are in his blood, Lee blood, and he is proud of it. It is an honor for me to marry this man, Father. Can't you see that?"

His eyes wandered to the window, that window that he had looked out on with such pleasure for over thirty years. "I suppose I do, Mary," he said at last. "You're right, of course. I've known Robert all of his life, and perhaps I have grown so accustomed to him that I have forgotten his finer qualities as a man." He turned back to her and continued in a tone now tinged with worry. "But Mary, he is poor, and I can't help but worry about that, and I addressed my objections to Lieutenant Lee. You've never been poor, child, you've no idea what it's like. You, living in officer's quarters in a fort? I tried to tell Lieutenant Lee that I would like to be allowed to help, but he—"

Mary burst out laughing. "Oh Father, dear Father. For a moment there I really thought you were coming to understand us. Don't you know Robert E. Lee at all? Don't you know *me*? Neither Robert nor I would ever accept your charity under any circumstances. And no, we didn't discuss this last night. Of course we talked about Fort Monroe and economies that would have to be made and so on, but neither of us ever mentioned asking you for help. We didn't have to. We both knew that it was impossible."

"But Mary, a fort?" he protested weakly.

"Yes, a fort," she said firmly. "And in spite of my ignorance, I happen to know that there are many people that are much worse off than that. I am so blessed, so exceedingly blessed, and I'm so happy! I want you to be happy for me, too, Father. I believe that in time you'll find that Robert will be just as treasured by you as if he were your own son."

He sighed. "That may be. He is a man that I admire, I freely admit. But it may take some time for me to be positively giddy about your marriage."

She squeezed his hand. "Not too much time, Father. Because I have told Robert that I've waited for him long enough. I refuse to have a long engagement. We're going to be married next month."

the SURRENDER

❧

On June 30, 1831, Robert E. Lee married Mary Anna Randolph Custis at Arlington House.

It was a stormy day, and the Episcopalian minister had arrived soaking wet through and through. Mr. Custis loaned him some clothes that were ill fitting, but his vestments gave him an appropriate grand solemnity.

Robert waited by the fireplace in the formal drawing room. Six of his friends stood with him. About forty people, all of them relatives to one degree or another to the Lees and the Custises, were in attendance. He looked expectantly past them to the door into the dining room, where his bride, with her six attendants, was to enter.

Jack Mackay, his old friend from West Point and Cockspur Island, leaned forward and whispered, "Robert, it's the first time I've ever seen you look pale. Are you all right?"

Lee looked slightly surprised. "I'm pale? How very odd. No, I'm fine. I thought I would be more excited than this, but I feel only calm."

Mary's attendants started coming through, but Robert only had eyes for his bride. Somewhat to his consternation, she looked very nervous. He mentally made a note to write of this day later to a friend not in attendance:

> The minister had few words to say, though he dwelt upon them as if he had been reading my Death warrant, and there was a tremulousness in the hand I held that made me anxious for him to end.

But Mary recovered from her jitters as soon as the ceremony was over.

The happy couple stayed at Arlington for a week then started making the rounds of nearby friends and family, all of whom had large estates and gracious homes.

Robert E. Lee was the happiest of men. He and Mary had played together as small children, when he had come to love her as part of his extended family. They had teased each other and argued with each other and flirted with each other all through their teenage years. And now he was a man, and in the footsteps of the immortal Paul, he had put away those childish things.

He loved Mary Anna with a devotion and loyalty and respect so deep that it would never waver, never falter. He knew he was blessed, for he had married the greatest love of his life.

Mary Anna had to admit that, despite her insistence of her worldly knowledge to her father, life at Fort Monroe came as a great shock to her. The enlisted men who were assigned to the artillery school were a raucous, belligerent bunch of men who got drunk as often as possible and fought with each other, reeling drunk or rock sober, almost every day.

Looking up from her book, she watched Robert with affection. He sat at his small camp desk, lit by a single lantern, sketching out mechanical drawings for breastworks. His handsome face was a study in total concentration, but it was not indicated by frowning or chewing his lip or any other facial gesture. He was expressionless, except for his intense gaze, and he was motionless except for his drawing hand.

The room was small, a tiny parlor that barely held a sofa, two armchairs, and Robert's desk. At the other end of the room was the kitchen, which consisted of a cookstove, three cabinets, and an oak table that served both as a worktable and a dining table. The door on the right-hand side of the room led to their bedroom, the only other room in the apartment. This shabby little second-floor flat was as far from Arlington House as two structures can possible be and still be called houses. But Mary didn't care about the house. To her, home was where Robert was, and that made her happy.

Robert finally looked up from his work. He rose and smiled

at his wife. He came to kneel by her chair and took her hand and kissed it. "You know, I knew that our home would be happy, no matter how much of a setdown it is from Arlington. But what I didn't really realize was what a good soldier's wife you would become. This life is so different from your world."

"You are my world, Robert," she said simply. "You have been my whole world for a long time."

He studied her then said warmly, "I love you, Mims. I thank the Lord for giving you to me. You are my treasure."

She smiled at him. "Robert, how would you like to have another treasure?"

"Hm? What?"

"An addition to our world. A small, noisy one that I fervently hope looks like you."

He took both her hands and stared up at her, his eyes so dark they looked ebony. "You're pregnant? We're going to have a baby?"

"Yes, we are," she said happily. "In September, I think."

Robert E. Lee laid his head down in her lap and, in quiet reverent tones, gave thanks to the Lord.

He was born at the fortress on September 16, 1832. They named him George Washington Custis Lee.

To Mary's joy, even as a newborn, the boy had the aristocratic male handsomeness of the Lee men. Mary bore the birth well, and Custis was healthy.

In her journal she wrote:

> *The voice of joy, and the voice of gladness,*
> *The voice of the bridegroom, and the voice of the bride,*
> *The voice of them that shall say,*
> *Praise the Lord of hosts:*
> *For the Lord is good;*
> *For his mercy endureth forever.*

CHAPTER THREE

Life at Fort Monroe was pleasant for Robert and Mary. Robert's immediate superior was a man named Captain Andrew Talcott, and they made fast friends. He married one of Mary's cousins, a girl named Harriet Randolph Hackley, and the two couples enjoyed many good times: picnics in the summer, riding to Hampton Roads, and dinner parties.

But extremely good news came to the Lees in the fall of 1834, when he was assigned to Washington as assistant to the chief of engineers. That meant that they would only be across the Potomac River from Arlington. Though Robert tried to find suitable lodgings for them in Washington, it was impossible to find a nice home for a couple with a son in the overcrowded city. So he rode back and forth to work every weekday from Arlington, and though it was difficult, he and Mary were blissfully happy to be back at the gracious home.

Although Lee was happy with his home situation now, he intensely disliked his work. The politics in Washington—the bickering, the petty dislikes, the favoritism, the double crossing—

irritated to the extreme his finer sensibilities. And he was exceedingly bored with office work.

In the spring of 1835, a boundary dispute arose between Ohio and Michigan, and the young lieutenant eagerly applied to the Topographical Department to be assigned to the survey team. To his delight, his old friend Captain Talcott was commanding the team, and he immediately left Arlington for the Great Lakes.

Mary and two-year-old Custis were sorry to see him leave, but Mary knew very well how he felt about his clerk's position in Washington, though he never complained. She was pregnant again, right at six months when Robert left, but she was in good health. Custis was a strong and energetic child, and they were in the tender care of her parents and, of course, Bathsheba, who was like a lion with her cubs. And so Mary was happy for Robert, that he was able to get out in the field, which he loved.

The surveying mission lasted the summer, and the final determination wasn't made until late September. Robert had enjoyed the mission intensely; it was interesting, complex work, and Captain Talcott was a lively, obliging friend. They had even begun a friendly "rivalry" concerning their children, for the Talcotts had had a boy soon after Custis Lee's arrival, and then in winter of 1834, both Harriet Talcott and Mary Anna found they were expecting. Lee was "betting" he'd have a girl and Talcott would have another son, while the good-natured Talcott bet the opposite.

Robert E. Lee won the bet. In July, news reached him that Mary had given birth to a girl, whom they named Mary Custis Lee. Robert was concerned because the child was a bit earlier than they had predicted, and Mary's letters said she had not had such an easy time as before, with Custis. But she wrote that the baby was thriving, and though Mary was ill, it was nothing serious, and she was recovering.

In September, Robert brooded over her latest letter. The tone of the letter was lighthearted, with descriptions of the leaves turning their glorious fall colors, with Bathsheba's latest vocal antics, with descriptions of Custis's mischief and baby Mary's beauty. But Robert knew his wife as well as he knew his own soul, and he worried over the last paragraph:

> *I am not recovering as quickly as I would wish, for Dr. Waters says I have some sort of infection, and it vexes me to the extreme, for on some days I must remain bedridden. On the good days I enjoy little Mary and even Custis' rowdiness so much, I hate to miss a minute of their days. But don't trouble yourself, please, Robert, for I'm sure that by the time you're back home I shall be my old cranky self.*

Both Robert E. Lee and Mary regarded complaining as a personal weakness, and so he suspected that Mary was downplaying her illness. When he received his orders to return to Washington in October, he was much relieved.

Mary stared at her reflection in the mirror. She was now twenty-eight years old, but she looked fifty-eight. Her face had gotten so thin in her prolonged illness that she looked positively gaunt, with deep purple shadows under her fever-dulled eyes. Her complexion had no hint of color; she was deathly pale.

Sighing, she looked at her hair. Not one strand could be cleanly pulled from the mass of tangles, no matter how long Bathsheba and her mother tried to brush it out. Her mouth tightening, she picked up a pair of scissors, grabbed a huge tangled mass, and cut it off. In only a few minutes she was surrounded by great hanks of hair, and what was left on her head stood up in bizarre spikes of different lengths.

"I don't care," she said defiantly to her sickly reflection. "It feels so much better." But walking from her bed to her dressing table—all of four steps—and cutting her hair had exhausted her. She rested her forehead on her hand for a few minutes before she made the effort to go back to bed.

The door opened and Bathsheba flew to her side. "Oh, Miss Mary! Look what you done! Oh, Miss Mary, how could you have cut all your pretty hair!"

"It wasn't pretty. It felt like I was lying on a scratchy wool rug," she retorted. "I'm glad I cut it. I already feel so much better, and I want it washed right now."

Bathsheba crossed her arms against her massive breast and said knowingly, "Mm-hmm. You look like getting your hair, or at least your head, washed right now. I better git it done in a hurry 'fore you fall over dead. You just had to get up and come over here and cut all your pretty hair off, didn't you? Me and your mama tole you ten thousand times not to try to get out of bed by your own self!"

Mary said wearily, "I am sorry now, Bathsheba, I admit. I'm not feeling too well. Would you please help me back to bed? Maybe after I rest awhile I'll feel more like having a bath."

Bathsheba almost carried her back to bed, which she could have done easily since Mary probably weighed no more than ninety pounds now. Tucking her in, Bathsheba clucked over her much as she had when Mary was a child. "You rest now, baby girl, and I'll go have Cook fix you some sweet creamed rice, and then we'll get you cleaned up, and I'll give you a nice alcohol rub. You know, Mr. Lee is comin' in tomorrow, so maybe you'll get a good night's rest and feel better when he gets here."

"I'll feel better when he's here anyway," Mary said. "I've missed him terribly."

"I know dat, and I know Mr. Lee's missed you something fierce, too," Bathsheba said soothingly. "So you just stay in this here bed, Miss Prance-About, till I come back to sit with you."

"I will," Mary promised.

Bathsheba bustled out, and Mary immediately fell into an exhausted doze.

She only rested for about half an hour, however, and woke up knowing that her temperature was rising, and that in about an hour she would have a debilitating fever. In her melancholy, a sudden thought came to her. She visualized her husband riding up to Arlington—his handsome, clean-cut features, his immaculate uniform, and the gladness and appreciation so plain on his face every time he came home.

And then she remembered that awful reflection in the mirror. She looked twice his age, old and ugly, and now her hair was grotesque. Even a ruffled housecap wouldn't cover the bald forehead and sides. What expression would she see on Robert E. Lee's "Marble Model" face then?

Robert E. Lee loved his mare, Grace Darling. She could walk all day long over the roughest terrain and never jolt him. But she wasn't a racer; she couldn't travel at a strong canter for long. Nevertheless, he pushed her as soon as he reached the Arlington property and galloped right up to the wide portico.

A servant came rushing out of the house to take his horse, followed by Mr. and Mrs. Custis. They greeted him warmly, but he could tell that they both looked strained, and his heart plummeted.

Mrs. Custis said, "Please, Robert, come into the drawing room before you go up to see Mary. We'd like to talk to you."

He followed them into the room, and a maid offered him lemonade or a cordial, but he asked for iced water. Molly Custis seated herself on the sofa and patted the seat beside her for Robert to take. Mr. Custis stood in front of the fireplace, fiddling with the ornaments on the mantelpiece.

After Robert had had a few sips of water, Molly Custis said quietly, "Mary is very ill, Robert. She was adamant that when we wrote to you none of us would give you a hint about exactly how grave her condition is."

In a voice of pure misery George Custis said, "Dr. Waters says that she—that this infection—that—" He choked slightly.

Robert turned to his mother-in-law. She looked straight into his eyes and said, "Dr. Waters has prepared us for the worst."

Robert's eyes closed in pain, but in only a few moments he looked back at Molly. "No, I don't believe that Mary will be taken from us," he said firmly and clearly. "Deep in my heart I've always known that when God gave her to me, we would have a lifetime together." He stood up and went over to lay his hand on Mr. Custis's shoulder. "Sir, Mary has the strength of heroes' blood in her veins, and she has fire, and she has heart. Please don't mourn. Just pray for God's assurance and comfort."

Mr. Custis's head was down because he was fighting tears, and it embarrassed him. But he nodded.

George Custis had had a complete turnaround about Robert E. Lee in the three years that he had been married to his daughter. Mary's prophecy had been right. To him Robert had proved to be the best in a son—honorable, loyal, and as dutiful toward him and Molly as any son of blood could be. Robert even helped him tremendously with his complicated business affairs.

Robert asked, "But how is baby Mary? How is she faring?"

Molly smiled. "She is thriving, Robert. She's just fine. Apparently this infection that Mary is suffering from had nothing to do with her pregnancy or the birth, and it didn't affect baby Mary. Dr. Waters is of the opinion that Mary would have these abscesses whether she was pregnant or not."

Overwhelming relief washed over Robert like a dunking in clear, cool water. He felt guilty enough being away when Mary was ill, but if it had been caused by her pregnancy, he thought he would never be able to recover from the remorse. But his face merely showed relief, and he managed a small smile. "Then I'll go up to see my Mary now."

Molly said, "There's just one more thing, Robert, that I think I should tell you before you see her. Yesterday she cut her hair. It was terribly tangled and matted. Bathsheba and I both kept working on it, trying to get it combed out, but Mary didn't have the strength to let us brush it for long. Apparently it was so uncomfortable that she just cut it herself."

George Custis had recovered enough to say, "Looks like she whacked it off with a hatchet. Impetuous girl, always has been."

"And always will be, I suspect," Robert said. To the Custises' surprise, he looked amused. "But thank you for telling me first." He went upstairs to their bedroom, and the door was open.

Mary was sitting up in bed, wearing a pretty white ruffled bedjacket and a morning cap. She held her arms out, and he hurried to sit on the bed and pull her up into his embrace.

"How I've missed you, darling Mims," he whispered, kissing her cheek, her mouth, her forehead. "I try not to be impatient, but it seemed the days were endless, waiting until I could hurry home."

She pulled back from him and searched his face hungrily. Then she opened her mouth, tried to speak, but couldn't make the words come out. Swallowing hard, she tried again, and tears filled her eyes and began running down her cheeks in a flood. "I cut my hair!" she said, almost sobbing.

He gently drew her to him again, and she wept against his chest. She felt as fragile as delicate china. She was so thin, and her bones so small, yet her tiny body threw off heat because she had a fever. "I'm glad you did, my dearest, because I'm sure you're more comfortable."

"You are?" she asked dully. "But I look—"

"As beautiful as ever to me. Mary, you are the light of my life. How could I see anything but beauty when I look at that light?"

She cried a little more against his breast, but Mary was not a woman that dissolved into tears very often. Finally she pulled away from him and sat back against her pillows. "All of that salt water is going to tarnish your shiny brass buttons," she said drily. "I would hate for the impeccable Lieutenant Lee to have dull buttons on his uniform."

"So would I," Lee admitted. "But in this case I think you may be forgiven for tarnishing my buttons. Now, where is my daughter? I'm going to take care of you, my dear, from now on, but first I must see little Miss Mary Lee."

"I'm sure Bathsheba is listening outside the door," Mary said in a loud tone. "She'll take you to the next bedroom."

The door opened slightly, and Bathsheba said in an offended tone, "I was just waiting to make sure you didn't need anything, Miss Mary. Hello, Lieutenant Lee. We've just put the baby in the spare bedroom next door, and Master Custis is waiting to see you, too."

The sturdy three-year-old Custis ran to his father and grabbed him around the knees.

Lee bent to hug him fiercely. "Is this my son? This big sturdy lad? Let me look at you. You are a fine-looking boy, aren't you? Have you been a good boy?"

"I'm good sometimes," he said in his little-boy lisp. "But Mother says sometimes I'm not, sir."

"I see," Lee said. "Well, now that I'm home, we can talk about all of that, man-to-man."

Custis brightened. "Yes, sir. Please, sir."

Lee went over to the crib where the sleeping baby lay. She was four months old now, and already Lee could see the long thin nose and the stubborn chin. She opened her eyes and considered him gravely. He picked her up, and she kept her eyes trained on his face.

"Come along, son," he said to Custis and went back into Mary's bedroom and sat on the bed.

Mary managed a smile at her son and patted the other side of the bed. Eagerly he climbed up. "How do you feel, Mummy?" he asked worriedly.

"I am already feeling much, much better since your father is here," she said, glancing at Robert. "I know I haven't been able to see you much lately, Custis, but soon I'll be well and we'll be able to go out in the sled when we have our first snow, and we can visit your friends, and we'll have a wonderful Christmas."

"That's right," Robert said. "Baby Mary's first Christmas is going to be a happy one. She's just beautiful, Mary. She looks like you."

Tears welled into her eyes again but didn't fall. "Thank you, Robert," she said simply.

"No, thank you, wife," he answered. "Now, as soon as you feel strong enough, Mims, we're going to Berkeley Springs, in Bath. I think it will be so good for you. I don't know much about the medicinal properties of the springs, but I know that a holiday in the mountains will be a treat for all of us."

"All of us?" Custis repeated quickly. "May I go, too, sir?"

"Of course," Robert answered. "All four of us, my beloved family, are all going. I've been away so long I couldn't think of being separated from you again anytime soon."

Mary was very ill indeed, and it was the next year before she was able to travel to the old hot springs resort. The town was named Bath after its English sister city, founded by her father's grandfather, George Washington.

In all the long months of her illness, Robert E. Lee had cared for her day and night, just as he had cared for his mother for most of his teens and early twenties. These two women, though they were weak and sickly in body, imparted to Robert E. Lee some of the most forceful and virtuous qualities that are found in the best of men. He learned self-sacrifice, the highest form of that virtue in that he was never conscious of it. Putting others before himself became such a natural part of the fiber of his being that it was difficult for him to recognize a lack of it in others.

Though his father, "Lighthorse" Harry Lee, had been a man of audacious courage and fiery élan, Harry was an undisciplined man, flighty and careless in business and in caring for his family. He had died when Robert was eleven, and during Robert's life he had barely known his father, for Harry Lee was always traveling and had spent more than two of those years in debtor's prison. Anne Carter Lee had raised her children practically single-handedly. In stark contrast to her husband, she was intelligent, level-headed, dutiful, and loving. She taught Robert frugality without being poor-mouthed; the visceral rewards of always fulfilling any duty, no matter how small, to the utmost; a Christian warmth and care for others; and above all, self-control.

For all his life, when Robert E. Lee's closest friends were describing him, the two words they most often used were *honor* and *duty*. These two excellent virtues were the primary forces of Robert E. Lee's character.

The years of 1835 and 1836, when Mary was so ill, became a clear turning point in Lee's life. Always before he had had a lively disposition, much given to teasing and laughing heartily at jokes he found funny, his demeanor generally bright and cheerful. After the Lees returned to Arlington from Bath, a friend wrote, "I never saw a man so changed and saddened."

But because of his unselfishness and his iron self-control, Lee never showed any hint of distress or upset to Mary or his children. With them he was always happy, buoyant, playful, and merry.

It was with others that his demeanor, while not cold, became more dignified and decorous. Always gallant with the ladies and unfailingly delighting in the company of children, he nevertheless had an air about him that set him apart from other men. And because of the noble qualities that had been so firmly set in him by his mother, and the genuine deep love and caring that he had learned from his life with Mary, he did indeed become a man above other men.

CHAPTER FOUR

Mary Lee wrote in her journal:

July 1, 1848. Although Robert only returned two days ago, he has been ceaselessly playing with the children. Tonight, again, he is allowing them to stay up very late, telling them stories.

She looked up from her writing to watch her family. Mary had borne Robert seven children in fourteen years. Now Custis, the eldest, was fifteen years old, while baby Mildred was only two. Blissfully "Milly" sat on her father's lap, resting her head against his broad shoulder. It was the first time she had met her father.

As Mary's gaze rested on her daughter, Mary Custis, she sighed. At thirteen Mary was blooming, and she was turning into a lovely young girl. She was hearty, too, the healthiest one of the four girls. It was odd that she had been born so strong, since her birth had been a nightmare for Mary. It had been after Mary Custis's birth that Mary had cut her hair. A small smile touched her lips as she recalled that even then Robert had insisted that his wife was beautiful.

the SURRENDER

Custis and Mary sat on side chairs next to Robert's armchair. The other children, except for Milly, sat on the floor around their father's footstool.

Rooney was eleven, a fine strapping boy who from the time he was first able to talk had insisted he was going to be in the army like his father. When he had been eight years old, they were stationed at Fort Monroe, and Rooney had decided he was going to go to the stables, where they were bringing in a load of hay for the horses. He proceeded to grab a straw cutter to help trim the stalks and managed to cut off the tops of his left forefinger and middle finger. It was an hour and a half before a doctor arrived. He had sewn the tips of Rooney's fingers back on, and they had mended with no muscle damage or nerve damage. The officers present had marveled at the young boy, who sat stoically on a hay bale waiting for the doctor, bleeding profusely, without a word of complaint or any sign of pain. He was very much like his father, and he was as handsome as Robert E. Lee, too.

Next in ages had come "The Girls" as the family called them, for they were only eighteen months apart in age, and Robert and Mary had purposely named them as one might name twins: Annie and Agnes. Annie had been born with a reddish-pink birthmark on her face, and Mary reflected that that might have made a girl very shy. But her father affectionately called her "Little Raspberry" and told her all the time how pretty she was, so she had grown to be outgoing, vivacious, and mischievous unfortunately. At five years old she had been playing with a pair of scissors and had sliced part of her left eye and eyelid. Her vision was not much damaged, only the peripheral vision in that eye, but the accident had left a ropelike scar on her eyelid and socket. Still, it seemed that her father had made her feel so secure that she didn't seem to let her disfigurement affect her. She had been delighted when her sister Agnes was born. In fact, Annie had left off playing with any of her dolls, for Agnes had been her "baby doll" until she was a year old. The two girls were as close as twins.

Robert E. Lee Jr. was now five years old, and of all her children, Mary knew he was going to be the most trouble for her. In fact, he already had been the rowdiest child, ever since he started to walk at ten months old. From that day he was into something, anything, hiding from servants and his mother and grandparents, running in the house, yelling at the top of his lungs, balking at food he didn't like, often attempting to hide green peas under his plate. However, on the rare times his father had been present, Rob behaved perfectly.

Now Rob was taking his turn tickling his father's feet. Robert loved taking off his slippers and socks and having the children tickle his feet as he told stories. They liked for him to read to them, too, but they enjoyed it most when he dramatized the stories. On this warm July evening he was telling them the grand story of "The Lady of the Lake," basically paraphrasing the poem by Sir Walter Scott, for the language was too difficult for the younger children. However, he often quoted memorable simple passages.

Mary thought that this poem, above all, represented all things that Robert loved. It was a story of chivalry, of true nobility, of familial love and loyalty, of self-sacrifice, and of course, of bravery and courage in war.

Just then Robert lifted his head and quoted in deep ringing tones:

"And the stern joy which warriors feel
In foemen worthy of their steel!"

Mary thought with a touch of regret, *That's the part of him I will never understand—the warrior. He is so gracious, so warm and kind, so gentle. I suppose no person, man or woman, who is not born a soldier can understand that stern joy.*

All at once, Rob, Agnes, and Annie all started talking loudly. "Papa, don't stop! More story about Ellen and Roderick and Malcolm! Please, Papa!"

With mock gravity he said, "Rob has been lax in his duties. He stopped tickling my feet. No tickling, no story."

Mary laughed with the children, marveling at the difference in Robert E. Lee's public persona and his playful demeanor with his family. No matter what problems arose, no matter what the circumstances, he was unfailingly jovial with them, teasing her as much as he ever did when they were young, playing even infantile games with the youngest children, laughing with delight at their antics.

Rob resumed his duties, and Agnes pitched in by taking one foot while Rob took the other. Lee started his spellbinding story again.

Mary returned to her journal:

> *Robert is telling the children the story of "The Lady of the Lake," and my thoughts went back to the nightmares I've had for the last twenty months since Robert went to fight the Mexican War. I always knew that being a soldier's wife would mean moving often, postings to strange and lonely places, being away from home. But what I didn't understand until 1846 was what it was like to be a soldier's wife when he was in war. It was agonizing, struggling daily—sometimes hourly—to stop thinking of Robert getting wounded or even killed. I pray, dearest Father God, that my husband will never have to fight a war again. Thank You, my Lord, for this homecoming was of all most blessed.*

Even as she wrote the words, she thought that this time may actually have been the most difficult for Robert himself. Mary, who had never been completely healthy in the years since Mary Custis had been born, had grown steadily weaker in body in the last two years. Though she had downplayed her decline in her letters to Robert—as she always did—by the time he returned, rheumatism had so drastically invaded her right side that she was barely able to walk, and often she couldn't write or paint.

She knew it had been a shock to him when he had first seen her. But the only way she knew it was because she was his wife, and in the seventeen years they had been married they had in many ways become two halves of a whole, and she knew him as well as she knew her own soul. His face showed nothing but joy and love when he greeted her, but deep in her spirit Mary knew he was grieved. As she was, for she knew that Robert had spent most of his young life caring for his invalid mother. And now his wife was an invalid. But Mary was determined that she would do all that she could, for as long as she could.

Though the servants and the older children had begged her to get a wheeled chair, she flatly refused. She knew that day was coming, but until it did, she courageously either walked with help or even with crutches on the days she was strong enough to manage them. She was even beginning to teach herself to write with her left hand, though on this night she wrote in a strong script with her right. In fact, she had felt very well the last couple of days—probably because Robert was home.

Idly she leafed back through the previous pages of her journal. Mary didn't write in it every day. By nature she was a gregarious person, taking after her father, who loved having a busy social life. Mary took great interest in all her friends and extended family, and she loved receiving visits from them and visting them. She concerned herself with all parts of their lives, not in a busybody way but because she truly cared for their well-being and wished happiness for all of them. She also loved nature, taking long walks, studying the flora and fauna of the Park, and tending all the gardens, even the kitchen vegetable patch.

Her painting was probably her favorite pastime, and she was extremely talented in landscapes and still life, both in oils and watercolors. It irritated her that she had no aptitude at all for portraiture, but then she thought wryly that perhaps that was a good thing, for if she were good at it, she would probably never do anything but portraits of her handsome husband.

the SURRENDER

Mary was an active, busy woman, and oftentimes her journal was the last thing she thought of, especially since Robert had left for Mexico. During that dark time the only private thoughts she had were of fear, and she had no desire to journalize such things. She turned back to 1847, where she had written a short entry:

This was reported in the Richmond Times.

A newspaper clipping was pressed between the pages:

General Winfield Scott, commander of the Army in Mexico, is quoted here in an excerpt of his battle reports to the War Department in Washington. Colonel Robert E. Lee, married to Mary Randolph Custis Lee of Arlington House, was particularly singled out by his commanding officer:
I am impelled to make special mention of the services of Captain R. E. Lee. . . . This officer, greatly distinguished at the siege of Vera Cruz, was again indefatigable during these operations, in reconnaissance as daring as laborious, and of the utmost in value. Nor was he less conspicuous implanting batteries and in conducting columns to their stations under the heavy fire of the enemy.

The only other entries Mary had made during the Mexican War were:

Commissioned August 1846, Major, for gallant and meritorious conduct in the battle of Cerro Gordo.

Commissioned August 1847, Lieutenant Colonel, for gallant and meritorious conduct in the battle of Churubusco.

Commissioned September 1847, Colonel, for gallant and meritorious conduct in the battle of Chapultepec.

And now, she thought with satisfaction, he was showing his gallant and meritorious conduct to his family, at his own home.

In a couple of months, Mary took her journal and sketchbook and paints and crutches to Baltimore, where Robert was stationed for construction of a new fort on Soller's Flats, which would become Fort Carrol. He was pleased Mary enjoyed their time there—which turned out to be four years—for they were close enough that they could visit Arlington often, and they had many friends and the ever-present Fitzhugh, Carter, Hill, and Lee cousins in Baltimore.

In September of 1852, Colonel Robert E. Lee was appointed as superintendent of the United States Military Academy at West Point. He was a superb administrator, but he was an even better leader of young men. The classes that were fortunate enough to attend the Academy during his tenure were better educated, better disciplined, and had a more deeply ingrained sense of honor and duty than ever before. Mary loved it, too, for she mothered all of the young cadets, while her husband was to them the best in a father, strict but always fair.

The only thing that marred their three years there was the death of Mary's mother, Molly Custis. Since Robert had been young, she had loved him like a son, and now he mourned her almost as much as he had mourned the loss of his own mother twenty-four years earlier. The entire Lee family missed her terribly, and Mary and the older girls made several prolonged trips to Arlington to take care of her father, who was desolate.

But 1854 was a good year, for in June George Washington Custis Lee—Robert and Mary's eldest son—graduated from West Point at the head of his class. Both of them were very proud of him, for he had become a brilliant scholar; a dedicated, well-disciplined cadet; and a strong and purposeful man. All these qualities made Robert E. Lee especially proud of his son. He never realized that all of Custis's best qualities were mirror images of his own. Born to follow in his father's footsteps, he immediately joined the Engineer Corps.

Though he thoroughly enjoyed his role as an educator and life-teacher of young men, Robert E. Lee's second love, after his wife and family, was the army. In 1855, because of the increasing Indian uprisings in the West, Congress authorized the formation of two new regiments of infantry and two of cavalry. Colonel Robert E. Lee had high hopes, though he said nothing to his wife. On March 13, 1855, Albert Sidney Johnston was named colonel of the new 2nd Cavalry, and Robert E. Lee was named lieutenant colonel, as his commission as a colonel was brevet only.

To Lee, service in the line meant a healthful, vigorous outdoor life, which he loved. The superintendency at West Point was a high honor, but it was mostly confining and dull office work.

In April, Mary and her younger children moved back to Arlington. Though he would miss his Mary, for the 2nd Cavalry was to be sent to Texas, he was glad his family would be back at Arlington House. Although Robert and Mary had made each little place they had lived into their own home, they both now regarded Arlington as their true home, the center of their family, regardless of where they lived or where Robert was assigned.

Since Molly's death, George Custis had been terribly lonely, and he often complained that he didn't feel well. He was in very good health, however, so Mary and Robert knew that his ailments were mostly from emotional upset. Robert did not, perhaps, love his father-in-law as deeply as he had loved Molly Custis. But he was very devoted to Mr. Custis and felt a son's duty toward him. He, too, was glad that his wife and girls would be at Arlington House with his father-in-law. As a conscientious and caring son, he determined that George Washington Parke Custis should never again be left alone.

The Indians were courageous and daring fighters, but they were not stupid. They would attack small villages and single homesteads and a group of farmers that might be daring enough to hunt them. But they weren't foolish enough to attack a numerous force of trained professional soldiers in the field. In April of 1856, when Colonel Robert E. Lee reached what he was to call his "Texas home"—desolate and crude Camp Cooper, more than 170 miles from the nearest fort—all the Comanches had disappeared, fleeing farther west to hide in the mountains.

At this time Lee was charged with the most unpleasant and troublesome task he ever knew in the army: court-martial duty. Dispensing justice, which must at all times be perfectly fair and impartial, was an onerous burden for a man like him.

Robert E. Lee was apparently born with true aristocratic sensibilities, without the usual accompanying qualities of superciliousness and vanity. He believed that all men were created equal before God, but he also knew that all men must be governed by rules.

Robert E. Lee's rules were in truth a high and noble code of honor, which few men could ever attain, but because of his modesty he never realized that. In his mind men made choices, and often the choices they made were not the correct ones, and then they disobeyed the rules and must bear the consequences. But they, like he himself, were simply on a journey toward harmony with the Lord, and people were in different places along that long road. At heart he was a simple man.

"I believe that Texas dust is probably the best, most comprehensive and complete dust there is," Major George H. Thomas announced grandly.

Colonel Lee chuckled. "Do you, now? I was unaware that it was of such exalted quality, although I'm sure I've dealt with a ton or so of it about my person and belongings in the last two and a half years."

"Oh yes, it has to be the ultimate, as dust goes. It comes in all colors, from orange-red to dull gray; all textures, from gravelly grit to the finest sand. Regardless of its composition, it's able to invade every single object that exists, from your mouth and eyes and ears to your books and clothes and coffeepot. And it never dies. It only disappears temporarily when you brush it away and then returns as soon as you put your brush away."

"The same dust, you think?"

"And its cousins."

They rode in silence for a time. Both men were saddle weary, for this was their third day of hard riding. George Thomas, at thirty, was a full twenty years younger than Robert E. Lee, but he slumped in the saddle, his shoulders rounded wearily, his hands limp on the slack reins. As always, Lee kept a beautiful, erect posture in the saddle, and his eyes and face were alert and watchful, continually scanning the empty desert landscape.

Now Lee stood up in the stirrups, shielding his eyes from the blazing setting sun on his right. "I think I see the willow bank ahead. It should be Comfort Creek."

"Thank heavens!" Thomas exclaimed. "The little pool there is the only place within five hundred miles of here to get a good bath." Sitting up straighter, he said, "What do you say, Colonel? I think the horses may not mind a little gallop for a long cool drink of water."

The two broke into a canter that brought them to the creek, a welcome oasis on the hard-bitten plains of south Texas. Willows lined the banks of Comfort Creek, providing a cool, freshly scented shade beside the bubbling cheerful stream. An old tributary splashed over a six-foot-high ridge to form a pool that through the ages had gotten to be several feet deep. It was indeed the most welcoming stop for weary travelers between Fort Mason and San Antonio.

When they reached the banks, both of them dismounted and let the horses wade out into the cool water. They knelt, splashing their faces and drinking deeply.

Through Lee's silver beard, droplets of water trickled, turned crimson by the glare of the dying sun. He stood and faced due west, narrowing his eyes. "The dust is cruel, Major Thomas, but I think that it is the reason for these spectacular sunsets. I've never seen anything like them."

"Neither have I," Thomas agreed, wetting his gold neckerchief and scrubbing his face with it. "And I'll treasure the day I see the last one of them in this country."

Lee waded over to his horse, the solid, hardworking mare named Grace Darling, led her to the bank, and began unsaddling her.

Thomas joined him. "Don't you agree, Colonel Lee? Surely of all of us you have the most reason to despise this place."

"I? The most reason? Why should that be?" Lee asked, puzzled.

Thomas grimaced. "Because of this court-martial duty. I know it must be most distasteful to a man of your sensibilities."

Lee shook his head, easily lifting the heavy saddle from the mare's back and placing it up against a deadwood log on the bank. It would be his pillow for the night. "Somehow you've got the wrong idea, Major Thomas. The only sensibilities I have about being a tribune are the responsibility I feel for the men being tried, and that their rights are fully respected, and that justice, fair and impartial, is done them. This is my duty as I see it, and there is no question of finding an honorable duty distasteful."

Thomas put his saddle next to Robert's, and they began currying the horses. Both the mare and Thomas's gelding were covered with foam and grit. Thomas said, "But wait, Colonel. You said your responsibility to the men being tried? What does that mean? Surely you feel no responsibility to those men? You don't even know them!"

"That makes no difference," Lee said. "God has placed me in a position of authority over them. Having authority over another person makes you responsible for them. Certainly there are degrees of responsibility, according to the situation, but one must always be mindful that with any power comes grave responsibility."

"But what can you do?" Thomas demanded. "You can't possibly influence these men in any way or even help them."

Lee said quietly, "I can pray for them."

After a short silence, Thomas rasped, "Oh. Shot me right between the eyes, Robert. Again."

Lee grinned. "You're just a bumptious youth, and you need advice from your elders."

"Hmph!" Thomas grunted. "You never gave anyone advice in your life, and now I guess I can see why. The responsibility, eh? Aw, I don't want to talk about this anymore. The trouble with you, Colonel Lee, is that you refuse to complain. It's just like with the dust. I spend half my time here grumbling about it, and all you have to say is that it makes for beautiful sunsets. But you can't possibly like it here. Can you?"

"I don't like anywhere that's away from my wife and family," Lee said quietly. "And I like anywhere I am with them. If they were here, I would be perfectly content."

They finished brushing out the horses and let them graze on the raggedy prairie grass growing underneath the willows. Both men bathed in the pool, spluttering and shivering a little.

It was the first week in October, and although the days were still burning hot, the nights were cool. They made a campfire, and Major Thomas fixed them some gravy in a small frying pan he carried. One of the ladies of Fort Mason had given them a dozen biscuits for the five-day ride to San Antonio, and in this arid country they kept well.

After eating and doing the little bit of washing up, they spread out their bedrolls, leaned up against the saddles, and gazed up at the millions and millions of stars in a perfect moonless night.

"This is another thing I like about Texas," Lee murmured. "This land, it's so flat that the sky seems to go on for eternity. Very little of earth, much of the heavens."

"Despite all that nonsense about you being my elder, I have learned a lot from you, Colonel," Thomas admitted. "There is a certain stark beauty here, if you look. I guess I haven't bothered. But I will."

Lee nodded. "Then you'll see it. And it helps a man to know

there's beauty around him, especially when he's lonely."

"So you are lonely?"

"Oh yes, there's no shame in that. A man's not complete without his wife and children with him. Anyway, by the time we get back, I should have several letters waiting for me," he finished, smiling. "The next best thing."

Two days later, on October 21, Robert reached headquarters in San Antonio, and the first thing he did was check his mail. He only had one letter waiting for him, and it was not the next best thing. His father-in-law, George Custis, had died suddenly on the tenth of October after a short severe illness. Colonel Robert E. Lee asked for leave and started the long journey back to Arlington.

CHAPTER FIVE

It was the saddest homecoming of all.

Robert E. Lee reached Arlington on November 11, 1857, a month after his father-in-law had died. The funereal pall cast by George Custis's death still remained over Arlington. Even the slaves mourned.

Mary, dressed in black from head to toe, was melancholy in her greeting to her husband. "It was so abrupt," she said as they talked in the family parlor. "I still feel much of the first shock. Countless times a day I think that he's still here."

Lee took her hand—her left hand. Her entire right side had become so crippled by arthritis that she was almost paralyzed, and she was in constant pain. The realization had been an additional blow to Robert, for she had, as always, downplayed the severity of her condition in her letters to him. He hadn't seen Mary or his children for twenty-one months. Sadly he realized that his wife was now an invalid.

"It's not surprising that you still feel him here. He was such a part of this home, our home," he said. "I think that we'll always be

738

reminded of him here, and I know that in time the Lord will give us His perfect comfort so that the memories will be joyful. But it will take time, dearest."

She nodded and grasped his hand tightly. "You're right, of course. Oh Robert, in spite of the circumstances, I'm so very glad you're home! I've missed you terribly. This is the longest time we've been separated since we were married, you know."

"I know all too well. I've been very lonely without my Mims. But now I'll be here for a long while. I've been granted six months' leave, and I promise you that I'll work very hard to make sure Arlington remains our beloved home."

A quick spasm of pain crossed her face as she moved to stroke his hand with her swollen, misshapen right hand. But she managed a small smile. "Robert, wherever you are is my most beloved home."

Six months' leave was not nearly long enough. George Custis had left an extremely complicated will, and Robert E. Lee was the executor. Custis had several other properties besides Arlington, and he was what was called "land poor," a common condition when people had large tracts of land and sometimes several homes but had very little ready cash.

Mr. Custis's will also stipulated that all his slaves be freed within five years of his death. Lee approved of this in principle, but he found it impossible to implement immediately. As it turned out, Lee had to take over two years' leave to straighten out the Custis legacy, and it took all his time, energy, and the meager savings he had managed to accumulate. Those two years, from winter to winter, 1857 through 1859, were perhaps the bleakest of his life.

Although he was on extended leave, Colonel Lee was, by General Winfield Scott's order, considered on "active duty" because he still held the position of a military tribune and attended several courts-martial in the two years at Arlington.

Late in May of 1859, he returned from a trial at West Point, and to his surprise and pleasure he saw that Mary was sitting out on the veranda, and she had shed her mourning clothes to wear a light blue muslin dress with satin trim. He rode up and dismounted and hurried to lift her hand to his lips and bow to kiss it. "Mrs. Lee, you look as pretty as nature herself today!"

"Get on with you, silly man," she scoffed, but her expression was pleased. "Such foolishness."

"I have many faults and failings, but I don't believe I'm a fool," he said lightly. "I'm going to wash and change. Do you think that you'll be able to wait here for me?" He could still be quite boyish, at least with Mary.

"I'm staying here until night falls," she said firmly. "Perhaps it's the benevolent weather, but I feel much better today, and I want to enjoy the outdoors as long as possible."

He hurried off and soon returned. Arlington had several cane lounge chairs and glass-topped tables for the veranda, and he and Mary sat companionably close together by a table that held lemonade and tiny sandwiches. Robert ate two of the triangles then reached for a third. "Is this one that fish kind?" he asked, lifting it to his nose.

"Can't you tell? They do have such a distinctive odor," Mary teased.

"Yes, I know, but after you've had one you can't smell them anymore. I forget, what is this fish kind?"

"Anchovy paste. This half of the platter is anchovy paste, and the other is cucumber for me. Don't worry, I'm not going to take your sandwiches, Robert, and I'll thank you to stay out of mine."

"Yes, ma'am," he said obediently.

They both ate for a while, and then Mary asked, "How was the trial?"

Robert grew sober. "It was disheartening, Mary. I suppose they all are. But when the defendants are officers, and supposedly gentlemen, I find it so distresses me. It is very difficult for me to understand how these young men can behave so irresponsibly."

"Yes, Robert, I know that you find it difficult to understand," Mary said quietly. "That is because you have never done an irresponsible thing in your life, and I doubt that you ever will. In fact, I doubt that you could even think of something feckless to do. It's not in your nature."

"I could be feckless," he said mockingly. "I can be, right now. Watch this." He took one of the little triangular sandwiches and threw it out onto the drive. "See? See how irresponsible and capricious that was?"

Mary laughed, and Robert reveled in it. Though she was not ill-tempered, she rarely laughed out loud, mainly because she was so clever it took something very witty or absurd to amuse her.

"It was, Robert, and I am shocked to the core of my being!" she said, her dark eyes sparkling. "I'm so proud of you!"

"Are you? Gracious, I must be monstrously boring if it takes something like that to make you laugh."

"Don't worry, I laugh at you all the time, dear. You just don't know it," she said slyly. "No, you are not at all boring."

"I'm gratified to hear it."

"Good. Now that I've complimented you for the day, I'm going to proceed with telling you what to do."

"Now I know that we have indeed returned to normal." He sighed. "What can I do for you, my dear?"

She looked out over the gracious Park. "Do you remember when Father used to have the spring sheepshearing here?"

"Of course. It was such fun. And he would always use President Washington's tent and display all of the artifacts."

"Yes, and we did it for so many years. I know that Father truly enjoyed the party, but I don't think he could actually bring himself to have such a large party after we got married, and I wasn't here to help."

"I'm sure that's true," Robert agreed. "He did love social events, parties and dinners and outings, but I know that you and your mother were always the ones to plan and organize them. So, Mims, you want to have a sheepshearing?"

"No, I don't think people have sheep as they used to. But I would like to have a party in the Park, with dancing at the pavilion. And like the old sheepshearing days, I'd like to make it semipublic, instead of simply by invitation. You know, word used to get around quite easily. I think if we choose the date carefully, we can get the boys here."

All four of the Lees' daughters were at Arlington, although thirteen-year-old Milly was attending daily academy in nearby Alexandria. Custis was in the army. Rooney had married, and he and his wife were living at White House Plantation, a property left to him by George Custis. Rob, now sixteen, was at boarding school.

"I long for us all to be together again," Robert said. "Christmas was so wonderful this year."

Mary looked down, and her crippled hands clasped in her lap. "And I think we both would enjoy a big party and seeing all of our friends and family, Robert. To forget for a while our troubles."

He nodded. "You're right, Mims," he said quietly.

His eyes searched the city beyond, across the Potomac River, and he thought of the chasm of differences between the politicians there, the underlying hostility between abolitionists and the men representing the Cotton South. Lee abhorred politics and paid as little attention to the political matters of the day as he could possibly manage and still stay knowledgeable. But he could see that the slavery issue was slowly going beyond politics, and the chasm was growing dangerously wide and deep. It was beginning to dawn on him that that rift may in fact cause a tearing asunder.

He dreaded to think of it, and he shunned too much reverie on the subject. And so he agreed with his wife, though the troubles he wished to escape from were not just those of managing Arlington and in fulfilling all of George Custis's last wishes. He wished to escape the creeping fear that it may be his world that was in danger of being torn asunder.

❧

"Marse Robert," Perry said apologetically, "I found Miss Mildred over there in the apple orchard. And she's climbing a tree."

Robert merely sighed, but seated next to him Mary rasped, "Good heavens, Robert! How is it that all of our children are full-grown, but they're still like a flock of wild geese!"

It was an exaggeration, for Custis was performing his duties as a host admirably by dancing with every lady attending the party. Rooney, his wife Charlotte, and Mary Custis were sitting on a pallet right next to the Lees' lounge chairs. "The Girls," Annie and Agnes, were also dancing, although eighteen-year-old Agnes had disappeared from her father's hawklike gaze, and Robert had asked Perry to find her along with Milly and Rob.

"Did you find Rob?" he asked Perry, his manservant.

"Yes, suh. He's right with Miss Mildred, a-egging her on."

"All right, I'll come," he said resignedly.

But Rooney got to his feet, grinning. "Never mind. I'll go get them, Father. And Mother, I'm a little surprised at your indignation. What was that story again about the fall from the apple tree. . . ?"

"Never you mind that, Rooney," she sniffed. "I was only a child. Milly is thirteen and should comport herself in a ladylike manner."

"I believe you were twelve years old at the time," Robert said innocently.

"Twelve is not thirteen. Rooney, stop standing there gawping and grinning. Hurry up before she falls and breaks her head."

Rooney went across the plantation road in the direction of the apple orchard.

Mary returned to her knitting, and her pleased composure returned. "Oh Robert, this is wonderful. I'm so glad we decided to have this party. We simply must start entertaining again."

"It does seem to be a success. It's good to be back in touch with the family." Between Robert's family and Mary's family, they were related to practically all the First Families of Virginia. Although they had literally hundreds of cousins, neither Robert nor Mary viewed any relation as "distant" or "close." If people were related to them in any way, they were family.

Rooney soon returned with his younger brother and sister in tow. Milly and Rob came to stand in front of Robert and Mary, their heads bowed, their hands crossed in front of them. Robert reflected with amusement that they looked guiltier than many criminal defendants he had seen.

Mary said in an even tone, "Milly, what were you thinking? Climbing a tree?"

Without looking up, she said in a small voice, "But Rob said I couldn't, and I knew I could, but I had to prove it to Rob."

Rob faced his father, his cheeks crimson. "It's true, sir. I teased her into it, and it's all my fault."

"But it's not," Milly argued. "I decided to do it. It's my fault."

"You're both right. Both of you are responsible, and I'm glad to see you own up to it. Now go on with you. It's too pretty a day for me to be fretting over my children acting like circus monkeys." Mary settled back in her chair again, her mouth twitching.

"How do you know what circus monkeys do?" Robert asked. "You've never been to a circus."

"I've read about them," Mary said indignantly. "And I wish I had seen a circus. If there is ever one near here, Robert, I would very much wish to go."

"You never fail to surprise me, Mims," he said with amusement. "You, at a circus! But if one does come here, it would be my honor to take you, my dear."

Perry appeared again and slid in front of Robert. "Marse Robert, suh, Miss Agnes, she's in one of them little sailboats, chasing around in circles and giggling, it appears to me."

"Is she by herself?" Robert said alertly.

"No, suh, there's a young gentleman with her. I b'lieve it's that Taliaferro boy."

Robert relaxed. "That's fine then. Thank you, Perry."

Mary Lee hummed. "Circus monkeys."

Mary had chosen a glowing day for the party. The dance pavilion that George Custis had built many years before had received a new coat of white paint, and it gleamed brightly in the benevolent sunshine. They were at the foot of the hill that Arlington House was built upon, on the banks of the Potomac River. Just across the road was the apple orchard and the stretch of actual farm fields belonging to Arlington.

During George Custis's time they had lain fallow, for he was not a man to be a dedicated farmer. He was interested in agriculture, and often had grand plans for crop rotations or watering systems or new methods of fertilization, but implementing these imaginative ideas was too mundane for a man with such a mercurial mind.

In the previous year, however, Robert E. Lee had managed to bring in a corn crop that actually made the estate some money. Now the corn plants were only knee high, but they were verdant and shone as if they had been polished.

Just by the dance pavilion was Arlington Spring. It was not at all connected to the river, for the water bubbled up clean and icy cold. Cheerily it splashed into a small pool that had an underground outlet, for the pool stayed always about six feet in diameter.

George Custis had collected large rocks and had made a border around the fountain-like spring and pool, arranging them artistically rather than functionally. It was the kind of project he loved and would stick to until the end.

For the party, Robert had had low benches built to set around the pool, and now at least twenty young people sat there, catching mugs of water to drink and sometimes splashing each other. "I think there must be about fifty people here," he told Mary.

"I'm sure more will come along," she said with satisfaction. "All I did was tell the Fitzhughs, the Bollings, and two of the Carter families to spread the word, and I see many more of our cousins here."

Most everyone had arrived by boat, for sailing and punting on the river was a favorite entertainment of the young people that lived on both sides of the river. Arlington was a well-known stopping point, to get a drink of the refreshing spring water and rest or picnic in the shade of the pavilion. George Custis had always intended the landing to be semipublic, for he had enjoyed visiting with anyone who happened to stop at the landing.

It was not just young people who had come, however. So far there were four carriages lined up behind the tea tent next to the barn. Close by Mary was her aunt Fitzhugh, who lived in the fine country home of Ravensworth; her cousin Melanie Byrd; and another cousin Katrina Page. Other older couples were dancing or were sitting on one of the many canvas pallets that Arlington provided. Though the sun was bright, it was not hot even at high noon.

Mary glanced up the road and then shaded her eyes. "There's a crowd coming up the river road now, Robert. I wonder who that could be."

"Six people, one of them a black boy," he murmured after searching the distance. As they drew nearer, Robert said, "Oh, it's Edward Fitzhugh and his two daughters. I haven't seen him for at least two years. I must go and meet them."

He got to his feet, but before he walked away he gave Mary a sly glance, and she almost, but not quite, made a face at him. This was the Edward Fitzhugh who had been courting Mary for two years before Robert E. Lee had become her fiancé. He had seemed gravely disappointed when he found out that Mary was engaged to Robert, although Mary had never given Edward the least reason to suppose that she would consider marrying him. Even now, twenty-eight years later, Robert still gently teased her about Edward Fitzhugh.

He went to meet his guests and saw that Edward's two daughters were riding, both dressed in attractive riding habits. A man on a giant black horse accompanied them, along with a black boy riding a fine mare.

The company turned up the plantation drive road. Edward and the other two men dismounted, and Edward greeted Robert with obvious gladness. Shaking hands heartily, he said, "Robert, it's so good to see you. I didn't even know until last week, when Aunt Fitzhugh told me about this party, that you were still here at Arlington. For some reason I'd got muddled and thought you were back in Texas. Certainly we would have called before now. You remember my daughters, Frances and Deborah? And may I introduce to you our friend, Mr. Morgan Tremayne? Mr. Tremayne, this is Colonel Robert E. Lee."

Robert shook hands with him and "took his measure" in the few seconds their eyes met, a gift of discernment he had that he was completely unaware of until he had been told he possessed it.

Tremayne was about twenty-five, with a slim build but with wide shoulders. He was distinctly patrician in looks and bearing. His auburn hair was thick and carefully styled, his dark blue eyes were well spaced under neatly arched brows, his nose was thin and high-bridged, and his mouth was as full and well shaped as a woman's. However, he was as tanned as a farmhand, and the hand that clasped Lee's so firmly was rough and calloused. His eyes were keen and quick, surveying Robert and the surroundings alertly.

"Welcome to Arlington, Mr. Tremayne. Edward, please, come sit with us. Mary is anxious to see you, and Aunt Fitzhugh is here. Miss Frances, Miss Deborah, are you ladies going to ride the bridle paths or come to the party and dance?"

The girls looked gratified at Colonel Lee's courtliness. Their father, Edward Fitzhugh, was very plain, and he still had his cast eye, but he was a kind and gentle man, and he had won the heart of a beautiful woman. His two daughters took after her, with lush chestnut hair, heart-shaped faces, velvety dark eyes and complexions like magnolia blossoms. Frannie was nineteen, and

Deb was seventeen, and they were very close.

Frannie said, "Oh, Colonel Lee, I simply must show off my new mare, so I don't want to disappear into your lovely forest. May I ride her over on the other side of the spring?"

"I want to show mine off, too," Deb said. "May we ride them over there, sir?"

"Of course, if you feel confident of controlling them," Robert answered. "They are both very handsome, I must say." Admiringly he stroked Frannie's mare. Her coloring was distinctive, a uniform silvery gray, which was rather unusual. Deb's horse was a dark chestnut, almost a mahogany-red color, with dramatic black points. Both mares had small neat heads and petite alert conformation.

Edward murmured, "Oh, I don't know, Frannie. You've only had them for two days."

"Father, we've been riding since we were four years old," Frannie said lightly. "And besides, Mr. Tremayne's horses are so well trained and behave so admirably, I'm sure there won't be a problem."

"All right then." He relented.

Morgan turned and said to the black boy in a low voice, "Go with them, Rosh, and bring them up to the barn when the ladies are through with them."

"Yes, sir," he said and handed the reins of both his horse and Tremayne's stallion to Morgan. Then discreetly he followed the ladies around behind the gatherings of partygoers and the tea tent.

"Those are your horses, Mr. Tremayne?" Robert asked, puzzled.

"They were until two days ago, sir," Morgan answered good-naturedly.

"I bought them for the girls," Edward said. "Both of them love to ride, and I admit I'm proud of them. They are excellent equestriennes."

"They are," Morgan agreed. "It makes me very happy to know when my horses have good owners."

"Come," Robert said, "I'll walk with you to the barn. In the back is a lean-to roof where we're tying up the horses." He loved horses. Everything about them interested him, and he wanted to talk to Morgan. "Edward, will you walk with us?"

"By your leave, Robert, I would like to go visit with Mrs. Lee and Aunt Fitzhugh. And, I admit, have a nice cup of tea. Mr. Tremayne, would you mind taking care of Rutherford?"

"Not at all, sir," Morgan replied, taking the reins of Mr. Fitzhugh's horse.

"Go on then, Edward. We'll join you shortly," Robert said, and he and Morgan turned toward the barn.

Morgan Tremayne was glad he was getting an opportunity to look over the horses of all of those present. In his business, it was important to know what horses people liked and thus bought.

Eyeing the stamping, snorting stallion behind them, Robert asked, "And so you are in the business of selling horses, Mr. Tremayne?"

"I have a horse farm, and yes, sir, for the last two years I have done well," Morgan answered.

"That great brute behind us is one of your horses, I take it."

"Yes, sir. This is Vulcan. He's my prize sire. The mare is from my farm, too." Vulcan tossed his head so far that Morgan almost lost all of the reins he held.

Hastily Robert said, "Here, Mr. Tremayne, perhaps I'd better take Edward's horse." After fumbling around until the reins were straight, he went on, "I assume Vulcan is acting up because of the mares."

Morgan rolled his eyes. "Sir, for Vulcan this is not acting up. This is fairly calm for him."

"Really? You must have spent many hours training him, if he's this manageable around mares. He's quite a striking horse. If you're selling his bloodline, he must be very good advertisement for you," Robert said shrewdly.

"Yes, sir, he is, when he behaves like a civilized horse," Morgan said. "That chestnut mare that Miss Deborah is riding? Vulcan is her sire, by a fine brood mare named Bettina that I have. In my opinion, their offspring are the best of my breedings."

They went on talking as they watered the three horses then tied them up in the shady lean-to. Morgan quickly checked the other four horses there and saw with satisfaction that they were geldings. Vulcan wouldn't be too pleased with his company, but at least there were no other stallions. Morgan knew that Vulcan would almost certainly start a fight if there were.

Robert led Morgan back under the great spreading live oak tree where the lawn chairs had been placed for the older people. Robert said, "Mary, I want you to meet Mr. Tremayne. He is a friend of Edward's. Mr. Tremayne, this is my wife, Mary."

Morgan bowed over her hand and said all the usual pleasantries.

An empty chair was next to Mary, and she motioned Morgan to sit down. "Welcome to Arlington, Mr. Tremayne. I'm so pleased that you came today. Edward was telling me that you sold those two excellent mares to him for Frannie and Deb."

"Yes, ma'am, it was my distinct pleasure to be able to provide the Misses Fitzhughs with what I believe to be superb saddle horses," Morgan said enthusiastically. "And I was just telling Colonel Lee that it always gives me great pleasure to sell my horses to someone I know will be a good, caring owner."

Mary nodded. "Yes, Edward was telling me that you flatly refused to sell any of your horses to one of the planters in your area. It seemed you found the care they would receive was not up to your standards."

Awkwardly Morgan said, "Um—er—I apologize, Mrs. Lee, but you caught me quite off guard. I wasn't aware that the details of that little incident were generally known."

Her mouth curled upward in a small smile. "All of northern Virginia is like a small town, Mr. Tremayne. Generally everyone knows everyone else's business. I understand that you are from Fredericksburg?"

"No, ma'am, I have a horse farm outside of Fredericksburg, about ten miles west on the Rapidan River. My family is originally from Staunton, in the Valley."

"And how did you come to these parts, sir?" Mary asked politely.

"My mother inherited a townhouse in Richmond, and the family travels there quite often, because we have many old friends there. Actually, I inherited my farm from a great-uncle on my mother's side. She was a Carter, and my property was in the Carter family for almost fifty years."

Mary's face lit up. "Oh, is she one of the Richmond Carters?"

"Yes, ma'am."

"Why, then you're family, Mr. Tremayne! Please, you must tell me all about your mother's family. And your father's, too, for since you are surely my cousin I must hear all about this new connection."

Her delight and interest was obviously genuine, and Morgan readily began to explain his mother's genealogy. They had not been talking for very long when Morgan saw out of the corner of his eye that the Misses Fitzhughs had come up to them and made their curtsies to Mrs. Lee.

As it was unheard of for children to interrupt their elders, she kept talking while the girls stood patiently waiting. ". . .and later I shall determine if you and my husband are actually third cousins or third cousins once removed," she finished thoughtfully then turned to the girls. "Good afternoon, Frannie, Deb. You both look lovely. Are the riding habits new?"

"Oh yes, ma'am," Frannie gushed. "Father bought us horses, saddles, tack, spurs, and riding habits. Which do you prefer, Mrs. Lee, my blue one or Deb's green one?"

But Mary ostensibly knew these two girls too well to fall into that trap. "In my opinion, that deep shade of blue particularly complements your complexion, Fran, and that dark green flatters yours, Deborah."

"Thank you, ma'am," they said in unison, though they obviously were dissatisfied with Mrs. Lee's diplomacy.

SURRENDER

"Anyway, Mrs. Lee, we wondered if we might steal Mr. Tremayne," Deborah said mischievously. "Everyone wants to know all about Serafina and Delilah, and also we were hoping that he would get Vulcan to do his tricks."

"Just who, pray tell, are Serafina and Delilah?" Mrs. Lee demanded, her brow lowering.

"That's what I named the mares, ma'am," Morgan said hastily. To the girls he asked, "You aren't going to name them? They're very intelligent, you know. They would catch on quickly."

"No, no," Fran replied. "We like their names. So, Mr. Tremayne? Will you come meet everyone and tell them about Serafina and Delilah? And then will you and Vulcan please perform?"

"I'll be glad to talk horses with anyone anytime, ladies. But I doubt very much that Mrs. Lee wants a circus starting up at her nice party."

"I gather that Vulcan is that great black horse you ride, Mr. Tremayne? And he does tricks?" she asked curiously.

Morgan grimaced. "Well, I would say that he shows off when he wants to. If he doesn't want to, then he just balks and sulks."

Mrs. Lee laughed.

Morgan thought that she had a very youthful laugh for her age. He couldn't quite tell how old she was, because he could see that she was sickly. He only thought that she looked older than Colonel Lee.

Mrs. Lee said, "As a matter of fact, Mr. Tremayne, I was telling Colonel Lee just awhile ago how much I wished to see a circus. So please, if Vulcan agrees, I would love to see you perform. I assume that the drive will do?"

"Yes, ma'am," Morgan said resignedly. "We don't require three rings."

"Hurrah!" Deborah cried. "Please go ahead, Mr. Tremayne, and get Vulcan. We'll introduce you to everyone after."

Morgan went to the barn and untied Vulcan, who showed his annoyance at being crowded into a lean-to with other lesser horses by irritably chewing on his bit. Morgan checked the saddle, the cinch strap, and the bridle, to make sure they were secure. Then he led Vulcan out onto the plantation drive.

To his bemusement, most everyone at the party lined the wide gravel road. He saw Colonel Lee standing behind Mrs. Lee, and realized with a start that she was in a wheelchair and had evidently wanted to come have a ringside seat.

He stopped in the middle of the drive and stepped in front of the prancing horse. He put his hands on both sides of Vulcan's head, just under his ears, and stepped very close to him. "Listen, Vulcan. I know you've never performed for a crowd before, but there's no reason to be nervous. Just do what I've taught you, okay? Okay?"

To Morgan's relief, he bobbed his head enthusiastically, as if he were saying, "Yes." It meant that Vulcan was in a good mood. He hoped.

He swung up into the saddle easily and sat motionless, the reins slack, for a few seconds. Vulcan shifted, bobbed his head again, then stood perfectly still.

Morgan steadily pulled the reins back tight. Under him the horse rose until he was in a picture-perfect rearing stance. Morgan heard "Ooohs" from the crowd. Vulcan pawed the air once, twice, then came back down in a collected stand. Then he began his gaited trot.

It had taken Morgan many, many hours to teach Vulcan this tightly choreographed gait, and this time Vulcan did it perfectly. He lifted his right hoof, brought it up until it almost clapped against his chest, then kicked it out smartly. It was a proud gait, and Vulcan arched his neck while holding his head perfectly straight. Morgan reflected that he had never done so well. Perhaps he ought to have an adoring crowd all the time.

Morgan reached the crossroad then pulled on the right rein. Vulcan made a sharp about-face and landed, still in his gaited trot, heading back up the drive smoothly. When he reached their starting point, Morgan pulled on the left rein then pulled on both simultaneously. Vulcan turned, reared again, then came back to a show horse stance.

The crowd applauded and shouted. Mrs. Lee was smiling with delight.

Morgan dismounted, said another word to Vulcan, then led him to stand in front of Mrs. Lee. "He does one more trick sometimes, Mrs. Lee," Morgan said. "I hope he shows you the proper respect now." Morgan bowed, and after a second, Vulcan tossed his head, bent his left leg back, and bowed.

Mary Lee said, "Thank you so much, Mr. Tremayne. I will never forget this day."

Morgan did meet everyone, all fifty-seven of them.

Soon after Fran and Deborah Fitzhugh started introducing him, they got sidetracked and disappeared when he was dancing with Miss Mary Custis Lee. He thought the Lees' eldest daughter was charming and vivacious, and he soon found out that all their children were warm and gracious, much like Mrs. Lee.

Colonel Lee was certainly a courteous, gallant gentleman, but in many ways he stood apart. Part of it was that Robert E. Lee had an innate reserve, and part of it was that he inspired such a great deal of respect that it bordered on awe. At least that was the way Morgan saw him, but he could see that Lee laughed much more when he was talking to his family, so he could tell that he was much more approachable to his wife and children.

Morgan had danced with Mary Custis, Agnes, and Anne and had just finished a vigorous Virginia reel with Milly when he begged a chance to have a cup of tea.

As he was heading to the tea tent, Colonel Lee fell into step beside him. "I find tea to be so much more refreshing than coffee in warm weather," he remarked pleasantly.

"I agree, sir." A jolly-faced black woman served them tea in fine china cups.

Lee took an appreciative sip then said, "Mr. Tremayne, will you sit with me for a minute? I'd like to talk to you."

"Of course, sir."

They went to two lounge chairs that were set apart from the ladies and settled into them. "That was quite a performance you and your horse put on, Mr. Tremayne," Lee said, his eyes lit with amusement.

"Thank you, sir, but it is Vulcan that does the performing," Morgan said. "He just allows me to sit on his back while he shows off."

Lee nodded. "He is spirited, I can see. A fine stallion. And really, Mr. Tremayne, that is what I wanted to talk to you about, your horse farm and your horses. You see, I am considering buying a horse, maybe two."

Morgan blanched. "Oh, sir—Colonel Lee—please don't think that I put on that show just as a. . .a. . .vulgar sales pitch! I assure you—"

Lee held up one hand, shaking his head. "No, Mr. Tremayne, that is not what I think at all. If it were, I certainly shouldn't be interested in buying anything from you. No, I have been talking to Mr. Fitzhugh, and he gives you the highest recommendations. Truthfully I have been thinking of buying a good saddle horse for the girls, and now that Rob is sixteen, I think he's ready for his own horse. So I would like for you to consider if you have any three- or four-year-olds that would suit."

With vast relief, Morgan said, "Sir, I have eight three-year-olds that would suit."

"Good," Lee said, settling back in the comfortable chair. "And I will tell you, Mr. Tremayne, that Mrs. Lee would never allow me to buy a horse from a stranger. But she has assured me that you are either our third cousin or third cousin once removed, so she has given me permission to purchase two horses from you. In fact, I think that if she were still riding, she would try to buy Vulcan from you."

SURRENDER

Morgan grinned boyishly. "Colonel Lee, I will never sell Vulcan. But I would give him to Mrs. Lee."

A small smile lit up Lee's face. "Don't tell her that, please, Mr. Tremayne. It's better for all of us if she doesn't know."

PART TWO

PART TWO

CHAPTER SIX

Morgan Tremayne pulled Vulcan to a stop to look up at his house. He had named his property Rapidan Run Horse Farm, for the house was plain and functional and not nearly grand enough to warrant a fancy name like so many of the large plantation homes in Virginia. Still, he felt a sense of deep pride when he surveyed the house, prettily situated on a rise above the Rapidan River, the manicured grounds cool and green under sheltering oak trees. The house rose above, a two-story rectangular box set on its end. The windows were exactly spaced above and below, and a modest gabled pediment was above the front door. The only nod to any whimsy was that the clapboard house was painted red.

Morgan had inherited the farm four years ago, on his twenty-first birthday, and he had been surprised and somehow pleased to see the faded red paint on the house. In the next two years he had enlarged the barn, added stables with fifty boxes, a carriage house, and two servant's cottages. He had painted them all red.

"Let's go, boy," he said to his horse and rode up the small hill by the path that led to the back door.

the SURRENDER

On this glorious spring morning in June 1859, the double doors to the detached kitchen were propped open, and even before Morgan rode into the yard he could smell pies baking. He had a keen sense of smell—in fact, all his senses were sharp—and he guessed a peach pie and a cherry pie.

His servant Amon hurried out of the paddock as he dismounted, and at the same time Amon's wife, Evetta, came out of the kitchen, drying her hands on her apron. Both of them started talking at once as they neared him.

Amon said, "That there little filly outta Dandy is just as sweet as she kin be, Mr. Morgan. Not like her daddy—"

Evetta said, "You been wandering out in that Wilderness again like some wild man in Borneo, I guess, and without breakfast, too—"

"—'cause I see he's been running you, that Vulcan devil, 'stead of you ridin' him—"

"—which you need breakfast, Mr. Morgan. Haven't I told you ten thousand times to eat something—"

"—Even Ketura could break her, she's so nice and polite—"

"—my peach pie and cherry—"

"I knew it!" Morgan said, grinning as he handed Vulcan's reins to Amon. "I could smell those pies all the way in the Wilderness. You say the little filly—is it that pretty dappled gray one you mean?"

"Yes, sir," Amon said.

Morgan nodded. "I want to come see her work out. Go on and tend to Vulcan, Amon, and I'll come out to the paddock as soon as I've had some coffee. Er—can I have some coffee, Evetta?"

"I suppose so," she said ominously. "Since I made a big ol' pot of it for *breakfast*."

Over his shoulder Morgan said, "Just coffee right now, Evetta. I'll make up for it at dinner. I'll have a peach pie."

He went into the house and upstairs to his bedroom, shrugging off his black frock coat. It had been chilly in the predawn when he had left for his morning ride. He quickly washed his hands and face and combed his thick auburn hair. He was by nature a neat and tidy man, though he was neither a fop nor was he finicky.

His bedroom reflected this. It was spare, with a plain oak bedstead and bed precisely made, a sturdy armoire, and washstand with toilet articles meticulously arranged.

Hurrying back downstairs, he went out to the kitchen, where Evetta was standing at the worktable, kneading dough. Evetta was a black woman of thirty-five, small and sturdy. She looked up when he came in, and he saw that she had apparently swiped her forehead, for a white flour streak lay across it. One eyebrow was white.

She started to say something, but Morgan, hiding a smile, told her, "I'm just going to get a mug and go watch Rosh and Santo working the two-year-olds." He got an oversize white stoneware mug and poured a steaming cup of strong black coffee.

"I don't s'pose you're planning on eating today, then?" she said sarcastically, pounding the dough with vengeance. "Tomorrow, mebbe? Week from Thursday?"

"Aw, Evetta, you fuss like a mama goose. I'll eat at dinnertime. I'm fine until then."

"Not no 'just peach pie,' neither," she grumbled.

"Okay, not just peach pie. And I'm going over to Mr. Deforge's later on this afternoon. For tea, he says, about four o'clock. So I'll have a late supper, okay?"

She nodded. "Glad you told me, Mr. Morgan. We need to send them a couple of chickens. I'll have Amon take care of that."

"Why am I always taking dead chickens to Deforge's?" Morgan complained.

Evetta's mouth drew into a straight line. "Cleo says that Miss Jolie don't like chicken."

"She doesn't? Mr. DeForge doesn't either?"

"I wouldn't presume to know nothing about that," Evetta answered primly.

"But if they don't eat chicken, then why am I always taking them chicken? But wait—they have chickens of their own. I've seen them! Or are those just for the eggs?"

Evetta gave a careless half shrug.

Morgan rasped, "This is very confusing. But if Miss Cleo wants chickens, I'll take them to her." He went to the door and turned. "You know, Evetta, I think I'd better get a mirror to put in here."

"Wha—?"

He went out to the enclosed paddock and stood up on the bottom railing to see over the high fence. Sipping his coffee thoughtfully, he watched Amon and Evetta's two sons, Rosh and Santo, as they worked two mares. Though they were only eighteen and sixteen years old, both of them were very good horsemen, like their father. That was the main reason Morgan had asked Amon and Evetta to come to Rapidan Run to help him.

They had been servants at Tremayne House, Morgan's family's farm in the Shenandoah Valley. Amon and his sons had worked in the livery stables there, and Morgan had seen how expert they were at handling horses. They had agreed to come work for him, and they were one of the main factors contributing to the success of Rapidan Run Horse Farm. That and the fact that Morgan had chosen to breed American Saddlebreds, a relatively new equine strain.

The Tremaynes had cousins in Kentucky who had begun breeding them in the 1840s, when the superiority of the bloodline was just beginning to be recognized. Morgan had gotten all his breeding stock from his Tremayne cousins at a very reasonable price. Without exception he had found them to be wonderful horses. As saddle horses, they had comfortable, ground-covering gaits and were sure-footed, but still they were stylish, flashy horses that were beautiful for harness, strong enough for farm work, and fast enough to win races.

After four years, Morgan now had eleven brood mares and three stallions, eight three-year-olds ready for sale, ten two-year-olds, six yearlings, and nine foals less than a year old. All the two-year-olds were good horses, trainable, and generally all of them had good temperaments. Vulcan's progeny had a tendency to be high-strung, though generally not to the degree that he was. With Morgan's and Amon's expert care, they molded these nervy tendencies into high-spirited, lively horses.

Ketura, Amon and Evetta's daughter, suddenly popped up beside him. "Can I watch, too, Mr. Morgan?"

"Sure."

She was thirteen years old and was in that awkward stage between being a child and being a young woman. She was skinny, with long legs and arms, and had a tendency to be clumsy. But she was a comely girl with a dazzling smile and enormous dark eyes. Supposedly she was training with her mother to become a housemaid and cook, but for the last year or so Morgan had noticed that she liked to spend much more time with the horses than in the house or kitchen. Evetta continually fretted about it, even though technically Ketura was Morgan's servant, and he didn't care. Even as he was reflecting on this, Ketura cast a cautious look behind her toward the kitchen. Morgan decided to talk to Evetta. If Ketura would rather help with the horses, that was fine with him.

After a while she asked, "Mr. Morgan, did you go riding in that Wilderness again this morning?"

"Sure did. I didn't go too far inside, though. I mostly rambled along the river."

"Ain't you scared?"

"No, of course not, Ketura. What's the matter? Have you heard tales about the Wilderness?" He had heard that people thought it was haunted.

The Wilderness was aptly named. It was seventy square miles of second-growth forest, which meant that many of the trees were stunted and covered with parasitic vines, and the ground was a snarled undergrowth of weeds and brambles. The north side of the Wilderness was bordered by the Rapidan River, and the land along the riverbank was low and clear. But the ground in the Wilderness itself was treacherously uneven, with rock outcroppings, low craggy hills, and ravines, and it was crisscrossed by dozens of streams and brooks. When the area had heavy rain, in several places it became a pestilential dead marsh.

"Yes, sir, people say there's ghosts and monsters in there," Ketura answered, hugging herself.

"I've ridden all over it in the last four years, and I haven't seen one ghost or one monster," Morgan said gently.

"But it is spooky."

"Maybe. But I like it."

"Mama says that's 'cause you like being alone," she said casually. "Is that right?"

Perplexed, Morgan thought over the girl's innocent question. His first impulse was to answer, *Yes, I like being alone. I prefer living alone, riding alone, staying up late at night to read alone.* But if that were true, why did he want to get married so badly?

Six months ago he had started "courting" a girl from Fredericksburg, Leona Rose Bledsoe. He was beginning to think that she was the woman he wanted to marry. Morgan was a rather bookish, commonsensical, levelheaded man, and he had never put much stock in "being in love." He believed that a man and a woman should marry if they suited each other, amused each other, and were approximately equal in intelligence, and Leona Rose Bledsoe fit all these requirements. He could easily imagine being married to her, so he assumed he must "be in love" with her. At least, that's what one part of his mind insisted. Another part of him knew that he was a solitary man, and that it was by his own choice.

Ketura was watching him curiously, so he finally replied, "I do enjoy exploring the Wilderness by myself, Ketura. So sometimes I do like to be alone."

She opened her mouth, and Morgan could see that more questions were coming.

But he was saved by Evetta shouting at Ketura at the top of her lungs. "You there perched up on the paddock railing like a crow-bird! Yes, miss, I'm talking to you. I'm going in the house this here minute, and let me tell you something, if that downstairs dusting and polishing ain't done, I'm gonna pinch your head clean off!"

Ketura jumped down and scampered to her.

Morgan turned back, searching beyond the paddock to his pastures, four of them, planted with Bermuda grass for summer and ryegrass for winter. In the near pasture he could see several newly-weaned foals running and hopping and playing on their still-spindly legs. Morgan thought that that sight, this day, this home gave him feelings of peace and contentment he had never known. Even though he was alone.

Rosh, the older boy, was working with the filly Amon had spoken of. She was out of Vulcan by Bettina, Morgan's favorite mare. The filly was a pretty silver gray, with highlights of darker gray in her coat so that she was the color called "dappled." Rosh had her on a long tether, walking her around in tight circles, and Morgan could see that she was going to be naturally gaited. The distinctive, showy trot was more pronounced in some horses, and this filly would be one of those, he could see.

He decided to name her Evie. He couldn't remember each of the foals until he named them, and then he could always remember their sire and dam. It was a double-edged sword, though. Once he named them he was loath to sell them. At heart he loved them all.

Dismissing his meandering thoughts, he called out, "Amon, would you turn all the two-year-olds out to pasture and then bring in the three-year-olds two at a time?"

"Sure and certain, Mr. Morgan," he replied.

In a few minutes, Rosh and Santo brought out two colts and walked them around the paddock, first in file and then abreast. Amon joined Morgan on the fence as he studied the horses. They were both chestnuts, one with black points and one with a white face and socks on his front feet.

"Here's what we need, Amon," Morgan said thoughtfully. "Colonel Lee has four daughters, from twenty-four years old to thirteen years old. They all like to ride, and from what I saw they are fairly accomplished. Two of the daughters are somewhat frail, though, so I don't want them to have anything too high-spirited. Now the son, Rob, is sixteen, and he's a handful, I can see, but he can ride. He even rode Vulcan."

Amon's brows shot up. "He did? And howsomever did that go?"

Morgan shrugged. "For some reason Vulcan was on his best behavior at the Lees'. I don't know why, but he's made up for it since we got home yesterday. Tried to nip me this morning. Anyway, he was just as cool as a breeze when Rob Jr. mounted him. Plodded around in a circle like he was the pony ride at the fair."

"Can't never tell about that horse, though, Mr. Morgan," Amon said darkly. "He was jist as likely to toss him as he was to carry him."

"I know, but I couldn't very well tell Colonel Lee that my own horse is unridable, could I?" Morgan said.

At one time or another, Vulcan had bucked off Morgan, Amon, Rosh, and Santo during his early training. Now he didn't throw them, but he was an excitable horse. The entire time Rob Jr. had been riding Vulcan, Morgan's heart had been in his throat.

"Anyway, I'm already thinking about Diamond Jack for Rob," Morgan continued. "But I haven't made my mind up about the ladies' mounts. I want them to have the very best I've got."

Amon thought for a few minutes then said, "What about Roebuck, suh? I know you were thinking about keeping him, but all together I'd have to say he's the best of the three-year-olds. Did they want a mare in perticklar?"

"No, Colonel Lee left it completely up to me," Morgan answered. "But Roebuck, it would be hard to part with him."

Roebuck was a three-year-old out of Vulcan and Bettina, and he was that very unusual color, a palomino. He was a creamy-golden color, with white tail and mane. He hadn't inherited Vulcan's temperament, though he was a big horse like his sire, almost fifteen hands. Instead he was sweet tempered, patient, and calm like his dam. Morgan had been considering keeping him strictly because of his unusual coloring, but suddenly he knew that the Lee daughters would take just as much care of him as he himself would.

"Right," Morgan finally said, "you're right, Amon. Get Rosh and Santo to saddle up Roebuck and Diamond Jack. Let me see them do a workout."

The boys brought out the two geldings, the graceful and collected Roebuck and Diamond Jack, another gelding out of Vulcan by a spirited bay mare named Lalla. Diamond Jack was solid glossy black except for a blaze on his face that was in the exact shape of a diamond, hence his name. He was showy like Vulcan, prancing and preening and proudly tossing his head.

Morgan got his portfolio and took notes as he watched the boys work the horses, and then he rode both of them himself, a short ride up his dirt drive to the woodline where he got them both into a gallop. Both of them were magically smooth runners.

Rejoining Amon, he told him to come into the house, and they went into Morgan's study. The floor plan of the house was timeworn and simple: a hall down the middle with a parlor on one side and dining room on the other, and on the second floor four square bedrooms, each exactly the same size. Downstairs, Morgan had converted what was supposed to be the parlor into a study/library with a comfortable seating area in front of the windows. He took his seat in one well-worn overstuffed leather armchair and motioned for Amon to sit down on the other side of the small cherry tea table between the chairs.

"You know, Amon, I haven't told you yet how much I appreciate your advice about the Fitzhugh girls. Even though I had met them, I didn't realize how important it would be to them to have different horses. I just thought—sisters—close in age—same horses."

Amon grinned, a wide, delighted smile that lit up his entire ebony face. "Back at home, you 'member, Mr. Morgan, Evetta had three sisters. I knows how they fight and argue and try to top each other. I figgered them two highfalutin Fitzhugh girls were much the same. Seems like women everywhere are kinda like that."

"Are they?" Morgan asked with honest surprise. He had very

little experience with women. Growing up he had one younger brother, Clay, and he had twin sisters now, but they were only five years old. Morgan barely knew them. "Guess I'll have to take your word for it. I could sure see when I delivered Serafina and Delilah that it would never have done to have given them the two chestnuts. They each started right in about how much prettier their horse was than the other. So thank you, Amon. I appreciate the advice. I'm going to give you a small bonus on that sale—five dollars."

"Thank you, Mr. Morgan," he said with dignity.

"You're welcome. That kind of brings me around to what I wanted to talk to you about. Now that Rapidan Run is making some money, I'm going to do what's called profit sharing with you, Amon. Beginning today, you and your family are going to make one percent of my profit on each sale and each stud fee. I know you realize this, because you've learned every aspect of the business, but I do want you to make clear to your family that one percent of the profit is not one percent of the sale price. Even though I sell the horses for two hundred fifty or three hundred dollars, what I'm actually making on them is about half that."

"Yes, sir, I knows that. And I knows you wouldn't be making near that much if you didn't farm your own forage," he said shrewdly. "That's right kind of you, Mr. Morgan. I can promise you me and my family will work all the harder, knowing that we got us a share."

"I don't see how you could work any harder than you do, all of you," Morgan said warmly. "And it's not any charitable virtue on my part, Amon. It's only right and fair."

"Maybe, but it ain't what you'd call commonly done, profit sharing with servants," Amon said. "Me and Evetta, we haven't met any other servants here, only slaves."

Many years ago, when Morgan's great-great-great-grandfather had settled in the Shenandoah Valley, he had been Amish, and he had abhorred slavery. Though it was his forebear who had eventually married a girl outside of the Amish faith and had become an

Episcopalian, he kept his Amish sensibilities. None of the Tremaynes had ever had slaves. Morgan himself hated the institution, and so naturally Amon and Evetta, along with the other black servants at Tremayne House, were employees.

"Yes, I know, Amon, but you know you and yours will never have to worry about that," Morgan said firmly. "So, since you're getting a percentage now, I have to tell you that I lowered the price of two horses when I quoted to Colonel Lee. I'm only charging him two hundred apiece for them."

"For our two best geldings?" Amon said doubtfully. Normally Morgan charged three hundred for geldings, two hundred fifty for mares.

"Yes, Mr. Fitzhugh told me something of the family problems the Lees are having. I'm glad he did, for I certainly would never have known it from talking to Mrs. Lee or Colonel Lee. Apparently, Mrs. Lee's father, who owned Arlington and several other properties, left his affairs in something of a mess, and Colonel Lee is the executor. Mr. Fitzhugh said that Colonel Lee has been using his own money to try and fulfill all the bequests in Mr. Custis's will. When I saw what kind of people they are, I decided to give them the best price I could."

"Fine with me," Amon said. "I b'lieve the good Lord's gonna bless us, and this place, Mr. Morgan, with whatever you decide to do. So when are you taking the geldings to Arlington?"

"I'm going to leave on Friday," Morgan said. "Taking Vulcan on the train left me, Serafina, Delilah, Rosh, and Calliope all to bits and pieces. That horse would drive a saint insane. I figure we'll stop at Alexandria on Sunday and spend the night to recover before I take Diamond Jack and Roebuck to Arlington."

Amon grimaced. "So you're a-going to take that Vulcan on the train again."

"Going to try," Morgan said. "He's got to learn."

"Mebbe so, mebbe not," Amon said darkly. "Why don't you just ride Laird, Mr. Morgan? He's one fine-looking gelding and got a lot sweeter temperament than that Vulcan."

"Because Vulcan is good advertising. You know that, Amon. So far this summer I've got him booked out for four studs. People see him, they want a foal from him."

"That is true," Amon admitted. "He's a big showoff, prancing about and preening and tossing his head. Anyways, if you're set on it, I'll give him a bath tomorrow and use that mane and tail cream and shine him up."

"No, I'll do it," Morgan said. "I need to take every opportunity to show that horse who's boss."

Amon's face worked.

Finally Morgan laughed. "All right. I know, I know. So I need to take every opportunity to show that horse who *wishes* he were boss."

"Yes, sir," Amon said with amusement. "If you're set on it— and if that Vulcan will let you. Good Lord watch over you an' keep you, sir."

CHAPTER SEVEN

The brilliant sunshine of June caught Jolie DeForge full in the face as she stepped out of the house and then crossed the porch. Though she was thirteen years old now, the face that the golden sun lit up was more like a ten-year-old's, for with her wide-spaced dark eyes and tiny nose, mouth, and chin, she looked very much like a little kitten.

No one would ever suspect that she had black blood. Her skin was of an unusual shade, a very light olive, and her complexion was pure and smooth. Her hair was black and shiny, but instead of coarse curls, it was satiny, as her mother's had been. Since she was so young, she still wore it down, flowing around her shoulders, with the top and sides pulled away from her face with a sky-blue ribbon. She wore the dress of a young lady of good family, a fine-quality muslin of blue and green stripes, with a satin sash that matched her hair ribbon.

Jolie went to the enclosure around the chicken house and scooped out some feed into a five-gallon bucket and started lightly spreading it around. The chickens came running and at once began pecking at the feed. Jolie watched them with a smile. "Ophelia, don't be so greedy. Let Juliet have some of that seed."

She had named the hens after characters in Shakespeare, which Cleo, the housekeeper, had long ago warned her not to do. "If you name them, you'll get to thinking they're pets, Jolie. Just don't do it, chile."

Jolie had found that to be true, and finally, after many broad hints to Mr. DeForge, DeForge House no longer had chicken for supper. They had loads of eggs, but that was because no chickens were ever killed and Box and Cleo kept them "broody" so they wouldn't have little chicks.

After she'd fed the chickens, calling each one of them by name, she went back to the summer kitchen, which was in back of the main house, connected by a bricked, covered walkway. DeForge House, a majestic Greek Revival home looming above the banks of the Rapidan River, had an enormous kitchen in the cellar that was used in the winter, because it gave the big house additional heat.

As Jolie thought of this, she wondered for perhaps the thousandth time about her benefactor, Henry DeForge. He was 59 years old now—Jolie could always recall his age because he was born in 1800, and so the math was easy—and he obviously had a lot of money, because he had bought this plantation, and only he and Jolie lived in the fifteen-room house. He wore nice clothes, she knew, and she always had nice clothes, but that seemed to be the extent of Mr. DeForge's extravagance. He had a business in Baltimore; he had been teaching Jolie some of the basics of bookkeeping, and so she knew that his company, DeForge Brothers Import & Export, Ltd., made quite a bit of money. But Mr. DeForge had no horses and no carriage, he never entertained, and he never bought new furnishings or accessories for grand DeForge House. Besides the necessities, the only other thing Jolie had seen him purchase was books.

Jolie entered the stifling kitchen. Cleo had an enormous bowl underneath her left arm and was whipping the batter so vigorously she could have powered a boat. "Sponge cake for tea?" Jolie asked as she put on a stained and worn canvas bib apron. "Mr. DeForge will be so happy. Do you want me to help you, Cleo?"

"No! No'm, it's fine. I kin do it," Cleo blurted out.

Jolie had tried three times before to make sponge cakes, Henry DeForge's favorite food. All three times she had neglected to beat the eggs and sugar enough to give the cake its airy texture, and twice she had yanked the cake out of the oven to test its doneness, which made it promptly fall into a gummy mess.

"You go ahead and work out in the garden, Jolie. Box weeded them tomato plants just three days ago, but I swear it looks like they're gettin' took over again."

"I'll put a stop to that," Jolie said briskly, forgetting all about the sponge cake or helping Cleo in the kitchen. She would much rather be outdoors. She liked working in the gardens, for DeForge House had a rich and plentiful, varied kitchen garden, and the flower gardens around the house were gorgeous.

Humming softly to herself, she knelt down by the first staked tomato plant in the row and started working out the weeds with a claw. Two of the field slaves were working the kitchen garden today, two boys in their teens. Jolie talked to them as they worked, desultory things like the weather, how tall the corn was growing, what vegetables they would take to the farmer's market on Saturday in Fredericksburg. The boys mostly just mumbled yes'm and no'm, but Jolie knew them by name and knew their families, and she talked to them as if they were school friends.

By one o'clock, her back was aching, her fingers were sore, and she was very hungry. She went back to the kitchen to beg something from Cleo.

"I'm a-makin' this mayonnaise for tea," Cleo said impatiently. "You can help yourself to whatever you want, Jolie, but I don't have time to stop right now to fix you something."

"That's all right," Jolie said hastily. "I see you've got some of that ham left. I'll just have a couple of slices of that with some cheese."

"Good thing we don't have no hogs what you named, or we'd never have the likes of bacon nor ham," Cleo muttered.

Ignoring her, Jolie put a slice of ham and a chuck of cheese on a stoneware plate, poured herself a mug of apple cider, and went outside to sit on the bench by the door. She ate slowly, staring into space.

She was reflecting upon her age. She had turned thirteen two months previously, and for some reason she had thought that she would be very, very different once she was in her teen years. But she didn't feel any different, and she sure didn't look any different. She was still thin and gangly with no hint of a womanly shape.

Her life was exactly the same as it had always been. Mr. DeForge taught her lessons five days a week in the mornings. In the afternoons she went outside to work in the gardens or take long walks or go down to sit on the riverbank and read and nap. Sometimes, when Mr. DeForge felt well enough, he would go with her, and they would have a picnic at teatime. Either she would read aloud to him, or he would read to her. These times were treasured by Jolie.

She ate very slowly, and she wasn't yet finished when Cleo appeared at the door, hands on hips. "You know you look like a field hand, Jolie. Ain't you going to have tea with Mr. DeForge and Mr. Tremayne?"

Jolie jumped up, scattering plate, ham, cheese, and cider. "Mr. Tremayne's coming for tea? Why didn't you tell me?" Turning, she started running toward the house, skirts flapping.

As Morgan rode to the DeForge place, he wondered about two things: the chickens and Jolie.

When Morgan had inherited his farm in the winter of 1855, he had immediately traveled here and surveyed the property, assessed the state of the house and the outbuildings, and checked on the one-hundred-twelve acres of fields that went with the property.

Also, as soon as he could, he had called on all his neighbors. Henry DeForge was his nearest neighbor, as it was only about five miles along the river to DeForge House. Mr. DeForge had received him most cordially, and in the four years since then they had become fast friends.

Mr. DeForge had, in the course of time, told Morgan that he and his brother had a successful import/export business in Baltimore, Maryland. In 1840, Henry DeForge had been diagnosed with consumption, and that was when he semiretired from the business, bought this property in Virginia, and moved down here. He was very much a recluse. He never traveled; he didn't even own a horse and buggy. He had made arrangements with various shopkeepers in Fredericksburg to have his supplies shipped to him by boat on the Rapidan.

As far as Morgan knew, he was the only visitor to DeForge House, and that was strictly by invitation only. Though he knew that DeForge was a good friend, he was a rather formal, insular man, and each time Morgan visited, Mr. DeForge would make an appointment with him to visit the next time.

In four years of long visits, Morgan and DeForge had talked about their lives, their families, their plans for the future, politics, religion, books, and public figures, but Henry DeForge had never spoken once about Jolie. On his first visit, Morgan had been introduced to the nine-year-old child with Old World gallantry. Mr. DeForge had said, "Mr. Tremayne, it is my honor to make known to you Jolie. Jolie, may I introduce you to Mr. Morgan Tremayne." The child had curtsied prettily but had not said a word, and DeForge had gone on visiting with Morgan. Since then Morgan guessed he might have heard her speak a dozen times.

Morgan Tremayne was not inherently a curious man. He firmly believed that the world would be a much better place if people minded their own business, and he set about doing that very thing. But sometimes he did, in passing, wonder about Jolie. It seemed she had no last name, but only slaves had one given name. Jolie wasn't a slave, that much was obvious, but apparently neither was she a DeForge relative.

"None of my affair anyway," Morgan grunted to himself. Still, he couldn't help but wonder about the chickens.

He let Vulcan have his head, and instantly the horse started galloping wildly, an all-out run. Vulcan did love to run. Morgan wore spurs, but he never *ever* used them on Vulcan. He might have to touch his sides with his boots to get him to turn, but Morgan fancifully believed that if he actually spurred Vulcan to a gallop, the horse would probably jump six feet straight into the air, buck him off, and streak away like a red-hot railroad engine. Very soon Morgan was at the bottom of the hill at DeForge's.

The plantation house was built like most on the river: the drive came up to the back door, with an unspoiled lawn in the front sloping gently down to the riverbank. On Morgan's left were DeForge's farm fields, where he raised cash crops only: corn, peanuts, sweet potatoes, tomatoes, beets, and turnips. Bordering the house on the left were two orchards, cherry and pecan. Directly behind were all the outbuildings, the barn, a storehouse, the creamery, the smokehouse, and the slave cottages. Henry DeForge only had the old couple, Box and Cleo, as house slaves. He had about twenty working field slaves, and Morgan guessed there might be around thirty slaves on the property counting the women and children.

There was a hitching post and watering trough in the yard, and Morgan dismounted and began to tie up Vulcan when a young boy came running up. Morgan remembered his name. "Hello, Howie. You going to take care of Vulcan for me?"

"Yes, suh, if'n he'll let me," the boy said, but he took the reins, and Vulcan meekly allowed him to lead him into the barn.

Morgan was amused; he knew that Vulcan liked visiting here because the slaves gave him lumps of sugar and sweet cherries, no matter how many times Morgan warned them not to do it. Every time he visited DeForge's, he was always afraid Vulcan would be sick the next day.

He walked up the gravel path to the back door, raising his head to catch the scents. Anywhere on DeForge's grounds it seemed one could smell jasmine and roses. It amused Morgan to see the kitchen garden, which grew exactly the same crops that were grown on the farm. But in time he had come to learn that Mr. DeForge was a generous man and apparently didn't need money, because he allowed his slaves to take most of the cash crops to market and sell them. The kitchen garden supplied the home produce. Morgan noted the herb garden and saw that it was thriving. Someone on the place was a good gardener.

Box, a tall, angular black man, met him at the back door, bowing. "Good afternoon, Mr. Tremayne."

"Good afternoon, Box." Morgan gave him his hat and gloves and said, "I've got two chickens in that canvas sack on my saddle. I forgot to tell Howie to bring them up here. Evetta says they're for Cleo."

"Yes, suh. No, suh. It's all right, suh. I'll fetch 'em, and I know Cleo will want to thank you personal. Mr. DeForge is out on the veranda, Mr. Tremayne."

"Thank you, Box. I can find my own way." Morgan went to the front door, passing the butler's pantry, the storage pantry, the formal dining room, the parlor, the music room, and the sitting room, and finally went out onto the veranda.

DeForge and Jolie were seated around a white wrought-iron table, sipping lemonade. Henry DeForge was a tall, distinguished-looking man with thin silver hair and thick side whiskers and sharp blue eyes. However he was ill, and he had good days and bad days. Morgan could see this was a good day. He wasn't nearly as pale as he had been on Morgan's visit two weeks ago, and his shoulders weren't weakly slumped. Jolie looked fresh and pretty in a mint-green dress with a green ribbon in her hair.

He shook hands with DeForge, and Jolie offered hers, dropping her eyes shyly. Morgan bent over it, remembering a couple of years ago, when she had jumped to her feet and curtsied when he had come into the room. DeForge had gently told her, "Jolie, you are a lady, and Mr. Tremayne is a gentleman. Ladies do not rise to greet gentlemen. In fact, it is supposed to be the other way around. Gentlemen are supposed to rise when you enter or leave a room. I know that I don't do that, but that's because I'm old and tending to laziness."

Morgan seated himself and accepted a glass of lemonade from Jolie. "Thank you, ma'am," he said. "Mm, I see you still have ice, Mr. DeForge. Delicious, I got rather heated riding Vulcan, and it made me thirsty."

"How is that devil of a horse?" DeForge asked.

"Devilish," Morgan said lightly and told DeForge about how he had shown off at Arlington. "But it was a good visit, I think. Colonel Lee is going to buy two horses from me."

"Excellent," DeForge said briskly. "Business is good, eh? What about your spring plantings?"

Henry DeForge had three hundred acres that had lain fallow for almost twenty years. After he had gotten to know Morgan, DeForge had leased the acreage to him to raise forage crops for the horses, and with three hundred acres, there was plenty to sell. Morgan had also hired ten DeForge slaves to work the fields, paying them by the day. Unlike other slaveholders who leased out their slaves, Henry DeForge wanted no money for himself.

"The oats and alfalfa already look strong and healthy," Morgan told him. "That's some good soil in your fields, Mr. DeForge. My winter rye and barley was a bumper crop, and the soil shows no sign of weakening. Next year, of course, I'll rotate to legumes and corn, but I think I'll go ahead and do another winter rye and barley."

They talked about crops and weather for a while; though Henry DeForge was not a farmer in the proper sense of the word, he was interested in agriculture, as he was interested in many things.

"Mr. Ballard says that we are to have a blue moon this season," DeForge said, his eyes alight, "and that Widow Tapp's cow gave birth to a white calf. These are, I understand, very good omens for farmers."

"Hope so," Morgan said. "But speaking of livestock, may I ask you a question, sir? Every time I come to visit, Evetta makes me bring Cleo a chicken or two. Is there something wrong with your chickens?"

DeForge chuckled and glanced at Jolie. Her cheeks flamed, and she dropped her head. DeForge said, "Jolie has named all of the chickens, and so they have become her personal pets. Naturally I can't execute a pet. I don't really mind one way or another, because chicken is not my favorite meat, but I understand that Cleo takes great exception to it."

"It's the stock," Jolie said in a small voice. "She says you must use chicken stock in lots of dishes."

"Mm, true. It's unfortunate that you still have to kill them to get the stock," Morgan said lightly. "Don't worry, Jolie. I'll tell Evetta to make sure Cleo has plenty of anonymous dead chickens."

"Thank you, Mr. Tremayne," she said, her face still downcast.

"Jolie, would you please go check on Cleo?" DeForge asked. "I'm about ready for my tea." Jolie rose and went through the front door.

Morgan didn't rise when she left the table. To him she was very much a child, and gentlemen weren't constrained to show the same politeness to children as they were to adults.

DeForge said, "Speaking of omens, have you kept up with the news out of Washington, Mr. Tremayne?"

"Somewhat, sir. I admit I've been so very busy that sometimes I let the newspapers pile up for days."

DeForge frowned. "I see some very bad signs for the future of this country. Arrogant hotheads, who normally would never be paid any attention by sane persons, seem to be the dominant forces on both sides of the Mason–Dixon Line. And it's not just Washington and New York in the North, you know. From Maine to Minnesota they're all getting up in arms."

"But surely you don't think we'll go to war, do you?" Morgan asked, shocked. He knew Mr. DeForge, though he never traveled, kept up with national news every day. He took newspapers from Fredericksburg and Richmond and also Washington, New York, Chicago, Indianapolis, New Orleans, and Austin, and once a month he was delivered papers from California. He was a very sharp, intelligent man.

"Last year at this time I didn't think so," he said quietly. "This spring I do think so. I don't believe it will be next spring, because next year is election year. But I'm afraid spring of 1861 will not be nearly this peaceful and sweet."

Morgan sat and stared into space, stunned. Of course he was aware of the growing tensions between the slave states and the free states. He knew that in many ways, "bleeding Kansas" was symbolic of the entire nation, with "free staters" battling proslavery "border ruffians" in a series of ugly violent incidents that had begun five years ago. But to actually believe that the United States of America would be dissolved and any state would ever consider secession had not entered the darkest recesses of Morgan's mind.

He wondered now if DeForge was suffering from some worry that had ballooned into a big fear. Morgan thought that sometimes happened to older people. But quickly he pushed the thought away. Henry DeForge was not a man to suffer from baseless fear, nor was he given to exaggeration.

Morgan frowned. Perhaps it was he who was blind, refusing to see the disaster looming so clearly in the forefront of his friend's mind. "What would you do, sir, if there was a war?" he asked.

DeForge shrugged. "I know that Maryland is considered a border state, but I'll never believe she would secede. Personally, I have great sympathy for the South. I've lived here for almost twenty years, and I love it here. I've been happier living here than any place I've ever been. If Virginia seceded, I would stay here and face the consequences."

Jolie rejoined them and slipped back into her seat. "Cleo will be here in a few minutes with tea, Mr. DeForge."

"That's fine, child," he said absently. Then he continued

speaking to Morgan. "But are you asking what I would do, in the practical sense, if we were at war?"

"I suppose so," Morgan said. "I'm still trying to imagine such a terrible thing."

"Yes, you may think I'm just an old worrywart," DeForge said with a smile. "But for a few moments let's talk as if I'm in my right mind. If I knew that I was going to be caught in a war, I would start hoarding. I would hoard gold, first of all, because it is truly a universal currency. Then I would hoard all of the necessaries I could gather. Foodstuffs, wood, coal, tools, nails, fabrics such as wool and cotton, soap, candles—anything and everything I could think of that I would need to run my homestead."

Morgan frowned. "But surely we will always be able to buy such things as food and clothing. I mean, those are the absolute necessities of life. Surely we wouldn't end up back in the Dark Ages!"

"Before I became ill, I traveled all over," DeForge said calmly. "I've been to the Far West, to Maine, to Florida, all over the Midwest. Let me explain something to you, Mr. Tremayne. The Southern slave states will never be able to win a war against the industrialized North. I have an import/export business. In the North and the Midwest they import and export everything. They have thriving industries, they have disposable incomes, they are not land-poor like so many planters are. The South exports cotton, period. And they have to import everything else." He shook his head. "I could be wrong about the coming war, certainly. It may not come in a couple of years. It may not come to that at all. But one thing I do know, Mr. Tremayne. If it does come, the South will end up desolately poor and naked. It's simple economics."

Jolie's gaze had been darting back and forth between Morgan and DeForge as they spoke. Her eyes were huge and luminous, her expression one of deep distress. DeForge focused on her, then took her hand in his. "I apologize, Jolie. Children shouldn't have to listen to such things, especially just an old man's ranting."

"You're not old," she said. "And you never rant."

"Exactly," Morgan said in a low voice. He was all too afraid that Henry DeForge knew exactly what he was talking about. He quickly pushed the unwelcome thoughts aside and forgot them.

But later, with deep regret, he was to recall every word that Henry DeForge had said.

Jolie was curled up and seemed almost boneless with her legs tucked under her and her body bent. She was sitting on one side of the enormous fireplace in the parlor, while Henry DeForge sat on the other side.

In spite of the fact that it was a warm night, DeForge had ordered a big fire built, and he wore a wool shawl. Occasionally he coughed, a painful racking sound that made Jolie wince. Still, she kept reading aloud:

> "'We are friends,' said I, rising and bending over her,
> as she rose from the bench.
> 'And will continue friends apart,' said Estella.
> I took her hand in mine, and we went out of the ruined
> place; and as the morning mist had risen long ago when I
> first left the forge, so, the evening mists were rising now,
> and in all the broad expanse of tranquil light they showed
> to me, I saw no shadow of another parting from her."

With a sigh, Jolie closed the volume. "I just love *Great Expectations*."

"It's always been my favorite of Dickens's novels. Oh Jolie, you're not crying!"

Quickly Jolie wiped the tears from her cheeks. "But it's sad. Pip had such a hard life and then lost the girl he loved."

"Why, he didn't lose her, child," DeForge said. "Look at that last sentence. 'I saw no shadow of another parting from her.' They didn't part from each other. The two shadows stayed together, so it's a happy ending."

Jolie managed a weak smile. "Why, it's so, isn't it? I'm so glad. I think it's awful to lose someone that you love."

"Yes, it is," DeForge said quietly, staring into the flames. "It is truly awful."

After a few moments, Jolie said hesitantly, "Mr. DeForge? May I ask you a question?"

"Of course, Jolie."

"Well, you see, I am thirteen now. Do you—would you be able to tell me about my parents?"

"That's right," DeForge said with surprise. "I forgot. You did turn thirteen in April, didn't you, Jolie?"

"Yes, sir. And you've always said I needed to be older before you told me about my parents. I just thought that maybe thirteen is old enough."

"I see. You may be right, Jolie. Maybe thirteen is old enough." He shifted in his chair, which brought on a coughing spell.

Jolie wanted to run to him and hold him, but she knew he didn't like gestures of tenderness such as that.

Finally the coughing subsided, and he went on in a weak voice, "I will tell you about your mother. She was a quadroon. Do you know what a quadroon is?"

"No, sir."

"It means she was one-quarter black and three-quarters white."

"So I'm black?" Jolie asked with no visible surprise.

"You are one-eighth black, yes. But you are not, and never will be, a slave," DeForge said firmly.

Jolie digested this for a while then asked, "My mother, what was she like? Was she nice?"

"She was a very beautiful woman, inside and outside. She was sweet and kind, and she was very religious, although I know that doesn't mean much to you, since I haven't brought you up that way." A curious half smile touched his lips. "She would be very angry with me if she knew I had neglected that part of your education."

"She would?" Jolie asked, astonished. "But she was a slave, wasn't she? If she was black, she had to be a slave. Surely she couldn't get angry with you!"

"Yes, she was a slave. But still she was angry with me at times."

"Do you—is there a picture of her, Mr. DeForge?" Jolie pleaded. "I would love a picture of her more than anything."

DeForge hesitated for a long time. Finally he turned to stare back, unseeing, into the fire. "No, there is no picture of her."

"Oh. No, I guess there wouldn't be, not if she was a slave," Jolie said sadly. "But Mr. DeForge, what about my father? Did you know my father?"

In a curiously dead tone he said, "Yes, I knew your father. He was not a good man. He was not good to your mother. She died in childbirth, having you, Jolie, and he was bitter and angry because of that for a long time."

"You're saying 'was,'" Jolie said. "Is he dead?"

"I hope so," DeForge said angrily. "I truly hope so. I don't want to talk about him any more, Jolie. In fact, I'm very tired. I'd like to go to bed now."

"Of course, sir. I'll get Box," she said, jumping up.

Later, as Jolie lay sleepless in her bed, she figured out what had been wrong with the conversation she'd had with Mr. DeForge. It had had a false ring to it, and now she knew why.

It was the first time he had ever lied to her.

CHAPTER EIGHT

The next year was very good for Morgan. Rapidan Farm thrived and prospered. Morgan had at last been accepted in Fredericksburg, which was an insular, proud little town.

He visited the DeForge place regularly, as he was invited, and even though there was such a difference in their ages, he thought of Henry DeForge as his closest friend.

Somewhat to his surprise, he also kept in close touch with Mrs. Robert E. Lee at Arlington. She wrote him regularly, and every time he had business in the northern part of the state, he stopped by to see her. Colonel Lee had returned to active duty in Texas in February of 1860, and it seemed to Morgan that she was always particularly glad to see him then, because she was alone at Arlington. The girls traveled a lot, and when Millie turned fourteen, they had sent her to boarding school in Winchester. Morgan always stayed long hours with Mrs. Lee, talking about family and also about business things concerning the plantation, for Mrs. Lee was now running Arlington by herself, as she had done for so many years as her father grew older.

November 7, 1860, was a fine, icily clear day. Morgan and Vulcan made their way along the worn path between the two farms to DeForge House. The week before, Henry DeForge had purposely asked Morgan to come to tea on the day after the election. Morgan was troubled. Abraham Lincoln, an ardent abolitionist, had been elected. For the most part he had ignored politics, as his own life seemed so settled, so safe and secure. Even now he didn't much want to think or talk about slavery or secession or the Union. He hoped that Mr. DeForge didn't want to talk about it either, but he thought very likely that would be the topic his friend wanted to discuss.

When he reached DeForge House, he saw the black buggy in the backyard and immediately recognized it. It was Dr. Travers's buggy. The doctor had a little homestead just downriver from DeForge House. Morgan sprang out of the saddle, threw the reins around the hitching post, and ran into the house.

Cleo met him at the door. "He had a bad spell. It's the first time he's tole us to call the doctor," she said, troubled.

"Is the doctor with him right now?"

"Yes, sir. If'n you'd like to wait in the parlor, Box has got a good fire in there."

"Thanks, Cleo. I'll wait. I'd like to see him if I could."

"Yes, sir. He 'specially said he wants to talk to you, Mr. Tremayne."

Morgan nodded and went into the parlor. He walked up to the fireplace and stripped off his gloves to warm his hands. Silently he stared down into the flames, wondering just how ill DeForge was. Morgan had seen that he had grown visibly weaker in the past year, and the coughing fits he suffered seemed to come more often. But he still had been alert, interested in all of Morgan's news of the farm, knowledgeable and articulate about current events. He never complained.

Morgan became aware that someone was watching him, and only then did he see Jolie sitting in a chair up at the front of the room by the window. She was sitting bolt upright, her hands restless in her lap. She looked terrified. "Hello, Mr. Tremayne. I'm sorry I didn't let you know I was here, but I just couldn't get the words out somehow."

"It's okay, Jolie," he said soothingly. "How is he? Tell me what happened."

"He was fine, just fine this morning," she said, obviously bewildered. "He ate a good breakfast, and we played chess. He asked Cleo for sponge cake for tea. But then he started coughing, and it seemed like he couldn't stop. He got out of breath, and we got scared. Finally he told Box to go for the doctor."

"I know Dr. Travers. He's a good man. Maybe this is just a touch of catarrh."

She shook her head. "His handkerchief. . .there was blood."

Morgan didn't know what to say. He himself was extremely healthy, as was his entire family. It was true, he did know Dr. Travers because he had made it his business to know all his neighbors. But he had never had to call him for medical reasons.

They waited in silence for what seemed a long time. Finally they heard footsteps on the marble stairs, and Dr. Travers came in. He was a young man, in his early thirties, with sandy brown hair and kind brown eyes. He had two children, a boy and a girl, and another one on the way, Morgan knew. He also knew that Dr. Travers was poor, for although he was the only doctor for miles around, the small farmers couldn't afford to pay him much in cash. Instead, they paid him in chickens or tomatoes or canned jam or sides of bacon. Morgan himself had recommended him to Mr. DeForge when the slaves had gotten influenza that spring.

Jolie jumped up when he came into the room then stood, her hands curled into tight bloodless fists at her side. "How is he?" she asked in a strangled voice.

"He's sleeping quietly," Dr. Travers answered, stepping up to warm himself at the fire. "I gave him a sleeping draught. He didn't want to take it, but. . ." He made a helpless little motion with his hand. "Hello, Mr. Tremayne," he said. "One reason Mr. DeForge didn't want to take the medicine was because he insisted that he had to talk to you. But—I'm sorry, Jolie, but I guess you probably already know this. Mr. DeForge has consumption, and that, unfortunately, is an incurable disease. The best thing I can do for him is give him something to stop the coughing and help him sleep."

Morgan asked, "But how is Mr. DeForge. I mean, where is he in the course of the disease?" Morgan didn't want to ask if he was dying in front of Jolie.

Dr. Travers seemed to understand the question very well. "We don't know much about why the disease progresses at different rates in different people. But I feel optimistic about Mr. DeForge for several reasons. One is that he's had this disease for many years, and so it's obviously progressing very slowly in his case. I personally think that moving here, away from Baltimore or any other large industrial city, has likely helped him. Most big cities have a noxious atmosphere. Here the air is clean and pure. Another thing that encourages me is that Cleo tells me that his appetite is good," he said, glancing questioningly at Jolie.

"Oh yes, sir," she said eagerly. "He eats well and eats regularly. I make sure of that."

"That's good, Jolie. One of the first signs of a terminal stage is a loss of appetite and refusal to eat. If he still wants to eat and eats good, nourishing food, then I would say that we have nothing to worry about just yet," he finished warmly.

Jolie took a deep breath and sat back down, obviously relieved.

Morgan was still worried. "Dr. Travers, I was planning on going back to my home in the Shenandoah Valley tomorrow for Christmas, so I plan to be away for at least a month. Does Mr. DeForge. . .that is, do you think he'll be all right?"

Cautiously the doctor replied, "No man knows his appointed time, Mr. Tremayne. But based solely on what I've seen and heard here today, I see no reason why Mr. DeForge shouldn't recover quickly. Barring any complications, that is."

"You're going away for a month?" Jolie exclaimed. "But that's such a long time!"

"Yes, I know," Morgan said thoughtfully. "It's the first time since I've moved here that I've felt able to take a long holiday."

"Oh, I see," Jolie said slowly. "You would want to be with your parents and your brother and sisters for Christmas."

For a moment it jarred Morgan, thinking of Jolie and Henry DeForge here alone during the holiday season. But it wasn't really his concern, was it? His primary responsibility was with his own family. "I'll give you my address, Jolie," he said with a reassuring smile. "I'd like it if you and Mr. DeForge would write to me."

"Of course," she said stiffly.

"You say Mr. DeForge is asleep? How long will he sleep, do you think?" Morgan asked Dr. Travers.

"I hope through the afternoon and all night," he answered. "I'm leaving more laudanum with Cleo just in case he needs another dose. I think if he rests quietly for the next twenty-four hours he'll be much better."

Morgan nodded. "Jolie, please tell Mr. DeForge I'm sorry we didn't get to talk today, but as soon as I get back, I'll come by and get caught up on all the news. Good-bye for now, Jolie, and God bless you and Mr. DeForge."

"Thank you, Mr. Tremayne," she said.

Morgan smiled at her as he left. He thought of how small and defenseless she seemed in that big armchair. When the cold brisk air touched his face and he heard Vulcan's welcome nicker, he felt the burden of worry for his friend lift. He said a quick prayer for Mr. DeForge and Jolie and then turned his thoughts to his trip home.

Morgan lifted the brass lion's-head door knocker and rapped sharply twice.

the SURRENDER

The Bledsoes' maid, Nance, answered the door and made a quick, awkward curtsy.

"Hello, Nance. Is she in the parlor?" Morgan asked as he handed her his hat and gloves.

"Um, yes sir, but, um. . . ," she stammered.

Morgan ignored her and went into the parlor with the ease of a longtime caller. He had been seeing Leona for almost two years now. He went into the small but elegantly furnished sitting room and stopped in surprise.

Leona was there, seated on one end of the long camelback sofa. On the other end of the sofa sat Wade Kimbrel.

Leona looked up, and Morgan thought for a moment that she looked angry, but then her expression smoothed out, and she rose, coming to him with her hands outstretched. "Well hello, Morgan. This is a surprise. I thought you were leaving for the Valley."

"Yes, I am. I'm taking the 5:00 train," he said, eyeing Wade Kimbrel, who remained seated. He made a quick bow over her hands, and she motioned him to an armchair by the fireplace.

Leona Rose Bledsoe was now twenty-one years old. Morgan had actually met her back in 1855, when he had moved to Rapidan Run. Although his family had connections in Richmond, Morgan had wanted to be a part of nearby Fredericksburg, and so he had formed all his business associations there, including getting his own lawyer. He had decided to go with the largest firm in the wealthy little town, Mercer & Bledsoe, and Leona's father, Benjamin Bledsoe, had been his lawyer for the last five years. He had started attending St. Andrew's Episcopal Church upon Benjamin Bledsoe's recommendation. At church Morgan had gotten to know the family: Mrs. Eileen Bledsoe; Gibbs Bledsoe, Leona's brother, who was one year younger than Morgan; and their daughter, Leona. But she had been only sixteen at the time, and he had dismissed her as a child.

In January of 1859, Morgan had turned twenty-five, and though he didn't really consciously know it, he began to feel that he should settle down. He knew several pleasant girls in Fredericksburg, and he knew even more in Richmond. But it was then that he noticed that Leona Rose Bledsoe had become a striking, vibrant young woman. She was not pretty, in the conventional sense. Tall, with strong features and flashing dark eyes, she had a rather imperious manner. But she was extremely intelligent, and she was an interesting woman. In the previous year, to Morgan's amusement, she had begun to hold what would be called a "salon" on the Continent. She had many callers, men and women both. Every Friday evening she had a musicale, when she would play the piano and sing, and others would perform, too. All of her friends were from the oldest, finest families of Fredericksburg.

Except for Morgan. He had persistently courted her for a year before she would allow him to see her alone, without her mother in attendance. Yet here she was, with Wade Kimbrel, and Eileen Bledsoe was obviously not in the parlor.

Kimbrel remained insolently seated, one leg crossed over the other, his arm laid comfortably along the back of the sofa. When Morgan sat down, he merely nodded and said, "Tremayne."

"Kimbrel," Morgan said shortly. To Leona he said, "I wasn't aware that you were such close friends with Mr. Kimbrel."

"Morgan, I'm surprised at you," she said dismissively. "It's rude to speak in the third person when that person is present."

"Got a burr in your saddle, Tremayne?" Kimbrel drawled. "Mr. Bledsoe has been my family's attorney for twenty years now. Of course I'm friends with Leona. I've known her all her life."

Morgan frowned. Leona had given him permission to use her given name only four months ago, and she had agreed to call him Morgan. Still, when he was speaking of her, he called her Miss Bledsoe out of respect.

But Kimbrel's intimate use of her name wasn't the only thing that bothered Morgan. Wade Kimbrel was his nearest neighbor, aside from Henry DeForge. Just across the river from both of their farms was Wolvesey, an eight-thousand-acre cotton plantation that John

Edward Kimbrel had established in 1780. The Kimbrels had had slaves ever since then, and now Wade Kimbrel had over seventy slaves.

Wade had inherited the property from his father, who had died when Wade was only twenty. He was now thirty-two and had never married. He was a fine-looking man—tall, burly, with jet-black hair and a ferocious mustache. The talk around town was that he had courted several women, but it seemed they could never quite bring him to the point of marriage. He was considered to be something of a rake.

And Morgan knew, because he had seen firsthand, that Kimbrel mistreated his slaves. He had called on Kimbrel not long after he had moved to Rapidan Run, and as he had passed through the miles of cotton fields, he had seen Kimbrel's overseer beating a slave until he passed out. Morgan had not questioned Kimbrel about it, feeling that it was none of his business, but when Wade Kimbrel had wanted to buy a horse from him, Morgan had flatly refused. "You mistreat your slaves, you'll mistreat your horses," he had told him. He and Kimbrel had been enemies ever since then.

Now Morgan made himself calm down. He didn't often lose his temper, and he disliked it when he did. He felt it showed a lack of self-control. "I apologize, Kimbrel. Of course I know you're friends with the Bledsoes. I was just a little surprised, that's all."

Kimbrel shrugged carelessly.

After an awkward silence, Leona said brightly, "I was surprised, too, I admit. I had no idea you were still in town, Morgan." Morgan had told her on Sunday as he was walking her home after church that he would be going to Staunton on Wednesday.

"I wouldn't have thought of leaving without saying good-bye," he said somewhat stiffly.

"Good-bye, then," Kimbrel said.

"Oh! Wade, you are wicked. I thought you were leaving anyway," Leona said with amusement.

"I've decided to stay for a while. Why don't you invite me for supper?"

"I suppose I might as well. Father will be home any minute, and I know he will anyway," she said.

Morgan felt confused, embarrassed, and apprehensive. It was as if he weren't even there. Somehow he had taken for granted that he and Leona had an unspoken agreement between them, and that their relationship was special. Even as he thought it, he realized how vague this supposition was, and obviously he was very much mistaken about Leona. He was so perturbed that he wanted to get away, get some fresh air, and think. He shot out of the chair, and both Leona and Kimbrel looked up at him in surprise. "I have to go," he said hurriedly.

Leona rose gracefully and took his arm. "I'll see you out," she said. She walked him to the door, then turned and rested her hands on his shoulders. "You must come see me as soon as you get back," she said. "I will miss you."

"I'll miss you, too, Leona," he said unhappily.

She kissed him lightly on the cheek and said, "Good-bye, then, Morgan. God be with you."

Morgan returned on the first Saturday of the new year. As the train neared the station in Fredericksburg, Morgan looked out the window at the so-familiar landscape and smiled to himself.

In the month that he had been gone, he had completely cleared his mind of the confusion he'd felt at his last meeting with Leona. He had made some crucial decisions, and now he felt that his course was set. He would ask Leona to marry him after a short engagement. Perhaps they could be married in the spring, he thought. That would give him time to fix up the house, buy some new furnishings. Leona was good at that kind of thing, and he was sure that she would be excited to furnish and decorate her new home.

Idly he reflected, as the train hurtled on, on the surprise he had felt when he had realized that he was actually homesick for Rapidan

Run. He had always regarded Tremayne House as his home. But he supposed it was a sign that he was a man, and that it was time to start his own family apart from his parents. His spirits grew even more buoyant.

Leona will make an excellent wife, he thought with satisfaction. *Mother and Father will love her. Mother, especially. They have so much in common.*

Again he smiled as he thought of the surprise he had for Leona. He was bringing home a carriage, a fine four-seater landau with a folding top. True, it was secondhand. His father had just bought his mother a new barouche box, and originally Mr. Tremayne had intended to sell the old landau. But Morgan grabbed it up—though he did pay his father for it—because he knew that Leona would need it. It was fine for him to travel into Fredericksburg on horseback, but a lady needed a carriage.

He had telegraphed ahead and instructed Amon to bring Ace, a big brown gelding that served as their work horse, when he came to meet him. Ace pulled the farm wagon, and Morgan thought, considering Ace's placid temperament, that it wouldn't spook him or make him nervous in the new experience of pulling a carriage.

The long shrill whistle sounded, and the conductor began his chant: "Fredericksburg! Coming into Fredericksburg!"

Out his window Morgan saw Amon and Rosh waiting. Amon waved then bent to speak to a slight man standing with him and pointed to Morgan. The stranger looked up at Morgan searchingly.

Morgan stepped off the train steps and hurried to the three men waiting for him. "Hello, Amon, Rosh. I can't tell you how good it is to be home."

"Yes, sir," Amon said gravely. "Mr. Tremayne, this gentleman is Mr. Silas Cage. Mr. Cage, this here is Mr. Morgan Tremayne."

Cage, a short, thin, earnest-looking young man with spectacles, shook Morgan's hand. "I'm very glad to meet you, sir. I know this is unorthodox, but it is extremely important that I speak with you."

"Right now?" Morgan said with astonishment. He had just had a fifteen-hour train ride, and he had some complicated arrangements to make to get himself, his luggage, and the carriage home.

"Yes, sir. I am an attorney, and I have an extremely urgent matter that requires your immediate attention, Mr. Tremayne."

"Is something wrong at home?" he demanded of Amon.

"No, sir, everything is fine. We's all fine, and all the horses is fine," Amon reassured him.

"Thank heavens," Morgan said with relief. "All right, Mr. Cage, I'll be glad to speak to you as soon as I've made some arrangements."

"Would you come to my office?" he asked. "It's right on Dalrymple Street, just off Main. The one-story red brick with the wrought-iron gate."

"I'll be there as soon as possible, sir," Morgan assured him.

Cage hurried off.

As they walked to the yard to collect the carriage, Morgan asked Amon, "Do you know what that's all about?"

"No, sir," Amon said uneasily. "What I mean is, he come to the house two days ago, looking for you. He told me he needed to see you right quick, but he didn't tell me why."

"But you know something about it, Amon, I can tell," Morgan insisted.

"Not for sure, Mr. Tremayne. Alls I know is that old Mr. DeForge, he died three days ago."

"What!" Morgan said, halting abruptly. "He died! But no one wrote me, no one telegraphed me!"

"I think that Mr. Cage did think to send you a telegram, but it appears you ain't got it, huh?"

"No, I didn't," Morgan said thoughtfully. Tremayne House and farm were about eight miles outside of Staunton. It was conceivable that a telegram had come there and it might not have been delivered to the farm until after he left.

Morgan resumed walking, his head bowed. His friend had died, and he hadn't been there. He did not think that Henry DeForge was actually a lonely man; his reclusive tendencies seemed to be voluntary. But now Morgan heartily wished that he had been here the last month. He would miss Henry Deforge terribly.

Numbly he instructed Amon about taking the carriage home. He and Rosh had brought Vulcan, so Morgan said, "You two go on home. After I speak to Mr. Cage, I'll be along."

It was a short distance to Cage's office, so Morgan didn't ride. He took Vulcan's reins and walked slowly. Even though it was just after noon, it grew dark and started to snow, a wet, heavy snow. Morgan was so beset by grief that he barely noticed.

He knocked on the door of the small house, for when Morgan found the place he realized that Mr. Cage must have his office at his home.

A young sweet-faced woman answered the door. "Mr. Tremayne, please come in. I am Mrs. Cage. My husband is in his office, if you'll follow me." She ushered him down the hall to a tiny room with every wall filled with books.

Cage sat behind a work-scarred desk. He rose to shake Morgan's hand again. "Please, sit down, Mr. Tremayne. I know you must be very tired after your journey, and again I apologize for intruding upon you in this manner. My wife will bring us tea shortly."

"That would be very welcome," Morgan said. "I've gotten into the habit of having afternoon tea. In fact, it's because of my friendship with Henry DeForge that I formed the habit. He always had what he called high tea."

"Yes, I know," Mr. Cage said sadly. "I was not as close a friend as you obviously were. I was his attorney. But I will miss him, too." He took a deep breath, leaned forward, and clasped his hands together on the desk. "I assume that your servant told you of Mr. DeForge's death."

"Yes, I didn't know of it until just now," Morgan said. "He didn't write me while I was gone, but I didn't think that too unusual. He was ill when I left, and I thought that perhaps he simply didn't feel like corresponding. But his death is a shock. I understood from Dr. Travers that his condition at that time wasn't critical."

"Dr. Travers was right," Cage said. "He did recover nicely from that downturn he took in November. For the rest of that month and until the last two weeks in December, he was as well as I've ever known him to be. But just before Christmas the consumption worsened again, and Dr. Travers attended him, with the same instructions, to get plenty of rest and take laudanum to ease the pain and coughing. The problem was that he developed pneumonia. That's actually what killed him, not the consumption. And it was fast. Dr. Travers diagnosed pneumonia four days after Christmas, and he quickly grew worse and died on January 3rd. It was a great shock."

"How I wish I'd been here," Morgan said quietly. "I considered Mr. DeForge my closest friend, almost like a father to me, though I'm not sure he returned my regard in the same manner."

"Did he think of you almost as a son? Yes, he most certainly did," Cage said, to Morgan's surprise. "I'm sure you realize by now that I need to speak to you because of Mr. DeForge's will. He has left you some—bequests."

At that moment a soft knock sounded on the door, and Mrs. Cage entered with a tea tray. Morgan thought that Cage looked relieved, and he wondered why. Mrs. Cage efficiently served them tea and then slipped out of the room.

With clear reluctance Cage continued, "First of all, Mr. DeForge willed you the three hundred acres that you've been leasing from him."

"He split that out from the estate?" Morgan said with surprise. "Well, that was very generous of him."

"Er—yes." Cage took a sip of tea. "Mr. Tremayne, Mr. DeForge's will is a bit complicated. I was there two days before he died, and I was with him for several hours, finishing up the details of his final wishes. He dictated a letter to me, and it is to you." Slowly he took a long envelope from a drawer and handed it to Morgan.

My dear Morgan,

I know that I have little time left, and so this letter must necessarily be short and to the point.

When I bought my property, which was then known as the Strickland place, the slaves were included in the purchase price. I fell in love with a beautiful quadroon girl named Jeanetta, who was one of my maids. She was my mistress for five years, and we were carefree. But in the sixth year, she became pregnant, and in April of 1846, she died giving birth to Jolie. I never gave Jolie my name, just as I never gave Jeannetta my name, and now I am bitterly ashamed of it.

I know that it is too late for me to regain my honor and make things right for Jolie. So now, in my last days, I am asking you to help me make amends.

I have been setting money aside for Jolie and have accumulated ten thousand dollars. For this reason I have appointed you as Jolie's guardian. Use whatever is necessary to educate her until she is eighteen and then give her what's left.

But Morgan, I'm afraid I must ask you to do even more. It is my dying wish that Jolie would be protected and nurtured, and yes, even loved. Can you find it in your heart to do that? I can't demand that you do so or make it a provision of my will. I can only hope that the generous and kind heart that I've seen in you will dictate what is right. I know you to be a man of honor, and I beg you to make a vow to God to be faithful to my daughter.

The letter was simply signed, "Henry DeForge."

For a long time Morgan couldn't speak, he was so stunned. He simply sat there, staring blankly into space.

Cage, with compassion written on every feature, sat quiet and still.

Morgan had no idea how long he sat there, speechless, but finally he roused a bit. "This is a great shock," he said gutturally. "I had no idea. Tell me, Mr. Cage, was this decision about me being Jolie's guardian something that he decided just before he died?"

"No, it wasn't. I made up this will four years ago. I understand that he had known you for about a year, and he designated you as Jolie's guardian then. Of course," he said, taking off his glasses and polishing them with his handkerchief, "at that time he was only thinking of you being a trustee for the money. He always intended to speak to you about taking Jolie into your home. He's told me through the years that he felt so well, and he didn't feel that his time was near, and so he didn't think it was the right time to burden you with it. Who knows? He might have lived well past Jolie's eighteenth birthday, if he hadn't come down with pneumonia."

"Maybe that was what he wanted to talk to me about in November," Morgan said wearily. "Maybe he had some idea even then."

"It's true, he did. He told me at the last. He so regretted that he'd never talked with you about it, found out how you feel about it," Cage said, eyeing Morgan shrewdly. "So how do you feel about it, Mr. Tremayne?"

Morgan shifted uncomfortably in the hard chair. "Shocked. Bewildered. And—yes, angry. This is a terrible burden to ask a man to bear."

"It is. And Mr. DeForge knew it. He did make provisions just in case you felt you couldn't act as Jolie's guardian. He knew full well that you might refuse. In fact, he said that you should," Cage finished with an odd look on his face. "I think that might have been the last joke he ever made."

Morgan ignored this; he didn't feel any lightness in this conversation at all. "What alternate arrangements did he make for Jolie?"

"He asked me if I would be a trustee for her inheritance. He instructed me where to send her to school, to purchase a house for her, and to finance her if she thought she may be able to open some sort of shop," he said. "Jolie is clever, you know. Mr. DeForge thought that she might very well be able to find her own way, when she's older."

"But he didn't ask you to take her in," Morgan said bluntly, with some bitterness.

"No, he didn't. You see, Mr. Tremayne, my wife is only eighteen. It's awkward. My wife is still very young herself to take over any responsibility for a fourteen-year-old girl."

"Jolie is fourteen?" Morgan said, astounded. "I had no idea. Somehow I still think of her as a child. She still looks like a child."

"She will be fifteen in April. And yes, she is petite and still childlike," Cage agreed.

Morgan threw the letter down on Cage's desk and began to pace. "Fourteen! That's even worse! I'm single, you know. How am I supposed to have a fourteen-year-old girl living with me alone? And I hope to be married soon. How can I ask my fiancée to take Jolie into our home? It's impossible! The whole thing is just impossible. It can't be done!"

"It can be done, sir," Cage said mildly. "The question is whether you are willing to do it."

Morgan's head snapped toward the attorney, and he saw the kindness and understanding on his face. Resignedly Morgan sat back down. "I don't suppose I have much time to consider it, do I?"

"It would be hard for Jolie. Mr. DeForge is to be sent to Baltimore tomorrow, and Box and Cleo are returning with him. He brought them from Baltimore when he moved, you know, and to them it's still home because they have family there. So Jolie would be at DeForge House alone."

"Tomorrow?" Morgan passed his hand across his forehead. "Of course, he died three days ago. It's just all happened so fast, to me. Yes, I see what you mean, Mr. Cage. I'll go get Jolie tomorrow. First thing in the morning. I apologize, sir, but I'm extremely tired now, and I'd like to go home. May I make an appointment with you later to discuss the details?"

"Certainly, Mr. Tremayne. I'll be happy to see you at any time," he said courteously. They rose, and Morgan started toward the door, but Cage said, "Mr. Tremayne? There is one more thing I should tell you now."

"Yes? What is that?"

"In my last conversation with Mr. DeForge, he told me to tell you this: that he knew he had never been able to show it, and he could certainly never say it, but he loved you. He loved you as if you were his own son."

❧

The next day was a dreary, depressing day indeed. It had snowed throughout the night, and Morgan had slept very little. He was awake for most of the night worrying. A darkened dawn brought more lowering gray clouds, a portent of more snow to come.

He called Amon and the family together after he picked at his breakfast. "I don't know how to say this, except just to say it. When Mr. DeForge died, he named me as Jolie's guardian. She's coming to live here. Today."

None of them were surprised. Evetta nodded and said, "Lawyers might be tight-mouthed, but servants ain't. Cleo and Box knew, and they told us."

"Guess I must have been the last to know then," Morgan said dryly. "So I'm sure you see that it's put me in a bad position. I didn't even realize until yesterday that Jolie is almost fifteen. To me she's just a little girl. Anyway, I can't possibly have her living here with me alone. Evetta, Amon, would it be all right with you if Ketura moves in, and she can serve as our maid? I guess it might seem silly to you, since you just live right out the back door, but to me it makes a difference who's under my roof."

"We allus knew something like that, Mr. Tremayne," Amon said. "Ketura, here, she's already volunteered to be Miss Jolie's maid. It ain't silly, neither. It might only look more proper, but there you are. It looks more proper."

"Good," Morgan said with relief. "That's one problem overcome.

Now for the big thing. How are we going to get Jolie and her things moved here? You know I'll have to bring her bedroom furniture. None of the three spare bedrooms have anything. Oh—Ketura, do you have a bed?"

"Sure I do, Mr. Tremayne," she said, smiling. "My daddy made me a nice bed and my very own chiffarobe. It even has a long mirror on the door. Don't you 'member? You bought the mirror for me, a long time ago when I was little."

Vaguely Morgan recalled helping Amon, Rosh, and little Santo build furniture to furnish their two cottages, though he couldn't recall about the mirror. "Okay, Amon, can you and the boys go ahead and quick-quick get Ketura's things moved in here? I'm going to put Jolie in the bedroom just across from me, and Ketura's will be next to hers. The reason I'm hurrying you is because I'm afraid it's going to start snowing again," he said, casting a cautious look out the window. "I can't figure out how to get Jolie and her things moved here." He closed his eyes and rubbed his forehead. "It's hard for me to think straight."

"Mr. Tremayne, we'll git that little girl here today. Don't you worry. And her furnishings and stuff. Me and the boys'll get Ketura moved in, and then we'll bring the wagon over to DeForge's and load her up."

"How? There's already six inches of snow on the ground. You know, Amon, that the only path over there is a bridle path. How can we get the wagon over there and back with a heavy load of furniture?"

"Muscle it through," Amon said. "Me and Rosh know that we can double-team Ace and Calliope, and they can do it."

"I hadn't thought of that," Morgan admitted. "Yes, you're probably right. But still, what about Jolie? She can't ride, and it might take us hours to get the wagon through."

"It might. You're just going to have to go fetch her," Amon said. "She can ride back with you. But you better take Philemon, sir. You know that Vulcan devil ain't gonna allow no two human bein's on his back."

Morgan managed a small smile. "I'm glad you're thinking, Amon, because I'm sure not. I worried all night about this and just couldn't reason it out. Never been so muddle-headed in my life," he added in an undertone. Rising, he said, "Then I'm going right over to get Jolie. Seems like all of you are ready, even if I'm not."

Evetta said, "Me and Ketura are cooking up some good solid food for dinner, Mr. Tremayne. You bring that child straight on home. She don't need to be rattling around in that dead house by herself not one minute longer than she has to."

Morgan got his heavy overcoat and wool slouch hat. When he went out the back door, he saw that Amon apparently had already saddled Philemon, which was his own horse, a big gentle chestnut gelding. Morgan marveled again at how much his servants knew and how clear-headed they were thinking, while he felt like he was wandering around in a stupor. "Thanks, Amon. See you shortly."

Morgan was much preoccupied during the short ride. The Wilderness bordered both his and DeForge's properties, and the ride between the farms skirted the northern edge of the forest. Normally he would be enchanted by the snow scene, but on this day he barely looked around.

When he reached DeForge House, he noted that there was not one slave out anywhere. All of the slave cabins' chimneys had threads of smoke coming out of them, so Morgan figured they must all still be there. No one came to take his horse.

He made his way to the house and knocked hesitantly. Immediately the door flew open, and Jolie stood there. "Oh, you've come," she cried. "I–I've been afraid—afraid."

Morgan came in and shed his overcoat, hat, and gloves.

Jolie took them and carried them as they went into the parlor. Absently she sat down on the sofa, still holding them.

Morgan went to the fireplace, glad to see a healthy, glowing fire built. "I'm so sorry, Jolie. Sorry about Mr. DeForge, sorry that I wasn't here, and I'm sorry you've been afraid. Don't be. You do know about the arrangements Mr. DeForge made for you?"

She nodded, but her eyes were filled with uncertainty. "Mr. Cage told me that you are going to take care of me now. Is—is that true?"

"Yes, that's true. You're going to come live at my house, at Rapidan Run. Ketura is going to be your maid."

"My maid? Ketura? But she's my friend, the only friend I have that's my own age. I don't need a maid, anyway," she said fretfully.

"Oh, but you do," Morgan said with an attempt at lightness. "You're a very wealthy young lady now, you know. Mr. Cage told you about the money Mr. DeForge left you, didn't he? Of course he did. And wealthy young ladies must have a lady's maid."

"Oh. Then I suppose I will, if that's what you want."

"It's not what I—oh, never mind. We can talk all about everything later. Right now I think I'd better go ahead and take you to my house, Jolie. I'm afraid it's going to start snowing any minute, and I don't want you to have to ride in a freezing snowstorm."

"I'm ready," she said eagerly. "Just let me get my cloak. I already have my winter boots on." She practically ran out of the room.

It struck Morgan that Jolie might have been sitting there for days, in her winter boots, waiting for him or someone, anyone, to come help her. He determined he would be more welcoming, warmer toward her. He was still in a state of disbelief that his life had been turned upside down in this way, and he realized that he had a distracted air.

She came running back in, practically breathless, pulling on a long, luxurious wool mantle in a deep shade of pine green. It had a hood lined with dark gold satin, and when she pulled it up, it framed her face perfectly. Looking up at him, she seemed very young and innocent, with her wide tragic eyes and cupid's bow of a mouth. "I didn't take too long, did I?"

On impulse, Morgan bent and gently hugged her. He noted that she grew stiff, and so it was a very brief light caress, and then Morgan stepped back again. "Here I am, having to apologize again, Jolie. I'm hurrying you, and it's not really necessary. We'll make it home just fine. Amon and the boys are on their way with the wagon, and I'd like it very much if you would show me your bedroom and whatever else in the house you would like to take."

Vast relief washed over her face, and she slowly pushed back her hood and took off her cloak. "Thank you, Mr. Tremayne. I did wonder about my things, but I didn't like to ask."

Morgan ventured to touch her again. He reached out, and with his forefinger gently pushed Jolie's chin so that she would look up at him. "Jolie, I want to tell you right now, you never have to be afraid to ask me anything at all. I made a promise to Mr. DeForge that I would take very good care of you, and I will. I want you to know that."

Her eyes filled with tears as she stared up at him. It made her enormous, dramatically dark eyes positively luminous. "Oh, Mr. Tremayne, I'm so glad you've come. Now I know I won't have to be afraid."

"Never again," Morgan said firmly.

"Never again."

CHAPTER NINE

On December 20, 1860, South Carolina had seceded from the United States of America. Morgan had given it very little thought, because he was at home in the peaceful, quiet Shenandoah Valley. The heated politics of northern Virginia and Washington, DC seemed far away.

On January 9, 1861, Mississippi seceded from the union. Morgan didn't notice. On that day, Jolie had been at his home for exactly three days.

Early that morning Evetta had told him in a most accusatory manner that Jolie had no clothes. About halfway through the diatribe, Morgan managed to grasp that it wasn't that Jolie actually had no clothes, but that the clothes she had were unsuitable. Apparently Henry DeForge could see Jolie no better than Morgan could, for she was still wearing little-girl outfits—one-piece dresses that came about halfway down her shin, with lacy pantalettes underneath.

According to Evetta, this was outrageous. "There she is, that poor chile's got no idea that she's walking around a-showing her ankles!

And there's her hair, all down with baby ribbons in it! She shoulda started putting her hair up already! Shame on you, Mr. Tremayne!"

On January 10, 1861, Florida seceded from the United States. Morgan didn't notice because he spent the entire day in Fredericksburg, frantically searching for a dressmaker that could make Jolie some new clothes. Quickly.

On January 11, 1861, Alabama seceded from the union. It escaped Morgan's attention because that was the day that he found out that Wade Kimbrel had bought Henry DeForge's property. Wade Kimbrel came by Rapidan Run early in the morning to crow over Morgan.

Just after noon, two of DeForge's field slaves, the boy Howie and his brother Eli, came running up to the farmhouse. They pleaded for Morgan to buy them.

He was still trying to explain to them that he couldn't do such a thing when Kimbrel's overseer rode up. He was an ugly great brute named Gus Ramsey. He told the boys they were going to be beaten within an inch of their lives, and if they ran again, he'd kill them. When Morgan protested, the man threatened to have him arrested for harboring runaway slaves. He could do it, too. It was the law of the land. Morgan was depressed all day long.

On January 19, 1861, Georgia seceded; on January 26th, Louisiana seceded; and on February 1st, Texas seceded. Morgan did at last begin to take note of what was happening outside the borders of Rapidan Run.

But it wasn't until February 4th that he fully realized how deeply he was involved in these events. On that day, the Confederate States of America was formed. Jefferson Davis was elected president by the representatives of the states that had seceded, and Montgomery, Alabama, was named its capital.

The following morning, February 5, 1861, Morgan was sitting in his study after breakfast reading the newspaper, poring over the details of the events from the day before. The joining together of the seceded states, naming the association, electing a president, all of these things made it become jarringly real to Morgan. He realized that war was surely coming.

No, Virginia had not seceded—yet—but he knew she would. And like thousands of other men throughout all the states, he wrestled with making the choice of what he would do. Fight? Fight against the United States, his homeland? It was unthinkable. But the alternative was also inconceivable. Fight against Virginia? To Morgan, as to others, Virginia was more of a home to him than the rather intangible union of states that had been formed almost a hundred years ago. Virginia was much more than the simple geographic location of his house. Virginia was his motherland.

Abruptly Henry DeForge's voice invaded his thoughts. *"If I knew that I was going to be caught in a war, I would start hoarding. I would hoard gold, first of all, because it is truly a universal currency. Then I would hoard all of the necessaries I could gather. Foodstuffs, wood, coal, tools, nails, fabrics such as wool and cotton, soap, candles, anything and everything I could think of that I would need to run my homestead."*

With another jolt, Morgan realized that he had responsibilities now. He was no longer a single man who could make any decision he wanted and it would not affect anyone else. Everything he did now would deeply affect another person, besides his family. He was solely responsible for Jolie DeForge.

Whatever I do, I have to make sure she's safe, that she's secure. I promised. . .

The promise was made posthumously, of course. Once Morgan decided to take Jolie, he swore a solemn oath in his heart to God, and to the memory of Henry DeForge, that he would take care of her to his utmost for as long as he lived. Morgan was that kind of man. Once he gave his loyalty to someone or something, he would brave any evil to defend that bond.

And that's exactly how I feel about Virginia, about my home, he realized with sinking heart, for then he knew that he would, he must, fight for his home. Then he thought, *But I need time. . .time to make sure Jolie is well provided for, that her future is secure. Do I have enough time? Please, God, grant me the time. . . .*

Just then Jolie came in, interrupting his dark reverie. He looked up and managed a smile. "Hello, Mouse. Had breakfast yet?" "Mouse" was a joke between them. After Jolie had been with them a couple of weeks, Morgan had told her that she looked like a kitten, but she was as quiet as a mouse. Sometimes he called her "Kitten" and sometimes, as when she came unexpectedly into the room, he called her "Mouse."

Morgan realized she was wearing one of the new dresses he had bought her, a simple brown wool dress trimmed with coral-colored satin ribbon. The dress had puffed sleeves and wide skirts. Ketura had dressed her hair. It was parted modestly down the middle and made into a simple bun at the nape of her neck. But to Morgan these things didn't make her look any more mature. He thought they just made her look like a little girl playing dress-up.

"Yes, sir," she answered. "Are you ready to help me with my geometry?" Morgan had continued teaching her in the mornings, as Henry DeForge had done since Jolie was five years old. Morgan had been pleasantly surprised at how educated Jolie was. She knew American history, English history, European history, she was conversant in French, she read many novels and nonfiction such as biographies, letters of note, and prominent men's journals that were very much beyond the normal comprehension of a fourteen-year-old. She was skilled in arithmetic, and DeForge had even taught her the basics of bookkeeping.

But she was weak in geometry, because Henry DeForge had been weak in the higher mathematics, and he had no interest in trying to school himself. Also, Jolie was not at all "accomplished" in the sense that was usually meant to describe young ladies. She had no musical talent at all, aside from a clear, sweet soprano voice, and she couldn't draw. Also, she couldn't seem to learn the very basics of cooking. She was a passable seamstress and seemed to be determined to better her skills. Much to Morgan's surprise, he had found that she was a formidable chess opponent. It took all his concentration to keep her from beating him.

Now he said vaguely, "Sorry? Oh yes, you said geometry." He folded the paper and slid it across his desk to her. "I think that today we'll put off geometry. There are some serious things I need to talk to you about, Jolie."

She scanned the banner headline: CONFEDERATE STATES OF AMERICA IS BORN! PRESIDENT ELECTED—VICE PRESIDENT ELECTED—MEMBER STATES DESIGNATE MONTGOMERY, ALABAMA, AS THE CAPITAL.

She sighed deeply. "This means there will be a war, doesn't it?"

"I guess so," Morgan said quietly. "I've tried to ignore the whole thing, but it's just not going away like I want. So there are some things we need to settle."

She bit her lower lip, and Morgan hurriedly added, "No, Jolie, don't be afraid. We just have to talk about your future, that's all. Remember, I promised you that you'll never have to be afraid again. And that's what I need to make sure of now. How best to take care of you."

"But I can stay here, can't I?" she pleaded. "You aren't going to try to send me away again, are you?"

When she first moved in, Morgan had suggested that she might like to go to boarding school. After all, she could afford the very best. But the thought had so obviously terrified her that Morgan had told her to forget it and had never mentioned it again. It had taken him a while to see it from her point of view. Of course she would be frightened out of her wits, to be sent to a strange place, with strange people, when her entire life had been spent with a loving, indulgent father. No wonder she had been terrified.

"No, no, Jolie," he said soothingly. "I know now that is not feasible. No, the problem is that I need to make sure you are safe here. That Rapidan Run is safe, and that Amon and his family are safe. I need to make plans. I need to do some things to prepare."

He found himself groping for the words to explain, when to his surprise Jolie said, "It's because of what Mr. DeForge said, isn't it? On that day you were talking about if a war came."

"You were there?" he said blankly. Though he recalled every detail of Henry DeForge's worn face and all his words, he had no picture in his mind of Jolie being there that pleasant spring day on the veranda. A pained look came over her face then vanished.

Evenly she said, "I was there, and I remember what he said. About hoarding gold and food and other things. That's what you're worrying about, isn't it? Making sure that Rapidan Run has food for us and the horses stored up in case the war makes it hard for us to buy things?"

"That's it exactly, Jolie. You're a smart little mouse, you know." He shifted in his seat and rested his chin on one hand, studying her face. "Do you remember about Mr. DeForge's will, Jolie? Not about your money or me taking care of you. Do you remember me telling you that you have a personal line of credit at Mr. DeForge's company for life?"

"Yes, I remember."

"Do you know what it means?"

"Yes, because Mr. DeForge taught me a lot of things about business," she said confidently. "A line of credit means you can buy things and pay for them later."

Morgan nodded. "I thought it was kind of odd at the time. But now I'm beginning to think that maybe Mr. DeForge could foresee a lot of things that others, certainly including myself, could not. I would like your permission to use your line of credit at DeForge Imports & Exports, Ltd. Though the debt will be in your name, of course I will repay it all."

"That's okay, Mr. Tremayne. I know what you're going to buy with the credit line. But let me ask you something. I have so much money, Mr. Tremayne, why don't you use that instead? I don't mind you using my credit line, but you don't have to run up a debt."

It amused Morgan that she was talking in such a grown-up manner, while to him she still looked very much like a tiny little kitten. "No, I'm not going to use any of your money at all, Jolie. That is your legacy, and it's meant to last you all of your life if it has to. Besides, it's all in gold, which is another thing that I thought was odd of Mr. DeForge to do, and once again he's proved to be much smarter than I. Do you remember what he said that day?"

"About gold? Yes, I do. He said he would hoard it first of all, because it's the universal currency." Her smooth brow wrinkled a bit. "I don't really understand what that part means."

"It means that the actual value of paper money may rise and fall, and sometimes in emergencies, like a war, it can lose its value. In other words, what you can buy with it can change, and change quickly. One day you may be able to buy a pair of shoes for a dollar, and the next day that same pair of shoes might cost you five dollars. That means that the dollar has lost much of its value."

"I see," she said slowly. "But that doesn't happen to gold?"

"No, never. Gold is precious. Any man, woman, business, state, king, or government will take gold in payment for goods."

"Then we'd better hoard my gold," she said soberly. "One day we may need it."

"I hope not," he said emphatically, "and I pray not. But I'm going to prepare as if that day is coming, Jolie. Like I've promised, I never want you to be afraid again."

She smiled sweetly. "With you, I'm not afraid, Mr. Tremayne. Now that I know you've promised to take care of me, I don't worry any more. My—father"—she still stumbled over it—"always said that you were an honorable man, and I know that means you keep your promises. So I know I'll never have to be afraid again."

CHAPTER TEN

Colonel Robert E. Lee stood in the twilight, still and unmoving. His eyes were focused across the lazy river below him on the city only three miles distant. As he watched, the lights began to glow, thousands of streetlamps and thousands of lamps in the windows of homes and offices. Washington was lit up as if there were a celebration.

But there was no celebration. In spite of the festive appearance, the city buzzed with dark and dangerous business. Men who represented the United States of America were making life-and-death decisions about their rebellious brothers, joined together into the Confederate States of America. And Robert E. Lee was enmeshed in his own momentous struggle.

It was March 1, 1861. Lee had been recalled to Washington from his post in Texas, and he had reached Arlington on this day. He and Mary had talked for hours. As always, he could confide fully in her, and only to her. It helped him to see the way clearly.

Earlier in February he had written to a friend:

The country seems to be in a lamentable condition and

may have been plunged into civil war. May God rescue us from the folly of our own acts, save us from selfishness, and teach us to love our neighbors as ourselves.

But no matter how closely Robert E. Lee adhered to these principles, other men did not. He knew now that war was certain.

Wearily he told Mary, "In the event of Virginia's secession, duty will compel me to follow. We are loyal Americans, Mary, but we are Virginians first. To raise my hand against my home, and my family, would be dishonorable. My heart, my hand, and now to my sorrow, my sword is with Virginia."

On April 12, 1861, shells burst on Fort Sumter far away in South Carolina. Two days later, the federal fort surrendered to P. G. T. Beauregard, brigadier general of the Confederate States Army. On the following day, Lincoln issued his proclamation to a nation gone mad. He called for seventy-five thousand troops of volunteer militia to "suppress treasonable combinations" and to "cause the laws to be duly executed."

Lee was still waiting in trepidation, hoping against all hope that Virginia might not secede. He was a simple man with an innocent heart, and he couldn't see that it was impossible that Virginia would remain neutral. The North and the South were at war. She must choose.

On April 17, he received word from Richmond that the convention had gone into secret session, and he then knew his fate. On that same day he received a letter and a message. The letter was from General Winfield Scott, the general commanding the Federal Army, requesting Lee to call at his office as soon as possible. The message was delivered by one of Lee's cousins, the young John Lee. Francis P. Blair asked him to call the next day. Blair had been the editor of *The Congressional Globe* for many years, and now he was a "kingmaker" in Washington.

On the morning of April 18, 1861, Colonel Robert E. Lee called on Francis Blair at his son's home on Pennsylvania Avenue. Blair received him personally and wasted no time. "Colonel Lee, a large army is soon to be called into the field to enforce the federal law; the president has authorized me to ask if you would accept command."

For over an hour Blair used all his considerable skills to try to persuade Lee to stay with the Union. Lee remained firm; his course was set.

Of the conversation, he later said, "I declined the offer he made me to take command of the army that was to be brought into the field, stating as candidly and as courteously as I could, that though opposed to secession and deprecating war, I could take no part in an invasion of the Southern States."

After his interview with Blair, Lee went to General Scott's office. He had known General Scott for many years, having served under him in the Mexican War. He had always been the old general's favorite. Without delay Lee told him about Blair's interview and his answer.

"Lee," said Scott sadly, "you have made the greatest mistake of your life, but I feared it would be so."

Lee returned to Arlington and to Mary's always-comforting presence. He was disheartened and said little except that he had been offered the command and had refused it.

The next day, on April 19th, he learned that Virginia had seceded from the Union. He spent many hours that day pacing in his and Mary's upstairs bedroom and kneeling before his Father, fervently praying aloud. Finally he came downstairs.

Mary was waiting patiently for him.

"Well, Mary," he said calmly, "the question is settled. Here is my letter of resignation and a letter I have written General Scott."

She nodded. "Robert, I know that you have wept tears of blood over this terrible course that the country is set on. But you have made the right decision. As a man of honor and a Virginian, you must follow the destiny of your state. Only I know what this has cost you. Aside from loving you as my own dear husband, I esteem you as an honorable, courageous man. You always have been, and I know that you always will be the best man I've ever had the privilege of knowing."

By April 25th, Robert E. Lee was a brigadier general in the Confederate States Army.

Morgan lifted the now-familiar lion's head knocker, and as usual Nance opened the door. He greeted her then handed her his hat and gloves.

"Mr. Tremayne, Mr. Bledsoe's waiting to see you in the parlor."

"He is?" Morgan said with surprise. Leona had sent him a note asking him to call.

"Yes, sir." The maid offered no more information, so Morgan followed her into the parlor and waited for her to introduce him. "Mr. Bledsoe, Mr. Tremayne's here, sir."

"Come in, Tremayne," Benjamin Bledsoe called out.

Morgan walked inside, feeling awkward at the unaccustomed formality. Normally Leona was waiting for him when he called, alone in the parlor. But he admitted to himself things between them had been very strained since he had taken Jolie as his ward. Somehow he hadn't been able to tell Leona about her, even though four months had gone by. In fact, he hadn't seen Leona much at all in those months. And when he did, he knew there was a growing distance between them. He had felt helpless, not knowing how to get close to her again. Morgan was feeling buffeted by many things these days.

Benjamin Bledsoe was standing with his back to a small but warm fire when Morgan entered. He was a tall man with a commanding presence. He had thick silver hair, carefully styled, and a sweeping silver mustache. His eyes flashed sharply at times. Leona was much like him.

"Come in, Tremayne. Sit down, sit down," he said, waving toward an armchair.

When Morgan sat down, Bledsoe loomed over him in a most intimidating manner. Morgan was sure it was on purpose.

"I need to talk to you, Tremayne. You've been scarce around here lately. Leona's wondered at it. What are you up to these days?" he demanded. It was not a rhetorical question.

"I've had some changes in circumstance you might say, sir," Morgan said with difficulty.

"Not with your business, I hope," Bledsoe said sharply.

"No, sir. That is. . . .Rapidan Run is doing very well."

"That's good, Tremayne. After all, I know that you're very keen on my daughter, and I would never allow her to waste her time on a pauper."

"No, sir. I am not a pauper."

Bledsoe clasped his hands behind his back and stared down at Morgan with narrowed eyes. "Are you aware that Gibbs joined the army last week? He went to Camp Lee in Richmond and volunteered for Jeb Stuart's cavalry."

"No, sir, I wasn't aware. I have heard of Jeb Stuart, though. My brother—"

But impatiently Bledsoe interrupted him. "I would like to know what your intentions are concerning this war, Tremayne. Surely you aren't still wavering like some of the insipid weaklings I know. Virginia needs all her loyal sons to defend her now. Don't you believe that?"

"Yes, sir, I do. But there are some things I must do, some affairs I must settle before I can think about joining the army."

"What can possibly be more important than fighting this war? It's all going to be over in no time, anyway. Southern men, particularly Virginia men, have more dash and courage than ten Yankees. If they dare to cross the Potomac River, we'll send them back running like whipped pups!"

Morgan had heard this, and other declarations like it, countless times in the last year or so. *"One Southern man can beat three Yankees, five Yankees, ten Yankees. We're dashing and courageous and brave and valiant, and they are nothing but whelps with no honor. Hurry up and join up, or the war will be over."* Morgan was heartily sick of it.

Now he struggled to keep the distaste out of his voice. "Sir, I'm afraid I can't completely agree with you there. I believe that it is going to be a long, terrible war, and I believe that people on both sides are going to suffer. Victory is not inevitable, as so many people seem to think, and a quick victory is highly unlikely."

Bledsoe's mouth tightened. "So that's your opinion, eh? And you have more important things to do right now? That makes you look like a coward, Tremayne. I never thought I'd say that. I've always regarded you as a sensible, forthright gentleman. But now I'm not so sure."

"But sir, if I could just explain—" This time Morgan cut off his own words. How could he explain? How could he explain the terrible burden he felt for Jolie, and how bitterly he regretted not heeding DeForge's warning and preparing himself for war? Since that momentous day of February 5th, Morgan had worked himself half to death trying to make Rapidan Run into a fortress, a self-sustaining stronghold, a place that he could be sure would withstand the desolation of war. Suddenly now he was feeling the weariness that plagued him each day. He finished dully, "It's just that I have so many responsibilities now. There are some things that I simply must do before I can join the army."

"Sounds like lame excuses to me," Bledsoe said. "You're a single man with a profitable business, and there's sure no reason it couldn't continue to be profitable. I know your man Amon has been practically running it for a couple of years now. There are thousands of men, men with wives and families, who haven't hesitated to join up to fight for their land and homes." He stopped talking, watching Morgan carefully.

But Morgan could think of nothing to say.

"Well, I know Leona has invited you for supper, Tremayne. I suppose I can forget this unfortunate state of affairs—just this once. But after this, I don't think you need to see my daughter anymore. You're not the man that I thought you were."

"Don't you think that it's up to Leona who she sees?" Morgan argued heatedly. "She's a grown woman, and she makes her own decisions."

"That she does," Bledsoe said with grim amusement. "Don't be surprised if she makes a decision that you won't like, Tremayne. I know her better than you do."

The meal was pleasant enough.

Morgan could not take his eyes off of Leona Rose. She wore a rose-colored dress, her favorite color, and the pale alabaster of her shoulders and the rich coloring of her cheeks caused him to stare at her. She rebuked him once saying, "You're just staring at me, Morgan."

"Well, a mummy would sit up and stare at you, Leona."

"Oh, you foolish boy!"

Gibbs Bledsoe said very little during supper. He was wearing the uniform of a cavalryman and proud of it. He was a fine-looking young man with blond hair and blue eyes, slim and handsome. He was an imaginative fellow, full of dreams and often practical jokes. As a matter of fact, Morgan had always been fond of Gibbs.

When they had finished supper and retired to the parlor for after-dinner coffee, however, Gibbs said, "You'll notice that I joined Jeb Stuart's cavalry."

"Yes, I know. My brother Clay tells me he's probably the finest horseman in Virginia except, perhaps, for General Lee."

"Yes, he is, and he's a fighting man, too."

Gibbs had been drinking wine steadily, and now he said rather rudely, "I've always thought you were a good man, Morgan, but I hear talk that you're not going to support this war."

Morgan sighed. "As a conscientious man, I do find it hard to support war."

"Well, man, what's holding you back? We're being attacked. The Yankees are going to send their armies down here. Wouldn't you defend your native state?"

"It may come to that."

"It's slavery, isn't it?" Benjamin Bledsoe spoke up. "I know you and your family have never had slaves, and that you actually pay your free blacks like employees."

"That's true, and yes I'm opposed to slavery. I think it's a foolish economic system."

"What do you mean by that?" Gibbs lashed back. "We've done very well in the South using slaves."

"I'm not sure we've done all that well, but we could have done better using free labor. Look at it, Gibbs. A good field hand costs as much as three thousand dollars, and he might drop dead the day after you buy him. At the most you might get a few years out of him, and then you've lost your capital."

"There's no other way to raise cotton."

"Well, as for that, I think we're making a mistake."

"What do you mean? A mistake about what?" Gibbs demanded.

"We're a one-crop country. Look at the North. I don't admire many of their manners, but they are inventive. They have shipyards, foundries, factories manufacturing everything from tinned peaches to cannon. We can't fight those cannons with cotton. And now, with the blockade, I doubt if we can even sell it."

"We'll sell it to England."

Morgan had thought this out a great deal. "Maybe. But how are we going to get anything in? We can't eat cotton, our horses can't eat cotton, and we can't build our houses with it. In two years, we're going to be hungry, Gibbs."

Now Gibbs brought up the ancient argument. "This war will never last for two years. We'll send them packing, probably within six months. Our men are more outdoorsmen than the Northerners.

They don't know anything about hunting, and that's all it is, really. It's just that we're hunting Yanks instead of deer."

Morgan gave up. "Gibbs, I really don't think it's that simple. I guess we'll just have to agree to disagree."

Finally Leona spoke up. "Morgan, it's just hard for me to understand you. Don't you see that this war is going to be our moment? It will be in the history books forever, how the Confederate States of America declared their states' rights and the rights of all the people in those states to live as they please. Our children, and all of our descendants, will see that we are heroes! We fought and died for the Glorious Cause!"

Morgan was astounded. Never in his life had he thought that Leona Bledsoe would be so blind. It was alien to him that she would have such romantically shallow sentiments. Numbly he shook his head. "Leona, I don't think you've actually thought this through. No war can be glorious. Especially civil war, brother against brother. 'A house divided against itself cannot stand.'"

"Great heavens, Morgan, I've never known you to be so dreary!" she said heatedly. "You, who can claim a friendship with General Robert E. Lee himself. I'm sure he would give you a commission, and you could be an officer, maybe even on his staff! But here you sit, mouthing self-righteous platitudes. Is it possible that my father is right? Morgan, are you a coward?"

That question began to haunt him, and he knew he must find the answer soon.

CHAPTER ELEVEN

When President Lincoln had issued his call on April 15th, for a seventy-five-thousand-man militia to subdue the treasonous Southern states, he had given the Southern forces twenty days in which to "disperse and return peaceably to their respective abodes." Morgan, along with the Confederate government and military, took this to mean that President Lincoln would wait until May 5th to begin active military operations against the South. Morgan knew this meant that after that fateful day, he would no longer be able to buy supplies—or at least have them delivered. He was sure that the Northern blockade would become effective, deadly effective then.

Since February, Morgan had traveled to Baltimore twice, to place complicated orders with DeForge Brothers Imports & Exports. Henry DeForge's brother was older than he was and had long retired, but the general manager of the firm was a professional, helpful man named Paul McCray. When Morgan explained his connection to the firm and his guardianship of Jolie DeForge, Mr. McCray then personally helped Morgan with all his needs. Morgan ordered foodstuffs, household supplies, farm supplies, tools, leather, textiles, and hardwood lumber from all over New England and the Midwest. McCray obligingly made the arrangements to have them shipped to Richmond, and Morgan knew rivermen who could deliver to Rapidan Run. Mr. McCray even helped Morgan with purchasing the things that he needed that could be found in the South, such as smoked hams, coal from western Virginia, beef from Texas, and fruit from Florida. Morgan, of course, had always simply purchased such things from a general store; he had never bought in bulk. Mr. McCray's help was invaluable. Morgan had to build a storehouse and a smokehouse, and by the end of April every single building, including the house, was stocked full of everything he could think of that Jolie might need. . .in case something happened to him.

Morgan's winter crop of barley and rye did very well, but at harvesttime in March he was discouraged. He had three hundred acres of crops, and only four men to bring it in. He knew there would be no affable leasing of slaves, with daily payment to them, from Wade Kimbrel as he had with Henry DeForge. Kimbrel would charge Morgan, certainly, and he would never let a slave of his have one penny. Furthermore, Morgan knew that any former DeForge slaves would run the minute they set foot outside of Wolvesey property, so he was sure that Kimbrel would stipulate that they could only work under his cruel overseer's supervision. It was just an impossible situation.

But again, as he had done so many times before, Amon saved the day. "Mr. Tremayne, I know about a dozen free men and boys livin' in shacks in that ol' Wilderness. I'll git 'em to work, whether they want to or not." Sure enough, Morgan was able to employ fourteen sturdy field hands to bring in the crops. And this year, instead of selling what he wouldn't need, he stored it all in dozens of metal-lined barrels, another item that Mr. McCray had known where and how to order.

On the first day of May, Morgan received something of a shock.

SURRENDER

A letter arrived from Mary Lee, from her home at Arlington. The tone of the letter was light and rather careless. One part read:

> *The rose garden here is perfectly lovely this spring. I've been able to paint it on these warm sunny days. Twice I have had good results, I think. Perhaps the next time you visit, Cousin Tremayne, you may give me your opinion of them.*

Morgan was horrified that Mrs. Lee would still be sitting placidly at Arlington. After May 5th, he thoroughly believed the property would be behind enemy lines. The very next day he headed out to Arlington, with Amon driving the carriage and Rosh and Santo driving the wagon. By May 14th, he had moved her, with some of the family belongings, to her Aunt Fitzhugh's home in Ravensworth.

General Lee was in Richmond during this time, and he had sent her many letters trying to get her to leave her beloved home. He could not go to her, of course.

Morgan didn't even try to consult with General Lee. He just went to Arlington and took charge of Mrs. Lee and then returned home. He did send a brief note to the general explaining what he had done and reassuring him that Mrs. Lee was well and safe for now.

General Lee sent a courteous note of thanks back to him.

Morgan continued working hard at Rapidan Run. As always, running a horse farm was a tremendous amount of labor. And once the harvest was over, it was time to plow and ready the fields for spring planting. To Morgan, May, June, and the first two weeks of July, 1861, seemed to flash past him in a blur.

But on Tuesday, July 16th, Morgan rejoined the world, his world that was at war. Over thirty thousand men in gray were coming together and marching north.

On June 20, 1861, a great comet appeared in the sky. It lit up the night; the stars paled in comparison. Many thought this was an ill omen, a foreshadowing of war and blood and desolation.

It was rumored that an elderly slave named Oola, who belonged to some close friends of Mary Todd Lincoln and her husband, Abraham, could conjure spells. She was a tall, large woman with eyes like gimlets and gray-black skin drawn tight over her grim face. She said of the great comet, "You see dat great fire sword blaze in the sky? There's a great war coming, and the handle's toward the North, and the point's toward the South. And the North's gonna take that sword and cut the South's hide out. But that Lincoln, man, chilluns, if he takes that sword, he's gonna perish by it."

Lincoln had already taken up that sword, as had hundreds of thousands of men, North and South. The young men of the North flocked to enlist. Lincoln had called for seventy-five thousand, but he could have tripled that number and not been disappointed.

At the time the whole thing looked like a big picnic—to men who were not soldiers and knew no better. One young private in the Union Army wrote home about

> *the happy golden days of camp life where our only worry*
> *was that the war might end before our regiment had a chance*
> *to prove itself under fire. The shrill notes of the fifes, and*
> *the beat and roll of the drums. That's the sweetest music*
> *in the world to me.*

It was true, the sound of jaunty military marches sounded everywhere. Boys whose recruit roster was not full rode about the country in wagons with drummers and fifers seeking recruits. They rode into the towns with all hands yelling, "Fourth of July every day of the year!"

The training these recruits received was very sketchy indeed. Almost all of them, including most of the officers, were amateurs, and it was not uncommon to see a captain on a parade ground consulting a book as he drilled his company. Most of the privates had been recruited by one of their acquaintances, and the volunteer companies elected their officers. Naturally they had been on a first-name basis with their lieutenants and captains all their lives, and these men could see no point whatever in military formation, drill, and particularly discipline.

For many long frustrating months, General Lee, the consummate soldier engineer, fought to overcome the prejudice by Southern men that digging earthworks was beneath them.

President Lincoln was a man bowed down with care. The government offices were packed with office seekers, as they always were with a new president. Abraham Lincoln was not a brilliant military strategist, and he knew it. He chose his war cabinet with care, but it was hard for him to discern exactly the right course to take, the voice to listen to, the man to trust with so much at stake.

In a meeting with the war cabinet, General Scott, the brilliant soldier who had won the Mexican War, became angry at those who said the war would be easy. He almost shouted, "You think the Confederates are paper men? No, sir! They are men who will fight, and we are not ready to engage the enemy at this time."

Edwin Stanton, secretary of war, stared across the room with hostility in his cold, blue eyes. "General, we've been over this time and time again. I concede that we are not as well prepared as we would like to be, but neither are the rebels. And I must insist that we have here more than a military problem. Surely we all realize that our people must have a victory now. If you do not know how transit and changeable men are, I do! If we do not act at once, the issue will grow stale. Already the antiwar party is shouting for peace, and many are listening. We must strike while the iron is hot!"

The argument raged back and forth until finally President Lincoln stood up, his action cutting all talk short. Every man in the room was alert waiting for his word. He said firmly, "Gentlemen, I have listened to you all, and I have prayed for wisdom. I presume that Jefferson Davis is praying for that same quality. We have little choice. I feel that from the military point of view, General Scott is absolutely correct, but as Mr. Stanton has pointed out there is the matter of the people. They must agree to this war, and they must have something immediately. Therefore, the army will move at once. General McDowell will be in command, and he will be ordered to march as soon as possible and engage the enemy. Some of you disagree with this decision. I can only ask you to put aside your objections and join with me in prayer for our union."

Thus it was that the first great battle of the Civil War was set in motion. The objective of McDowell's army was Manassas Junction. If this could be taken by the North, the railway system of the South would, for all intents and purposes, be wrecked. So the army marched out of Washington, led by General McDowell, who was the President's choice. Practically no one else thought him at all a capable soldier, much less a capable commanding general.

Still, the Union forces invaded the South. Young men in blue faced young men in gray across a little creek in northern Virginia called Bull Run. That night many of them still felt great bravado; the Yankees had sightseers coming to observe the festivities, and the Rebels believed that they would each and every one of them beat three or four Yanks.

Shortly after dawn, even the most naive of them knew that this was to be a day of fire and blood. Sheets of flame lit up the bright spring air as the cannons exploded and the muskets blasted. As for General McDowell, he had been in only one battle in his military career, in the Mexican War, and he had not particularly distinguished himself. Mostly he was famous for his Homeric appetite. Once he ate an entire watermelon which he pronounced "monstrous fine."

But on the morning of July 21st, the General did not find the situation at Bull Run Creek monstrous fine. First he tried throwing his men directly across the creek and meeting the enemy head-on. But to his shock, he found that the Rebels were a murderous and implacable enemy. He tried to flank them, and he found that the Confederate commander, General P. G. T. Beauregard, hero of Fort

Sumter, had moved his men to again face the now-ragged blue line dead-on.

All of that endless day, the two armies maneuvered and struck, maneuvered and struck. The Union Army, who had believed that this would be little more than a military drill and an opportunity to show off, began to disintegrate. A few men began to run, and the inevitable happened in the mob mentality.

The panic spread. First squads threw down their muskets and ran, and then companies, and finally almost the entire rabble, were fleeing back toward Washington. The seasoned officers could not stop them, and they themselves tried to retreat in good order, but it was impossible. An artillery caisson was turned over on the Bull Run Bridge, blocking the way to safety, and it only fueled the madness. With a few exceptions, the entire Union Army was in full flight. The spectators in their fine carriages turned and ran for the safety of Washington, too.

And so the boys in blue were soundly beaten and had, as so many had predicted, turned tail and run away in disgrace. In a way it was unfortunate that the Confederates had won First Bull Run. It only served to reinforce the strongly-held belief that it would be a short war and an easy victory.

But to Abraham Lincoln, it meant something altogether different. He had no need of any military adviser to tell him that old General Scott had been right. The Confederate Army was by no means a paper tiger. It was going to be a long, tragic, costly war.

The line of ambulance wagons, the walking wounded among them, seemed endless.

Morgan, on the side of the road south to Richmond, watched with horror. In his head he had known this would happen. But having a mental certainty and seeing the reality were two very different things.

Then a sight galvanized him. He saw two of his friends,

brothers, walking down the road. The older brother, Blair Southall, had a bloody bandage around his head, and his left arm was in a crude sling. He was supporting his brother, Nash, who was barely able to limp along. His right pants leg was bloody from the thigh all the way down to his shoes.

Morgan jumped off Vulcan and pulled him over to the two men. "Blair? Nash? Here, get up on my horse. I'm taking you home."

Blair looked up, blinking because of the blood smeared in his eyes. "Morgan? That you, my friend? What did you say? You think I can ride that devil of a horse?"

Beside him, Nash gave an odd half sigh, half moan and crumpled to the ground, his face bloodless and sickly white.

"Mount up, Blair," Morgan ordered and helped the injured man step into the stirrup then pushed him up into the saddle. He picked up Nash Southall with newfound strength and lifted him up. Between them, he and Blair managed to get him mounted behind Blair, completely collapsed against his back. Morgan took Vulcan's reins and whispered to him, "You know what's going on, boy. Be easy; go easy." The slow ride back to Rapidan Run was probably the lightest, smoothest walk Vulcan had ever done.

Amon, Rosh, Santo, Evetta, Jolie, and Ketura all came running down the drive to meet them.

Tightly Morgan said, "These are friends of mine, Blair and Nash Southall."

Evetta said, "Git 'em in the house. Jolie, Ketura, you come on right now and help me."

"There are more," Morgan said. "Many more. I'm going to take the wagon back and bring home as many as I can. Understand?"

"Well, don't just stand there. Hurry up," Evetta said, throwing her arm around Nash Southall, who had come to, and helping him as he stumbled toward the house.

Quickly Amon said, "Mr. Tremayne, I'll drive the wagon. You, Rosh, and Santo ride. We can double up two men again like you just did. Evetta's got good sense. She'll have them girls getting the barn ready so's we can take as many as we can."

"You're a good man, Amon," Morgan said, remounting Vulcan. "I thank God for you and your family." He turned and sped off toward the Richmond road.

By nightfall there were eight wounded men in the house and eighteen in the barn. Morgan paused for a moment to watch Jolie as she went to each man's pallet and knelt down. She was checking bandages, giving them water, promising hot soup and fresh bread, smiling at them, reassuring them. She looked up and saw him and got to her feet to come over to him.

Morgan said, "You're a fine young woman, Jolie. Not many young ladies would do this. Not many of them could."

"I just want to help them, sir." She sighed. "I wish we could have taken them all."

CHAPTER TWELVE

"Evetta's made a treat for us all today," Jolie said, bringing an enormous steaming platter into the dining room and setting it in the center of the table. "Roast beef with carrots and potatoes and turnips. I love turnips," she added, so childlike that the men at the table exchanged amused glances.

Unaware, Jolie took her seat at the foot of the table and said, "Mr. Southall? Would you take Mr. Tremayne's seat at the head of the table, please?"

Morgan had gone to Mrs. Mary Lee's rescue again. She had written him that her rheumatism was bothering her some, and Morgan had known that meant she was hurting a lot. He had left this morning to take her to the Hot Springs, in Bath County. She had been there before and swore by the healing properties of the waters.

Blair Southall now took Morgan's seat, and the other six men, including his brother, sat down. Blair said a short blessing, and the men began to dig in. Seated by Jolie, Nash Southall rolled his eyes. "Gentlemen! Bunch of rooting hogs, that's what you look like. Get your big paws off that platter and pass it down here to me so I can serve Miss Jolie."

Shamefaced, Blair started the platter down the table. But he and the others then started helping themselves to the bread, the cornbread, the stewed apples, the celery sticks, the sliced tomatoes and cucumbers, and the corn relish.

Jolie marveled at them. Henry DeForge and Morgan were finicky eaters. It wasn't that they disliked certain foods; they both liked a wide variety of meats and vegetables and fruits. It was just that they ate sparingly. Jolie had never seen a robust, hungry man eat before. She herself could hardly eat for watching them.

These seven men were all that was left of the original twenty-six men they had taken in. Over the last two weeks the others had recovered, probably much quicker than they would have in the overcrowded hospitals in Richmond. Evetta, Ketura, and Jolie were all excellent nurses, and thanks to Morgan's hoarding, they had good food and plenty of it.

This was the first time they had all sat down to eat in the dining room, however. Until this morning they had been fifteen, but today Dr. Travers, who had joined the army and was now a captain, had pronounced eight men fit for duty, and they had returned to Richmond to join their units.

Jolie watched Blair Southall, a big bear of a man six feet tall with a barrel chest. He was Morgan's age and handsome, she supposed, though he was tough looking, with thick black hair and a full mustache. Nash was only eighteen and was built more like Morgan, though he wasn't as tall. He was slender, with sandy blond hair and expressive brown eyes. Both of the Southall brothers were keen outdoorsmen, and Morgan had many times taken them hunting in the Wilderness and fishing on the Rapidan. If they had been surprised to see Jolie living in his home, neither of them showed it. They were well-brought-up, gallant young men.

During the next week, Dr. Travers came by twice and finally certified all the men fit for duty.

On the morning the Southall brothers were leaving, Jolie was surprised to see Nash Southall come find her in Morgan's study. Since the wounded men had been recovering, she had resumed her lessons, whether Morgan was there or not. She looked up as Nash came in and said, "You aren't leaving yet, are you? I was coming to tell you good-bye."

"Blair's still polishing up his brass," Nash said, coming to perch up on the corner of Morgan's desk by her. "He thinks since he's a lieutenant that he should look like a peacock on parade all the time."

Jolie giggled. "Nash, you're one to talk. You're the natty one in the family. You can't fool me, you know. I'm the one who had to mend your uniform, not once but twice."

"Guess you're right," he admitted. "I can't help it. I don't like to get dirty. I can see I'm going to have a little trouble with that in this man's army. Anyway, Jolie, I want to ask you something. How old are you?"

"I'm fifteen," she answered, mystified.

He nodded. "I thought so, but when you were nursing all of us, you seemed so much older, so much more mature. But you sure don't look older. Morgan said he's your guardian. Is that right?"

"Yes, my father died a year and a half ago, and Mr. Tremayne was kind enough to take me in."

"I see. So that's all there is to it, then?"

"What do you mean? Oh wait, I think I see. Between me and Mr. Tremayne, you mean? He's my guardian, Nash," she repeated with some vehemence and some bitterness.

Nash asked quietly, "Then do you have a sweetheart, Jolie?"

Jolie's cheeks turned a delicate shade of peach. "No, I don't have a sweetheart, Nash."

He grinned. "Good. Then I'll be back, Jolie. I'll be back to see you just as soon as I can. Er—that's all right with you, isn't it? I mean, you don't think I'm an ugly toad or a dead bore or anything, do you?"

Jolie smiled. "No, I happen to think that you're handsome and interesting. Yes, I'd like for you to come visit me, Nash. Whenever you can."

～

Morgan returned on the last day of August. He rode in late that afternoon, tired and dusty and world-weary. Everywhere he had looked he had seen the machinery of war, whether it was men in uniform or cannon or overflowing hospitals or women rolling bandages.

I'm not even a part of it. I haven't even joined the army, he reflected grimly. *How can I be so sick of it all? And after only one major battle? What am I going to do? What is the right thing to do, Lord?*

He caught sight of his neat red house up on the hill, and his spirits lifted. He would talk to Jolie about it. She never said much, but Morgan had found her to be a good listener. When she did say anything or offer her opinion, it was always thoughtful and intelligent. He spurred Vulcan to a fast canter.

When he got onto the grounds, he saw Jolie in the training paddock, mounted on Calliope, Rosh's dependable mare.

Leading the mare around in circles and laughing up at Jolie was Nash Southall.

Morgan leaped out of the saddle and stamped up to the paddock. "What's going on? Jolie, what are you doing, perched up there sidesaddle, without a sidesaddle? You're going to fall off and break your silly head!"

Jolie and Nash turned, both of them with looks of surprise. Jolie called, "Hello, Mr. Tremayne! Welcome home! And I won't break my silly head. This is the fourth time Nash has helped me ride this way."

Nash led the mare to the fence where Morgan was standing. "Hello, Morgan. Why are you so upset? Miss Jolie's doing very well. If she had a lady's saddle, she'd be galloping along before you know it. Besides, I'd never let her fall." He smiled up at Jolie.

"I'm not upset," Morgan snapped. "I'm just surprised. I've been teaching Jolie to ride, and I didn't think she was ready to try sidesaddle yet."

Nash stepped back and held his hands up. Jolie jumped into them, and gently he set her on the ground.

She came to Morgan and said, "But sir, you know I can't ride astride, bareback, all my life. And you're much too busy to teach me the proper way. I just thought I could try sitting sidesaddle, and if I could do it, maybe you could order me a lady's saddle."

"I can do that, certainly," Morgan said in a calmer tone. "When I'm sure you're ready. Nash, how is it that you're not back with your unit yet? You look all healed up and fine to me."

"Sure I am, Morgan. Blair and I went back last week. I just came by to see Miss Jolie."

"You did? Oh. Oh, I see. I guess," Morgan said uncertainly.

"He can't stay for supper. He has to be back in camp tonight," Jolie said. "Do you mind if I ride just a little more, Mr. Tremayne? Nash has to leave soon."

"I guess that'll be all right," Morgan said. "Nash, it's good to see you. I'm glad you and Blair are all fixed up. But I'm really tired. I think I'm going on in and getting a nice, long, hot bath."

"Go ahead, Morgan. I won't keep Miss Jolie long," he said easily. "See you next week."

Morgan went back into the house and had an hour-long soak. Jolie came in for supper and told him all about the men and how they had recovered so well in that last week they'd been there. Morgan let her chatter on.

When they were finished, he said, "Jolie, would you mind coming into the study with me? I need to talk to you."

"Of course."

Carrying his coffee cup, Morgan went and seated himself behind his desk, instead of sitting in the chairs by the windows.

Jolie sat across the desk from him.

"Jolie, I have to admit I was shocked when I saw you and Nash this afternoon," he said evenly. "Do I understand that he is court-ing you?"

"I think so," Jolie answered with some difficulty. "I'm not too educated about these things, Mr. Tremayne. He asked me if I had a sweetheart, and when I said no, he asked if he could visit me. That's courting, isn't it?"

"Yes. But Jolie, it's not fitting. You are much too young to have men courting you."

"But I'm fifteen! Evetta says that lots of girls get married at fifteen, or even fourteen."

"Married! Good gracious, Jolie, you can't be thinking of marriage!"

"Of course I am," she replied with a tiny smile. "I'm a fifteen-year-old girl. But I'm not thinking of marrying Nash Southall, nor is he thinking of marrying me. We just like each other, that's all. He's sweet and fun, and he makes me laugh. What's wrong with that?"

Morgan frowned, and it was some time before he answered. "There's nothing wrong with that, of course. It's just that you've led a very sheltered life, and you're very innocent. I don't think you're ready for beaus yet, Jolie."

"Mr. Tremayne, most girls are innocent at my age, aren't they? I mean, they should be. Am I so odd, so bizarre, because I'm an octoroon and because my father wouldn't dare claim me while he was alive?" She spoke passionately, and her eyes filled with tears.

"No, no, Jolie, that's not it at all," Morgan said quickly. "Please don't cry. I don't know what to do when ladies cry. My mother never cried in front of me. It makes me very nervous."

Suddenly Jolie smiled through her tears. "You called me a lady. Even you know deep down that I'm not a child anymore, Mr. Tremayne. I am a young lady, and having Nash Southall visit me shouldn't scare you at all."

"No, it shouldn't," Morgan said, almost to himself. "All right, I guess I won't kick Nash off the property when he comes to see you.

But you just watch yourself, Jolie. I don't want to see you get hurt."

"I won't," she assured him.

Summer passed quickly; fall lingered sweetly, it seemed to Morgan. It didn't get really cold until the last of October, when the first snowfall, a light, pretty one, blanketed northern Virginia.

The two vast armies were huddled in their winter camps. Abraham Lincoln and his war cabinet were planning their spring campaign. Jefferson Davis and his generals were trying to figure out what Lincoln was planning, and General Lee was working hard to push for an offensive campaign beginning in March of 1862.

Morgan felt as if he had suddenly come to a halt and had breathing space. He felt no anguish over whether to join the Confederate Army or not, for he knew that there would be no great battles during wintertime. He had winter crops to plant and horses to train. In the spring, he would make his decision. He must make his decision. . . .

PART THREE

PART THREE

CHAPTER THIRTEEN

Jolie heard the sound of a bird outside her window and slowly opened her eyes. March had just come and, as always, the spring was a delight to her. Slowly she got up, stretched, and then swung her feet out of bed and moved over toward the window.

She stared at the bird nibbling at the sunflower seed that she had put out. It was a medium-sized bird with a ladderback design and a red head. "I thought I knew all the birds," she murmured, "but you don't look like a woodpecker to me." She watched the bird until he evidently had eaten his fill then leaped into the air and flew away.

Jolie went to her armoire and for a moment could not decide what to wear. She finally selected a well-worn blue cotton dress. Sighing, she put it on. She had to struggle to pull it down. Close to turning sixteen, it seemed as if her figure had developed overnight. Every dress and blouse she owned was too tight across her chest, the sleeves were too short, and most of her skirts were too short.

Leaving her room, she walked through the house and went out to the kitchen where Evetta was rolling out dough, preparing to make biscuits.

"You can't wear that dress, Jolie. It ain't modest." Displeasure was in Evetta's face, and she added, "Go put on something decent."

"All my dresses are too tight. I don't know what I'm going to do."

"Well, you're going to have to have new dresses. That's what you're gonna do. You tell Mr. Morgan that you got to have some new clothes."

"I don't like to ask for things."

"You're just too proud. That's what's the matter with you, child. Now, you do like I says."

Amon came in, moved behind Evetta, then put his arms around her and lifted her off the floor. "My, it's fine to have a good-looking wife."

"You put me down!" Evetta protested, even though she really liked the attention.

Amon set her down but gave her an extra squeeze. "My next wife, she's going to be more loving than you."

"Never mind your next wife. I'm all the wife you needs."

The outside door opened, and Morgan came in. "Good morning," he said cheerfully. "Do I smell bacon and eggs?"

"You sit down there, Mr. Tremayne," Jolie said, "and I'll get your coffee."

Morgan sat down. Amon, Rosh, and Santo joined him, and they talked, as always, about horses. Ketura came in, and she and Jolie helped Evetta finish and serve the men. Finally breakfast was on the table.

They all bowed their heads, and Morgan asked a quick blessing; then he filled his plate and began eating hungrily. "Good cooking, Evetta, as always. Thank you." Morgan was always courteous, showing his appreciation to Amon and his family.

"You're welcome, Mr. Tremayne. You know, sir, she don't like to say, but Jolie really needs some new clothes. She's outgrown just about everything you got her last year."

Morgan looked thoughtful. "All right, Jolie. We can go into

town to Sally Selden's and order you some things. Would you like to do that?"

Jolie eagerly said, "Oh yes, sir, please. And may Ketura come, too?"

"Of course. In fact, I'll bet Ketura could use a new dress or two. We'll make it a shopping day for the ladies. Be ready to go in about an hour."

Morgan drove the wagon into Fredericksburg, and Jolie thought he seemed carefree and confident, not weighted down and burdened as he had so often been since the war started. He made jokes and teased Jolie and Ketura unmercifully. "So I guess I'm taking you two ladies to the mill, to buy you some flour sacks for new dresses, isn't that right?"

They giggled and cried, "Oh no! No, sir, Mr. Tremayne! Please, please!" Their high youthful voices on the gentle spring air seemed to please him.

Despite all his teasing, he stopped the wagon on Main Street, just in front of a small, neat brick shop. Over the door was a sign that read: SALLY SELDEN, DRESSMAKER AND MILLINER. Morgan jumped out of the wagon and came to gallantly help Jolie and Ketura down.

Instantly they went to look in the shop window. In it was displayed a cambric dress, white with a print of tiny yellow daffodils. The mannequin had a straw hat with a wide graceful brim. It had a yellow ribbon around the crown, tying underneath the chin. The hat was trimmed with real daffodils and white baby's breath.

"Oooh, that's just beautiful," Ketura breathed. "That would look so, so pretty on you, Jolie."

"It would on you, too, Ketura," Jolie said wistfully.

Standing behind them, Morgan said, "Tell you what. Both of you order yourselves that dress and hat. You pick out the material you want. I don't guess you'd want the same thing. Seems like ladies don't like it when that happens for some reason. Anyway, go ahead and order a couple of nice dresses each, and let's see, maybe three dresses for everyday. How does that sound?"

"Really?" Ketura said, her big brown eyes as round as saucers. "Even me, Mr. Tremayne?"

"Even you, Ketura. And by the way, you'd better order a nice new hat for your mother, too, or we'll all be in big trouble."

Jolie went up on tiptoe and kissed Morgan's cheek. "Thank you, Mr. Tremayne. Being able to get something for Ketura makes me almost as happy as getting new clothes myself."

"I know," he said lightly. "That's one thing that makes you a very unusual girl, Jolie. Now I've got a couple of errands to run, and I'm going to stop by the Club Coffee Shop to get the papers and the latest news. You two don't go wandering around, do you hear me? When you get finished, you come straight to the coffee shop. Jolie, do you remember where it is?"

"Yes, sir." She pointed down the street. "It's just down there, across the street. I can see the sign from here. We promise we'll only go there."

"Okay. Have fun. And take your time. I know girls like to do this stuff for hours and hours." Morgan climbed back up into the wagon.

Jolie called out, "Mr. Tremayne?"

"Yes?"

"Um—maybe—perhaps—two hats, sir? Each?"

"Minx," he said affectionately. "Two hats. And don't forget Evetta."

Morgan went first to the wheelwrights, because he thought that one of the wagon wheels was jinking a little. He left the wagon there and walked to the bank and made a deposit. Vulcan had already gone out to stud and ruefully Morgan sighed as he handed over the Confederate money to the teller. Already fifty dollars in Confederate money was equal to about ten dollars gold. As he had predicted, the blockade was working all too well. Coffee was a dollar a pound, tea five dollars, a pair of shoes were anywhere from ten to fifteen dollars a pair. Morgan knew that it was only going to get worse.

From there he stopped by Silas Cage's office and gave the attorney an update. He had made friends with Cage in the time since Henry DeForge had died. Pretty, young Mrs. Cage had given birth to a little girl just before Christmas, and Morgan duly admired the new baby. After they finished discussing his new daughter and Jolie, Cage took off his glasses and polished them with his handkerchief. By now this was a familiar sign to Morgan. He knew Cage was going to tell him something important.

"Morgan, I've decided to join the army," he said quietly.

"I see," Morgan said. "That's going to be real hard on Mrs. Cage, isn't it?"

He put his glasses back on. "Yes. But it's something I have to do. I love this country. I mean Virginia. I have to fight for her. It's just that simple. Maybe I'm presuming on our friendship, but I would like to know. Are you planning on joining the army, Morgan?"

"Yes," he said instantly. His quick definite answer was something of a surprise, even to Morgan himself. Now he realized that all winter he had, in the deepest recesses of his mind, firmly decided to join. "But I'm not sure when I'm going to join up, Silas," he temporized. "You know that I've spent the last year making preparations, planning, stocking up, so that Rapidan Run, and Jolie, will be safe if something happens to me. Oh, I'll just say it. In the back of my mind I've always known that I was doing all of those things in case I was killed in battle. So right now I've got just a couple more things to do. I've got spring planting, and I've got ten three-year-olds that are just about ready to be sold. And of course I'm selling them to the Confederate Army. I did just want to make sure they're trained and ready before I do."

Silas nodded. "I understand. I think you've been very wise, Morgan. I know it's been hard, because I know all too well how people think you're a coward if you don't join. But I determined I was going to wait until after my daughter was born before I left her and my wife. It was the right thing for me to do, and I'm sure you've done the right thing for you, too."

The men parted on good terms, and Morgan went on to the coffee shop. It was a gathering place for the men of the town, some of whom came first thing in the morning and stayed until dinnertime. All the newspapers were sold there, and the men gathered and talked and discussed the latest news for hours at a time. Morgan joined three men sitting at a table, all acquaintances of his: young Asa Cooke, whose father was a railroad engineer; Bert Patrick, who owned the largest general store in town; and Will Green, who was Morgan's favorite saddler.

Bert said as Morgan sat down, "Hello, Morgan, good to see you again. It's been a couple of weeks since you've been in town, hasn't it?"

"Three weeks, in fact. Guess the war's put a hitch in river deliveries, because I haven't seen Dirk Jameson or his boys for the last week." Jameson had a sturdy twelve-foot boat, and for years he had delivered the newspapers and other supplies to Henry DeForge and Morgan.

"They all joined up, even Old Jameson himself," Asa said eagerly. He was a bright boy with red hair, freckles, and a toothy smile. "I'm joining up, Morgan, this very day!"

"You're too young," Morgan said shortly. "You need to stay at home and take care of your pretty mama and your sisters, Asa." Morgan knew the family. Asa was the only son, and he had five sisters.

"Nope, my papa told me I could join up when I was seventeen, and today is my seventeenth birthday. My mama and my sisters are all real proud of me, Morgan. They want me to fight for the Glorious Cause. I'm glad I'm seventeen now. I was getting worried I might miss the whole thing!"

"You're not going to have to worry about that, boy," Will Green said. He was an older man, in his fifties, and he was one man who was in complete agreement with Morgan about the war. He had no illusions of glory, and he knew that the South was going to be fighting against almost impossible odds in the long run. He and Morgan had agreed that it was likely to be a long run, indeed. "You're going to have plenty of time, and chances, to get your fool self killed."

"Pshaw," Asa said disdainfully. "I gotta hurry up and get my five Yanks, Mr. Green, before they all scoot back to Washington for good, like they did at Bull Run."

Bert Patrick said, "The news hasn't been that good since then, has it? Morgan, you know about Fort Henry and Fort Donelson, don't you?"

"No, the last paper I got was around February 12th."

Bert shook his head. "Fort Henry in Tennessee was captured by federal gunboats. And then a new young whippersnapper they got, name of Ulysses S. Grant, of all the outlandish things, took Fort Donelson. Word is that he demanded, and got, an unconditional surrender. Made those Tennessee boys look pretty bad, except for a hotshot cavalryman we got out there in the West, General Nathan Bedford Forrest. He refused to surrender, and somehow he snuck out of Fort Donelson right under Grant's nose. Him and about two hundred of his men. But that's two pieces of real bad news right there. We lost control of the Tennessee and Cumberland Rivers"—he snapped his fingers—"right there, just like that. Not to mention fourteen thousand fighting men at Fort Donelson."

"Only good news I've heard tell lately is that President Davis has recalled General Lee to Richmond," Will Green said soberly. "I know he's an experienced engineer, and he's needed to shore up the coastal defenses in the Carolinas and Georgia, but he's a Virginia man. We need him here."

Morgan knew that Mrs. Lee hadn't seen her husband for over a year now. She had written him in February, telling him that she was going to go to the White House, one of George Custis's holdings on the Pamunkey River that he had given to his son Rooney in his will. Morgan hadn't been needed to move her this time, as

Rooney had managed to get a leave to pick her up from the Hot Springs, where she had wintered, and take her to his plantation. The White House was just west of Richmond, and Morgan thought that he would be able to take the carriage and bring her to Richmond if the general wanted him to. "When is he due back?" Morgan asked eagerly.

"Any day now," Will answered. "And a good day it'll be, I'll say. Joe Johnston is a good man, but in my opinion, His Excellency would do well to look to Robert E. Lee to command this army."

The table agreed, for Lee was a famous man in Virginia, a favorite son. Even Asa said, "I hope he comes today. I'd sure like to know I was going to be one of Robert E. Lee's boys. That would just be the icing on the cake."

Privately, Morgan thought, *I have to agree with the boy there. When I join, I'd like to know that General Lee is my general. Maybe it's time. . . .*

❧

As Morgan had foreseen, it took Jolie and Ketura two hours to pick out fabrics, decide on the dress patterns, try on hats, and for Mrs. Selden to get their measurements. "I'm so glad Mr. Tremayne brought you into town, Jolie. Every time he orders something for you, sight unseen, I just shudder, thinking it can't possibly fit you. You're not a little girl like you were when you were with Mr. DeForge. You're turning into a young woman now. And a very pretty one, too."

"Thank you," Jolie said. "But Mr. Tremayne thinks I'm still twelve years old, I guess. I wonder that he's not still ordering me pantalettes."

Mrs. Selden laughed. "No, I think I would put a stop to that." Sally Selden had been making Jolie's clothes ever since Jolie was born. When Jolie turned two, Henry DeForge brought her in, and once a year, every year, after that. Naturally Morgan had had to confide in Mrs. Selden when he took Jolie after Mr. DeForge died, and he kept ordering clothes from her.

Morgan had still not made it public knowledge that he had taken guardianship of Jolie, but Fredericksburg was, after all, a small town. Mrs. Selden had always kept her friends and neighbors updated about the exotic octoroon child that Morgan Tremayne had taken in. Morgan hadn't even found a way to tell his own family about Jolie. And he had never mentioned her to Leona Bledsoe.

And so it was rather a cruel trick of fate that Gibbs Bledsoe was walking down Main Street and was right in front of Mrs. Selden's shop when Jolie and Ketura came out, arm in arm. Gallantly he stopped and lifted his hat and let them pass, thinking, *What a lovely girl she is, and her maid's a pretty sight, too.*

Then he heard Jolie say, "Oh dear, Ketura, we've been here for two hours! Hurry, hurry! I hope Mr. Tremayne isn't getting impatient with us."

Bledsoe's mind clicked! And he knew who she was. Taking two long strides, he caught up with them and fell into step beside Jolie. She looked up at him with surprise. "Well, well, well," he drawled. "So this is the big secret that Morgan's been keeping from my sister. Pardon my rudeness, Miss Jolie DeForge. My name is Gibbs Bledsoe, and my sister's name is Leona Rose Bledsoe. Do you know that name, by any chance?"

"Yes, sir," she said stiffly, looking straight ahead. But Gibbs saw that she clutched Ketura even closer with nervousness.

It amused him. "You are one fine, handsome young woman, Jolie. My sister's not going to be happy to hear that. I think she had more of a picture of a little black girl in her mind."

"I am part black, sir. But I don't think you should be talking to me like this. It's not very respectful," Jolie managed to say. She hurried hers and Ketura's step, but Gibbs easily kept up.

"Morgan should know better than to let a pretty girl like you wander around with just your maid to accompany you. Here, take my arm. I'll escort you, and you, girl, you can walk behind like a proper maid does."

"You don't have to do that," Jolie said desperately, trying to pull away from him.

But he insistently took her hand and tucked it around his arm. "No, I want to. We should get to know each other, Jolie. In fact, maybe I should come out to Rapidan Run and visit you sometime. Maybe you could accompany me to the town hall for the next dance."

"No, sir. Mr. Tremayne would never permit that."

"He wouldn't? Stodgy old Morgan. Keeps you hidden and won't let you loose."

"No! It's not like that!" she said desperately. She tried again to pull away from him. "Please, Mr. Bledsoe, let me go. Mr. Tremayne is right over there in the coffee shop. Ketura and I can cross the street by ourselves."

"Nonsense," he said then pulled her out into the busy street, dodging carts and buggies and riders.

Jolie looked back to make sure that Ketura was following them, which she was, a dogged look on her face.

They got onto the plank boardwalk, and Morgan came storming out of the coffeeshop. "Gibbs, stop hauling on her like she's a side of beef! What are you doing anyway? You shouldn't impose yourself on young ladies you haven't met. Mind your manners, boy."

Gibbs Bledsoe had a fiery temper and growled, "Don't you ever call me 'boy' again. And it's your fault that I haven't met Jolie, Morgan. You know very well you should have told me, and particularly Leona, about her a long time ago."

"Maybe I should have, but I'm not going to stand out here on the street and argue with you. In spite of what you think, or whatever vicious gossip you've heard, Jolie and Ketura are ladies who deserve respect, and I intend to make sure they get it."

Gibbs glared at him. "Maybe you'd better make sure you're really the gentleman here, Morgan. At least I acknowledged that I know Jolie." With that parting shot, he turned on his heel and hurried off.

Morgan turned to the two girls. "I'm sorry," he said helplessly. "I'm so sorry, Jolie."

She answered spiritedly, "You have nothing to apologize to me for, Mr. Tremayne. I just want to forget this whole thing. And please, sir, don't ever tell me you're sorry for anything ever again. It's just not right."

Morgan gave in. "All right, Jolie. For now at least. So, are you ladies ready to go back home?"

"Yes, please," Jolie said, brightening. "But we have some—things we need to pick up at Mrs. Selden's."

"What things? She didn't have any ready-to-wears, did she?"

"No. At least not dresses," Jolie said, taking Ketura's arm again as they walked down the street to the wheelwright's. "It's—um—hatboxes. Six hatboxes."

"Six?" Morgan repeated.

Jolie said, "Remember, you said we could get two hats. Each. And of course we couldn't forget Evetta."

"Ah yes, it's all coming back to me now. I do recall getting ambushed just as I was leaving, and something about lots of hats," Morgan teased her. "Six hatboxes, you say. Guess Calliope can handle that."

When they were on their way out of town, they passed the town square.

About twenty young men and boys were there, drilling in new gray uniforms. At least they would march two steps then hoist their rifles to their shoulders and pretend to shoot. "Got one Billy Yank!" one of them cried. "Got four more to go for my quota!" The men laughed, and one of them shouted, "How 'bout we all decide to get ten? No graybelly is any match for a Virginia fighting man!"

Morgan sighed deeply as they passed.

Jolie looked up at him curiously. "Mr. Tremayne?"

"Hm?"

"You're going to join the army, aren't you." Though it was in the form of a question, the tone of it was not. And she sounded sad.

"Not today, Jolie. That's all I can tell you. Not today."

❧

The next day Morgan came back to town and called on Leona. She was having tea with her father and mother in the parlor, and Leona cordially asked him to join them.

Morgan had been unsure of her reception. He knew that Gibbs had surely told the family about meeting Jolie.

But as soon as Leona had served him tea, Benjamin Bledsoe started in. "Morgan, Gibbs told me about meeting your girl yesterday. We've heard about her, of course. I was wondering if you were ever going to own up to it," he said disdainfully.

"It?" Morgan repeated sharply. "Sir, Jolie is not an 'it.' She's a young woman, a well-brought-up, respectable young woman, I might add. It is true I haven't discussed her with you, or with anyone else for that matter. I had no idea that everyone was so interested in my private affairs."

"Perhaps you may truly be that naive, Morgan. But surely you see that you should have told Leona about her a long time ago."

"Maybe," Morgan said doubtfully. "Then again, as I said, this is a private matter. In fact, it's a private *family* matter. I am Jolie DeForge's legal guardian, and in my view that makes me her family. I, for one, wouldn't be interested in knowing all of your family business, Mr. Bledsoe. I wouldn't think I had the right."

Benjamin Bledsoe took the mild rebuke with surprising equanimity. "Maybe you're right, Morgan. Adopting a child is a very personal thing. How old is the girl?"

"She's sixteen."

"She is part black, isn't she?"

"She's an octoroon."

Leona Rose had been listening carefully with a neutral expression. But now she said, "You sound very high and noble, Morgan, but most people aren't. They talk, and the fact is that you have a young girl—a very pretty young girl, Gibbs tells me—living with you. Looking at it objectively, it's pretty scandalous."

Stung, Morgan retorted, "That is nowhere near an objective view, Leona. It's a malicious and skewed version of a situation that is perfectly innocent. This, in fact, is exactly why I don't talk about Jolie very much. I don't want to hear it." He had never spoken so sharply to Leona, and she looked thoroughly taken aback.

Gibbs came in and looked around. "You all look as solemn as a bunch of owls. Hi, Morgan. I'm still angry with you, in case you didn't notice."

Morgan said, "Gibbs, I'm sorry we had that altercation, but let me ask you this. Suppose a man had taken the liberties with your sister that you did with Jolie. What would you think of that?"

Gibbs Bledsoe had a hot temper, but really he was a fair-minded young man. He shook his head ruefully and answered, "I'd do exactly what you did. I'm too touchy." He winked at Leona. "Like my sister."

"Let's put it all behind us then," Morgan said with relief.

But Leona Rose Bledsoe was far from relieved and far from amused. She rose to her feet and snapped her fan shut angrily. "Men! The things you get away with! Well, you're not going to just pat me on the head and brush me off, Morgan. You're so worried about your responsibilities to that little black girl, and you never seem to think about your responsibilities to me!" Majestically she sailed out of the room.

Nervously her mother followed her.

Morgan, Gibbs, and even Benjamin Bledsoe looked guiltily at each other.

Gibbs gave a low whistle. "You fell into it this time, Morgan. Glad I'm not in your shoes."

"You could help me out here, Gibbs," Morgan said helplessly. "Can't you go talk to her, tell her not to be mad at me?"

"Not me, brother. I'm no coward, but I'm not squaring off against my sister."

Benjamin Bledsoe cleared his throat. "Er, Morgan, Leona is a little upset just now. Usually it's best to leave her alone until she gets in a better—I mean, until she feels better. Maybe you'd better go and come back tomorrow. Or even the next day."

"Right," Gibbs said forcefully. "You better stick your head in first, Morgan, to make sure you're not still in the bull's-eye."

"Maybe I'll come back on Monday," he said uncertainly.

"Maybe that's best," Mr. Bledsoe said with relief.

Morgan went toward the door then turned around when Benjamin Bledsoe said, "Morgan?"

"Sir?"

"I called you a coward once. I'm sorry for that. Any man that's determined to hold his own with my daughter is no coward."

"No, sir," Morgan heartily agreed and hurried away.

CHAPTER FOURTEEN

Throughout the Civil War, the major problem of the South was that the North could quickly forge an arsenal of weapons. The industrial power that had been built up in the Northern states was immense. Unlike the wealthy elite of the South, who were only interested in growing cotton, businessmen in the North were interested in capital investment, in utilization of natural resources, of machines and equipment and factories. Quickly the North was able to turn their industrialized cities into factories that could turn out the implements of war. Ironclad ships, muskets, cannons, and ammunition all came like a flood once the North geared up. The South had nothing to compare with this. Many of their weapons were those captured from the North, of necessity.

The North outnumbered the South tremendously. The North was thickly populated, whereas the South had many fewer citizens and many blacks, who were not permitted to fight. This was starting to become a factor, but at the beginning, on both sides of the Mason–Dixon Line, young men, and older men as well, rushed to join the respective armies of the Union and the Confederacy.

SURRENDER

But it was not a matter of armament or soldiers that made the difference in the two foes, at least not until the end. The real problem the North faced was finding generals who had the courage, the nerve, and the quality of bold leadership of all great military men. Though the rhetoric of the South was high and overblown, the fact remained that many Southern generals and colonels were exactly that kind of man. It was not so in the Union Army. Throughout the history of the Civil War, generals such as Pope, Burnside, McDowell, Hooker, and others knew how to build armies but lacked the killer instinct of sending these armies into the fierce cauldron of bloody battle.

One such man who arose was General George Brinton McClellan. He was thrust into a difficult position. After the Bull Run disaster, the armies of the North, as well as the citizens and the government itself, felt that trying to subdue the Southern states was well-nigh impossible. There was a peace party, well populated by those who clamored for peace at any cost. The newspapers that had once been screaming, ON TO RICHMOND, were now begging the government to turn to peace.

General McClellan, who before the war had been the president of a railroad, was summoned to Washington and rode sixty miles on horseback to the nearest railway station. When he arrived in Washington, he found the city almost in a condition unable to defend itself. To his shock, McClellan found himself looked up to from all sides as a deliverer.

He wrote to his wife that evening:

I find myself in a new and strange position here. President, cabinet, and General Scott are all deferring to me. By some strange operation of magic I seem to have become the power of the land.

When asked if he could help rescue the cause, McClellan replied proudly, "I can do it all."

He set out at once to reconstruct the Army of the Potomac.

Rigid discipline was the order of the day, and something new came into being. Little Mac, as the soldiers called this man, transformed the army from a whipped mob into a hot-blooded army that seemed to have never known the taste of defeat.

He was a young man, only thirty-four, his eyes were blue, his hair was dark auburn, parted on the left, and he was clean-shaven as a rule, except for a rather straggly mustache. He was of average height, robust and stockily built with a massive chest. The newspapers began to write about him, and the name "The Young Napoleon" became his journalistic title. And, indeed, he did have a Napoleonic touch. The soldiers liked him. They understood that he was firm, a strict disciplinarian, but he was fair.

Within ten days of his arrival in Washington, he could say proudly, "I have restored order completely." The army seemed to be reborn. Reviews were staged, with massed columns swinging past reviewing stands. Equipment was polished new and gleaming, and there was a camaraderie in the Army of the Potomac that had been lacking from the beginning.

Yet in the small hours of the night, it seemed, McClellan had grave doubts. "I am here in a terrible place," he wrote. "The enemy has from three to four times my force." This was not guesswork. These numbers came from Allen Pinkerton, the railroad detective, who was supposedly a master spy. Later it would seem that he had invented numbers in his mind rather than sent spies.

In addition to feeling he was being overwhelmed with Southern forces, McClellan had to fight his way in Washington against Lieutenant General Winfield Scott, who had been a great man in his day. McClellan saw him merely as an old man who had not the strength nor the wisdom to fight a war. "He understands nothing, appreciates nothing." McClellan spoke of General Scott. "I have to fight my way against him." Later on he said, "General Scott is the most dangerous antagonist I have."

Lincoln, desperate in the hope of finding a fighting general, did everything that McClellan requested. Finally General Scott retired, and McClellan was appointed to fill his place in command of the army. He spoke so positively that Lincoln wondered if McClellan was as aware of the the monstrous burden of responsibility as he himself was. "The vast labor weighs upon you, General," he said, half chiding.

"I can do it all," McClellan said confidently. Indeed, he had made a prediction: "I shall crush the Rebels in one campaign." Still, his constant bickering with politicians bothered him.

He wrote to his wife:

The people think me all powerful. . . . I can't tell you how disgusted I'm becoming with these wretched politicians.

He did not include Abraham Lincoln, who showed a great deal of deference to General McClellan. But Lincoln, who had been boning up on the science of war, was chafing for action, and McClellan kept putting him off and putting the country off. When someone said that McClellan did not show him the proper respect, Lincoln responded, "I will hold McClellan's horse if he will only bring us success."

Little Mac finally made a decision. He had never enjoyed the concept of a full frontal battle on the plains, as McDowell had done at Bull Run. He came up with another plan of campaign. He would load his soldiers aboard transports, steam down the Potomac in the Chesapeake Bay, then south along the coast to the mouth of the Rappahannock. There he would be less than fifty miles from Richmond, his objective. Without loss of a man, he would have cut his marching distance in half and would be in the rear of the enemy, who would be forced to retreat and fight on grounds of McClellan's choosing.

Unfortunately, he ignored the details, including the assembling of transports for the 150,000 men he planned to invade with. Then the rains came in the middle of his campaign, and the fields were turned to quagmires, and the roads were axle-deep in the mud.

This gave him another excuse for not attacking.

Now Lincoln saw that he was looking at a general who was not the man to lead the Army of the Potomac. But what was done was done. No matter how Little Mac delayed, surely battle would come.

"I wish you didn't have to go, Robert. I know that in many ways this is your dream, but I still wish you could just stay here with me." Mary reached up and put her hand on her husband's cheek. Anxiety was in her expression, and when he leaned forward and kissed her, she held on to him tightly. "I'm so afraid for you," she whispered.

Mary Lee had finally wended her way to Richmond and was living in a rented house on East Franklin Street. Lee had come to bid farewell to her. McClellan was approaching at a rapid speed, and everyone knew that there was going to be a life-and-death struggle over the city of Richmond.

"I have to go, dearest," Lee said, "but I won't be the commanding general. I'll be way back in the lines, so you needn't worry. Just pray for me."

"Of course I will. I always do that."

"Then, Mary, you know that all will be well, no matter what happens. The Lord will protect you and me, always."

Lee left the house, mounted Traveler, and rode to the outskirts of town. There he met with Joe Johnston, who was an old friend of Lee's and was the commanding general of the Confederate forces in the east.

With him was President Jefferson Davis. Davis's thin aristocratic features were tense. "You're sadly outnumbered, General Johnston."

"I think you are correct, but there is nothing we can do about that. We must all fight as best we can."

Lee said nothing, but he stayed close to Jefferson Davis. In truth, he had been kept from a higher position in the army because he was the only man who could get along with Jeff Davis. Other generals were short with him or were egotistical, and since Davis fancied himself a fighting man, as he had been in the War of Mexico, instead of a political figure, the clash was inevitable.

Although he was not outwardly resentful toward his president or his old friend from both West Point and Mexico, Joe Johnston was rather arrogant, and he kept his council and plans much to himself. He only gave Davis and Lee the bare outlines of his strategy. Eventually Johnston politely suggested that General Lee ride out on the field and said that he hoped he could soon send some much-needed reinforcements. Of course, Jeff Davis could not bear to stay away from a battle, and so both he and Lee witnessed the Battle of Seven Pines.

The battle itself proved to be the worst-conducted large-scale conflict of the entire war. What it finally came to was a military nightmare. The Southern troops had little contact with each other, and therefore Johnston could not get them to move as he ordered. He was never able to position his divisions properly. Casualties were high, and the gain was small. But the most significant casualty was General Johnston himself. He was hit in the right shoulder by a bullet. As he reeled in the saddle, he was wounded a second time when a shell fragment struck him in the chest and unhorsed him.

They were trying to get the wounded general back behind the lines to an ambulance when he bade them stop. Weakly he said, "Would someone go back and see if they can find my sword? I would not lose it for ten thousand dollars."

A courier went back under fire, found the sword and his pistol, and returned. Finally the ambulance drove away toward Richmond. A courier hurried to President Davis and General Lee with the news that General Johnston had been wounded, perhaps fatally.

That night Davis and Lee rode around the field of battle, surveying it and talking to the senior officer on the field, General Gustavus W. Smith. He had been ill, and he was showing great battle strain.

They rode on in the darkness. The only account of their conversation was Jefferson Davis's: "When riding from the field of battle with General Robert E. Lee. . .I informed him that he would be assigned to command of the army. . .and that he could make his preparations as soon as he reached his quarters, as I should send the order to him as soon as I arrived at mine."

Lee tackled his monumental task. After he took charge, he immediately organized an offensive. It came to be called the Seven Days' Battle, but it was really a series of battles: Gaines' Mill, Savage's Station, Frayser's Farm, and Malvern Hill.

Lee did his best, but his troops were untrained, and he himself had not had an opportunity to teach his officers how to maneuver quickly and effectively and how to keep constant lines of communication open to the commanding general.

The last battle took place on Malvern Hill. The Union troops under McClellan were up at the crest of the hill, and Lee felt he had the Army of the Potomac on the run. He then made one of the most serious mistakes of his career. He ordered a charge, and as his troops swarmed up the hill, they were mowed down by the artillery and musketry entrenched there.

Thus, the Seven Days' Battle ended, and McClellan's grand Peninsular campaign was ended. It was, however, a great victory for Robert E. Lee. He had broken up the Union army, cowed them with his masterful offensive, and once again, the Northern troops fled back to Washington in defeat.

McClellan was promptly relieved of command. Lincoln simply could not understand how a man who had vast superiority in both troops and artillery could lose against a smaller, less well-armed force. Once again, he started searching for a capable commander.

But he did not have General Robert E. Lee.

❧

"I have a present for you, Jolie."

Jolie looked up from her book and saw Morgan beckoning her. Obediently she followed him out the back door. There she saw a new gleaming sidesaddle on the hitching post. "Oh, Mr. Tremayne! Thank you, thank you!" she said excitedly, running to it to feel the soft leather and studying the leg hook and single stirrup.

"That's not all the present," Morgan said, grinning. He gave a short sharp whistle, and Rosh came out of the stables, leading a three-year-old mare.

She was a beautiful horse, a deep chestnut that was almost a mahogany red, with black points. She was small but was the perfect size for a small lady like Jolie. Her head was neat, her eyes were soft and sweet, and she was proud and alert in her stance.

Jolie had seen the mare, but it had never occurred to her that Morgan would give her such a valuable gift. "You mean she's mine?" Jolie whispered.

"All yours. One of the finest mares I've ever bred."

Jolie threw her arms around Morgan crying, "How can I thank you, Mr. Tremayne? Oh, I can't believe it!" She became aware then that he was slightly pushing her away, and Jolie realized that he was becoming more aware of her developing figure. She stepped back hurriedly and asked, "Can I go for a ride?"

"Of course you can. She's your horse. You can go any time you want. Just be sure that somebody at the house knows."

"I'll saddle her all by myself. I know how," Jolie said excitedly. She saddled the mare quickly. In a fast, agile motion she mounted, positioned her right leg in the leg hook, and caught the stirrup securely with her left foot. Primly she arranged her skirts.

"You look like you've done that a hundred times," Morgan said admiringly. "When you first came, I didn't think you'd ever be a rider. Especially such a good one."

"That just shows that you don't know everything," Jolie said sassily.

"Guess I don't," Morgan said mildly. He had already saddled Vulcan, so now he mounted him, and the two cantered down the drive.

❧

When they reached the river path, Morgan laughed when he saw Jolie gamely kick the mare into a gallop. Vulcan kept up with them easily, and Morgan watched her ride with a critical eye. He knew horses, and he knew riders. Some people had a natural affinity for riding, and Jolie was one of those. She kept a beautiful erect seat and instinctively knew just how to control the spirited mare.

After a good long run, they slowed down and walked along the path, skirting the river on one side and the Wilderness on the other. It was a delightful time for both of them.

Only the setting sun made Jolie want to return home. "I don't want to be in the Wilderness after dark," she said, casting a dire look at the thick forest. "I would be so afraid."

"You promised me once that you'd never be afraid again," Morgan said quietly. "And I promised you that you would never have any reason to be. Do you remember?"

"Oh yes, I'll never forget that day, Mr. Tremayne," she said in a low voice. "That was the day you came for me and brought me here. You brought me home."

"I'm very glad I did, Jolie."

"So am I, sir. So am I."

When they returned, Morgan waved away Rosh and Santo. "We'll see to the horses. Jolie needs to get used to taking care of her mare." They unsaddled then started brushing down the horses. "You know we've just always called her Little Chestnut. What are you going to name her, Jolie?"

"I'm going to call her Rowena, after the beautiful princess."

"Pretty name for a pretty horse."

They finished up and took the horses into the stables. "I know you're tired, Jolie. Your first ride is always the hardest. Let Rosh and

Santo grain them. Let's go on inside."

"First, I want to thank you again, Mr. Tremayne," she said, holding her hand out. "It's the most wonderful present anyone has ever given me. You're very, very good to me, and I'm grateful."

Morgan caressed her hand, savoring the softness of her skin. He stared down at her, searching her face, her wide, clear forehead, her warm eyes, her tiny straight nose and perfect mouth. She really had grown up, he saw clearly for the first time. Still, she was very young.

Morgan knew when he was an old man he would still have this picture in his mind. The young girl with glossy black hair and enormous dark eyes, staring up at him, filled with gratitude. He knew that he had done the right thing. Not just in giving her the horse, but in everything. For the first time since that cold January day, he knew in his heart that he had done a good thing, a righteous, unselfish thing, and it was good.

For the first time in a long time, Morgan was at peace.

CHAPTER FIFTEEN

After the Seven Days' Battle, the Army of Northern Virginia took the next six weeks to refit and reorganize.

Jolie received letters from Nash Southall when he had time to write. He wrote proudly how he had served with distinction during the constant battles and skirmishes of June and July and had received a promotion to second lieutenant. He said as soon as they returned to Richmond, he would get an extended leave and would return to his home outside of Fredericksburg. The first thing he promised her he would do was go to Rapidan Run to see her and show off his dashing new uniform.

Jolie was thrilled for Nash and his promotion. She was also excited about seeing him again, but when she tried to decide if she was excited to see a good friend or a charming suitor, she had no answers. She hoped seeing him would reveal her true feelings for Nash Southall.

When Nash rode up on a hot morning in the middle of July, Jolie met him at the door, smiling. "You're getting earlier and earlier, Nash. I'm a lady of leisure, you know. You come much earlier, and I might not even be up yet."

"I know that's not true, especially since you got Rowena. You know, Jolie, you don't have to muck out her stall every day," he said as she led him into the study/sitting room. "That's what servants are for."

"I want to do it," Jolie said with emphasis. "She's my responsibility now, and I want to take care of her."

"So many heavy burdens for one so young," he teased.

"You don't make fun of me, Nash Southall," she said, sitting on the sofa beside him. "It wouldn't hurt you to get those manicured hands dirty doing some real work for a change."

"Nah, a gentleman of my station does not do manual labor," he said lazily. "At least, that's what my father's always told me. Say, Jolie, do you think Evetta's got any coffee? I have to admit that I'm still kinda groggy. I was in such a hurry to see you I got up at dawn's crack and galloped off without breakfast."

"I'm sure we can find something for you, you poor, starving, sleepy boy. C'mon. We've all had breakfast hours ago, but Evetta's usually got some biscuits left over. Maybe you can get her to take pity on you and fry you some eggs."

They went out to the kitchen, and although it was with much grumbling, Evetta fixed Nash a full breakfast and a fresh pot of coffee.

After he finished, he asked Jolie, "Would you go for a walk with me? Down to the river?"

"Of course, I know the breeze is much cooler down there." Jolie got her pretty straw hat, and soon she and Nash were walking down the little hill that the farmhouse was perched on to the small landing on the Rapidan. She sat down, took her shoes off, and let her feet dangle in the cool water.

Nash threw himself down beside her, lying on his side and propping one arm on his bent knee.

Jolie said, "Tell me about the battles, Nash. It must be terrible."

A frown marred his smooth features. "Yes, it is terrible. Much worse than I had imagined. It's kinda hard to talk about. You can't explain it. I think only people that have been in a battle really understand what it's like."

"Oh," she said in a small voice. "I apologize, Nash, I didn't mean to make you uncomfortable."

"You couldn't do that if you were trying to," he said warmly. "I'm always comfortable with you, Jolie. You're smart and fun and sweet, and I like being with you very much. Jolie, I wanted to ask you something today. Would you come to my home this weekend and meet my mother? My father, you know, is a major, and he's at camp in Richmond. But I've told my mother and my sister all about you, and they want to meet you."

Instantly Jolie became alert. This sort of thing, she had learned, was serious business. A Southern gentleman didn't invite a young woman to meet his family unless the lady was considered marriageable. And as to her queries of her true feelings for Nash, seeing him had not defined them as she had hoped. "I–I'm not sure, Nash. You've sort of taken me by surprise."

"Please come," he urged her. "You'll like my family, I'm sure. We've got a big house, plenty of servants, and a bridle path in the woods nearby. You can bring Rowena," he said slyly.

"I'll have to ask Mr. Tremayne. I don't know if he'll give me permission."

"Sure he will. Morgan knows my family. It's all perfectly nice and proper. How about if I bring the carriage Friday morning? I'll bring a groom to ride Rowena. And you can stay the night, and I'll bring you back Saturday morning. You'll enjoy it, Jolie. You'll see. My mother's kind of stuffy, like old Morgan, but my sister is lots of fun. And of course, I am superbly entertaining," he finished loftily.

She punched him lightly on the arm. "Silly thing. All right, Nash. If Mr. Tremayne gives me permission, I'll come."

They went back into the house, talking a mile a minute. Morgan had several maps in his study, and Nash showed Jolie where his family's plantation was.

After another half hour, Morgan came in from his morning ride. "Morning, Nash. What are you two cooking up?"

"Nash has asked me to come meet his family this Friday and Saturday," Jolie said excitedly. "May I have permission to go?"

Morgan stared at Nash, considering. "So you want to take Jolie to meet your mother and sister. I assume Major Southall and Blair are still in camp."

Nash nodded. "But it's perfectly proper. You know that, Morgan. My mother's anxious to meet Jolie."

For a moment Jolie thought that Morgan intended to say no. She had learned to read his expressions so easily, and now she saw that he was opposed to the idea of her going.

He looked at Jolie and asked abruptly, "Is this what you want to do, Jolie?"

"I think it would be nice. . .if it's all right with you."

Morgan hesitated, studying them thoughtfully. Finally he shrugged and said, "All right then, you may go. Nash, I'm warning you—"

Nash held up one slim hand and said, "I know, I know. If anything happens to Jolie, you'll kill me in some awful way. She'll be fine, Morgan. I'll take good care of her."

"You'd better," Morgan rasped. "I mean it."

"I know," Nash said, now soberly. "I mean it, too. I'll take good care of her. After all, she's my girl."

The grand five-glassed barouche pulled up in front of Maiden's Way, the Southall mansion, and Jolie was impressed. It was a beautiful home with tall white columns along the wide portico of the main hall, which was two stories. Two long, low graceful wings were on each side.

A dignified woman with snowy-white hair and a young blond

woman with an hourglass figure came out to meet them.

Nash helped Jolie down and performed the proper, intricate introductions.

Mrs. Southall immediately took Jolie's arm, and his sister, Leila, took the other. "I'm so looking forward to finally getting to know you, Miss DeForge. I've heard so much about you from both of my boys. They tell me that you are an excellent nurse. And you're the first young woman that Nash has ever brought home," Mrs. Southall said.

Leila said, "Yes, we were very surprised. Nash has had several lady friends, as young as he is. But this is the first time he's shown much interest."

Jolie thought this was said in a somewhat snobbish manner, but she didn't want to judge Leila Southall after ten seconds of acquaintance. "Nash is a fine young man. I know you must be very proud of him, and Blair, too."

A shadow crossed Mrs. Southall's face, and she replied automatically, "Of course we are proud of our sons. Major Southall knew they would make fine soldiers."

Too late, Jolie remembered that it wasn't considered ladylike to call young gentlemen by their given names. She was beginning to think that this might not be as much fun as she had thought it would be.

They entered the grand foyer. A flying staircase with an ornate black wrought-iron banister soared up to the second floor. A maid in a black dress, white apron, and white cap curtsied as Mrs. Southall led Jolie to the foot of the staircase.

"Lindy will show you to your room, where you can freshen up, my dear. I've had a light luncheon prepared, so we'll expect you back down in about half an hour."

"Yes, Mrs. Southall," Jolie said and followed the maid upstairs. Her room had an enormous grand tester bed, an armoire that would hold a year's wardrobe, and a dressing table with a triple mirror mounted on it. Jolie took off her bonnet and jacket, splashed her face with the cool scented water in the washbowl, and patted her hair. Nervously she wondered how many minutes had gone by, and she decided to venture back downstairs right away.

Lindy was waiting for her and silently conducted her to a grand dining room.

The table seated eighteen, and Jolie saw with a sinking heart that she was stranded in the middle, across from Leila, while Mrs. Southall was at the head and Nash at the foot. He seemed miles away. But he smiled reassuringly to her then said a blessing.

As soon as he finished, Mrs. Southall began questioning Jolie. "I've only met Mr. Tremayne once, when he came to a large party here at Maiden's Way. I'm afraid I wasn't able to talk to him extensively. Tell me, dear, are you in fact a blood relative of his?"

"No, ma'am. My mother died in childbirth, and my father, Henry DeForge, died three years ago. At that time, Mr. Tremayne became my guardian."

"I see," Mrs. Southall said, although it was plain that she didn't. "And was your father able to leave you any kind of legacy?"

Jolie thought that this was positively rude, so she merely said politely, "Yes, ma'am."

The silence after this was very awkward for a few moments, but Jolie didn't care.

Finally Nash spoke up. "You know, I brought Jolie's mare. We're planning on going riding after luncheon. Leila, would you like to go with us?"

"Good heavens, no. It's much too warm for such physical activity. I'm going to take a nap," Leila answered in a bored tone.

Mrs. Southall said thoughtfully, "I think I'll just pop over and visit Amelia Blankenship this afternoon. If you don't feel I'm neglecting our guest, Nash."

"She's my guest, Mother," Nash said with a touch of impatience. "Don't worry. We've got a busy afternoon planned."

"Do you," she said evenly. "That's fine. Just please don't be late for dinner, Nash. Eight o'clock sharp."

"Just like it's been my whole life," he said, grinning crookedly. "I think I've got it now, Mother. Eight o'clock sharp."

Finally they finished the sandwiches and slices of tart apples with cheese, and Jolie and Nash were able to go riding. They rode around some of the cotton fields. Already they were beginning to bloom. Everywhere Jolie looked, she saw orderly rows of the dark shrubs with their virginal white flowers. It amused Nash that she thought cotton fields were pretty.

The woods that were part of the plantation were carefully manicured, and Nash and Jolie dismounted and walked for a long time. Jolie picked long vines of the wild jasmine and trimmed her hat with them. The sweet scent filled the air wherever she went.

At about six o'clock, they started back toward the house. When they came up the long drive, Nash said, "I don't see a servant in sight. Oh, well. You go on in, Jolie, and I'll take the horses around to the stables."

As Jolie went inside, she could hear Mrs. Southall and Leila talking in the parlor.

"I tell you, Leila," Mrs. Southall was saying, "it's the same girl."

"It can't be, Mother!"

"I tell you it is! Mrs. Blankenship told me, and you know she knows about everybody and everything in the county."

"And she said what about this girl?"

"Her mother was black."

"I can't believe it! She looks as white as we are."

"But she's not. She's an octoroon, Amelia said. In fact, she says that she told me all about Henry DeForge and Jolie when he died, and that Morgan Tremayne had taken her in. But somehow I suppose I didn't connect the story with the girl Nash has been telling us about, until this afternoon when she named Mr. DeForge as her father. Good heavens, Nash can't possibly know the girl has black blood in her!"

Jolie heard all she needed to hear and went at once to her room. That night at supper she could barely speak. She suffered through the evening and went to bed, and the next morning she insisted that Nash take her home, very early before his mother and sister had even gotten up.

Nash noticed that Jolie was disturbed, and he asked, "What's wrong, Jolie?"

"I don't want you to come and see me anymore, Nash."

"What have I done?" he asked with amazement. "I haven't hurt your feelings somehow, have I?"

Jolie knew that he would have to know the truth. "I'm an octoroon. You didn't know that, did you?"

Nash swallowed hard. "You—you're part black?"

"One-eighth black, and your mother found out about it yesterday. I'm not welcome here, Nash. I would never be welcome here."

"I don't care if you're an octoroon," Nash insisted. "That doesn't make one bit of difference to me."

"That's very sweet of you, but you have to consider your family. So, find you a nice young woman who has no black blood and court her. Like I said, I don't think I want you to come visit me again, Nash. It's just not meant to be."

CHAPTER SIXTEEN

"Why, it's you—Miss Jolie, isn't it?"

Jolie had come into Fredericksburg without Morgan for the first time. She was determined to buy a gift for Morgan, since he had given her Rowena and her saddle. She was peering into the window of a tailor's shop when she heard her name called.

She turned and saw a Confederate officer coming toward her. "Why, Colonel Seaforth, it's good to see you."

At Bull Run, Colonel Seaforth's two boys, Edward and Billy, had been wounded, and they were two of the men that Amon had loaded up into the wagon and brought to Rapidan Run. Colonel Seaforth had come by to thank them all for taking such good care of his sons. "It's good to see you, too, Miss Jolie."

Jolie saw that the colonel's face was marked with strain, and she knew at once that something was wrong. "Is something troubling you, colonel?" she asked quietly.

"I'm afraid it is. My youngest boy, Billy. He was wounded in action three days ago."

"Not seriously I hope."

Seaforth dropped his eyes and stared at the ground as if he was trying to find exactly the right words, and finally when he raised his head, misery was in his eyes. "It's very serious, Miss Jolie. He's here, at the hospital."

"Where is he wounded?"

"It's a stomach wound."

Jolie did not answer for a moment for an alarm sounded in her spirit. She had heard enough talk about wounds to know that a stomach wound was almost always fatal. "I'm so sorry," she said. "I'd like to go see him. Do you think that would be all right?"

"Oh, yes. He needs somebody to cheer him up. His mother is here, and we take turns, but my wife isn't too well, and this has just almost killed her."

"What about Edward?"

"Oh, he's fine. He's off at Chattanooga right now with his unit, so he can't be here. Could you come now, do you think?"

"Why, of course I could, Colonel. My friend Amon is just down the street, waiting for me with the wagon. Let me go talk to him." She went and told Amon, "I'm going to go to the hospital to visit Billy Seaforth. You remember him? He's wounded again, and it sounds serious this time."

Amon nodded. "I know where the hospital is, Miss Jolie. I'll take you and wait."

Jolie climbed up into the wagon, and Colonel Seaforth paced his horse alongside. He was silent, and Jolie knew that this was indeed likely to be a trying visit.

Colonel Seaforth pulled his horse up in front of the hospital. "If you'll go on in, Miss Jolie, I'll go hitch up my horse and show your man where to park the wagon."

Jolie went inside and was shocked by the odor. The place was a beehive of activity, with doctors and nurses scurrying from one patient to the other. Colonel Seaforth joined her, and Jolie said, "Why, there are some patients out in the hall, Colonel."

"It's that way in every hospital in Virginia," he said sadly. "I wish we could have gotten Billy a room, but there's no such thing anymore."

They made their way through the hospital until finally they arrived at a corridor divided off into wards. "Right in here, Miss Jolie," Seaforth said. They went inside, and Colonel Seaforth led her through the maze of beds. He stopped and said to the woman sitting beside a soldier, "Amy, this is Miss Jolie DeForge. You remember, she took care of Billy and Edward when they were wounded. This is my wife, Amy."

"I'm so sorry about Billy, Mrs. Seaforth," Jolie said. Her eyes went to the figure of the young man on the bed. She was shocked at the pallor of his face. He had a sheet over him, but she could see that the blood had seeped out from under the bandages and stained the sheets underneath him.

Amy Seaforth looked up, her eyes filled with tears. She was a frail woman with silvery hair, and she looked thin and gaunt.

"You look absolutely exhausted, Mrs. Seaforth. Why don't you go and get some rest, and you, too, Colonel. I'll stay right here with Billy."

Colonel Seaforth said with relief, "I've been trying to get her to do that. Come along, dear. Miss DeForge is a wonderful nurse."

"All right. I do think I could rest a little," she said.

"You take as long as you want," Jolie said firmly. "I'll be right here."

The two left, and Jolie sat down beside Billy. His face was flushed, and she put her hand on his forehead. *He's got a fever. I need to bring that down if I can.*

She'd had this problem when she'd taken care of the the wounded men. She knew that the only cure for fever was to take cool, wet cloths and bathe the body. She waited until an orderly went by and said, "I need to get some clean water and some cloths to try to bring this man's fever down."

"Yes, ma'am," the orderly said. He had a harried look on his face and was carrying a filthy mop and a bucket. "You'll have to see

Mrs. Franklin for that."

"Where will I find her?"

"That's her right over there. See? The little woman." He added with a grimace, "With the fussy look on her face."

Jolie did not know the woman, but she found out that Mrs. Beverly Franklin had gone straight to Jefferson Davis and gotten a letter from him that said, "Mrs. Beverly Franklin will be in charge of Unit B. Medical personnel will give her full cooperation." The physicians in charge resented her. The orderlies hated her. But she had given good service and had collected a group of women from town who helped her.

"Mrs. Franklin?"

"Yes, what is it?"

"My name is Jolie DeForge. I would like to try to bring Billy Seaforth's fever down if I could. All I need would be some water and some cloths."

Mrs. Franklin stared at her. "Are you a nurse?"

"No, not really, but I took care of Billy and his brother Edward when they were wounded before."

"At the hospital?"

"No, ma'am, we took them home."

Beverly Franklin's voice was strained, and she was pale with exhaustion. "If you really want to take care of him and you have a place, then I suggest that you take him there."

"Out of the hospital?"

"Look around you. You see how little personal care each man gets. We have to go from one to the other." She hesitated and then added, "He's gravely wounded. The doctors don't offer much hope."

Instantly Jolie made up her mind. "Yes, ma'am. I'll bring my driver in, and if you can get some help, we'll load him in the wagon. We'll take good care of him at our house."

"That would be best. I wish we had a place like that for all the seriously wounded. If you like, I'll send a messenger to Colonel Seaforth to let him know that you've taken Billy to your home."

"Thank you, ma'am."

Thirty minutes later Jolie was in the wagon. She had made a bed for Billy in the back, and instead of riding in the seat next to Amon, she sat down in the wagon bed and put his head in her lap. As they left the hospital, she leaned over and whispered, "Billy, you're going home with us."

"Who is this?" Billy muttered.

"It's Jolie."

"Jolie? You're going to take care of me?"

"Yes, I am, Billy. Now you just lie still and rest. We'll be at Rapidan Run soon."

The sun was low in the sky when Amon pulled up in front of the ranch house.

Morgan came out at once and took one look at Jolie in the back holding the soldier's head in her lap. "What's this, Jolie?"

"It's Billy, Billy Seaforth. He's been badly wounded, Morgan. He wasn't getting any care in the hospital, so I brought him home."

"You did the right thing. Amon, we'll put him in the spare room. Bed's all made up. Will that be all right, Jolie?"

"Yes, if you'll bring him in, I'll get some cool water and some cloths. I need to bring his fever down." She moved inside and told Evetta what she had done.

"That poor young man," Evetta said. "You say he ain't got much chance?"

"That's what the doctors say, but I'm going to pray that he'll be all right." She got the cool water out of the well and several clean cloths. When she got to the room, she found that Amon and Morgan had put the young man in bed. She said, "I'll take care of him now."

"You let me know if you need any help, Miss Jolie," Amon said and left the room.

Morgan stayed and looked down at the pale face. "Well, Billy," he said, "are you awake?"

"Yes. . .yes, sir."

"I'm sorry to see you like this, but we'll do the best we can for you. You know what a good nurse Miss Jolie is."

"Yes, sir, I know that."

"I sent a message to your parents, Billy. They'll be out as soon as your mother is rested up," Jolie said.

"You're too good to me, Miss Jolie."

"Not a bit of it. Now, we're going to get that fever down."

Jolie arched her back for she was tired. Billy had grown worse in the two days he had been there. His parents had moved in to the house. She had grown to love Mrs. Seaforth, and it hurt her to see how the parents were suffering.

She looked out the window and saw that the moon was high in the sky, a silver ball that casts its beam down on the earth. She went over to look out the window and tried to pray, but it seemed she had prayed herself out. The whole household seemed to be quiet in a strange sort of way, as if the wound of the young man had infected them all.

It was half an hour later when she heard Billy crying out in a feeble tone. Quickly she went to him and said, "What is it, Billy?"

"I don't know. I feel. . ." He could not say any more.

Jolie felt his pulse. It was rapid and irregular, and this frightened her. Several times she called his name softly, but he did not respond. Quickly she left the room and went to knock on the door where his parents were. "Colonel Seaforth, Miss Amy, you'd better come."

The colonel opened the door, pulling on a dressing gown. Behind him, Amy said fearfully, "Is it Billy? Is he worse?"

"I think so. I didn't know what to do, but I think you should be there."

They hurried down the hall to Billy's room.

Morgan stepped out of his bedroom and asked, "Is Billy worse?"

"I think he's dying."

Morgan bit his lower lip. "Poor boy. I wish we could do more for him, but you've done all you could, Jolie. If he passes on, you won't have a thing to reproach yourself for."

Jolie said, "Maybe so, but I still feel so helpless."

"So do I. This is the worst of war. So many young boys rode out with high hopes and excited about being in a war, being soldiers, and so many of them have died."

Finally they crept inside Billy's room and hovered just inside the door.

Amy was weeping already, and Colonel Seaforth was standing straight, as if he were before a firing squad.

The minutes passed slowly, and then Billy opened his eyes. He cried out, "Mother, is it you?"

"It's me, Billy."

"I'm glad you got here." He turned to face his father and said, "Sir, I hope I've been a good son."

"The best son in the world, Billy. The very best." Colonel Seaforth's voice was husky, and it broke at the last.

"Thank you, Father. Tell Edward I love him and. . .tell him. . . good-bye. . . ." His voice faded. He took a deep breath, but he did not seem to expel it.

Colonel Seaforth moved around the bed, leaned forward, and kissed his son's forehead. "Good-bye, Billy," he whispered.

Amy Seaforth fell on her son and held him as best she could.

Morgan turned to leave the room, and Jolie followed, knowing she couldn't possibly help the Seaforths in the depths of their grief. When she and Morgan were in the hall, Jolie said, "I can't help crying."

Morgan said, "I could cry myself. Maybe I will." But he didn't.

Jolie knew he was trying to be strong for her.

The rest of the saga was simple. The Seaforths arranged to take the body of their son away, and as they were leaving, they told Jolie and Morgan when the service would be.

Jolie watched the family leave, and sadness gripped her heart.

Morgan did not speak except to say, "We'd better get some rest."

Jolie nodded and retired to her room. She had learned to love Billy Seaforth, as if he were her brother. It was a completely new feeling, and it overwhelmed her.

Jolie finally went to bed and cried herself to sleep.

It had been a week since Billy's funeral, and Jolie had been very aware that Morgan was brooding. His morning rides were getting longer and longer, and when he returned he was unusually silent.

He came back from one of those rides and found her in the stables, currying Rowena. He dismounted and walked over to her.

She saw that there was determination on his face. "What is it, Morgan? You've been so troubled, I know it."

"Jolie, I can't let other men fight for me and for my land. It's time. I have to join the army."

Fear came to Jolie then. "I was so hoping that this day would never come," she said miserably. "I wish you never had to leave me."

"You're a sweet girl, Jolie." He put his arms around her and held her. She knew that it was the action of a man not with romantic overtones but simply with the desire to comfort her.

Desperately she clung to him and thought, *I love him so much, and he doesn't know it and probably never will.*

He released her.

She reluctantly stepped back and asked, "When will you go?"

"Going to leave tomorrow. I've got to get this thing done."

"We'll wait for you to come back, and we'll believe that you will."

Morgan smiled at her. "You're strong, Jolie. I'm proud of you. I always will be."

CHAPTER SEVENTEEN

The following morning, Morgan packed his things, left his room, and found Jolie waiting for him.

"Do you have to go now?"

"Yes, I do, Jolie." He saw that she looked troubled and felt a moment's guilt. "I hate to leave you like this."

"I don't understand. I thought you were against the war."

Morgan shrugged his shoulders. "It's hard to explain, Jolie. I expect there are lots of men like me who hate slavery but have to defend their native states. As I told you yesterday, I just can't let other men do my fighting for me." He saw that she was afraid and said, "You remember now, if I don't come back, you know where your money is. Amon and Evetta will take good care of you and help you."

"All right." She hesitated and then asked, "Have you told Leona about signing up?"

"No, I'm going to do that right now."

"When will the army be leaving?"

He smiled briefly and shook his head. "I don't have any idea,

Kitten. To tell you the truth, I'm probably going to be stuck in Richmond since I'm volunteering for the quartermaster division. So don't worry too much."

"I can't help it. You've already said that the whole Army of Northern Virginia will be going out to meet the Yankees."

"I guess we will. They've got a new general named Pope. Nobody knows much about him, but he can't whip Bobby Lee, as all of our men call the general." He leaned down and kissed her cheek. "I know I don't have to tell you to pray for me."

She threw her arms around his neck and gave him a desperate hug. "No, you don't. I'll pray for you, Morgan. Always."

Jolie watched Morgan ride away and felt a tremendous sense of emptiness. She had felt loss before, when her father died and when Billy died. But now there was anger mixed in with her grief, and she knew it was directed toward Leona Bledsoe.

He loves that woman, and she's nothing but a flirt! She likes to play with men just like a child plays with dolls, and Morgan can't see it. He's a fool where that woman is concerned!

She reveled in her anger for a few minutes. But then she remembered what Morgan had said, and she said a prayer for him instead. Her anger dissipated like dandelion fluff on a strong summer wind.

"Morgan, I'm so glad to see you."

Morgan had arrived at the Bledsoe residence and had been greeted by Leona, who had answered the front door.

"I was watching out the window, and I saw you ride up. Can you stay long?"

"No, I've got some news, Leona."

"What sort of news?" Her eyes grew larger. She looked beautiful, her complexion glowing, her eyes luminous. Her wine-colored dress set off her figure admirably.

"I'm joining the army, Leona. Today."

Instantly Morgan saw that the news struck Leona as being something absolutely wonderful. She hugged him then pulled him by the hand toward the parlor. "I'm so proud of you! Come on, we have to tell my family."

Morgan allowed himself to be pulled inside, and soon he was in the drawing room with Mr. and Mrs. Bledsoe.

"We've got news!" Leona said excitedly. She paused for dramatic effect and said, "Morgan's joining the army."

"Wonderful!" Mr. Bledsoe exclaimed. He came forward with a huge smile to shake Morgan's hand. "I'm pleased to hear it, my boy. Very pleased indeed!"

Leona said, "Sit down, Morgan, and tell us all about it. Have you spoken to General Lee yet?" She patted the sofa for him to sit close beside her.

Morgan sat down and said slowly, "No, I have no intention of talking to General Lee. I'm just going into Richmond and volunteering for the quartermaster's division. It's hard to explain, but in the last year I've had lots of purchasing experience. I figure I'll make a pretty good scrounger."

All of the bright smiles around him faded. Leona repeated, "Scrounger?" as if it was in a language she had never heard. "But— Morgan, what will be your rank?"

"Private, I'm sure," he said as lightly as he could. "I'm no military man, and I'm sure no officer."

Benjamin Bledsoe was now frowning darkly. "Let me get this straight. You're telling us that you know General Lee and Mrs. Lee personally, and he might even be said to be in your debt for the times you helped Mrs. Lee move around, and you aren't even going to go to him and ask him to give you a commission? He could do it so easily, and he should do it!" When he finished, he was almost shouting.

Morgan said stiffly, "Mr. Bledsoe, I don't mean to correct you, but you're just wrong with that whole speech. General Lee owes me nothing. I helped Mrs. Lee because I'm her friend. And—and—you're just wrong, sir. Wrong about him, and wrong about me."

Leona said indignantly, "What are you talking about, Morgan? You're not making any sense. Of course you deserve a commission. There's nothing at all wrong with seeking that. It's done all the time, by all kinds of honorable men! It shows courage and ambition."

"No, it doesn't, Leona," he retorted. "How can I explain it to you? I can't even believe that we're arguing about this."

"I can't either," Leona said, her dark eyes flashing dangerously. "Morgan, it's really very simple. If you insist on joining the army as a private and your highest aspiration is to be a scrounger, I really have nothing more to say to you."

He stared at her in disbelief. "You mean, we've been together all this time, and suddenly you're telling me that I'm not good enough for you?"

"That's what she's telling you," Benjamin Bledsoe interjected. "I've had my doubts about you for a while now, Morgan, and I was right to have them."

Morgan never took his eyes off Leona.

She met his gaze defiantly. "I'm sorry, Morgan, but I don't think we should see each other anymore. You're just not the man that I thought you were."

He stood slowly. "If you think I'm the kind of man to smugly ask for political favors of a man that I respect more than any man I've ever known, then I'm happy to tell you that you're right. I'm definitely not that man." He left the Bledsoe home without another word.

He mounted Vulcan and rode south toward Richmond. After about a mile, his anger faded and was replaced with depression. *I've lost Leona, and now, of all times! When I'm going to war!* He felt sorry for himself for a while, but then he reflected, *It's not that I just lost Leona. I don't think I ever really had her. I don't even think I ever really knew her even.* This comforted him somewhat.

But lingering in his mind all the way to Richmond was the wish that he could talk to Jolie. She would comfort him; she always did. But now it was too late. He had an appointment to keep.

CHAPTER EIGHTEEN

Morgan went into Richmond, signed up, and requested the quartermaster division. When he told the recruiting officer of his background, the man had immediately assigned him to it. He'd been given a desk in crowded headquarters and told to find horses, horses, and more horses.

Three days later, he got word from his amazed lieutenant that he was to report to General Lee's office. Morgan had to wait for three hours in an anteroom that was like an anthill, but finally a young corporal called him into Lee's office.

Lee stood up and came around his desk to shake Morgan's hand. "Private Tremayne, it's good to see you. Please sit down."

Morgan sat on a plain straight chair in front of Lee's desk, which had many papers on it, but they were all arranged neatly.

Lee sat down and said, his dark eyes alight, "I had to hear from my wife that you had enlisted. Then I had a time chasing you down. I was a little surprised to hear you were crammed into a corner somewhere shuffling papers."

"Important papers, sir," Morgan said. "You see, I know where to find horses that no other man can find. In this army, that's real job security."

"Yes, sir, it surely is," he agreed. He regarded Morgan steadily for long moments. "As I said, I was a little surprised to hear that you had enlisted, Private Tremayne. I've certainly had many other men, to whom I owed a much lesser debt of gratitude, come to consult with me when they joined the army."

"You don't owe me any kind of debt at all, sir. It was a pleasure for me to help Mrs. Lee. I enjoy her company very much."

"Yes, so do I," he said drily. "I understand that you specifically requested the quartermaster division. You feel that is where you can best serve?"

"Sir, I would really rather be taking care of horses, as I obviously love to do. But under the circumstances, I thought I would be most useful in procurement and forage."

Lee nodded. "That's thoughtful of you, Private Tremayne. Many men never seem to be able to understand exactly where they fit in. However, I would like to make a request of you."

Surprised, Morgan said, "Anything, sir."

"I would like for you to consider volunteering as my aide-de-camp. I can think of no other man better suited to take care of my horses and those of my staff. Also, I know that you know this country, and you're probably a very good scrounger. That may not be an oft-used title, but it's certainly an important one."

"Sir, I think I'd be an expert scrounger. It's an honor to serve you, General Lee, and I accept your offer, with thanks," Morgan said happily.

"Good. Now, I suppose you'd better have a rank. The general commanding's staff usually does," Lee said reluctantly.

"Oh no, sir, no. I can't possibly accept that," Morgan said and saw the relief flood Lee's face. "I don't want to pretend to be an officer. I don't have the training or the knowledge. And it seems to me, sir, that the general commanding can have anyone on his staff that he likes."

Lee gave him his wintry smile. "Come to think of it, you're correct, Private Tremayne. Very well. Please report to my chief of staff, and he'll outline your responsibilities."

"Thank you, General Lee, for your faith in me," Morgan said simply and then took his leave.

❧

Watching the battle unfold, Morgan had been amazed at the daring of General Robert E. Lee. He had known the man as a person of infinite tact and patience and of great calmness and serenity of purpose. But Morgan hadn't realized that Robert E. Lee was daring, too.

Early in August, Lee had sent Stonewall Jackson on a mission that had defeated part of Pope's army. Pope had lost that skirmish but had assumed that Lee would remain near Richmond. After all, Pope had forty-five thousand men against Jackson's twenty-four thousand.

By shifting their troops around, Lee and Jackson had an army that outnumbered Pope five to four. Unfortunately, a copy of Lee's attack orders was carelessly lost by one of Lee's officers.

When General Pope saw the order that was brought to him, he exclaimed, "With this paper, if I can't beat Bobby Lee, I'll retire."

In two days, Lee realized that Pope would have seventy thousand men, and shortly after that, when he was joined by other Union forces, he would have over a hundred thousand. In the face of this emergency, Morgan was shocked, as was the entire army, when Lee divided his army into two forces. He sent Jackson on a large march completely around the Union right flank, and on August 26th, Jackson struck with all his force. The Union troops had no idea that Jackson was near, and they were fragmented.

By August 30th, Pope had made every wrong move that a general could make. Well-placed, massed Confederate artillery broke the Union assault. When Longstreet hit the Union forces, the battle was lost completely, and Union forces retreated into the defenses of Washington yet again.

In the North, they called it Second Manassas. In the South, they called it Second Bull Run. Everyone called it a solid Confederate victory.

The troops returned to Richmond once more. As it was after every battle, the hospitals overflowed with wounded men. Again they were quartered in private homes and warehouses and barns. There were funerals every day, which were a taxation on the spirits of Richmond citizens.

General Lee gave Morgan a two-day leave of absence, and Morgan spurred Vulcan to an all-out gallop all the way to Rapidan Run.

Jolie must have been watching for him, because as he neared the stables, she flew out of the back door. He barely had time to get off his horse before she threw herself at him.

He caught her up and smelled the freshness of her hair and was shocked at the firm roundness of her figure. He had to remind himself again and again that she was a woman now and not the little girl he had first known. "Aw, Jolie, don't make so much of this," he said.

"I will if I want to!" Jolie cried. He saw there were tears in her eyes. She tugged at his arm. "Come on into the kitchen. I know you're starved."

"I could use some of Evetta's good cooking, that's for sure."

Soon everyone was in the kitchen, and Morgan was eating and, between bites, telling of the battle and what it was like being on General Lee's staff. After lunch he said, "Come on, Jolie. Come walk with me. I want to go see my horses."

The two went out and walked along the fenced-in pastures. It was a pleasant day. Summer was dying slowly and reluctantly, and the air was heavy like old wine.

For Morgan it was a time of joyful relaxation. On the way to battle and in the midst and fury of it, his nerves had been pressed to the limit. Now he soaked in the sight of his horses, the mares contentedly grazing, the new foals playing, the geldings running just for the fun of it. All thoughts and images of war and battle faded away. "It's good to be home," he said quietly.

"It's good to have you home."

Jolie stayed close to him all afternoon, as he talked to Amon and went through the stables, looking over every horse and checking the tack and the feed. Finally she said, "Let's go in, Morgan. You probably need to take a nap before supper."

"Sleeping in my own bed sounds really good. I think I will."

Morgan slept until supper, got up, and ate like a starved wolf. "I had forgotten what a fine cook you are, Evetta. This is delicious."

"Nothing but barbequed ribs."

"Always my favorite, you do them so well."

Evetta smiled and, in a rare show of affection, came and brushed Morgan's hair back from his eyes. "We done miss you around here, Mr. Tremayne. We surely have."

"I've missed all of you, Evetta. You've done a good job, Amon, you and the boys. The place looks great."

After supper, Evetta and Amon left, and Ketura went up to her bedroom.

Morgan and Jolie went into his study and sat quietly for a long time, watching the small cheerful fire that Morgan had built. Morgan felt a sense of peace soaking in.

After about an hour Morgan said, "You know, I'd like to have some popcorn. You have any?"

"Yes, I'll make it." Jolie got up quickly and found the corn and the long-handled covered pan they popped it in. Soon the homey sound of corn popping filled the room. She poured it into two bowls then sat down and started munching.

Morgan looked down in his bowl and said, "I wonder why

some corn pops and some doesn't. We always called these that didn't pop 'old maids.'"

"Why do you call them that?"

"I don't know. Because they didn't do any good, I guess."

"Not very fair to women. Some women can't be wives. Nobody asks them."

He grinned at her and said, "And old bachelors just get to be crusty old complainers. Like me."

"Not like you," Jolie said firmly. "Oh, I just remembered, I have a letter you'll want to read." She went to the desk and got it. "It's from Colonel Seaforth."

Jolie watched his face as Morgan read it. When he had finished, Jolie saw that he was grieved.

"They miss that boy of theirs, don't they?" Morgan said quietly.

"Of course they do. He was such a sweet boy. Such a loss!"

They munched for a while in companionable silence.

Jolie finally asked, "Are you sorry you joined the army?"

"I can't say I'm sorry, no. I know it was the right thing to do. But it's hard, Jolie. It's the hardest thing I've ever done."

She considered him. The lamplight fell across the surface of his cheek, darkening and sharpening the angles of it. She saw in him those things his friends and the people who knew him loved—the tenacity, the faithfulness that never wavered, the fierce loyalty, the determination to always do the right thing. He was a man to stay by his friends, for good or bad, to the end of time. These were qualities that people admired in Morgan, and Jolie admired them, too. It had nothing to do with the feelings she had for him. She just recognized him for what he was, an honest, honorable man.

"I wish you didn't have to go back. I wish this war was over, and you could stay home," she said. Her voice was so low it was almost inaudible.

"I wish that, too. But you do understand, don't you, Jolie, that this is something I have to do?"

"I do understand. I know that's just the kind of man you are."

"Sometimes I wonder what kind of man I am," he said regretfully. "But one thing I do know, it was time for me to join the army and fight. Fight for this place, for Amon and Evetta and their children, for my family, and for you. I'm just glad that you know that, Jolie."

"There's something else I have to ask you, Morgan. Are you going to marry Leona Bledsoe?"

Ruefully, he answered, "No, I'm not. Or rather, Leona Bledsoe isn't going to marry *me*."

"What?"

Morgan shrugged. "She decided that she didn't want to have anything to do with a lowly private."

"But you love her, don't you? Did you—are you terribly hurt, Morgan?" Jolie asked anxiously.

"I was, but somehow now it doesn't seem to matter quite so much. I haven't forgotten her, but no, it doesn't hurt anymore."

Jolie felt a rush of overwhelming relief wash over her. Then she had a thought that shocked her. *I could make him want me. I could lean against him and kiss him and make him forget Leona Bledsoe once and for all!* Jolie immediately chastised herself, angry that she would even think of using such wicked feminine wiles to trap Morgan.

She was distracted for the remainder of their conversation, and when Morgan said good night, she hurried upstairs before he kissed her on the cheek. She definitely didn't trust herself.

As she lay in bed, wide awake, she thought, *I have to be better than that. Morgan is too good a man to have me use cheap tricks on him like Leona did. But oh, how I wish he would love me! I know I'll never love another man in my whole life.*

Please, God, keep him safe. Keep him safe. . . .

She finally fell asleep, still praying for the man she loved.

PART FOUR

CHAPTER NINETEEN

Private Tremayne stuck his head inside the brightly lit tent.

Captain John M. Allen, assistant quartermaster forage, did not look up from his camp desk. He was scribbling furiously. "Yes?" he said absently.

"Sir, I'm reporting back from leave and ready for duty," Morgan said, stepping inside the tent and saluting.

"Hm?" He finished a sentence with a flourish and a final period then looked up. He was a young man, only twenty-nine years old, but he was balding and wore thick spectacles that glinted oddly in the light. And his demeanor was that of a much older man. He was grave and always seemed distracted, as if his mind was racing ahead of the moment to the next order, the next column of numbers, the next inventory report. "Oh, it's you, Tremayne. Yes, yes, go on. You know what you should be doing better than I." He went back to his scritch-scratching.

Morgan ducked back out of the tent and headed behind the line of officers' tents that surrounded General Lee's modest tent headquarters. The horses were picketed there in neat rows underneath a stand of oak trees.

Morgan frowned as he passed them. He saw that someone had put a nervous, flighty gelding right next to Traveler. He would have to remedy that right away.

A good-size tent was pitched nearby, and Morgan went there first. It was not lit, and as he neared, he could see in the darkness that two figures sat on camp stools just outside the tent flap. "Hello, Meredith, Perry. I'm back, as I guess you can see."

Both men murmured, "Good evenin', Private Tremayne."

Perry was General Lee's body servant. A tall, solemn black man, he had all the dignity such an exalted position should bestow upon a man.

Meredith was Lee's cook. He was average sized, of average height, but his wide grin was like a summer sunburst. He was much more jovial than Perry, but then he wasn't actually in General Lee's presence very often. Morgan suspected that when Meredith talked with the general, he was like everyone else was, pretty much: on his best, most dignified, most polished behavior. General Lee brought these finer qualities out in a man. Meredith said, "I wanted to burn your camp stool for kindling 'cause you didn't scrounge me enough rich pine to get a hot quick fire going this morning. But Perry wouldn't let me."

"You rascal," Morgan said as he popped into the tent, retrieved his stool from underneath his bunk, and popped back out again. "Right over there, on the west side of this field, is a pine forest. You should have gone out there and found your own rich pine for the general's breakfast."

"Was too late by the time I knowed I was short on it," Meredith said lazily. " 'Sides, that's your job."

"Yes, guess it is," Morgan admitted. "That's my title these days. Aide-de-Camp, Scrounging. And Private Tremayne-my-horse-needs-blank. Make up any ending you choose."

It was true, but Morgan was not displeased with his duties. Far from it, he was doing exactly what he wanted to do. He helped

Captain Allen find forage for the horses all over the South. He knew every farm, every barn, every storage shed and storehouse in northern Virginia, and he could always find chickens, beef, eggs, bacon, flour, cornmeal, and sugar for General Lee and his staff. But mostly he took care of Traveler, General Lee's beloved horse, and all of the staff officers' horses.

These staff officers had deeply resented Morgan at first. Word had gotten around that he was the only person General Lee had personally requested as an aide-de-camp. But Robert E. Lee would never in his life show favoritism to any man under his command, and his staff came to see that he treated Morgan with the same courtesy and respect that he treated everyone else, whether a general or a servant.

Morgan made an effort to show Lee's officers that he had no ambitions for promotion or recognition. From his very first day in the field, he wordlessly groomed every officer's horse, checked each animal regularly to make sure it was in sound health, paid endless attention to each horse's preferred diet, checked the shoes of each, and even brushed each horse's teeth. Without being asked, he took care of all the tack, keeping the saddles clean and well-shined, the stirrups set just right, even the saddlebags and rifle sheaths polished.

Soon it was true. Everyone, from young couriers to assistant adjutant generals, was coming to him and saying, "Private Tremayne, my horse needs. . ." Anything from shoeing to liniment to a tooth check to a hoarded apple filled in the blank.

In those first few hard and lonely days, as they marched to engage the enemy, Morgan had also started helping Perry and Meredith with the general's supply wagon. In spite of the fact that General Lee's camp tent was not very large and his furnishings were simple and few, both men were constantly anxious that they should have everything perfect for him. A clean tent, clean sheets for his cot, clean uniforms, polished boots, adequate lamplight, plenty of wood for his camp stove, a good stock of food staples, seasonings, coffee, tea, and fresh fruit when they could find it.

Morgan helped them with his expert scrounging, and he helped them to organize everything in the wagon so they could quickly load up and move or unload and camp. He had his own little tent, of course, but Meredith and Perry's was actually a four-man tent, and eventually he just sort of moved in on them. They had the room, and it seemed so much trouble to pitch his own tent. It suited Morgan just fine, though it caused some whispers among the officers, particularly the ones who were slaveowners. Morgan didn't care.

Now, as the three men sat on the little stools looking out at the sweet Virginia night, Morgan said, "I brought us two tins of tea and some coffee and sugar. How's the general's stock holding out?"

"Jest fine since you been with us, Mr. Morgan," Meredith answered.

"Good. In a couple of weeks, I'm going to have three hundred acres of rye and barley ready to harvest, so the horses will be fixed up, too. Maybe Captain Allen will give me and about ten stout fellows leave to go harvest it."

Perry pursed his lips. "We'll have to see 'bout that. 'Cause we're heading up North, you know. To Maryland."

"We are?" Morgan said with astonishment. "When?"

"Day or two, I gather," Perry answered. He didn't purposely eavesdrop on Lee's councils of war, but like most people who were accustomed to having servants, General Lee rarely took note of their presence.

Morgan jumped up. "I better get to seeing to those horses right now. I've been gone two days. I'll bet they're in an unholy mess. Did you know that some idiot picketed Colonel Corley's fidgety gelding right next to Traveler?"

Perry and Meredith exchanged amused glances. "No, sir, Mr. Morgan, I sure didn't know that," Meredith said solemnly. "You'd better get to tendin' to that right now."

"I sure better," he grumbled, heading off toward the horses. But he heard his two friends talking as he walked.

"I ain't never seen the like of a man that loves horses so much," Perry observed.

"Oh, yes you have, Perry," Meredith said. "His name is Marse Robert E. Lee."

Morgan couldn't help but grin as he continued toward his favorite task.

The only way in which Morgan had insisted on insinuating himself near to General Lee was because he was determined from the beginning to follow the general when he was in the saddle. It was Lee's habit, as the army marched, for him to ride with them, passing through the ranks of cheering men to encourage them. And he constantly rode around the battlefields, surveying the ground with his field glasses, watching the masses of men and artillery as they maneuvered. Normally when General Lee was on the move, only two or three of his most senior staff and a few ready couriers accompanied him.

On August 15th, when General Lee left Richmond to face General Pope, Morgan saddled up Vulcan and moved up behind the three couriers who were following General Lee and his officers. The first time Lee stopped for a short rest, Morgan dismounted quickly and pushed his way rudely up to Lee and took Traveler's reins without a word as Lee dismounted.

"Good afternoon, Private Tremayne," Lee said, the first words he had said to him since that day two weeks previously in his office.

"Good afternoon, sir," Morgan replied.

General Lee walked to the side of the road and stretched a bit, slapping his gauntlets into one palm, a habit that he had.

Morgan gently led Traveler and Vulcan to the side of the road and stood, waiting.

Colonel Robert H. Chilton, Lee's chief of staff, stalked up to Morgan and said in a severe undertone, "General Lee did not request that you accompany him personally, Private Tremayne."

"No, sir, he didn't," Morgan said. "But it seems to me that you and the other officers would appreciate someone just to see to the horses while you're conferring with the general."

"Oh," he said, his severe expression lightening just a bit. "I see. Perhaps you're right, Private. But be sure you remain quiet and unobtrusive. General Lee does not appreciate any fussing and flapping in his presence."

"No, sir," Morgan said respectfully. "I will be quiet, sir, and I'll keep the horses calm."

"See that you do," he snapped then thrust the reins of his horse into Morgan's hand.

Soon Morgan was holding the reins of five horses: Traveler, Vulcan, two belonging to colonels, and one belonging to a major. Quickly Morgan improvised. He tucked Vulcan's reins into his belt, casting a cautious glance back at his temperamental horse. Vulcan seemed to stare back at him with disdain and tossed his head, but he didn't attempt to pull away. Morgan then gently pushed Traveler to his right side, followed by a colonel's horse. Morgan looped Traveler's reins around his thumb and forefinger and the other set of reins around his ring and pinky fingers. He did the same thing with the horses on his left side and jockeyed the reins around the same way. This way, two horses were on one side of him, two on the other, and Vulcan behind. Morgan kept up a soft, reassuring nonsense conversation to keep the horses still and calm, hoping that it wouldn't be in the same class as fussing and flapping.

When General Lee and the three officers returned to retrieve their horses, General Lee merely said, "Thank you, Private Tremayne." But Morgan saw a quick gleam of amusement in his eyes, and he knew that General Lee had overheard Colonel Chilton and was amused, probably about the fussing and flapping. Of course, Lee could never single Morgan out by having a light conversation with him; there were about a hundred thousand men who would love his doing just that with them, and it would cause untold jealousies if one man was that lucky. Still, Morgan knew that he and General Robert E. Lee had just shared a private joke. Morgan knew it would be a treasured memory to him all of his days.

Morgan saw the reality of Meredith's comments about Lee's love for horses as they neared that all-important boundary, the Potomac River.

It had been raining steadily for three days and two nights, and the roads were like mucky bogs. In some places the artillery caissons sank to the wheel hubs.

Morgan was following Lee and his officers, having pulled up closer behind than usual because the general was riding right through the marching men. They always pressed him, the boldest reaching out to simply touch Traveler, who always bore such adulation with great dignity. Many times the men would fall into step behind General Lee, and Morgan had been obliged to push through them so that he wouldn't fall far behind.

They passed the marching infantry and began to ride alongside the road because the artillery wagons were strung out in a long line. The second caisson they approached was stuck, its left wheel canted down into a deep rut, the cannon muzzle pointed crazily up toward the nearby hills.

Morgan heard shouting and cursing, and as he came around the caisson, he saw a man beating a horse. Instantly he spurred Vulcan and flew to a stop just beside the man. Morgan opened his mouth to shout at him, but behind his left ear he heard, "You, sir! Stop beating that horse this instant!"

Morgan saw the man freeze, stick in midair, staring in horror, his mouth open.

Morgan turned to see General Robert E. Lee, his eyes flashing dark fire, his mouth set in a thin grim line. Righteous indignation seemed to form a red aura around him. It grew strangely quiet.

General Lee spoke again, and his voice was quieter, but his face was still flushed with anger. "You are doing no good to your horse, your men, or your army, Sergeant." Sharply he turned Traveler and rode past the caisson.

After a moment, Morgan recovered himself and followed him. He looked back at the man, whose face was such a tragic mask that he looked more like he'd been gut-shot than reprimanded. Morgan knew exactly how he felt but had little sympathy for him. Mostly he was happy that the man had suffered such shame. Personally Morgan thought all men who beat horses should be beaten themselves.

All that long march, Morgan reflected upon the incident. It was a side of Robert E. Lee that he had never seen, never even imagined. To him, Lee had always been the perfect picture of a gentleman, unfailingly courteous, diplomatic, tactful, gallant to women, patient and kind to children, and longsuffering with the burdens of being a leader of men.

Finally Morgan came to realize that, yes, Lee had all those virtues, but he must also feel the heat of strong emotions, because he would not be a whole man if he did not. He just kept his temper tightly controlled, because that was the kind of man that he was. It was very rare for Lee to allow that temper to show, and Morgan was convinced that when he did, it was because he chose to do so. Morgan valiantly swore to himself that he would never *ever* do anything to deserve that kind of treatment from Lee. He had seen that there were worse things than beatings after all.

The Army of Northern Virginia marched into Maryland, fifty thousand strong. General George McClellan, back in command, marched south with ninety thousand men. They met at a little town called Sharpsburg. By it ran a lazy stream, Antietam Creek. After three days in September of 1862, Sharpsburg in the South and Antietam in the North automatically conjured up visions of piles of dead bodies. September 17th came to be known as the Bloodiest Day.

General McClellan, true to form, could not bring himself to

order his troops to fight the fast-maneuvering Confederates in a large-scale attack. He threw in his men piecemeal. He sent Joe Hooker in here, and Stonewall Jackson furiously beat him back. McClellan ordered Burnside to cross Antietam by that bridge, and his troops were mercilessly slaughtered. Two fresh divisions arrived over there, but McClellan said they should not engage until they had received "rest and refreshment."

No one could ever figure out why McClellan simply would not order his army to fight the kind of all-out battles that were crucial for victory in the field. It was not that he was personally a coward. He had served with distinction in the Mexican War. He had even served briefly with Robert E. Lee, surveying Tolucca. For his service he was twice brevetted.

Little Mac did have a tendency to procrastinate and dawdle, but this still did not explain why, when he finally did have a superb army fielded, he would not fight the enemy. Some suggested that he was simply intimidated by Robert E. Lee, and this may have very well been true. But particularly at Sharpsburg, where he had the advantage in numbers of almost two to one, it would seem that he could have rock-solid confidence enough to simply overrun the ragtag horde of screaming rebels.

But he did not, and after three days of fighting, Lee was withdrawing back across the Potomac, his walking wounded and ambulances and slow supply train completely unmolested.

General Lee's plan of invading the North had failed. Though the Army of Northern Virginia had a tactical victory over the Union Army, they could not hold the ground, and so in reality the outcome was inconclusive. The North had won a strategic victory because the rebels had to withdraw.

And so General Lee led his men back to blessed Virginia, to the fertile and peaceful Shenandoah Valley to rest and refit. It was fall when they came back home, and it was beautiful. For this, and for many other things, General Robert E. Lee gave simple thanks to God.

SURRENDER

❧

Morgan Tremayne found himself in a singular position in the Army of Northern Virginia. He was certain that no other private was as fortunate. As they readied to march, he reflected that the thousands of lowly privates, corporals, and sergeants couldn't possibly be as well-informed as he was. He knew exactly where they were going—Fredericksburg—and exactly what they were facing—125,000 Yankees. He knew that again General Robert E. Lee was outnumbered, because Morgan understood that once the two corps of the thinly-stretched army gathered together to face this new threat, there would barely be seventy-eight thousand Rebels.

The average man in the field never had such information until he was looking across some creek or pasture at another average man in blue. In fact, Stonewall Jackson was so secretive that even his brigade commanders sometimes did not know where they were going. Stonewall had a habit of going around, loudly asking if anyone had good maps of the roads to X when their destination was actually Y.

"Hit don't fool nobody no more," Meredith had told Morgan with amusement. "Wherever Ol' Blue Light's axing for maps, they knows that's the place where they can't be found."

"True, but I guess they still don't know the place where they can be found," Morgan had said, chuckling.

Meredith and Perry were half of the reason Morgan was so well-informed. Most of the officers had their own cooks, and cooks talk. Morgan reflected wryly that if a spy was smart, he'd forget trying to infiltrate the upper echelon of officers and just become a cook. They heard everything, and they told each other everything.

Perry, on the other hand, was stubbornly closemouthed. He heard practically every meeting that General Lee had at his head-quarters. For months he wouldn't tell Morgan anything, and it frustrated Morgan to no end, but he finally gave up trying to weasel information out of the silent, somber man.

However, Morgan was as fully dedicated as Perry in ensuring that General Lee never had to worry about his clothing, personal equipment, and supplies. Morgan made sure that Perry had chalk for white gauntlets, boot polish, leather soap and conditioner, valet brushes, laundry soap, plenty of needles and thread, and brass and silver polish. Whenever Morgan had time after caring for the horses, he would help Perry mend or launder General Lee's clothing, linens, and blankets.

It was during these quiet nights in winter camp that Perry began to talk to Morgan about the events of the day. Morgan determined to keep Perry's confidences and never spoke to anyone else about things Perry had told him, not even Meredith.

And, too, Morgan himself became party to many of General Lee's talks with his officers. Lee rode Traveler every day, and often his commanders and staff accompanied him. Over time they began to regard Morgan much as they did Meredith and Perry, as a useful servant tending the horses but not as a person that would have any interest in matters above their station. They talked freely while he stood, mutely holding the horses or riding just behind General Lee and overhearing every word.

When he wrote to Jolie, Morgan was always extremely careful never to reference exactly where the army was, and particularly any future plans that he learned of. He knew all too well that this, not enemy spying, was the way word got around the country about the army's movements. The mail was running faithfully, and practically every home, plantation, or shack in Virginia had someone's mother, father, sister, or brother there. Men who would rather die a torturous death than betray the Confederacy unwittingly mailed out all kinds of information every day. Morgan made certain that he was never guilty of this.

On October 6th, General Lee got word that the Yankees had crossed the Potomac and were heading south. That day Morgan wrote a long letter to Jolie, telling her all about the beautiful fall hardwoods in the mountains and about all the horses he cared for.

But on November 6th, when Perry told Morgan that the Army of the Potomac was at full strength and heading for Fredericksburg, Morgan agonized over the letter he wrote to Jolie that day. He ached to warn her that apparently a big battle was going to be fought just ten miles from Rapidan Run. At the end of the day, his letter was all about the gallons of maple syrup he'd found at a nearby farm and the kind farmer who had happily sold it to him for practically worthless Confederate money.

On November 9th, it was reported to headquarters that for some reason the Union army had come to an abrupt stop in their march to the Rappahannock River. The next day—within twenty-four hours after the Army of the Potomac itself had found out—Lee knew the reason for the halt. Little Mac had been replaced by General Ambrose E. Burnside, and the transfer of command had taken place on that day.

As they washed General Lee's dishes that night, Perry told Morgan, "Gen'ral Longstreet had supper with Marse Robert tonight, you know."

"Yes, I saw him ride up," Morgan said. "How is Old Pete these days?"

Perry appeared to be considering a very complex question, for he sucked on his lower lip for a time then said, "D' ye know, Marse Robert calls him 'My Old War Horse.'"

"No, I didn't know that," Morgan said with interest. Such were priceless tidbits that he often gleaned from Perry.

"Yassuh, he does," Perry asserted. "Marse Robert, he can talk to Gen'ral Longstreet easier than some of them younger, flightier officers. They say Gen'ral Longstreet is slow, but I'm of a mind that he's careful. Anyways, Marse Robert tole him tonight at supper what he thought of this new man Mr. Linkum is a-throwin' at him now."

Perry had very complex unwritten and unspoken rules for his conversations, and Morgan knew them now. If he showed too much eagerness to hear this conversation repeated, Perry would stubbornly clam up. If, however, Morgan showed only mild interest, Perry would repeat the conversation or the comment, sometimes word for word. So Morgan kept vigorously scrubbing a pillowcase on the scrubboard and said carelessly, "Is that right."

"Dat's right. Gen'ral Longstreet tole Marse Robert that this man named Burnside is the Yankee gen'ral now, and he was glad 'bout it. Said this Burnside weren't near as good as Gen'ral McClellan. But seems like Marse Robert was sorry to hear him go. 'We always understood each other so well. I fear they may continue to make these changes till they find someone whom I don't understand,' said Marse Robert."

Morgan almost smiled. It was a typically genteel comment Robert E. Lee would make about a deadly enemy. It was funny, too, because whenever Perry quoted Lee, his speech became flawless, as Lee's was. Morgan liked the old servant and had come to enjoy his company greatly, whether he was telling Morgan crucially sensitive information or just discussing which kind of laundry soap he had found most effective.

Somewhat to Morgan's surprise, he realized that he thought of Perry and Meredith not as servants or as two more of hundreds of black men he had known but as valued friends.

The Army of Northern Virginia left the pastoral hills around Culpeper and marched east. On the storm-swept afternoon of November 20, 1862, General Lee handed Traveler's reins to Morgan and took half a dozen steps up to the crest of a hill. He took out his field glasses and studied the ground.

Below him lay the old picturesque hamlet of Fredericksburg, nestled in neat squares along the flat west bank of the Rappahannock River. The east bank rose up into a range of hills called Stafford Heights, and this was where the enemy was encamped. But behind Fredericksburg, the land sloped up gently to this long wooded ridge that was about the same elevation as Stafford Heights. Lee knew that Union artillery could not reach his army, but they could rain down mortars on the town below. Lee wondered if this could possibly be a feint, but the numbers arrayed on the hills across the river convinced him that it was not. Still he was puzzled. What could this new general be thinking?

Even Morgan, who knew nothing of military strategy or tactics, wondered the same thing. It was simple, really. The Yanks were on the offensive, so they were going to make the first move; they would attack. But that meant that somehow Burnside would have to throw tens of thousands of men across the river, and then they would be down in a valley with Robert E. Lee holding the priceless high ground above them.

Morgan reflected that perhaps the generals might know something that he did not, and he stopped wondering about it to turn and look longingly to the north. *If I were a bird, and I flew straight north, I would fly over the plains and the Wilderness until I got to the Rapidan River, and then I would see Rapidan Run and Jolie.* Even though he was so close to home, naturally Morgan wouldn't ask for a leave. Battle was coming.

General Lee's headquarters tent was pitched underneath a stand of Virginia pine trees that soared forty feet, forming a lush green bower. The staff tents sprang up like mushrooms around him.

Morgan was glad to find that about thirty feet behind the tent line was a long row of smaller trees, perfect for picketing the horses. He, Meredith, and Perry pitched their tent close by.

It was about midnight when they were awakened by a persistent hissing from the tent flap opening. "*SSSSTTT! SSSSTTT!* Is dis you, Mr. Tremayne?"

Meredith and Perry looked up quizzically, but Morgan jumped out of his cot and ran to the opening. "Rosh! I thought that was you!" He hugged the boy hard. "What are you doing here? How'd you find me?"

"I almost didn't," Rosh said mournfully. "I've had about fifty people yellin', 'Halt! Who goes there!' at me in the last two hours. Took me longer to get to this tent than it did to get to the camp."

"I'm surprised they let you through," Morgan said, throwing his arms around Rosh's shoulders and pulling him into the tent. "General Lee's headquarters are just up there, on top of the ridge. Here, give me that oilskin and your hat. Come over here and stand by the stove."

It was still raining, a cold, cutting November storm, and Rosh's cape and hat were dripping. Morgan shook them, scattering icy drops, and hung them up on the clothesline they always kept up behind the stove. Meredith and Perry were already asleep again, with Meredith snoring softly.

Morgan said anxiously, "How's Jolie?"

"She's doing real good, Mr. Tremayne, considering. We all worry 'bout you all the time, of course." He pointed to the east. "All them fires over there on the other side of the river. That's Yankees, isn't it?"

"Yes, it is," Morgan said soberly. "I don't know when they're going to cross that river, but for sure they are."

Rosh nodded. "Figured that. Daddy came to town this morning and saw 'em over there like a big ol' anthill. He rushed back home, and we loaded up the wagon to bring you some things."

"That's good of you, Rosh, but there's going to be a big battle here any time now," Morgan said worriedly. "I want you to go back home and help take care of the farm."

Rosh's face wrinkled with worry. "You—you don't think them Yankees is going to get to Rapidan Run, do you?"

"No," Morgan said vehemently. "I think General Lee is going to stop them right here. But still, with over a hundred thousand bluebellies wandering around, I want you to be at home to take care of everything just in case."

"Yes, sir," Rosh said, sighing. "Do you want me to go ahead and unload the wagon and go on back tonight?"

Morgan saw that he was exhausted and said, "No, no. Is Calliope pulling the wagon? She still hitched up?"

"Yes, sir, I still wasn't sure which of these hunnerd tents you was in," Rosh answered with annoyance.

Morgan nodded. "C'mon, we'll go rub her down and get her with the other horses. They stay warmer that way. Unloading the wagon can wait until morning. When we get Calliope settled, we'll get a cot for you, and you can sleep for whatever's left of the night."

They got Calliope bedded down, and then Rosh bedded down. Morgan went back to sleep instantly as soon as he lay down. He had found that, like any good soldier, he slept hard when he could.

In the morning, he was delighted to find that Amon had mixed up twelve buckets of hot mash for the horses. Morgan and Rosh heated water on the camp stove and fed the horses first thing. Meredith fussed at them and made them sit down and eat breakfast, for Rosh had also brought four dozen eggs, a side of bacon, grits, a wheel of sharp cheese, and two smoked hams.

"Best breakfast I've had for a while," Morgan said with appreciation. "How are the stores at the farm holding out, Rosh?"

"Still seems to me like we got as much as we ever started out with," he said with a big grin. "Daddy says we're livin' in the Land o' Goshen."

Morgan had intended to send Rosh back as soon as the wagon was unloaded, but Rosh said, "You know, Mr. Tremayne, now I can see my hand in front of my face, they's lots of big branches that got blowed down in the storm. It wouldn't take me and you but a coupla hours to build a brush shelter for them horses, with the wagon to haul and all."

"That's a great idea, Rosh," Morgan said gladly. "I hate having to picket horses out in the open. Let's get to it."

It took them more that two hours, but as they started working, they found themselves constructing an arbor that was almost as weatherproof as a snug log cabin.

They were still poking small evergreen branches in the cracks and holes when Meredith came out, nervously drying his hands on his dirty apron. "Mr. Morgan, you said you was from around these parts, didn't you?"

"Yes, my farm is just about fifteen miles from here, due north. That town down there, Fredericksburg, is the nearest, so it's sort of like my hometown," Morgan replied. "Why?"

"Marse Robert had a bunch of officers to dinner, and Perry heard 'em talking. Seems like one of them heathern Yankee gen'rals over there tole the mayor of Fredericksburg that he was mad at 'em, 'cause some boys was snipin' at 'em acrost the river, there. And 'cause they been millin' flour and grain and manufacturing clothes and the like to give to bodies in rebellion 'gainst the US gov'ment. He demands they surrender the town, yes, suh."

"Did he say what he was going to do if they didn't? This Yankee general?" Morgan demanded.

"He said he was gonna blow up the town to pieces," Meredith answered with disdain. "Shame on him is what I say. Ain't no soldiers left in no town in Virginia. Bound to be a bunch of old folks and slaves and women and children down there. Anyways, Marse Robert says he's not going to be able to take the town, 'cause something about the ground down there. But he's not going to let the Yankees just dance in there and take it, neither. So he told the mayor that there was going to be fightin' there, one way or t'other, and that they better 'vacuate."

Morgan exclaimed, "Evacuate!" With distress Morgan stared toward the river, though he couldn't see the town because they were on the far side of the hill. After long moments he said, "Thank you, Meredith, and thank Perry for letting me know."

"Yes, sir, Mr. Morgan, sure 'nough." He turned and hurried back up the hill.

Morgan dropped his head and paced back and forth.

Quietly Rosh went down the row of horses, stroking their noses, murmuring endearments. As usual, Vulcan wouldn't let Rosh touch him. He temperamentally shook his mane and backed up a step.

SURRENDER

It was a full ten minutes before Morgan stopped pacing. He stared at the wagon, then at Calliope, the faithful sturdy mare that did most of the hard work around the farm. His face changed, hardened. He had come to a decision. "Rosh, listen to me," he said. "I want you to go back to the farm just as fast as you can. Calliope's going to have to rest, so double-team the wagon with Lalla and Esmerelda. Hitch up Antoinette and Bettina to the carriage. I know there are only four brood mares left, and they all four have foals, but the situation is getting desperate."

He continued, "Get Amon to drive the carriage into town, to Mr. Benjamin Bledsoe's house. Have him tell Mr. Bledsoe that they can come stay at the farm tonight, and then we can take them somewhere else farther behind the lines if they want, or they can stay at Rapidan Run.

"Then I want you and Santo to take the wagon into town. Go to Sally Selden's, you know she's a widow and has those two kids. Then go to Silas Cage's house, you know where that is, don't you? Good. His wife is there with their child, and I think her mother may be there, too. Then go by the general store and see if Bert and Maisie Patrick need somewhere to go, and then go to the saddler's. I know Will Green probably still has his old mare, but I don't know if he has anywhere to go. That's—that's all I can think of right now. But Rosh, if you've got room left, take any woman and her children. Now listen to me. You're only going to have time to make one trip. Don't come back to Fredericksburg. It's going to be a war zone."

CHAPTER TWENTY

It was already three o'clock in the afternoon when Amon drove the carriage into Fredericksburg. Throngs of people were in the streets, but they were orderly. There was no panic, no shouting, no pushing or shoving. In fact, an unearthly quiet lay like an oppressive fog over the town. Everyone cast anxious glances to the thousands of fires across the river. Almost all the refugees were women with children and older people. They carried little bundles, usually a blanket tied up and containing clothing and more blankets and perhaps some prized possessions such as silver and jewelry. Sadly Amon thought that the thin women wouldn't be able to carry the family silver very far. It was surprising how quickly two pounds could get unbearably heavy.

Amon had come in on the east–west River Road, and he had not met a single soul. It appeared that everyone was going north, perhaps to Falmouth, or south, toward Richmond. They were walking. He saw several single riders on horses, but not one cart or wagon or carriage. He supposed the ones who were fortunate enough to have those were long gone. As he passed, people looked up at him and inside the empty carriage, but no one said a word. They seemed to be numbed into silence. They were all white people. To Amon they looked hollow-eyed and haunted.

He went down Main Street, for the Bledsoes' home was only one block over. He was passing the Club Coffee Shop when he heard a churlish shout that seemed to echo abrasively in the silence.

"Hey, you, boy! Here, boy!" He turned and saw the tall figure of Benjamin Bledsoe come running out of the coffee shop into the street and grab the horses' harness. Antoinette and Esmerelda took great exception to this. They were cosseted mares who had never heard an angry shout in their lives, and they weren't used to strangers. Both of them started violently, and Antoinette reared and knocked Bledsoe down into the filthy, stinking, freezing mud of the street.

I'm in for it now, Amon thought with dread. He jumped down, grabbed the crosspiece of the harness, and started talking soothingly to the nervous mares.

"What's the matter with you? Help me up!" Bledsoe said, slipping as he tried to rise. Of course, Amon couldn't attend to him for a few moments or the horses would have bolted. Bledsoe obviously knew this, but it didn't help his temper any.

Finally Amon got the horses quieted, and he helped Bledsoe to rise. Immediately he said, "That's Morgan Tremayne's carriage. Are you stealing it, boy? Because I'll have you hanged if you are!"

"No, sir," Amon said patiently. He had known this was going to happen. "Mr. Tremayne sent word for me to come to town to get you and your family, Mr. Bledsoe."

"Huh? He did? Oh. Quite right, too. What took you so long, you simpleton? It's going to be dark soon," he growled. "Help me up, up onto the seat. I'm not sitting in the carriage. I'm filthy. Hurry up, boy."

Amon got him situated, climbed up, and they started down the street. Bledsoe neither looked at him nor said a word as they drove. He was occupied with trying to wipe off his shoes with his handkerchief.

When they arrived at the Bledsoe house, he jumped down himself and hurried into the house. Amon sat for a moment, stifling his anger. He had met the Bledsoe family before, when he had driven Morgan into town to take them on rides and picnics. Amon loved Morgan Tremayne and believed that he was the best man he had ever known except for his father, Caleb Tremayne, but he had never been able to understand how Morgan could be so blind about the Bledsoe family. As far as he was concerned, the Bledsoes and other people like them were perfect examples of why the phrase "white trash" had been invented.

Guess he's so crazy 'bout Miss Leona that he's done blinded his own self about these people. I thought he was through with that woman, but it 'pears now he's not. Rosh said he thought about her first.

He climbed down and went to soothe Antoinette and Esmerelda some more. Esmerelda was a good-natured horse, normally very mannerly, but Antoinette was saucy and snobbish. She was still snorting and stamping impatiently.

Leona Bledsoe came out of the house and stamped down the brick walk. "Amon, where's the wagon?" she demanded.

"Rosh and Santo are bringing it into town, to get some of Mr. Tremayne's friends."

"What? Nonsense! Morgan cannot possibly have meant for us to leave town in just the carriage. What are we supposed to do with all of our furnishings, our paintings, our china and silver, our linens?" she snapped.

Obviously Amon could not answer that, so finally she said, "Oh, very well. Come with me and get our trunks now, when we see Rosh and Santo we'll just tell them to come fetch our things."

Amon said politely, "No, ma'am, I'm 'fraid the boys can't do that. They got strict orders from Mr. Tremayne 'bout picking up some folks and taking them out to the farm."

"Fine. Then they can just turn right back around and come back here," she argued.

"No, ma'am. Mr. Tremayne said once we got everyone to the

farm, on no 'count was we to come back to town."

"Mr. Tremayne said this and that! What if I *order* you to come back and pack up this house!" she said, her dark eyes flashing.

Amon merely regarded her gravely. He was not a slave, and Leona Bledsoe knew it.

She looked at him with such rage that he thought she might strike him. But then the moment passed, she took a deep breath, and when she spoke again it was in a normal, if rather stiff, tone. "Very well. Come into the house and fetch the trunks. As soon as my father changes clothes and I can get my mother to stop screeching, we'll leave."

It was somewhat of an exaggeration. Mrs. Bledsoe was not exactly screeching, but her voice was so shrill that it made Amon grit his teeth with every word as he followed Leona up the stairs to the bedrooms. "Benjamin! What about Mama's tapestry? I am not leaving this house until that tapestry is safely wrapped in oilcloth and put in the wagon!"

Mr. Bledsoe growled loudly, "Then I guess you are not leaving this house, Eileen!"

"Oh! OHHH! How can you say such a thing to me! I notice you're taking your portrait. That was the first thing you packed! I'm not—"

Leona opened the door of her parents' bedroom, stuck her head in, and said, "There is no wagon. Just the carriage. Are your trunks ready?" She turned to Amon and said, "Two trunks in here, and mine is in the bedroom just down the hall."

Two fine brassbound trunks lay in the bedroom, both large and bulky—and heavy. Amon picked up one and headed downstairs, thinking wearily, *Now she is a-screechin',* as behind him Mrs. Bledsoe started arguing with her husband and Leona about the wagon. It was stupid, of course, but Amon was just glad that she wasn't arguing with him. At least Leona wasn't stupid. When she was beaten she knew it, and she just cut her losses and moved on.

Amon returned and got Mrs. Bledsoe's trunk and stacked it

on top of Mr. Bledsoe's on the back carriage rack and lashed them down. There wasn't room for another trunk on the slender wooden board, so Amon was going to have to put the trunk inside.

He went back inside and found the family in the parlor, putting on their capes and gloves and hats. "Miss Leona, there's no more room for your trunk on the back. I can put it inside, but it's going to crowd you a bit."

"What! Why can't you lash it to the top?" she asked.

"It's a cloth top, with light wood bows so's you can fold it down," he answered.

"But what about our big trunk, with the linens and silver?" Eileen wailed. "Benjamin, we cannot possibly leave that here! The Yankees, with the Bledsoe silver? No, no—"

"Be silent, woman!" he said with gritted teeth. "I would try to explain to you again, but it wouldn't do a whit of good. Amon, go get Leona's trunk and let's go! It's dark already. It looks like the rain is turning to sleet, and *the Yankees are coming*! So everyone just shut up and get in that carriage!"

Amon passed Rosh and Santo on the north side of town. He cringed a little as the boys called out to him, hoping the Bledsoes would not hear. "You got 'em Daddy? The Bledsoes? Who's that up there with you?"

Amon gave up and pulled the carriage to a stop alongside the wagon. "I got the Bledsoes, and these is some ladies and two chilluns that's half froze to death. I'll introduce everyone proper when we all get home. Now you boys don't argy-barge around. You fill up this here wagon and git on home." The raindrops that were falling now were large and made slushy plops on Amon's hat. The rain was beginning to freeze.

"Yes, sir," they said in unison and moved the wagon along.

Out of the corner of his eye, Amon had seen Mr. Bledsoe pop his head out of the carriage window, but he said nothing and almost instantly pulled his head inside again and closed the shutter.

Amon sighed with relief. He'd had just about enough of listening to Mr. Bledsoe call him boy, and Mrs. Bledsoe's shrieks, and Miss Leona's complaints. The volume on all three of them had gone up considerably when he had stopped to pick up the Archers.

When they left Fredericksburg, it was full dark, so Amon lit the carriage lanterns. Even though the rain was so steady they couldn't light the way for him, somehow he found the yellow globes of light on each side comforting. He passed many people, still walking slowly out of town. Each time he did he felt a little stab of guilt, but he knew he couldn't take all of them. How could he choose to take this lady or that limping old man and not the next one?

Then he came upon an old lady who was standing up very straight but was walking with a noticeable limp. She used a walking stick with her right. A young woman had her arm entwined with hers and was holding the hand of a young boy, who was holding the hand of a very small girl. None of them, even the children, looked behind as the carriage neared. But as he drew up with them, the little girl looked up at the lanterns, pointed, and smiled. The young woman saw her and smiled back at the child.

It was the only smile Amon had seen on that dark day, and his heart melted. He jerked the reins, shouted, "Hup," to the horses, and brought them to a sudden stop. Jumping down, he came to stand in front of the two ladies. Doffing his hat, he bowed as if they were in a drawing room. "How d'ye do, ma'am, miss. My name is Amon, and this here is Mr. Morgan Tremayne's carriage. I'm taking some folks out to our farm. Would you ladies need me to take you someplace? Or if you've a mind, we'd welcome you at Rapidan Run."

The older woman, whose face was drawn in pain, and the pretty younger woman just stared at him. The boy was looking up at him in bewilderment, and the little girl's mouth was a round *O*.

Behind him, he heard the shutter crash, and the Bledsoes all started talking at once. Loudly. Rolling his eyes, he said, "Please don't pay no mind to these folks. They're just upset with the 'vacuation and all. I'm afraid there won't be room in the carriage, but if you do need a ride or would like to visit us for a while, I b'lieve I can make room for you up on the driver's seat."

The two women exchanged glances, and the older lady said with great dignity, "God bless you, sir. We have nowhere to go, and if you could take us in for a day or two, we would be most grateful."

The younger woman asked doubtfully, "Are you sure we can all get on that seat?"

"Yes, ma'am, I'm sure," Amon said firmly. "Your boy can squeeze up right next to me, and if you can hold the little girl in your lap, we'll make it just fine."

Behind him he heard Bledsoe roar, "Boy, you don't even know what kind of people they are! And I strongly protest. My wife and daughter are getting chilled while you stand there and chat with strangers!"

In a low voice, Amon said, "I'm sorry, ma'am, miss."

The younger woman smiled at him. He thought that she had the purest, sweetest smile he had ever seen, except for maybe the little girl's. "I don't know what you mean, Amon. I didn't hear anything at all. Now, if you would be so kind as to help my mother-in-law up, we'll be on our way."

It took them over three hours to reach Rapidan Run. Along the river, a single rider could make it to Fredericksburg in an hour. But the River Road ran south, looping around the Wilderness and then east, so it was about five miles farther. Amon had to go very slowly, because the night was as black as a coal mine, and the road was muddy and slippery.

The young lady introduced everyone. The older lady was her mother-in-law, Mrs. Archer. She was Connie Archer, and her ten-year-old son's name was Sully. The little girl was Georgie. Amon liked Connie Archer immediately, because she spoke to him like Morgan Tremayne did, as equals with no hint of the strain that white people showed even when they were kind. Mrs. Archer said very little, but Amon thought that may be because she was obviously in pain. Every time the carriage went over even the slightest bump, she pressed her lips together and closed her eyes tightly.

Finally they drove up the path to Rapidan Run and then the drive that led straight to the back door. Every window in the house was lit, the kitchen windows were bright, and Amon could smell fresh bread baking. He thought that perhaps a homecoming had never been so welcoming.

Jolie stood at the back door waiting.

Amon helped the Archers down first, which enraged Benjamin Bledsoe, but Amon was long past caring. In just a little while, he could go into his own house, have a cup of hot cider, sit at his own fire, and forget about the Bledsoes.

Poor Jolie, he thought as he handed down Mrs. Bledsoe and Leona. *Wouldn't be surprised if she and Ketura don't come to my house looking for shelter themselves.*

Jolie didn't waste any time with social convention. She immediately took Mrs. Archer's arm and called, "Please, everyone just come in. Follow me."

The Archers went in first, and behind them Mrs. Bledsoe harrumphed, "Dreadful manners that child has."

They went into the house and down the hall, but as they came to the foot of the stairs, Leona said, "Jolie? That is who you are, isn't it? I would prefer to be shown to my room immediately, and I'm sure my parents would, too. We've had quite a trying day."

"Of course, Miss Bledsoe," Jolie said politely. "It's upstairs, the second room on the left. Mr. and Mrs. Bledsoe, your room is right across the hall from Miss Bledsoe's." Jolie turned and led the Archers into the parlor.

"Just a moment, Jolie," Leona said curtly. "We are going to need some hot water and brandy. And my mother and I will need your assistance with unpacking and attending us."

Jolie said evenly, "Soon we'll have supper. Evetta and Ketura are cooking right now. After supper I'll be glad to take you out to the kitchen, so that you will know where the pots for heating water and the cookstove are. Mr. Tremayne does keep brandy in the house, but it is strictly for medicinal purposes. However, warm mulled wine will be served at supper. Perhaps that will do. And Miss Bledsoe, I plan on doing everything I can to help all of our guests here at Rapidan Run. But I am not your maidservant. I'm afraid you and your mother will be obliged to look after yourselves while you are here."

As Jolie spoke, Leona's face grew stormier with each word. When Jolie finished, she said in an ominous tone, "We will talk about this later, Jolie."

"Yes, Miss Bledsoe," she said and turned again.

Mrs. Bledsoe was aghast. "What did I just say? What did I just say! That child is not fit for polite company! The impudence! I would say to her—"

"Mother," Leona said between gritted teeth, "shut up."

Jolie worked hard getting the Archers warmed up and their little bundles of clothing sorted out. She sat Mrs. Archer in a rocking chair right next to the fire and fetched hot bricks wrapped in flannel for her feet. "I would like for you to take one of the other bedrooms," she told Connie Archer. "One has a generous double bed, and we could fix comfortable pallets for the children."

Mischievously Connie looked upward to the second floor, where they could hear a muffled high-pitched constant drone coming from the bedroom upstairs. "Thank you, Jolie, that's very generous, but I think we'll be much more comfortable down here."

"I can't possibly walk up the stairs anyway," Mrs. Archer said with ill-disguised relief. "I never thought I'd be glad of that, but there you are. The Lord can turn even the rheumatism into a blessing in disguise."

It was after nine o'clock when Rosh and Santo got back with

the wagon. They brought six adults and six children with them. Will Green, the saddler, rode his mule. All told, there were twenty-six people that found Rapidan Run a blessed haven on that terrible night.

Jolie was surprised, but she found the next few days enjoyable. She had never been around a group of women, and she had never been around children. She immediately found that she loved children, and she hoped that she might have four or even six children herself. It was also a revelation that the company of genteel, kind women was pleasant and an education in itself. Jolie, of course, had never had a mother or sister. Cleo and Evetta had been mother substitutes, but they weren't the real thing. Ketura had become much like a sister, but she was exactly the same age as Jolie, and so she didn't know the benefits that an older sister might bring.

The refugees at Rapidan Run were a varied group. There was Bert Patrick of Patrick's General Store, and his cheerful, garrulous wife, Maisie. The Patricks had never had children, and it had come about that they had virtually adopted a neighbor's son, Howie Coggins. Howie was twenty-eight now, and he had been in the army and lost a leg at First Bull Run. He had a wife, Greta, and three children. Bert and Maisie's wagon had been stolen the previous night, and they had gotten stranded in the city.

Jolie's dressmaker, widowed Sally Selden, had come with her four-year-old son, Matthew, and six-year-old daughter, Deirdre. Silas Cage's wife, nineteen-year-old Ellie, whose daughter was now eight months old, had wept with relief when Rosh and Santo came to get her. Old Will Green, the saddler, had decided to stay in Fredericksburg and tough it out, but then he decided that he didn't want the bluebellies to get his mule, Geneva, and he had saddled her up and plodded along with the wagon.

Jolie especially enjoyed Connie Archer, an average, rather plain woman with mousy brown hair and weak eyes. But she had a smile that positively made her face glow, and she was gentle and kind. She cared for her mother-in-law with the utmost tenderness, though Mrs. Archer was a rather stiff, formal woman who complained when her arthritis was especially painful. However, Mrs. Archer melted and became positively jolly with her grandchildren, Sully and Georgie. She seemed a different woman when she was with them.

Within three days they had established a routine. Everyone except the Bledsoes got up early. The women helped Evetta with breakfast, Mrs. Cage and Mrs. Archer kept all the children, the men helped Amon and Rosh and Santo with their chores.

Jolie managed to keep the dawn for herself. She still went out and mucked out Rowena's stall and exercised her and then groomed her. Her cooking skills had not improved much, and Evetta was happy to excuse Jolie from it. Jolie got back at breakfast time.

The women ate in the farmhouse, and the men ate in the kitchen. After the washing up, Maisie and Sally Selden helped with the baking and roasting meat and other cooking for dinner and supper, while Jolie, Ketura, and Connie Archer cleaned the house and did the laundry. After dinner in the afternoon, they all sat at the dining room table and sewed.

Jolie would have been very happy during this time if it were not for two things: the constant worry over the war and the Bledsoes. Basically the family would have nothing to do with any of them. They came down to eat, heat water for washing up, and to get tea or coffee. That was all. All three of them stayed in their bedrooms all day. The only exception to this was that Leona sought out Jolie once or twice a day to make demands on her.

"Jolie, it's ridiculous for my parents to have to come down to simply get a cup of tea. I assume Morgan has a tea service. Where is it?" she said the day after they arrived.

"It's in use, Miss Bledsoe. We keep tea available to everyone in the afternoons. You will find the teapot and cups on the sideboard in the dining room."

"Jolie, I need these petticoats ironed."

"Jolie, my mother says that her sheets are scratchy. Don't you have any finer-quality linens?"

"Jolie, it is simply impossible for us to carry enough hot water for baths. I insist that Amon and those two boys provide us with hot water for baths every other night."

"Jolie, Mrs. Cage's baby kept us up half the night last night. Why doesn't she stay in one of the servants' cottages? There are two cottages, and only five in that family. Why are we all stacked up in here like tinned sardines?"

And on and on. Jolie always politely refused her demands, and she was puzzled that Leona never argued. She simply turned on her heel and stalked back upstairs. She was relieved, however. Regardless of how much she told herself that Leona was a hateful snob and that she didn't have to cater to her or her caterwauling mother, Leona still intimidated her frightfully. Jolie was only sixteen years old and had no sophistication or cleverness about people. And Leona was a very striking woman.

Two years ago, after she had gotten to know Amon and his family well, she had asked Amon about her.

"Is she very beautiful?" Jolie had asked wistfully.

Amon shook his head. "Nah, she's the kind of woman that white men calls handsome. Don't ask me why. That's just white folks for you, I guess. Mebbe it's cause she's tall and proud and has those kinda eyes that spark. And she dresses like the Queen o' Sheba, too."

Jolie had to agree with all of that. Leona was five feet ten inches tall and slim. She stood with her head held high, her neck long and graceful. She had rich, abundant hair and always wore jeweled combs and hair ornaments. Her clothes were all of the finest fabrics, her tailoring exquisite.

She made Jolie feel like a little ragpicker, for once again Jolie had blossomed out since the previous winter, and all of her blouses were too tight. Her work shoes were worn, and her nice shoes were too small. Most of her skirts were thin from hard wear and constant washing. Jolie had four nice wool ensembles, but they couldn't compare with Leona's clothing. And Jolie never would have worn them on the farm anyway. It wasn't practical. She determined that she would keep out of Leona's way if possible, though she wasn't about to hide on her own farm.

But on the fourth day, Leona sought her out for the "talk" she had promised on the night of their arrival. Though the Bledsoes never came downstairs until breakfast was on the table, Leona must have been awake to see that Jolie went to the stables early in the morning. It was, in fact, the only time she was alone.

She had just started clearing the soiled hay out of Rowena's stall when Leona came into the stables, wearing a gorgeous chocolate-brown hooded mantle with black grosgrain trim. Throwing back the hood, she said with apparent gaiety, "So here's where you get off to every morning, little girl. Mm, such hard work. Your hands are going to be as rough as Amon's. Come here, Jolie, I want to talk to you." She looked around, up and down the long row of boxes. "Isn't there anywhere to sit in this place?"

Resigned, Jolie said, "In the tack room there are some stools." She threw her shawl back around her shoulders and led Leona to the far end of the stables. The stove was next to the tack room, and it was warm and smelled of leather and horse. Jolie liked it, and she was sure that Leona hated it.

Leona bent and dusted off the stool with one gloved hand, then sat and regarded Jolie for long moments.

Jolie became very uncomfortable under such scrutiny. Nervously she clutched her shawl tighter and hooked her boots on the stool's rungs and smoothed her skirt over and over.

She looks amused. . . . She's laughing at me, Jolie thought bleakly.

Finally Leona cleared her throat with a tiny, delicate sound. "First, Jolie, I must apologize for my and my parents' behavior the last few days. I assure you, we are normally polite, well-spoken people. It's just that we were in such shock, with the Yankees threatening to bombard us, and then having to leave all of our possessions. In particular, my mother is suffering, which explains why she's been so impatient and cross."

An apology, no matter how insincere and incomplete, threw Jolie completely off guard. She swallowed hard. "I—it's fine, Miss Bledsoe. You don't have to apologize."

"Perhaps not, but I do, anyway. Now. I have come to see in the last few days that I don't quite understand your role here, Jolie. Please explain it to me," she said peremptorily.

"I—I beg your pardon? My role?" Jolie repeated, bewildered.

"Yes. You don't know that word? I mean, your position in Mr. Tremayne's household."

Jolie knew what the word *role* meant perfectly well, but it seemed silly to bluster about it now. "I don't know about a position," she said slowly. "He's my guardian."

"Has he formally adopted you? Legally?"

"No, that is, I don't think so," Jolie said with difficulty.

"So basically he took in a penniless orphan, as an act of charity," Leona said with a condescending smile.

Stung, Jolie started to fling her inheritance in Leona's face. She was far, *far* from penniless. But a tiny little voice in her head suggested that it was none of Leona Bledsoe's business, and she shouldn't try to fight Leona on her own ground. She was sure to lose. It startled Jolie to realize that she was, somehow, in a fight with Leona. Though Leona was speaking pleasantly, even warmly, she was definitely attacking Jolie. What did she want? What was she trying to win? Jolie had no idea.

She was quiet for so long that Leona continued, "That is so like Morgan. He's a generous, charitable man. But I must admit that I'm rather surprised he chose to take in an octoroon. Heaven knows there are many poor white children who desperately need a benefactor."

"It's—not like that," Jolie said in confusion. "Mr. Tremayne was very good friends with my father, and he—helped me because of him."

"Ah, I see," Leona said. "Yes, Mr. DeForge, I remember him. I believe that he didn't actually tell you that he was your father? Yes, now I recall Morgan telling me that Mr. DeForge was quite embarrassed to have a black child on the wrong side of the blanket, as it's said."

Jolie stared incredulously at Leona. Then her eyes filled with scalding tears. She dropped her head, buried her face in her shawl, and sobbed.

Leona stood and patted her lightly on the shoulder. "Don't cry, dear. I'm sure Morgan has made up for all of that. I know he must be a wonderful father to you."

"He is not!" Jolie cried. "He's—he's not old enough to be my father!"

"Yes, of course," Leona said soothingly. "Calm yourself, Jolie. There's really no need for such dramatics. I can see that you have had a good life here. Why should you be crying when so many people are suffering so much more than you are?"

"Yes, that's true," Jolie said woefully, making a valiant effort to stop the helpless flow of tears. "Mr. Tremayne has taken very good care of me. And I am grateful and happy. Usually."

"Yes, Morgan has taken care of you, but he's a single man, and he has no idea how to raise a little girl," Leona said, smoothly taking her seat again. "You see, Jolie, Morgan has obviously indulged you, and it's made you proud and rather smug. Such unattractive qualities in children. I mean, you seem to think that you are fit to be a hostess for Morgan's household! It's preposterous to see you, a little black girl, lording it over me and my parents. No, no, Jolie. I'm sure that Mr. Tremayne would be extremely upset if he knew of your behavior since we arrived here."

Jolie was horribly confused. She had tried to do her best to make everyone feel welcome and to make sure that they were comfortable and well fed. True, she had refused to be Leona's house slave, but surely Morgan never meant for her to be that! Did he? She had thought she knew exactly what Morgan would expect from her, but now she wasn't sure.

Leona was watching her coolly.

Jolie said, "Maybe what you say is true, Miss Bledsoe. I'm just not sure. I need time to think. But anyway, I have some questions, too."

"Yes, I'm sure you do, but I'm certainly not going to be interrogated by you," Leona said, rising and pulling up her hood. "As you said, you do need to take some time and think this through. I would hate to have to tell Morgan that you insulted me and my family while we were guests in his home." She started toward the door but then turned back, and now Jolie saw the touch of malice in her. "I will answer one of your questions, Jolie, because you apparently have a very mistaken idea of my relationship with Morgan. He is in love with me. He has been for years. That's why I have much more right than you do to say what happens in this house."

"No, you don't," Jolie said, too loudly, she knew. In a less panicky tone she said, "Besides, Mr. Tre—Morgan told me that you and he weren't together anymore. That you told him you didn't want to be with a private. You wanted him to be an officer, and you got mad at him when he wouldn't, and you told him you didn't want to see him anymore."

"Lover's squabbles," Leona said, waving her hand. "You can't possibly understand the complex relationships of adults, particularly since you're black. Besides, just think, Jolie, who did he think of first when the whole city was in danger? Me. Do you doubt me? Ask Rosh. And know that this is the last time I'll make any explanations to the likes of you." She whirled around, her mantle billowing, and walked out.

CHAPTER TWENTY-ONE

Jolie," Ketura whispered, laying her hand on Jolie's shoulder gently, "are you crying?"

The two girls were sleeping under the dining room table. Jolie had worked out the sleeping arrangements. Ellie Cage, with her eight-month-old daughter, Janie, had the spare bedroom upstairs, and Bert and Maisie Patrick, who were in their sixties, had taken Ketura's bedroom. The Bledsoes were in Morgan's room, while Leona was in Jolie's. Will Green and Howie Coggins slept in the barn. The other women and children were all sleeping in Morgan's study/sitting room.

Although there had been room in the study for Jolie and Ketura—it was the largest room in the house, taking up over half of the first floor—they had decided to sleep in the dining room, finding that under the table, right by the fireplace, was a cocoon of warmth.

Now Jolie turned over, and by the golden flicker of the flames Jolie could see her friend's concerned face.

"You are crying," Ketura said. "I've never seen you cry, Jolie, not even with everything you've been through. Whatever is wrong?"

"I don't think I can talk about it," Jolie said helplessly. "Every time I think about it I just cry. I hate to cry. It gives me a such a headache."

Ketura sat up and crossed her long legs. "Sounds like you better talk about it. Maybe if you can tell someone, you won't cry anymore. You can tell me anything, Jolie. You know that."

Slowly Jolie pulled herself up into a sitting position, hugging her knees close under her chin. "I know. I'll try, but it's all kind of like this big red blur." Jolie did cry as she told Ketura about her conversation with Leona Bledsoe, but by the time she was finished, she had stopped weeping. Her headache had even lessened.

Ketura's big round eyes grew more and more distressed as Jolie talked. "Oh Jolie, what are you going to do?" she asked anxiously.

"Do? I don't know what to do! You've got to help me, Ketura! I'm—I'm afraid!" Jolie said, grabbing the girl to her and hugging her close.

Ketura clung to her, then pulled back and wiped the remnants of tears from Jolie's face. "I don't know what to do, Jolie. That lady scares me, too. Maybe we should go talk to one of the ladies, tell her what Miss Bledsoe said and did to you. I know, what about Miss Connie? She's the nicest, sweetest lady I've ever met, and she's smart. She'd know what to do."

"She is nice and she's so kind, but I barely know her. I had a hard enough time telling you, Ketura. I couldn't possibly tell a stranger all this. Besides, she doesn't know Morgan, she—she couldn't help me decide what he wants and what he means for me to do. Why don't we go talk to your mother? She's smart, too, and she knows Morgan. Evetta could help."

"I don't know," Ketura said slowly. "Mama's smart, but she doesn't have much use for mean white ladies. I think she'd just tell you to ignore Miss Bledsoe and get on about your business."

"Maybe," Jolie said, "but even just that might help. I'm so awfully confused."

The girls got up and put on heavy dressing gowns and went outside. They had thought that they would go to Amon and Evetta's cottage and wake her up. But they saw that the kitchen lamps were blazing, so they went to find Evetta there.

When they went in, they were surprised to see Connie Archer standing over a big pot on the stove, stirring the boiling syrup that gave off the sticky sweet aroma of hot peaches. Two more pots were on the range. Six piecrusts were lined up along the wooden counter on the back wall. Evetta was just shaping up the last one. They looked up as the girls came in.

"Oh. Hello, Evetta. Hello, Miss Connie," Jolie said awkwardly. "We didn't know you were here."

"Guess you musta, since you come in," Evetta said crisply. "Now Jolie, I don't need you in here twitchin' around and making me forget every one thing I'm doing. Besides, you girls need your rest. Go back to bed."

"But I wanted to talk to you, Evetta," Jolie said nervously. "Please?"

"Then talk."

Jolie's eyes slid to Connie Archer, and she fidgeted. A knowing look passed over Connie's thin face, and she said, "Girls, why don't you sit down? I was just going to make myself some cocoa. Why don't I make three cups, and we'll share? Evetta, would you like some cocoa?"

"No, thank you, Miss Connie, but you go right ahead and take you a little break," Evetta said in the warmest tone Jolie had ever heard her use. "Everything's ready. All's I got to do is pour up these pies and pop 'em in the oven, and I can do that by myself, thank you."

When Connie had poured up three mugs of the warm, creamy chocolate, she brought them over to the worktable and sat down on the stool next to Jolie. "What a great luxury to have chocolate for Christmas! Do you know that the Patricks haven't even been able to get it for the last couple of months. We all owe Mr. Tremayne a very great debt of thanks."

"Yes, we do," Jolie said dully. "He worked very hard in the last two years to make sure that we didn't want for anything here at Rapidan Run."

"I don't know him, but I feel as if I already do," Connie said quietly. "I know that he is a courageous man, because he's gone to fight in this terrible war. He's a kind man, because I can see the love you all have for him. He's a charitable man because we're all here, all of us. And I know that he's a generous man because I, a perfect stranger, am sitting here drinking his valuable cocoa."

"He's all of that and so much more," Jolie said.

Connie nodded. "I'm sure he is, and I so look forward to the time that I might get to know such a man. But for right now, Jolie, I'd like to get to know you. You see, I'm thirty-two years old now, but I can remember when I was sixteen. It was very difficult. I didn't understand my place in the world. I didn't understand what people wanted of me. It seemed I never knew the right thing to do. I had lost my parents, you see, and I felt I had no one in the world to help me. But the Lord sent me someone, a teacher, a lovely woman who didn't do a thing except listen to me. And that helped me more than anything in this world. So, Jolie, may I be your teacher? It might only be for this one night, I don't know. But I do think now that the Lord sent me and my family here for a purpose. I think He sent me here for you, Jolie."

A moment of profound silence came when Connie's soft voice faded on the air. Then Ketura breathed, "Oh Jolie, you've got to talk to this lady. If you don't, I will."

"No, I—I'll try," Jolie said. "I believe you, Miss Connie. But I'm so confused, so upset. I don't even know if I'm making any sense or not. Somehow I just want to cry, and whine, I guess, and just go on and on about how Miss Leona Bledsoe was so mean to me. But I know that's childish, and feeling sorry for myself won't solve anything."

"That already shows a great deal of maturity on your part," Connie said. "Especially for a sixteen-year-old girl. But I'm not at all surprised, Jolie. I've only known you for four days, and I've already seen that though you may look like a young girl, you have a love in your heart that makes you wise and good much beyond your years. Now, why don't you just try to set aside all the emotions you feel and tell me what Miss Bledsoe said to you?"

Jolie was able to do just that. Her account of the conversation was much more coherent than when she had told Ketura. She hadn't been able to say much more than that Leona had been horrible to her and had made her feel like she was childish and selfish and arrogant.

But after that cleansing outburst, and particularly after Connie Archer's soothing, restful assurances, Jolie felt calm and clear headed. She was able to remember the conversation practically word for word and could articulate Leona Bledsoe's attitude that had made it so much worse than the actual words she had said.

"We were in the stables, you see, and when she left I thought that she'd made me feel as if I was like the horse droppings she was so careful not to step in. That's how low I felt," Jolie finished painfully.

As Jolie had talked, Connie Archer had kept her eyes fixed on Jolie's face, and she hadn't said a word.

Ketura had murmured, "Oh, no," a couple of times, hearing the story again.

Behind them, Evetta was busily making pies and putting them in the oven, but she let her feelings be known several times by derisive grunts. Now she said, "Huh! I'm surprised that hussy knows what horse droppings even is, 'cause she don't know the upside of a horse from the backside. She's so scared of 'em she won't even look at 'em."

"She is?" Jolie said with surprise. "I didn't know that."

"No, you didn't," Connie said firmly. "But that's the thing about Leona, you see, that most people don't realize. She's frightened. She is frightened out of her wits. And I don't mean just of horses, either."

SURRENDER

Ketura said with disbelief, "Miss Bledsoe, scared? I didn't think she was frightened of anything. She's so scary herself."

"She sure is," Jolie agreed forcefully.

Connie studied them. "You really think she is scary? So, you're actually frightened of her? Like you're frightened of snakes, or of being in a strange dark place, or of fire?"

After long moments, Jolie said, "No. . .no, not like that."

Evetta muttered, "Mebbe like the snakes."

Connie said, "No, you're not frightened of her. What you are is intimidated. That's a very different thing. It's much easier to overcome feelings of intimidation than it is to overcome true, real fear."

"Maybe," Jolie agreed halfheartedly. "But I don't know how to keep from feeling like—like—"

"Like she's better than you?" Connie supplied quickly. "Like she's prettier than you, like she's smarter than you, like she knows Mr. Tremayne better than you, like she deserves more respect, more love than you? That's what intimidation is. And you can get out from under that easily, Jolie, and you, too, Ketura, just by recognizing what she's doing. She's deliberately making you feel that way, because it's her weapon, and a very weak and pathetic one it is, too. Attacking people where they are most vulnerable is a coward's tool. And she is a coward, because she is so afraid, and instead of facing her fears and overcoming them, she belittles other people to make herself feel powerful."

"But what is she afraid of?" Jolie demanded. "I don't understand. She *is* beautiful, she *is* smart, she *is* rich, and it seems like men just fall in love with her so easily! What can she possibly be scared of?"

"All right, let's consider everything you just said, Jolie," Connie said, "which is pretty much exactly what you see when you don't know Leona like I do. Beautiful? Maybe, although I'm not so sure that exactly describes Leona's looks. She's exotic and striking, yes—"

Loudly, Evetta interrupted, "I think that her face is hard enough to dent an ax handle."

A quick look of amusement passed over Connie's face, and she continued, "And she is extremely intelligent. She's smart enough to realize that a woman's looks don't last forever. She's only twenty-five now, but for years she's been using expensive lotions and exotic ointments and bathing perfumes and herbal preparations for her hair and skin.

"And that brings me to your next point. Leona is not rich. As a matter of fact, she is poor. The Bledsoes have been broke for a long time, and Benjamin Bledsoe was in debt up to the ceiling of their expensive two-story house before the war even started. After that, of course, there was no one he could borrow from. Leona's had to do without her expensive creams and milk baths for a long time now. Believe me, she's scared to death. Scared of losing her looks, scared of being poor, scared of having to do without, but mostly scared because now there's no one to coddle her, adore her, fulfill her every wish. All those men who fell in love with her so easily are gone now."

After long moments, Jolie said in a low voice, "I see what you're saying, Miss Connie, and I guess you must be right about Miss Bledsoe being scared about her looks and being poor and all. But you're wrong about one thing. All those men aren't gone. Morgan Tremayne hasn't deserted her."

"No, I know he hasn't. And I'm not surprised. He strikes me as the sort of man who is very loyal to his friends."

"But do you think that's all it is?" Jolie asked desperately. "He thought about her first, Rosh told me! Morgan sent the carriage just for her! Don't you think he must still be in love with her?"

"I don't know," Connie said calmly. "He may be. Men can be so blind, so terribly ignorant, when it comes to women like Leona. But even if he is, it shouldn't make any difference to you, Jolie."

"But it does! It's—it's everything. It's what frightens me most of all!" Jolie cried passionately.

A sudden look of recognition came over Connie's face, and she reached over to take Jolie's hand. "I see," she said quietly. "I will pray about that, Jolie. But I meant what I said. When Mr. Tremayne left, he entrusted you and Ketura and Amon and Rosh and Santo with this place, with his home. He obviously believed you would be faithful stewards. And you have been. You have taken in strangers and cared for us, shared all of your worldly goods with us, sheltered us when we had no home. You have all demonstrated true godly love, for you knew that we could give you nothing in return."

"That is what Morgan intended all along," Jolie said slowly. "I know him."

Evetta shoved the last pie in the oven, slammed the door shut, and came to stand in front of them, flour-covered hands firmly planted on her hips. "Well, you don't know all about him. You didn't know he made out a new will afore he left to go help Gen'ral Lee. Yes, sir, he did. He left this place to us, to all of us, to my family and to you. He left us equal shares in the farm, but he left the big house to you, Jolie. So the way I sees it, this place is ours, no matter where Mr. Tremayne is, 'cause that's what he wanted us to know by doin' that."

Jolie absorbed this then said, "So Miss Bledsoe was wrong, after all. I really do have much more right than she does to decide what happens in this house."

Evetta sniffed. "Thass right. So you need to quit stewin' your frilly little britches about whatever bugs crazy white ladies got in their addled brains, 'scuse me Miss Connie, and git back to goin' about your business."

Ketura sighed, "Told you so."

Jolie managed a smile. "And it did make me feel better. But it was mostly you, Miss Connie. Thank you so much for helping me," she said simply.

"You're welcome."

"But there's something I'd like to ask you, Miss Connie," Jolie said, puzzled. "You seem to know Miss Bledsoe really well. But I know she hasn't spoken one word to you since you all came here."

"No, she wouldn't," Connie said quietly. "The reason I know her so well is that she—she—" For the first time she faltered and searched Jolie's and Ketura's faces as if she were trying to read their minds. Then, with a regretful sigh, she continued, "I suppose I can tell you. It's a shame, but in these times children have had to grow up much too fast and know terrible things that no child should have to face. Leona Bledsoe had an affair with my husband. That's the reason why I know her so well."

Even Evetta paused in her work and stared.

Connie continued, "It was in the spring, three years ago, just when we were all realizing that war was coming. My husband was Mr. Lucien Lewis's personal secretary. Mr. Lewis was president of Merchant's and Planter's Bank. I say that Martin and Leona had an affair, but really it—they were only together twice. Leona seduced him, you see, because she wanted him to persuade Mr. Lewis to loan her father money. Martin told her that it was impossible, as he had no such influence over Mr. Lewis. Then Leona tried to persuade him to embezzle money for her."

"What's 'bezzle?" Evetta demanded, still frozen with a spoon in her hand.

"Steal it," Connie answered shortly. "It's funny, I guess, in a way. A man can be seduced by a woman, and it's as if he sort of gets sucked into that sin slowly, like sliding into a bath that's almost too hot. But stealing, particularly when you know you would get caught, is quite jarring. Apparently it can bring even the most deluded of men to their senses. Martin knew then what kind of woman she was, and he realized what a terrible thing he had done."

Evetta banged the spoon against a pot and then stirred it with repeated dull clangs. "A flyswatter can swat spiders as good as they swat flies." Somehow they all knew what Evetta meant.

Jolie asked, "And so Mr. Archer told you? He confessed to you?"

"No, he didn't have the chance, really," Connie answered, and the pain of the memories showed in her face. "Leona told me. I mean, she sent me a note. Hand-delivered, so that she could be sure that Martin was at work so he wouldn't intercept it. It was a terrible shock, and things were very bad for us for about a year."

"That is horrible!" Jolie said compassionately. "So much worse than those stupid things she said to me! Oh, how did you bear it, Miss Connie?"

"I didn't bear it at all for a long time. I made Martin pay for it. Every day, all day, I punished him. But finally I realized that I was hurting myself as much as I was hurting him. I forgave him then. It took much longer to trust him again, but finally I did. And I thank the Lord Jesus for giving me that spirit of forgiveness," she said, tears springing to her eyes.

"When I told Martin good-bye when he was leaving to march into Maryland, it was the last time I ever saw him. He died at Sharpsburg, and he's buried there. But we parted with love and sweetness, and I'm so thankful to God. Because that's what gives me joy, and strength, to this very day."

On the night of November 25th, as Jolie poured out her heart to Connie Archer, Morgan Tremayne walked through a hard, cold rain to the top of what was beginning to be called Lee's Hill. It was not the highest point of the ridge of hills that ran behind Fredericksburg, but it gave the best vantage point for the battle that was coming.

The Yankees were concentrated directly behind Fredericksburg, to the south for about three miles, just along the Rappahanock River. Lee's Hill was prominent, as it was a slightly lower prominence and was almost directly in the center of the Union dispositions. Morgan knew that Longstreet's corps ranged out to his left and two of Jackson's divisions to his right. He suspected that as soon as General Lee was sure that the battle was to be here, he would call on his most trusted general, Stonewall Jackson, to fortify the line.

Two days later, Lee became certain that Burnside's attack was here, no matter how unlikely it seemed to him. He sent for Jackson, who marched his men 175 miles in twelve days. He arrived on December 1st.

By then General Lee, and indeed the entire army, was puzzled. Why did Burnside not attack? His men had been on the field for over two weeks. What was he doing?

The answer could not have been made known to General Lee by even the best of spies, because even the Union Army did not know why Burnside tarried. He had ordered pontoon boats to build bridges across the river, and somehow the orders had been misunderstood, or not communicated correctly, and then due to the heavy rains and the swollen creeks and rivers the delivery of them had been delayed. Then Burnside had decided to change his attack to a crossing eighteen miles downstream, called Skinker's Neck. But Lee had anticipated this possibility, and all others, too. Burnside hesitated when he found out that thousands of Confederates waited for him downstream.

The next few days he seesawed in an agony of indecision. Finally he decided to go with his original plan, to build five bridges across the river and to pour his men into Fredericksburg. He envisioned tens of thousands of men in blue sweeping through the little empty town, across the plains beyond, up the gentle little hills, and overrunning the Confederates with ease.

But that was not the vision that General Robert E. Lee had, at all. Finally, on December 11th, at 2:00 a.m., the engineers began building their pontoon bridges. They learned, first of all, of the plans Robert E. Lee had for the battle. It was to slaughter every man who tried to cross that river. General Longstreet had posted Brigadier General William Barksdale's tough Mississippians, including some of the best sharpshooters in the army, in Fredericksburg to delay the Union advance as long as possible. They waited all along the waterfront, behind walls, in rifle pits, in basements, on roofs. When dawn came, the slaughter began. Engineers, using tools to build bridges, were unarmed. The sharpshooters sent them back time and time again, all that morning and into the afternoon. Finally the

Yankees brought their artillery down and began shelling the town.
That worked until about 2:30 that afternoon. When the Yankees
ceased firing the artillery, the sharpshooters came out of hiding and
began picking off the engineers again. Eventually Burnside ordered
that infantry be rowed across the river in the pontoons. They finally
managed to get a foothold on the waterfront and began moving
through the town. The Mississippians fought them fiercely; for
every foot of ground that they gained, men died. But finally the
Confederates were safely ensconced on Marye's Heights, and the
Union Army occupied Fredericksburg.

It was about 4:30 p.m. On Lee's hill, General Lee advised
couriers to send the word to commanders to be ready for an attack.

But when night fell, he was still watching the river, where
more and more men were pouring across. But the frozen night
was not dark, for the entire scene was lit with a lurid orange glow.
Fredericksburg was burning.

General Lee finally retired to get some rest, telling his aides to
awaken him at once if it looked as if General Burnside was making
a move. But General Lee could have slept late on the morning of
December 12th, if he had chosen to. On that day he stood on Lee's
Hill and watched through his field glasses as thousands of Union
soldiers vandalized and looted the little town.

Appalled, Morgan tied up the horses and came to the crest of
the hill to use his own field glasses. The looting was vicious. Every
house still standing was broken into, and everything of value was
stolen.

But it was the vandalism that was so needless and cruel that
it became almost bizarre. Soldiers dragged furniture out into the
streets and built huge bonfires. Pianos were danced on until they
fell apart, and some were filled with water to use as horse troughs.
Paintings were dragged out and slashed with bayonets and then
stamped on. Large alabaster vases were smashed to bits. Even picket
fences surrounding little gardens were yanked up and set on fire.

Morgan was so angry that he made an inarticulate growling

sound in his throat then quickly looked guiltily at General Lee, who was standing only a few feet from him.

Lee's face showed no anger. Instead he looked disgusted, as if someone had said an obscene word to a group of ladies.

The looting went on all day, because it took all day for General Burnside to get his eighty thousand men across the Rappahannock, and it became evident that that was the only plan for December 12th.

The next day dawned, a cold, foggy morning. About 10:00 a.m. the fog lifted and the Union assault began. All day long, at every point along the battle line, waves of Union soldiers tried to advance the heights, and they died. Again and again they came, long lines of them bravely marching into the face of artillery and thousands of muskets. They fought as they had been commanded: to walk toward the enemy, and when within range, to fire their rifles, then reload and march forward again. Thousands of them never got within firing range. More thousands of them never got the chance to reload.

Far to the right it seemed as if at last Union forces had found a weak spot, a heavily wooded shallow valley, part of Stonewall Jackson's line. The atmosphere on Lee's Hill was tense, as they all strained to see any indication of the men in blue streaming back away from Jackson's line. But no such welcome sight met their eyes. They couldn't hear because of the throaty continuous roar of the cannon.

But then, distinguished only as a soprano note to the artillery's bass, they heard the high, quavering Rebel yell. One Union chaplain reported that it was an "unearthly, fiendish yell, such as no other troops or civilized beings ever uttered." Even as their hearts rose at the eerie cries that were so welcome to them, they saw Union troops running out of the woods, throwing down their rifles, and staring behind them in terror. Then behind them ran ragged men in gray, screaming their banshee song, insanely joyous in pursuit.

Morgan felt a thrill of triumph as he watched. He had not

fought in a battle. He had never even fired his rifle. But at this moment, for the first time, he understood men of war.

General Lee turned to General Longstreet and said, his dark eyes flashing, "It is well that war is so terrible—we should grow too fond of it!"

On and on they came, dashing themselves to pieces against the entrenched might of the Army of Northern Virginia. They fought until a dense gray twilight fell. It was bitterly cold, and the Northern Lights, which were rarely seen this far south, colored the air with a surreal display. Over nine thousand men had been wounded on this day. Many of them died of their wounds, lying on that bloody field, and many of them froze to death.

General Lee fully expected Burnside to renew his attack in the morning, but it did not come. In the morning, sharpshooters picked off some men on the field below and scattered Yankees who were collecting their dead and wounded close to their lines. Those were the only shots fired that day.

On the next, Burnside asked for a truce for the burial of the dead and the relief of the wounded. Lee agreed. All day long, surgeons, ambulances, and burial details were busy on the body-littered fields. There was no blue or gray now. Surgeons attended wounded men, no matter their uniform, and burial details interred Billy Yanks and Johnny Rebs side by side. No shots by the men of war were fired on this day.

On the next morning, December 16th, Burnside was nowhere to be seen. The Army of the Potomac had melted away in the night.

CHAPTER TWENTY-TWO

Jolie, Ketura, Evetta, Rosh, Santo, and Amon waited as long as they could. As the days turned into weeks, and still no tidings, no newspapers, no mail, and above all no sound of distant battle came to Rapidan Run, Jolie finally said to Amon, "I cannot stand this one more day. We must have some news! What has happened? Did we dream it? Did they decide not to fight, and everyone just packed up and went somewhere else?"

"That ain't it," Evetta assured her. "Them armies is still there, all right. I guess they's just making scary faces to each other 'crost the river. But she's right, Amon. We got to know something. I know Mr. Tremayne didn't want you to get caught in the battle, but maybe if you could get some idea of when that might be, we'd know to stay away."

"I've had it up to here, too, sitting around and waiting," Amon admitted. "I'll go as close as I can, but not till tonight."

"Then you gotta take me, Daddy," Rosh said. "I know exactly where Mr. Tremayne is, just in case it seems like we can go on in."

So Amon and Rosh set out for the battlefield at twilight. As far as they knew, all the Yankees were on the other side of the Rappahannock, but they were still cautious. They decided not to take the River Road. Rosh knew the way across country that would take them to the southernmost point of the line of hills above Fredericksburg. "Can you find your way at night?" Amon asked hesitantly.

"Yes, sir. Mr. Tremayne taught me," Rosh answered confidently. "He could find his way around this country blindfolded. One of those nights we were out camping he showed me this way."

But they didn't need to know the way. When they had traveled about a mile south of Rapidan Run, they began to understand the glow in the sky they were seeing ahead. Fredericksburg was on fire. Sadly, they returned to the farm.

Everyone, even the Bledsoes, were waiting in the house for Amon and Rosh. When they finally returned, Jolie could tell from their demeanors that the news was not good.

"I'm sorry, folks, but it looks like there's a real big fire in the town," Amon told them quietly.

"What? What's on fire?" Leona demanded.

With compassion, Amon repeated, "It's a real big fire, ma'am."

"You mean you don't know? Are you telling me that you didn't go into town and see what was burning? And try to help?" Mrs. Bledsoe cried in outrage.

"Ma'am, when we left, they wasn't anybody left in that town," Amon explained patiently. "And that means that there's prob'ly just Yankees there now. I don't hardly think I'm gonna go help 'em put out the fires they started anyways."

"How dare you speak to me like that!" Mrs. Bledsoe shouted, her voice shrill with hysteria.

Jolie wanted to rail at the woman, but she didn't. She couldn't. Regardless of how Mrs. Bledsoe was acting and how outrageous her behavior was, she was Jolie's elder, and Jolie wasn't about to show her any disrespect.

But she wasn't Maisie Patrick's elder, and Maisie's view at that moment was that Mrs. Bledsoe didn't deserve an iota of respect. She stepped in front of Mrs. Bledsoe defiantly and said, "Eileen, everyone here is sick to death of your shrieking and wailing and the way you're treating all of us respectable people. Calm down. If you can't calm down and act like a civilized person, then go to your room. Benjamin, I'm surprised at you. How can you let her embarrass herself in this way?"

He looked disconcerted. He had lost his bluster, which was practically the only way he knew to deal with people. In the last two weeks, he had become a parody of himself, a mumbling, indecisive, fumbling old man.

Leona, her head held high, stepped up and took her mother's arm. "You have no right to speak to my mother that way, Maisie. Just leave us alone."

"I'll be glad to," Maisie retorted, "if you'll go away."

Leona whirled around and, practically dragging her protesting mother, flew up the stairs. Benjamin, after one shamefaced look at the others, hurried after them.

Maisie turned to them and said defiantly, "There are probably a hundred thousand men out there who are going to try their best to kill each other in the next day or so. Half of them are our families, our sons, our husbands, our brothers. For anyone to be hysterical over their parlor or their china or their Grandma's portrait right now is just shameful. I don't regret what I said one little bit."

It wasn't the next day. On that day, eighty thousand Union soldiers crossed the Rappahannock, while the ones already landed destroyed Fredericksburg.

Everyone at Rapidan Run was so anxious with anticipation and dread that each avoided in-depth conversations with any other. Evetta burned a pudding and volubly called her own self a variety of colorful names.

So it was a kind of release when the sound of artillery came to them late the next morning. All day long they heard it, like a constant rolling roar of far-off thunder. After dinner they all gave up any pretense at working. Wherever they were in the house, or out on the grounds, they constantly searched toward the south. Of course they couldn't see Fredericksburg, ten miles away. But they could see the death-gray smudge rising and growing in the southern sky. It was smoke from Confederate cannons and a hundred thousand muskets. The distant din didn't stop until nightfall, and then the sky was lit with the strange aurora.

Jolie stood for hours out on the tiny front porch, staring up, wondering if it was an evil omen. If that's what it was, she was sure Morgan must be dead.

The next day and the next were eerily quiet. Again they were utterly mystified. Amon didn't wait for Evetta to prod him this time. On December 17th, he said, "I'm going. It's so quiet I'm wonderin' if they ain't every last one of 'em dead. That's how crazy I'm a-gittin'."

"It ain't just you, Amon," Evetta said. "Not knowin' will make a body a lot crazier than knowin'."

Amon and Rosh again set out early that evening. It was two o'clock in the morning before they returned. Again, all of them were sitting up waiting. Mrs. Bledsoe was truly ill now. She had been shocked out of her hysteria by Maisie's sharp words and had finally mentally rejoined the real world—the one where her only son was fighting in a war. She had been suffering heart palpitations and near-fainting spells, and Jolie had finally given her a bottle of brandy. She suspected that Benjamin Bledsoe and Leona had partaken, too, from the high, hectic color on Leona's sharp cheekbones to Mr. Bledsoe's bleary eyes. She didn't care. She didn't even care who had won the battle. All she could think about was Morgan Tremayne.

When Amon and Rosh came in, she didn't have to ask or say a word. She could tell from their faces that Morgan Tremayne must be alive and well. Before they had even said a word, Jolie sat back in the straight chair, put her head back, closed her eyes, and took a deep, trembling breath.

The others crowded around them, firing questions at Amon and Rosh both. Finally Maisie raised her voice above the insistent cries of the women and the hoarse, rapid-fire interrogation by the men. "I'm telling my own self to shut up now," she said loudly. "And I suggest you all do the same. Let the men tell us what they know, and maybe then they can answer our questions." Finally it was quiet.

"Mr. Tremayne's alive and fine, jist fine," Amon said with a broad smile. "He says to tell you all that he's so glad you're all here together, with me and my family and Jolie. Friends need to stick together real close in these dark ol' days." The smile faded, and the big man looked distressed. "We won, all right. Yes, sir, we did. I couldn't see those lowlands 'tween Marye's Heights and town, but Mr. Tremayne says there must be a thousand men buried down there, most all of 'em Yankees. He says it looked like ten thousand of 'em got wounded. And now they're gone. Not a Yank in sight on either side of the river from Falmouth down to Massaponax."

"Have they sent out the lists of wounded and killed yet?" Ellie Cage asked with anguish.

"No, ma'am. Mr. Tremayne says that's gonna take some days, always does."

"What about Gibbs? My son, Gibbs Bledsoe?" Mrs. Bledsoe asked in a weak, fearful voice. "Morgan is friends with him. Surely he knows whether—surely Morgan knows how he is."

"Mr. Tremayne sends his 'pologies to you, ma'am, 'cause he knows you must be worried to death about your son. But Mr. Tremayne says he only knows that General Stuart was far, far down the river, guarding the army's right flank. He said he'd seen General Stuart at headquarters, but he didn't know about any of his men."

"Did he send me a message?" Leona demanded, her eyes brilliant and her mouth tense.

"Uh—not personal, no, ma'am. He just ask who all was here, and like I said, to tell everyone how welcome they was, from him. He didn't hardly have time to send word to everyone," Amon said in a very gentle voice. "The battle might be over, but they was still all scurryin' around, busy as beetles. And Mr. Tremayne hurried us off, like he wanted us to get word back to everyone."

Leona seemed mollified with Amon's diplomacy and tact and said nothing more.

Connie Archer said softly, "And so the Yankees are gone. Does that mean that we can go home now?"

"Yes, ma'am," Amon answered. "Mr. Tremayne said that he don't know much about the town, 'cause he ain't been down there yet. All he knows is that there's no Yankees there. So whoever wants to go home, me and Rosh and Amon will be glad to take you."

On Christmas morning of 1862, Mary Custis Lee sat in her rolling chair at the front windows and watched the snow fall. It was a pretty sight, but as soon as the feather-flakes hit the earth, the scene became grimy and dreary. East Franklin Street in Richmond was always busy, as were all the streets in the heart of the capital city. The humble rented house had a generous covered front porch, but no garden or yard, so it loomed right up over the street.

Soldiers dashed up and down, some on foot, some on horseback, always hurrying. Even in the dry heat of summer, the street was always a mire of mud and horse droppings.

Still, in good weather, Mary sat on the porch hour after hour, day after day, knitting socks of Confederate gray. But in the cruel winters, she was in so much pain she could barely sit up at all, and when she did, she huddled close to a hot fire.

Today, however, she had decided to brave the icy drafts around the window to watch the charming snowfall as she opened her special Christmas presents. They were Robert's letters.

Mary Custis Lee was not a sentimental woman. She was

intelligent, clever, forceful, plain-spoken, and pragmatic. She had saved Robert's letters through the years, because they documented so well the times and events in his life, but she rarely visited them. It had only been in April of 1861, when her husband had become General Robert E. Lee of the Confederate States of America, that she began to treasure them. Last Christmas she had started her tradition of giving herself the best Christmas present: rereading Robert's letters.

Opening one letter that crackled with age, she began to read and was transported back to those heady days of their youth, when he was a lonely second lieutenant at Fort Monroe and she had wintered at Arlington. She saw again the wonderful years there when Robert was working in Washington. She relived the terrible two years of the Mexican War and the joy of his homecoming. Then there were the blessed peaceful years, at Baltimore and West Point. The death of her father was still sorrowful to her, though it was muted now, and she remembered how her grief had been mixed with joy that Robert had been at Arlington with her for two years. Then he had gone back to Texas, but only for a short time. The events after March 1, 1861, when Robert had returned to Arlington, seemed fast and frantic.

Grimacing with pain both physical and in her soul, she opened Robert's letter of October 20, 1862, only three months ago:

> *I cannot express the anguish I feel at the death of my sweet Annie. To know that I shall never see her again on earth, that her place in our circle, which I always hoped one day to enjoy, is forever vacant, is agonizing in the extreme. But God in this, as in all things, has mingled mercy with the blow, in selecting that one best prepared to leave us. May you be able to join me in saying, "His will be done."*

Mary looked up, now sightless with hot tears stinging her eyes. No, she had not been able to join Robert in his acceptance of God's will. She did not think it was merciful that Annie, their sweet Little

Raspberry, had died. She was angry, and she was bitter. Hers and Robert's only grandchildren were dead. Robert E. Lee III, Rooney and Charlotte's son, had died the previous June. He was only two years old. Charlotte had given birth to a little girl in November, and the child had died on December 2nd, only twenty-three days previously.

No, Mary thought savagely, *I am not him. I am not like him! No one could be so humble, so forgiving, so ready to accept such grievances and call them merciful! I cannot say, "Your will be done!"* All that was within her raged for a long time.

But Mary Lee had known the Lord for many, many years. He had been her love, her companion, her most faithful friend long before Robert E. Lee was. And she realized this, and she knew her love for the Lord Jesus was stronger than her anger, stronger than her bitterness, stronger even than her love for Robert and her children. Her heart broke, and she surrendered.

After a time of tears, she dried her eyes and opened her last, most treasured letter, though it was not the last one in time. It was dated June 22, 1862, when Robert had just named the Confederate army in the east "The Army of Northern Virginia."

> *I have the same handsome hat which surmounts my gray head. . .and shields my ugly face, which is masked by a white beard as stiff and wiry as the teeth of a card. In fact, an uglier person you have never seen, and so unattractive is it to our enemies that they shoot at it whenever visible to them.*

Mary looked up again, but instead of seeing a galling darkness, she saw her husband's face. He had always been the most handsome man she had ever seen, and this was not the rosy imagination of an adoring wife. Men and women alike remarked on Robert's fine and noble countenance. Even one of the newspapers had crowned him "the handsomest man in the army." But she knew that Robert's lines, in his mind, were simple unvarnished truth. There was not a shred of vanity in him.

And then she read her favorite lines Robert had ever written:

> *But though age with its snow has whitened my head, and its frosts have stiffened my limbs, my heart, you well know, is not frozen to you, and summer returns when I see you.*

She looked up again, a dreamy smile transforming her pain-wracked, drawn face into the vivacious Mary Custis of Arlington. It really was a beautiful snow.

It snowed on Christmas morning, a pretty, light snow of big flakes. After dinner Jolie sat in the rocking chair, looking out the study windows on the grounds that sloped down to the river. All the sharp edges of nature were softened. The world beyond the borders of Rapidan Run may rage in fire and blood and death, but here all was clean and silent and tranquil.

"Hello, Mouse."

Jolie's eyes widened. Then she jumped out of the chair and leaped into Morgan's arms. For long moments they hugged, holding each other tightly.

Then Morgan lifted her up and swung her around in circles, laughing. "I'm glad to see you! I've missed you!" he said.

Breathlessly, Jolie said, "Put me down, Morgan! I'm so dizzy I can't see straight!"

He set her down, and she smoothed her skirt then felt her hair. "Is it standing on end? Feels like it. I've missed you, too, Morgan. Very much. Welcome home. And Merry Christmas! How long can you stay?"

"Let me at least take off my hat and coat and sit down. Hm, a real chair. Not sure I remember. . ."

Jolie took his snow-soaked slouch hat and heavy overcoat.

"Silly moose," she said. Once when she had been little, her father had called her a silly goose. The next time she used the phrase herself, she had transformed it into 'silly moose,' and that's what she had said ever since then. "Sit down. What do you want, tea, coffee, cocoa?"

"How about if you sit down with me for a minute and stop fast-firing questions," he said good-naturedly.

Jolie went and hung up his hat and coat, then returned and obediently sat on the sofa across from his old armchair.

He cocked his head to the side and studied her. "You look different. You're growing up. And it seems like every time I don't see you for a while, I'm always surprised by how pretty you are. And you're filling out. You don't look so much like a gawky little girl anymore."

"I was going to thank you for the compliment," Jolie said with mock wrath, "but now I think I'll pinch you instead. But I don't want to talk about me, Morgan. I want to know everything, everything about you, and General Lee, and the horses, and the Yankees—"

A shadow crossed his face, and now Jolie saw that when he wasn't smiling weariness and sorrow marred his smooth features. "Jolie, I wish I could give you everything that you want right now," he said with an attempt at lightness, "but I can't talk about me right now. All I want to think about, and talk about, is home. Please?"

"Of course, Morgan," she said quickly. "I'm sorry. I didn't think. Why don't we go to the kitchen and get mugs of hot coffee, as we used to do, and then go to the stables?" She smiled slyly. "I know you're going to pretend you came home to see us, but we all know you too well. You only came home to see the horses."

"I did not!" he said with indignation. "I missed you all so much, and I'm dying to see everyone. Right after I check on the horses, of course."

They spent the entire afternoon seeing the horses, the stables, riding around the pastures, inspecting the barn and the storeroom and the root cellar and pantry. "Looks like we've still got plenty of stores," Morgan said with relief. "For both the humans and the horses."

"I'm glad horses can't eat meat and vegetables," Jolie said mockingly, "or the humans would be eating oats and barley."

Morgan requested that Amon and the entire family join him at supper at the dining table in the farmhouse. "And that means you, too, Evetta," he said sternly. "No hopping up and down and serving us. I want you to sit down and eat with us like a Christian woman."

"I'll do that, but I s'pect only till they's something you want out in the kitchen," she said suspiciously.

"If there is, I'll get it myself," he said. "If there's one thing Perry and Meredith have taught me, it's that I am most definitely not Marse Robert, so I can wait on my own self along with all of the other lesser beings in the world."

They had supper late, and true to her word, Evetta sat down like a Christian woman. Morgan said a heartfelt prayer of thanks for their family and for the great bounty of their meal. Everyone else had, without being told, understood Morgan's need for a time free from dealing with worries with life-and-death consequences, and they kept the conversation airy and cheerful.

As they were finishing up with pecan pie and coffee, Morgan said, "Now tell me all about everyone from Fredericksburg who stayed here after the evacuation. I'm not even sure who was here."

Everyone turned to Jolie, and she swallowed hard. But she managed to say blithely, "You know about the Bledsoes, of course, and Ellie Cage and Mr. and Mrs. Patrick and Will Green. But you didn't know the Cogginses, did you? Or the Archers. First, let me tell you all about Connie Archer. She's just a wonderful woman. . . ."

Jolie went on telling Morgan about the good things, the funny things, the odd little quirky things that one didn't know about people until living with them. She said very little about the Bledsoes, and what she did say was kind.

Jolie noticed that Amon and Evetta were listening to her with approval written all over their honest faces. Evetta even smiled at her.

They all sat at the table laughing and talking for over two hours. Even when Evetta finally rose to clear the table, everyone, even the men, helped her. They all trooped out to the kitchen, and Evetta made a fresh pot of coffee.

At ten o'clock, Morgan suddenly yawned hugely. He looked vaguely surprised, as if he'd been ambushed by a practical joker.

Jolie and Ketura giggled.

"I must be getting old. Next thing you know I'll be dribbling soup down my chin and forgetting where I put my teeth," Morgan grumbled. Then he grew sober. "But before I go to bed, there's something I have to tell you all."

They all grew very still.

Morgan went on, "I have to go back, first thing in the morning."

"Oh, no," Jolie whispered, but it sounded loud in the quiet kitchen.

"I have to, Jolie," he repeated firmly. "And this may be the last leave I'll have for—well, I can't know for how long, because I'm not requesting leave anymore. You see, I thought about it the whole time I was riding here. It's not fair. In fact, I feel guilty, almost dishonorable, taking a leave right now. There are thousands and thousands of men who are far away from home. They can't just saddle up and ride to their farms in an afternoon. Some of them haven't been home in two years. In good conscience, I can't come home and then go back and face them."

"But they would do the same thing if they were only ten miles from home!" Jolie cried. "And I'm sure General Lee would give them a leave, just as I know he must have given one to you, or you wouldn't be here!"

"He probably would, if in fact we all asked him for leaves, which of course we don't," Morgan said, taking the sting out of his words by speaking very gently. "But in any case, General Lee himself won't even take a leave to go home. I know that President Davis urged him to visit Mrs. Lee in Richmond, but he refused, and I know why he did. It's because he believes that he must set an example for his men and also because he very consciously shares the hardships of his men. It's the same thing when people send him food or ask him to stay at their homes. He sends the food to the hospitals and eats our rations. Unless he's so ill he has to stay in bed, he lives in his tent. Even that is plain and simple and without any luxuries. The only frill he has, if you can call it that, is a little brown hen named Abigail. She lives under his cot and lays him an egg every morning," Morgan finished with an oddly sad smile.

"But I still don't understand," Jolie said stubbornly. "That's all very admirable of General Lee, but like you said, Morgan, you're not Marse Robert. You're not responsible for setting an example for tens of thousands of men."

"But I am," he said slowly. "We all are."

Jolie decided to leave Morgan in peace for the night, but she knew that she simply must ask him about Leona Bledsoe before he left in the morning. She tossed and flailed around, turning her bed into a mare's nest trying to think of how to ask him about Leona without upsetting him or worrying him. Finally she thought, *If he's not in love with her, then nothing I say will upset him, and if he is in love with her, then nothing I say will worry him. Now I'm the silly moose.* Finally she slept soundly.

She must have awakened as soon as Morgan did, in a glowing dawn. Quickly she dressed then ran downstairs to wait for him.

He came down about five minutes later.

She met him at the bottom of the stairs, saying, "I knew you'd try to sneak out, but you're not going to get away with it, mister."

"I wouldn't try to sneak anything past you, Jolie," he said, grinning. "You're too smart for me. In fact, I'm finding out that most ladies are." He took her arm and started toward the back door.

Jolie plucked at his sleeve and asked, "Now that you've

mentioned it, could I talk to you for a minute before we go get breakfast?"

"Sure," he said, doing a quick turn and leading her into the study. "Mentioned what?"

"Ladies," Jolie said as carelessly as she could. "I wanted to ask you about one."

"Ah, I bet I know who. Leona Bledsoe, right?" he said playfully as he handed Jolie onto the sofa, and he settled into his old shabby chair. "I forgot to tell you yesterday. Well, I guess I forgot to tell you because there's nothing to tell you."

"Morgan," Jolie said, summoning all her patience, "make sense."

"That's just it. I can't even really tell you why I got so weird about Leona," he said, obviously perplexed. "Just minutes after I had sent Rosh off that night, I started wondering about my silly self. I kept thinking, why send the carriage after the Bledsoes? They're a wealthy, prominent family with loads of friends and resources. Why not send the carriage for Ellie Cage and the baby? Or the Patricks?" He shrugged. "I guess it was just some throwback gut reaction. 'Send the carriage for the Bledsoes.' Kind of pathetic of me, I feel like now."

Jolie was so enormously relieved she almost felt dizzy. She felt silly and rather pathetic herself, letting Leona Bledsoe make her so miserable. She knew Morgan Tremayne as well as she knew herself. In fact, she probably understood Morgan better than she did herself. Morgan could never love and honor the woman she had seen here, in those difficult weeks. Jolie didn't know what Leona had been like before, and she didn't care. Now Morgan was here, and now Jolie knew that he loved her deeply. He may not love her in the way that she loved him—with a deep, desperate longing and passion—but he certainly did not love Leona Bledsoe in that way, either.

Morgan was watching her curiously, and finally he asked, "Jolie? Leona didn't insult you, did she? Amon was telling me that she was the worst harridan that ever lived while she was here. I can't imagine Leona acting like a snarling fishwife, but apparently she did. So, did she say something ugly to you, Jolie?"

Jolie smiled radiantly. "I hope never to lie to you, Morgan, so I will tell you that yes, she did. But I also will tell you that I don't care about that now, not in the least."

"Good," he said with relief. "Because after what Amon told me, I realized that Leona is far beneath your notice. You're a nobler, more honorable person than she has ever been. She's not the grand lady, Jolie. You are."

In an hour Jolie stood holding Vulcan's bridle, looking up at Morgan. *Do not cry*, she told herself sternly, *until after he leaves.* "I'll miss you, Morgan," she said softly, her dark eyes like rich velvet. "I'll pray for you always. Good-bye." She let go of Vulcan's bridle.

"Good-bye, Mouse," he said.

She watched him until he disappeared into the snowy woods.

CHAPTER TWENTY-THREE

Although the Battle of Fredericksburg had been a ghastly defeat for the North, and the Army of the Potomac had crept away in the middle of the night as they had done before, this time they didn't retreat all the way back to the safety of Washington. They stayed on the far side of the Rappahannock River, ranging up and down in their thousands, looking for another way to get at the apparently unbeatable team of Robert E. Lee, Stonewall Jackson, and James Longstreet. And so, General Lee and his army settled into winter quarters in his old tent on the hills behind Fredericksburg.

When Private Morgan Tremayne reported back for duty on December 26, 1862, that is where he went. In the coming months, although his gaze and his mind often went fifteen miles to the northeast, he was determined not to ask for leave until Robert E. Lee did.

On January 20th of the new year, General Ambrose Burnside, who had been devastated both personally and publicly by his ignominious defeat, again marshaled his army to cross the Rappahannock River to attack the Rebels. It rained for four days and four nights. The army became so mired down in Virginia sludge that they had to give up and retreat. It was dubbed Burnside's Mud March, and this debacle finished off Burnside. He was replaced on January 26th by General Joseph Hooker as commander of the Army of the Potomac.

By the end of January, Morgan was beginning to see that being in the army did not mean going from glory to glory in a series of battles. What it meant was weeks and months in camp, resting and refitting from the last battle and preparing for the next one. Morgan was lucky, he knew. He was never bored because he had his horses. He could, and did, spend all day feeding them, grooming them, exercising them, shoeing them, diagnosing and doctoring them.

He was riding Vulcan one bright morning when he came upon some troops from Georgia and Texas who whooped and hollered as they played in the snow. It was obvious that they had never seen such a phenomenon. As delighted children invariably do in a good sticky snow, a snowball fight started. Morgan walked Vulcan around for hours, because by early afternoon he estimated there must have been at least five thousand men, spread out for miles around, in snowball fights. He grinned so much that his face hurt that night.

Morgan had told Amon that he could come to camp twice a month as long as the Yankees stayed on the other side of the Rappahannock. Each time he came, he brought food for Morgan and hot mash for the horses. Morgan shared the food with Meredith and Perry and all the other officers' lowly privates and servants. But he jealously gave the hot mash only to Traveler and Vulcan and the staff officers' horses.

Amon also brought good news from Jolie and from Rapidan Run. The horses and foals were doing very well, and the army had sent two dozen men to harvest the winter forage crop. At the end of February, Morgan asked hesitantly, "Does Jolie ever ask to come with you?"

"No, sir," Amon replied. "I think she knows that'd prob'ly worry you too much."

Morgan was relieved. He hadn't forbidden Jolie to come to camp, because he wanted no shadows of war to dim that perfect Christmas day. But he had hoped that she would comprehend that it would be a hardship for him. He began to realize how very mature and wise she had grown to understand that.

At the end of March, General Lee grew ill, and for the first time he agreed to be moved to a private house near Fredericksburg. He wrote to Mary:

> *I am suffering with a bad cold as I told you, and was threatened, the doctors thought, with some malady which must be dreadful if it resembles its name, but which I have forgot.*

The doctors called it an inflammation of the heart sac. It was a very serious condition.

April came; spring came; warm weather came; and with it came the Army of the Potomac. They crossed the Rappahannock above Fredericksburg, over 138,000 strong, and marched west then south. They came to the Rapidan River and began their crossing at Germanna Ford and Ely's Ford. The roads from the fords led into the Wilderness, and by May 1st, they were concentrated in the largest clearing in that blighted wood. The only three roads in the Wilderness intersected there, and because of that the clearing with the one old house was called Chancellorsville.

Morgan felt as if every single nerve ending in his body were raw when he found out that the Yankees had crossed the Rapidan and were invested along the south banks all the way to where it flowed into the Rappahannock. That meant that Rapidan Run was now behind enemy lines. Dread and fear overcame him, but only for a few moments. The reality was that he could not help Jolie and Amon's family by going to them, even if it had been possible. The best thing he could do was pray for victory and deliverance. After a short wordless prayer to that effect, he turned his mind to those things that he could do: he took care of the horses and followed General Lee.

Morgan had never put himself forward to General Lee, but he did so the night of May 1st. General Lee had come to the edge of the forest south of Chancellorsville to consult with General Jackson. Before Jackson arrived, General Lee pored over a crude map with several of his officers. Morgan stood nearby holding the horses, as usual, but in the close woods he was nearer to the conference than usual. He heard one colonel say, "Perhaps we can find a local who knows the country, General Lee."

Without thinking, Morgan sprang forward and said, "General Lee, sir? I know these woods. This is very near my home."

General Lee turned to look at him quizzically then recognition dawned on his face. "That's right," he said quietly. "I remember, Rapidan Run Horse Farm. Tell me, Private Tremayne, can you tell me if we are looking at this map upside down or right side up?"

In fifteen minutes Morgan had improved their map greatly, and then Stonewall Jackson arrived. Morgan withdrew back to the horses, and the two men moved away from their officers to lay out the map on the ground and study it. This meeting was memorialized by the humble name of the "Crackerbox Meeting," because that's what Lee and Jackson sat on as they decided the disposition of the entire army. The conversation ended with three simple words so typical of General Lee. "Well," he told Stonewall, "go on."

The next morning Hooker's Union forces advanced. . .and successfully. But once again, the fey fear that seemed to strike Union generals who faced Robert E. Lee assaulted the swaggering "Fighting Joe" Hooker, and he ordered all to fall back to Chancellorsville and hold a defensive position. This, of course, gave Robert E. Lee what he loved most: the initiative.

The fighting was fierce on May 2nd and 3rd, and on that day, they broke the Union line, and Hooker withdrew a mile. By May 6th, the vast army had fled back across the Rappahannock. Lee had beaten them with only sixty-two thousand men, and those split up into three forces.

When he heard that the Yankees had withdrawn from the Rapidan, Morgan was so relieved he felt weak. But even though he was only about seven miles from his home, he didn't see Rapidan Run. General Lee quickly gathered the wounded and the men in the field, and the march back to the heights above Fredericksburg began.

Morgan had heard on May 3rd that Stonewall Jackson had been wounded somewhere in the Wilderness, shot by his own men because of the overlying spirit of unease and confusion that seemed to rule in that place. He was anxious and disheartened when he heard the news.

On Sunday, May 10th, General Jackson crossed his last river to rest under the shade of the trees. Morgan was deeply saddened, and he saw many battle-hardened veterans weep unashamedly at the news. The entire South mourned.

General Lee, however, had little time to weep, even for his most beloved comrade in arms. In June, the Army of Northern Virginia would invade the North for the second time.

Morgan was always acutely aware that his view of the war was vastly different from that of other soldiers. As he wrote Jolie, "I hold the horses while the real soldiers fight the war."

He had never been in battle. He had always observed it from afar, standing behind General Lee and talking softly to Vulcan and Traveler. Sometimes it was not so "afar" that Morgan didn't feel the hot rush from artillery shells screaming over his head or the sharp whistle of a rifle round close to his ear. Robert E. Lee liked to get as close to the battle line as possible and still retain a coherent view of the field. Sometimes that was close to people shooting at each other, indeed.

Of course Morgan saw the aftermath, the grisly bodies, the little creeks and streams running crimson, the horror of wounds of war. But though these images were the most vivid and graphic, they were but a small fraction of his memories. Most of the pictures that loomed large in his mind were very different, of quiet evenings with Meredith and Perry, of the few times that General Lee had groomed Traveler while Morgan groomed Vulcan, and they talked of little inconsequential things, of the strange predatory exultation he had felt on Lee's Hill above Fredericksburg.

Two little incidents that happened on their march north imprinted on Morgan's mind, and he knew for the remainder of his life they would become part of his most vivid recollections of Robert E. Lee.

On June 25th, General Lee, riding his beloved Traveler, crossed the Potomac River into Maryland. On the Yankee side of the river, a group of ladies holding umbrellas in the drizzly rain were waiting for him. They stepped in front of him, and General Lee courteously dismounted to doff his hat and bow. As always, Morgan slipped forward to take Traveler's reins.

The ladies were on a mission. They had an enormous wreath of white roses for Traveler to wear as a garland. General Lee was silent for a fraction of a second, and behind him Morgan thought, *He's horrified. I can almost hear him thinking. . .things like that are all fine and good for General Stuart, but. . .* Morgan had difficulty keeping a straight face.

At a stand, the general balked. But the ladies were very insistent. Still General Lee declined the honor. Finally Morgan stepped forward slightly, doffed his hat to the ladies, and said, "General Lee, perhaps I may have the honor of carrying this magnificent garland and walking beside you and Traveler."

Though reluctantly, the ladies assented. Morgan walked into

Maryland by General Lee's side, holding a rose garland in his arms, Vulcan's reins tied to his belt. As soon as they were out of sight of the ladies, General Lee said, "I believe you may mount up again, Private Tremayne."

The next day, in the afternoon, they crossed into Pennsylvania. At the head of the column rode General Lee, his uniform immaculate, his seat on Traveler perfect, as nobly handsome as when he was the Marble Model.

As the army marched through a small town, a group of well-dressed women stood on the walk in front of a large house to watch the invaders. A young girl stood in front of the women, defiantly waving an American flag. When she saw General Lee, she lowered the flag and said loudly enough for a hundred men following the general to hear, "Oh! I wish he was ours!"

Lee's plan was to draw the Yankees into battle at Harrisburg, which would enable him to cut their east–west communications. On their way out of Chambersburg, General Heth heard of a supply of shoes in nearby Cashtown, and he sent a brigade for them, since many men in the army were barefoot. They found themselves engaged by Union cavalry. Within the next two days, following the capricious tangents of war, the two armies found themselves in the little sleepy town of Gettysburg.

People remembered the fields of battle at Gettysburg. Soon everyone in the South and in the North knew the Peach Orchard, the Wheat Field, Devil's Den, Round Top, Little Round Top. But the one that Southern people always recalled with anguish was Cemetery Ridge. Here was where they charged when Major General George Pickett led his division of thirteen thousand Rebels and seven thousand of them fell.

On that hot, dusty afternoon, General Lee took his hat off and rode with the remnant as they streamed back to the safety of Confederate lines. "This was all my fault," he said. "It is I who have lost this fight, and you must help me out of it the best you can."

On July 4, 1863, the defeated Army of Northern Virginia

retreated back toward the Potomac River and the safety of Virginia soil. The train of wounded stretched more than fourteen miles.

❧

After Gettysburg, the army quartered south of the Rapidan, about twenty-five miles west of Fredericksburg. General Lee established his field headquarters at Orange Court House. Morgan wished valiantly for the old quarters on the hills above Fredericksburg. One reason was that the brush shelter he and Rosh had built for the horses had proved to be as sturdy and almost as weatherproof as a log cabin. The other reason was that he was too far away from Rapidan Run for Amon to be able to come to camp.

For the first time since he had joined the army, he was homesick. He missed Jolie, and he missed Rapidan Run. His homesickness always took that form in his mind, in that order, and it interested him when he realized it. He missed Jolie terribly, perhaps even more than he missed his home. Why was that? How had that happened? In his disheartened state, he honestly didn't know. All he knew was that it was true, and this revelation only made him more forlorn.

In August, when they finally settled down in the fields and pastures around Orange Court House, bleak news from the western theater greeted them. In May and June, a rising star Union general named Ulysses S. Grant had besieged the vital city of Vicksburg, Mississippi. On July 4th, the day the Army of Northern Virginia had begun their retreat from Gettysburg, Vicksburg had surrendered. Longstreet was sent west, to help in the defense of Chattanooga.

In September, they were elated when they heard of a resounding victory by Confederate General Braxton Bragg at Chickamauga. In November, they were utterly downcast when the news of Chattanooga's surrender reached them.

Even though life in camp could be monotonous, Morgan was glad that the army fought no great battles in the winter of 1863–1864. They could not recover so readily from the defeat at

Gettysburg, the first they had known. And they were hungry, they were short of blankets, they were threadbare, and they were ill-shod. Morgan spent much of the time helping the quartermasters as they implored Richmond for supplies and searched desperately for new sources.

But as surely as the dawn follows the darkest night, renewed hope and strength come in springtime. By March of 1864, the army was still poorly fed and many were still barefoot, but the days were warm and the air was scented with jasmine. Men found renewed vigor in their hearts and minds and renewed strength in their reverential loyalty to Robert E. Lee.

Darwin's theory of evolution was hotly argued in some quarters of the camp. But one carefree spring day, an earthy veteran told the debating scholars, "Well, boys, the rest of us may have developed from monkeys, but I tell you none less than God could have made such a man as Marse Robert."

In May, the Army of the Potomac crossed the Rappahannock again. This time they didn't poke along as they had under General McClellan, they didn't procrastinate for days as they had under General Burnside, and they didn't swagger in a parade as they had under General Hooker. They marched fast and relentlessly now, for they had a new commander, Ulysses S. Grant, and he was a true man of war.

Grant's orders were identical to Hooker's in one area alone. He ordered the army to cross at Germanna Ford and Ely's Ford and to march into the Wilderness. On May 3rd, Morgan stood by the side of the Plank Road, holding the horses while General Lee conferred with General Longstreet, thinking grimly that it had been exactly a year since he had looked at that dark forest. Again sickening dread assailed him when he thought about Rapidan Run, in danger of being overrun by the Union Army.

He deliberately eavesdropped on General Lee's conversation

this time. Lee knew of the Union crossings at the fords on the Rapidan, but he did not yet know the exact disposition of the Union Army. "I believe he will make a feint around on my left," he told Longstreet, "but I believe the main attack will come on our right. I wish that we had a clearer picture of their concentrations, but the dispatches come fast and furiously, and they are often hazy and confused."

Morgan stepped up to the two men, saluted, and said, "General Lee, I would like to volunteer to scout out the Federal concentration on your right."

Lee studied him. "I believe that you would be an excellent scout, Private Tremayne, for I've seen before how well you know this country. However, you are not a trained soldier, and through no fault or reluctance of your own, you have no experience in battle."

"That's true, sir. But I assure you that I can find the easternmost Yankee pickets, and I will take great pains to assure that they do not find me," Morgan said forcefully. "If they do find me, though, I will strive to do my duty, sir."

Lee nodded as if that were obvious, but he argued in his gentle manner. "In the morning I will send my two best observers, who have performed this same sort of covert task for me many times. I believe that would be the better course."

But Morgan was determined. "Sir, there is just one more thing I would like for you to consider before making that your final decision."

"And what is that, Private?"

"I can find them in the dark."

Just as twilight descended, Morgan mounted Vulcan, said a quiet good-bye to Perry and Meredith, and headed across the plains toward the southern border of the Wilderness. He was challenged several times, because Confederates were camped all over the roads and fields and pastures, waiting to be told exactly where to march to engage the enemy.

Each time he was challenged, Morgan replied, "Scout from headquarters" and started to retrieve his orders from General Lee. But not one man looked at it. After seeing him clearly they waved him on. Morgan didn't realize it, but he was a well-known figure because he rode with General Lee. They called him Marse Robert's horsemaster.

He went to a southeast point on the border of the woods and without hesitation plunged into the dim gray shadows of the Wilderness. After Vulcan had trotted forward a few steps, Morgan pulled him to a stop. He knew that if he waited and made himself relax for a few minutes, his eyes would adjust to what seemed like impenetrable blackness. Slowly the darker shapes began to form themselves into recognizable things—trees and boulders and an earth mound and a tangle of vines. Morgan could see. He gave Vulcan the lightest of kicks, and the horse walked slowly forward.

Morgan reflected that his mission would seem like the worst of folly to anyone else, and rightly so. Men got lost in the Wilderness in glaring daylight, and finding one's way at night seemed impossible. But to Morgan it was not. He had good night vision and sharp instincts for place and direction, but that was not what gave Morgan confidence at night in the Wilderness. It was because he knew this place so well, because he had taught himself. In the years that he had been at Rapidan Run, he had ridden into some part of the forest bordering his land almost every day. He had regarded it as a self-imposed challenge, to learn of this place. He had spent nights traveling through the woods, constantly mapping the place in his head, until he found a good place to camp. He wasn't afraid of the Wilderness, because he knew it.

But other men would fear it, because even courageous men feel vulnerable and apprehensive in a thick forest at night. Morgan was pretty sure he knew where the small squads of outlying pickets would be. About midway on the east side of the Wilderness were three little clearings, all roughly in a line from east to west, separated by the uneven ground of ridges and ravines, some of the dozens of small streams that traced all through the woods, and piles of sharp boulders and rocks. Morgan knew that three or four men alone at night in this place would want any open space they could find, instead of trying to sleep in a hostile jungle of stunted scrub pine, thorny tangles of vines, and tall misshapen oaks looming over them.

He sensed, rather than calculated, that he was nearing the first clearing, and he dismounted. "Be very, very quiet," he whispered to Vulcan. He began to creep forward. It was eerily quiet. The only noise was the occasional *shreep, shreep* of a cricket, its cheerful call odd and jangling in the portentous silence. Morgan was careful to gently pull any branches and vines away so that he and Vulcan could pass quietly.

Ahead and on his left was a group of white boulders, the biggest of them almost six feet tall. They gleamed dimly in the scant starlight, and Morgan was glad to see this landmark. About a hundred feet past the boulders in a straight line was the first clearing. Confidently now, Morgan made his way to the large boulder. At exactly the same moment he stepped around it, he heard a hoarse whisper.

"We aren't ever going to find—"

He came face-to-face with two Yankees.

The next few moments Morgan remembered as if he were a bystander, for he moved and acted on pure instinct, without conscious thought. He reached behind him and grabbed his rifle from the saddle sheath. In a smooth, swift movement, he twirled it to hold it like a club and hit the nearest man across the head. He reeled then fell hard, and Morgan heard a sickening crack as his head hit a rock.

Directly behind the first man, the second soldier raised his rifle and fired point-blank at Morgan's stomach, but either the rifle was not loaded or it misfired. To see that rifle barrel right at his gut made Morgan pause for a fatal second. The Yankee was quick, and now he grabbed his rifle barrel, reared back, and planted a vicious blow right across Morgan's left temple.

The lurid sight before his eyes instantly began to fade to black, and Morgan could feel himself falling but couldn't seem to stop himself.

He barely registered that Vulcan rushed to him, rose up, and hit the soldier with both hooves right in the chest. The man was knocked backward several feet and lay on his back, all breath gone. Vulcan moved forward to rear over him and stamp him, but the man rolled to his right and crawled away into a thick tangle of undergrowth. Vulcan neighed, a screaming trumpet sound, nose pointed to the sky, galloped headlong into the jungle of vines and shrubs, and disappeared from the death scene.

The blackness finally claimed Morgan.

It seemed to Morgan that he regained consciousness in one heartbeat, because the blood pushed through his head was hot and burning as if he had liquid lava in his veins. Each throb of his pulse was a second of agony. He lay still and motionless, thinking that if he didn't move, the pain would lessen. But it did not.

Resignedly he decided to open his eyes and try to sit up, for he was uncomfortable lying on the rocky ground. He opened his eyes. At least, he thought he had opened his eyes. But he saw nothing at all but featureless black, no shadows, no murky outlines of trees and boulders. He squeezed his eyes shut, which felt like an explosion in his head, then opened them again. Still nothing.

Panicky now, he scrabbled with his feet and pushed up with his hands until he was kneeling. He reached up to feel his eyelids, frantically thinking that they would not open, and his fingers gouged right into his eyeballs.

His eyes were wide open, and he was blind.

For an eternity, it seemed, he knelt there, his eyes straining and popping out of his head. He swiveled his head around in a futile effort to see. His brain said, "You're blind," but his body fought it. Every muscle was as rigid as stone, his mind was a single energy screaming a single word over and over: "See! See! See!"

But the strain overtaxed Morgan's shocked system, and he grew weak and limp, and his thoughts became thick and murky. He drew in a deep shuddering breath and began to feel again the horrendous pain in his head. He put his shaking hands to his temples, then slowly his fingers went to his eyes, and he deliberately closed his eyelids. With a jaw-hardening effort of will, he made himself calm down and concentrate.

Morgan had always been a man of action, but in different ways than that term usually denotes. He was a fixer. If he faced a problem, he formulated a plan then went to work and fixed the problem. If he had a monumental project, he broke it down into manageable steps and worked until he had finished completely. He could not bear passivity. To him it was the same as stagnation, and he must always be moving forward to accomplish the task in front of him. That was why, with no combat experience and no natural aggressiveness to speak of, he had instantly attacked the Union soldiers the moment he saw them. They were a problem, and he fixed it.

As these thoughts slowly plodded through his mind, Morgan decided to shift into a more comfortable sitting position, and he put his hands down to steady himself. His hands rested on a man's chest.

Morgan shot up and took a step backward, tripped over a rock, and fell sprawling on his back. It knocked the breath out of him, and again he panicked as he struggled to pull air into his chest. But as he started breathing the panic subsided. *I killed him,* Morgan thought with a strange indifference. *He's dead. I killed him.*

And now Morgan's tidy, efficient mind simply took over and compartmentalized all the jumbled thoughts and shocking images and deep fears, even the pain. It was as if a shutter closed, hiding all the confusion in another part of his brain, leaving him in a small, tightly controlled and clear and logical place.

He sat up and felt around him for a support, but there was nothing but small rocks and ground-covering vines surrounding him. He crossed his legs and thought, *I'm in the Wilderness. I was scouting for the pickets, and I came upon those two soldiers.* He could remember hitting the one and hearing his head crack savagely on a rock. But he remembered little after that. He wondered why the other soldier hadn't killed him. Then he wondered if he had killed the other soldier, too, but he wasn't about to go crawling around, feeling his way, trying to find another dead body. It wouldn't help anything. He was alive, and he was alone in the Wilderness.

He thought of Vulcan, but after considering it, he wasn't at all surprised that the horse had bolted. Vulcan was high-strung, but he was smart, and after all, they were only about three miles from Rapidan Run.

That thought took Morgan's breath away even quicker than his headlong fall had done.

Only three miles. Only three miles! It might as well be three hundred, or three thousand! I am blind. I cannot find my way home!

Perilous weakness hit him again, his head felt as if it were splitting into little jagged pieces, and he was nauseated. Trembling, he got to his hands and knees, crawled a couple of feet, and vomited. And then he was sick again and again until he knew his system was completely empty.

He half-fell as he turned away, then went down and crawled on his belly a few feet. Letting his head fall into his hands, he thought with anguish, *I always did something. I always figured out how to make things right, how to make them work, how to accomplish everything I set out to do. But now my worst fears have come to me, I'm helpless. Utterly, completely helpless.*

Morgan wandered in the darkness, both physical and spiritual, for a long time. He found himself praying with a desperation he had never known. *Oh God, what can I do? Please, please, tell me.*

Show me something, anything! Please, let me see a way out!

Very gently, as if God had barely touched his shoulder, Morgan felt the answer. There was no task he could accomplish. There was no way out. There was nothing he could do.

Nothing except surrender. For the first time in his life, scalding tears sprang to his sightless eyes and fell into his hands as they cupped his face. It was the hardest thing he had ever done, to do nothing. Calmly now he prayed, *I am in Your hands, Lord. Thy will be done.*

Morgan marveled at the feeling of the presence of God, a sharper, more vivid sense than sight alone could ever give. He rested and meditated and prayed and was completely at ease.

Only a few miles away, he heard the opening salvo of big guns and the sharp constant crackle of musket fire began. Abruptly Morgan remembered that he was in the Wilderness, and probably less than a mile to his left was the flank of a force of about seventy-five thousand Yankees. It was daytime, he suddenly realized. Because he saw only darkness, he had, quite naturally he supposed, assumed it was still night. *I may not be able to see where they are, but I can sure run away from the sound of the guns.*

But no, he couldn't run anywhere, he would surely fall with each step. Morgan could find his way in the dark, certainly, but only if he was walking or on horseback, scanning the entire scene in view. He didn't know every rock and ravine in the Wilderness.

In another reluctant surrender, he thought, *I guess it would only be sensible to sit here and hope I don't get shot and let the Yanks take me prisoner.* But on reflection he saw that would not be a sensible course at all. Coming from the east, assuming that the battle even swung this far over, the Union soldiers would see their dead comrade first, and there would be Morgan, sitting placidly by, an easy target for a soldier in heated battle mode. "The term 'sitting duck' comes to mind," Morgan said ruefully to himself. Aside from that, it went utterly against Morgan's every instinct to let himself be taken prisoner.

I know, Lord, that I can't solve this situation, that by myself I can't fix this. But I don't think You just want me to sit here and die. Isn't there some way, something You could do to help me?

This humble plea was much more heartfelt than his indignant demands to God before. But there was still no answer. Morgan decided to crawl. He got up on his hands and knees, turned so that he was facing away from the nearby battle din, and began. He cut his hand on the first rock, but he kept crawling. He knew he was moving so slowly that it was just about hopeless, but doggedly he kept on.

Morgan was already aware that his hearing had sharpened since he couldn't see, and he heard the soft tread of a shoed horse. Then a warm muzzle hit him on the shoulder so hard he fell over. Lying on the rocks, he murmured, "Vulcan? Is that you?"

Vulcan answered with a sarcastic snort and another blow to the shoulder. "Okay, okay," Morgan muttered, "take it easy. I'm blind, you know. It's not going to do you any good to knock me around."

Vulcan shifted his front hooves and impatiently bobbed his head. Morgan could hear the jingle of the bridle rings and the creaks of the leather very close to his ear. "Don't step on me, you big ninny. Let me think." Morgan pictured himself standing up, feeling for the stirrup, and swinging up into the saddle. And then he would be sitting there on a feisty horse, blind. That was crazy.

But it was better than crawling.

He pushed Vulcan's insistent nose away then, teetering a little, managed to stand up. He reached out with both hands and felt the horse's hot, muscular shoulder. He kept on. He felt the stirrup strap. In a move he had done thousands of times, he grabbed the saddle horn, put his left foot in the stirrup, kicked up and over with his right foot, and he was on horseback.

The minute he was sitting up there he felt horribly vulnerable, not only to bullets but to low tree branches and overhanging rocks. Helplessly he bent over and clasped his arms around Vulcan's strong neck. "I can't do it, boy. You're going to have to do this by yourself.

Please just take me somewhere, away from here."

Vulcan started walking slowly along, picking his way. Morgan's head began to pound again, and the sickening rolling of his stomach started up. He felt as if his whole body was spinning around, like a child's top, and vaguely he thought how odd it was that being dizzy felt so different when he couldn't see. The whirling sensation grew stronger, and Morgan fell unconscious again. This time he welcomed it.

CHAPTER TWENTY-FOUR

Morgan opened his eyes and said sadly, "Still nighttime. . ."

A low-timbred, rich voice answered, "Yes, it is." He felt a cool, soft hand smooth back his hair and smelled a faint, poignantly familiar scent of chamomile.

"Am I dead?" he asked curiously.

"No, no, no, Morgan, you're not dead. You're just injured."

He digested this for a while. "Are you Jolie?" he finally asked.

"What?" she exclaimed, though she kept her voice low and calm. "Of course it's Jolie. Don't you recognize me, Morgan dear?"

"I can't see you," he said quietly. "I'm blind."

The hand stroking his forehead stopped for only a moment then resumed. "I didn't know," she said simply. "You've been unconscious since you got here. This is the first time you've opened your eyes."

"Since I got here. . . You mean Vulcan brought me home?" he said, weakly incredulous.

"Yes, he did. And I cannot imagine how you stayed in the saddle. You were collapsed over his neck, arms hanging down. He must have come very slowly and carefully from wherever you were."

"We were in the Wilderness," he said wearily. "What day is it?"

"It's Thursday," she answered. Then seeing that it meant nothing to him, she added, "It's May 5th. The battle in the Wilderness started this morning and went on all day long until about an hour ago. It's about nine o'clock at night now."

"May 4th," he said, "that night. That's when we rode into the Wilderness, and I—there were some Yankees, and—something happened. I can't remember—"

"Ssshh, don't worry about that right now," Jolie said. "You'll remember in time."

"My head hurts," he said, reaching up and feeling the enormous swelling on the left side of his head.

Jolie took his hand in both of hers, settled it onto his chest, and patted it. "I'm going to get you some medicine."

He heard the tinkling of a glass and smelled it even before she pressed the glass to his lips. "Laudanum," he said, wrinkling his nose. "Don't we have any brandy left?"

"No, I'm sorry, we don't," she said. The two bottles of brandy that Jolie had stored away in the pantry had disappeared back in December, the day the Bledsoes left Rapidan Run. "But laudanum is better for severe pain, anyway. Drink it, please, Morgan. You'll rest, and that's what you need."

Obediently he took two gulps of the strong medicine. With a heavy sigh he lay back on the pillow and closed his eyes. His right hand groped for her, and Jolie took it and held it. "I'm so tired," he murmured.

"I know. You just relax and sleep, Morgan dear. You're home now, and you're safe."

This time, when the blackness overtook him, it brought a peaceful rest.

Jolie held his hand until he was taking long even breaths and his grip on her hand relaxed. Silently she rose and went downstairs, leaving Morgan's bedroom door open.

Amon, Evetta, Ketura, Rosh, and Santo all sat at the dining room table, waiting.

When she entered, she put her finger to her lips to stop the questions she saw coming. "He's sleeping, and I left the door open so we can hear if he wakes up." She slid into her chair and stared down at the table. "He doesn't remember what happened. He just said that he was in the Wilderness last night."

"Last night?" Amon echoed. "Oh, ain't no tellin' about him. But Evetta says he wasn't shot or anything." Evetta and Jolie had taken off his filthy clothes, quickly bathed him, and put him in a comfortable, light linen nightshirt. His hands and knees were scratched and scraped, but other than the appalling bruise on his head, he didn't appear to be seriously injured.

"No, he wasn't shot," Jolie said. "But obviously something, or someone, hit his head hard. It's swelling up and turning bluer every minute. And—and—" She swallowed hard then continued, "He's blind."

A stunned silence lay heavy on the room.

Evetta said, "We gotta get a doctor."

"There's no doctor," Jolie said painfully. "There won't be any doctor, except in the field hospitals and then in Fredericksburg, or wherever the army ends up after this battle."

"Then what are we gonna do?" Amon asked worriedly.

"There's nothing we can do, except watch him and give him laudanum to help him rest so he can recover," Jolie said firmly.

No one said it, but the thought was almost tangible and audible in the quiet room: *If he recovers.*

Jolie and Ketura took turns sitting with Morgan throughout the night. Evetta was willing, but all three of the women decided that it would be best for Jolie and Ketura to take care of Morgan.

Evetta was a magnificent cook, but she was a dismal nurse. In her kitchen she moved quickly and purposefully without a wasted moment or movement. In the sickroom she fumbled and ran into the bed and almost hit Morgan's ear when she was adjusting his pillow. Gladly she banished herself to the kitchen.

At about three o'clock in the morning, Jolie was sitting in the easy chair Amon had moved upstairs to Morgan's bedside. It was a tattered old armchair that had been in the corner of the study, unused except when Jolie wanted to snuggle up in it on winter nights. But it was soft and comfortable, the contours of her body well worn into it, and she could sleep in it.

Now she awoke from a light doze and stared at Morgan. All through the night he had been sleeping so heavily that she began to worry that he was unconscious again. She tensed up because she wanted to shake him awake, but then she realized how foolish that was. If he woke up, he woke up. If he was unconscious, shaking him wouldn't do any good anyway. After a while she dozed again, uneasily.

At four o'clock, Ketura came in and whispered, "I'll sit with him now, Jolie. Go get some good sleep."

Morgan still slept soundly. He hadn't even moved.

Jolie was still worried, but she knew she would have to get some sleep if she was going to be able to take good care of Morgan, so she went to bed.

Just an hour later, the roar of cannon shattered the quiet sunrise. Jolie jumped up and ran to Morgan's room without even pulling on her dressing gown.

Ketura, too, had stood up in alarm at the sudden crashing booms. "That's closer than yesterday," she said, her eyes big and round.

Morgan turned his head toward the west and the Wilderness. His eyes opened, but it was obvious from their emptiness that he wasn't seeing. "Artillery," he murmured dully.

Ketura went across the room to look out the window, but

it faced north. Even if it had faced west, she couldn't have seen anything except a dingy gray smoke from the cannon rising.

Jolie hurried to his bedside and, seeing the condition of his face, didn't want to even touch his forehead. She took his hand and stroked it. It felt cold, and Jolie herself felt a chill, for it was a warm morning. "Yes, it's sunrise, Morgan. It's begun again."

He licked his dry, swollen lips.

Jolie berated herself, for he obviously had a raging thirst. Quickly she poured him a glass of water then gingerly slipped her hand behind his neck. "If you can raise your head just a little, I have some water,"

"It hurts so badly," he whispered, but he did manage, with Jolie's help, to get up just enough to drink.

"Small sips, Morgan. Don't gulp," she warned him.

But it was too late. Jolie grabbed the basin just in time for Morgan to be helplessly sick.

Ketura rushed back but then stood there, unable to do anything.

"He's falling, help me," Jolie grunted, pushing on Morgan's shoulder.

He had leaned over the bed when he knew he was going to throw up, and he was so weak he was sliding out of the bed head-first.

Ketura grabbed his other shoulder, and between them they managed to push him back onto the bed.

"So. . .so sorry," he whispered, squeezing his eyes shut.

"No," Jolie said firmly. "No. Don't be sorry. Don't ever apologize. Now I want you to just lie back and relax, Morgan. Try to make yourself relax." She sat down in the chair and took his hand, then began lightly stroking it and murmuring softly to him, "It's me, Jolie, dear Morgan. You're home, and we're all going to take very good care of you. Just be calm, clear your mind, take nice even breaths. . . ." She kept up the soothing undertones until it seemed that he slept. But now it was different from the night before. He twitched, and he frowned. She saw his eyes moving erratically underneath his eyelids. "Oh, Morgan," she whispered to herself with anguish.

Jolie had forgotten about Ketura, but now the girl touched her shoulder lightly and bent down to whisper, "Jolie, you slept less than an hour before the cannon woke you up. Go on, go back to bed and at least get another hour or two of sleep. Go on, you're still in your nightdress."

"It doesn't matter," she said distantly. "He can't see me anyway."

"It does matter," Ketura said firmly, "and you know it. Besides, it won't do Mr. Tremayne one bit of good for you to sit here and pass out in that chair, which is what you'll do if you don't get some rest. Now is as good a time as any. I'll come wake you if there's any change."

"Come get me if he wakes up," Jolie insisted. "I don't care if it's ten minutes from now."

"All right, I will," Ketura promised.

Jolie tried to go back to sleep, but it was impossible. Battle raged near, and something was wrong with Morgan, she knew it. Something new. After about half an hour, she gave up, rose, and dressed. She went downstairs and out to the kitchen, where she knew Evetta and Amon would be. The boys were there, too.

"How is he?" Amon instantly demanded.

"I—I don't know. Something's wrong," Jolie said hesitantly. "I mean, of course something's wrong, but I mean he's not resting as well as last night, and it worries me."

Evetta's face was grim. "Jolie, we don't know how bad his injury is, really. It may be that—"

"No, don't say it!" Jolie said loudly. "I know it, Evetta. Just please don't say it."

Evetta nodded with understanding.

Amon shook his head. "Y'know, those guns there is closer than they was yesterday. We might end up in the middle of a big ol' bloody mess."

"I know, but what can we do?" Jolie said. Then her face changed. "Oh, Amon, Amon. Of course you need to get your family out of here. You all take the wagon and go now, before they get any closer."

Amon frowned darkly. "We thought of that, but we ain't gonna do any such thing. First place, I know you wouldn't let us move Mr. Tremayne, and you'd stay here with him, and that can't be. Second place, Mr. Tremayne, he'd kill us if we runned off and left his horses. And where are we gonna go, anyways? 'Crost the river? There's a big bunch of Yankees over there, and prob'ly in Fredericksburg and everywhere else 'round here they're crawlin' around. Onliest reason I said anything is to ask if you want us to hole up somewheres else, like the barn or the stables, maybe."

Jolie frowned. "I don't know, Amon," she said at last. "You and Evetta would be able to decide that a lot better than I could."

Amon's fierce visage softened. He, like everyone else, had forgotten that Jolie was only eighteen years old. "I think the Lord's going to have to watch over us whatever comes, and we might as well be comfortable in our houses as in a barn."

"Good," Jolie said heartily. "Maybe they won't get this far east," she said hopefully. "But if they do, you're right, Amon. I can pray for protection here as well as somewhere else." She hurried to the door.

Evetta sternly called after her, "I'm bringin' you up some breakfast, missy, and you're going to eat it."

"Yes, ma'am," she called over her shoulder.

The battle did not rage at Rapidan Run. The two armies clashed all day long in the Wilderness. Jolie reflected that she wasn't getting used to the continuous thunder of cannon and the spiking racket of thousands of muskets, but somehow she shut it out of her mind, and so she didn't really hear it. Besides, she was so concentrated on Morgan that she was barely aware of anything else at all.

At about noon, he suddenly started shivering uncontrollably. As lightly as a snowflake, she laid her hand on his forehead and knew that he had a fever. She started laying cool, wet cloths on his forehead, though he still shivered convulsively. His fever got so high, and the heat given off him was so intense that the cloths were too warm only seconds after she had applied them to his forehead. She worked steadily, methodically, continually wetting a cloth and wringing it out and replacing the warm one and starting again. Ketura came in, and Jolie only looked up at her and said darkly, "No."

After about an hour he stopped shivering, but then he started talking and thrashing about. "Not going to cold-shoe him. I've got to set up that forge," he said clearly, his eyes open and glaring but obviously unseeing. "Have to move that mare. She's too restless for Traveler." He was restlessly making odd motions in the air with both hands, and fitfully he tossed his head from side to side.

Jolie held his wrists and began to wonder desperately if she might be able to force some laudanum down his throat when he abruptly calmed down. His arms dropped limply to the bed, and he lay still against the pillow. After a few moments, his eyes slowly closed. He began to murmur, but he spoke so weakly and softly that Jolie couldn't understand anything he was saying.

Like an automaton, she began putting wet cloths on his forehead again, for he still gave off waves of heat from his entire body. She could feel it emanating from him when she bent over. Though outwardly she looked calm and controlled, inwardly she was ravaged by fear.

Is this brain fever? I've heard of it, and don't people always die from it? Oh, God, no, no, no! If he dies I'll kill myself!

No such dire thought had ever entered Jolie's mind, and she drew herself up with alarm. "That's not true," she whispered to herself. "I'm so sorry, Lord. I'm so sorry. . . ."

It was hard for her to gather her thoughts, but finally she was able to pray. *Oh Lord, You know my heart, You know how much I love him and how much it frightens me to think that he might die. I don't know if I even really mean this, Lord, but I say now to You: Your will be done. I pray for his healing, I pray that he will live, I pray that I'll have the chance to tell him how much he means to me, how he is my whole life. But if. . .if. . .You take him. . .Your will be done.*

She repeated these words and variations of them many times over, all afternoon into the evening. Ketura came in every half hour or so, but Jolie rarely even looked up, she was so absorbed in her prayers and attending Morgan. When Amon came in as night fell, she looked up and said with wonder, "They've stopped firing."

He nodded. "Artillery stopped after only coupla hours. The onliest reason we could hear the muskets this far is 'cause there must have been 'bout a hunnerd thousand of 'em blasting all at the same time. He crossed his muscular arms and said quietly, "The Wilderness, it's on fire."

"Is it close?" she asked anxiously.

"No, thank the Lord Jesus for another mercy on this day," he said fervently. "Them two armies stayed all bunched up 'bout four miles over, and that's where the fire is. I guess it might get over this far, but I doubt it. Calm night tonight, no wind, and it'd have to jump a coupla pretty good streams, Rosh and Santo tells me."

"Thank You, Lord," she said simply.

She had not thought it possible, but Morgan's fever seemed to go even higher as night fell. Every once in a while his whole body jerked, and he would say something she could hear, though his voice was thick and sluggish. Once he blurted out, "Tell Ketura I was wrong. It is haunted." Mostly he muttered things about caring for horses. An hour later he said, "Scout from headquarters, here's my pass." Still later, "Meredith, Perry, we've got to strike the tent."

Finally he got so quiet and still that Jolie, for a heartwrenching moment, thought that he had died. She knelt by his bedside and grabbed his hand, which still burned, to her great relief. Tiredly she laid her head down beside their clasped hands. *If he lives, I'm going to tell him. I have to. I won't while he's feverish and not able to understand. I'll wait until he's better. He'll get better. . .and I'll tell him, first thing.*

His fever lessened, but he sank visibly into a deep stupor. Jolie watched him hour after hour, clinging to his hand. She thought that she could actually see him wasting away. He seemed to be getting thinner, his jawbones and cheekbones on the uninjured right side of his head appeared to be more prominent. She was afraid to leave him, because she was terrified that each long breath was his last.

When the north windows grew into a light gray instead of charcoal gray, she knew it was dawn, and she thought that she was so agitated that she might be getting a fever herself.

The sun rose again, and the light now streaming through the windows seemed offensively bright and cheerful. Jolie rubbed her gritty eyes and stared back at Morgan. Then she leaned forward and laid her hand on his forehead then against his chest. There was no mistake, he was definitely cooler. In fact, he felt a little clammy, so she pulled the sheet up and gently arranged his arms outside it with his hands resting on his chest. He looked more natural that way.

Ketura came and went a couple of times.

Jolie thought it had been a couple of hours since dawn when Morgan slowly opened his eyes and then licked his lips. "Here, Morgan," she said, lifting his head and holding the glass to his lips. He took several small sips then laid back, seemingly content.

Jolie set down the glass and leaned over close to him. "Morgan, dear, it's Jolie. Can you hear me?"

"Sure," he whispered weakly. "Hi, Jolie."

"Hi," she said awkwardly. "I need to tell you something."

"Okay."

She stood up, leaned over, and cradled his face between her hands. She looked straight into his eyes, though she knew he couldn't see her. "Morgan, I love you. I love you so very much, with everything that is in me. I loved you when I first met you, when I was nine years old. I loved you with a child's love for years, until I knew that I loved you as a woman loves the man of her dreams. That's what you are to me, Morgan. You always have been. The best man I could ever dream of."

His eyes widened as she talked. When she finished, she let go, sat down in her easy chair, and took a deep breath. *I did it, Lord, and no matter what he says to me, I'm glad I did.*

Morgan turned his head as if he were watching her. "Jolie, are you sure?" he asked in a deep voice, much stronger than before.

"I'm sure. I've been sure for a long time."

"But I'm blind," he said darkly. "How could you love a blind man?"

"I don't love some blind man. I love you."

Her simplicity delighted him, and he managed a small smile. "I love you, too, Jolie."

"You do?" she said, astonished. "But how do you know? When did you know?"

"I'm not too sure about how I know," he admitted. "But I knew it for sure and certain when I woke up and you were there. I was so happy. I was so thankful that I loved you and you were with me that I thought I had died and gone to heaven."

She dropped to her knees by his bedside and pressed her lips to his hand. "No, you didn't die, and you didn't go to heaven. You just came home. Home to me."

That day they heard no artillery, and if there were muskets firing, there weren't enough of them for the sound to travel to Rapidan Run. Morgan slept off and on all day and slept soundly and quietly for twelve hours that night. Two mighty armies only four miles away marched south.

The next day the armies clashed again at Spotsylvania. For two weeks, combat would rage all around Spotsylvania Court House.

Morgan was able to sit up enough to sip some beef broth boiled fortified with red wine.

Evetta had brought up a bowl and spoon, and Jolie started to feed Morgan.

A quick spasm of pain crossed his face, and he said, "Please, no, please don't feed me. Put it in a mug." He managed quite well.

For the next two days, fighting raged in a salient that came to be called the Bloody Angle. The men in blue and the men in gray locked in vicious hand-to-hand combat for twenty hours.

Morgan was able to sit up longer and gained strength to talk more. He asked Jolie to read *Great Expectations* to him. On the fourth night he was there, he didn't need any laudanum to help him sleep. The next day he asked Amon to help him get out of bed, and he sat in Jolie's chair for nearly an hour. He continued to improve daily.

On May 21st, Ulysses S. Grant, after battering futilely against the entrenched and fortified Army of Northern Virginia, disengaged from Spotsylvania and continued his advance south, toward Richmond. Lee parried him again at Cold Harbor. On June 3rd, the Union lost seven thousand men in one assault, a hopeless and needless engagement that Grant later heartily regretted. By June 15th, he had seen that the approaches to Richmond were too well defended, and so he shifted his army south toward Petersburg.

On that day, Morgan and Jolie sat outside on the front porch steps, holding hands.

"Morgan," she said decisively, "we have to get married."

He turned to her. Even though he still could see nothing at all, he always responded by turning to the speaker. "What?" he stammered. "Get married?"

"I am speaking English, you know," Jolie said very slowly and deliberately. "Yes. We have to get married. As soon as possible."

"But—but why do we have to get married?" Morgan said, bewildered.

"Don't make it sound like I'm telling you that you have to dig a ditch or something," Jolie said impatiently. "Don't you want to marry me?"

"Well, well, yes, sure. You just kind of took me by surprise. Uh—okay. But what's the hurry?"

Jolie rolled her eyes heavenward. "You know. I told you that I loved you, and you told me that you loved me. So that means that we want to be together forever and ever. And that means that we're engaged to be married. But I'm living with you, in your house, and that used to be all right, but now it's not. So we need to get married *fast*."

Morgan listened to this undeniable progression of logic with amazement. Then he threw back his head and laughed. It felt good, and he thought that he couldn't remember the last time he had laughed out loud. "Hm, I'm beginning to see that you're going to be way ahead of me on some things."

"A lot of things, probably."

"A lot of things. So I guess you don't want to take a little time and think about it?"

"No, I don't have to because I've been dreaming about it since I was thirteen years old. And you can't use that excuse either. You've always been a man to go ahead and get done whatever you've decided to do."

"Like digging ditches," he said, "and now getting married. Okay. But I'm also a man that wants to do things right." He reached around to get his bearings, half stood, then groped until he could figure out how to kneel in front of Jolie on the step below her. He took her hand in his and said, "Jolie DeForge, I, too, love you with my whole heart. Even though I'm in darkness, when I'm with you I feel as if I'm standing in radiant light. Would you do me the very great honor of consenting to be my wife?"

And now Jolie was speechless.

Morgan leaned forward, and Jolie clasped him to her eagerly to kiss him for the first time. All the desire and longing coursed through her, and Morgan responded with his own long-denied passion. The kiss lasted for a long, long time.

They were married on July 1, 1864, at Rapidan Run. The Reverend Melzi Chancellor, whose family owned the big house that had given its name to Chancellorsville, consented to come to the house to perform the ceremony. Their only witnesses were Amon and his family, and Jolie and Morgan couldn't have been happier.

"My family's going to kill me," he had said, "but they're just going to have to come to understand, as I did, that it was an emergency."

They were blissfully happy. It seemed that they were on an island, with their closest friends and their horses. War and sorrow and fear seemed far away.

In the middle of the month, they were in the stables early in the morning. Jolie was happily mucking out Rowena's stall, and Morgan sat on a stool. He faced her, and Jolie thought that if she hadn't known he was blind, she could swear he was watching her. He had lost that stark glare he'd had when he first came home. It had slowly gone away, along with the terrible swelling and bruising on the left side of his face. Now, a month and a half later, the only remnant was a slight swelling just on Morgan's left temple, behind the hairline.

As if he were reading her mind, he asked abruptly, "What do I look like?"

She smiled as she looked up, and she noted with interest that Morgan's frown lightened and the corner of his mouth twitched upward. *Maybe he is watching me,* she thought with amusement. *Somehow, in some way we don't understand. It's a miracle that he's here, and that I'm his wife. I'll believe in any gift You give me, Lord.*

"When I was nine years old, I remember the first day you came to DeForge House. That night I told Mr. DeForge that you were pretty."

"Pretty? No man wants to be pretty!" Morgan exploded.

"That's what he told me, but he was nicer and quieter about it," Jolie said severely. "But you are, in a way, you know. What I mean is that your face is fine, your features are clean-cut and clear, not heavy and thick like so many other men. You're not feminine, Morgan, but you are pretty."

"I'm not—oh, forget it," Morgan grumbled. "All I meant was did I still have bruising around my eye and cheekbone."

"No, you don't. Now get off that stool and get over here and help me curry Rowena," she said bossily.

He got up, felt his way over to the stall, found a curry brush hanging on a peg, and started on Rowena's right side while Jolie did her left. "I've wished a thousand times that I had seen you sometime during that year and a half I was away. I've still got stuck in my mind a little girl, looking up at me wide eyed and worried. And that Christmas day, when you were sitting in that raggedy old armchair, hugging your knees, looking out at the snow. . . You looked like a little girl then, too, peeping through a window out onto a fairytale land. I know you're no little girl, Jolie. I know you're a grown woman, and I know you must be beautiful," he said wistfully.

"Four hundred ninety-five days," she said. "I didn't see you for four hundred ninety-five days. Anyway, you can picture me in your mind, Morgan. And it will probably be better than I actually am."

"I doubt that," he said.

"Hand me the mane comb, would you? I'm going to really give her a going-over today," Jolie said. "And you're going to help me."

"Yes, ma'am," he said obediently, handing her the comb.

"You know, I was so worried about being black that I asked Evetta if it was even legal for us to get married," she said conversationally. "Everyone says I don't look—what's the matter?"

Morgan had stopped brushing the horse, and his eyes seemed to be focused on her face. He had an odd expression, half puzzlement, half amusement. "I forgot. I had forgotten that you are an octoroon."

"Had you? I'm not surprised," Jolie said airily. "I forget sometimes that you're blind."

"I don't, but I'm learning to live with it. But this reminds me, Jolie. I didn't marry some woman with black blood. I married you."

In the first week of August, Will Green came riding up on his old mule, Geneva. They all greeted him joyously, for he was the first person they'd seen since April.

After a flurry of welcomes, Morgan said, "Come on, let's sit out here where it's cool, and Evetta will bring us something cool to drink. We're all starving for news."

Morgan had a cane now, hand-carved by Santo, who was turning into a skilled wood sculptor. He had formed the head of the cane into an eagle. Morgan took Will's arm and led him up the drive onto the grounds. "I can tell as soon as I get under this shed roof. The temperature drops about twenty degrees," he said.

Will stopped and looked around in wonder. Amon and the boys had built a low shed roof onto the front of the kitchen, which faced east. They had also built a long, heavy oak table and benches. "This here's new," Will said.

"Yes, we never really had a good place to sit in the back of the house," Morgan explained. "And I don't like to sit in the front yard. I like it back here, where I'm close to everything."

"But I mean, you still got nails? And planed boards and everything?" Will asked, slowly sliding onto the bench facing Morgan and Jolie.

"Yes, we've still got a lot of supplies and food, too," Jolie said. "Thanks to Morgan. People thought he was a coward because he didn't join the army right when the war started, but he spent that year traveling all over, getting everything we'd need."

Will shook his grizzly head. "You mean you ain't had no Yankees out here to clean you out? That's a miracle, pure and plain."

"The Lord's worked a lot of miracles in my life lately," Morgan said. "I'll tell you all about it, but first we'd like to hear all the news."

In his picturesque way, the saddler told him about the series of battles beginning with the Wilderness. "Caught on fire that second day of fightin'," he said, his old rugged face grieved. "Some men, they had their legs busted up and couldn't git out of the woods."

"Oh, no," Jolie said with horror.

"Thank God I got out of there the night before," Morgan said fervently. "Thank God."

Will went on to tell them of Spotsylvania, of the Bloody Angle, of Cold Harbor. "Now Marse Robert's dug in at Petersburg, and the bluebellies are diggin' in all around it. Looks like it's going to be a long time, them snipin' at each other in ditches."

Morgan sighed. "I feel so guilty because I haven't reported that I was wounded and unfit for duty. We just haven't had any way to communicate. I was afraid to let Amon or the boys go into town."

"You was listed as missing at the Wilderness when the lists come out last month. That's why I was real s'prised to hear Reverend Chancellor telling me all 'bout how he married up you and Miss Jolie. Don't blame you for bein' missin', and I mean that, Mr. Tremayne. Even if you sent one of the boys to town, it's occupied now by the bluebellies. They ain't carin' where you are, long as you ain't behind them earthworks at Petersburg."

"I can't say that I wish I was, exactly," Morgan told Will, his brow wrinkling. "But I do feel like I should be."

Jolie put her arm through his. "And you would be, if you weren't blind," she said quietly. "I'm sorry, Morgan. I wouldn't wish it on you, but as long as this war is on, I'm not going to be very regretful that you are."

"Y'know, it's a funny thing," Will said, staring at Morgan. "You look like you can see. You look at a body when they're talkin' to you, and it just seems like you're lookin' 'em straight in the eyes. I keep forgettin' that you're blind."

"That's funny," Jolie said with a smile. "So do I."

CHAPTER TWENTY-FIVE

The winter that year was hard and grim. Cold weather and icy rains set in the very first day of September, and it was winter, with no joyous autumn season. It snowed a lot that winter. Most of the time it was dark, portenous days with heavy merciless snow piling up in drifts sometimes six feet deep.

The men, including Morgan, worked hard to keep the snow at bay. Morgan could find his way all around the farm. He had begun by memorizing the number of steps to take, but after a couple of months, it became instinctive.

Rosh and Santo went into Fredericksburg once a week, unless the snowstorms were too bad. News from Petersburg wasn't good. The armies were stalemated. Still, battles erupted as Grant kept attacking, attacking, always pushing to try to finally defeat Robert E. Lee. But now, as before, it seemed he could not beat even the starving, ragged, decimated Army of Northern Virginia.

One freezing night in February, Morgan and Jolie sat in their favorite chairs close to a hearty comforting fire in the study. The boys had brought back some newspapers that day, and Jolie had been reading them to Morgan. She had just read that they estimated that Ulysses S. Grant now had about 125,000 men around Petersburg, while General Lee had 52,000.

Morgan said sadly, "It's all going to come down to the numbers in the end. There's just too many of them. They could probably go on replacing every casualty for the next ten years. But I guess we can't replace even one anymore. At Fredericksburg, I realized then that this was going to happen."

"Really? But that was such a great victory for us," Jolie said.

"It was. But I watched it from the hills above the battlefield, so I could see it, but I wasn't really in it. I saw lots of blue dots, long lines of them, come across that field of death, again and again. Tens of thousands of them marching, standing up proud, aiming, firing. . .falling. Then thousands more would come, marching right over the ones who'd been killed and wounded, marching slowly, aiming, firing. Sometimes they would even get to reload, but they all fell. At the end we found bodies piled up seven and eight deep.

"But then I saw, as clearly as if it was a painting in front of my eyes, that if they had just thrown that whole army at us then, and all eighty thousand of them had rushed up those hills in a bayonet charge, they might have just overrun us by sheer weight and momentum. They would have died, yes, but I doubt that their casualties would have been much higher than they were. They probably would have been lower. But no general had the guts to do that. . .until General Grant came along."

"But he hasn't done that at Petersburg," Jolie argued.

"No, but once again General Lee outsmarted him. Fighting against an enemy that's on a level plain with you, behind earthworks, is different from storming a hill. Those trenches are about thirty miles long. Even General Grant doesn't have enough men to rush a thirty-mile line." He sighed deeply. "But what he does have is enough men to eventually encircle General Lee and the army. It will happen. I know it. I can see it."

"You said you can see it," Jolie said softly. "And I know that's true."

"Mm. Jolie?"

"Yes?"

"It is truer than you know. I can see red," he said almost casually. "I can see the fire."

Meredith and Perry, for the first and last times, came to the front of the tent and stood by the flap opening to watch General Lee. The date was April 9, 1865.

Lee came out, bowing to get through the low opening, then naturally resumed his stately erect posture. He looked at his two servants and nodded courteously to them but said nothing. His face was a study of sadness.

He wore a new uniform, Confederate gray with the graceful sleeve insignia of a general and the embroidered gold stars on his collar. His trousers were pressed to perfection with a gold stripe down the sides and a ruler-straight crease front and back and tucked into his glossy black cavalry boots with heavy gold spurs. His gauntlets were spotless white. His hat had new gold braid and tassels surrounding the brim. At his waist was a gold satin sash. At his side was a heavy sword, with jewels on the hilt and an icy blue steel scabbard that glittered in the weak sunlight as if it had been fashioned from sapphires.

An aide brought Traveler. Lee mounted, and without a backward glance, he rode down the dusty road that was lined with thousands of silent soldiers.

Perry had stayed up all night long readying General Lee's uniform and boots and sword. His face was tired and tragic.

Meredith was openly crying. "I'd give my right arm and right leg if Marse Robert didn't have to give hisself up," he said miserably.

"Me, too," Perry said quietly. "But one thing I've found, that the Lord don't want arms and legs. He wants sacrifice and surrender.

SURRENDER

Marse Robert's done sacrificed all his life, and now it's time for him to give up and let the Lord take keer of him."

When General Lee reached the McLean house, the agreed-upon meeting place, General Grant had not yet arrived. Lee went inside and entered a parlor with fine but plain furniture typical of a middle-class farmhouse. He selected a marble-topped table and cane chair that was in front of the window. He would be able to see Grant arrive.

There was a flurry of horses and heavy boots on the porch. Grant came in dressed for the field. He was about five eight and sturdily built but slightly stooped. His hair and beard were thick and nut brown, with no sign of gray. He wore a plain blue coat with only shoulder straps to indicate his rank, a dark blue flannel shirt, unbuttoned and showing a black waistcoat underneath. His trousers were tucked into ordinary top boots, mud-spattered and worn.

General Lee stood and crossed the room to shake his hand. The contrast between the two men was remarkable. General Lee was six feet tall, fifty-nine years old, and immaculate. Grant was much shorter, he was fully sixteen years Lee's junior, and he was untidy. If it had not been for the gravity with which he conducted himself, he would have looked like a careless, rowdy second lieutenant.

General Grant took a seat at a small table in the middle of the room, while General Lee resumed his seat across from him. General Grant opened the conversation. "I met you once before, General Lee, while we were serving in Mexico, when you came over to General Scott's headquarters to visit Garland's brigade, to which I then belonged. I have always remembered your appearance, and I think I should have recognized you anywhere."

Politely, Lee said, "Yes, I know I met you on that occasion, and I have often thought of it and tried to recollect how you looked, but I have never been able to recall a single feature."

Grant went on reminiscing about Mexico, seeming to enjoy his recollections and encouraging Lee to talk of it, too.

General Lee was, as always, courteous, but finally he determined to bring the conversation around, though he dreaded saying the words more than anything he had ever done in his life. Still, he spoke in the most natural manner, in the soundest tones, and his deep smooth voice seemed to echo in the somberly quiet room. "I suppose, General Grant, that the object of our present meeting is fully understood. I asked to see you to ascertain upon what terms you would receive the surrender of my army."

CHAPTER TWENTY-SIX

Morgan came around the corner of the kitchen porch, and for a moment Jolie was horrified because she saw that he was using his cane again. But then she saw that he was stumping along with a limp, trying not to put any weight on his left foot. Heavily he sat down on the bench.

"What happened?" Jolie demanded.

"That horse stepped on my foot. Again. And good this time. I think he did it on purpose," Morgan grumbled.

"He's tired of everybody else riding him, you know that. He blows out his sides like a great fat man when they try to cinch him, and if they can get him saddled, he deliberately runs right against the fenceposts to try to shuck them off," Jolie said with frustration. "He's getting worse every day. You know you're the only one who can control him, Morgan."

"I'm doing a real good job at that. My broken foot is a sure sign."

"Is it really broken?" Jolie asked with sudden alarm.

"No, but it really hurts."

"Shame on you, you big baby-muffin. You scared me. You need to stop this whining, Morgan, and get on that horse and ride him. That's all there is to it."

Morgan frowned. "Am I really whining?"

"Well, kind of."

"I'm sorry about that. I'll try not to whine anymore, but really, Jolie, it scares me. I can see up close, yes, but far off everything's blurred, and it makes me a little bit dizzy. I just don't want to fall off and—and—"

"Hit your head," Jolie completed the sentence for him. "And maybe go blind again."

"Yes," Morgan said resignedly.

Jolie came around the table and sat down in Morgan's lap. She put one finger under his chin and tilted his head up to look straight at her. "Look at me, Morgan."

"With pleasure," he said, lightly kissing her lips. "You're even more beautiful than I imagined. You're alluring and exotic and radiant. Since spring has come, it seems that you've bloomed along with the flowers."

She smiled, and it was indeed dazzling. Jolie had grown into a gorgeous woman, with smooth rich olive skin with a golden cast, dark eyes slightly uptilted at the corners, a wide generous mouth, and perfect white teeth. "Evetta tells me that's another symptom. She said ladies always glow."

"What? What are you talking about?"

"You know that thing we've been hoping for, and praying for, ever since we got married?" Jolie asked with a hint of mischief.

"You—you mean, for a baby? That we'd get pregnant?" Morgan asked with excitement.

"Morgan, I was horribly sick yesterday morning and this morning! Evetta said it's got to be a baby!" she cried, throwing her arms around Morgan and pulling him close.

He almost smothered her, returning the hug, and finally she pulled back, breathless. "Don't smush me. You might smush little

Jeannetta," she warned him.

"Or little Lee," he reminded her, his face lit with a foolish grin.

"Or little Lee," she agreed placidly. Then she grew grave and said, "So, what are you going to tell him, Morgan? That your big bad horse is too scary to ride? No, no, Morgan. You've never been scared of a horse in your entire life. Horses, and in particular Vulcan, are like a part of you. I may not really understand the kind of love that you have for them, but I see it, and I recognize it. Vulcan is missing you, and you're missing him."

"After what you told me, I feel like I could ride a storm! You're right, Jolie. As usual you're so right. Would you come with me now? I'm going to saddle up that old devil and make him see the error of his ways."

They walked to the stables hand in hand. Morgan still favored his left foot, but he could put weight on it now. He went in to saddle Vulcan, and Jolie went to stand on the fence rail around the paddock, as they had done for so many years.

It took so long that Jolie began to doubt that Morgan had been able to saddle the horse. But finally she heard Vulcan's heavy, prancing steps at the stable doors opening out into the paddock.

Morgan came out, sitting high and proud in the saddle, holding one rein in each hand, as he did when he wanted Vulcan to be collected. Stamping, tossing his head, snorting, Vulcan took two steps out into the paddock and then, with a slight movement of Morgan's hands, stopped completely still.

The great black stallion reared, pawed the air once, twice. He landed neatly then began a perfect gaited trot to the far end of the paddock. There he turned, a quick smooth whisk around, reared, and came back to a collected stance.

Morgan dismounted, took the reins, and led him to Jolie.

And then Morgan and Vulcan both bowed.

Robert E. Lee was revered in the South and reviled in the North.

In the North the press was merciless and vile. But no matter whether it was a personal attack, a criticism of his tactics or strategy or leadership, or even attacks against his family, he refused to respond, not privately and especially not publicly. He was that kind of man. In all the trials, tribulations, and tragedies that he suffered throughout his life, he never lost his sense of goodwill toward others, his self-control, or his dignity.

His fame was because he was a man of war, but others remembered his excellent service at West Point. In August of 1865, the trustees nominated him for the presidency of Washington College in Lexington, Virginia. On October 2nd, he was inaugurated in a modest service, and the final phase of his life began.

It was a good life. Lee was sensible of the honor of educating the young and worked as hard to make the college an excellent place of higher learning as he had in planning any campaign. Finally he was settled with Mary, and he knew he would never have to leave her again. They had lost sweet Annie, but the six children, including the three boys that had all served the Confederacy, had come through the war and prospered.

During the Christmas holidays, they were often all together at Lexington. Lee must have felt that it was a quiet, peaceful life, and a rewarding one. But after the war, he could never again be characterized as a happy man. In many ways he was solitary and withdrawn, and though his eyes would sparkle with good humor, he rarely smiled. The phrase "grave dignity" best described his last five years.

On September 28, 1870, he went to a vestry meeting at his church on a wintry wet evening. When he came home, he fell ill, seemingly alert one minute and then dozing off into apparent unconsciousness. His final enemy had attacked.

He seemed to be aware that each moment may be his last, and he accepted it quietly and without complaint. Steadily he worsened as days went by, and October came. He rarely spoke, and often when he did it was an unintelligible murmur. By the ninth day, it was clear that he was traveling down his last road.

Mary sat by him and held his hand.

As men of war so often do, he returned to the battlefield as his time ran out. "Tell Hill he *must* come up," he said sternly, so plainly that all in the chamber could hear.

But all battles come to an end, and Robert E. Lee's long battle did, too. "Strike the tent," he said firmly. It was his last surrender, and he finally went home.

ABOUT THE AUTHOR

Award-winning, bestselling author Gilbert Morris is well known for penning numerous Christian novels for adults and children since 1984 with 6.5 million books in print. He is probably best known for the forty-book House of Winslow series, and his *Edge of Honor* was a 2001 Christy Award winner. He lives with his wife in Gulf Shores, Alabama.

Other books by Gilbert Morris

The Appomattox Saga Omnibus 1
The Appomattox Saga Omnibus 2
The Appomattox Saga Omnibus 3

WESTERN JUSTICE SERIES

Rosa's Land
Sabrina's Man
Raina's Choice